BY DEMI WINTERS

THE ASHEN SERIES

The Road of Bones

Kingdom of Claw

Roots of Darkness

Dawn of the North

DAWN OF THE NORTH

DAWN OF THE NORTH

THE ASHEN SERIES

BOOK THREE

DEMI WINTERS

DELACORTE PRESS | NEW YORK

Delacorte Press
An imprint of Random House
A division of Penguin Random House LLC
1745 Broadway, New York, NY 10019
randomhousebooks.com
penguinrandomhouse.com

Hardcover ISBN 978-0-593-97565-7
Ebook ISBN 978-0-593-97566-4
International ISBN 979-8-217-30098-3

Printed in the United States of America

1st Printing

First Edition

Book Team: Production editor: Christa Guild • Managing editor: Saige Francis • Production manager: Meghan O'Leary • Copy editor: Laura Jorstad • Proofreaders: Julie Ehlers, Alissa Fitzgerald

Book design by Betty Lew
Map design by Megan Wyreweden
Endpapers by Scuttlekid

For Ben, and your unfounded
confidence in everything I do.

Author's Note

Dawn of the North takes place in a dark fantasy world and is intended for mature (18+) readers. Some scenes may make certain readers uncomfortable. A full list of content warnings is available at:

demiwinters.com/trigger-warnings/

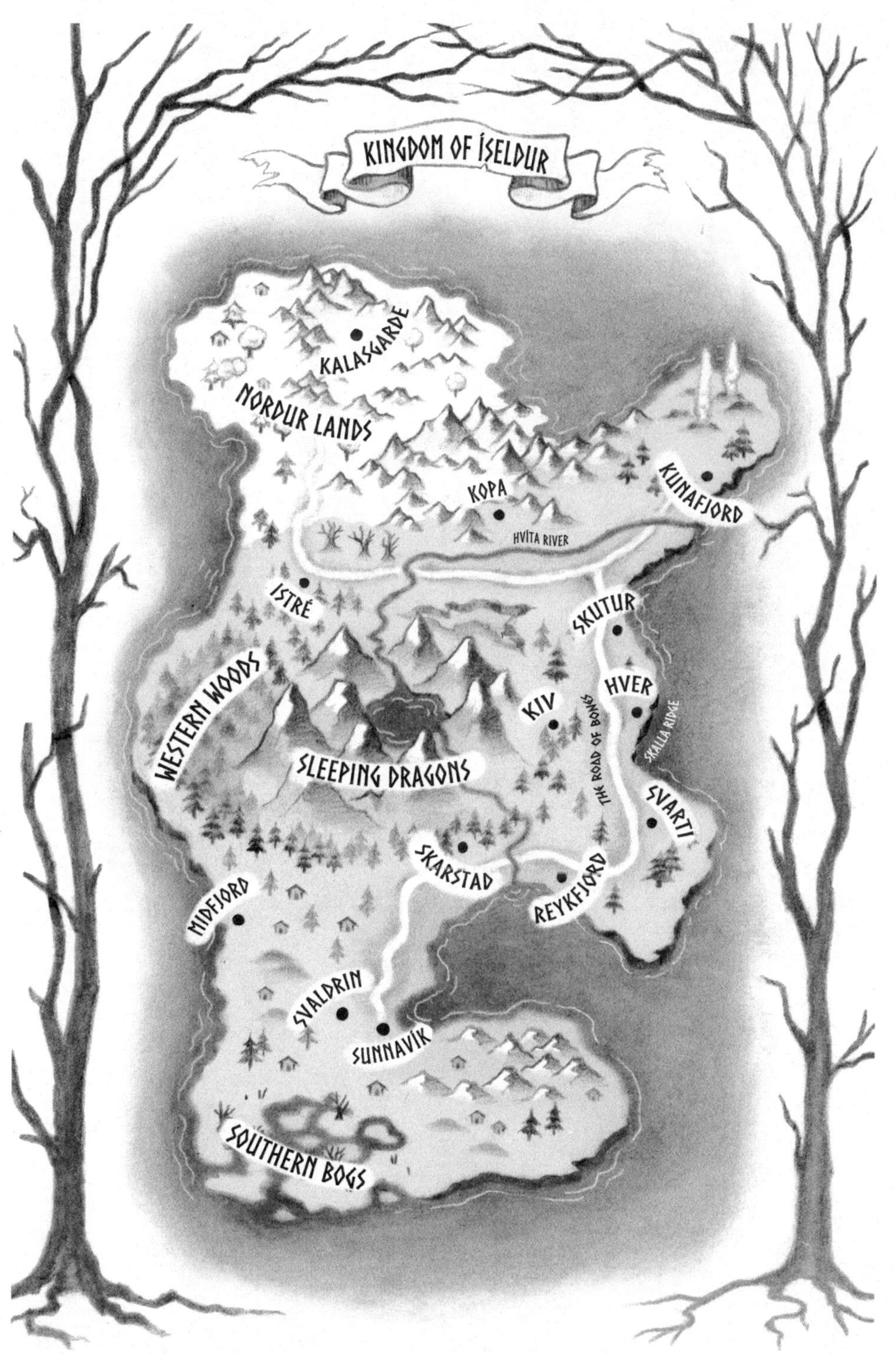

KINGDOM OF ÍSELDUR
KALASGARDE
NORDUR LANDS
KOPA
KUNAFJORD
HVÍTA RIVER
ISTRÉ
SKUTUR
WESTERN WOODS
HVER
KIV
SKALLA RIDGE
THE ROAD OF BONES
SLEEPING DRAGONS
SVARTI
SKARSTAD
REYKFJORD
MIDFJORD
SVALDRIN
SUNNAVIK
SOUTHERN BOGS

Kingdom of Claw Recap

Silla

Fleeing from the queen's warriors, Silla hides in the Bloodaxe Crew's wagon, and, upon being discovered, convinces them to take her to Kopa. The Bloodaxe Crew, meanwhile, are assigned the biggest job of their careers—to travel to the village of Istré where a deadly mist terrorizes its citizens.

Jonas "The Wolf" Svik begins a secret romantic affair with Silla, but when his younger brother Ilías is killed in battle, Jonas turns against her. Jonas drugs and kidnaps Silla, before handing her in for a reward. Meanwhile, the leader of the crew, Reynir "Axe Eyes" Bjarg, comes after them and helps Silla escape Kopa. Together they flee to a shield-home in Kalasgarde. In the process, they learn the truth about each other—Silla is Eisa Volsik, the princess long thought dead, while Rey is Galdra, and the murderer who'd been burning people along the Road of Bones.

Silla begins magic training with Rey's grandmother, Harpa, while Rey helps hunt down a monstrous serpent terrorizing the town. In the confines of the small shield-home, Silla and Rey are unable to ignore their attraction to each other.

After discovering Saga has almost taken her own life, Silla and Rey leave Kalasgarde to find help for her, but they are ambushed by Jonas and a warband. They battle, and Silla and Jonas are trapped under an avalanche.

As Saga's magic matures, a dormant curse awakens in the sisters' blood—a shard of Myrkur, the god of chaos, is activated. In order to survive the avalanche, Silla gives Myrkur access to the heart of her Ashbringer magic. Silla emerges black-eyed and ruthlessly kills all remaining Klaernar before turning on Rey. He pricks her with a galdur-quelling needle (hindrium), then strangles her until she's unconscious.

She awakes in Kopa to discover that Rey has been dosing her with hindrium to keep Myrkur from accessing her Ashbringer source. The story closes with the revelation that Saga is missing.

Saga

Saga lives in Askaborg Castle with the king and queen who killed her parents. She's betrothed to their thirteen-year-old son, and struggles with anxiety, particularly when trying to set foot outdoors. After learning that her younger sister Eisa is alive, Saga vows to stop Queen Signe from capturing her.

Saga has a panic attack after struggling to leave the castle, and a mysterious man comes to her rescue. She soon learns he's Kassandr Rurik, a lord from Zagadka in Íseldur to negotiate a grain treaty. Saga also meets Ana, a woman who works for the Uppreisna (a rebel group seeking to push King Ivar from the throne) and begins working with her.

Queen Signe, having discovered Saga's satchel in a room where she's been performing experiments on the Galdra, has Ana executed. Frightened, Saga makes plans with Rurik to escape the castle. But before they can enact their plans, they're caught kissing.

When the Zagadkians flee without Saga, her engagement is changed from Bjorn to Magnus, and she almost jumps from her balcony. A mind-to-mind conversation with Eisa (Silla) changes her mind.

At her engagement feast to Magnus, Signe slips the catalyst in

Saga's wine, making her lose control of her Sense. She retreats into her mind, where she meets Silla/Eisa (unconscious due to the avalanche). Saga goes through her Cohesion Rite and comes into her full power, which awakens a bargain made by her mother with the god of chaos. Saga grants Myrkur access to her magic and the god causes an explosion of black flame in the hall.

Saga wakes on a boat, Rurik sitting by her bed. After explaining what had happened, he takes her to the ship's hull, where Magnus is tied up. Magnus provokes Rurik, making him lose control and reveal himself as the Beast of Zagadka. Terrified, Saga flees.

The book closes with Rurik's revelation—he will take her to Zagadka, and not to the city in Íseldur as they'd agreed.

Roots of Darkness

Hekla and the Bloodaxe Crew are in Istré, trying to solve the mystery of the mist with a heartbeat. Frustrated that Istré's chieftain continues blocking her attempts to investigate, Hekla has a passion-fueled night with a stranger who's recently arrived to town, only to discover the next day that the man is Eyvind Hakonsson, Rey's childhood friend who's been sent to help with the job.

While investigating the forest, Hekla is trapped in the mist, then saved by a squirrel-turned-grimwolf. The squirrel takes to following her around, pestering her to free his mistress.

After disobeying Eyvind's orders, Hekla discovers that the chieftain has kept the human victims of the mist chained up in a barn, and that they've been Turned into draugur, undead creatures who do the mist's bidding. After discovering her betrayal, Eyvind is forced to throw Hekla off the job. She sneaks back in and partners with the Bloodaxe Crew and, reluctantly, Eyvind and his retinue, in order to evacuate the town.

Hekla risks her life to distract the mist so the citizens of Istré can escape, but when an explosion rocks the village square, Eyvind shields them both with his fireproof cloak. They abandon the city, and Hekla considers resuming her romantic partnership with Eyvind, only to overhear that he's been betrothed to a woman named Liv all this time. Upset, Hekla prepares to flee back to Kopa, but encounters the squirrel, who begs her to return to the woods and free his mistress. Hekla vows that she will return with more men.

DAWN
OF THE
NORTH

PROLOGUE

Signe did not flinch as the High Gothi's dagger slid across the thrall's throat. A crimson trickle quickly grew to gushing, rhythmic throbs as the Gothi's acolytes rushed forward with cups to collect the girl's lifeblood. Signe watched the thrall's blue eyes go from wide and panicked to dull and unseeing as the low, undulating tones of the High Gothi's voice met her ears.

A hundred or so figures had gathered on the southernmost dock on this sullen, overcast day. Askaborg Castle loomed behind them, Sunnavík harbor's many piers stretching out before them. Gulls called overhead, the smell of seaweed so pungent it nearly overwhelmed the acrid scent of burnt corpse.

Nearly.

All morning, Signe's moods had wavered between disbelief and brutal, aching grief. It had to have been a mistake. The corpse in the ship docked at the end of the pier wasn't Yrsa. Surely her girl was just missing. Hiding perhaps. The chaos in the great hall had been so very frightening, after all. Any minute and her Yrsa would appear and reassure Signe that it had all been one big misunderstanding.

The High Gothi's voice shifted to guttural rhythmic chanting as he poured the thrall's blood over the altar stone. Signe charted its course over the deep grooves carved into the stone; watched as it pooled in the trough below. When the thrall's lifeblood had drained from her, acolytes wrapped bear cloaks around her naked body before carrying her to the end of the pier and lowering her into the ship.

As Signe's gaze fell upon the figure in the center of the boat, tears tried to claw forth. The resplendent silks wrapped around the corpse could not hide the fact that the body was nothing but charred flesh and blackened bones.

Her baby.

Her Yrsa.

Signe's hand curled into a fist as she stared at what remained of Yrsa. Never again would she kiss her daughter's cheek. Never again would she hear the sounds of her laughter.

"Mama?" A small hand prodded her balled fist.

Signe forced herself to exhale and unclench her fingers, reaching for Hávar's hand.

"Not much longer, my darling," she said in a low voice.

Little Hávar had seen only three winters, and it was unlikely that he understood what was going on. In the days that had followed the explosion, he'd asked countless times for Yrsa, wrenching Signe's heart anew. But it was worse than merely her heart. It felt as though a piece had been torn from her very soul.

The next thrall was yanked forward, her ice-blond hair marking her as Norvalander. Beside Signe, Ivar loosed an impatient sigh. She ground her teeth together. *Get on with it,* that sigh seemed to say. *I've important matters to attend to.* It was no secret that Ivar favored his sons above all else, but Signe had dared to hope he'd *pretend* to mourn his daughter.

Hávar's hand squeezed Signe's as the thrall girl wailed and thrashed before the High Gothi. Her elbow collided with one of the acolytes, sending the man staggering backward into an ornamental brazier. But the thrall's attempt to flee was fruitless; three more acolytes rushed forward and seized her. The High Gothi ended her with a slash of brutal efficiency, the wound on her neck opening like a crimson smile.

By the end of this service, five maidens would lie alongside Princess Yrsa to accompany her on the journey to Ursir's Sacred Forest.

Signe hoped that the thralls and treasure heaped upon the ship were sufficient to allow her girl an afterlife without wanting for anything.

Her girl.

A sob broke low in Signe's throat, catching her by surprise. She turned away from the procession, trying to gather herself.

"Mother." The crackle of Bjorn's voice—not quite a man, yet no longer a boy—came from her right. He stood beyond Ivar but leaned behind his father to place something soft into her free palm.

Signe opened her hand and stared down at a clean square of linen. Such a thoughtful boy, her Bjorn had proven to be, and his kind gesture gave Signe the strength not to crumble.

She dabbed at a rogue tear, then faced forward once more. The latest thrall girl was lowered onto the ship, nestled between a bushel of apples and a cask of heather mead left over from Yrsa's birthday feast.

Ivar stepped forward, commanding the attention of all those present. Clad in a fine red-and-gold tunic, her husband cut an imposing figure. Ivar might once have been the most handsome man Signe had ever seen, but now . . . now, half his face was a patchwork of oozing burns and peeling flesh, his once-striking beard singed short.

The beard, Signe knew, maddened her husband nearly as much as what he now dubbed the assassination attempt. The Urkans saw beards as a sign of male potency, and Ivar Ironheart's formerly chest-length beard was now so short, he could not even braid it. It was little solace to Signe on this day, though. Not with what came next.

The High Gothi passed an unlit torch to Ivar, who dipped it in the flames of a sacred brazier. With swift, efficient steps, Ivar strode to the end of the pier.

One more moment, Signe wanted to beg. *One more moment with my baby.*

But Ivar did not hesitate. He threw the torch onto the ship. Turned without ceremony.

Signe watched the flames catch—first on the hay padding the edges of the ship, then on the rich silks strewn throughout. The

High Gothi cut the rope securing the boat to the pier, then worked with his acolytes to give the carved prow a gentle shove. The flames danced higher, higher, licking the skies.

Signe watched the boat drift away through a fog of tears.

But Ivar didn't see any of it. He strode past Signe. Put his hand on Bjorn's shoulder. "We have plans to make, son."

Ivar Ironheart left without watching the moment his only daughter departed the realm of the living.

Signe sat in an armchair arranged near the enormous glass windows of the king's bedchambers, a goblet of wine clutched in her hand. The clouds had lifted as the day progressed, and so Signe had ordered the room made dark so that she might gaze at the star-speckled skies. And as she stared listlessly up, she could have sworn one star blazed brighter before streaking amid the others. But as she blinked, it was gone, and with the amount of wine she'd already consumed, Signe couldn't be certain of much right now.

Her younger sister would have been able to name each constellation in the sky—would have been able to recite the Norvalander folklore stories behind them. Not a day went by when Signe didn't think of her, but here, now, her sister haunted her thoughts more than ever.

"I miss you," Signe murmured, then shook her head at the wasted emotion. She'd put her sister—had put all things Norvaland—behind her almost two decades ago.

Signe refilled her cup with an impatient breath. When would Ivar return from his meetings? All afternoon he'd been gone, busy preparing for retaliation against the Zagadkians. The fool of a man was convinced Kassandr Rurik had orchestrated the explosion in the great hall; that the Zagadkians had used the treaty as a ruse to gain access to Ivar and end his life. Had the man not seen Saga Volsik with his own eyes? Had he not known what the unnatural dark blue of her veins had meant?

Of course the dim-witted man had not. But Signe understood the significance of those veins—they meant that Saga Volsik had not acted alone. Because with them, in that room, Signe had sensed the presence of her old friend. Her secret friend. The one she'd grown to love and to trust over the years. Why had Signe's friend given themselves so wholly to Saga, when Signe had been so dutiful? And to kill her Yrsa . . . it was a betrayal so deep that it hurt her to even consider it.

Signe drank a large gulp of wine, forcing her mind back to Ivar and his foolish plans. He was adamant that Saga Volsik had acted with the Zagadkians, that she could not have done it alone. Saga was, as Ivar put it, "only a woman."

Her chest ached for what could never be. Yrsa's wedding to a high-ranking cousin of Ivar's. A quiet, safe life for her girl among the verdant fjords and rocky shores of Norvaland. Within a few short months, Yrsa would have been protected. Instead, she'd perished before Signe's very eyes.

Because of that ungrateful little *serpent.*

Signe swallowed a large mouthful of wine, desperate to dull the sharp pain of her grief.

Thankfully, the door to the bedchamber swung inward, diverting her attention. Ivar, it seemed, had finally returned. Signe set her cup aside and made to stand, but paused as a petite blond woman entered first. She recognized her at once as Eldrún, Ivar's favored concubine.

The queen's fingers curled around the arms of her chair as Ivar pushed Eldrún against the wall, groping her with the finesse of a drunken troll. Signe ought to have expected this—she hadn't, after all, warmed Ivar's bed in some time. But after Yrsa's funeral, such things had been far from her mind.

Clearly, it hadn't hindered *Ivar*'s lechery. Anger burning low in her stomach, Signe decided she'd seen enough. She stood and cleared her throat loudly.

Ivar whirled, his hand going to the sword belted at his hip.

"Signe." He exhaled in clear relief, but even in the dim light, she could see fear lingering in Ivar's brown eyes. Ever since the explosion, he'd grown paranoid that someone would make another attempt on his life. It would have amused Signe had it not come at the price of her daughter.

The queen's eyes fell upon Eldrún—scant years older than Yrsa. Her amusement quickly kindled into anger.

"Out."

The girl scampered away.

Ivar fetched a torch from the corridor, glancing at his wife in irritation as he used it to ignite the braziers in the room. Light danced along the walls and across the enormous carved bed that dominated the space. "I did not expect you to grace my bed tonight, Signe."

"And I," said Signe, "cannot fathom how you could take *anyone* to your bed the day your only daughter was sent to the Sacred Forest."

Ivar bristled as he slid the torch into a sconce. "What do you want, *wife*?"

Signe strolled toward her husband, his gaze hard and flat as he leaned against the wall.

Reaching him, Signe caressed his forearm with soft fingertips. Once she'd admired the toughened muscle of these arms. Once she'd admired *all* of her husband. Had desired him above all others. But the years together had hardened her tender heart. She forced herself to look past her husband's ruined face and meet his dark eyes.

"Vengeance, Ivar," she purred. "That is what I want."

Ivar pulled away, and though it shouldn't hurt after all these years, pain twinged in Signe's chest.

"You know I do not concern you with the affairs of men, Signe."

Ivar strolled to the table where Signe's unfinished jug of wine rested. Finding a goblet, he filled it, then turned to face her. And for the first time in *years,* Signe found traces of softness in her husband's gaze.

"But today, perhaps, I can make an exception. Will it ease your grief to know we plan to sail to Zagadka within a fortnight?"

A fortnight. Signe's mind raced. A fortnight was not enough time to muster all their forces, nor for Ivar's father to arrive from Norvaland with his fleet. Fear twisted in her gut as she thought of Bjorn. She'd just lost a daughter. Signe could not lose her Little Bear, too.

"But your father's fleet—" With the winter ice floes between Íseldur and Norvaland, it would be some weeks before King Harald arrived. "Surely you can wait a little longer. With those numbers, you'll be unbeatable—"

"We *cannot* wait, Signe. The Zagadkian scum tried to assassinate me—"

"You do not know it was them," Signe interjected.

Ivar took a menacing step forward. "Do not interrupt me, wife."

Signe clamped her mouth shut, berating herself for reacting, as Ivar would say, *emotionally.* But when it came to her children, she'd always struggled to hold her tongue.

"You worry for Bjorn, that much is clear," said Ivar, coldly. "Do you not know your worry weakens him in his men's eyes? He must see battle, Signe. Must sharpen his skills. Yes, this is happening sooner than we'd anticipated—"

"It is foolhardy!" The words burst from her before Signe could stop them.

Ivar's hand lashed out, slapping her hard across the face. Her vision exploded with white, burning pain, and Signe stumbled back, clutching her cheek. Ivar tossed his wine back in a solitary gulp, leveling a hard look at her.

"I warned you not to interrupt me, wife."

Signe forced her lips together. Swallowed the vile words trying to push up her throat.

"We sail two weeks from today. When my father's fleet arrives, they will join us. But I do not think we shall need them at all." Ivar's gaze grew distant and hungry. "We have some . . . battle innovations we are eager to use."

Signe's anger had grown to a living, breathing thing, and it took every ounce of her will not to release it on her husband. Instead, she focused it on the one person she despised above all others.

"I ask only one thing of you, husband." A deep breath eased her raging heart. Signe straightened her spine. Faced the beast of a man before her unflinchingly. "Bring Saga Volsik to me. Alive."

Ivar raised a quizzical brow.

Signe answered him with a queenly smile.

"I want to watch as the light fades from her eyes."

PART I

SEEDS

When ill seed has been sown, so an ill crop will spring from it.

—NJÁL'S SAGA

CHAPTER 1

Kopa, Íseldur
One week after Kingdom of Claw

A bead of sweat trickled down Silla's brow as she stood before the largest pair of doors she'd ever seen—as tall as three warriors stacked up. Knotwork was carved into thick oak planks that were secured on enormous iron hinges. If the doors were this massive, she wondered how big the council room beyond them would be.

Silla blotted her forehead with the sleeve of her dress, then paused. Would *Eisa Volsik* wipe sweat on her sleeve? She could not recall discussing how a queen was to deal with such things during her daily etiquette lessons. More likely, a queen did not sweat at all. But bother that, Silla was melting. The secret council room used for Uppreisna gatherings was deep beneath Ashfall Fortress. And given that the fortress was built into a slumbering fire mountain, it was sweltering.

She glanced over her shoulder at Rey. Half a head taller than Runný and her other queensguard, Rey was rather hard to miss. Torchlight caught on his tight black curls and gave his brown cheekbones a bronzed glow. But as her gaze slid to his tunic—a shade so red, the word *violent* came to mind—laughter escaped through Silla's nose in a decidedly unqueenly sound.

"Quiet, woman," grumbled Rey, folding his arms and looking away.

Jarl Hakon had insisted that, in his second son Eyvind's absence, Rey must wear House Hakon's colors and take a seat of honor with his family. Though Rey had protested valiantly, the jarl had won out in the end.

"You look so . . . festive," Silla teased, glad for a distraction from her frayed nerves.

"I look like a rowan berry." Those gold-flecked eyes landed on her, sliding down her body like the softest silk. "And you," he said in a low voice, "look like a goddess."

Silla was certain she flushed right down to her toes. "I feel . . . strange. Unlike myself." She looked at her gown. Beautiful it was—sumptuous emerald silks contrasted with stunning embroidery and elegantly draped cuffs that reached to the floor. This was the kind of garment Eisa Volsik wore. But *Silla* couldn't shake her disappointment—there were no pockets!—nor could she keep herself from wondering how many mouths the sales proceeds would feed.

Silla tried to focus. In a moment, she would stride through those mountainous doors and present Eisa Volsik to the most powerful households in Kopa. It was the first step of many they'd concocted—unite the jarls of the north under a common banner; gather allies in the south and abroad; amass enough might to keep the Urkans at bay and prevent the god of chaos from bringing fire and death to the realm.

That last item knocked her off-kilter. "It's only the twilight of days," she muttered to herself, a statement that did nothing to ease her discomfort. Though if she were being honest, Silla had not felt comfort since the moment she'd woken in Kopa unable to sense the source of her magic.

Daily doses of hindrium smothered her Ashbringer galdur—an unfortunate necessity to keep the god of chaos from accessing it as He had in Svangormr Pass. *A life for a life,* Myrkur had vowed. But without access to Silla's magic, He seemed to have lost interest in her. Though she could sense Him slumbering low inside her, the god had remained quiet since that horrid day. She remained vigilant all the same, searching relentlessly for a way to escape this ill-worded bargain of her mother's.

Silla stared at the doors, trying to ease her nerves. Despite her desire to rip the dangling sleeves from this dress and run off to the stables to take Dawn for a ride, she could not give in.

That, she decided, would definitely be unqueenly.

"If you run, I run," warned Rey.

"Don't tempt me," she teased back, unable to keep from imagining the pair of them tearing away from the fortress on horseback, the ridiculous garments flapping behind them in the wind. Sadness panged inside her chest at the impossibility of the idea.

A loud creak echoed in the corridor, making Silla jump in her skin. The enormous doors swung slowly outward, and her heart raced ever faster. With a deep breath, she forced her feet forward. She felt like an imposter. She *was* an imposter. It was Saga who was rightful heir to the throne—Saga who ought to be standing before these doors. But for now, Eisa would have to do.

And so, Silla would do her part. Would play queen for a while. And when Saga was found and brought to Kopa, everything would change.

"This is only temporary," Silla recited to herself as she gathered her courage and strode through the doors.

As expected, the room was cavernous, with an enormous arched roof held up by towering black columns. Silla walked along the central walkway flanked by golden braziers. Stone benches climbed up on either side of her, hundreds of people seated upon them. Silla thought she might be smiling, but couldn't be certain—she was too busy trying to remember if she swung her legs and arms at the same time or not.

At last, she reached the dais at the end of the walkway, but the stairs leading up to it made her nerves spike.

They're stairs, she told herself, grinning like a wildcat. *You've climbed stairs a hundred times. You won't trip.* As her slippered foot came down on the first stone step, Silla exhaled. She could do this. She wouldn't—

She tripped on her ridiculous dangling cuffs.

The crowd gasped as Silla tumbled forward. Rey's arms snaked around her from behind just as Atli Hakonsson lunged forward, catching her forearms. She blinked up at Jarl Hakon's heir, humiliation flaming at her cheeks.

Atli's smile was kindly, but as his gaze drifted over her shoulder, it quickly fell. Rey's low grumble had Atli releasing her and backing away with an exasperated look. Rey hauled her upright, keeping hands clamped on her waist until she'd regained her footing. Well. This was not the first impression she'd hoped for, but as Jarl Hakon rushed forward, she tried to push it from her mind.

Slightly stockier than his son, Jarl Hakon wore elaborate red robes that brushed the floor. With golden rings on each of his fingers and silver cuffs in his beard, there was no question he was a man of wealth and status. The jarl cocked his head at Rey, who, after a long-suffering sigh, strode to Eyvind's vacant seat on the dais.

Jarl Hakon turned Silla gently toward the crowd, and for the first time, she found herself slightly emotional. *Queenly,* she urged herself, reciting the attributes of Eisa Volsik. *You must inspire their confidence.*

"For the first time in seventeen years," Jarl Hakon proclaimed, "a Volsik will lead the offering!"

The crowd shouted in approval, and Silla caught more than a few damp eyes among them. But then Atli was beside her, handing over a platter of boar steaks. His dark eyes glinted, a reassuring smile on his chiseled face telling her, *Just like we practiced.* With a deep breath, she stepped toward the enormous brazier lit to the side of the dais.

"Oh Bright One."

"Louder," whispered Atli.

"Oh Bright One!" Silla tried with a bit more zeal. "We offer you meat."

She tipped the boar steaks into the flames, jumping back as the fat hissed and spattered.

"Mead!"

Atli handed her a golden goblet, which she poured into the flames. A bead of sweat clung to her temple, and Silla did her best to ignore it.

"And our finest weapon!"

At last, Atli produced a finely wrought dagger that looked to have cost a fortune. She hesitated, wondering how many sólas this weapon would fetch, but after Jarl Hakon impatiently cleared his throat, she tossed it into the brazier with the rest.

The crowd stood with a roar, stomping their feet. Silla hazarded a glance over her shoulder at Rey, wishing he was standing beside her. Instead, she found him glaring at the crowd as though every one of them had wronged him.

"Now!" exclaimed Jarl Hakon, "I present to you, Eisa Volsik!"

The banging grew to a cacophony, and Silla's heart felt as though it had grown wings. Tears clouded her vision, and she wrung her hands, trying desperately to keep her emotion at bay. *Temporary*, she reminded herself. *Soon this will all belong to Saga.*

"Take a seat," whispered Atli, directing her to the chair beside Rey's. She fell into it, glad that her part in this meeting had ended. Her instructions were to keep a demure, queenly smile upon her lips for the rest of the gathering. Rey's hand slid over, squeezing her knee.

"Did I not tell you that you'd do well?" he whispered.

"Did you not see me trip?" was her reply.

Rey's lips twitched in amusement. His gaze drifted to Jarl Hakon, now standing at the front of the dais, one hand raised. Within a few measured breaths, the crowd had quieted and taken their seats.

"I've received word from our spy in Askaborg."

The hair on Silla's arms stood on end, and her heart raced. *Finally,* she thought, *news of Saga.* Surely the mystery of her whereabouts would be revealed.

"I'm certain you've all heard of the explosion that rocked the castle a fortnight past." Heads nodded among the crowd. "Strange tales have emerged. We continue to hear that Princess Saga was the cause of the explosion. That black flames shot from her palms and caused the destruction."

Silla's gaze found Rey's hand, still resting on her knee, and she slid her own under it, desperate for comfort. There could only be one explanation for the explosion of black flames in Askaborg Castle: Saga had given Myrkur access to the heart of her galdur. Worry knotted tightly in her stomach, and Silla instinctively probed inward in an attempt to communicate with her sister. But with her galdur quelled, contacting Saga was impossible.

"Princess Saga's whereabouts are yet unknown."

Silla's heart plummeted into her stomach as Jarl Hakon's words sank in.

"She was not among the dead, nor is she in any Uppreisna safeholds," continued Jarl Hakon. "Our spies continue their search and shall not rest until every shield-home in the realm has been examined. We *will* find her."

Jarl Hakon glanced over his shoulder at Silla as he said this, but it did nothing to ease her frantically racing mind. Where was Saga? Was she in danger? And how could Silla simply sit here without knowing—without *doing* something?

But the jarl had turned back to the crowd. "Ivar has recovered from his injuries, and now he plots to retaliate against Zagadka. Despite reports of the black flames coming from Saga, the king accuses the Zagadkians of the attempt on his life."

Confused murmurs slid through the room, but Jarl Hakon continued. "It does not take a Weaver to see the threads of fate coming together before us. With Ivar's eyes on Zagadka, he won't look so carefully at his northern lands. This, paired with Eisa Volsik's return, tells me it is time."

Jarl Hakon paused for effect. "Time to return to the old ways of Íseldur, where we can worship the gods of our ancestors and use the blessings they granted to us!" A cheer rose, but Hakon's voice rose higher. "Eisa Volsik vows to champion the old ways! To banish the Klaernar from these lands! To tear down the pillars where so many of our kind have died!"

Silla's mind raced somehow faster. This was not how it was supposed to go. It should be *Saga* Volsik, not Eisa. The people of Íseldur deserved a true queen, not some placeholder. But Jarl Hakon's words had built excitement in the crowd. Warriors stood, some shouting and others banging their weapons on the floor. And in the middle of the dais, Jarl Hakon stood, arms spread wide, bathing in the moment's glory.

Once the room quieted, Hakon continued. "We will have to act quickly to solidify our northern alliance." His gaze swept the crowd. "As you know, Jarl Agnar has been the source of many violent incursions along my eastern borders. All attempts to talk sense into the boy have failed. Before the north can raise banners for the Volsiks, peace must be secured among us."

Silla wrangled her mind to the troubles with the mysterious Jarl Agnar. She'd listened to Rey and Jarl Hakon discuss the young jarl over the daymeal this morning. Between the number of warriors oathsworn to Agnar and the ports he controlled in Kunafjord, it was clear he was a man of significant power. What would Saga do if she were here? Broker peace between Hakon and Agnar? Yes. Surely she'd pen a letter, perhaps meet the jarl face-to-face . . .

Shouting beyond the chamber doors yanked Silla from her thoughts. Her gaze darted along the walkway, fear prickling down her spine. She did not need to be reminded that discussions of treason would land every person in this room a brutal execution on the pillars.

The doors flew open, and five figures strode briskly down the walkway. The dim light of the meeting hall made it difficult to make out their faces, but as their voices grew louder, one rose above them all. Silla shot to her feet. She knew that voice.

"Hekla!"

Tears filled Silla's eyes as she stared at the figure at the front of the group. Black hair was braided along the top of her head, and her metallic hand glinted as she stormed toward the dais. Gods, but she was glad to see her friend. There had been no communication from Istré in some time, and Silla's worry for the Bloodaxe Crew had grown each day. But here they were, Hekla and Sigrún, and oh—there was Gunnar, bringing up the rear! They were hale and apparently as vivacious as ever.

Rey scrambled to the edge of the dais, and Silla was on his heels.

The group reached the end of the walkway, bickering among themselves, and Silla examined the pair of warriors she did not know. But then her gaze flitted to Hekla's amber eyes, and emotions chased themselves across her friend's face—surprise, relief, and utter delight.

Silla imagined her own expression looked rather the same.

"Eyvind!" bellowed Jarl Hakon. "What is the meaning of this?"

Silla's gaze found the warrior in question right away, his likeness to Jarl Hakon and Atli impossible to miss. But Eyvind Hakonsson's black hair was singed and sticking up at odd angles, and bright-red burn marks marred an olive cheekbone. Despite it, Eyvind was clearly a handsome man, tall, with vivid hazel eyes. Silla examined him with curiosity. So this was Eyvind Hakonsson, younger son of Jarl Hakon, and the childhood friend Rey had sent to Istré to help the Bloodaxe Crew.

"Istré has fallen," Hekla proclaimed.

The words reverberated through the room for a long, weighted moment.

"What?" breathed Rey, so quietly only Silla heard him.

"What do you mean, 'fallen'?" exclaimed Jarl Hakon. His gaze swept the crowd, as though searching for someone.

"She means," said Eyvind, speaking at last, "Istré has burned to the ground."

Whispers raged through the room, but one attendee stood from a bench and bellowed, "Burned! You let it burn?" Silla examined the furious, gray-haired man with curiosity. He boorishly clambered over attendees to reach the walkway.

"We did not *let* it burn, Loftur, you utter blockhead," seethed Hekla, glaring at the man as he tried to squeeze past a disgruntled woman on the second row of benches.

What in the eternal fires happened in Istré? Silla wondered.

"Loftur hid vital details about the mist from us and brazenly endangered the entire village!" Hekla continued, glaring at a mad-eyed Loftur as he reached the walkway. "'Twas a miracle we got them out alive."

Whispers whipped up in the crowd, but Jarl Hakon grew very still, his gaze falling on the warrior beside Hekla. "Eyvind," he growled. "I do not understand this ill-tempered woman. Explain."

Rey took a menacing step toward Hakon, but Silla grabbed his hand to hold him back. The last thing they needed was a brawl.

On the walkway below, Hekla's cheeks turned a furious red, while Eyvind ran a hand through his hair. "It did not go as planned, Father. I'm afraid it was far more complicated than we'd expected—"

Jarl Hakon threw his hands up in the air. "I should have known to send Atli."

Silla's incredulous gaze whipped to Jarl Hakon. What kind of a father spoke of his son like that?

"This *woman* is to blame!" Silla's attention was drawn back to the one named Loftur, pure loathing in the man's expression as he stormed toward Hekla. "Stubborn and reckless, and endlessly meddlesome—"

In a move that was casually threatening, Eyvind stepped between Hekla and Loftur. Silla's eyebrows rose. "I was there, Loftur," he said in a firm voice. "She was not reckless. In fact, I believe many hundreds of people—including yourself—owe her their lives."

The man was not cowed. He tried to dodge Eyvind to get to Hekla, whose face was now a furious shade of red.

"What good are our lives if we cannot feed our families?" growled Loftur. "Centuries, my kin have lived in Istré, and now it is all gone, all burnt because of you—"

Silla gasped as the man took a swing at Hekla. But Eyvind caught his fist, twisting until Loftur screamed.

"Do not," said Eyvind through clenched teeth, "touch her."

Silla lifted her eyebrows even higher. Twice now, Eyvind had protected Hekla.

"Eyvind!" exclaimed Jarl Hakon. "Loftur is a respected member of this community! Release him at once!"

Whispers whipped through the room as Eyvind released the man's fist, and Loftur stumbled away. "Loftur," said Eyvind, every word laced with deadly intent, "you and I both know there were no *people* in that barn, nor was there a cure for their ailment."

"Gods' sacred ashes, can *someone* speak plainly?" muttered Rey, scratching his head. Silla nodded, wholeheartedly in agreement.

Hekla sent them a wary look. "The mist Turns all living beasts—humans and woodland creatures alike—into draugur."

Silla blinked at the word "draugur," trying to recall the meaning of it.

"The restless dead," Rey said numbly, and a cold sensation crept down Silla's spine.

"Aye," said Hekla. "And the gods damned chieftain of Istré had all the human victims locked in a barn, hidden away from prying eyes. Loftur tried to perform some ritual to convert them back to the living but—" She shook her head. "It was the mist's trickery. It would have killed them all had we not evacuated in time."

"It might have worked!" Loftur clutched his injured hand indignantly. "I had to try!"

"And after the double black moon," continued Hekla in a booming voice, "the mist has grown strong enough to escape the confines of the woods. We were able to restrain it long enough to allow the people of Istré to escape, but now that it's loose . . ." A muscle in Hekla's jaw flexed. "The mist will spread and feast on all mortals in this kingdom. It will not rest until we are all Turned."

Silence spread in the wake of Hekla's words, but Silla's mind spun with renewed speed.

"How do we stop it?" she blurted.

Hekla's amber eyes met hers, lit with determination. "We must seek the mist's origin, somewhere deep in the Western Woods. And then we must destroy it."

"Well, what do you ask of us?" demanded Jarl Hakon.

"More men," said Hekla simply. "More resources." She folded her arms, waiting expectantly.

"The bulk of my warriors are busy quelling the violence on the eastern borders," said Hakon. "I do not have the resources to send more warriors to Istré." Hakon grew eerily still before turning to Rey.

Silla's heart stuttered as time seemed to slow. And she knew what the jarl would say before the words left his mouth. *Not him!* she wanted to scream. Anyone but him. But she knew how badly Rey wanted to complete this job. Knew how he'd worried for the Bloodaxe Crew during those long weeks in Kalasgarde.

"This was your job, Galtung," said Jarl Hakon. "It is time for you to see it through."

CHAPTER 2

Kovograd, capital of Zagadka

Saga Volsik's charcoal stick smudged shadows into the shallow cleft of the man's chin. The relaxing effects of drawing were in full effect—her insides were warm and calm, and she could almost forget that she'd been stolen and locked away in this drafty room in Kovograd Fortress for the past two weeks.

Saga paused, then held her drawing board at an arm's length to examine the portrait. Kassandr Rurik's bold brows were arched, the corners of his lips curved up in mischief. And those eyes seemed to burn at her from the vellum.

"It will do," Saga murmured to herself. She stood from the wooden, fur-draped bench, then made her way to a bare patch of wall where a tapestry had once hung on the lone nail. The beams and wooden trim in her room were intricately painted in vivid red bird and floral motifs—a sight that might cheer some, but only reminded Saga how far from home she was. Frowning at the thought, she pushed the vellum onto the nail.

After retreating several paces, Saga examined her drawing from afar. Pride gathered in her stomach as she realized how well she'd captured Kassandr's likeness. Saga reached down her bodice and retrieved the dining knife she'd stolen several meals past.

Holding the handle between her thumb and forefinger, Saga

drew her arm back, then flicked it forward. The knife sailed through the air, landing with a dull thud a good foot wide of Kassandr's face.

With an exasperated sigh, she fetched the knife and returned to her place to try again. Again and again, Saga threw her knife at the vile man before her. The man who had stolen her away and kept her locked in a room "for her safety." The man who was, as it turned out, the Beast of Zagadka—a monstrous creature with a penchant for tearing out throats. Saga hated that the part that hurt worst was Rurik's betrayal of her trust.

For a moment in time, she'd thought she had someone who cared for her. Someone she could rely on. But Rurik had only used her trust against her. And now she was caged away yet again, this time in a frightening foreign land. Saga had reexamined her every interaction with Rurik time and time again, searching for the signs she'd missed—some hint at his treachery—but each time, she came up empty.

Now she scowled at the drawing of Rurik, gripping her stolen knife as she imagined the man standing there in the flesh.

"I hate you!" she hissed, then let the knife fly. This time, the dagger landed in the very center of Kassandr Rurik's left eye. Saga's lips spread into a smile, and she sauntered to the drawing before tearing it free. Her face fell. "You deserve worse."

She crumpled the drawing, then tossed it into the hearthfire. With a sigh, Saga flopped onto the bench before it and watched the vellum curl and blacken. Drawing Rurik's likeness and using it for target practice had become a morning routine for her. Though her knife skills hadn't improved much, her moods certainly had.

Saga knew she was imprisoned in Kovograd Fortress, a stronghold nestled in the center of Kovograd city. But aside from that, she knew little about the fortress itself and even less about the Kingdom of Zagadka.

She gazed about her room in frustration. Her chambers were no smaller than they'd been in Askaborg, yet everything about them was different. For one thing, this entire gods-forsaken fortress was made of timber, which lent the place a rather musty smell. The beams groaned at night, and there was a constant draft flowing through the space.

Saga supposed the room would be a comfort to most. The bed was large and heaped with furs and blankets. The hearth provided warmth, and she had a handmaiden who replenished the wood. And there was an enormous bookshelf on the far end of the room, filled with tomes. In the days since her arrival, Saga had flipped through them all, examining the strange drawings of animal shifters and seasonal gods, of monsters she'd never seen before, and, most curious of all, winged horses. If only she could read Zagadkian and understand the words written in the books, perhaps she wouldn't be so gods damned bored.

Leaning back on the bench, Saga closed her eyes and retreated into the safety of her mind—the place where she'd last spoken to her sister.

Eisa! she called out. But as it had been since she set foot on this isle, Saga's mind was still and dark. Where had Eisa gone? Saga worried her bottom lip, thinking of her sister buried under a mountain of snow. It was impossible to keep the question from pushing forth—what if Eisa hadn't made it out of the avalanche?

"I must get back to Íseldur," Saga said to the hearthfire. Her mind raced for a plan, but it was impossible. She was thousands of miles from home, utterly cut off. There were no allies for her here. No one to help her escape. No way to get to her sister. Saga pushed against the hopelessness building inside her.

In addition to Eisa, she wondered why she could not feel that strange creature deep in her chest—the one that had pulled her darkest wants to the surface and caused that explosion in Askaborg's great hall. But after two weeks with no sign of it, she wondered if it had all been a conjuring of her mind.

It made no sense. Saga was certain she'd felt traces of the new power Eisa had helped her awaken while aboard Rurik's boat, but everything had grown more and more muted as they neared Zagadka's shores. And since she'd set foot on Zagadkian soil, there was no trace of it at all. Worse than that, she'd discovered she could not use her Sense to listen in on anyone's thoughts. It was as though even her galdur had abandoned her in these foreign lands.

Saga found herself longing for the dark creature—longing for the power it had granted her, if only for a moment. Perhaps together, they'd be able to free her from this place . . .

"Stop," she told herself, Yrsa's brown eyes filling her mind's eye. She grieved for Yrsa, who'd died that day in the great hall. Logic told Saga it had been that dark creature that had caused the explosion, yet she could not forget the hunger she'd felt to make the whole room suffer. *That,* she knew, had been entirely her.

She pressed a hand to her stomach to quell her nausea, and pulled a fur around her shoulders. Saga felt the faint stirrings of another crisis building within. "You're safe," she reminded herself. "Magnus is dead. He cannot harm you."

But she'd been in this strange place for two weeks, and there was no way out. No exit. Gone were all of Saga's comforts; gone was the advantage she'd held in Askaborg—knowledge of the sprawl of tunnels beneath the castle. The hand of panic squeezed, sending Saga's heart skittering.

He's dead, she chanted inside her mind. Her fingers found the hard wood of her bench and began tapping slowly and rhythmically. *He cannot hurt you.*

But she knew it was no use. The crisis gripped her in earnest, her heart trying to hack its way out of her rib cage as every fear she'd tried to suppress surged forth. She was going to die here, so far from home, and without fulfilling her promise to Eisa that they'd meet. No one would ever know what had happened to her.

The crisis passed with torturous slowness, leaving Saga shaking. In the weeks since she'd arrived, she'd suffered dozens of the attacks. To her great chagrin, the tapping ritual Kassandr had taught her helped the attacks pass more effectively than anything else she'd tried.

Still, she eyed the door to her balcony warily, but the mere sight of it sent her heart skittering once more. *Not today*, she told herself. But one day soon, she needed to step outdoors. She'd made such progress in the weeks before she'd been taken from Íseldur, and she did not want to lose her nerve. Besides, if she wanted to leave this gods-forsaken isle, she'd need to get used to open skies. But before that, it would be wise to learn the layout of this sprawling fortress. Learn what secrets and advantages it might have for her.

Her shaking subsided, and Saga fortified herself for what would come next. The knife lay heavily beneath her bodice, and soon Kassandr Rurik would arrive, as he did each morning.

And for the first time in a week, Saga was ready to face him.

It was Saga's handmaiden, Alasa, who arrived first, knocking lightly three times before entering. Saga didn't know what the point of knocking was when a door was locked from the outside, but she kept her irritation to herself. It was not Alasa's fault.

Her handmaiden backed into the room, clutching a large tray. Clad in a dress of heavy blue fabric that was secured with an ornamental crimson belt, Alasa wore a kerchief tied around her black hair. Saga averted her gaze, wondering what the poor girl had done to be assigned to serve her. Alasa never complained, but she also never smiled, performing her duties with a no-nonsense air. The tray thudded onto the table, Alasa efficiently unloading its contents.

Saga thought of the books filled with Zagadkian words, and pointed at the bowl of porridge-like substance, asking, "What is this called?"

Alasa's brows furrowed in concentration as she tried to glean her meaning. But as her gaze followed Saga's to the bowl, understanding settled in her expression. "*Kasha,*" she answered brusquely.

"*Med.*" She tapped a small carafe of honey.

"*Smorodina.*" A bowl of blackcurrants.

"Róa?" Saga asked hopefully.

The girl looked at her blankly, then nodded. "Róa," she replied with a curtsy, then left.

Saga sighed, staring down at the table. She knew she ought to be grateful for what she had; that the people of Íseldur were going hungry amid a grain shortage. But this *kasha* was not the same as Íseldurian porridge, and the blackcurrants were strange and tart. And róa . . . gods above, what she'd give for a nice cup of spiced róa to warm her from the inside out.

"Perhaps you might like the Zagadkian *sbiten,*" drifted Kassandr Rurik's voice from the doorway.

Saga gripped the table's edge, trying to ease the jagged beat of her heart.

"Or if you are truly missing Íseldurian róa, we can heat water and throw in some sticks to give to you the bitter taste of it."

Saga knew he was baiting her, but she could not keep herself from reacting. Her nostrils flared and her gaze flew to him. Kassandr looked irritatingly handsome as he leaned in the doorway—his posture so casual it was easy to forget the predator lurking beneath. But Saga refused to forget. She lifted her eyes to his, and a jolt ran down her spine.

Green.

Green like the beast that had stared her down in the depths of that ship.

Green like the man she'd thrown caution to the wind for.

Gods, she was such a fool. How could she not have realized this man's nature was anything but human? There was the way he'd smelled her blood the day they'd met; the strange growl that had scared Jarl Skotha's hound away. And then there were the impossible moves he'd displayed while fighting Thorir the Giant. If she'd missed such glaring signs, could she really trust her own intuition?

"What do you want?" Saga now asked, loosening her grip on the table.

The moment of silence in the wake of her words told Saga that Rurik had expected her to send him away as she had every other time he'd come to see her. But the man recovered quickly. "I want many things," he drawled, pushing off the doorway and strolling into her chambers.

Saga tried to ignore how his structured jacket emphasized the breadth of his shoulders; how the power of his strides hinted at something barely leashed within. She stared at his hands, searching for any sign of those strange, creeping tattoos, but there was nothing but sun-kissed skin marred by the occasional scar.

The clank of boot buckles punctuated each step he took, and Saga's foolish heart instinctively took off at a gallop. She silently cursed herself—the man could likely hear her heartbeats with his inhuman abilities.

His fingertips landed on the table, and Rurik leaned closer. "Above everything, Winterwing, I wish to know how you fare. Is room to your liking?"

He sank into the chair across from hers and folded a leg over his knee.

Nothing about you stealing me is to my liking! she wanted to scream. Instead, Saga scowled, and asked, "Must you lock my door?" She forced herself to meet those green eyes. *Cunning and dangerous, much like a mountain cat's,* she'd once thought. Little had she known, she was not far off.

Kassandr took the small pot of honey, leaning over the table to drizzle it over her bowl of *kasha.* "As I have said." Rurik reached for the bowl of blackcurrants next. "It is for your safety, *moya koroleva.** Until you meet the high prince and have his protection, none may enter your chambers but myself, Rovgolod, and Alasa."

He spooned the blackcurrants over her *kasha* before nudging the bowl closer. "Eat." Rurik leaned back in his chair, and Saga could finally breathe.

Begrudgingly, she took a tentative bite. The sweetness of the honey contrasted with the sour berries, all mixed with the chewy, nutty grains. It was nice enough, but still . . . it wasn't home.

"What about you?" Saga asked after swallowing. "You're not safe for me, either."

Kassandr cocked his head to the side. "If you wish for me to apologize, I'm afraid I will not. I took you to keep you safe. Here, you are under my protection."

* My queen.

"Here, I am caged!"

The words came out louder than she'd expected, echoing off the timbered walls.

A frown marred Kassandr's stupidly beautiful face. "I am sorry you think that, Saga. Perhaps, in time, you will see truth."

Saga trembled with rage as she stared at the man before her. But her anger quickly fizzled to despair. Because with those words came the realization—this sculpin truly thought he was doing the right thing.

"I must return to Íseldur," she said quietly. "I need to find my sister."

She could feel Kassandr's assessing gaze upon her, but the irritating man ignored her pleas. "The high prince is wishing to meet you. I have told to him you are ill from sea voyage, but with each day, he grows more . . . eager."

"You mean," she seethed, glaring at him, "the high prince wishes to see his new pet."

Kassandr's expression hardened, and he leaned across the table, taking her hand in his. "You are no one's pet, Saga."

His thumb smoothed along the scarred back of her hand, and for a moment, she was back in a rain-swept garden, letting him hold her, kiss her, comfort her. But the moment passed, and Saga jerked her hand out of his grip. "You took me from my home, against my will. Keep me in a locked room. Just what do you think that makes me?"

He pursed his lips, gaze skimming over her reverently. "You, Saga, are a queen without her throne."

Words escaped her, and Saga stared at him blankly.

"You are fierce," continued Kassandr, "and beautiful, and one day, I will see a crown upon your head. But first, we must plan. We must be clever. First, you must come to speak with high prince. Explain to him about the Urkans. You will need to be convincing to get them to act. My father will be upset, but perhaps his anger can be tempered."

Saga struggled to comprehend, a thousand questions battling for dominance. Explain what about the Urkans? And what, precisely, did his father need to be convinced of? But the words that fell from her lips were "Tempered how?"

Immediately, she regretted her question. And when Kassandr's gaze shifted to mischief, she wanted to snatch it right back.

"Saga Volsik," he said, "rightful queen of the Kingdom of Íseldur, most beautiful woman I have ever met, I ask for your hand—"

Saga leaped to her feet, her chair toppling back behind her. "I hate you!"

Kassandr cocked his head to the side. "*Ty pytayesh'sya menya soblaznit?*[*]" he said with a sly smile.

"What does that mean?"

His smile remained, yet something flashed behind his eyes. "It means I wish for you to become my wife."

"I will *never* marry you!"

"If you marry the heir to Zagadka, none will act against you in violence—"

She picked up the bowl of blackcurrants and flung it at him. Kassandr dodged it with irritating ease, and the bowl smashed against the wall, dark berries smearing the weathered planks.

"You missed," he said with a smirk that snapped something deep within her.

Before she knew what was happening, Saga was around the table, the knife from her bodice gripped in hand. She was a being of pure emotion, fueled by a week's worth of pent-up rage. She wanted to show this arrogant man he could cage her, he could take away her freedom, but he would *never* control her. Saga drove the knife into the flesh of his shoulder.

She'd expected a reaction. A cry of pain, perhaps. But Rurik's face flickered with amusement. And then his hand wrapped around her own, pushing the knife even deeper.

"*Teper' ty tochno pytayesh'sya menya soblaznit,*[†]" he rasped.

"What does that mean?" she demanded in a shrill voice.

* Are you trying to seduce me?

† Now you are truly trying to seduce me.

"It means, '*Again, you have missed.*' "

She gaped at him. "I stabbed your shoulder!"

A slow smile crept across his face. "It seems you have not the heart to kill me." He glanced at the knife and tutted. "We must get for you better knives. Come with me to red room at end of corridor. There you can choose from many."

Saga stored the detail about the red room away for later and made to yank her hand free from him, but Rurik's unyielding grip slid to her wrist. His eyes darkened as they caught on something, but they met hers again and Saga couldn't look away. Slowly, he lifted her hand to his lips, his tongue sliding along her index finger. For a single, disorienting moment, Saga felt the wet heat of his mouth in places she should not.

But then her senses swarmed back, and she yanked her hand away.

"You must be more careful," Rurik said, nodding at her hand. A thin trickle of blood ran down her palm. Saga identified the source as a small nick on her index finger. The index finger Kassandr had just licked.

Cradling her hand to her chest, Saga backed away from him. He'd just licked blood from her finger, and it was the reminder she needed that he was half beast—that he was impulsive and violent, and always got what he wanted. Her despair returned with new force. She was in a foreign land without allies. She could not speak the language. Could not reach her sister mind-to-mind.

A small whimper broke free at the realization: She was trapped.

Rurik's gaze was unreadable as he moved toward the doorway. "Tell to me when you are ready to say yes, Saga. I will marry you that very day."

A scream built low in her throat, and Saga didn't think. She reached for the bowl of *kasha.* Hurled it at him with all of her strength. But it only collided with the closed door.

And as the sticky grains slid to the floor, the dead bolt scraped shut.

CHAPTER 3

Kopa, Íseldur

Hekla trailed a serving woman through Ashfall's corridors, each turn revealing more opulence than the last. From the black stone archways to the shimmering brass doorplates and crimson tapestries bearing House Hakon's dragon sigils—it all made Hekla's face twist in distaste.

Her bones were weary, yet her blood ran hot in the wake of her confrontation with Jarl Hakon and Istré's chieftain, Loftur. She'd had enough of Loftur to last a lifetime. To think he still thought himself in the right when he'd fallen for the mist's trickery, and all of Istré's citizens had nearly paid for it with their lives.

She supposed relaying the news to Rey and Jarl Hakon had gone about as well as she'd anticipated. At the very least, Istré's problems—Íseldur's problems, Hekla corrected—were out in the open. The poisonous mist was a danger to every citizen in this kingdom. If left unchecked, it would spread and grow more powerful; it would feast on every human and creature in this realm and Turn them draugur.

The serving woman paused before a door, drawing Hekla from her dark thoughts. "Your chambers, miss."

With a nod, Hekla entered the room, then paused. Her gaze bounced from the ornate chandelier, shimmering with dozens of candles, to the luxurious bed with crimson silk spilling from an utterly ridiculous canopy. A fire burned in an enormous obsidian fireplace to her right, fur-lined benches and chairs arranged around it, and at the back of the room, glass-paned windows stretched nearly to the roof.

"I think there's been a mistake."

The serving woman looked about nervously. "No, miss, this is the room His Lordship ordered readied for you—"

"Which 'Lordship,' exactly?"

"Why, the second jarl-in-waiting. I'm sorry, miss, if 'tis not to your liking—"

Though her insides prickled with irritation, Hekla did not want the serving woman to get caught in this mess. She forced a smile to her face. "No, no. It is lovely. My thanks."

But as the woman curtsied, it took every ounce of Hekla's willpower not to snort. Curtsied—to *her*? Thankfully, the woman departed, leaving Hekla alone in the monstrosity of a bedchamber. So Eyvind bloody Hakonsson was behind this. Did the fool truly think he could win her forgiveness with palatial living quarters?

A squeal from behind her had Hekla whirling toward the open doorway. And then, she was running; was wrapping the curly-haired figure in a single-armed embrace. Hekla wasn't usually fond of hugs, but in the aftermath of everything, this one felt better than ever.

"You're really here—" The muffled voice made Hekla realize her sooty lébrynja jacket was pressed against Silla's fine gown.

Reluctantly, Hekla released her friend, but held her at arm's length. "Look at you!"

Gone was the wild hair and homespun apron dress. Silla's glossy curls were interspersed with small, silver-cuffed braids, and her gown looked made of silk or some fine material like it. Silla's cheeks flushed pink, her emerald skirts rippling like water as she shifted. "I feel like a child playing dress-up," Silla whispered loudly.

"No, you look lovely. Gods, I am so glad you're safe, Sil—er—Eis—"

"I'm still Silla, in private at the very least." The fierceness in her friend's voice made Hekla breathe a little easier. She might look a little different, but some things, it seemed, remained the same. And Silla's warm reception told Hekla that beneath it all was the optimistic and caring woman she'd met on the Road of Bones.

Hekla grinned. "Silla, then."

"Hekla, I'm so sorry—"

But Hekla only held up a hand. "Do not apologize, dúlla."

She and Silla hadn't parted on good terms. Ilías had been freshly buried and the truth of Silla's situation brought to light. Back then, Silla's withholding of details had felt like a betrayal. But time had given Hekla new perspective. She knew what it was like to be a woman in a man's world. Safety was never a thing to be taken for granted, and trust was a hard-earned thing. And it hadn't escaped Hekla's notice that the moment Jonas had learned Silla was Eisa Volsik, he'd handed her in for a reward. It made complete sense why Silla would keep the name hidden, even from her friends.

"You were only trying to survive." Hekla's tone made it clear she would accept no argument.

Relief washed over Silla's face, and a thousand questions sprang to Hekla's mind—had Jonas truly drugged her and given her over to the Klaernar? How had Silla escaped from her cell? And did both she and Rey truly have Galdra powers? But it felt like too much for this moment—a thing to ease into.

"I hope you can learn to trust me with your secrets," Hekla said instead. "Istré . . . put a lot of things into new light for me." Such as the fact that Galdra, including Silla, Rey, and Eyvind bloody Hakonsson, existed in far greater numbers than she'd ever thought.

Silla nodded, then drew her to the benches near the fireplace and grinned like a cat. "I cannot believe you're sitting across from me. Tell me everything, Hekla. What happened in Istré? Why did Loftur—what an absolute arse—take a swing at you? And Hekla . . . who is *Eyvind*?"

Hekla did not like the way Silla had spoken the name "Eyvind," nor the mischievous glint in her dark eyes. Inwardly, she cursed Hakonsson for playing the protector when Loftur had come at her. Had Hekla not proven to him already that she was no damsel?

"Where do I start?" Hekla ran a hand down her face. "The part where Istré's chieftain, Loftur, blocked my every attempt to investigate the mist? The part where he kept his kin—kin Turned draugur by the mist, might I add—chained up in a barn? The part where I took Axe Eyes' replacement to bed—"

"What?" Silla leaned forward eagerly. "That part!"

The serving woman returned to the chambers, setting a tray of refreshments down before them.

"Our thanks, Eilif," Silla said to the woman. "How fares your sister?"

"Oh, far better, Your Highness," replied Eilif, bowing low. "She's sewing a token of her appreciation for you."

Silla waved a hand. "It is not needed. To know her condition is improving is enough for me."

Eilif ducked her head once more, then departed the room. Hekla quirked a brow. "What was that?"

A flush stained Silla's cheeks. "I had some medicinal herbs prepared by Ashfall's healer for Eilif's sister." She folded her arms over her chest. "Do you know, I've been told it's unseemly for me to know the names of those serving me?"

Warmth suffused Hekla as she stared at her old friend. "Gods, but I missed you, Silla."

Silla's smile was warm and wide, and for a moment, the two simply grinned like fools.

But the scent of róa called to her, and Hekla poured a steaming cup for them each. When she handed one to Silla, there was a mischievous look in her friend's eye. "I believe you owe me a salacious story, Rib Smasher."

Leaning back on the bench, Hekla sighed. "I took Eyvind bloody Hakonsson into my bed, but I swear to you, Silla, had I known who he was, I'd have stayed far away. The man wasn't due to arrive for three more days!"

Silla quirked a brow. "And?"

An exasperated breath escaped Hekla. "And then I had to pretend I did not know him, lest his warriors think I was trying to earn some sort of favor. Taking the crew leader to bed is a quick way to lose the respect of your fellow warriors."

Silla looked ready to protest, but Hekla continued.

"Do not think too much of it, Eyvind is a serpent. As it turns out, he's betrothed to some woman named Liv—"

"Liv?"

At the note of recognition, Hekla eyed her friend. "Do you know her?"

"Liv is one of my so-called ladies-in-waiting but—" Silla chewed her lip, clearly perplexed. "She's never once mentioned a betrothal."

Hekla mulled this over for a moment, then swiftly changed the subject. "And Gunnar must have knocked the wits from his skull, because the eelhead asked for my hand in marriage!"

"What?" Silla sat forward, róa sloshing onto her fine emerald gown. "Porridge," she muttered, blotting it with her sleeve, then giving up. "And what did you say to Gunnar?"

"I am not proud of this." Hekla stared at her steaming cup, unable to meet Silla's gaze. "I asked for time." She ran an irritated hand along her braid. "Gunnar suffered from dark moods after Ilías's death and had only just returned to himself. I cannot be the one to send him back to the gloom."

Silla's eyes shone with compassion. "I see."

Hekla sighed. "Istré was a complete, utter mess." And then she told Silla everything—how she'd grown frustrated with Loftur blocking her investigation and Eyvind's restrictive rules. How she'd stormed into the woods and been caught in the mist. How a squirrel-turned-grimwolf had rescued her and had then taken to pestering her to "free his mistress."

And Silla, in turn, told Hekla of Kalasgarde—how she'd learned how to express her galdur and had battled a giant serpent. How Jonas and a battalion of Klaernar had showed up and trapped them with an avalanche. Silla's voice faltered when she reached the part about her mother's bargain, and how a fragment of the god of chaos now lurked within her.

A month ago, gods and bargains gone awry were merely things of myth and story. But Hekla had seen too much in Istré. Now she didn't question a single word that came from her friend's mouth.

Silla's gaze had grown distant, a solemn air settling over her. "I can . . . *sense* Him inside me, and yet ever since Svangormr Pass, He only slumbers. I would hope that He's lost interest in me, but that would be too easy. And the longer He's silent, the more restless I get. I can't help but feel a sense of anticipation . . . like He is only biding His time." As Hekla's brows raised, Silla forced an overbright laugh. "I'm certain I'm reaching," she said breezily. "Besides, it is only temporary. We search for a cure, and soon, we'll find one. I can just feel it."

"Dúlla," said Hekla on a heavy breath. "That's a lot to weather."

"Yes, well, thankfully I've not had to weather it alone," Silla continued. "And while we search for a cure, we've agreed that it's best to keep the details quiet. Jarl Hakon thinks Eisa ought to solidify her place at court before adding in such . . . complications."

Hekla opened her mouth to ask why Silla referred to Eisa as though she were someone else, but decided against it.

"Which means more lies. I suppose it's only temporary. Soon Saga will come back to us and take her rightful place as queen." Silla sighed, flopping back. "Ashes, but a lot has transpired since we've last seen each other."

"Aye." Hekla's arm throbbed where no limb existed—the phantom pains that had once plagued her seemed to have returned on the ride back from Istré. Exhaustion was weaving itself into Hekla's bones, her cravings for a bath and a long nap growing.

But her gaze caught on Silla, who watched her carefully. "Hekla, there is more." Silla chewed on her lip, wrestling with something inwardly. "Something unexpectedly wonderful happened in the shield-home—"

Curiosity prickled Hekla's skin, but before Silla could continue, the door to the chambers burst open and people filed into the room.

Hekla leaped to her feet and rushed at a startled Axe Eyes, throwing her left arm around him and slapping him on the back. It seemed she was a hugger today.

"You're a sight for sore eyes," she said, drawing back. Trying to hold the Bloodaxe Crew together in Istré had been empowering, yet utterly exhausting. Hekla was glad to hand the reins back over to Axe Eyes.

"As are you." Rey's lips twitched, and he nodded at her. That singular expression was worth more than Hekla could explain—a smidge of the old amid so much new. "Istré has long been on my mind. I am sorry I could not be there with you and that things went badly. But I am glad to see you whole and hale."

Movement behind Rey caught Hekla's eye. Eyvind Hakonsson sauntered into the room, freshly bathed and dressed in a fine-spun tunic that looked far too good on him. His once-glorious black hair was now singed and smoothed back, and the burns on his sharp cheekbones reminded Hekla of how he'd risked everything to save her from the explosion in Istré's town square. An ache bloomed in her chest, and she forced her gaze away.

How could he have hidden this *Liv* from her all this time? Her anger at Eyvind's deception was a low simmer, but the anger she directed inward burned far hotter. What Hekla could not bear to tell Silla was that she and Eyvind had grown close. That she'd convinced herself that perhaps they could be more than a mere roll in the furs. Thank the gods she'd discovered his betrothal before she did something wholly humiliating.

"They've set you up in a palace!"

Gunnar strolled into the room, his locs woven into a thick braid, and his beard neatly trimmed and oiled. He greeted Hekla with an unexpected kiss to the cheek that had her reeling back, her gaze accidentally locking with Eyvind's. Those hazel eyes smoldered, a muscle in his jaw twitching, and Hekla quickly refocused her glare on Gunnar.

We have much to discuss, Gunnar's amused look seemed to say.

She opened her mouth with a sharp reply, but a group of warriors she did not recognize entered the room.

"This is Runný, Kálf, Hef, and Erik," Rey introduced. "Galdra from my hometown who're now on queensguard duty."

Hekla shook each of their hands. Gods, this was strange. Not only being surrounded by Galdra, but being in the presence of a queen—even if Silla did not think of herself as such.

Thrand, Eyvind's second in command, led Eyvind's retinue into the room and closed the door behind them. Suddenly, Hekla's chambers didn't feel quite so large.

"Right!" boomed Rey, and conversations among the twenty or so warriors died a swift death. Silla sidled up beside him, and together they waited for the other warriors to gather around. "We're here to discuss Istré. There is more to it than many of you know. I am not certain if my letters reached Istré at the end, but I'll repeat the information for all present."

A feeling of anticipation settled over the room.

"I believe—" Rey cleared his throat, and Silla slid her hand into his, squeezing gently. Hekla's brows drew together.

"*We* believe—" Rey ratified with a strange expression so near to a smile that Hekla nearly fell over.

We?

"—that Rökkur is coming. It is a thing of legend long lost. The twilight of our days."

Murmurs rippled through the room, but Hekla was too busy examining Silla and Rey's joined hands. When last she'd parted from them, they were constantly at each other's throats. Rey couldn't wait to rid himself of Silla. But then he'd gone after her when Jonas had taken her.

Something unexpectedly wonderful happened in the shield-home, Silla had said. Could it be? No. There could not be a more unlikely pairing than these two.

"Rökkur," continued Rey, "is said to begin with frost and end with fire. We believe the long winters we've suffered for the last several years fulfill the frost part of the legend. And we believe that when the Sleeping Dragons awaken, we shall have fire. Yet all that lies between is unknown."

"While we were in Kalasgarde, an enormous serpent entered our realm through a crack in the earth," Silla chimed in. "Rey's grandmother is a Weaver. A type of Galdra able to weave the threads of past, present, and future into a tapestry," she added helpfully for Hekla and the other non-Galdra in the bunch. "Harpa wove a tapestry with four images: a serpent, a dragon, a tree, and a queen."

An ominous prickle ran down Hekla's spine.

"The serpent makes sense to us," continued Silla. "And the dragon—surely that is the one called Kraugeir. He who sleeps among the slumbering fire mountains. But we wonder—could the tree refer to Istré? Harpa said that dark creatures would emerge from the *deep-rooted woods of the west.* Surely, she's referring to your job in Istré?"

"Perhaps." Goosebumps formed on Hekla's skin at the sound of Eyvind's voice. "I'm afraid we know little of the mist." She felt the touch of his gaze like a caress. "Hekla," he said thickly, "knows it best of all."

There seemed to be hidden meaning in those words—an apology, perhaps, for all that had transpired in Istré. Hekla's jaw shifted as she tried to drive such thoughts away.

After a moment, she straightened her spine and looked at Axe Eyes. "What we know of the mist can be listed on one hand." She lifted a finger on her left hand. "The mist emerges with the sound of a beating heart coming from somewhere distant in the forest." She lifted a second finger. "Any creature—beast or man alike—entrapped in the mist is Turned draugur." *Except me,* she did not say. Hekla added a third finger. "It is repelled by fire and moonlight."

"'It'?" asked one of the Kalasgardian warriors—Kálf, if Hekla recalled correctly.

A fourth finger rose. "We believe the mist is alive."

This caused a chorus of whispers to whip up among the gathered warriors. "What do you mean?" someone called out.

Hekla shivered, thinking of the way the mist had spoken to her through one of its enthralled draugur. "It is strategic and cunning. It manipulated Loftur. Convinced him he could earn Sunnvald's blessing by holding a feast on the double black moon, which proved to be a trap. The double black moon was when the mist's power was unrestrained and it could fully escape the woods."

The silence in the room was absolute. For the thousandth time since she'd begun working on this job, Hekla cursed Loftur. He'd hidden the truth from her. Had barred her from entering the forest. They could have known so much more about this enemy had she been allowed to investigate. Instead Istré had burned to the ground and now, apparently, the mist had grown stronger.

"Rey defeated the serpent, and we killed many of her hatchlings. Does that not prove that Myrkur's creatures can be vanquished?" Silla's voice was small in the large room, but it was like a sudden summer breeze, lifting the mood in an instant.

"Aye," said Rey, squeezing Silla's hand, then turning back to the group. "You've been there, Hekla, you know this thing. What do you suggest?"

Hekla met his gaze, warmth again flooding her chest—she'd forgotten what it was like to be listened to and respected. After a moment of stunned silence, she spoke. "We need more men and replenished supplies. And we need to go into those woods."

"Before," said Rey, looking from Hekla to Gunnar and Sigrún, "you did not know the true nature of what you faced. Your hands were shackled by rules and restrictions. You made the best of what you had. We shall return to Istré armed with numbers and knowledge."

The group settled on the benches surrounding the hearth, and they began to plot the details of the mission. Though the thought of returning to Istré had been demoralizing at the start of the hour, by the end, Hekla was reinvigorated. She was eager to face down this foe and vanquish it for good.

Eventually, warriors all around stood and prepared to leave. From the corner of her eye, Hekla spotted a lone figure seated at the bench. It was Silla, staring listlessly at the fire as flames danced in her glassy eyes.

"Dúlla?" Hekla's left hand clasped Silla's wrist, intending to rouse her friend from her daze. But her fingertips met ice-cold skin, and when Silla's blank eyes locked onto hers, Hekla gasped.

In that instant, she knew it was not her friend looking back at her at all, but something altogether *other*. The hairs on her neck lifted as Hekla reached back out. Tapped Silla gently.

Silla's head jolted forward, and she seemed disoriented. "Oh! The meeting has ended." She glanced around the room. "I must have fallen asleep."

Hekla observed her. "You seemed wide awake to me."

Silla's brows furrowed. "Oh, no. I'm certain I fell asleep. How embarrassing." She offered a smile, but it fell as she took in whatever was revealed on Hekla's face. "What is it, Hekla?"

"I'm not sure," Hekla answered honestly. She searched her friend's face for any hint of the presence that had lurked behind her eyes, but there was nothing to be found. Hekla shook her head. A cautious smile spread across her lips as she helped Silla to her feet. "I think," said Hekla, "I need a bath and a very long nap."

Silla yawned in agreement.

CHAPTER 4

Kovograd, Zagadka

Kassandr Rurik braced against the whip's stinging lash. Wildfire raced across his bared back, and he jerked against his leather restraints. Within him, his beast snarled and lunged, desperate to be let free. But that's what his father wanted, and Kassandr would not give him the satisfaction of losing control.

His father and half brother had gathered in the red room, a smaller, more intimate setting than the grandiose great hall, to witness this special punishment. As its name would suggest, the room was red, from the hand-painted walls to the carved, arched roof. Between the flickering light from the hearth and the dozens of candles lit about the space, the room seemed to glow. But Kassandr could think of nothing but blood.

A dais was located on the west side of the room, where his father, the high prince of Zagadka, sat with Kassandr's half brother Oleg. While the high prince watched Kassandr's whipping with stern displeasure, Oleg seemed to revel in it, drinking wine from a jeweled goblet, and snacking on grapes imported from the Southern Continent.

Avoiding his father's disapproving eyes, Kassandr focused his gaze on the three arched windows behind the man. Their frames were carved with red swirls and botanical patterns, reminding him he was back in Zagadka. Kassandr used this comfort to keep his mind from the fact that he was clad in naught but his breeches, his wrists cuffed to twin posts.

But it was impossible to forget Kresimir with the whip at the ready, pacing restlessly. The whip dragged across the floorboards, and Kassandr decided that anticipation of the next lash was a punishment all of its own.

As he gazed out the window, a russet leaf drifted by. The Autumn Crone's reign was ending, with Father Winter's stirrings felt in the timber flooring beneath Kassandr's bare feet and in the dank, chill air. Despite this, Kassandr's back was aflame. He shifted, trying to relieve some of the pressure from his wrists, but no position brought him comfort. That was the point of this, after all.

Again, Kassandr's beast yowled, urging him to burrow down within himself, away from the pain. But he couldn't go there now, not without handing control to the raging beast inside him. And that would mean they won.

"Tell me again, son, why you think yourself wiser than me?" The fury in his father's voice had been a slow-building storm throughout this ordeal, and now it neared its crescendo.

"They took Nostislav."

Kassandr's throat was so scratched from bellowing that he scarcely sounded like himself. It was maddening, this game they must play. Did his father truly think Kassandr's answers would change? No matter how many strips of flesh Kresimir's whip tore from his back, they would remain the same.

While Kassandr described Nostislav as "like a brother," the truth was far more complicated. The love Kassandr held in his heart for the man was far from brotherly. And though Nostislav had never shown any inkling of returning his affection, Kass had never given up hope that one day, that might change. But no matter how one-sided Kassandr's longings might have been, when Nostislav was taken, it hadn't been a question. Kassandr would do whatever it took to get him back.

To return from Íseldur without Nostislav was the worst sort of pain. At the very least, he had answers. Nostislav was buried in the place called Svaldrin, Magnus had told him. It was little consolation that Kassandr had torn the vile man's throat out a few minutes later. It was too easy a fate for those who'd killed Nostislav.

And yet Kassandr hadn't returned from Íseldur empty-handed. He'd returned with a chilling understanding of precisely what fate Zagadka would suffer should they remain complacent. After the time he'd spent in Íseldur, Kassandr understood—Zagadka needed allies; it needed to ready itself for the inevitable. Sooner or later, King Ivar would come for them.

But more than all that, he'd brought *her.*

The brush of air against his blazing back had Kassandr bracing against the whip's brutal onslaught. His roar of pain echoed off the red walls as his vision bloomed white. Heaving for breath, Kassandr fought back his beast as it lunged and snarled within him.

Kill, it growled. *Kill. Kill!*

"Do you know"—the high prince's voice pierced through pain's veil—"we have received a letter from Íseldur. From King Ivar himself."

His beast faltered at that, and Kassandr's brows drew together.

"He accuses us of treachery. Of playing at diplomacy while plotting his death. Did you know that, my son?" The fury in his father's voice broke free in the last few words.

"We did nothing of the sor—" Kass's breath seized in his lungs as Kresimir's whip tore across his back. The beast inside him raged, clawing at its cage. But Kassandr allowed the pain to engulf him, unwilling to grant them victory.

"We must send the girl back," came Oleg's nasal voice. Kassandr longed to sink fangs into his half brother's flesh. Of course Oleg would side with their father—he'd made no secret of just how unsuited he thought Kassandr as the heir.

It was not supposed to be like this. The throne was meant for Kass's older brother, Radomir. In truth, Kass would have abdicated were it not for Oleg, who shared his father's belief that Zagadka could remain safe by keeping to the old ways. They had no interest in modernizing, nor in gaining allies. But Oleg did not know what

Kassandr did with new, frightening certainty—there was no hiding from these Urkans. They would come, and the only question was, would the Zagadkians stand and fight, or would they flee?

"We will not send Saga back—" The whip cracked against his back, cutting through Kassandr's words as easily as his flesh. Pain screamed through him, becoming his world, and his beast shoved with increasing desperation. How much longer could he keep it at bay?

Sucking in a breath, he forced out, "We must do what is right."

"When have you ever done what is right, Kassandr?" Oleg, again, the spite so evident in his voice. "You do only what pleases you. You see a pretty thing and you take it for yourself, with no concern for the safety of your people."

Despite Oleg's words, Kassandr was unshaken in his choice. Taking Saga had been much like chasing after Nostislav—he felt down to the marrow of his bones it had been the right thing to do.

"The Urkans will come for us," Kassandr argued, bracing as his beast threw itself against his rib cage. "Who better to have by our side than the one who was raised by them? Think of the knowledge she—"

"King Ivar thinks Zagadka tried to *kill him*!" exclaimed his father, rising to his feet and beginning to pace.

"If we send the girl back," said Oleg, "we might prove our innocence. Perhaps with an extra boatload of grains; a tribute of ore and silver. Let us try for peace before we resort to violence."

The rage of his beast melded with Kassandr's own. "You are no fool, Father. The Urkans will come for us now, or they will come for our children. Better we die fighting than throw our descendants to the wolves."

Silence followed in the wake of his bold words, but Kass could sense his father's anger gathering. Even Kresimir paused in his pacing, as though readying himself for the high prince's wrathful order.

"It seems my son has not learned his lesson!" bellowed his father. "He shows no remorse for bringing danger to our doorstep. Another ten lashes, Kresimir."

Boots thudded, and Kassandr managed a single deep breath before losing himself to the whip's fury. His beast yelped and howled, snapping its jaws and gnashing its teeth. He was so lost in the pain, he could not find his way through it. The slavering beast grew louder, stronger. Tattoos pulsed and stretched out along his bare arms, and Kassandr knew he was losing the battle to his beast. But the whip suddenly stilled, leaving him disoriented.

Before he could question why Kresimir had stopped, her scent hit his nostrils, so potent it was dizzying.

Saga Volsik's Íseldurian rang through the silence. "Oh, I . . . I must have the wrong room."

Kassandr blinked, trying to claw his way back to himself.

Mine! howled his beast, ceasing its thrashing.

He was strung to a pole, his back a pulpy mass of hot agony, and Kassandr winced. She'd followed the clues he'd left for her—the mention of the red room when last they'd met; the strategically lit torches leading her straight here. Saga must have discovered her unlocked door; that her guards were not at their usual post. But he hadn't meant for her to find him like *this.*

"Excuse me," she said tremulously, and the door clicked shut.

Kassandr gritted his teeth as he tugged against his restraints. Had she left?

But the door swung open once more, determined footfalls striking the floor. "No. I—I cannot leave him like—" Saga sighed in frustration and tried again. "You must release him. Let him see a healer."

"What does she say?" asked his father in Zagadkian.

"She tells you—to release me," was Kassandr's broken reply.

His father's laughter was like knives in his skin, and Kassandr could feel Saga's apprehension. It had taken much courage for her to leave her rooms and reach this place, and now, because of Kassandr's poor planning, she'd be further distressed. His beast let out a plaintive wail. He longed to comfort her. To let her know the ruination of his back was nothing he hadn't faced many times before in his life.

"What is happening here?" Saga pressed on as Kassandr interpreted for his family. A man with ordinary hearing might think her unaffected, but he heard the racing of her heart, the quickness of her breaths.

"Deceivers must be punished," spat Oleg, "and this man's deceptions are deeper than the ocean."

"Saga Volsik," said the high prince blandly. "I have wanted to meet you for many days now."

Kass interpreted for Saga. Her breaths were shallowing, and though he could not see her, Kass could hear the gentle tapping of her fingers against her palms. Inwardly, he smiled, glad to have taught her this useful trick. "I cannot—" Saga protested, and she made to leave again.

Kassandr's heart gave a heavy lurch, but his keen hearing picked up on the moment she paused in the doorway with a breath of resignation. "I will meet with you once he's freed."

"You are not in a position to argue, girl," warned his father after Kassandr interpreted.

Protect, hissed his beast, now reduced to a needy, restless creature.

Kassandr had ordered Rov to follow Saga, and knew his friend would be lurking beyond the doorway, yet he did not like the thought of Saga facing his father and Oleg alone. He yanked against his restraints, the iron rings clanking in the quiet room.

The silence stretched on, and he prayed to all the seasonal gods that she found that fire she'd shown Kassandr on so many occasions. As the high prince let out a long-suffering sigh, Kass's smile spread. His Saga was so brave. So fierce. She'd needed no prayers from him.

"Release my son," ordered the high prince.

Kresimir scowled as he freed Kassandr's hands from the leather restraints, no doubt irritated he'd been robbed of the pleasure of drawing out the beast. Kass's knees buckled, and he landed hard on all fours, hair falling over his sweat-slicked brow. After several deep breaths, he pushed to his feet, then limped to a wooden bench set before the dais.

Perched in the seat to his father's right, Saga Volsik was clearly uneasy. Her fingertips tapped furiously, her complexion wan. This . . .

was not ideal. A moment of doubt struck Kassandr. Had he pushed too much, too soon? But time was a luxury he did not have. And as Saga's eyes met his, her uncertainty quickly morphed into a scowl. Good. There were the embers of her fire.

Her gaze drifted to his father, and Kassandr tried to see him through her eyes. With his impressive height and broad shoulders, the high prince still cut an imposing figure. But his once-dark hair was now shaggy and gray, and he increasingly relied on his walking staff. To Kassandr's dismay, the lines around his father's eyes were deeper than before he'd stowed away on that Íseldur-bound ship.

Oleg had their father's dark hair and green eyes, but lacked his height. Instead, he took after his mother's shorter, more stocky line. Oleg wasted no time in calling for an Íseldurian interpreter, lest Kassandr mistranslate anything Saga said. The pulse at the base of Saga's throat told Kass she was deeply uncomfortable, yet thankfully currently not in the grips of her panic. He wished he'd been better able to prepare her for this moment—because what he needed right now was Saga Volsik, rightful queen of Íseldur.

The moment Oleg's ruddy-faced interpreter entered the room, the high prince wasted no time in addressing Saga. He pulled a piece of parchment from his jacket and unfolded it carefully. "The Urkans think we joined your attempt to murder King Ivar," he said in a deceptively calm voice. Perhaps he, too, had noticed Saga's nerves—the way she flinched when the interpreter's words reached her ears. "They have ordered we send you to them. Tell me, what do you think of this?"

"It was not my intention," his Saga replied stonily. "I-I am sorry it looks that way." She shot an icy glare at Kassandr.

"I won't apologize for bringing you to safety," Kassandr told her in Íseldurian, ignoring his father's scowl as his words were interpreted. "But Winterwing, I need you to tell him what Ivar will do."

Saga's pulse thrummed faster, her fingers resuming their taps. "I f-fear that is bad news, Sire. If Ivar believes you tried to kill him—" She swallowed, her gaze darting to Kass then quickly away. "—the Urkans will be honor-bound to seek revenge."

Kassandr's chest warmed as the interpreter conveyed this in Zagadkian. This was what his father needed to hear. Zagadka needed to ready themselves for war.

"Father," said Oleg, eyeing Saga with clear disdain. "How do we trust in her words? She is a stranger."

Kassandr's beast opened one eye and growled as Saga's shoulders tensed. He wished to shelter her—wished she need not expose herself like this—but she *must* understand what was at stake.

Saga met Oleg's gaze, resigned. "Your fate was sealed the moment you stole me," she replied. "Though I know Zagadka played no part in the explosion, if Ivar believes it, he will come for you."

Oleg pushed to his feet, taking a threatening step forward. "*We* did not steal you." He gestured at Kass. "It was this fool of a man who does not think with his head!"

As Saga recoiled, Kassandr's beast grew lethally quiet.

"Perhaps we should not return her to Íseldur!" Oleg shouted, spittle flying from his mouth. "Perhaps we should enact justice on King Ivar's behalf! String her from the walls! When the Urkans come, they will see where we stand. A tribute in grains and silver will appease them. Keep peace in our lands."

If Kassandr hadn't just spent two hours using all of his will to hold his beast at bay, perhaps he'd have been able to prevent what happened next.

Oleg took another step nearer to Saga, and Kassandr's beast erupted with pure primal rage that caught him by surprise. Tattoos struck forth, claws bursting from his knuckles. Sharp spines broke the skin along his back. The beast took hold of Kassandr, and he lost himself to the frenzy.

As Kassandr lunged at Oleg, Saga leaped to her feet with a scream that only heightened his beast's anger. In an instant, Oleg shifted into his gray lupine form, absorbing his brother's bulk and rolling them across the dais. His father shot to his feet, shouting in anger, but it was all in vain. Oleg would have her killed, would string her from the walls. Dodging a powerful lashing paw, Kass buried his fangs in his brother's shoulder. Oleg howled and the taste of copper flooded Kass's mouth.

Kill, snarled his beast, jaw clamping harder as he shook the wolf. *Protect. Kill!*

Claws raked across Kass's chest, but the pain was nothing compared with the ever-present burn of his back. Kass and Oleg raged on, rolling across the floor. Kass heard his father's furious bellow, but it was so distant from the need to destroy Oleg.

Time grew slippery when Kass was in a frenzy, but at some point, Kresimir produced the snare. It wrapped around his throat and tightened until he could not breathe. Kresimir yanked on the pole, heaving Kass away from Oleg. Incensed, his beast lunged against the snare, jaws snapping. He needed to finish what he'd started. Needed to show Oleg he could not touch her.

"Enough!" bellowed the high prince, but there was a distinct note of victory in his voice.

Immediately, Kassandr was filled with the shame of having lost control, before Saga, of all people. His gaze roamed, finding her backed into the darkest corner of the red room, eyes wide and fingers tapping furiously.

You've frightened her, he thought in despair.

His beast whimpered, ceasing its fight at once. Slowly, Kass's humanity grew stronger, at last seizing control from the creature. With a shudder, he shifted back into human form, uncaring that his breeches were torn and barely hanging from him.

"You think with the wrong body part, brother," Oleg growled, his eyes yellow with the remnants of his wolf form. "And your actions will doom us."

Kass swallowed against the snare's sharp bite at his throat.

"Kassandr," snapped his father, displaying his full, towering height. "Your actions have dishonored me. Oleg is right—you have brought danger to the kingdom. You will go to the golden oak and make an offering to the four gods."

Panic filled Kassandr's chest. The golden oak was three days' travel each way. In any other circumstance, he would not argue against his father's decree, but this meant leaving Saga in Kovograd.

"But, Father—"

The high prince held up a hand and turned to Saga. Kassandr was glad to see she'd emerged from the shadows, that the pulse in her throat had calmed ever so slightly. Still, he did not like the fear in her eyes as she glanced his way. Today had gone all wrong, and Kassandr knew he was to blame. He'd pushed her too hard. Had lost control, and in doing so, had only fed her fears.

"You, Lady Saga," his father was saying, "will write a letter to King Ivar, accepting full responsibility for the attempt on his life. And you will assure him Zagadka played no part in it."

Kassandr's heart felt heavy as iron as the interpreter relayed his father's words to Saga. He tried to find solace in the fact that the high prince had not agreed with all of Oleg's plan, yet he could not help his disappointment that Saga had not convinced his father to raise arms.

Saga could not hold the high prince's gaze as she answered in Íseldurian. "I will do it. But I ask you, Sire—no—" Her voice wavered, and she shook her head. "—I *beg* of you. Please, I must return to Íseldur. My sister is in danger. I must help her."

"After you write the letter," said the high prince, "we will discuss it." And with that, the high prince strode from the room. As he watched his father leave, Kassandr's chest grew tight with worry. He could not bring Saga with him to the golden oak—not with her struggles with the outdoors. But how could he leave her in Kovograd?

As though summoned by Kass's thoughts, his half brother laid a hand on his shoulder.

Kass glared into those yellow-tinged eyes.

"Do not worry, brother," said Oleg. "I will look out for the Lady Saga in your absence."

CHAPTER 5

Kopa, Íseldur

Rey stared across Ashfall's sparring grounds as he leaned against the armory building. The chill wind scraped across his cheeks, carrying the promise of more snow. It had been a constant thing in recent weeks, making him feel as though winter had lasted an eternity, when in truth they'd yet to celebrate the Shortest Day. Not that he'd be in Kopa to join in the celebrations, given they'd depart for Istré tomorrow.

The very thought of it caused unease to burn in his gut. For so long, he'd been certain of his place in this world, and had been content to be a weapon in the Uppreisna's arsenal. But everything had changed in Kalasgarde. *Frightened together,* they'd vowed. How did they do this together, when Rey was being pulled to Istré, and Eisa Volsik was needed in Kopa?

Pushing such thoughts aside, Rey adjusted the wolf's pelt wrapped around his shoulders, gaze drifting to where Hekla and Silla stood at the edge of the sparring grounds. The tightness in his chest eased as he laid eyes on Silla. Each time he saw her, it was like finding a coveted belonging he'd lost a long time ago. Like his head was in the clouds, but his feet were on the ground. How unsettling it was that a person could have such an effect on him.

Today, determined to embody Eisa Volsik, Silla had opted for a thick, fur-trimmed cloak over heavy woolen skirts, her hair artfully styled into complicated braids. But he saw the envious way she now eyed Hekla's lébrynja armor and wondered if she regretted her choice.

Hekla handed Silla her wool-wrapped blade, and Rey watched in amusement as Silla moved through the attack routines he'd taught her under the shadow of Kalasgarde's mountains. Her skirts inevitably grew tangled, and she grumbled as she righted herself. Her exasperated expression tugged at his heartstrings, but he ought to have seen it as a warning. It wasn't until she turned on her heel and stormed around a stack of hay bales that Rey knew she was up to something. He was halfway across the yard, ready to chastise her for leaving his field of view, when she reappeared with the elegant furred cloak draped over—her own set of lébrynja armor. His feet faltered and he rubbed his chest in relief.

Rey shook his head at himself. He was a gods damned fool for this woman. But as he studied her newly donned armor, he soon grew perplexed. Had she worn it under her gown? Hekla hooted in delight and pulled Silla close, the pair conversing in low tones.

Reluctantly, Rey returned to his post by the armory building. He tried to ease the jagged beat of his heart. But when it came to Silla, he was always on alert; always watching for danger. How could he not be, when she'd been hunted so relentlessly? All it would take was one misplaced blade; one sly arrow.

Silla reclaimed the wool-wrapped blade, and Rey watched as she worked through the routine once more. Seeing her clad in her lébrynja made Rey's blood heat. It was impossible to forget their morning sparring sessions in Kalasgarde. His body certainly remembered the feel of hers as he'd adjusted her hips and the grip on her sword.

Silla's movements were fluid, the wool-wrapped blade arcing through the air with confidence, and pride bloomed inside his chest. She was strong—capable of defending herself. He had to trust in Silla and in himself for teaching her to the best of his abilities.

He forced his gaze elsewhere, lip curling when it landed on Atli Hakonsson sparring with his retinue. The burn in his stomach had him quickly moving on until he found a black-clad Sigrún facing off against Runný.

Earlier in the day, Sigrún had approached Rey and apologized in handspeak for her "shameful failures" in Istré. As Rey blinked, dumbfounded, Sigrún had explained that old fears had gotten the best of her, but she would not let it happen again. She'd stroked the scarred flesh on her cheek, and Rey tried to put the details together. Istré had gone up in flames, and Sigrun's marks looked an awful lot like burn scars. The petite woman had never spoken of her injuries, and Rey had never asked. But now he felt the need to put her at ease.

"You need not apologize, Sigrún," he'd replied, signing as he spoke. "But if ever you have worries you wish to speak of, you can confide in me."

She'd sent him a strange look, and Rey realized it was entirely out of character for him. A month ago, Axe Eyes would have simply grunted. It seemed Kalasgarde had softened some of his rough edges. He'd been shown that kindness was not weakness, and that speaking of old wounds could be healing. He still wasn't sure how he felt about this. And as Sigrún peered curiously up at him, the old urge to keep people at arm's length kicked in. "What I mean—that is to say—" Rey cleared his throat. "You can tell *Silla.*"

Sigrún pursed her lips, glancing in Silla's direction. Then she'd smiled, knowingly. *You're a far better match,* Sigrún signed, before striding off and leaving Rey feeling out of sorts.

Movement in his periphery alerted him to Eyvind's presence, and he turned to greet his old friend with a handshake and a slap to the back.

"Well met, old friend," Eyvind drawled with a smile.

Clad in Hakonsson red, Eyvind had been busy mustering more warriors to join them on the trip to Istré, and Rey had not seen much of him in the past days. Eyvind's wavy black hair had once fallen around his shoulders. Now it was cut short to tidy the disorderly singed ends acquired in Istré. Yet Eyvind, who had been known to preen over his mane, seemed utterly unbothered.

He slumped against the wall with a long sigh, a small smile playing on his lips. Rey followed his friend's line of view to where Hekla and Silla sparred, and his brows shot down at once.

"Good to be back, even if only for a few nights," mused Eyvind, his gaze never leaving the women.

Rey grunted. "I must thank you for stepping up . . . for leading my Crew when I could not."

Hekla twisted behind Silla, sweeping her feet out and taking her down. With a cackle of glee, Hekla pinned Silla to the ground and straddled her hips. Rey made the mistake of glancing Eyvind's way. His old friend had never been good at concealing his emotions, and right now, Eyvind's eyes were filled with hunger.

"She's spoken for," Rey grumbled, stepping between Eyvind and the sparring women.

Eyvind's hazel eyes met Rey's in disbelief, followed swiftly by anger. "She said nothing of the sort to me."

Rey's heart lurched. "What?"

"She told me that she does not form attachments. And I don't think she'd appreciate you, as you say, *speaking for her*."

Rey was momentarily stunned by the hardness of Eyvind's voice. Then his mind raced with questions—when had Silla and Eyvind become acquainted, and why would she tell him such things? Rey retraced this morning's daymeal. He'd arrived late to find Eyvind jostling with Gunnar for a spot beside Hekla—

He stared back at the sparring women, and at last he understood. Rey huffed in amusement. "Is there something you need to tell me, Fire Breath? Did something transpire between you and a certain clawed warrior?"

Eyvind glanced at the sparring women and seemed to comprehend. A mischievous smile curved his lips. "Perhaps. And is there something you need to tell me about Kalasgarde, Soot Fingers?"

Rey shrugged. "She was cold."

"Cold?"

"Aye." Rey folded his arms over his chest, resuming his position against the armory's wall. "I . . . warmed her up."

Eyvind watched him with utter delight.

"And you, Fire Breath?" Rey bit out. "I sense there's a story?"

As Eyvind's eyes drifted back to Hekla, they seemed to soften. "A beautiful woman who can knock me on my arse and is not afraid to speak her mind? What's not to like?" But there was something buried behind his words . . . something almost like bitterness.

Rey looked between Eyvind and Hekla, then shook his head in disbelief. Never would he think they would be a pair well matched. Then again, Rey would never have guessed he and a woman like Silla would be, either.

"I'm glad for you, friend," he said, clapping Eyvind's shoulder.

But Eyvind drew away with a glower. "Don't be. I ruined it before it could start." He sighed. "I didn't think to tell her of Liv, because, well—"

It took Rey a moment to recall that Liv was the name of Eyvind's betrothed. "Isn't she—"

"Aye."

"It sounds," said Rey cautiously, "as though a conversation is in order."

Eyvind kicked a stone. "Hekla won't speak to me. Won't give me a chance to explain."

Rey considered this. "Perhaps you can win her favor back. Might I suggest baby chicks?"

"Chicks . . . as in *chickens*?"

"Aye." Rey opened his mouth to elaborate, but a flash of raven-black hair diverted his attention. He felt his *axe eyes* settling into place, his moods souring in an instant as a familiar tall woman sauntered across the yard.

Eyvind huffed a breath. "Question for you, Galtung. Did you tell Kaeja about your new . . . attachment?"

Rey's gaze found Atli, then darted quickly back to Kaeja. Black hair swept into a long braid; her lithe frame was encased in lébrynja armor. "I haven't spoken a word to her since I carved her from my life."

As a rule, Rey thought of Kaeja as little as was possible, and if you'd asked him an hour ago, he'd have said she had no effect on him. But seeing the woman he'd once thought would be his wife brought a rush of unwelcome emotions to Rey. His skin felt itchy, his stomach knotting tight. Was it his imagination, or were heads bowing together, eyes darting his way?

He breathed deeply, trying to shake the unsettled feeling gaining strength inside him, but it was to no avail. Suddenly Rey couldn't wait to leave this place and its gossip behind. Couldn't wait to get back on the road. To get normalcy back in his life.

But as Kaeja marched toward Silla with concerning determination, his discomfort shifted to worry. Silla turned and greeted Kaeja with a pleasant smile, and Rey scrubbed a hand down his face. He should go over there, yet his feet were not eager to move.

"Coward," murmured Eyvind, evidently reading Rey's expression.

Silla and Kaeja clasped hands, then chatted animatedly. Inwardly, Rey cursed. A better man would go over there. A better man would have warned Silla of Kaeja.

Rey folded, then unfolded, his arms. "What in the eternal fucking fires do they have to talk about?"

But the women parted, and Silla drew her wool-wrapped sword with a determined smile. Rey could only groan.

"It appears they intend to spar," said Eyvind brightly. "This shall be entertaining."

His traitorous friend pushed off the wall and joined the other warriors crowding around the pair. A hush had fallen over the sparring grounds, warriors gathering around the women. As Rey caught his name on a whisper, a sharp breath hissed through his teeth. Reluctantly, he made his way closer.

Kaeja removed her cloak and began wrapping her weapon in raw wool, though this did little to temper Rey's nerves. The blades might be protected for practice, but that did not mean injury could not be had. The worry in Rey's gut only tightened when Kaeja found him in the crowd and smiled. It was a smile he'd once fallen for, a smile he now knew held a thousand hidden knives.

When weeks had passed in Ashfall without sight of his former flame, Rey had foolishly thought Kaeja had found another court to haunt. Of course he was not so lucky as that. And now he cursed himself for not warning Silla about her. Because if there was one thing Rey knew about Kaeja, it was that she would cheat.

The muffled clang of steel signaled the start of their sparring match. Too late, Rey thought, as he pushed closer. Their match started amicably enough—the women trading blows with little force behind them. But when Silla's blunt blade struck Kaeja's hip, she retaliated with a rough shove to the chest. Silla stumbled, regaining her balance barely in time to parry Kaeja's incoming blow. Their blades cracked together, and Silla blinked at the power Kaeja had thrown into it.

"Keep it friendly!" warned Hekla.

But Kaeja didn't have a friendly bone in her body. Taking advantage of Silla's confusion, Kaeja rained blow after blow upon her. On the defensive, Silla was forced backward, bobbing and ducking the ever-quickening slashes of Kaeja's blade. Her boot got tangled in her long cloak, and she stumbled onto her backside, Kaeja's blunted blade pressing into the hollow of her throat. Silla glared up at her opponent.

As the whispers whipped back up in the crowd, Rey clapped his hands to rally Silla.

"Remember what we practiced!"

Silla shoved to her feet, determination blazing in her eyes. "Again," she demanded, unhooking the golden pin securing her cloak in place.

Rey's chest filled with pride, an illogical thought settling in his mind. If Silla could beat Kaeja, it would give the gossipmongers in Kopa something to truly talk about. Perhaps it would show them who had come out the better from their parting. It was a petty thought, one he was not proud of. But Rey focused on Silla with new eagerness.

After shrugging out of the fine garment, Silla returned to the center of the circle and squared her shoulders.

Kaeja smirked, joining her. "Perhaps we are not as suited in the ring as I believed."

Silla pushed a wayward curl from her forehead, taking the attack stance Rey had drilled into her. "Again."

"As you wish." Kaeja shrugged.

They had barely begun circling each other when Silla launched a quick attack. She was far from the girl who could barely hold a blade a few months past, yet Silla was not privy to Kaeja's secret skill. After parrying a blow, Kaeja burst with galdur-fueled Harefoot speed and twisted behind Silla. With a brutal kick to the back of her legs, Silla went sprawling, her blade skittering out of reach.

Kaeja put a foot on Silla's spine, her blade poised at the back of her neck.

"Yield," ordered Kaeja.

A growl built low in Rey's throat, but he could not let it loose. If he stepped in, it would not only bring dishonor upon Silla, but would further spur the whispers. He saw the determination in her eyes, and his chest inflated with pride. Kaeja had thrown the gauntlet, and Silla would want to see this through now more than ever.

"Again," snarled Silla. As Kaeja blinked in surprise, Rey's lips curved up in a savage smile. Kaeja might know her way around the sparring ring, but his girl knew how to get back up.

Hekla shouted her encouragement, the crowd joining in.

"You don't know when to quit, do you?" muttered Kaeja, offering a hand up.

Silla sent her a sweet smile. "I *don't quit.*"

Rey's heart sang at this proclamation, and he watched with eagerness, ready for Kaeja to learn the lesson he had long ago—that Silla was *not* to be underestimated.

Angered, Kaeja yanked Silla up with excessive force, sending her stumbling. The moment she regained her balance, Silla whirled on Kaeja, who'd lunged at her with Harefoot speed. Silla's blunted sword parried blow after blow, dodging and twisting away from Kaeja's brutal onslaught. But her regular speed was no match for that of a Harefoot, and she did not even see the kick that swept her feet out from beneath her. Silla landed hard on her back, eyes widening as she fought for breath. But Kaeja was on top of her, her forearm shoving into her neck as she pinned her to the ground.

Rey's chest squeezed tight, his feet moving without thought. He stumbled into the circle just in time to hear Kaeja's low voice. "You don't know him like I do. You will never replace me."

Shock rippled through him as her words settled in place. Hábrók's hairy bollocks, had Kaeja taken a blow to the head? He was so dumbfounded that he could not form words.

But Silla, it seemed, had words for the both of them. She leveled a fierce glare at Kaeja. "Explain to me why I do not even know your name. Could it be because you mean so little to him?"

Any other woman might have let Kaeja seed doubts in her mind. But not his girl. She knew him. *Trusted* him.

Kaeja screamed in rage. Drew her fist back with full Harefoot speed. Then slammed it forward, right into the packed earth.

But Silla was not there. In a flash of movement too quick for Rey to see, Silla had rolled free and lunged at Kaeja, knocking her to the ground. Silla triumphantly placed a boot on Kaeja's back.

"Yield," ordered Silla.

Rey was filled with petty glee at seeing Kaeja bested, but he shoved it aside to make room for his pure, blinding pride. He felt light as air. Watching Silla take this victory felt better than any *he'd* ever achieved. The crowd erupted in cheers, and Rey grinned like a fool, even as he replayed the event in his mind. How had Silla bested a Harefoot in speed? It made no sense. But at this moment, with Silla looking at him with fire in her eyes, Rey didn't care. She stepped away from Kaeja and strode toward him. Silla paused before him, lifting onto the tips of her toes. And then, before the whole yard of warriors, she slid her lips against Rey's.

It was an obvious statement of ownership.

And Rey had never been so turned on in his gods damned life.

"But—" sputtered Kaeja. Now sitting, she stared at her palms.

"How did you—" Her crystalline blue eyes bored into Silla, and she pushed to her feet before striding toward her. "I know what you really are," she said in a voice too low for anyone but Silla and Rey to hear. "You're nothing but a filthy little *thief*."

And with that, Kaeja stormed from the sparring yards.

CHAPTER 6

The moment Silla kicked the door to her bedchambers closed, Rey's lips crashed down on hers. Anger and jealousy and raw lust churned through her veins, and Silla tugged at Rey's thick curls as she urged him on. They collided with the wall and sent a tapestry tumbling to the floor. Silla pulled back with a laugh, but Rey's lips quickly recaptured hers. His mouth was soft, but his kiss was hard and domineering.

And Silla understood that the morning spent sparring had been the most torturous form of foreplay for Rey as well. With Rey's eyes on her the entire time, it had been impossible to forget their morning routine in Kalasgarde—those large hands landing on her hips, tilting them just so; the press of his warm chest against her back as he'd restrained her lightly. She'd thrown herself into her practice, but her body had only grown tighter with need.

Now those hands landed possessively on her hips as Rey walked her backward. Her legs hit the bed, and Silla was falling, pulling Rey down with her. Though he braced himself carefully on his forearms, the sheer weight of him pressing her into the feather mattress was utterly delicious. But it also made her acutely aware of just how many layers of clothing separated them.

Silla fumbled with the fastenings of Rey's lébrynja armor, desperate to feel his bare skin against hers. Anger from the sparring grounds lingered in her bones, exacerbated by thoughts of that *woman* who'd not only tried to humiliate her, but also clearly marked herself as Rey's past lover. The very thought of the woman's hands on him made Silla's anger flare hotter. Well. The woman hadn't gotten the best of her in the sparring yard, and she certainly wouldn't get the best of her in the bedchamber.

Hooking her leg around Rey's hip, Silla took advantage of his surprise, heaving them both to the side. She twisted on top of him, then settled on his hips. Gods, he was hard as stone beneath her. Rolling against him, she tried to satisfy her cravings, but it wasn't enough. Her heart pumped at an alarming rate as she shimmied down his thighs and tugged at his breeches.

"*Silla*." Rey's voice was a living thing, skimming along her skin but catching on every notch of her spine.

Silla raked her curls over one shoulder, looking deep into Rey's eyes as she pulled him out, hot and firm and wholly enticing. "Did you enjoy it?" she asked, stroking him slowly. "Watching me spar?"

Rey's hips gave an involuntary jerk. "Gods above, woman," he growled, sounding half pained.

Silla's lips curved into a smile. She did not know what Rey's history was with that woman, but she did know she'd make him forget her.

"I think you did."

Lowering her head, Silla licked the tip of him and felt Rey's low groan all the way to her toes. A whimper escaped her, but she tried to cover it by taking him as deep as she could. Her eyes watered, but the flex of his hips only encouraged her. Silla began to move, noting the strain of his stomach muscles, the smoldering intensity of his gaze. His eyes fell shut on a curse, and inwardly she smiled.

"Silla," hissed Rey, his fingers threading into her curls and pulling her up. "Wait."

Silla wiped her mouth on the back of her hand, scowling at him. "I don't want to wait."

His passion-glazed eyes seemed to darken further. "Ever impatient." Sitting up, Rey cupped her jaw, one thumb caressing her cheek. But Silla turned her head, capturing his thumb with a gentle suck. "Gods, woman. I won't last if you keep this up."

Having control over such a large, powerful warrior sent warmth unfurling low in her belly. Releasing his thumb, Silla leaned downward, but Rey moved with preternatural speed. Before Silla knew what had happened, she'd been flipped onto her back, Rey looming over her. Scowling, she reached for the length of him, but he caught her wrist and pinned it above her head.

"Trouble," he muttered, forcing her other arm up and securing both wrists with one hand.

For a long, measured breath, he stared down at her reverently. Then, Rey slowly worked his breeches off before reaching for his tunic. As he shifted hands on her wrists to pull the garment over his head, Silla's legs hooked around his hips, and she shoved against the weight of him. She rolled him easily—too easily. And when she tried to clamber atop him, she cried out in surprise as momentum kept them rolling. Rey landed atop her, a victorious look in his eyes.

"Are you trying to spar with me, Silla?"

She was too distracted by the expanse of tattooed skin above her to answer. Inky-black scales against warm, brown skin. A barbed tail twisting down one arm, a burst of flames twisting down the other . . .

As the scent of smoke met Silla's nostrils, she blinked out of her stupor. Rey had expressed a thin ribbon of smoke and was now looping it around her wrists.

"What—" Before she could finish the thought, the smoke tightened, pinning her hands on either side of her head. A shiver rolled through her at the feel of the smoke—hot and prickly, yet not to the point of discomfort.

Rey sat back, both hands now freed. The man was beyond pleased with himself. "Better."

"Unfair," complained Silla, writhing against her smoky binds. "You know I cannot use my own galdur!"

But Rey was unfazed. He reached for her lébrynja jacket and unfastened it with excruciating slowness before pulling it free around her restraints. Rey repeated the move with her undertunic, her boots, her breeches. When at last Silla was bare, Rey's gaze raked over her form.

"Do you enjoy it," he rasped, a large, warm hand sliding up her rib cage, "when I tease you?"

"No!"

But he only chuckled. "Liar."

"*Your* liar," she breathed.

"My liar," Rey agreed, and then his mouth was back on hers.

This kiss was slow and deep, so decadent it made Silla's head spin. Callused fingertips scraped along the curve of her hip, the flat of her stomach, then lower. As they slid through her center, Silla knew he would find her ready. Gods, she'd been craving this for hours now; she was half wild with need.

He dipped two fingers in, working rhythmically until she writhed beneath him. Her muscles flexed as she tried to urge him faster, harder, but Rey's smoke held her firm. With slow, languorous movements, he stoked her need higher, deeper, until she was desperate to reach that pinnacle and break apart.

But Rey drew back. Withdrew his fingers. And as he slid down her body, Silla had a moment of apprehension.

"Rey, I was just sparring," she protested.

"I know," whispered Rey, throwing her leg over his shoulder.

"But I *sweated.*" She whispered the last word in warning.

"I *know.*" Rey's eyes were fever-bright as he looked up at her. "Please," he rasped, reaching down to adjust himself. Was he . . . aroused by this?

"Oh, very well—I—oh!" Silla gasped as his tongue slid through her, and all her inhibitions burned to ash. There was only feeling. Only the scrape of his beard and his coarse curls against the sensitive skin of her inner thighs. Only the thrust of his fingers, the delicate touch of his tongue. Her feet pushed down against his back, trying to urge him closer, trying to get the pressure just right . . .

"More," she begged, tugging against her binds to no avail. The realization that she was at his mercy—that she gladly relinquished complete trust and control to him—only made her pleasure coil tighter.

"Patience," he rasped, yet his voice betrayed a hint of his own impatience. And as Rey reached down to adjust himself once more, Silla knew she was not alone in her frustration.

Rey pulled the tenderest part of her into his mouth with a gentle suck, and Silla bowed off the bed with a cry.

"Yes!" she urged him on, her heels digging into the thick muscles of his back. "Please!"

And finally, the man obliged. A curl of his fingers. A twist of his tongue. Another gentle suck, and it was enough. The tension inside her broke free, her pleasure a living thing thrashing ferociously through her. On it went, Rey's merciless fingers never letting up. Silla spasmed and clenched until it had run its course. Then she lay panting, clutching her hands to her forehead as she stared up at Rey.

His brows were drawn. "How did you do that?"

"Do what?"

"Free yourself—"

Silla blinked, then stared at her freed wrists. "I don't know. Did you not free them?"

He shook his head slowly. But Silla was quickly distracted by the sight of his unfulfilled desire.

"Need—" she whispered, freed hands reaching for him.

Every muscle in Rey's body seemed rigid as he took himself in hand and pumped. And not for the first time, she thought he looked much like a malevolent god. Slowly, Rey pushed into her. Silla clasped his arms as her body gradually accepted him. The room was quiet save for the sounds of their mingling breaths as Rey worked himself in with deliberate, insistent thrusts. As he reached the deepest part of her, Silla's body clenched around him, and they stared at each other.

But neither could bear to exist in such a state for long, and when

Silla, ever impatient, wriggled against him, Rey began to move. As he found a rhythm, her pleasure quickly spiraled anew, tightening with each increasingly erratic thrust of his hips.

"You drive me mad, woman," he muttered, and Silla wasn't sure if it was praise or a complaint. "Did you enjoy kissing me in front of all those warriors?"

"Y-yes."

Rey's eyes flared wide at her response, his hips surging forward with yet more speed.

"I wanted them to know—" Silla gasped as he again reached the deepest part of her.

His hand slid behind her nape, drawing her gaze back to his. "Tell me."

"You're mine."

Rey's low groan was all it took—pleasure crashed over Silla with violent intensity. Tremors burst through her, her spine arching off the bed. Her fingers grew bloodless with the force of her grip on Rey's arms, and he pumped into her with a crazed desire she'd not yet seen. Silla could not find her voice, could only gasp, could only hold on through wave after wave of sharp, brutal pleasure that darkened her vision.

Rey made a throaty sound as he found his own pleasure, but he seemed distant—as though Silla were underwater and he was above. Wrung out, Silla's mind was a hazy, drifting thing. Wings ruffled gently within, a low deep purr that softened her further.

"Silla."

But it wasn't a purr, it was a low, deep snarl. It was talons sinking into the mind of an old, weak king. It was weathered fingers wrapping around a white-hilted dagger. It was a blade, tearing into the flesh of the young, but not *deep* enough . . .

"Silla!"

Her eyes flew open to Rey hovering over her. Sweat slicked his brow, and his tattooed chest heaved with his exertion, but his eyes were filled with concern.

"Where did you go?" he asked, smoothing a tendril of hair from her forehead.

"I'm right here." Was she? Her heart and mind raced as she tried to shake off the echoes of the dream—had that been a dream?

Rey collapsed onto the bed, then rolled to face her, fingertips skimming along her cheek. "Are you certain?" he prodded, studying her face. "For a moment, I thought Myrkur—"

"He's not there," she assured him, sliding a fingertip along the tattooed dragon's taloned wing. Inwardly, she probed for the god, trying to detect any hint of His presence. But as He had for weeks on end, the god of chaos remained curiously silent.

"Good," Rey replied, though the line between his brows lingered.

They stayed like this for some time, naked and content and enshrouded in silence. Silla hadn't fully appreciated the solitude of Kalasgarde—the peace and simplicity of it all. And she hadn't anticipated that in Kopa, they'd each have duties keeping them apart. Rey's day was filled with meetings with the Uppreisna chieftains as they scrambled to salvage his careful integration into Magnus Hansson's network. Silla, meanwhile, had gown fittings and tutoring sessions on top of her daily etiquette lessons with Jarl Hakon's friend and confidante, Lady Tala.

And then there were the meetings she had with Jarl Hakon and his advisers. There were endless discussions on how best to capitalize on the sudden reappearance of Eisa Volsik. There was talk of raising banners for the Volsiks once more; talk of marching south and driving the Urkans from the kingdom.

Silla found herself disagreeing from time to time. She wanted to ask of their plans for the people of the north in the face of the poisonous mist and a grain shortage. And yet she was only a placeholder for Saga. The truth was, Silla didn't want to get too invested in the affairs of ruling. Aside from the fact that she was completely unsuited, getting too involved would only make it more difficult to let go when her sister arrived.

But she hadn't been able to refrain from asking Jarl Hakon what course of action he'd take regarding Rökkur.

"One thing at a time," Jarl Hakon had reassured her.

Though Silla and Rey had told Jarl Hakon everything they knew about Rökkur, it was clear he was not fully convinced. Silla didn't blame Jarl Hakon. Violence on his eastern border; the Urkan enemy in the south—these were tangible things. Problems to be solved with solid solutions. The twilight of days was too big, too murky, simply too *much* to consider all at once.

After countless meetings, Silla, Rey, and Jarl Hakon had agreed their priority was to unify the north. Silla would play the role of Eisa Volsik, and when the jarls arrived for the feast of the Shortest Day, she would be formally presented to the most powerful leaders in the north. Then Eisa would meet with the jarls and convince them to raise their banners for her sister.

Jarl Hakon thought that Rökkur and the bargain living inside Silla ought not to be mentioned. Once the jarls were won over, then they would tackle these more challenging topics. Though her insides rebelled at keeping such details hidden, she could see the merit of this plan. And so, for the time being, Silla's goal was to mold herself into the kind of leader the hardened jarls of the north would follow.

But news of Istré had knocked her plans astray. Silla wanted to go to the Western Woods—wanted to fight with her friends. And yet she knew that was not Eisa's fate. Silla knew without a doubt that Rey was aware of this. Was certain he, too, had been avoiding this topic.

She released a weary exhale and forced the words out. "I cannot go to Istré."

"I know." Rey twined her curls between his fingers. "Your work with the northern alliance is too important. And you must continue your search for a cure for Myrkur's bargain."

Silla smoothed a finger between his brows. "And your place is in Istré. I know this job has haunted you. Know you must see it through."

Rey nipped at her finger. "It is only for a time."

She nodded. All of this was temporary. Rey's job in Istré. Silla's job as queen.

His rough palm slid up her spine, and Rey pulled her to him. Closing her eyes, Silla drew in deep pulls of his scent; counted his heartbeats.

"The Kalasgardians will stay as your queensguard," Rey said into her hair. "Keep them by your side no matter what."

Silla nodded as tears burned her eyes. "I'll miss you."

"And I you." His lips found hers, so soft and lush, but he drew back suddenly. "I have something for you." Rey rolled off the bed, and as he crossed the room, she stared unabashedly. He turned and caught her looking, his eyes darkening as he sauntered back to her. Silla was so distracted, she scarcely noticed what he'd handed her.

"Keep this on you at all times." He paused. "And be careful who you trust here."

Trying to blink the lust from her gaze, she stared at the item. An ivory hilt protruded from a supple leather sheath attached to a strap that looked far too small to fit her hips. "I don't think—"

"Like this," said Rey, his voice rough and deep. He took the sheath from her and slid the leather strap over her foot before dragging it upward.

"A thigh sheath," she breathed, gasping as his fingertips brushed the sensitive place behind her knee. When he reached mid-thigh, Rey tightened the strap into place. Then he sat back on his haunches to examine his work. A smile curved his lips. "Perfect," he murmured, eyes grazing down to her toes and back up again. "Show me," he said huskily, "how you'll use it."

Silla's hand slid along her stomach, then down her thigh, as she watched the black of his eyes expand. Her fingertips reached the ivory hilt, then wrapped around it. The blade made a soft *shick* as she pulled it free.

"Good," said Rey, taking the blade from her hand and tossing it to the floor. His eyes were black pools as he covered her body with his own.

"Promise me," he muttered, pressing kisses down her throat. "Promise me you'll wear it."

"I promise," she whispered. "Promise me you'll write."

Immediately, Silla felt like a fool. The man was heading into danger—he had far more serious things to worry about than *writing letters.* Besides, with Istré burned to the ground, how would that even work?

But Rey didn't so much as pause in his ministrations. "Every day."

Silla blinked in surprise. "You will?"

Rey drew back so that he could look her in the eye. "I'll bring falcons with me. Will send one daily." His unyielding gaze dared her to question him.

A tentative smile crept across Silla's face. She was relieved to have this discussion behind her. She arched like a contented cat. "You know, Galtung, your ex-lover is a real kunta."

Rey blinked, then rolled onto his side, chuckling. Gods, she loved his laughs, and prided herself that they came more frequently now. "I think you're being generous," he said.

Silla snickered, then gasped. "Kraki! When we played the drinking game with him in Kiv, he mentioned her." She searched her memory, trying to recall. "I asked you about her and you responded—"

"The spawn of Myrkur," finished Rey. "I stand by what I said."

Silla shook her head incredulously.

"You do know that Kaeja cheated."

Her gaze snapped to Rey. "What?"

He reached out. Smoothed a thumb across her lower lip. "She's a Harefoot, Silla. Did you not wonder how she was able to move so quickly?"

A "Harefoot," as Silla recalled, was the type of Galdra who could generate great bursts of speed. And as she thought back on their battle, she recalled several instances when Kaeja had moved impossibly fast.

"Her aim was to humiliate you," Rey continued with pride, "and in that, she failed."

Silla lifted a hand and frowned at it. If Kaeja had inhuman speed, how in the gods' ashes had Silla been able to maneuver past her? "She called me a *thief*."

Rey snorted. Fingertips slid beneath her chin, tilting it toward him. "You cannot steal something that already belongs to you."

And with that, his lips slid against hers, and every thought in Silla's head evaporated.

CHAPTER 7

Sunnavík, Íseldur

The clear light of a winter sun crept beneath the window coverings and crawled across the fur-draped bed. Grumbling, Jonas threw an elbow over his face to shield his eyes. He'd been having the most incredible dream—he was running through golden fields toward a towering elm tree, chased by his younger brother's laughter. The remnants of happiness clung to him for a singular, perfect moment. But then time rolled on and any cheer immediately dissipated as Jonas's reality settled in place.

He'd lost everything he cared for in this world. His brother. The Bloodaxe Crew. And frostbite had stolen the feeling from his leg and three toes from his left foot. That last thought had him swinging from the bed and yanking on his breeches. He had plans to see to and was eager to get away from this room. But Jonas caught a glimpse of the slumbering woman from the corner of his eye and his stomach clenched tight. Long, curly brown hair spilled across her pillow.

His gaze darted quickly away. Jonas pulled on his boots, then grabbed his cloak where it was slung over the back of a chair. And with that, Jonas strode out of the room, vowing to find new lodgings tonight. As he stalked down the stairs, the numbness in his left leg gave way to spears of sudden pain. Gritting his teeth, he leaned against the wall, massaging his thigh vigorously while failing to keep his mind from all that he'd suffered.

He'd woken in Svangormr Pass partially buried in the snow, the queen's Chosen lying slain all around him. The hard-packed snow of the avalanche track sported an impressive crater that led Jonas to believe he'd somehow been blasted free.

The week following had been long and excruciating. He'd ridden hard for an unending cycle of short days and long, brutally cold nights. By the time he'd reached Kunafjord, Jonas had taken one look at the blackened toes on his left foot and had known there was no saving them. The healer had removed them and sent Jonas on his way with little hope that his leg would ever heal. The frostbite he'd suffered while buried in the snow was simply too severe.

Clutching the wall, Jonas waited until the pain in his leg dulled, then slowly resumed his descent. The mead hall was drowsy with a midmorning crowd eating the daymeal, but seeing that woman in his bed had cured Jonas of any appetite. Instead of seating himself for a meal, he strode onto the streets of Sunnavík. It took a moment for his eyes to adjust to the sharp angles of the winter sun, and he relished its feel on his skin. Daylight hours were sparse at this time of the year, and it was best to appreciate them while they lasted.

But Jonas had tasks to accomplish, and his feet were soon carrying him down cobbled streets. The Sunnavík that Jonas now visited was not the same as the one he'd seen in years past. Everywhere he looked, the ravages of the grain shortage could be seen. Many shops and market stalls were boarded up. There had been riots here, he knew, and each day news of another brawl met his ears.

As he passed a hungry-looking boy whittling a stick, Jonas flicked a sóla the child's way.

"My thanks!" the boy called out.

But Jonas did not look back, and he continued his path toward Sunnavík's pier. When masts burst above the roofline and the pungent smell of fish tinged the air, he knew it wasn't much farther.

Sunnavík's harbor was the largest in the realm, with wide, wooden quays and hundreds of ships docked at any given time. From merchant ships to fishing vessels, it was usually a bustling hub of trade. Today, curiously, the normal jumbled assortment of masts and canvas was replaced by an orderly array of sails stitched with snarling bears.

Jonas made his way through a crowd, reaching the entry to the harbor grounds. It was barred, guarded by a squadron of unsmiling Klaernar warriors.

"What's going on?" Jonas asked.

"King Ivar's fleet prepares to sail," said a grizzled warrior to Jonas's right. "And it seems they plan on taking all of Íseldur's provisions with them."

Jonas craned his neck, trying to see past the Klaernar warrior. Wagons upon wagons were parked along the harbor's edge, barrels and crates hauled onto the ships.

"We're starving!" shouted a woman from somewhere down the road. "My family is ill. Surely you can spare a bag of oats!"

"Aye!" came a man's voice, rusty with age. "We starve while Ivar's soldiers gorge!"

"Silence!" bellowed the largest of the Klaernar warriors, his hand moving to his sword hilt. The crowd grumbled with discontent.

"Where do they sail?" Jonas asked.

"They won't say, lad," growled the old warrior, turning to examine Jonas. "But if whispers are to be believed, they sail for Zagadka. The king seeks retribution for the attempt on his life."

Jonas ran a frustrated hand along his hair, then yanked on his braid. He needed to get dockside.

"Either the Zagadkians never delivered the grain they'd promised," continued the warrior, "or not a grain of it has emerged from Askaborg Castle."

The desperation of those gathered at the harbor's entry was a low, hot simmer, and Jonas had a feeling it would soon build to a boil. Thankfully, the king's fleet was moored at the north of the harbor, the opposite side from his destination. He slid back through the crowd, finding a side street running parallel to the harbor, then making his way southward. As he reached the small southern pier, Jonas's heart leaped.

A slender figure crouched at the edge of the dock, laying a wreath of flowers down upon the sea. She was clad in mourning black, so it was difficult to be certain of her identity, but as the figure straightened, a lock of white-gold hair fell from beneath her veil. And if that didn't confirm Queen Signe's identity, then the twenty armed warriors guarding the pier surely would.

It had taken Jonas days to discover where he might meet the queen, and a full week spent scouting this very pier before the woman herself appeared. But now she was here, and Jonas's heart kicked up to a violent tempo. Pain shot down his leg, and he was filled with a foreign sensation—apprehension.

Jonas was a man of humble beginnings, but this was the gods damned queen of Íseldur. She could have him killed with a twitch of her smallest finger. Jonas's hand found the family talisman hanging around his neck, and he reminded himself of his purpose. He must restore his family's lands and avenge Ilías's death.

And so he gathered his courage. Forced himself to step out of the shadows and approach. The queen, apparently finished with her mourning ritual, walked toward shore in smooth, unhurried steps.

"Halt!" shouted one of her warriors, a black-haired brute half a head taller than Jonas.

Jonas slowed, all the words he'd carefully practiced emptying from his skull. "Your Highness—"

"If you value your head, I caution you not to take another step," growled the queen's enormous guard.

Swallowing, Jonas came to an abrupt stop, watching the queen beyond the warrior's shoulder. Queen Signe made no outward indication she'd noticed Jonas, yet he felt the piercing weight of her gaze from under her black veil.

"I would ask for a moment of your time, Your Highness," Jonas tried.

But the queen turned away from him as she stepped onto the cobbled street lining the harbor.

"Please!" Jonas's chest tightened with his rising desperation.

The queen's guards fell into formation around her, and they began the trek back up to Askaborg.

"Svangormr Pass!"

Slowly, the queen turned. Again, that unnerving black veil kept her reaction hidden, yet as she strode toward him, he sensed her anger. Swallowing, Jonas forced himself to stand his ground, even as the queen and her twenty-odd guards descended upon him.

Queen Signe stopped half a dozen paces from him—silent, as though examining him. "You were in Svangormr Pass," said the queen. "And yet you are not Klaernar."

Jonas shook his head. "I assisted Kaptein Ulfar."

"Kaptein Ulfar," repeated the queen with a clear note of distaste. She cocked her head to the side. "Your name, warrior?"

"Jonas Svik, Your Highness."

"Jonas," said the queen. "Now I have a name for the warrior who got a squadron of my most skilled warriors killed." She made a quick gesture, and half of her guards stepped forward.

Panic rose in Jonas's chest. "It wasn't like that. My plan would have worked, we had the upper hand, but—" His arms were wrenched behind his back and he was quickly disavowed of his weapons. "There was an explosion a-and . . . something happened to the Chosen. Decapitated, all of them—"

But the queen had turned her back on him. Jonas's heartbeat now seemed to crack against his chest. This wasn't how it was supposed to happen. He hadn't dragged himself from the wilds of Nordur for this . . .

"I would have you put to the pillar, *Jonas,*" spat Signe over her shoulder. "But I have something else in mind for you." Half of her guards had closed around her as they made their way down the harborside road.

"What do you want done with him, Your Highness?" asked the guard, now gripping Jonas's arm.

The queen did not so much as pause as she called out, "Take him to Volund."

CHAPTER 8

Kovograd, Zagadka

The balcony door nagged at Saga. She paced the confines of her room, trying to ignore it, but each time she passed by, her guilt burned hotter. She'd made such progress in Íseldur. Could not let herself falter now. And each day that passed without venturing outdoors made it just a little harder to rebuild her courage.

As it called to her now, she glared at the door. *Tomorrow,* Saga promised it. The truth was, she had no plans to leave this room today. Not after what she'd discovered days earlier—Kassandr Rurik being whipped before his father.

The sight had been shocking, and her initial instinct had been to flee. But those marks on his back had burned into her eyelids, and before she'd known what was happening, Saga's anger had eclipsed her panic. And so she'd stormed back into that room and demanded they release him. It wasn't until later that Saga realized the entire thing had been orchestrated by Kassandr Rurik—a plan to force her to meet with the high prince of Zagadka.

Initially, she'd been stunned to find her door unlocked and the corridors beyond unattended. And in that moment, Kassandr's casual mention of the red room—of the weapons to be found there—had come swiftly to mind. Saga had foolishly thought it a sign from the gods. But no. It hadn't been the gods at all, but that meddlesome man.

Worry twinged inside her, against her better judgment. She rubbed her scarred hands, wondering if Kassandr had applied ointment to his wounds; if they'd been bandaged properly.

Saga physically shook her head, as though that would dislodge the thought, then continued pacing. She'd now done as the high prince had requested and written to Ivar. Saga had taken responsibility for the explosion and assured the king that the Zagadkians had played no role in it. And she'd had a lump in her throat as she'd penned her apology for her role in Princess Yrsa's death. By the time Saga had handed the letter to Alasa, she'd been utterly dejected. Yrsa was innocent in all of this.

But now Saga had played her part, and it was time for the high prince to play his. He'd assured her they'd meet and discuss her return to Íseldur. Saga would request she be delivered to Midfjord, as Kassandr had originally agreed. From there, she would find the Uppreisna and try to track down her sister's whereabouts. But worry gathered in her stomach as she probed inward for any sign of Eisa. And for the hundredth time, Saga was met with utter silence. What if she was too late? What if Eisa had perished beneath the mountain of snow? She *had* to get back to Íseldur. Had to find out for certain what had happened to Eisa.

A gentle knock at the door had Saga's heart leaping in her chest. Instinct took hold, and she soon stood beside the trestle table where she took her meals, brandishing a silver candelabra.

The bolt rumbled, and the door swung open, and she readied herself to fight. But instead of the familiar pleated armor the Zagadkian warriors favored, red silk skirts whirled into the room. Saga's grip on the candelabra loosened.

It was a woman of average height, clad in resplendence that would put even Queen Signe to shame. Saga's gaze jumped from the enormous golden necklace draped along the woman's collarbones to her bright-green eyes. Oh. There was no doubt in Saga's mind that this woman was related to Kassandr.

"Greetings, Lady Saga," she said in heavily accented Íseldurian. "I am Elisava, sister of Kassandr."

Saga managed a curtsy through her shock. "I'm honored to meet you, my lady."

Now that Elisava stood before her, Saga realized it was not a dress the woman wore, but an ornate, fur-trimmed jacket in red. While parts of the jacket were ruched and embellished with red beads and embroidery, other patterns seemed to be woven right into the fabric itself. And her earrings—gods, Saga had never seen such extravagance. Delicate gold filaments accented with jewels, they dangled half a handspan long.

Elisava cleared her throat, and Saga's cheeks heated as she realized she'd been caught staring.

"How fares your brother?" Saga tried. "Has he finished his pilgrimage to . . ." She thought for a moment. "The golden oak?"

Elisava stared blankly, her lips pressing together.

"Er . . . have you had word from Íseldur?"

Elisava's tranquil expression rippled with irritation. She barked in rapid Zagadkian, then faced Saga with a startlingly demure expression. A heartbeat later, a familiar face peeked through the door, and Saga exhaled a relieved breath. Rov's dark, expressive brows sat above a slightly crooked nose, and dimples were carved into his brown cheeks. Kassandr's right-hand man loped into the room, hands thrust into the pockets of his armored jacket.

He replied to Elisava in jovial Zagadkian. "I told to her," said Rovgolod, switching to Íseldurian. "It will take much more practice to learn your language."

Elisava threw her hands in the air, retorting something that made Rov chuckle.

"You did well," Saga said to Elisava, touched that she had taken the time to learn what she had.

Elisava's exasperated expression softened, and she spoke to Saga in slower, lilting tones.

"Elisava says she will take the daymeal with you," said Rov, collapsing into a carved chair near the hearth, limbs sprawled across the arms.

Ordinarily, the prospect of dining with a stranger would have made Saga's skin itch. Yet she was so painfully bored, she found herself eager. And so she sank into a chair across the table from Elisava. Their gazes met, an awkward silence settling over the room. Elisava's gaze fell to Saga's folded hands, and she studied the branding marks with unabashed curiosity. Saga blinked, then tucked her hands beneath the table.

"I suppose you haven't news of Íseldur?" Saga said, just as Elisava spoke in Zagadkian.

Both women looked at Rov expectantly.

"She is curious to see what her brother hides so carefully from prying eyes."

Saga's anger was instinctive and visceral. Another person wanting a glimpse of the caged creature. But rather than ogle her like some sort of prized pet, Elisava propped her chin on her fists, as though settling in for a good story.

Thankfully, Alasa entered the room, saving Saga from answering. Rather than the *kasha* and blackcurrants Saga had grown used to, Alasa unloaded bowls of cold pork, fermented vegetables, boiled eggs, and flatbreads. She set down a metal carafe with steam drifting from a spout, curtsied, then departed.

Saga stared at the spread before her, then watched Elisava with apprehension as she poured the contents of the pot into the cups. Immediately, the smell of deep, rich spices hit Saga's nose, and she found herself leaning forward. It smelled different from the róabark from back home, yet was intriguing all the same.

"*Sbiten,*" said Elisava, handing a cup to Saga.

"Sbee-ten," repeated Saga, taking the cup and examining the purple liquid within. She took an experimental sip, her eyes widening. It was sweet and slightly fruity, with pungent, aromatic spices—ginger, cinnamon, cloves, and something else. "Oh!" Saga exclaimed, as spicy heat pricked her tongue and spread warmth across her cheeks.

Elisava sent her an amused smile as she picked up a small, red berry from the tray and showed it to Saga. She spoke in lilting Zagadkian. Silence filled the room, and both women turned expectantly to Rov, only to find his head resting against the back of the chair, eyes firmly shut.

A flurry of Zagadkian from Elisava had Rov's head jolting up.

"Elisava tells to you the story of this berry," Rov interpreted. "It is not to be eaten, as it makes one fall into a wakeful sleep. The stories tell that the Spring Maiden painted her lips with the berry's juices, making them red like rubies. She seduced Old Man Winter with a kiss, sending him to sleep and granting Zagadka an early and fertile spring. It is good luck to have such berries on your plate, but very bad luck to eat them."

Saga eyed the red berries with new apprehension. But her curiosity was piqued. She stood and crossed the room before selecting a book from the shelf. Saga returned to the table, flipping the book open to a page depicting four figures.

Elisava nodded, pointing to a young woman in the top corner of the page. Her lips were red as the berries, her blond hair woven into a crown of flowers.

"Spring Maiden," Saga murmured, her gaze then flitting to the young man in the bottom corner. Saga recognized the pleated armored jacket at once, but blinked at the headdress upon the man's head. "Are those . . . horns?"

Rov yawned. "Must be Brother Summer you look upon. They give him all manner of phallic objects. Sword, wheat, horns, and pouch of cow bollocks."

Saga cleared her throat. "I think you mistranslated—" But then she squinted closer, seeing the bulge beneath Brother Summer's jacket. "Is he—"

"Aroused?" asked Rov with amusement. "He is virile god and artists like to show him as such." Rov went on to name the last of the seasonal gods—Old Man Winter, with flowing white hair and a suit of thick reindeer furs, and the Autumn Crone, a stooped woman clad in reds and yellows.

Saga's blood enlivened as she drank in this knowledge. She flipped to the page she'd come back to countless times. It depicted a great battle, beasts and animals fighting misshapen, horned monsters. But it was the skies that had pricked Saga's curiosity the most. A legion of warriors flew upon winged horses, raining arrows down upon the battle below.

"Who are they?" she asked, stabbing a finger at the winged horsemen.

Elisava's expression hardened at once, and she exchanged a wary glance with Rov. When she spoke, her voice had a solemn air to it.

"Clans beyond the river," interpreted Rov. "This battle is many long years ago, when things in Zagadka were different."

Saga puzzled over his words, trying to make sense of them. But she was quite certain Kassandr had never mentioned the clans. "What happened?"

Rov relayed her question, but Elisava took another long minute before replying. "Would you like to see one of these horses, Lady Saga?"

Saga blinked as her mind scattered everywhere. "You—what—" Somewhere deep down inside Saga, a small child squealed in delight. All thoughts of never leaving this room again quickly vacated her. She gripped the table, staring at Elisava. "Yes!"

But Rov looked far from enthused as he and Elisava exchanged exasperated words.

Elisava waved off Rov's accusing finger, leaning forward on the table. A sly smile curved her lips. "*Ty khochesh' vstretit' Havoc?*[*]"

Rov folded his arms over his chest, apparently refusing to translate. Elisava's expressive brows arched, and she turned in her seat to send Rov a speaking glance. When he didn't budge, she pushed to her feet, sauntering toward the chair he lay sprawled across.

"*Uderzhi menya ot svoikh planov, zhenshchina,*[†]" he muttered, though Saga couldn't help but notice that the warrior seemed unable to look away from Elisava.

Elisava's elegant fingers slid around Rov's neck as she leaned down so that her lips hovered next to his ear. As she straightened,

* Would you like to meet Havoc?

† Keep me from your plans, woman.

Rov's head fell back and he groaned at the rafters. With an exaggerated sigh, he unfolded his long limbs from the chair and straightened the front of his jacket.

Rov's face was impassive, but his words seemed wrenched painfully from him. "I suppose is your . . . how do you say . . . *good fortune,* Lady Saga. Today you will meet the winged murderer they call Havoc."

The scent of straw and manure was heavy in the air, but the screams of the horse before Saga made it hard to notice anything else. Havoc was a majestic, yet terrifying stallion with a gleaming white coat. Enormous wings of iridescent feathers stretched out as the stallion reared and released another wrathful scream.

Saga's pulse had thundered as she'd left her chambers, but between Elisava's casual chatter and Rov's reassuring presence, she'd been able to gather the courage to continue. Rov thankfully understood the nature of her condition and assured her there was an alternative route to the stables. Rather than leading her outdoors, they'd navigated through a series of corridors before climbing down a spiral staircase—a back entrance.

Now she stared at the winged horse, torn between fear and wonder and outright anger. She glared at the manacle securing the creature's rear ankles.

"Why is it caged away?"

"Is secured," grumbled Rov, "so murderous beast does not kill another."

Saga's gaze slashed to Rov. "What?"

Elisava's small, warm hand landed on Saga's forearm, and she spoke gentle words, with Rov interpreting. "This horse is wild and dangerous," she explained. "We keep it only because the oracle has told my father we must."

Saga chewed her cheek, waiting for an explanation.

But Elisava only sighed, turning back to Havoc.

"Horse was . . . betrothal gift from clans beyond the river to high-prince-to-be," said Rov, taking over. "Was symbol of union of long arguing halves of Zagadka. But creature is dangerous and wild. Impossible to tame." He ran a hand through his hair, his gaze growing distant. "It kicked the high-prince-to-be, crushing his skull. The beast is cursed. Has robbed us of our heir and has brought discord."

"Heir?" Saga tried to comprehend. Wasn't Kassandr the heir?

Rov muttered something in Zagadkian before switching to Íseldurian. "Kassandr's older brother, Radomir."

Saga swallowed. "Kassandr was not meant for the throne?"

Rov nodded. "Always, it was to be Radomir. He who was gifted in speech and in combat, loved by even the oldest of crones. Is . . . how do you say . . . rather large boots for Kassandr to step into."

Saga was eager to hear more, but the horse minder appeared. After bantering with Rov in rolling Zagadkian, the minder entered the pen.

"We must be quiet while horse eats," whispered Rov.

Saga watched the horse minder walk slowly toward Havoc, speaking in soft, low tones. The horse's white nostrils flared and he hoofed at the ground, but the stallion did not rear back as the minder approached. The man set down a shallow bucket of grain, then began backing away from the horse. But his heel caught on a rogue stone beneath the hay. Fear clutched at Saga's chest as the man fell onto his rear, and Havoc screamed.

Saga's shock held her immobilized, and Elisava cried out in fear. But Rov, thank the gods, leaped over the fence and into the pen. Hands hooking under the man's armpits, Rov hauled him back. It was done without a heartbeat to spare—Havoc's hooves slammed down where the man had just lain, gouging the packed-earth floor. The horse whinnied, shaking his head, and his dark, malevolent eyes glared at the humans watching him.

Elisava backed away, murmuring in distress, while Rov went to comfort her. But Saga only stared into the pen at the beautiful, caged creature. She felt a strange sort of kinship with the horse.

The horse minder retched into the straw to her left while Elisava directed a torrent of angry words at Havoc, no doubt cursing it for trampling her brother and trying to do the same to this innocent horse minder.

But something fluttered deep in Saga's chest. In that moment, she couldn't help but remember the girl who'd locked herself away. Hadn't she wanted to fly from her cage? A new sense of purpose burned deep inside her. The balcony door she'd ignored for days was now at the forefront of her mind.

Saga turned away and, after a word with Rov, returned to her chambers.

Saga's heart beat riotously as her hand rested on the iron latch of her balcony door. The red-and-gold patterns painted on the door grew unfocused as she tried to slow her breathing, but it was impossible to forget what lay beyond it. Her balcony. Open skies. Her pulse leaped, but she reassured herself—it was only a few steps. She would leave the door open—an easy exit from the balcony.

Punished, rang Magnus Hansson's voice in her skull. *You deserve to be punished.* The screaming bears branded into the backs of Saga's hands throbbed, the smell of charred flesh vivid in her memories.

"You're dead," she spat. Magnus's screams and wet gurgles rang in her ears, and Saga latched onto that sound. Pulled it to her. "You're dead," she repeated, the tightness in her chest loosening just a touch. "You don't control me anymore."

She forced her thoughts to that night in Askaborg's gardens, when she'd felt rain on her skin for the first time in five years. For a moment, she'd felt hope. Saga would not lose the progress she'd made. Would not let her affliction rule her as it once had.

Before she could second-guess it, Saga lifted the latch. Pushed the door open. And stepped onto the balcony.

Her pulse was out of control, and she gasped for breath, but Saga reminded herself that she was safe. That Magnus was dead. That never again would she find herself trapped like she had that day in the stables when he'd branded her flesh.

She took another step forward. Breathed in the crisp wintery air.

Saga stepped forward again. And then she was gripping the wooden banister, closing her eyes, and tilting her face to the sky. Saga drew in a deep breath. Paused at the warmth kissing her cheeks.

The sun.

Her eyes flew open, but she slammed them shut against the intense light. But Saga laughed, incredulous, fingertips skimming along her cheeks in disbelief. The feel of the sun filtering through a window did not compare to the raw warmth of it bathing her skin. Saga cracked one eye open at a time, then squinted until she'd adjusted to the brightness.

Bathed in Sunnvald's light, she took in the sights before her. Saga's balcony looked over the fortress grounds. She saw frosted gardens stretching toward a curious-looking temple with tall wooden statues. She saw fur-capped workers bustling about and warriors patrolling the defensive walls. Beyond the walls of the fortress, the Kovosk River cut through the city of Kovograd. Saga gazed at the sprawl of peaked roofs and cobbled streets, all dusted with snow.

But a cloud drifted across the sun, and a raven called out, stirring memories of that day.

The screams wrenching from her throat. The ravens screeching from beyond the stables. The inferno of pain as the brand seared the backs of her hands. "Punished," rang Magnus's voice, and no matter how many times Saga told herself he was dead, she could not drive him from her mind.

Her heartbeats were now too quick to count, every muscle in her body urging her to return to her chambers.

"Just a little longer," she pleaded, fingers tapping rhythmically on her shoulder.

But the mystery of Zagadka, the strange beauty of Kovograd, could not make up for her air-starved lungs. Lights dotted her vision, and at last, Saga released her grip on the banister and stumbled back to her chambers.

After closing the door, she sagged against the wall and gasped for breath. Her entire body trembled, her heart racing as though her life were in danger. But a smile spread across her lips as she touched her sun-warmed cheeks.

The sun. She'd felt the sun on her skin. Had looked upon the great wooden city surrounding her. Saga had gone outdoors.

It felt like the first step toward something great.

CHAPTER 9

Kopa, Íseldur

Silla stood at the floor-to-ceiling glass-paned windows, watching the figures assemble in the courtyard below. They'd managed to recruit near two dozen warriors for the mission in the Western Woods. Silla sighed as she spotted Hekla securing the saddlesacks on her new gelding. Gunnar stepped forward, presumably to help her tighten the straps, but at a curt word from Hekla he raised his hands defensively and stepped back.

And then she saw *him,* the tall, black-haired warrior leading his white mare toward Ashfall's gates. Silla leaned forward, pressing her fingertips to the glass as Rey mounted Horse. An ache grew in her chest as he paused, then glanced over his shoulder, eyes lifting to the very window in which she stood. It was as though he knew she'd linger here, late for her etiquette lessons but desperate for one last glimpse.

He lifted one hand, hesitating for a long moment before turning back to his task. And as Reynir Galtung rode beneath Ashfall's gates, the ache inside Silla sharpened and spread.

She allowed herself a minute to wallow by the window. It felt like part of her heart had ridden off with him. Like she ought to fetch Dawn and ride on after them. After all the tumult in recent months, Silla felt like she'd found a sort of stability with Rey. But now he'd left, and she was alone once more.

Not alone, she chastised herself. She had Runný and her queensguard. Lady Tala and Atli and so many others. Silla blotted her tears with her gown's over-long sleeves. She pushed her shoulders back and turned to her queensguard.

"He's gone," she said miserably, as though they hadn't witnessed it all. "I suppose there's nothing to be done but get on with my day."

As Silla entered Lady Tala's sitting room, she hoped the lack of windows helped disguise her red-rimmed eyes. But between the golden braziers positioned in each corner and the lively fire crackling in the hearth, she was doubtful. Despite the space being windowless, Lady Tala had managed to give it a cheery feel with extravagant tapestries, bundles of dried flowers, and lush furs draped over chairs and on the floor before the fire.

A week and a half ago, Jarl Hakon had introduced Lady Tala to Silla as a chaperone who would help her transform into Eisa Volsik. At first, Silla was irritated at having to sit still and learn the names of each jarl in Íseldur. After all, it should be Saga learning these names. Saga who would be queen. Yet Silla understood the importance of these lessons. In Saga's absence, it fell on her to draw the jarls to their cause. And she had a lot to learn before they'd deem her worthy of following.

There was an air about the older woman that Silla struggled to name. Perhaps it was the confidence that came with knowing oneself to the very core. Or perhaps it was the conviction that came with a lifetime spent in a seat of power. Regardless, Silla strove for this magical thing Lady Tala possessed.

Wife of a late jarl, Tala had not remarried following her husband's death. According to Silla's maid, Hild, this was uncharacteristic for a woman of nobility and had won Lady Tala respect from some, disdain from others. Jarl Hakon, though, was a friend of Lady Tala's late husband, and had offered her a permanent seat at his court.

"Who rules her lands?" Silla had asked, trying to untangle the confusing muddle of landownership rules.

"Her eldest son," was Hild's reply, "though it's rumored that he and Lady Tala had a falling out."

As Silla now rushed toward the fireplace Lady Tala stood, then dipped into a curtsy. With auburn hair streaked with gray, Lady Tala wore a vibrant purple gown that complemented her pale coloring. Breathless, Silla pinched her silken skirts and dipped into a curtsy of her own.

Lady Tala's lips quirked up. "Remember, Eisa," said Tala with a kindly smile, "you need not curtsy to anyone. You will undoubtedly always be of the highest rank in the room."

"Oh," Silla said, flustered, "I keep forgetting that." How did one untrain twenty years of deferring to others? Twenty years of being the lowest of the low; of scrounging for every sóla she could earn; of fading into the background and never being seen?

Silla gave her head a shake and sank into one of three empty chairs opposite Lady Tala. "I apologize for my tardiness."

But Lady Tala raised a hand, shaking her head slowly. "A queen does not apologize for lateness, Eisa. Instead, you might say, *Thank you for your patience.*"

Silla nodded vigorously. "Oh, that's so much better." This was precisely why she met with Tala. And while she'd expected scorn, perhaps disdain at her upbringing, Silla had found Lady Tala to be kindly and maternal.

A cupbearer slipped through a servants' door, then lay a tray of róa and various accompaniments on a table nearby. Silla leaned forward to help the cupbearer arrange the cups, then stopped herself. She'd learned the last time to wait to be served, and though it felt contrary to her every impulse, she forced herself to remain still.

"Very good, Eisa," said Lady Tala as the cupbearer poured two cups of róa, then placed them before the pair.

"My thanks," Silla whispered to the cupbearer. The man paused, eyes darting to Silla. And with a quirk of his lips, he inclined his head before departing. She knew Lady Tala would not approve, yet this was a hill on which Silla would die. Kindness cost her nothing.

Lady Tala sighed, brows raised as she spooned honey into her cup. "They do not need to like you, Eisa," she said gently. "But they do need to respect you."

Silla pressed her lips together as she wondered how one rid oneself of the need to be liked? It was a thing Silla craved down to the very marrow of her bones. Right now, she was already thinking five steps ahead, considering what she might do to win Lady Tala's approval. On that note, *did* Lady Tala like her? Oh gods, did the woman roll her eyes at night, recounting Silla's many—*many!*—mistakes? Silla's pulse leaped at the very thought of it.

"Do not fret," said Lady Tala, as though reading Silla's thoughts. "It is not a thing to be learned overnight. We have time. And when the jarls arrive for the feast, they'll be met by a queen with iron resolve and a commanding presence."

Silla nodded, steeling herself with determination. She picked up her cup of róa and blew the steam from it.

"Liv has recruited a new lady-in-waiting," said Tala, carefully. "But I've asked them to wait until you and I have had a chance to speak alone."

"Speak?" repeated Silla dully, uncertain where this was heading.

"Word of your scuffle in the sparring grounds has reached my ears, Eisa."

Heat stung Silla's cheeks, and she stared at her hands like a child scolded. She should never have put her lébrynja armor on beneath her dress—should never have offered to spar with Hekla. And when the tall, beautiful Kaeja had challenged her, she most certainly shouldn't have agreed.

"I didn't think I needed to tell you, but it appears that I must." Tala's eyes bored into Silla's. "A king will earn honor and glory through deeds on the battlefield. But a queen—" She sighed. "It is below you, Eisa, to be rolling in the mud, throwing punches, and calling names. This is why you have warriors."

"But—"

"And it brings up another matter." There was a note of something in Tala's voice that made Silla brace for what was to come.

Tala sighed. "This is a rather tricky subject, but one that must be addressed." She took a sip of her róa, then met Silla's gaze. "You must know that there is one way to gain allies that is effective above all others, Eisa. Marriage."

Silla felt the blood drain from her face. "But I'm with Rey."

Tala pressed her lips together. "I mean this with every ounce of respect," she said carefully. "He's a soldier, dear. A handsome one, to be sure. But he has no lands . . . no standing. Marriage to him yields no benefit to Íseldur."

Anger churned in Silla's stomach. *He has no house,* she wanted to spit, *no standing, because Ivar stripped it from his family when they refused to turn on the Volsiks.* But in truth, his noble standing was beyond the point—what she and Rey had was . . . precious. A thing to be treasured. And yet it was still new, fragile—and completely untested. In Kalasgarde, they'd been sheltered from the realities of the world, but in Kopa, their delicate connection was exposed to dangerous elements.

"All I'm suggesting," continued Tala, "is to keep an open mind. Perhaps someone will catch your eye and you'll reconsider."

Silla bit down on an angry reply and forced herself to nod, then felt thoroughly guilty for it.

Tala leaned forward, clasping Silla's hand in hers. "I'm glad we had this talk, Eisa," she said quietly. "Now, would you like to meet your new lady?"

Silla nodded, trying to brighten her moods. But as she turned toward the approaching footfalls, her forced smile fell.

A pair of women swept into the room. She recognized Liv Eriksson at once; blond curls bouncing and cheeks rounded with a bright smile. It took her a moment to identify the lithe, black-haired woman to Liv's right. But as she met the woman's glowering blue eyes, Silla's stomach sank. It was the last person she wanted to see.

"Eisa," said Kaeja with exaggerated cheer. "How lovely to see you again."

"Can you believe it?" Silla huffed to Runný as they returned to her chambers several hours later.

"I don't know," said Runný thoughtfully. "The one named Liv is quite kind."

Silla's gaze swung to Runný. "Are you . . . blushing, Runný?" As the red flush on Runný's face swept down her neck, Silla bit down on her smile.

She'd spent a torturous afternoon practicing the art of conversation with Liv—the woman betrothed to Hekla's fling—and Kaeja, Rey's former lover. She hadn't missed Kaeja's rolled eyes and mutterings under her breath each time Silla had made a misstep. It had been a miracle she hadn't leaped from her chair and finished what she'd started with Kaeja in the sparring grounds.

Silla huffed.

Runný eyed her. "Do you need to visit the chicks again?"

Silla thought of the yellow fluff balls they'd snuck off to visit on multiple occasions, but suppressed a yawn. "Desperately. But I have the evening meal with Jarl Hakon, and I would rest my eyes for a few moments before it."

They reached the door to her chambers, and Silla felt for the dagger strapped to her thigh. The feel of it there was comforting, yet at the same time a disquieting reminder that Rey had left for Istré. Kálf, Hef, and Erik swarmed into the room to check for dangers. It was strange, this new routine, and Silla had yet to adjust to it.

Kálf soon appeared in the doorway, scratching his full beard. "Seems the jarl's magisters left more books for you." He gestured to the stack of books near the hearth.

"Oh, good!" Silla said with forced brightness, though truly, the prospect of thumbing through yet more books for clues of how to rid herself of the god of chaos made her temples throb. Weeks, she'd been at this, and with each tome she set aside, her optimism dwindled just a little more.

By the time the rest of her queensguard had cleared the room, the throb had intensified to a full-headed ache. The door clicked shut, and Silla flopped onto her bed with her limbs spread wide.

But a curious sound had her lifting her head. At first, she thought her headache had worsened, but then she realized it was fainter, higher. Silla rolled onto her back. It was a scratching sound, coming from the glass-paned windows next to her bed. The heavy velvet curtain had slipped free from its tie, and Silla pulled it gingerly back.

She stared at the iron plate secured to the outer window ledge. At Silla's request, Hild had brought offerings from the kitchen—one for the gods, one for the spirits. And where once had lain two cups of mead and the carcass of a fish, now stood an enormous bird. Cunning black eyes stared at her as the creature leaned forward and scratched its yellow beak along the glass pane.

It was a black hawk.

The omen of death.

She'd seen one minutes before her father had been killed, and again just before the Wolf Feeders had attacked in Kalasgarde. The gods had warned her both times before, and there was no question in her mind.

Long talons unfurled inside her, as though in recognition.

Death, whispered Myrkur, suddenly alert inside her. Goosebumps skittered down Silla's spine. *Death is coming.*

Silla opened her mouth and screamed.

CHAPTER 10

Kovograd, Zagadka

Kassandr Rurik flipped his dagger in the air and caught the hilt with ease. A smile curved his lips, his mood so jovial he began to whistle. He'd returned from his pilgrimage to the golden oak in four days—shattering his brother Oleg's record—only to discover that the high prince had taken leave to consult with the oracle, sparing him from further punishment. But the best part of his return was Rovgolod, informing him of all that had transpired while he was gone.

Not only had no harm befallen Saga in his absence, she'd requested Rov give her Zagadkian language lessons. And when Rov had reported she now took daily trips onto her balcony, Kassandr had been overcome. He'd leaped from his chair and kissed his friend, leaving Rov complaining and wiping his mouth. But Kass did not care. He could not contain his joy.

During his journey, Kass had dwelled on the disappointing outcome of the high prince and Saga Volsik's first meeting. He'd hoped she could persuade his father to act against the Urkans, but on further reflection, he realized he'd expected too much of her. His father and the Zagadkian elders were stubborn in their beliefs. It would take more than one meeting to convince them to raise arms against the Urkans.

But hearing that she spent daily time outdoors on her balcony reminded Kassandr of all that she faced. His Saga was fighting. Her fire was banked, not extinguished, and each day it would only grow hotter . . . brighter. He would bend low, would blow on those embers. Encourage their growth. Yes. It would work.

Now he strolled to Saga's room, flipping his dagger while whistling a jaunty song. Today, he would make her an offer she could not refuse.

As he reached her door, he nodded at the men of his Druzhina who guarded it. Though she might not know it, and certainly would not like it, Saga's door was guarded night and day. Her food was tasted before it was delivered. Trackers watched her balcony, surveying the yards and towers beyond for any sign of an assassin. When it came to her safety, Kass would not take chances.

After unlocking Saga's door, he pushed it open and sauntered in with a smile.

She leaped from the bench nearest to the fire, her drawing pad tumbling to the ground. But Kass could only look at her, resplendent in a blue Zagadkian brocade gown.

"*Krasavitsa,**" he murmured.

"Do you not know how to knock?" she demanded, much to his delight. "What if I had been unclothed?"

He closed the door, enshrouding them in privacy, then smiled. "It would have been to my great fortune."

A pink flush ran down her pretty neck, and Kass could not decide if she was angry or scandalized—perhaps both. He approached the hearth, bending low to retrieve her fallen drawing pad.

"That's mine," she snapped, lunging for it.

He let her grab it back, but not before he caught sight of his own likeness etched in charcoal. Inwardly, his beast gave a low, contented purr. "You were missing me?"

"Not in the slightest." Saga stormed to the wall, securing the vellum onto a nail.

Kass watched, intrigued, as she returned to the hearth, shoved

* Beautiful.

her hand down her bodice, and retrieved the all-too-familiar dining knife. She drew her wrist back, then flung the knife at Kassandr's portrait. It landed in the left side of his forehead. Kassandr's beast launched to his feet and howled in delight.

He sauntered to the drawing and pulled the knife free. "Impressive," he murmured, examining the blade. "But you are needing knives much sharper than this."

An incredulous sound came from behind him, and Kassandr turned toward his Saga. "Do you not recall that I stabbed you with that knife?"

"I recall that you *missed*." He flipped the knife and handed the hilt to her.

"Shall I try again?" she demanded incredulously.

Kass's smile was lazy and unconcerned. "Let me show to you a better way." He strolled behind her, pleased when she did not move away. The scent of her skin drove his beast into a near frenzy, and it took all of Kass's will to keep focused on his task.

"Lift elbow like so."

His hand slid along the back of her arm.

"And turn like this."

He twisted her wrist.

"Try again."

Against his beast's every wish, Kassandr stepped away. Though her back was to him, Kass could feel the intensity radiating from Saga as she focused on the drawing. She drew in a quick breath, then let the knife fly. It landed with a *thunk,* right between the eyes of his likeness.

Laughter boomed from Kassandr, and he clapped his hands loudly.

But Saga whirled on him, hands on her hips. "Why are you here, Kassandr?"

It pleased him beyond measure that she'd taken to calling him by his true name. Though he supposed she was now surrounded by many with the byname Rurik. It only made sense.

"Rov tells to me you wish to learn Zagadkian."

Her scowl was adorable. "That was not meant for your ears."

"Ah, my dear Winterwing," he said, settling down in a fur-draped armchair. "Everything you do in this place is meant for my ears."

"Do not bother yourself with my well-being," she seethed.

"I will teach to you," he said with a casual shrug. "But you must do something for me."

Saga laughed, a dry, humorless sound. "You *owe* me, Kassandr. You stole my freedom. Have kept me locked in this room for days!"

His beast's fur riled in indignation. "Saga," he said, low and deadly serious, "we both are knowing how badly things would turn if I had not taken you from that hall in Sunnavík. You would have been tortured. Executed in most vile of ways."

"But Midfjord—"

Kassandr leaned forward. Braced his elbows on his knees. "What about Midfjord, Saga? Who were you to meet? Where were you to go?" Her lips pressed into a thin line, and he knew he was right. "You know not a soul in Midfjord. You know only the name of the city—"

"At least it would be my choice!" Saga shouted, her face turning red. "You tricked me into thinking I would be free." Her voice broke on the last word, and something cracked inside Kassandr's chest along with it. "I will *never* forgive you for taking my choice away."

His beast let out a low, plaintive howl. "You may hate me for what I have done," Kassandr gritted out, "but I will never apologize for bringing you to safety." He was quiet for a long moment, allowing her to regain her composure. "My proposal is this: You will take daymeal with me each morning," he said, "and I will teach to you Zagadkian language."

Saga's hands clenched into fists, and Kassandr's beast whimpered in sympathy. It pained him that his reasons for bringing her here had not lessened her fury. Yet perhaps her anger could be useful if he directed it toward more productive things.

Kassandr's beast paced restless circles inside him as Saga remained silent for far too long. At last she released a long, deep breath.

"Fine," said Saga. She looked miserable at her choice, yet despite it, he saw the gleam of determination in her eyes.

"Good." Kass knew his smile was like salt in her wound, but he could not keep it hidden away.

Relieved to have this first obstacle out of the way, he called for Alasa. The door slid open and Alasa glided in carrying a tray with enough dishes to feed two. Saga glared at him, no doubt rankled that he'd guessed how she'd answer.

He moved to a chair at the table and gestured for her to join him. "First, we eat. Then lessons shall start."

The next several days proceeded much like the last. Kassandr took the daymeal with Saga, after which they spent several hours in Zagadkian lessons. In Íseldur, Saga had told him she had an aptitude for languages, but to see it with his own eyes—to hear it with his own ears—was truly astounding.

Though Kassandr knew that it was not merely luck. Alasa and Rov reported that Saga studied her notes long into the night; that she peppered them with questions about pronunciation and word choice. It seemed his Saga was quite motivated to learn the Zagadkian language.

What Kassandr hadn't anticipated was just how torturous those sessions would be for him. Enclosed in Saga's chambers, her scent was so potent it had his beast snarling to be near her . . . to feed and care for her. But he knew this was unwelcome, and it took every ounce of Kassandr's restraint to keep his beast's emotions at bay. It was hard when every small thing she did had taken an erotic turn. The slow slide of the spoon between those lips. Her scowl when she forgot a Zagadkian term. The fire in her eyes and the sharpness of her tongue when Kassandr's teasing went too far.

Which was how he now found himself leaning against the wall in the fortress's western wing. He could not take another day in her chambers, bathed in her scent while his beast went mad. Today, he would take her for a stroll in the fortress courtyard.

Saga had been hesitant when he'd first proposed it, but Kass had reminded her of the calming taps; that he would be there should she have a crisis. And perhaps she'd thought of that rainy night in Askaborg's gardens, when he had been there to help her through her panic, because eventually she'd agreed.

Alasa entered the landing, then curtsied before holding the door open. Saga scowled as she entered the space, but Kassandr forgot to breathe for a moment. Today, she wore a fur-trimmed jacket over heavy purple skirts, an ornamental belt of silver and gold medallions cinching it tight. His beast lifted its head and howled to the skies. His Saga looked like Zagadkian nobility.

She also looked ready to commit murder.

"You are"*—radiant, astonishing, like a goddess reborn—*"ready?"

Saga tugged at her elongated sleeves while glancing at the door. "Let us do this."

Kassandr offered his arm, but she shouldered past him and pushed the door open. His beast's keen senses tracked the rapid beat of her heart and smelled the fear on her skin, yet Saga did not let her nerves slow her.

He followed her outdoors, breathing the crisp, early-winter air while trying to see it through her eyes. The western wing of the fortress to their right, climbing three stories high. The gardens to their left, encrusted with heavy frost. The cobblestone footpath beneath their feet, winding around the fortress toward the garden temple.

And the blue skies yawning wide above.

Kassandr's muscles were primed and ready to catch her should his Saga stumble. Should she need the taps. He was not surprised when her feet faltered, her breaths coming in short, quick gasps. She needed a distraction. Luckily for her, Kassandr was an expert in stoking the flames of her anger.

He placed her hand in the crook of his elbow and casually asked, "I have heard it said women are less smarter than men, because of the smaller size of their heads. Do you think it true?"

His comment had the desired effect. Saga's gaze swung toward him, her expression incredulous. "You're certainly proof against this theory."

Kass was delighted at her tart reply. Already, her breaths were more even, the redness of her face less pronounced.

"My darling Winterwing," he drawled, patting his head, "what are you suggesting?"

"Only that your head is certainly not small, and yet I've questioned your wits rather often." Her lips quivered, then broke into a smile that made Kassandr's beast wag its tail. The moment she realized she was smiling, Saga turned to the pathway, not loosening her grip on his arm. "Where are you taking me?" she asked.

"To temple of seasonal gods." He eased her along the trail, and they walked at a gentle pace. Kassandr could not fail to notice her eyes darting in all directions. "*Stena,*" he said, gesturing to the defensive wall. "Is word for 'wall.' As you can see, is built on earthen ramparts."

Saga repeated the Zagadkian word, then pointed at a guard tower curiously.

"*Bashnya,*" said Kassandr. " 'Tower.' In Kovograd, we have two defensive walls—one around the city proper, and one around the fortress." Saga was silent, and so he continued. "The river—*reka*—flows through the city, and so there are four gates barring entry."

"Why are you telling me this?" Saga asked with suspicion.

"Because," said Kassandr, "King Ivar didn't answer to your letters."

The silence felt weighted, Saga's hold on his arm tightening as they walked toward the temple.

"You know he won't answer," she finally said, slightly breathless.

"No," agreed Kassandr, fingertips tapping on Saga's forearm. "He will not." He led her along the pathway, toward the frost-burnt gardens surrounding the temple. Red banners flapped from atop the temple tower, and the horned headdress of Brother Summer's wooden idol came into view.

"What will he do, King Ivar?" he asked casually, wondering if she understood this game they played.

Saga's breaths had slowed, her back more rigid, but when she spoke, her voice seemed far away. "Winter is coming, which will ice up the bay in Sunnavík. Ivar will need to act hastily to get his fleet safely out to sea."

It was much as Kassandr had figured, but hearing it from her own lips strengthened his resolve. He gazed toward the temple, now able to make out the raven perched on the staff of Old Man Winter's idol.

"But," continued Saga, "there is always the chance he'll call for his father's fleet from Norvaland."

His fingers ceased their tappings at that. "But surely this would take many long weeks. Do you think he would wait?"

A tremor ran through her, and his fingers resumed their rhythmic motions. "I do not imagine so," she breathed. "Ivar hungered for Zagadkian blood when he learned of the gardens."

His blood heated in remembrance of that night; the feel of her body was imprinted in his mind. And as Kassandr's keen hearing picked up the acceleration of Saga's heartbeat, he guessed she, too, thought of their kiss.

She cleared her throat. "I cannot imagine Ivar's wrath if he believes you tried to kill him." But the rapid beat of her heart did not ease; if anything, it grew ever faster. The panic she'd held at bay was wreaking havoc within her, and Kassandr held her steady as her knees buckled.

"Breathe, Saga. It is only us. You are safe." Her pulse was now furious, a hammering like Kassandr himself had never felt.

"You're dead," whispered Saga, eyes squeezed shut. "You cannot hurt me."

Kassandr's beast snarled in rage, and he wanted to kill Magnus Hansson all over again. Wanted to make it slower and far more painful. As he sensed Saga's panic fully grip her, Kassandr eased them both to the ground, his tapping fingers now also working to calm his own anger.

Together, they sat, surrounded by the frost-laced plants of the gardens as Saga's breaths puffed frantically out of her, pluming into the sky. The cobbled path beneath them was frozen, but the defensive walls surrounding the fortress broke the bitter wind, and the winter sun kissing their cheeks made it bearable. Saga's crisis passed in a matter of minutes, and as Kassandr helped her to her feet, he felt her exhaustion. Perhaps it was too much, too soon, to be out here.

Beside him, Saga gasped, and Kassandr braced himself for another attack. But she only bent low to pick something off the ground. As she lifted it to the sky, the corners of Kassandr's lips tilted up.

An iridescent black feather, most likely a raven's.

He watched her beautiful face as she examined the feather. Did his Saga think this a sign from the gods? A reminder that her cage was now open, and she could fly free? Kassandr could be certain of nothing except that Saga snatched his arm, and she now led *him* toward the temple.

"Tell me of the clans beyond the river," she said, fingertips digging into his skin. "What happened?"

Kassandr's brows lifted—now he was the one to be surprised. "Many things happened," he answered carefully. "Some small, some large. Long have there been arguments, but then . . ." He swallowed back his pain. "Then the oracle made a mess of things."

Saga's attention swung toward him, her blue eyes wide. "The oracle. The same one your father has gone to consult?"

He nodded. "It was *her* prophecy that we must unite with clans beyond river to keep our isle safe. And after a meeting, it was decided—my brother Radomir would wed a horsemaiden, uniting the two sides of the river. We sent to them great amounts of ore, only accessible from deposits in the east. And they sent to us the greatest winged horse to be born in a century.

"Oaths were sworn between my father and the clansmother, and it felt much like a fresh start. We were promised fertile lands in the west for some of our people to settle and farm. And clans beyond river were promised access to metal ore deposits in the east.

"Then oracle came to my father, unbidden. She told to him she'd seen another vision. That the white stallion must be kept safe no matter what. She saw that one day a great warrior would climb atop its back and usher in a new era of prosperity."

Kass shook his head with remembered sorrow. "Radomir—the fool—was certain *he* was great warrior she spoke of. He climbed onto horse and was thrown, and murderous stallion crushed his skull. Some believe it was planned by the clans. That they wished to rid us of our heir. Rebels slipped across river in dead of night and burned down one of clans' camps. After that, I fear, there was no peace to be found."

He sighed. "Oracle can see only small parts of the future, which means the coming to it is unclear. My father, though, he holds on to her word. Even after his heir's death, he believes that one day, the horse they call Havoc will accept a warrior. Is only reason foul horse has not been slaughtered."

"Have you tried?"

Kass scowled, his beast releasing a low, warning snarl against his rib cage. "Once I tried to mount insolent creature. Would not let me near. Not with my—" He thumped his chest. "—Not with beast." Kassandr blinked as he realized they'd come to a stop before the temple. Glancing at Saga, he found her staring at the four enormous idols of the seasonal gods. Surrounded by tall, frozen grasses glinting in the sunlight, and clad in Zagadkian brocade, Saga looked like she belonged in this place. Like she'd been destined to come here all along. Kassandr forgot how to breathe. For a moment, he simply stared.

"*Osennyaya Starukha,*[*]" Saga said, pointing to the Autumn Crone.

"*Khram.*[†]" She pointed at the temple building.

"*Sbiten.*" She pointed at the offerings plate, where cups of *sbiten* had been left in offering to Old Man Winter.

* Autumn Crone.

† Temple.

"*Khrabraya,*[*]" he murmured, watching her. "*Umnaya.*[†] *Prekrasnaya serdtsem i razumom.*[‡]"

Saga squinted at him. "I do not know these words."

A raven cawed overhead, and Saga flinched. Kassandr's enhanced hearing noted the acceleration of her heartbeat, and he steered them away from the temple. "Come, Winterwing, it is much for one day. Let us return to fortress, and I will tell to you the meaning of these words."

* Brave.

† Clever.

‡ Beautiful in heart and mind.

CHAPTER 11

The Black Road (east of Kopa)

Gunnar and Eyvind were getting on Hekla's last nerve.

Gaze trained on the darkening road before her, she tried to ignore the fact that Eyvind's white mare nudged ever closer to her left, while Gunnar refused to give any ground on her right. At some point, the pair had learned each other's intentions toward Hekla, and their antics had grown more childish with each passing day.

Last night, Gunnar had positioned his bedroll directly beside Hekla's—a move that would only have been more obvious if he were to whip his breeches down and start pissing on the trees all around them. But the bedroll had become mysteriously dampened during the evening meal, forcing Gunnar to string it up by the fire to dry. When he'd returned to set it back out, there lay Eyvind on his own bedroll, arms tucked behind his head.

Hekla knew that in avoiding conversation with either, she was being a coward.

Even Rey had stopped moping to watch Gunnar and Eyvind jostling to unsaddle and brush Hekla's horse. "How long will you let this go on?" he'd grumbled.

"Until I grow tired of it," she replied defensively. "When will you stop sulking about your woman, *Galtung*?"

When Rey's jaw hardened and he glared back into the fire, Hekla lowered her voice. “You hurt her, Axe Eyes, and you’ll have me to answer to.” Protracting her claws, she held them so they caught the glint of firelight.

To her great surprise, Axe Eyes threw his head back and laughed, leaving Hekla a little disconcerted. She could count the number of times she’d heard the man laugh on her lone remaining hand.

“If I hurt her,” Rey said, “I give you permission to shred my flesh into ribbons.”

“Good,” Hekla replied, studying him. She’d admit, the pair seemed unlikely. And after what Silla had weathered with Jonas, Hekla’s hackles were raised. But when she’d seen how disgustingly adorable they were together—not to mention the tenderness in Rey’s eyes whenever he looked at Silla—Hekla had wondered if there was something to be said about opposites.

Her gelding snorted, drawing Hekla from her reverie. She felt the weight of Gunnar’s gaze from where he rode beside her, but refused to look his way.

I kneel before you now to ask for your hand.

His words rang too loudly in her mind, her guilt burning hotter each day. She needed to find the words to let Gunnar down gently. But each time she looked into his eyes, they brightened with hope, and all she could see was the sullen man who’d been bed-bound for weeks after Ilías’s death. She couldn’t be the one to put him back in that dark place.

Hekla tried to drive all thoughts of Gunnar from her mind and refocus on the job ahead of them. Istré loomed ever nearer. Tonight, they’d bed down in a nearby village, and after a good night’s sleep, they would make the last leg of the journey.

They rounded a bend, and the village’s defensive walls came into view.

“’Twill be good to have a fresh pint of ale and a soft straw mattress tonight, eh, Smasher?” asked Thrand Long Sword, Eyvind’s second in command. Though he might have a highly punchable face and a rather ridiculous nickname, Hekla had discovered him to be a good man—a dependable warrior to fight alongside.

"I'll rest better once this gods damned job is complete," Hekla answered.

Limping away from the burnt ruins of Istré was not how it was supposed to go. But now she returned with more soldiers at her back and with renewed purpose. Now there would be no village chieftain to keep her from doing her job. They would find the source of the mist and destroy it. And though Hekla had not mentioned it yet to Rey, she had a promise she must fulfill—to a squirrel.

As they neared the village gates, disquiet grew in the pit of Hekla's stomach. Rey held up a fist, drawing them to a halt. The gate hung wide, yet Hekla could not spot a single warrior atop the defensive walls. She swallowed hard, but followed the group through the gate.

In a matter of moments, the air was thick with the smell of moldered things.

"The mist," Hekla said softly. "It has been here." Her mind spun as she tried to guess how far they were from Istré. Two hours? Perhaps three?

Warriors drew their swords, and Hekla readied herself for the sight of the undead. She could still see the draugur Loftur had kept chained in a barn in her mind's eye—gray skin, sharpened teeth and claws, and eyes that glowed like twin red coals.

But as they rode through the streets, no draugur lunged from the shadows. In fact, there was no movement at all. The timber homes were dark and still. For a moment, hope lifted in Hekla's chest. Perhaps the people'd had time to evacuate. Perhaps they'd found safety. But as Hekla stared at the weathered door of one home, the smear of a bloodied handprint turned her hope to ash. A moment later, her horse stepped over a severed arm.

There was no question that the mist had struck this village. Which confirmed it truly was growing stronger. Spreading farther. Her stomach burned with anger and regret. This never should have happened.

"Where have the townspeople gone?" asked Gunnar.

It was a good question. The smell alone was enough to confirm that they'd been Turned draugur. But where were they?

They reached the village square, half a dozen ravens watching them from atop the V-shaped pillars on the central dais. For a moment, Hekla thought she saw a red glint in their eyes, but it was only a trick of the light.

The group dismounted, milling about uneasily. Unthinking, Hekla climbed onto the dais and began barking orders. "We search the homes in pairs . . ." Her gaze found Axe Eyes and her voice trailed off. Hekla shook her head, inwardly chastising herself. "I forgot the Bloodaxe Crew's leader is back among us."

"Go on," said Rey, watching her with an unreadable expression.

Hekla cleared her throat, then launched back into it. "We search for survivors. If any are found, we'll want to speak to them."

"I'll go with Hekla," said Eyvind, determination in his eye as he moved toward her.

Her chest clenched—she was not ready to be alone with Eyvind.

"Actually," said Hekla, backing away, "I'll partner with Sigrún." She glanced at her old friend, whose mouth was drawn into an amused smile. "You ought to partner with Gunnar, Hakonsson."

Before either man could protest, Hekla grabbed Sigrún's arm and pulled her toward the northern quadrant. They kicked down door after door, battle thrill pumping through Hekla's veins. Any of these homes could conceal a draugur, ready to tear the flesh from their bones. But each home they searched was empty, with nothing to show save for bloodstains and claw marks, if one didn't count the boot with a foot still inside it. At last, they converged back on the village square with the rest of the group. It seemed no one had found a thing.

"I'd rather take my odds in the woods than slumber between these walls," Rey muttered. The chorus of agreement died off as a loud clang jolted the air. Collectively, they turned to the source of the sound.

Claws sliding out, Hekla eyed the building. "Who took the mead hall?"

"Group endeavor, I suppose?" said Axe Eyes. His sword unsheathed, he ambled to the hall. With a single, powerful kick, the door burst open, the moldered scent slapping them with sudden intensity.

"Gods," muttered Rey, throwing an elbow over his nose. "Worse than Gunnar's armpits."

"Worse than Siggie's cooking," Gunnar countered.

Worse than Hekla's boots, signed Sigrún.

"Worse than a dung heap," chimed in Thrand, clearly not understanding how this worked.

Rey retrieved a torch and lit it with his strange smoke magic, sending Hekla a sheepish look. He'd spoken to the Bloodaxe Crew in private and had explained the reasons for his secrecy. In truth, she had yet to accept it fully. But it was one thing to hear he was a so-called Ashbringer Galdra, and quite another to see it with her own eyes.

Cautiously, the group eased through the doorway. The mead hall had seen better days. Tables were overturned, chairs smashed to bits, crimson and black blood spraying the walls. Hekla stepped over a scalp, warrior's braid still attached, and scowled at a severed hand pinned to the wall by a dagger.

The rattle of iron chains broke the silence of the mead hall, and now Hekla was certain it came from out back.

"We mean you no harm!" Rey called out, jerking two fingers upward. Sigrún and Gunnar silently fell into step behind him. "We search for survivors."

A low, guttural sound was the only reply.

Rey nodded, and they edged through the doorway as a unit. Hekla slunk behind him, her heart a loud drumbeat in her skull. The smell was overpowering, forcing Hekla to breathe through her mouth and quashing any hopes of survivors.

A lone figure lunged for them with clawed hands and blood-red eyes. Gunnar made to swing his blade, but Rey held up a fist and he retreated. A chain fastened around the draugur's neck reached the end of its length, and the undead creature stumbled back.

And Hekla understood why this draugur alone remained in the

village. Perhaps the mortal man had been caught thieving and had been chained here to await his trial. Hekla supposed they'd never truly know. Because this thing, snarling with rage, was no longer a man.

"Where are they?" demanded Rey. "Where are the villagers—the survivors?"

Froth gathered in the draugur's mouth, its red eyes burning ever brighter. It threw itself against the chains with another incoherent hiss.

"I think it's saying something," said Eyvind, standing to her right with a pocket linen pressed to his nose.

Hekla's ears strained, trying to make out the draugur's voice through the clamor of its chains. "Rökksgarde," she repeated, exchanging a curious look with Rey. The draugur repeated the sound. "Rökksgarde, I'm sure of it!"

"What is Rökksgarde?" asked Thrand, scratching his forehead with the pommel of his sword.

Hekla searched her mind for any clues but came up short.

Rey snatched the creature's chains, yanking it forward. "Is this a place? Have the others gone to this . . . Rökksgarde? Where are they?"

But the draugur wrenched itself free, then threw itself forward. Rey bobbed backward out of its reach, but as the collar caught, it cut a deep gouge into the draugur's neck.

Rey let out a low sigh, and Hekla understood—the vile beast was now incapable of speech. After signaling for the others to back out of range, Rey hefted his sword and gripped it in two hands. And with a swift, brutal swing, the draugur's head was severed from its body.

"May Stjarna light your path," he murmured, staring at what had once been a man. Rey turned to face the group of warriors, a weary expression on his face.

"Rökksgarde," repeated Gunnar. "*Garde* means 'yard' in the old language, does it not?"

"And *Rökk*?" chimed in Thrand. "What does that mean?"

"'Twilight,'" said Rey dully. "I can only imagine this place is related to the twilight of days."

"Does that mean the other draugur have gone to this . . . Rökksgarde?" Hekla mused.

Rey wiped the black blood from his blade on the dead man's tunic before sheathing it. "It does not concern us at the moment." He paused, lips pulling down. "We will burn this man to ensure his death. And then we ride on."

Rey's gaze was hard as flint as he looked at the group and said, "We shall not stop until we reach Istré."

CHAPTER 12

Kopa, Íseldur

When Silla closed her eyes at night, she never knew what would meet her in sleep. She might see her foster father's face, those desperate last words gasping from him. She might see Rey's dimples or meadows of wildflowers as she galloped on Dawn. But tonight, when she closed her eyes, Silla saw something altogether different.

A desolate plain ruled by night. A river of poison, its beaches strewn with corpses. A hall made of bones, its roof of pointed swords and its floor a writhing mass of serpents. A figure sprawled across the high seat, glowering into the hearthfire. Despite the black flames flickering in the hearth, this place was cold and bleak. Worst of all, it was so very boring. Years and decades and centuries blended together, nothing ever changing, the monotony excruciating.

But then the flames sputtered. The figure sat upright. The flames flickered higher, and inside them the god of chaos saw it all—the Urkans' prowed ships landing on the shores of Íseldur. Berserkers charging the walls of Askaborg. Blood and death and so much chaos. Beneath His dark hood, Myrkur smiled. So long He'd waited for His opportunity, and here it was—a snarl in the webwork of His brother's orderly world.

The horrid vision vanished, and the canopy above Silla's bed blinked back into focus. Wings fluttered; talons retracted—the god was stirring inside her. Ever since she'd discovered the black hawk at her window, Myrkur had grown more active: restlessly shifting, prodding, scraping. It was unsettling, but she reassured herself her daily dose of hindrium kept Him from accessing her Ashbringer source.

Yet Myrkur's anger thrummed through her veins. And as the dark god burrowed deeper inside her, Silla was suddenly certain of two things: That hadn't been a dream, but a *memory,* and the god of chaos had not shared it freely.

She rolled out of bed, bare feet landing on cold stone floors. The hearthfire had burned low, so she padded over and added another log. Staring into the glowing coals, Silla tried to calm her racing thoughts, but it was to no avail. Instead, she settled beside the stack of tomes Jarl Hakon's magisters had provided and resigned herself to a wakeful night. For hours she thumbed through book after book, desperate for a way to evict the god from her body.

But by the time the sun rose, she had nothing to show for it but bleary eyes.

Silla could not stop staring at her lap. Never mind that the sapphire on her ring was the size of a boulder; the silk gown beneath her hand could fetch enough sólas to feed a family for a year. Yet surrounded by her self-appointed ladies-in-waiting in Ashfall's great hall, Silla didn't look out of place. To her right sat Lady Tala, whose violet gown had jewels sewn right into the bodice. And to her left sat Lady Liv, wearing so many strings of glacial pearls around her neck, it seemed a miracle she could hold her head up.

Today Eisa Volsik would meet the citizens of Kopa, and Silla was actually excited about it. Rather than memorizing the dynastic lines of Íseldur and the etiquette of a queen, today she'd speak to Kopa's everyday citizens. And if there was one thing Silla excelled at, it was talking.

But as she now gazed about, her stomach hurt with the opulence of the hall. Gleaming black pillars flanked a walkway to the dais, where a table was set with chairs and benches draped with furs. Fires crackling in golden braziers cast light to the high vaulted ceiling and made the scarlet tapestries lining the walls shimmer.

The table before her was laden with bowls of fruit and plates of sweet rolls, jugs of mead, and cups of spiced róa. Silla stared at it uneasily, questioning if this was, in fact, the best way to present Eisa Volsik to the people of Kopa. But Lady Tala's teachings had instilled in Silla the need to project an air of power and greatness. She needed the people to believe in her.

An enormous yawn burst free, and she blushed as she realized her ladies-in-waiting watched her expectantly. Had someone asked a question?

Silla's gaze fell quickly upon Lady Tala. "I . . . beg your pardon?"

"I asked how you slept, Eisa," said Tala, her green eyes drawn with worry. "You look a touch pale today."

"Oh," murmured Silla, suppressing a second yawn as she tried not to think of the dreams. "I'm afraid it was a restless night."

"Missing Rey Galtung, are you?" Lady Liv teased.

Silla glanced down the dais, to where Kaeja sulked. She'd tolerated Kaeja's presence among her ladies-in-waiting in some stubborn belief that people were more than their past actions. Or perhaps she simply wanted Kaeja to know her little *display* in the sparring yard had not unnerved Silla one bit.

"Liv Eriksson," chided Lady Tala. "Comport yourself."

Liv opened her mouth to protest, but quickly slid it shut. *Can you believe this woman?* her eyes seemed to convey to Silla. A cupbearer appeared at Silla's elbow, taking her untouched, cold cup of róa away and replacing it with a fresh, steaming one.

"Drink up, Eisa," Tala said now. "You'll need your strength. I'm told the queue winds all the way to the entry hall."

Silla tried and failed not to blink at the name. *Any day,* she told herself, *and this will feel as effortless as sliding on a well-worn glove.* But currently, being Eisa felt like pulling on a damp sock. Perhaps once she was reunited with her sister, everything would feel real. But as of this morning, there had still been no word of Saga's whereabouts.

"Best we get started," said Silla, forcing brightness to disguise her worry.

Lady Tala waved at Ingvarr, chief among Jarl Hakon's appointed queensguard. Ingvarr pushed the massive oak door open, allowing the first of Kopa's citizens entry.

The first woman to enter was tall, with silver streaks in her chestnut hair, and she clutched a satchel as she limped forward. Silla shifted. The woman had an injury—should she not descend from the dais to meet her? But Lady Tala had been clear that visitors must come to *her*. And so Silla kept herself planted in her chair.

At last, the woman reached the end of the walkway, her eyes widening as she studied Silla. "It *is* you," she breathed. "I would not believe it were it not for the proof before my eyes. You look so like your parents."

Silla's heart lurched, as it did each time someone remarked on this likeness. It seemed unfair that strangers knew things about her birth parents when she herself had been robbed of the chance. But the woman's shining eyes were precisely why Jarl Hakon had arranged this. To hear of Eisa's survival was one thing. To see her with their own eyes was another.

The woman's hand slid into her satchel, and a pair of Jarl Hakon's guards flashed forward. Soon their spear tips were poised at the woman's throat, and she raised her hands in defense.

"Oh, for the love of the stars." Silla gripped the arms of her chair to keep from leaping to her feet. "Stand down. She means no harm."

Reluctantly, the guards retreated, leaving the woman blinking uncertainly. After a moment, she produced a textile from her satchel, handing it to Ingvarr, who then delivered it to Silla.

It proved to be a square of fabric, the warp thread's coloring changing every few lines. It bulged in places and had gaps in others, but there was something endearing about the textile.

"'Twas woven by the children at our shelter home," explained the woman. "Each took a turn at the loom."

Silla's eyes widened, her heart expanding inside her.

"They were eager to make something for their princess."

Blinking furiously, Silla clutched the fabric to her chest. She was moved beyond words. "Where are they?" she finally managed. "The children, that is. I would like to thank them."

A tentative smile curved the woman's lips. "They are back at the shelter home," she replied kindly. "The children were not invited today."

Silla felt herself frowning.

"Your parents were good and fair leaders," the woman continued. "Long has it been since I've felt such hope. I feel as though I've gone back in time."

Silla tried to remain stoic. Tried not to let the woman's words affect her. Lady Tala shifted beside her, and Silla knew it was time for the next guest.

"What is your name?"

"Frida, Your Highness."

"I thank you for bringing this to me, Frida. And I ask the honor of visiting the children who made this thing of beauty."

Lady Tala shifted again, this time clearing her throat, and Silla blinked back her irritation.

"The honor would be all mine, Your Highness," said Frida, a smile cracking wide across her face. But Ingvarr was suddenly there, ushering Frida toward the exit.

"Such a way with the commonfolk," muttered Kaeja.

"Better than acting like I stepped in excrement," Silla shot back.

Lady Tala's sharp gaze had her slamming her mouth shut. She knew she ought not to rise to Kaeja's jabs, but it was so very difficult.

As Silla fought to control her irritation, a familiar figure strolled into the hall.

Tall, broad-shouldered, and with a pair of dimples that caused women to swoon—Silla had witnessed it with her own two eyes—Atli Hakonsson made his way toward her with a clutch of blue flowers in hand. Black hair falling to his shoulders, square jaw covered in a dark beard, and smooth olive skin. But where his brother Eyvind's eyes were a vibrant hazel, Atli's were midnight black. And they were, Silla realized, homed in on her.

"What are you—this is meant to be an opportunity for the public to—" Flustered, she looked at Tala, who merely raised her brows, as if to say, *Keep an open mind.*

Atli strolled past the guards, who dared not challenge the jarl-in-waiting, and climbed the dais steps with all the confidence of a man who'd never been told no. But rather than approaching Silla, he plucked two flowers from the bunch, handing them to Liv and Kaeja.

Liv seemed delighted by the gift, while Kaeja sent the man a cutting look that Silla did not quite understand.

Atli ignored it, strolling to Lady Tala. "I saw these flowers on my morning ride and could not resist."

At last, he reached Silla, handing her the largest flower in the bunch.

"That was . . . thoughtful of you, Atli." Silla smelled it, because what else did one do when presented with a flower?

"I shan't take any more of your time." Atli's gaze lingered on hers for a disorienting second before he *winked.* And before Silla could think of any good, smart reply, Atli was already striding for the exit.

"Did he have something in his eye?" she asked Tala, watching his retreating form.

Tala sent her a speaking glance, and Silla had to press her lips tightly together to stifle her laugh. Gods, she could not wait to tell Hekla . . . though perhaps, for the sake of Atli's pretty face, she would keep this incident from Rey. But before Silla could dwell on Atli's curious behavior, the next guest was entering the hall.

Deep inside her, Myrkur shifted.

It was an old man, stooped with age, and yet Silla could tell he had a warrior's build. As the man hobbled down the walkway, her brows drew together. There was something familiar about this man, something she could not quite put her finger on. With a grizzled beard that reached mid-chest and eyes bluer than clear skies, surely she'd have remembered him.

Myrkur's eyelids fluttered.

"Well met." Silla smiled, but as the man's gaze met hers, it faltered. "Have we met before?"

The dark god peered upward, preternaturally still.

The old man shook his head. "I've never had the honor, Your Highness. But I once knew your great-grandfather. I was a member of King Hrolf's retinue."

Her stomach gave a sudden, unsettling swoop. "Might I ask for your name?"

Deceiver, hissed Myrkur.

Silla blinked at the god's outburst, then refocused on the old man.

"I am Fallgerd, Your Highness."

And at last, Silla understood why she recognized him. In Kalasgarde, she'd seen him in a venom-induced fever dream. Her mind supplied her with the vision—a far younger Fallgerd, saving Princess Svalla from King Hrolf's dagger. Myrkur growled low inside her.

"You saved my mother." Before she knew it, Silla was on her feet, striding toward Fallgerd. Her guards closed around her, but Silla stepped through them.

Fallgerd's white brows lifted in surprise. "I—how did you know?" He swallowed, glancing around, and Silla realized her mistake—the attempt on Svalla Volsik's life had been covered up. No one should know about it.

Slayer of kings, growled Myrkur.

"I'm glad to meet you," said Silla, flustered.

She accepted Fallgerd's hand and shook it firmly. But the moment her palm slid into his, Myrkur shrieked inside her skull. Dark, membranous wings beat violently against her chest, and anger seethed through her blood with startling force. Fallgerd jerked his hand back as though he'd been burnt.

Staring down at his hand, the old warrior backed away. "I—I must go—" Turning on his heel, the man made a hasty exit.

But Silla scarcely noticed with the dark thing thrashing about within her. Desperately, she tried to subdue the god's hold on her.

Deceiver! hissed Myrkur. *Murderer!*

She was dimly aware of the guards closing back around her; of their murmured confusion as she clutched at her head. But her mind was a war field as the god of chaos rampaged inside her. Images flashed in her mind. A shadow on a wall. A bloodstained dagger. Little Svalla, clutching a wound on her neck—delivered by her great-grandfather, yet not deep enough. King Hrolf, felled by that meddlesome Fallgerd, thwarting their plans.

But the god's anger was a finite thing, and Silla could feel His grip on her waning. She forced her thoughts to butterflies; to feeding Dawn treats. She thought of the iridescent gleam of a black sand beach and cool salt gales rustling her hair.

With a last, pitiful thrash, Myrkur slithered back into His deep crevice, leaving Silla's mind completely to herself. She glanced at her guards, surprised to find them parted and Lady Tala at her elbow.

"Did that man say something unseemly to you?" Tala leaned closer.

"Say?" Silla tried to rub the goosebumps from her skin; tried to shake the echoes of Myrkur's screams from her mind. "N-no. It is—I've a sudden headache." She hated the lie, yet knew she must play the ruse. After a deep breath, she climbed the dais steps and sank into her chair.

"There's no shame in resuming tomorrow," murmured Tala, joining her.

"No." Saga would certainly not let a headache keep her from her duties, and neither would Silla. "These people have waited hours. I shall not have them wait any longer."

"Are you certain?" asked Tala.

"Quite."

And so the next guest was led into the hall, and for the next several hours, Eisa Volsik met the people of Kopa. She saw their disbelief shift to hope—saw the faces of those who suffered most in this kingdom. And though she tried desperately to keep it at bay, gradually Silla's imagination ran wild with thoughts of all the good she might do as leader of this kingdom. *No,* she chastised herself. That was for Saga. For the oldest sister.

But as she met the everyday people of Kopa, she also saw hollow cheeks and famished eyes staring at the spread on their table. By the second hour, Silla ordered her guards to gather the food up and distribute it among those waiting in line.

"Such a martyr," Kaeja muttered, too quietly for Lady Tala to hear. Silla gritted her teeth and turned to Tala.

"Is there no grain in Jarl Hakon's stores?"

"I'm told there's none to spare."

"But surely there is!" Silla chewed on her cheek. "Each meal served to me has had an abundance of breads." As Tala shook her head, Silla made a mental note to ask Hild and Eilif if they had insight into the kitchen stores.

In the third hour, a short woman entered the great hall. Dimples grooved her gaunt cheeks, and she twisted her auburn braid between fingers as she looked wide-eyed around the room. And as the woman's eyes landed on Eisa Volsik, they somehow widened further.

Then they rolled back in her head.

She collapsed to the floor with a thud that echoed off the high ceilings. For a moment, silence hung in the air. Then Silla was on her feet, racing down the dais and falling to her knees beside the woman. A guard's hand landed on her shoulder, voices urging her to hang back.

"It could be a ruse," grumbled Ingvarr, trying to pull her to her feet.

But the woman was now blinking up at Silla with fear and confusion in her eyes.

"You're safe," said Silla, shaking Ingvarr off. "What is your name?"

"Ástrid," the woman managed, slightly slurred.

"You're in Ashfall Fortress, Ástrid. You've had a dizzy spell. Come to the dais. A drink shall restore you."

Silla called for her guards to assist Ástrid and was glad when they did so unquestioningly. And despite a disapproving look sent Silla's way, Lady Tala vacated her chair, allowing the guards to settle Ástrid into it.

Silla snatched her untouched cup of róa and offered it to Ástrid.

Ástrid sipped from the cup, her gaze growing more focused. When at last she handed the cup back to Silla, her cheeks were flushed a bright shade of pink. "My thanks, Your Highness." Ástrid squeezed her eyes shut. "I've made a fool of myself, haven't I?"

Silla pressed her lips together. "Not one bit. I've been caught apologizing to a rock. I imagine that's far worse than a simple fainting spell."

Ástrid's eyes flew open, an incredulous laugh bursting from her. "Truly?"

"Truly."

But Ástrid's smile faltered, the vivid pink of her cheeks now spreading down her neck. As she fluttered a hand to her throat, concern slithered in Silla's belly.

"Perhaps some water—"

With a sudden gasp, Ástrid's spine arched off the chair and her eyes rolled back in her head. Before Silla could understand what was happening, Ástrid convulsed.

Panic broke out in the hall. Hands grasped Silla's arms, and she was yanked away from Ástrid's spasming body. Screams echoed off the vaulted ceiling, chairs and goblets knocked aside as her ladies-in-waiting fled the dais.

"Wait!" Silla cried, struggling. "Wait—"

Guards rushed from all corners of the room, and Silla tried to glimpse what, precisely was happening around Ástrid's prone form, but it was impossible to see.

"It's not safe," came Runný's voice, low in Silla's ear. "We must get you away from here."

"What do you mean? She's only fainted!"

Runný sent her a harsh look as she hauled Silla toward the exit. "I do not think she fainted. I believe that woman was poisoned after drinking from *your* cup."

Runný's words landed with jarring impact, and Silla grew pliant at once. As her queensquard fell around her, Silla's mind spun, landing on a single image—that cup of róa that she'd ignored all morning.

Had it been *poisoned*?

Silla was whisked back to her bedchambers in terse silence, her mind hazed with disbelief. Surely it was all a mistake. Surely they'd overreacted and would soon learn that Ástrid had only fainted again.

Runný ushered her into her chambers, then sat Silla down on a bench before her hearth. Turning to the queensguard, Runný ordered them all into position. But the door burst open and Ingvarr strode inside with the rest of Silla's Hakon-appointed guards.

Silla shot to her feet. "What news—"

"Dead," he said coldly. "She's dead."

Silence stretched through the room for a long, measured minute. Then her guards burst into action. Weapons were drawn, positions taken around the door, the window, any point of entry.

"It seems," said Runný, "that someone wants Eisa Volsik dead."

Silla's hand went to her throat, her thoughts jumping about wildly. Someone had tried to kill Eisa, but who? There'd been dozens of people in the room with her and hundreds of citizens who'd cycled through. It could have been any one of them.

But then her mind settled on the figure who'd darkened her window so recently. A dry, brittle laugh broke free.

"What is it?" asked Runný, eyeing her carefully.

"The black hawk," whispered Silla. Her gaze darted to the offerings plate secured outside the window. "The gods were trying to warn me." She swallowed.

"I should have listened."

CHAPTER 13

Sunnavík, Íseldur

Jonas's head thunked back against the wall of his prison cell. He stared listlessly at the silken web strung in the corner. A fly had landed in the center and now struggled against its sticky binds. As Jonas watched the spider looming ever closer, his numbness shifted to empathy.

Jonas had been in the bowels of Askaborg Castle for six nights now. Six nights since the queen had ordered him sent to the enigmatic Volund—a man he'd yet to meet. Six nights in this cold, dank cell, with nothing but gruel and foul-tasting water to sustain him. Men had once filled the surrounding cells, but one by one they'd been taken. None had ever returned.

The spider darted forward to sink fangs into the fly, and Jonas forced his gaze away. He could handle the cold and the hunger. What he could not bear was the insufferable boredom. Alone in this cell, he was powerless against the memories of better days. Bitterly, he wondered if his imprisonment was some trick of the gods. A thing to restore balance. After all, Silla had been thrown in the Klaernar's prisons because of Jonas.

Pain seared down his leg, and he muttered a foul curse. The pains in his limb had grown sharper during his time in this cell. He'd woken screaming the night before, every muscle in his body taut. Now he braced against the agony, forcing his thoughts to fields of golden wheat; smoke twisting up from a longhouse; an oak tree looming in the distance.

Do you ever think that our past is not our future?

Ilías's words rang in his ears, pain slicing down his leg with fresh vigor. A guttural sound slipped between Jonas's teeth as he weathered the torment of both his leg and his sorrow. He'd lost his brother and the Bloodaxe Crew, he'd lost three toes and the full use of his leg, and now Jonas had lost his freedom.

Gradually, the pain slipped away, leaving Jonas panting and wrung out. The sudden groan of iron hinges had his instincts quickly sharpening. Footsteps sounded from far down the hall—Jonas counted three pairs of them, accompanied by the jangle of manacles.

"Please," whimpered a man, young from the sound of it, "please, it's not what you think—"

"I'm sure," drawled a man, "the bread only *fell* into your satchel, aye, lad?"

The trio came into view—a pair of guards hauling a man of slight build. Blond hair hung lank over his forehead, a patchy, barely visible beard along his jaw. As Jonas took in the purpling bruise on the man's cheekbone, his eyes narrowed.

"N-no," pleaded the prisoner, "I paid for it—"

"A thief *and* a liar." The guard hauled open the door to the neighboring cell and, after removing the prisoner's manacles, shoved him inside. "You can rot in here for a few days, and then you'll pay your penance."

"P-penance?"

But the guards ignored him, moving to Jonas's cell. His heartbeat kicked up as Jonas glared at the men through the iron bars.

"Hands," ordered the larger of the guards.

Jonas had seen this next part play out enough times to know that refusal only resulted in a thorough beating. Resigned to his fate, he pushed to his feet and shuffled to the bars, where he slid his hands through a horizontal slot. Manacles were slapped on his wrists, and Jonas retreated, allowing the guards to unlock his door.

He sent a last fleeting look at the young man in the neighboring cell. His heart gave a sudden lurch as those brown eyes turned familiar. For a moment, it was Ilías beneath that lank blond hair, with a hint of a beard on his jaw. The guards yanked Jonas forward, and he stumbled to catch up. Heart beating like a war drum, he glanced back at the man in the cell.

Not Ilías.

Jonas exhaled, giving himself a mental shake. He kept a halting pace with the guards, trying not to think of all the prisoners taken and never returned. It was several long minutes before the hard-packed earth sloped upward. Muffled shouts reached his ears, followed by a screech that rattled the walls. Jonas's instincts sharpened further as he tried to parse what was happening.

The floor leveled out as they entered a landing. There stood a pair of stern-eyed warriors, armed with spears. Jonas could tell from one glance that these were the kind of warriors he'd spent a lifetime trying to avoid. They watched him with pure malice, and an excitement that he did not like. The taller of the two, an enormous black-bearded warrior with a wicked scar on his cheek, elbowed his neighbor and chuckled.

The guards released him from his manacles. As though on cue, an inhuman scream burst through the open doorway, setting the hairs on Jonas's arms on end.

"I give pretty boy five minutes in the pits," said the black-bearded warrior.

The pits. The name landed right in Jonas's gut. The pits were located deep within Askaborg Castle, renowned as the place where King Ivar had committed the worst of his atrocities against his enemies. And the ear-piercing snarl that came through the doorway told Jonas it wasn't kittens awaiting him.

He waited for fear to spike through him—waited for nausea. But there was only the blasted tingling of his leg, paired with a numb sort of resignation. And in that moment, Jonas realized he'd already lost everything he cared for in this world. There was nothing else left.

"Rules?" Jonas asked in a bored drawl.

A hand gave him a rough shove toward the doorway. "Kill," snarled the guard, "or be killed."

"Is that all?" Jonas rolled his neck and shook out his shoulders. And without a glance back, he ambled into the pits of Askaborg.

The arena was larger than he'd thought. A huge packed-earth floor stretched fifty paces across and wide, countless rows of stone benches surrounding it. Three V-shaped pillars were raised on a platform in the center of the pits, and Jonas knew this was where the Urkans held their executions. Indeed, people were secured to the pillars, struggling against their binds.

The doors slammed shut behind him, enclosing Jonas in the pits. He glanced to his right, eyeing the two hundred or so men filling the benches. It was more of the same—more brutish warriors watching him with chilling hunger.

"Are you here for a show?" drawled Jonas, spreading his arms and turning in a circle.

Clearly the men did not care for that, some sneering, others spitting on the ground. Pain jolted through Jonas's frostbitten leg, and he turned away to disguise his wince. Gritting his teeth, he examined the arena floor. Where was his opponent? What weapons would he wield? But there was only the dais and the pillars—

A snarl from that direction recaptured his attention. Jonas was alert for any signs of danger as he moved bracingly toward them. Three figures thrashed about upon the pillars, but before he could get a better look, the *thwack* of an axe preceded a shout.

"Attack!"

Their binds apparently cut free, the figures burst from the pillars, sending the warriors in the stands to their feet, shouting and stomping. The transition from silence to chaos was disorienting, and for a moment, Jonas could only stare. Or perhaps he was stunned by the humanoid creatures loping toward him on misshapen limbs. Bile rose in his throat as they neared, and he took in the grayish-blue hue of their flesh; their clawlike fingers; the strange marks carved into their foreheads. But their eyes chilled him most of all—they glowed a malevolent red. What *were* these creatures? What had happened to them? But there was no time to try to understand the strangeness of these beings, because they were upon him.

Jonas threw his shoulder into the belly of a lunging creature, and the putrid scent of mold and rotten things swarmed his senses. Immediately, he was back on the Road of Bones, facing down the forest walker with the same awful scent—and the same red eyes.

The warriors in the stands bellowed as a second beastly human threw itself at Jonas. He rolled beneath it, kicking a foot out to trip the third. His eyes watered with their overwhelming stench, but Jonas pushed through it, falling into his battle mindset—a place where only instinct existed.

Jonas drove his fist into a jaw and felt the bones crunch. But his opponent did not react to the pain, instead pivoting to lunge once more. Jonas blinked as he took in the beast's misaligned jaw, the teeth he'd punched out. It was no question—he'd just broken its jaw. The pain ought to be excruciating, yet this unnatural creature had not even flinched.

Jonas let his muscles guide him as he fought the three frenzied monsters, all the while searching for a weapon. From the corner of his eye, he spotted the braziers flanking the doorway he'd entered just minutes before. Each had three curved iron legs wrapped around a central bowl. If he could dislodge one from the ground, perhaps it would serve as a weapon. Driving his fist into one opponent's temple, he rolled beneath a launching figure, using momentum to propel him back onto his feet.

And then Jonas sprinted at the brazier. He was there within a few measured heartbeats, hope flaring in his chest as he pulled it from a slot in the ground with ease. But his opponents were hot on his heels, snarling and snapping their teeth as they charged. Jonas swung the brazier like a cumbersome sword, sending clumps of burning tinder flying through the air. He smiled as they landed—raw hemp fibers soaked in whale oil made excellent tinder, be it in a brazier or on the torn clothing of the beasts.

The creatures screamed as their clothing and hair caught alight, but Jonas's smile faltered as they staggered toward him. The brazier's bowl connected with the skull of one unnatural foe, sending it toppling to the ground. As the bowl fell free, Jonas was left clutching the tripod stand and facing down two more flaming creatures.

The air was a disgusting blend of charred flesh and rot, but Jonas did not let it slow him. He swung the heavy stand with all his might. It connected with a creature's head with a sickening crack, snapping it to the side. Jonas whirled with the brazier, letting its momentum carry him into the second foe's head. He became an instrument of death, cracking iron against the bones of his enemies. Black blood sprayed across the arena, the beasts finally showing signs of injury as they stumbled to the ground.

At least a dozen times, he'd landed blows that would kill any other foe. But each time he felled them, the wretched beasts got back up.

"Not on my watch," Jonas snarled, anger and righteousness coursing through him. He hefted the brazier overhead and brought it down on the felled creatures. Again and again, he brought it down, skulls crunching and black blood spattering the earth all around them. The fires had burned out, leaving blackened, charred flesh. Where ugly faces had once been was now only battered pulp. Yet still they moved, though feebly at best, and Jonas shook his head in disbelief.

"Why!" He brought the brazier stand down on a beast's skull.

"Won't!" He did it again.

"You!" Again.

"Die!"

The creature's skull cracked, and as Jonas hefted the tripod overhead once more, a voice boomed through the pits.

"Victor!"

Chest heaving, Jonas glanced around. The warriors in the stands had grown quiet, watching him with unexpected admiration. His lip curled, but he dropped the tripod and staggered away from the beastly creatures that would not die.

A warrior sitting front and center climbed from the stands and entered the arena. His hair was an equal mixture of black and gray, and his beard reached mid-chest. But there was something in the way this warrior carried himself that told Jonas he was a dangerous man.

"Well met, Jonas!" said the man in a gritty voice. "I am Volund."

So this was the elusive *Volund* to whom the queen had sent him. Jonas's eyes narrowed as the man approached, but Volund only smiled grimly. A necklace clinked from around his neck, and Jonas's stomach turned as he identified the strung objects as teeth.

Volund clapped Jonas on the shoulder, then faced the warriors in the stands. "Let us send a warm welcome to our newest brother-in-arms!" The warriors shouted, banging weapons against the floor. Volund turned back to Jonas and extended a hand.

"Welcome to the Corpse Bringers."

CHAPTER 14

Kovograd, Zagadka

Kassandr Rurik was late for their lesson.

With an exasperated sigh, Saga glared at the door, reciting the angry Zagadkian words she planned to unleash upon him when he finally deigned to cross the threshold. But minutes slid by and still the man did not appear, and Saga began to wonder if this was some twisted plan of Kassandr's. To get her used to taking the daymeal with him—to train her to anticipate his arrival like some sort of *pet*—only to yank it away like a toy?

Her stomach growled, and Saga wouldn't have been surprised to discover smoke pouring from her ears. She couldn't tell which source of her anger was greatest—Kassandr Rurik for his complete disregard for punctuality, or herself for feeling even the smallest measure of disappointment that her jailer had not yet come to visit.

The sunlight flowing through her windows grew ever brighter as morning progressed, and Saga's irritation reached a boiling point. She stormed to the door. Pounded on it with her fist.

"You tell Kassandr Rurik he can go jump in the river!" she shouted in Íseldurian. "I hope he has rocks in his boots every day for the rest of his life! That gnats buzz in his ear whenever he tries to find sleep!"

She paused, awaiting a reply in confused Zagadkian. But it was utterly silent beyond the door, a fact that only further incensed her. She was angry, damn it, and someone needed to know it!

Unthinking, she yanked on the handle. The door swung inward with ease, sending Saga sprawling backward on her arse. She scowled at the doorway, understanding slowly settling into place. This was not the first time Kass had left her door unlocked and unguarded.

"Again with the childish games, Kassandr?"

Apprehension knotted in her gut as she thought of what she'd stumbled across in the red room. Saga stood, then hesitated. She strode to her bed and pulled her new set of knives from under the mattress. Kass had delivered them to her on their second daymeal together and had proceeded to make her test them on her latest drawing of him. The irritating man seemed pleased as she'd impaled his likeness—was delighted to help her with small tweaks of her arm and her stance.

With a huff, Saga stowed one knife carefully down her bodice, and the other in her dress sleeve. Then she stepped into the hallway.

The fortress corridors had no windows to illuminate them, but normally there was a lit torch or two through this stretch. Saga blinked into the darkness as her eyes slowly adjusted. Down the farthest end of the corridor, she could just make out a faint bloom of light.

"I swear to the gods, Kassandr," she called, moving toward the light. "If it's not a ship ready to take me to Midfjord, I do not want to see it!" What did the featherhead have to show her?

As Saga reached the lit torch, the next one became distantly visible. She sighed, then began toward it. Countless unmarked doors flanked the hallway, and Saga wondered what purpose they served. The fortress was not as grand as Askaborg, yet it was equally sprawling, with countless wings and corridors.

Her mind flicked to the high prince. Had he arranged her ship yet? She'd come through on her side of the bargain. It was time he did, too. Gods, but if Kass truly had a Midfjord-bound ship readied for her, Saga might cry.

She reached the next lit torch, but paused, realizing that the door adjacent to it hung open. Saga glowered into the sparsely lit room, but as the scent of vellum and earthy pigments reached her nose, her heart quickened.

A gallery. Kass had drawn her to a gallery, and curse her foolish heart for swooping low in her belly.

Saga entered the room slowly and gazed around in wonder. To her left was a large worktable, an assortment of wooden idols and carving tools atop it. To her right, a second table. Saga stepped closer, her gaze trailing over pots of various pigments, stacks of parchment, and piles of quills. Pinned to a board on a slanted drawing surface was a partially restored image of the seasonal gods. She stared at the brilliant pigments the artist had applied. What had they used to create such colors?

She glanced to the far end of the room, where deep shadows pooled between enormous shelves stretching from floor to roof. Did the shelves contain more artwork, or perhaps painting supplies? Her irritation long forgotten, Saga strode deeper into the room, dreaming of new pigments; of new tools she might never have imagined—

The rasp of the door swinging shut made Saga jump in fright. But then her remembered anger rushed back, and she whirled with a glare.

"I do not enjoy surprises, you loaf-eater—" Saga blinked in confusion at the ruddy-faced man glaring back at her. "You're not Kassandr."

"No," said the man in heavily accented Íseldurian. "I am not."

Saga blinked in recognition. This man was no stranger—she'd met him before in the red room. Trepidation crept down her spine as Saga backed away. "You're Oleg's interpreter."

He bowed mockingly before taking a menacing step forward. There was no mistaking the malice in his expression; the sinister gleam in his eye. This man was at least a head taller than Saga, and her gaze darted to his battle belt, where half a dozen blades were sheathed.

"What do you want?" she demanded, letting her own blade slide down her sleeve and drop into her palm.

She brandished the dagger, but the man only chuckled, taking another threatening step forward. Saga took one back, and her spine hit a wall. But as the scent of an unwashed body met her nose and a thick forearm wrapped around her collarbone, she understood this was not a wall, but another warrior.

A dozen more forms coalesced from the shadows, encircling her, and a sick feeling built inside Saga. Kassandr hadn't left her door unattended. Hadn't brought her here to see the gallery.

These men had *lured* her here.

Whether the gallery had been selected intentionally or by accident, Saga could not say. Panic struck her like a violent storm, nausea churning as the air was stolen from her chest. She yearned for the safety of her room—to be locked back in her cage. Her hands throbbed in searing memory. Trapped. She was trapped. Surrounded.

You deserve to be punished, rang Magnus's voice. The sizzle of flesh. Saga's ragged screams. The bears branded into her flesh. Again. It was happening all over again, but this time, she'd pay with her life.

"Oleg wishes for you to know," said the interpreter in stunted Íseldurian, "that your corpse shall be strung from the walls for the birds to feast upon."

But Saga scarcely heard him. The room was spinning, her heart pounding viciously, and all she could do was try to hold on as panic thrashed through her.

"Have you nothing to say?" snarled the man, his eyes flashing a feline yellow. "You may choose now, outsider. Death by sword or by claw."

Saga choked out a dry laugh, and in a moment of pure insanity, she wished Kassandr were here, so she could tell him how wrong he was. *See?* she'd say. *You took me here to keep me safe! Where is my safety, Kassandr?* How, in her last moments alive, could she dwell on such a petty thing?

Distantly, she heard a flurry of confused Zagadkian, but it was secondary to her desperate need for air. The man who'd held her pinned to his chest had loosened his grip. This should be her chance to get free—to fight for her life—but all Saga could do was sway on her feet, choking for breath as her panic gripped tighter.

"What is wrong with you?" demanded the interpreter. When she could not reply, he said darkly, "I will choose for you, Íseldurian whore. Claw it will be."

Through her warped vision, Saga saw tattoos shifting on pale skin, claws bursting through knuckles. Beige fur. Vibrant yellow eyes. A mountain cat. She sensed the others shifting forms around her, but didn't dare tear her eyes from the feline.

Still, Saga could only swing her blade weakly as the enormous cat launched at her. An enormous weight collided with her chest, sending her crashing backward. Saga's head struck the wooden floorboards as the feline's full weight crushed what little air remained in her lungs. Claws pierced through her dress, gouging her skin, but Saga could only stare dazedly up at yellow eyes, angry as though he wanted her to fight back. It felt so strangely distant—like she was not even in her own body, but looking down upon this savage scene from above.

But some deep-buried instinct—a last shred of self-preservation—reminded Saga that this was real. Reminded her that even as she'd been knocked to the floor, her knife had miraculously remained clasped in her hand. The beast bared its teeth, readying to bury them deep in her throat. Gathering the shredded tatters of her strength and resolve, Saga shoved the dagger upward.

The mountain cat yowled, reeling back. Blood slicked down the hilt protruding from its chest and spattered Saga's face. She rolled onto her stomach and tried to wriggle away, but a scream tore from her throat as the beast's claws raked through her shoulder.

The pain was scalding hot, burning through her panic and incinerating her fear. It yanked her back into her body, and Saga was suddenly clear-minded and viscerally aware. She'd wounded the mountain cat, but not mortally so, and she knew it would attack again.

Rolling onto her back, Saga braced against the pain and pulled the second knife from her bodice. The cat surged at her, dagger-sharp fangs glinting. Saga shoved the knife upward. Readied herself to meet her fate.

When fangs and claws did not tear into her flesh, Saga blinked in confusion. A high-pitched shriek soon broke into a gurgle. Bones crunched and blood slapped the floor.

And then a deep growl resonated in the air, scraping up the hairs on her arms and all down the back of her neck. And in that moment, Saga knew this creature was the alpha of them all, that which even the apex predators feared.

The room grew utterly still. Saga hardly dared breathe. Slowly, her gaze lifted. Met eyes of a brilliant green. His gray fur stood on end, and his snout was drawn into a snarl, revealing exquisitely sharp fangs dripping with blood. The beast's limbs were grotesque and disproportionate—its forelegs long and angular, its back legs thickly muscled—and the spines along its back looked all wrong. But as Saga looked at Kassandr in his beast form, she could have wept with relief.

The beast leaped. Saga squeezed her eyes shut and curled into a ball, gasping as the wounds on her shoulder pulled. Howls and screeches she'd probably hear in her nightmares assaulted her, and Saga tried to find the dark, quiet place in the corner of her mind. But she couldn't escape it. She heard it all—squelches and bones popping; animalistic whimpers and Kassandr's answering roars. On it went, until she thought it would never end. But at some point, it must have.

A hand slid along her jaw, and Saga flinched away.

"They have hurt you."

On a long, slow exhale, Saga opened her eyes. Back in his human form, Kassandr now knelt beside her. His eyes held the same wildness as the beast's, his hair unkempt. A cut marred his cheek, and before she knew what she was doing, Saga's fingertips were skimming along it. He leaned into her touch, a low rumble coming from deep in his chest.

"You're hurt as well," she heard herself say. She could scarcely understand her own voice—it sounded raw and scraped. Had she been screaming that loudly?

"I am sorry, Winterwing. I was called away—a ruse, a stupid, foolish trick I should not have fallen for. And now you have paid the price."

"They were going to string my corpse from the walls," Saga murmured absently. A moment ago, she'd faced certain death, but now . . . now they were all dead. Before her, Kassandr vibrated with anger. He bowed his head, and her gaze traveled downward, then snapped rapidly back up.

"Where are your clothes?" It took all of her will not to confirm her suspicions. "Are you *naked*?"

Kass's head rose, amusement playing across his lips. "During shifting it gets . . . shredded."

Saga lost the battle, her gaze drifting downward across ridged, toughened flesh, past scars and a light dusting of dark hair. As it reached his navel, she slammed her eyes shut, cursing herself. "Your seamstress must hate you."

A low amused chuckle. "Very much."

Before she could ask him to find some gods damned breeches, his arm slid under her knees, the other wrapping around her back, and then she was being lifted into the arms of an extremely naked Kassandr Rurik.

"I can walk!" she protested, pushing against his hold. But as the gouges scored into her shoulder pulled, an agonized whimper slipped out.

"Stop fighting me, Saga. Let me to help you."

"That never goes well for me," she gasped out, but relented.

"Keep your eyes on me." Backlit by the torches, Kassandr's face was shadowed, yet those green eyes anchored her. "Do not look behind me."

Saga did not want to think of what carnage lay behind him. What he'd done to the mountain cat, to all of those shifters—

Kassandr strode toward the exit, then paused by a figure Saga had not noticed before. “String these men from the fortress walls, Rovgolod,” said Kass in Íseldurian. “Remind Oleg what happens when he crosses me.”

Oleg. The man’s name rang in her ears. He’d tried to have her killed. Would have had her corpse strung from the walls. Saga’s heart kicked up at impossible speed, her breaths growing quick and shallow.

“Not safe,” she whispered, squeezing her eyes shut. “I am not safe here—”

Kass strode through the doorway, carrying Saga back toward her chambers and whispering words that ought to soothe her. Yet nothing he said could assuage her fear.

The moment they reached her chambers, Saga ordered Kassandr to leave. He did as she bade, though the worried look on his face was telling enough. After the dead bolt slid into place, Saga rushed to the bench, swiping tears from her eyes. Fueled by desperation, she hauled it against the door to bar entry. She did the same to her balcony door with the second bench.

And with the last of her energy, Saga flung herself onto her bed.

Only then did she let herself truly fall apart.

CHAPTER 15

Kopa, Íseldur

Silla's knee bounced eagerly as she sat by the hearth. She knew she'd drunk too much róa, but hadn't been able to stop herself. After the attempt on Eisa's life, Jarl Hakon had appointed Eilif as her food taster, and Silla despised it. This morning, she'd watched despondently as the poor handmaiden had sampled her morning pot of róa and deemed it free from poison. Silla had wasted no time in consuming three full cups, desperate to keep her fatigue at bay. But it seemed the energizing properties of the róabark had done her nerves no favors. Or perhaps her nerves were due to the anticipation of what today would bring.

She would meet Jarl Hakon's Weaver and have the threads of her fate read.

As Myrkur shifted inside her, Silla tried to keep her moods bright, but gods, it was getting hard. Someone had tried to kill her. There was still no sign of Saga. The feast of the Shortest Day neared; her etiquette training was ramping up. And Silla could no longer deny that the god of chaos was growing more active.

Last night, she'd dreamed of what she hadn't in so long—the little blond girl's hand wrenching free from hers. "Don't leave me!" Saga had screamed as Silla was hauled backward and Urkan warriors swarmed the room.

As if that wasn't bad enough, the dream had soon shifted to Rökkur—the dragon Kraugeir waking from his slumber; the hot, orange lifeblood of the fire mountains spewing forth. Silla had woken drenched in sweat, the remnants of Myrkur's excitement coursing through her veins.

In that moment, she missed Rey more than she could say. There was no sleep to be found after that. Instead, she'd pored over every book in the stack the magisters had sent her and had found no hint at a cure to her mother's bargain. Weeks, she'd been at this—as had her queensguard and Jarl Hakon's magisters—and they were no better off than when they'd started.

A life for a life, her mother had promised Myrkur. The god had the power to take her life at any moment. So why was she still breathing?

At the very least, her daily hindrium doses blocked the god from her Ashbringer source. Yet He seemed unbothered. Instead, she felt Him prodding . . . as though He was searching for something.

Her desperation to rid herself of this god was growing by the day. And so she'd decided to take her search for a cure beyond books, to Jarl Hakon's Weaver. Perhaps there was something to be discovered in Weaving the threads of Silla's past, present, and future?

Now she sat with Liv and Kaeja in the Weaver's sitting room, an unnatural silence stretching out among them. Silla was so much more comfortable around Hild and the other fortress servants, but she supposed she must try with Kaeja and Liv, and so she blurted, "Ashes, but these dragons make me twitchy!"

Liv looked up from her embroidery in surprise, while Kaeja's face twisted into a look of derision.

"I mean—" Silla gestured to the enormous tapestry strung above the fireplace. "—there are simply so *many* of them in this place."

"Ashfall is built into a fire mountain," said Kaeja, as though Silla were a simpleton. "And the dragon is symbolic of both the fire mountain and House Hakon's might."

Heat rose in Silla's cheeks.

"They *can* be rather unsettling," said Liv, voice lowered conspiratorially. "Sometimes it feels as though I'm being watched, but when I turn around, it's only a tapestry."

Silla was glad to hear the telltale sounds of approaching footfalls signaling the Weaver's arrival, and her exit from this conversation. The Weaver looked to have seen four decades, and she was trailed by a pair of acolytes. The acolytes went to an enormous loom leaning against the wall and began untangling the warp threads, while the Weaver faced Silla with a demure smile.

"Your Highness," said the Weaver, before dipping into a curtsy. "I'm honored to Weave for you today."

Silla's stomach knotted and twisted as she considered the precise wording of her question for the Weaver. She'd been warned to keep her *affliction* within a tight-knit circle, and glanced at Liv and Kaeja, searching her mind for the etiquette lesson that would allow her to kick them out politely.

But the Weaver must have read her dilemma, for she turned to the pair and said, "My Weavings are done strictly in private."

Liv frowned. "But Lady Tala said—"

"You may wait in the antechamber," said the Weaver, her crisp voice brooking no argument.

Kaeja eyed Silla suspiciously, then moved toward the door with Liv in tow. The acolytes, having completed their task, trailed silently after them.

Once they were alone in the room, Silla shot the Weaver a thankful look.

"Have you had your threads Woven before?"

Silla wiped her palms on her skirts. "Not formally, but I . . . Harpa Galtung once read my . . . aura?"

The Weaver's eyes flared. "Harpa Galtung? She's not been seen in an age." She paused. "Well. I shall require a few drops of your blood to activate my galdur. Then I'll be able to sense your threads and Weave them into a tapestry." She gestured to the loom.

"I have . . . questions," Silla said apprehensively. The Weaver nodded, and she continued. "I would like to know what has befallen my sister, and where she might be. I would know who tried to poison me. And I would know if there is a cure for the bargain my mother made."

The Weaver's gaze drifted around her face.

"It is a lot, I know." Silla laughed bitterly.

"There is no guarantee I will find the answers," said the Weaver after a beat, "but I will keep my eyes and ears open while I Weave."

Silla nodded. The Weaver handed her a dagger, and with a quick breath, Silla slashed a shallow cut across her palm. As she watched the blood pool, she couldn't help but recall the vision of her mother slashing her own palm before summoning the dark god.

As though He were listening, Myrkur cracked an eye open.

The Weaver dipped her fingers in Silla's blood, rubbing it between forefinger and thumb. Silla had witnessed Harpa in her Weaving trance, and she knew to expect the milky-white sheen the Weaver's eyes would take on.

"I see your threads," murmured the woman, before turning to her loom. "I see . . . another. I see your sister."

Silla's pulse throbbed with excitement. "Where is she?"

The Weaver did not seem to hear her. "I see two bright threads, woven tightly together before splitting. Your sister's thread has diverged greatly from your own . . ."

Diverged greatly. Silla's mind raced. Where could she be? But the fact that Saga's thread was not yet cut surely meant she was alive. Silla clung to this fact with everything she had.

"I see threads of darkness woven in with each." There was a note of worry in the Weaver's voice. "I see . . . a battle."

The Weaver's magic thrummed in the air, while Silla's pulse kicked up with excitement. Myrkur yawned and arched His back. "A battle?" pressed Silla.

The stones weighing the warp thread knocked together as the Weaver worked at her loom. "Beneath a great tree—"

"And a cure?" she asked, leaning forward. "For my mother's bargain?" Hope and anticipation built inside her. Silla sensed she was on the precipice of a great discovery—

I think not, rasped a voice of sharp edges inside her skull, sending a prickle of alarm down Silla's spine.

At her loom, the Weaver inhaled sharply, then clutched at her throat.

"What—" Silla rushed toward the woman, then stumbled back.

Turning toward her, the Weaver's eyes were wide and completely black.

I'm not done with you, Eisa, purred Myrkur as the Weaver fell to her knees with a keening moan.

"No!" pleaded Silla.

Tremors shook the Weaver, spittle foaming at the corners of her mouth.

Yes, said Myrkur.

And as the Weaver toppled to the side and began to convulse, Silla's scream finally broke free.

Hours later, she sat at the long table in Ashfall's great hall, staring blankly at her plate. Silla was clad in a rich indigo gown, her hair woven into a sophisticated series of braids that bared her neck and showcased the ornate golden necklace she wore. The great hall was filled with Kopa's most important, gathered to greet the first of many jarls, who'd arrived ten days early for the feast of the Shortest Day.

Preparations for the feast were already under way. The hearth was being cleaned in preparation for the ceremonial log. And sprigs of pine and juniper had been strung from the antler chandeliers, scenting the air with their evergreen fragrance.

Tonight, they dined at a solitary table arranged in the middle of the great hall. Atli Hakonsson sat to her left while the visiting jarl's heir—whose name Silla had already forgotten—sat to her right. Across the table, Lady Tala was deep in conversation with the visiting jarl's wife, while Ladies Liv and Kaeja engaged his heirs-to-be. But though she was there in body, Silla's mind was leagues away.

After the Weaver had fallen, everything had happened so

quickly—the acolytes rushing in, Silla's queensguard ushering her away, and Myrkur cackling inside her skull all the while. Distraught, Silla had canceled her afternoon etiquette session with Lady Tala. But a message had returned explaining that one of the jarls had arrived early; that Eisa Volsik was expected at the evening meal.

Before departing for the meal, Silla had sent Kálf to inquire about the Weaver's health and was relieved to hear she was expected to make a full recovery. Apparently, Ashfall's healer had attributed the Weaver's symptoms to a "falling sickness" she'd been known to suffer from.

Only Silla knew the full truth.

I'm not done with you echoed endlessly in her mind, though the god Himself was silent and slumbering. Myrkur had done that—had harmed the Weaver to prevent Silla from learning more about her curse. Hopelessness filled her each time she remembered it. How was she supposed to cure herself of Him when He was privy to each thought in her mind?

Fingers squeezed her shoulder, and Silla's hand lashed out, nearly connecting with the goblet on the table before her. Thank the gods above, she'd missed. Trying to shake some sense back into her skull, Silla turned to Atli.

"I was just telling Helgi here—" Atli gestured to the jarl's heir, on Silla's right. "—about the meadows."

"The meadows?" Silla repeated.

"Aye," said Atli, and Silla gathered this was not the first time he'd explained it to her. "There's a trail climbing up behind the fortress. A tad steep to start, but it flattens out up top into a meadow. There you'll find winter-blooming flowers and a clear view all the way to the ocean."

"It sounds lovely," said Helgi, though his gaze was trained on her necklace—or was it lower?

Indignance rose within her, but Silla reminded herself she was Eisa Volsik tonight—that she must recall her etiquette lessons. "It does. Can you ride to the meadows?" She hung on to this thread of conversation for dear life.

"Aye," said Atli.

She didn't have to muster her wistful smile—Silla had lost count of how many days it had been since she'd ridden Dawn, and fresh air sounded positively divine. But that thought had her wondering how long it had been since Rey left—and how many days it had been without a single letter arriving. Gloom settled heavily inside her at that. It had been silly to ask him to pen letters in the midst of the danger they'd surely face. Yet Rey had been so sincere in his promise.

"Perhaps we might ride the trail, just the pair of us?" Helgi said in a low voice, his breath hot in her ear. He was far too close, and his hand on her knee made Silla jump in fright again. This time, her hand connected with the goblet, and she watched in horror as it tipped onto its side. Blood-red wine splashed across the table—and right onto Helgi's lap.

He leaped to his feet with a startled cry while Atli hauled Silla up and away from the dripping mess. Silence fell upon the hall, and Silla knew all eyes at the table were upon her.

"My mistake," said Atli, jovially. "Perhaps I ought to switch to ale."

Laughter burst around the table, though Helgi remained furiously silent as he blotted his tunic with a scrap of linen. As the conversation gathered back up, Helgi cast a single scathing glare at Silla before wordlessly turning on his heel and leaving the room.

"Barnacles," she muttered, snatching a linen from the table and mopping at her mess. "You didn't need to take the blame," she told Atli from the corner of her mouth.

He shrugged. "It was no trouble to me."

Eilif bustled up, taking the linen from her hand. Before Silla could protest, a second serving woman was at her elbow, pouring her a fresh goblet. Then, to her great distaste, Eilif sipped the wine to detect poison. Across the table, Kaeja glanced her way, whispering animatedly to Lady Liv.

Silla's skin prickled with humiliation. This was her first chance to make a good impression upon the jarls of the north, and already she was failing. Her gaze drifted across the table, where Liv and Kaeja conversed with Helgi's brothers. Kaeja's posture was straight but at ease, her fingers wrapped daintily around her goblet as she laughed at something one of them said. How did they make it seem so effortless?

Atli pulled her chair out, and Silla took a seat. "Thank you."

"Someone ought to have warned you," said Atli as he took his own seat. He lowered his voice. "Helgi might be heir to the Sveinar lands, but the man is a lecherous scoundrel."

Her fingertips trailed absently along her neckline. "I . . . had a curious sense about him."

"And perhaps my motives weren't entirely selfless." Atli picked up his goblet and swirled his wine. "If anyone shows you the meadows, it ought to be me."

Silla's gaze darted to Atli's, trying to find any hidden meaning in his words. She was not a *complete* fool. Atli was so frequently seated beside her at meals, and it was impossible to miss Jarl Hakon's frequent eager glances between the pair. Marriage to a man like Atli Hakonsson, heir to the largest landholdings in the north of Íseldur, was precisely what Lady Tala would deem "beneficial."

Silla lowered her voice, but held his gaze. "You do know that I am with Rey?"

Atli shrugged, his smile gleaming. "You're a beautiful woman. Surely you cannot blame a man for trying—" Atli ran his hand along his warrior's braid, glancing toward his father. He lowered his voice and leaned closer to Silla. "Let us be friends, then. I know Lady Tala can be rather . . . *zealous* in her teachings. If you'd like a break, the offer stands."

Silla could have sworn there was still a flirtatious glint in his eye, but she couldn't be certain.

Atli nudged her with an elbow. "Is that a yes to the meadows?"

A smile spread across her lips, and Silla nodded. "Yes."

But as her gaze drifted across the table, she caught Kaeja watching her and Atli. And while she could not read the look in her eyes, Silla was certain she did not like whatever it hinted.

CHAPTER 16

Ruins of Istré, near the Western Woods

Rey dreamed of Silla.

She reclined in the grass, moonflowers adorning her curls and starlight shining in her eyes.

"Together," she whispered, tracing the dragon tattooed across his chest. "Frightened together."

The words lit a hearthfire deep in his chest, heating him all the way through. Soft fingertips trailed up his biceps then slid into his beard before pulling him down to her. And when Rey's lips met hers, it felt like coming home.

He woke in a cold bedroll, a stone digging into his back and the scent of Istré's charred ruins heavy in his nose. Beside him, one of Eyvind's warriors snored loudly, and Rey stared at the darkness above, wondering if he'd ever felt so homesick in his life.

It was madness, of course. For weeks now, he'd longed to be here, in Istré, with his Bloodaxe brothers and sisters around him. It was his responsibility to finish what he'd started so many weeks ago. But now that he was here, he felt out of sorts.

Rey caught himself smiling at misshapen rocks, wishing Silla was here, pointing them out and humming incessantly. The crook between his arm and side where she liked to nestle ached for her. He'd lost his gods damned mind for this woman and needed to get his head on straight. Too many people depended on him to get this job right.

Yet Rey couldn't shake the feeling that something wasn't right. It was the strangest sensation—as though the once-straight threads of his fate had been rewoven into something meandering and ill-defined.

But he needed to see this job to the end. And the discovery that the mist had traveled so far from the Western Woods—that it had likely Turned an entire village draugur—had only solidified his decision. They had to discover the source of the mist and destroy it for good.

Rökksgarde, the draugur had said, and Rey could not stop puzzling over the name. Surely it was a location, and one linked to Rökkur. Where was it? And who was calling the draugur there?

It was pointless asking questions when there were no answers to be found. But Rey knew sleep would not find him again, so he dressed and made his way to the fire where Hekla sat on watch.

"Sent your falcon yet, Galtung?" She watched him from across the fire, and Rey had the sense she was testing him—trying to determine his suitability as a partner for her friend. After all Silla had weathered, Rey was glad she had a friend like Hekla.

He glanced to the cart Horse had pulled from Kopa, falcons dozing in the cage within. He'd bribed Jarl Hakon's falconer to borrow a dozen birds from the aviary. Had weathered endless teasing from those he rode beside. But Rey couldn't bring himself to care. He'd promised Silla he'd write and had done so each morning. And though Rey had raised the homing flag on the caravan, he had yet to receive a reply.

She was busy, he told himself. Was likely exhausted. And besides, *she* hadn't promised to write him back.

"Haven't given Gunnar an answer yet?" Rey shot back at Hekla.

Her sigh was weary. "You do not understand, Axe Eyes. You did not see him after . . . after . . ." She waved her left hand.

"You're right," he admitted, heaviness settling in his chest. When his identity as the Slátrari had been revealed to the whole of Íseldur, hiding in Kalasgarde had been the only option for Rey. He did not regret his choice, but he did regret that he hadn't been there for his Crew in the aftermath of Ilías's death and Jonas's betrayal. The Bloodaxe Crew was his responsibility and he'd let them down. Rey scrubbed a hand through his beard.

"Did Jonas truly . . ."

Rey met Hekla's amber eyes across the fire. "Truly orchestrate a plan to kill us?" He sighed. "His grief has changed him—has warped his perception of honor and justice. He's not the man we used to know."

Grief grabbed him by the scruff and shook him, leaving Rey disoriented. The coldness in Jonas's eyes had been startling. It was hard to reconcile the man he'd met in Svangormr Pass with the one who'd been his right hand for five long years. Now he mourned not only Ilías but Jonas, too.

A squirrel chittered from a tree overhead, and Rey stared up into the darkness. The horizon was now a faint sliver of blue, and he guessed that first light would arrive within the hour. Rey's eyes narrowed, then darted back to the source of the chatter. There had been no sign of any living thing on the road near Istré—unless one counted the Turned frost fox they'd swiftly dispatched.

"Patience," muttered Hekla, drawing Rey's attention. She'd pushed to her feet and now scowled up at the tree.

"What—" he started.

"It was not the right time to reveal it," Hekla snapped. "You must be patient. I said I would do it today."

And then Rey saw it—a small, twitchy figure, scrambling face-first down the tree. The squirrel paused, then unleashed a long string of chirrupy nonsense.

Slowly, Hekla turned to Rey. Raised her brows with a sort of weary acceptance. "This is Kritka. He wants to meet you. Says you have a curious smell."

Rey was torn between barking out a laugh and sending Hekla back to Kopa to have her head examined. But then the squirrel bounded cautiously toward him. Once. Twice. Rey stared in disbelief as the small creature sniffed his boot, then stood on hind legs and scented the air.

"It seems you've held some details back, Hekla," said Rey, unable to hide his amusement. He felt more than saw her scowl. "How long have you been able to speak to woodland creatures?"

Hekla released an exasperated sound. "Do you wonder why I did not tell you?"

"Curious, Hekla, I thought such skills were reserved for princesses in those tales from the Southern Continent."

"You have my permission to bite him, Kritka."

The squirrel hissed, launching itself upon Rey before he could react. Claws pierced through his breeches and into his flesh as it tried to climb him. With a shout of alarm, Rey toppled off his log, sprawling on his arse while trying to shake the creature free.

"That's enough, Kritka," said Hekla, looming over Rey with a satisfied smile. "I think the bjáni gets the point."

The creature thankfully bounded away, and Rey sent it a suspicious look as he accepted Hekla's hand up.

Hekla folded her arms, no trace of amusement left in her face. "When the mist trapped me, Kritka took the form of a grimwolf and saved me. Do not ask me how such a thing is possible, as I know it should not be. Now he seems to have . . . bound himself to me."

Rey examined Kritka's dark, beady eyes, ready to unsheathe his dagger should the rodent launch at him once more. Anyone else, and he might not believe them. Eternal fucking fires, a month ago he might not have believed it. But he'd seen Hekla command the creature to attack him, and knew his friend too well to doubt her words. Kritka turned to Hekla, making more vocalizations.

"I don't know why he smells like the Protector." Hekla looked at Rey and sighed. "I didn't tell you about Kritka in Kopa because I needed you to see him with your own eyes. Do you recall the Klaernar sent to Istré to help deal with the mist?"

"The ones that ended up dead and strung to the pillars?" Rey asked.

Hekla nodded. "The murdered Klaernar were, Kritka claims, his mistress's call for help."

"The Spiral Staves?" Rey murmured. He tried to recall what else Magnus Hansson had said while detailing this job.

Klaernar strung on Ursir's pillars by strange-looking vines . . . stabbed through the heart . . . a symbol written in blood, over and over. A Spiral Stave. He and Jonas had immediately suspected the Klaernar's killer was altogether separate from the murderous mist. The squirrel's story could fit.

"His mistress has since gone dormant, hiding herself in a tree. I know this sounds . . . mad . . ."

Rey quirked an eyebrow, and Hekla scowled.

". . . but he claims his mistress is older than the gods. That she has great powers and knowledge. He begs that we wake her."

"Who is your mistress, rodent?" Rey demanded, hardly able to believe he was talking to a gods damned squirrel.

Kritka released a flurry of rapid squirrel chatter, leaving Hekla throwing her hands in exasperation. "It is always the same—he gives me a dozen names that mean nothing to me. Wolf Mother and Pine Tree Hilda and the Forest Maiden—"

"Forest Maiden," Rey repeated, his mind latching onto the name and trying to glean meaning.

"Does it mean something to you?"

He scowled into the flames, trying to recall the stories Harpa had told him and Kristjan as children. His grandmother's stories had never been the comforting type to lull one into sleep. Instead, they'd been more likely to give one nightmares.

"She has tree bark skin and antlers on her brow," he murmured. "And a bristly tail much like a fox's. But her face is a thing of beauty, and she seduces men . . . leads them into the woods until they grow hopelessly lost and she can feast on their flesh."

Kritka chittered, and Hekla translated. "He says only the stupid ones follow."

Rey choked on a laugh. "I suppose so. But I thought she was only a story—a tale to keep children away from the woods and men from straying from their wives."

Hekla shrugged. "A month ago, I'd not have believed it. But I've seen too much not to consider that this irritating squirrel and his mistress might be allies. At the very least, they know the forest and might help us find the source of the mist."

She watched him expectantly, and Rey realized she was waiting for his take. He cleared his throat. "It sounds like a lead worth chasing," he said slowly. "What do you need from me?"

Hekla's eyes glinted in the firelight, her lips curving up at the corners. "You know, I think I might have missed you, Axe Eyes."

He snorted.

"No, truly. It's exhausting trying to keep all the arselings in line."

"I hear it was *you* needing to be put in line."

"Only because I refused to abide Loftur's bloody rules."

"'Tis a damned good thing you didn't." Rey smiled ruefully. "I think leadership suits you."

The moment he said it, the words felt right. He'd seen it when she'd taken charge in the village. Was this why he felt out of sorts? Like he no longer quite fit? But a baffled expression crossed Hekla's face.

"You held the Bloodaxe Crew together. Took charge of the situation in Istré." He thought of the camaraderie he'd seen between Hekla and Eyvind's retinue. She'd gained their trust and respect, a hard-won thing for a woman warrior. And he realized with sudden clarity what a natural-born leader Hekla was. Why hadn't he seen it before?

A twig snapped behind them, and a red-cloaked figure approached. Firelight caught on Eyvind's sleep-mussed hair, a pair of waterskins held in his hand.

"I filled your waterskins, Lynx."

"Lynx?" Rey asked, glancing between them. Hekla had grown rigidly still.

"You know, Galtung," said Eyvind, eyeing Rey. "The Bloodaxe

Crew's wagon is among Istré's ruins. You ought to go find it and have a look."

Rey's eyes narrowed. "If you want time alone, then just ask."

He pushed to his feet, but Hekla beat him to it. She snatched the waterskins from Eyvind, averting her gaze as she said, "I'll go look. You two stay."

Eyvind watched her retreat with a look of disappointment before sinking onto the log next to Rey's. "How long do you think it'll take her to give me a chance to explain?"

"Hekla is not as hard as she wants the world to see her." Rey picked up a piece of wood and nestled it into the fire. "And she knows how to hold a grudge."

Eyvind sighed, then smiled. "Then I suppose I'll have to be dogged in my pursuit. 'Tis a good thing I enjoy a challenge." He brightened. "What else did I miss?"

Rey released a long, slow breath. "Only that tomorrow we shall follow a squirrel into the woods and release his mistress from a tree."

Eyvind's gaze swung to Rey. "Ah," he said, without missing a beat. "You met Kritka."

CHAPTER 17

Kovograd, Zagadka

The wind was crisp and carried a piney scent, wicking Saga's fogged breaths up into the skies. She pulled her fur hat lower over her ears, timing her steps to the taps Kassandr Rurik's fingers made against her arm. During their walks, she'd learned to keep her focus on the surrounding curiosities. The Zagadkian soldiers with their fur caps, stationed at intervals along the defensive walls; the raw hides of reindeers stretched on racks before the tannery. Everything was bathed in a sharp, wintery light, a fact that distracted Saga from the tension in her stomach.

Her shoulder wound was quickly healing, but the attack in the gallery had been a setback. Saga had kept herself locked in her chambers. Had stopped venturing onto her balcony. This had gone on for days, until she'd found the raven's feather in her dress pocket. As she stared at this feather, discovered on her last stroll with Kassandr, Saga realized what she was doing.

It was a strange thing to acknowledge that your mind played tricks on you—that the things it perceived as peril were not always so. And while caging herself away might feel safe in the moment, it was a danger to her in the long run.

She could *not* go backward. Saga had to expose herself to dangerous elements—both the real ones, and those that were a product of her mind. And so she'd asked Kassandr to take her back to the temple gardens. And if she'd breathed a little easier when sliding her arm into his—if her blood warmed at the feel of his large body beside hers—Saga would never confess it. Because admitting that she trusted Kassandr Rurik with her safety felt like a betrayal of herself.

But she couldn't shake his words—*What about Midfjord, Saga? Who were you to meet? Where were you to go?* Because there was truth to what he'd said. Saga hadn't a clue what she'd have done in Midfjord—she and Ana had never gotten further than the location.

Saga's first walk with Kassandr had lasted a matter of minutes. Their next, a little longer. Each day, Saga was able to grow a little more used to those open skies; to the call of birds. The feather in her pocket helped her find strength on the days she felt like fleeing. It reminded her of those winterwing birds finally flying away from their cage.

Now they strolled through the west side of the fortress, a dozen of Kassandr's Druzhina warriors flanking them. A measure, Kassandr had assured her, in case Oleg got any more ideas.

"*Chto oni delayut?*[*]" she asked, pointing to a large vat. Four tannery apprentices stood on a platform surrounding it, stirring the vat with large paddles.

"*Eto osobyy tanin,*[†]" replied Kassandr in slow, measured Zagadkian. He switched to Íseldurian. "It makes the leather soft, yet impenetrable by iron."

Her brows furrowed as she thought of the conversation she'd overheard between King Ivar and Prince Bjorn over the daymeal a month or so past. They'd discussed a metal alloy the Karthians preferred and how it might be used for arrowheads as well. "Is vulnerable to steel?"

Kassandr cocked his head to the side. "*Nemnogo.*[‡]"

* What they do?

† It is a special tannin.

‡ A little.

"You plan," said Saga in rough Zagadkian, "for shields." She shook her head in frustration, wishing the words would come to her more smoothly. But Saga had to admit, the fact that words were coming at all was progress.

Still, Kassandr nodded in understanding. "We have many shields to deflect steel blades," he replied in Zagadkian, then paused. "If you were the high prince of Zagadka, what would you do right now?"

This was a frequent game they played while practicing Zagadkian. Saga eyed the defensive walls. Tall and sturdy, they were built atop earthen ramparts. Watchtowers were stationed every fifty or so paces, and the covered walkways between them would defend from projectiles. But there was one glaring weakness in this fortress—one that made Saga's pulse a little jagged.

Saga paused and sifted through her limited Zagadkian vocabulary. Realizing she was inadvertently staring at his chin, she cleared her throat and looked away. "Arrange for fire."

Kassandr nodded along.

There seemed to be a hint of stubble on his jaw. Had he shaved this morning? And did Kassandr do it himself, or have a servant do it for him?

"Beach rocks," Saga coughed out, trying to get her mind back on track.

He gave her a curious look. "Sand?" he guessed.

Saga nodded, trying desperately not to look back at his chin. "To kill fire. Also ocean plant."

His brow furrowed.

"Roof." Saga gestured to the fortress. Exasperated, she switched to Íseldurian. "Seaweed to cover the roofs!"

"Ahh." He stroked his jaw, and damn it, but her gaze was back, snagged on the shallow dimple in the center of his chin. Her fingers itched to trace it, so she balled them into fists.

"And—"

Kass cut her off with a raised palm. "In Zagadkian."

"Shield wall, no—" Saga shook her head in frustration. "*Protect* wall with ocean plant."

"What else?"

"Fire cup." She wrinkled her nose. "Fire *flask*."

"Projectiles?" he asked, switching to Íseldurian.

"The Urkans have clay flasks that erupt with fire when broken," she replied. "The liquid inside them cannot be extinguished by water." Saga could not keep the vision of Sunnavík's pier during the Urkan invasion from forming in her mind's eye. She'd been only five, yet she remembered it vividly—boats and piers and homes, all exploding with fire. Warriors caught aflame, jumping overboard, only to be picked off with arrows.

"I will ask my chieftains about this," mused Kassandr, rubbing his chin once more. "You are clever in such things, Winterwing."

His praise made her skin buzz . . . made her yearn to glance back at his chin. Gods, but there was something very wrong with her. Instead, she forced her gaze to the main gate of the fortress. Tall and thick, the studded double doors were topped with an enormous bell tower.

"You have considered what you will do after?" asked Kassandr in Íseldurian.

"After?"

"After you return to Íseldur. Find your sister."

Saga felt Kassandr's gaze on her face, and she was too weak—she gave up and stared at the groove in his chin before mapping the contours of his strong jaw. But as his words settled, an ache grew in Saga's chest and she looked away.

"If she's alive." She probed inward for any sign of her sister, but as always, there was nothing to be found. "I do not know." For so long, her life had been centered on simply surviving. How did she explain that she'd lived so long in the shadows of Signe and Ivar, that to conceive of a life of her own was too much?

"I see a queen in you, but more than that, I see a leader."

A laugh sputtered from Saga.

"No?" he asked, drawing them to a stop. "You do not see it?"

Saga scowled up at him. "You're mocking me, aren't you?"

"I would not jest about such a thing."

She pulled her collar tighter to ward against the chill. “My name might be Volsik, but it does not mean I am built for such things.”

Before Kassandr could form a reply, a male voice called out, and the Druzhina warriors tightened around them. Saga clutched Kassandr’s arm as she tried to see past the large men. But as Kassandr let out a low, deep growl, she had an inkling of who it was. Her shoulder wound throbbed, reminding her of how near this man had come to killing her.

“Dear brother,” drawled Oleg in slow, measured Zagadkian. “Call off your dogs. Unless you are feeling so insecure.”

Kassandr leaned down, his hot breath tickling Saga’s cold ear. “What do you wish for me to do?” he asked.

Saga tried to ignore the acceleration of her pulse, the shallowing of her breaths, but it was impossible. Oleg had tried to kill her, and seeing him now, so arrogantly unapologetic, made her blood simmer.

“Call down your men,” she said, forging steel into her voice and spine alike. Kassandr did as she bid him, and as Oleg’s smarmy face came into view, Saga refused to cower. She would show this preening turnip how little he’d affected her.

Oleg’s smirk was highly punchable. “Ahh,” he drawled in Zagadkian. “It is little pet of Ivar. Or should I say pet of Kassandr?”

“I am . . . my own,” Saga said darkly. Oleg’s startlement at her use of Zagadkian granted Saga a small victory. She wished she knew every Zagadkian insult so she could hurl them at him.

“She speaks,” he mused, watching her with predatory eyes.

“What do you want, demon?” growled Kassandr, the muscles of his forearm flexing and relaxing beneath Saga’s fingertips.

“I come from the armory,” said Oleg, slow enough for Saga to follow. “It seems they have set my commission aside in favor of large order of weapons. Do you know anything about this?”

“Forgive me, Oleg, for thinking our warriors might need sharp and durable blades in upcoming weeks,” said Kassandr.

Oleg’s brows dipped low, and he took a menacing step forward.

"They will not," he growled, "as we will avoid the need for it." His gaze slid to Saga, and a chill spread down her neck.

"Is your skull truly so thick?" asked Kassandr. "Do you think ore and grains will buy peace?"

"No," said Oleg. "*She* will buy peace."

Another low growl came from deep within Kassandr's chest, and as Saga looked down, she yelped in surprise. Inky black tattoos slid along his bared forearms and across the backs of his hands. And as she glanced at his eyes, they turned an inhuman green. The panic her anger had smothered quickly flared back to life, her heartbeat spiraling while Saga wheezed for breath.

As Kassandr glanced at her, he seemed to understand her inner turmoil. His fingertips found the crook of her elbow, and he tapped rhythmically while speaking to his brother.

"Understand this, Oleg. If your men come near her again, I will rip the limbs from your body and hang them for art on the walls."

Oleg's snarled reply was distant in Saga's ears as a dull ringing began. Air, she needed air, her shallow gasps doing nothing to fill her chest. Thankfully, Kassandr turned them away from his brother and ushered Saga back into the keep.

Away from Oleg and surrounded by the comfort of four walls, Saga stopped fighting her crisis. It was easier this way, giving in to the storm. She leaned into her panic—let it roll through her. Still, it took its toll on her, and when she came back to herself, she was panting and dazed, leaning into Kassandr's body as his fingers tapped along her back.

"You will not be given to Urkans, Saga," said Kassandr in Íseldurian. "I will not allow it." He watched her carefully with those too-bright eyes. There was something off-kilter about them—perhaps a little mad. Saga's insides squirmed with discomfort.

She glanced at his forearms, but only pale skin met her eyes. "Where are your tattoos?"

He blinked, then smirked. "They . . . show themselves during shifting." Kassandr disengaged his arm from hers, then tugged his sleeve up to reveal more of those thick forearms, and gods, but she might just like them more than his chin.

"How . . . far do they go? When they appear. Your tattoos." Even through the tumult of her mind, Saga could hardly believe she'd just asked that. Yet the tattoos—the brightness of his eyes—they all spoke of the strange dual nature of this man. And while the thought of him shifting into his beastly form filled her with dread, there was also now the thinnest shred of curiosity.

"Far." His voice was rough and hard, and Saga felt it all through her body. She couldn't help but wonder how the tattoos looked on his chest . . . down those muscled thighs . . . her cheeks flushed, and she looked away.

"We must be careful with Oleg, Winterwing," Kassandr murmured as she tried to regain her composure. "I fear he will whisper into my father's ears. Will poison the elders against our cause." He paused. "If we were to wed—"

A laugh choked out from her, her mind wrangling into a single, unified thought. "Being rejected once was not enough for you?"

"It will give you protection," he tried, an irritated edge to his voice. "If you were wed to heir of Zagadka, the elders could not give you to King Ivar—"

Saga folded her arms over her chest. "No," she said, her voice quiet and loud all at once. "And just so we're clear, Kassandr," she said, "I shall *never* marry you."

Turning on her heel, Saga returned to her chambers.

CHAPTER 18

Kopa, Íseldur

Silla stole from Ashfall Fortress under full sun, shocked that the guardsmen hadn't stopped her from leaving. With her queensguard flanking her on all sides, she was certain they'd be stopped—especially when they saw the bags of grain she'd commandeered from Jarl Hakon's personal stores. Yet with a quick word from Ingvarr, the guards had let her through.

Despite her exhaustion, Silla was exhilarated to feel the sun on her brow and wind on her cheeks, to see the beauty of Kopa up close. From her bedroom window, she could not see the iridescent sheen of minerals in the black stones, nor could she marvel at the intricate masonry. Now she gaped at the tall buildings and archways that defied nature—possible only thanks to the class of Galdra known as the Smiths. These specialized Galdra could forge and break the bonds of this world, allowing them to create stone cities and panes of glass, specialized textiles and so much more.

Despite Silla's constant stops to fawn over the marvels of Kopa, they eventually arrived at Frida's shelter home. She had no doubt that Lady Tala would frown upon Eisa Volsik coming to the shelter home—that she'd probably get an earful about how a queen doesn't go to her subjects, but waits for them to come to her. But she wasn't truly a queen, was she? And sometime in the darkest hours of the night, as Silla flipped through yet another tome, she'd come to a sleep-addled negotiation of sorts. Today, she visited Ástrid and the shelter home as *Silla,* not Eisa.

She smothered one last jaw-cracking yawn before entering. The children were a balm to her heart, refilling her bank of hearthfire thoughts and making Myrkur cringe deeper inside her. And Silla shed more than a few tears when Hef and Kálf handed bags of grain over to Frida.

She tried not to wonder how Jarl Hakon would respond when her raiding of his stores was brought to light. She hoped that his hoarding of grains while his people went hungry would bring so much shame upon the jarl that he simply would not broach the topic. And as Silla watched Frida wipe tears of relief from her cheeks, she didn't much care about any consequences she'd suffer.

The children crawled all over Silla—Ingvarr quickly gave up on trying to keep them off her—and squealed with delight when Silla provided them with gifts of her own. They were trinkets, really. Winter-blooming flowers from Ashfall's great hall; hairpins that had been lost beneath the bed. Then there were the charcoal sticks and bundles of parchment Atli had provided. Based on the conspiratorial wink he'd sent her while handing them over, she suspected he knew precisely who they were for.

Eventually, the winter sun reached its pinnacle in the sky and Silla knew it was time to move on. Her visit with the children had rather exhausted her limited energy, but a frazzled excitement buzzed in her veins. Next, she would visit Fallgerd.

Silla tried to keep her thoughts away from the old warrior. Tried not to divulge to Myrkur that she had not given up on finding a cure. Fallgerd had served King Hrolf during his darkest days—when the king had foolishly made his own bargain with Myrkur. If anyone in this realm might know of a cure, surely it would be Fallgerd.

As Myrkur ruffled His leathery wings inside her, Silla shoved her mind back to the children at the shelter home and her fresh hearthfire thoughts. She thought of the gap-toothed smiles and delight in their eyes as she'd told them the tale of hiding in the Bloodaxe Crew's wagon and tricking Axe Eyes into taking her to Kopa. With a hiss at her bright thoughts, Myrkur tucked His wings in tight and settled back down.

At the head of their procession, Ingvarr held up a hand, and they drew to a stop outside a small, nondescript home. Through the throng of guards, Silla could just make out Fallgerd's form filling the doorway.

"I would speak to Eisa alone," came the old warrior's voice.

Ingvarr laughed, shaking his head. "Not a chance, old man."

With an exasperated sigh, Silla wove through the crowd of guards to greet the former chief of her great-grandfather's retinue, Runný right on her heels. With a bright smile, Silla was careful not to extend a hand—she did not want a repeat of whatever had happened in the great hall.

"Well met, Fallgerd."

"Your Highness," said Fallgerd, glancing warily at Ingvarr. "There are matters we must speak of in private."

Silla examined the old man's face, searching for any hint of ill intent. Yes, someone had tried to poison her the day she'd met Fallgerd, but he hadn't gone anywhere near her cup. And besides, Silla couldn't help but see Fallgerd's much younger face, filled with worry as he'd applied pressure to Princess Svalla's neck wound. She sensed good in this man, and strong integrity.

Silla sent Runný a pleading look. Flicking her braids over her shoulder, Runný gave a long-suffering sigh. "We'll need to sweep your room," she told Fallgerd.

"Your Highness, I cannot allow this," Ingvarr interjected.

"Well, I *do* allow it!" Gods, but she was growing tired of the constant obstacles. Could nothing be easy? She breathed deeply, trying to temper her anger. "It is important I speak with Fallgerd alone. How can you best facilitate this?"

With a weary sigh, Ingvarr regarded Fallgerd. "Have you any weapons in your home?"

"Aye," the old man replied, but he moved aside to allow her guards entry. It wasn't long before Ingvarr and his soldiers emerged, carrying an assortment of blades.

"The home is clear," said Runný, leaving last. She paused near Silla and handed her a long-bladed hevrít. "Don't forget how to use this."

Silla accepted the weapon, then followed the old warrior into his home.

"I'll admit I relate to your young guardsman's position rather well," said Fallgerd, closing the door behind her. "Your great-grandfather could not stand his guards' fussing about, either. But it was my duty to ensure his safety."

His casual mention of her kin made Silla's heart crack open and spill warmth all through her. "Will you tell me of him?" she begged, following him to the hearth. "My—King Hrolf?" Silla settled on a bench, laying the hevrít across her lap.

A wistful smile spread across Fallgerd's face as he took his place on the bench across from her. "He was a good and just leader. One who put his people first."

Something flickered inside Silla at Fallgerd's words—a longing to sit in the seat of power. To bring true change to this realm. She, better than anyone, knew how the working people of this kingdom lived. But Silla pushed the thoughts aside. She could not let herself want such things when the throne was Saga's by birthright.

Fallgerd's expression grew troubled. "I fear he changed when your great-grandmother fell sick."

Myrkur rumbled low and deep within her, and Silla forced her mind to her sunniest thoughts while focusing on Fallgerd's words.

"When it became clear the queen was not recovering as she ought to, the king sent for healers far and wide—one traveled all the way from the isle of Karthia. Sadly, it was all to no avail. A month after falling ill, your great-grandmother succumbed to her sickness."

Fallgerd sighed, his gaze growing distant. "The king was never quite the same after that. Dark moods fell upon him. He could not climb out of bed some days. There was talk that he might abdicate the throne and pass the crown to his son. But one day, King Hrolf emerged from his gloom. He had a strange look about him. I asked what had happened, and he told me he'd had a dream."

"A dream?"

"Aye. He was vague about the details. Only that this dream had given him hope. Had restored his energy."

"Was he better then?" Silla asked, though she felt certain it had been no ordinary dream. Had Myrkur come to the king? Planted the idea of *a life for a life*?

"The king began giving us peculiar orders, often sending us on long, purposeless missions. I sensed that something was not right—that he was trying to rid himself of prying eyes. And so one day, I followed him." Fallgerd's gaze grew searching. "Do you know what he'd discovered, Your Highness?"

Candles flickering. The slash of a blade. Shadows coalescing on a wall. A book on a pedestal.

"A book," she breathed.

Fallgerd gave a long, weary sigh, looking much as though she'd just confirmed something. "I feared as much. When we—" His gaze dropped to her hands, folded around the hilt of the hevrit in her lap. And she knew in that moment, Fallgerd had sensed Myrkur in her when they'd first shaken hands.

Myrkur opened one eye, and Silla thought of Rey's large hands; the scent of woodsmoke that clung to his skin; the golden flecks that burned in his eyes.

"I tell you this," said Fallgerd, "because something tells me Hrolf would want you to know it." He paused, collecting his thoughts. "I was too late to keep your great-grandfather from making that foolish bargain. But Hrolf told me everything. How the Dark One had promised him a way to restore the queen's life. What it would cost him. He told me through tears how he'd searched through the book for an alternative, but the only thing he'd found was . . . impossible."

"But there *was* a way to cure himself of the bargain?" Silla leaned forward in her chair, ignoring the dark shiver vibrating low inside her.

Fallgerd rubbed his chin in thought. "Aye, but King Hrolf was simply too old to attempt—"

Myrkur's wings unfurled, His long neck craned upward, and it took Silla a moment to realize Fallgerd had stopped mid-sentence. His gaze flitted to the door in irritation as someone knocked impatiently.

"One moment, Your Highness. It must be my apprentice."

As he strode to the door, Silla gripped the arms of her chair, trying to calm her racing heart. Myrkur was now fully aware inside her.

Let me in, Eisa, purred the god of chaos.

Get out of my mind! she snapped back.

A low, dark chuckle slid through her veins. She searched for her hearthfire thoughts, but the god's presence muddled her focus.

Let me in, and together, we'll pull answers from him.

Silla blinked at the god's surprising suggestion, and for a moment, she found herself considering it. An end to the long nights spent searching through the books. An answer to the question that had been nagging at her for weeks. But even more enticing was the prospect of having her mind back to herself. She could contact Saga mind to mind. Discover her whereabouts and bring her to safety.

Yes, purred Myrkur, images sliding through her mind. Silla and Saga, reunited after seventeen long years. Silla and Saga, rallying the jarls of the north. The sisters on their horses, the Volsik banner snapping in the wind, as they marched south against Ivar Ironheart . . .

Lies, Silla forced out, trying to shove these illusions from her mind. Myrkur growled in frustration, but with it He slipped. A memory formed inside her mind—the queen's Chosen lying dead on the snow all around her. Rey's eyes wide with terror as Silla lashed out with her sword of black light. But what was most shocking of all was the anger Myrkur had felt while possessing her. Because though her cold Ashbringer light was fun to toy with, it was not what He'd been expecting to find.

You haven't found what you sought. Why would you help me banish you? Silla demanded.

Myrkur's shriek of anger was answer enough. The god wanted her to let Him in for some other purpose.

You are more clever than you seem, Eisa, hissed the god of chaos.

Silla was slightly offended.

I shall have to do this the hard way, it seems.

Fear rippled through her, but it was overshadowed by a great wave of fatigue. Countless sleepless nights caught up with her in an instant. Her blood churned thick and slow, sleep pulling her down, down, down, into its warm, syrupy embrace. Fighting was futile. It was inevitable. Silla rested her cheek on the back of her chair. Lost the battle to sleep.

Just for a moment, she told herself.

The Kingdom of Íseldur was in ruin. Lava spewed from the fire mountains as the black dragon Kraugeir spat flames of his own. Cities and forests and men burned. Ash and smoke choked the air, so thick Sunnvald could not shine down to the earth. Brothers and cousins slayed one another over the last scraps of food.

The scene suddenly darkened. Now Silla was in a room, a dark figure looming over her, a long-bladed knife held in hand.

"Queen Signe sends her regards," came a low voice. It was a familiar voice—one that left her momentarily surprised.

The blade glinted as it was raised overhead.

Silla awoke screaming, her heartbeat hammering violently in her ears.

He tried to harm us, whispered Myrkur.

Who? Silla asked, dazed.

Myrkur did not answer, and the heaviness of His exhaustion was a palpable thing. Perhaps she, too, might take a little nap. Silla's eyes fluttered shut. But there was more pounding, and for the first time, she realized it was not coming from her skull but from the door. Fists beat against timber as her guards shouted for Eisa. And above them all, Silla made out Runný's panicked voice.

"I'm here!" Silla called, suddenly alert.

Fallgerd. She was in Fallgerd's home. He'd stepped out to tend his apprentice and she'd . . . she'd nodded off. A stone landed heavily in her belly. She hadn't *nodded* off—Myrkur had forced her to sleep. And paired with the god's sudden brutal fatigue, an uneasy feeling fluttered low inside her.

It was the sight of the hearthfire—burned down to coals—that had Silla pushing jerkily to her feet. A loud clatter made her jump. She stared down at her feet—at the blade that had fallen from her lap. It was the hevrít she'd accepted from Runný, and it was coated in dark liquid.

Something was very wrong.

Silla's gaze darted to her dress, noting for the first time the red blotch on her skirts. Slowly, she lifted her hands, a low, keening wail coming from deep in her chest. Red smeared her palms, her fingers. A droplet slid over her wrist and under her sleeve.

"Get it off me," she whimpered, pawing at her bodice.

But even through her distress, Myrkur's words echoed in her skull.

He tried to harm us.

Who tried to harm us? she demanded of the god. But the god did not answer. He seemed to be slumbering, just as He had in the aftermath of Svangormr Pass. Whatever He'd just done had clearly drained His energy.

Silla tried to think. There was only one person who'd been in this room with her. One person, whose blood must be on her hands. She didn't want to look. Didn't want to see it. But Silla forced her gaze across the hearthfire.

"No no no," she pleaded.

Fallgerd's unmoving form was sprawled on the bench opposite hers. Widened blue eyes, devoid of life. Mouth opened wide in a silent scream. The front of his tunic was matted with blood. He'd been stabbed, repeatedly.

Silla looked from the blade on the floor to Fallgerd's wounds, then at the blood on her hands.

He tried to harm us.

Had Fallgerd lured her here to kill her? Could he have been responsible for the poison in her róa? But how, when he'd never come near her goblet—when she'd sensed such earnestness in him today. Silla had been certain he'd been about to tell her how to break the bargain . . .

The bargain.

You, she thought inwardly, revulsion and nausea battling within her. *Myrkur* had lulled her to sleep before she could glean answers. Had He seized control of her body? Attacked Fallgerd before he could reveal the cure to Silla?

Distantly, the sound of an axe splitting through wood met her ears, but Silla was too busy retching on the floor to think anything of it.

The door splintered into pieces and Ingvarr clambered through. Silently, he strode to Silla, put an arm under her knees, and lifted her. She felt as though she were in a dream, as though any minute she'd wake up to find this was all a big mistake. But as she caught sight of Runný's expression, she knew this was no dream.

"Did Fallgerd attack you?" asked Runný, panicked.

"He tried to harm us," Silla repeated dazedly. A wail built low in her chest, releasing as a sound more akin to a wounded animal than a human.

"Shields up!" barked Ingvarr, hefting Silla up higher in his arms. "Our job is to protect Eisa!"

Ingvarr strode out of the home and into the bright sunlight, but Silla only stared dazedly at his tunic. Up close, his pristine uniform was slightly less. A stain from spilled róa. A torn corner on his sigil badge. She focused in on these details. Tried to keep her mind from what lay back in that room.

Runný was on Ingvarr's left, Kálf on his right, their shields up and swords drawn as they jogged up the hill toward Ashfall.

"Hush now, Eisa," said Ingvarr, between heaving breaths. "We'll get you back to your chambers in no time."

CHAPTER 19

The Western Woods

A smile played on Rey's lips as he watched Hekla take charge of the contingent of warriors with a squirrel perched on her shoulder. First, she'd directed them to the burnt remains of Istré so they could search the Bloodaxe Crew's wagon. While the wagon and most of its contents were burnt beyond recognition, thankfully, the rhodium blades Magnus had provided them in Reykfjord had weathered the fire. This metal had proven particularly lethal to vampire deer and other creatures of darkness, and Rey guessed that they would be useful in the upcoming days.

After gathering the weapons, Hekla had ordered them to have their torches at the ready. And then they rode southward for an hour. This farmstead, Hekla had explained, was where she'd seen the first Spiral Stave carved into a tree and followed a trail of them into the grove where Kritka's mistress slumbered.

Rey stared hard at the symbol carved into the scaly trunk of a pine. The Spiral Stave was the Volsiks' sigil. When Magnus had first mentioned the symbol scrawled near the Klaernar's corpses, Rey had thought its purpose was to incense King Ivar's anger. Kritka, meanwhile, claimed the symbols were left by his mistress as a plea for help. But if this was true, Rey wondered who, precisely, the Forest Maiden had been calling for.

Long had the Western Woods remained a mystery. Much like

Harpa's tales of the Forest Maiden, her stories of the woods were equally mysterious—trails twisting until children grew helplessly lost, hollows leading to new worlds, and hills that proved to be slumbering giants. And then there were the groves of magical hjarta trees, so enormous that their roots burrowed down to the deepest depths, and their branches reached up like fingertips grazing the clouds. Rey didn't know if any of it was true. But as he stared into the shadowy veil of the woods, he knew for certain that there were things more ancient than the gods within.

Rey trudged after Sigrún into the Western Woods. For an hour, they followed a trail of Spiral Staves deeper into the forest. With each passing step, it became clear things in the woods were not right. Just as Hekla had described, the underbrush was dead, and though the taller trees lived, they were leached of all color. But most unnerving of all was the unnatural silence. Where were the chattering birds, the small woodland creatures? It was only their group, trampling dead foliage.

Finally they broke through a heavy thicket of brambles into a glade, and Hekla announced they'd arrived.

The clearing was carpeted with vibrant green grass, the air light and clean. It was obvious that whatever malevolence clung to the woods was excluded from this clearing.

Before them stood a tree. Thick-trunked, its twisted branches clawed upward, a few yellowed leaves clinging to them. Rey blinked in astonishment. The tree's gnarled bark was twisted into a central spiral with eight branching arms. It was, unmistakably, a Spiral Stave.

Rey's mind leaped immediately to Silla. If Kritka's mistress was calling for help, was it possible she called to the Volsiks? Nausea churned in his stomach as he thought of all Silla faced in Kopa right now—the weight of a kingdom on her shoulders, a missing sister and a god of chaos to contend with. Should he have brought her?

Kritka chittered from the tree's highest branch, and Hekla stepped forward. But Eyvind put a hand on her forearm, head bowing toward hers as he spoke in a low voice.

"Must it be you?"

Hekla shook Eyvind off with a glare. "I gave Kritka my word, and I shall see it through."

With a hard swallow, Eyvind drew his sword. "Then I give you mine that I shall guard your back."

A glowering Gunnar elbowed his way through the warriors, drawing his own weapon. "As shall I."

Rey struggled not to roll his eyes at the pair of fools. Instead, he focused his gaze on Hekla. She drew her dagger and slashed it through her palm. A long moment of silence stretched out as the blood pooled. And then Hekla began drawing symbols on the tree's trunk, checking for Kritka's approval at intervals.

At last, she stepped forward, placed her palm on the Spiral Stave, and spoke words that seemed quiet and loud, all at once.

"Wild One, we call to you."

Dry leaves rustled, like fingernails on wood. Wind whispered through the clearing, carrying the scent of damp earth and pine needles; of sunbaked rocks and frosted grass. A vibration built beneath their feet, the warriors calling out in surprise as it grew in intensity, building to a shuddering crescendo. The old tree groaned in protest, the last of its leaves fluttering to the ground. And then, with a sound like snapping bones, the tree split down the middle.

Several moments passed as Rey tried to get his bearings. Aside from the split tree, nothing seemed to have changed. But then a small sound escaped Hekla, and she crawled to the base of the tree. Eyvind cocked his head to the side and a groove formed between Gunnar's brows, but Rey couldn't see . . .

The vibration was back deep under his boots, shaking his bones. Rey glanced around, wondering if anyone else had felt it. But their gazes were fixed on Hekla, who now stood and turned. In her cupped hands was a tiny sleeping woman. Her green skin was patterned like tree bark, her clothing made of moss and woven grass. Miniature antlers sprouted from her brow, while a white foxlike tail curved around her back.

Rey's gaze flitted to Kritka, still, somehow, perched in the tree. "*This* is the Forest Maiden?"

Kritka chittered.

"It is only part of our mistress," Hekla translated. Her head whipped back to the squirrel. "Wait, *what*?" When Kritka did not reply, Hekla demanded, "Explain."

The air seemed to shiver. Rey glanced over his shoulder but found nothing amiss.

The squirrel chittered again, and Hekla raked a hand through her hair. "You did not tell me there was *another* part of her to awaken, you insolent creature!"

"Another part?" Eyvind scowled. "How many, rodent?"

Kritka's nose twitched. "One more," Hekla translated. Her expression turned thunderous. "The other part is *where*?" But the squirrel's head cocked to the side, and he held himself still, as though listening. "It knows," Hekla interpreted.

"What knows?" asked Thrand Long Sword, shifting nervously.

But the vibration beneath Rey's boots grew more pronounced, and he now realized it came in rhythmic throbs.

"The mist," said Rey. He swallowed hard. "The mist is coming."

CHAPTER 20

Hekla's pulse was in her throat as the telltale heartbeat of the mist grew louder, closer. Across the clearing, Eyvind straightened, then shouted orders to his men. Warriors jostled about, getting into formation. But Hekla was momentarily dazed, haunted by all that had happened before.

She'd been in this very clearing. Had heard the heartbeats. Had sensed the mist's anger . . . its need to consume. Back then, Hekla had done the only thing she could—she'd fled. But it had been too late. The mist had engulfed her, seeped into her lungs, permeated her skin. It had nearly Turned her draugur. But Kritka had appeared in grimwolf form. Had repelled the mist.

A nudge to her shoulder yanked Hekla back to the present. She turned and gasped at the enormous lupine face to her left. Clever yellow eyes watched her from above Kritka's gray muzzle. She hadn't seen him in grimwolf form since the day he'd rescued her from the mist. Fur raised on end, he thrashed his tail back and forth in agitation. Then the grimwolf cocked his head to the side, a motion so like a squirrel, she nearly laughed.

It senses my mistress, Kritka said into her skull. *We must protect her.*

Hekla glanced down at the tiny woman curled in her palm and scowled at the reminder of Kritka's trickery. He'd led her to believe she needed only to free his mistress from a single tree. Not *two.*

The heartbeat pounded louder, louder, and Hekla knew there was no time for such thoughts. Crouching low, she slid the tiny winged woman back into the tree's hollow. But as she straightened, she realized the other warriors had noticed Kritka's new form—had drawn their swords and backed away defensively.

"He's with us, you shite-beetles," she snapped. "And your swords won't do a thing against the mist. Fire is our only protection." Hekla pulled the twin torches she'd strapped to her back.

Gunnar fumbled through his pockets and pulled out a firestone. But Eyvind leaned forward, a flame cupped in his palm.

"Braggart," muttered Gunnar.

Hekla nudged her torch to Eyvind's flame until it caught, then frowned. Eyvind Hakonsson had revealed his Ashbringer skill to save her life during Istré's battle, but she'd yet to get used to it.

"Everyone has a gods damned secret, don't they?" grumbled Gunnar, and Hekla followed his gaze to Rey, smoke churning from his palms.

Hekla slapped Gunnar on the back. "Cheer up, Gunnar. Two Ashbringers will be useful in our arsenal." She turned to the group. "Keep your torches high. We fight back-to-back. Protect the Forest Maiden. Do not give the mist an opening."

"I thought the mist had left the forest," muttered Thrand, staring hard into the woods beyond the clearing. Their bones now rattled with each pounding heartbeat. "How can it have passed beyond the woods and yet still be here?"

"Clearly, we do not understand it at all," said Hekla. She could sense the mist's malevolent presence growing nearer by the minute, and was glad, at the very least, she didn't have to worry for the safety of Istré's citizens, now safely secured behind Kopa's walls.

"Shore up," barked Rey, gesturing for their group to tighten, their backs to the cracked tree and the forest spirit curled up beneath it. "Torches raised."

"Try not to burn down the forest, Soot Fingers," said Eyvind, far too jovially. Orange flames now crackled in his palms, but Hekla knew it was a bare hint at the power the warrior possessed.

Rey's reply was low, yet amused. "As I recall, *you* were the one to set Harpa's walls aflame, Fire Breath."

"How is your dear grandmother? Still as charming as a porcupine?"

"Focus, children," growled Hekla as a thick haze slid between the trees, swirling and eddying like the currents of a river. Hekla's heart raced in her chest, the urge to flee bone-deep. The smog slithered through the brambles, then paused. Recoiled.

Hekla felt its wrath as it sensed their torches. But as twigs snapped and low growls sounded, she understood well enough.

"It has not come alone—the mist has brought its army." Hekla's mind raced, but Eyvind's boot edged against hers. She hated that his presence was a reassuring comfort.

"Keep by my side," he growled, adding in a louder voice, "Rey and I will keep the mist at bay with our galdur while the rest of you battle the Turned creatures."

Hekla bristled at Eyvind's protectiveness. "Remember!" she shouted to their group, stamping out her torch and drawing her sword. "You must take their heads!"

Not a moment later, ember-red eyes appeared in the mist. The moldering scent of the undead swarmed at them from all sides.

A Turned grimwolf was the first to break through—mouth too wide, with dual rows of blade-sharp teeth, it surged forward on misshapen limbs. A vampire deer vaulted into the clearing, then charged at them with lowered antlers. Enormous Turned bears barreled through the brambles, elongated claws gouging into the soft earth. Ravens swooped down from above on torn, batlike wings, talons primed to rake through flesh.

Hekla's blood sang as the battle thrill took over. She became a thing of blade and claw, delivering death in lethal slashes. Black blood splattered her face—the putrid, moldering stench of the Turned beasts assaulting her senses. But Hekla did not care. Whenever one beast was felled, a new set of red eyes took its place a moment later.

Hekla and Kritka were a blur of swords and fangs and glinting claws. She was vaguely aware of Gunnar on her right, tirelessly defending her flank, and Eyvind behind her, keeping the mist at bay with controlled bursts of fire. These two might drive her mad, but she was glad to fight beside them.

Hekla buried her steel claws in the belly of a vampire deer as it tried to impale Kritka on pointed antlers. Warriors swarmed it, working together to hack its head from its neck.

Duck, came Kritka's command in her mind before he leaped over her to collide with a Turned bear. She'd never been so in tune with a fellow warrior.

Screams filled her ears, and Hekla was vaguely aware of one of Eyvind's men falling, of their circle tightening around the tree. It only spurred her on.

On and on they fought, Hekla losing herself to the dance of battle. She took a grimwolf's claw to the thigh, the beast's head rolling on the ground a moment later thanks to Gunnar's longsword. But as sudden as a clap of thunder, the wave of Turned beasts ceased.

Hekla scraped the hair from her face, chest heaving. Her senses were on high alert, blood churning furiously through her body. Something was wrong.

"Did the mist call them off?" asked Thrand, looking around.

"No," murmured Hekla. It was too abrupt to be natural.

A rapid series of clicks rattled through the air, sending a shiver down her spine.

"Wolfspider," muttered Rey.

Nausea rolled in her stomach. Hekla could handle the most putrid of vampire deer, the most violent outlaw. But gods, she despised spiders.

"Stay close," ordered Rey. "Shields up. We thrust together. Take it down from below."

Hekla took a fortifying breath, her boot edging against Gunnar's.

"Don't worry, Smasher," he said. "I won't let the little spider near you."

"Shut it, bjáni."

The wolfspider crashed through the brambles and Hekla's breath seized in her throat. It was larger than any she'd ever seen, as tall as three men and just as wide. Eight glowing red eyes burned down at them, fangs as long as longswords gleaming. The beast scuttled on legs as wide as tree trunks, crushing brambles and trees as though they were kindling.

Hekla was held immobile, some part of her recognizing that this being was ancient—a creature from the deepest part of the woods. The wolfspider came to an abrupt stop, and she could have sworn those beady red eyes looked directly at her.

You, it hissed in her mind.

Hekla stumbled back, trying to understand how she could hear this thing inside her mind.

Our mother has warned us of you. You won't escape us this time, taunted the spider. *Gjalla Eight Legs will taste you first. But we will end you last.*

Mother? Hekla vaguely wondered. It must mean the mist. But a series of rapid clicks burst from it, diverting her attention. Hekla was distantly aware of Rey shouting orders, but she could not hear him over the ringing in her ears. She was going to be sick . . .

The spider crouched low with a high-pitched shriek. Hekla fell to her knees, clapping her hands to her ears. Her sword fell free, but she could do nothing but hold on as the horrid sound burrowed into her skull and chewed up every thought in her mind.

At some point, the spider must have stopped screaming, but it echoed in her skull, rendering Hekla senseless. She was dimly aware of the spider surging forward, yet she was no longer in control of her limbs.

"Hekla!" someone bellowed as the spider surged at her with impossible speed, and Hekla knew she'd be too late to dodge it. Pinchers flashed through the air, and Hekla readied herself to feel them tear through her flesh. But the moment didn't come. A sword lashed out and steel cracked against the spider's chitinous fangs.

"Get back!" shouted Eyvind, and Hekla's senses rushed back to her in a torrent. She scuttled backward until hands hooked under her armpits and hauled her into the fold of a small shield wall.

Gunnar crouched before her, shaking her shoulder. "What's gotten into you?" he demanded.

"N-nothing." Gods, she needed to get her head on straight—needed to shake off her dislike of spiders. Hekla shoved to her feet and shouldered between a pair of warriors. "Eyvind," Hekla whispered, heart sinking into her stomach. She stared in horror at Eyvind, facing down the spider all by himself.

But Kritka shot out, teeth sinking deep into a joint in the spider's foreleg. The enormous wolfspider gave a shriek so earsplitting, Hekla's vision warped. Kritka's attack was enough to give Eyvind the time he needed to dart back to their group.

"Shore up, Kritka!" bellowed Rey. But when the stubborn beast did not relent—not even when the spider lifted its foreleg into the air and shook it roughly—Rey swore. "We rush the spider on the count of three."

Hekla reached for her sword, then cursed. It lay in the grass, near the spider's opposite foreleg. She drew her hevrít instead.

Rey counted them down, and they rushed as a unit. Hekla hacked into the carapace joints in the spider's foreleg, trying not to vomit as black blood coated her blade. Rey bellowed commands, urging the warriors to aim for the spider's underbelly, where its armor was not so thick.

The spider scuttled back, its voice rattling inside Hekla's skull. *Meddlesome little pests. Gjalla will string you up one by one. Savor your lifeblood over many long days.*

But their group was relentless, chasing the spider to the edge of the glade. Gunnar's sword sliced clean through a thick, hairy foreleg. Black ichor poured from the wound, and the spider gave one last furious shriek before crashing through the underbrush and into the greater forest.

Chest heaving, Hekla turned in a full circle. The scent of rot lingered in the air, but the crash of bodies through the greater forest was growing fainter. She blinked at the realization that the mist and its army were retreating.

Victory swelled in her chest, but it faded a touch as she took in the silent carnage in the clearing. Countless Turned creatures. Sigrún, bandaging her arm. Eyvind, kneeling over a pair of corpses—

both warriors from his retinue. Shame filled Hekla as she retrieved her sword. How could she have allowed herself to falter in the middle of such a battle?

But before she could dwell too long on her failure, Kritka—in squirrel form—clambered up Hekla's body and settled on her shoulder. "I told you to warn me before doing that, you tree demon," she bit out. But her anger soon shifted to worry as he flopped on his belly and lay still. "Are you hurt?"

Only tired, he said. *Our wolf form takes much strength. When Mistress is fully restored—*

At the thought of his mistress, Hekla whirled toward the tree. The tiny woman sat in the tree's hollow, grassy wisps of her hair swaying as she blinked at the scene before her. Hekla rushed forward, dropping to her knees before the Forest Maiden. Carefully, she pulled Kritka from her shoulder and lay him gently on the ground.

The antlered woman pushed to her feet, her foxlike tail twitching behind her. She looked from Hekla to Kritka with dark, verdant eyes.

"Who is *this*?" she asked, her voice reedy and thin, like wind whistling through a forest.

Kritka lifted his weary head. "Kritka has brought to you the Protector, Mistress. It took much convincing and proving of trust, but—"

"This is not the Protector!" The small woman's voice grew thunderous, echoing off the trees in the clearing. Hekla sensed the warriors gathering behind her, tension stirring in the glade. The Forest Maiden sniffed the air. "You have . . . *bonded* to this human, Kritka?"

Hekla's brows drew together. *Not* the Protector? After weeks of the squirrel telling her she was, she'd rather gotten used to the name. "I'm Hekla," she said, frowning. "I woke you—"

With a harrumph, the Maiden strode toward Hekla. Putting tiny hands on tiny hips, she scowled in disapproval.

Kritka's tail twitched nervously, and he finally pushed to his feet. "But Kritka did as you said, Mistress. We went south and searched for many long moons. In the strange, twisting woods, at last we found the Protector. But Protector was surrounded by predators. Kritka killed them all, but when we turned back, Protector had fled."

The Forest Maiden massaged her temples in a surprisingly human-like gesture. "You *lost* the Protector, Kritka?"

Hekla felt a pang of sympathy for the exhausted squirrel.

"Kritka searched for many long moons, Mistress, never giving up. We traveled very far north. And one day, we found the scent once more—the Protector had found Mistress's markings and followed them to your grove!"

Hekla puzzled over Kritka's strange story, trying to understand. South. Twisting woods. Surrounded by predators. "Do you mean the Twisted Pinewoods?" she asked, realization beginning to dawn. "That was *you* in the Twisted Pinewoods, Kritka?" Hekla dragged a hand down her face. "Silla fled through those woods. She told me that members of a warband had stolen her belongings—that a grimwolf had killed them all and she managed to escape." A caustic laugh fell from her lips. "She said it made no sense, but I'm beginning to understand. *Silla* is the Protector."

Crouching beside her, Rey cursed. Kritka bounded a few cautious steps toward him. "But this one also carries the Protector's scent." The squirrel's nose twitched as he scented Rey. "Why does he also smell of the Protector?"

"They carry the scent," said the Forest Maiden, "because they've been in *contact* with the Protector. You must fetch the true Protector. My woods are under assault, and the leech has grown too strong."

"Leech," Hekla repeated. "Do you mean the mist? What can you tell us about it?"

Tiny tail tucked up, the woman leveled her with a stern look. "It lives, yet it does not breathe. It is vast, yet small to the eye. It is the un-maker. It takes that which is natural and makes it . . . other."

"Chaos," said Rey.

The Maiden cocked her head to the side. "Unraveling of natural order. The corruption of bonds. The ruination of my forest. It is why I have called upon the Protector for help."

"Are you saying," said Thrand Long Sword, scratching his beard, "that the leech *is* Myrkur?"

The tiny woman's glare was fierce enough that Thrand retreated a step. "No, you fool. The leech is Myrkur's *progeny*. And thus the magic they carry is similar."

Rey's jaw hardened. "Chaos magic. This . . . leech has seeped into your forest from Myrkur's realm."

"The heartwood," murmured the Maiden. "It is the name of a grove of ancient trees in the Western Woods. Here the roots of the elder trees grow the deepest . . . this is where the leech climbed into this world."

"Elder trees. Do you mean the hjarta trees?" Rey's gaze grew distant. "They are blessed by Sunnvald."

The Maiden began pacing on the soft, verdant grass. "Yes, the Sun God's ashes fell upon these trees. The hjarta trees are the beating heart of the woods. Like mothers, they nurture those all around them through a lattice of threads beneath the soil. When the leech took the largest of the hjarta trees, it gained control of this webwork, pulling the life force from the trees and plants all around it.

"I tried to heal the hjarta tree, but it was too late. It is no longer as nature intended. Where once sweet, nurturing sap flowed is now thick, black ichor. Great burls grow and burst. The tree's sturdy wood is fortified by things I do not understand, all of it protecting the leech. Only the Protector can undo this great wrong."

"How does this tree tie into the mist?" Hekla asked.

"Mist!" spat the forest spirit. "Mist is the essence of the forest. *That* is not mist. It is the leech's progeny, seeking new hosts."

"Hosts," Rey repeated. "Are you saying . . . the leech *lives* in the Turned creatures?"

"It pulls the life force from the forest. Channels it into that deviant tree. And then it sends out seeds of destruction. When these seeds plant themselves, they grow and spread and seize control."

Hekla glanced at Rey. "If the leech controls the draugur, could

Myrkur do so, too? Is it He who has instructed them to travel to Rökksgarde?"

Rey's gaze grew distant as he rubbed his beard. "If so, then our need to destroy the hjarta tree is even greater than we thought. We must stop the leech from spreading its poison and Turning the good people of Íseldur to Myrkur's cause."

"The leech must have a weakness," said Eyvind. He turned to the Forest Maiden. "Fire?"

"An axe," suggested Thrand.

Poison, signed Sigrún.

The tiny winged woman pursed her lips in distaste. "The tree the leech inhabits is impenetrable. All I know is that I was once warned by Sunnvald to call upon the Protector should seeds of chaos ever be sown in my forest."

"I can fetch the Protector," said Rey cautiously, "although she cannot come straightaway."

Hekla's gaze snapped to him, but his expression was unreadable. Axe Eyes was beyond an asset to this mission. He was a fount of knowledge on monsters and battle tactics; a leader whom all looked up to. Was he truly suggesting he might not see this through?

But as a groove formed between his black brows, Hekla guessed he was thinking about the weight on Silla's shoulders—the bargain living in her blood, and her need to unite the jarls of the north. Sympathy twinged in Hekla's chest, and she was mildly disappointed that she was not, in fact, the Protector—that she could not take some of the burden from Silla.

"I *will* bring her," said Rey. The confidence in his voice told Hekla a decision had been made. She glanced about to see if the others felt the same trepidation she did, but they did not seem to be fazed in the least. "But," Rey continued, "how, precisely, is she to defeat this foe? She shows Ashbringer intuition—"

The Forest Maiden lifted a hand. "I know nothing but that the Sun God granted the Protector some weapon. A thing to wield against His trickster brother." She closed her eyes, growing silent for a long moment. "I have few eyes left in these woods, but some of the trees still heed my call. They tell me of a great gathering in the heartwood. There the leech assembles a vast army of the un-made. In order to reach the tree, we will have to battle through thousands of its soldiers."

Kritka let out a strange, squirrelly howl.

"Thousands?" muttered Thrand, putting a hand to his forehead.

"The trees have shown me the breadth of the leech's army, and I tell you this, mortals." The winged woman looked about. "Your numbers are not great enough to stand a fighting chance. You'll need more—many more able-bodied warriors."

Silence stretched out in the wake of her words until Rey cleared his throat. "I will return to Kopa to fetch the Protector," he said. "And while I am there, I will muster more warriors."

"Talk to Atli," suggested Eyvind. "He'll be able to help."

The groove between Rey's brows was back, his lips pulling into a look of distaste. But before Hekla could ponder it, Rey's *axe eyes* had landed on her. "It is clear to me," he said slowly, "there is one more suited to leading the task in the woods than I. This duty and great honor I pass to you, Rib Smasher."

Hekla stared at him, doubt brewing inside her. Had he not just seen her cower before the great spider? She'd faltered when these warriors had needed leadership the most. Hekla glanced around, trying to read the group's reaction. But rather than apprehension or doubt, they seemed in agreement of this plan. As she met Eyvind's gaze, lit with pride, determination sparked to life deep inside her. This was her chance to see this job through. To prove to men like Loftur what she could truly accomplish.

Hekla squared her shoulders. "Are you all on board?" She examined all those standing in the glade—Gunnar and Sigrún, Thrand and the rest of the warriors from Kopa. As the chorus of *ayes* filled the glade, her determination only grew.

"Then it is settled," said the Forest Maiden to Hekla. "You, the one to whom my foot soldier has bound himself. You will bring me to the southwestern reaches of the woods, to the place where the other fragment of my being lies dormant."

Hekla's chest clenched as she saw Íseldur's map in her mind. It was as far away as one could get in the Western Woods. "Southwestern . . . but that is an impossible distance."

"Not with my magic," said the Forest Maiden. "Once I am fully restored, then I'll be able to call to my children—those forest creatures who escaped the boundaries of the woods before the leech could claim them—and awaken the forest spirits. We will gather an army of our own. And then we will meet the Protector in the heartwood and do battle with the corrupted."

The Maiden glanced at the skies. "The leech is weakened by the light of the moons. It would be to our advantage to do battle when Marra is next at her fullest."

"But that is . . ." Rey thought for a moment. "Just over three weeks from now. And factoring in travel . . ." He paused. "That leaves me a fortnight to muster an army."

"Yes," said the Maiden, unconcerned. "And the longer we wait, the stronger the leech grows. It will create more un-made. Venture farther from the woods. Its hunger will never be satisfied—it will feast and feast until all plants and creatures in this realm have succumbed to it. We must act quickly."

Kritka's eager howl filled the woods, and it was infectious. Despite the impossibility of the task before them, Hekla's spirits lifted.

At last, they had a plan.

CHAPTER 21

Kopa, Íseldur

Silla's knee bounced uncontrollably as she sat at the sunlit table near her glass-paned windows. Myrkur was silent, slumbering deep within her as He had since Fallgerd's death. Before her sat an empty jug of róa and the deconstructed ruins of a sweet roll. The sight of them made her stomach turn over. She'd had no appetite since leaving Fallgerd's home the day before, and had not allowed herself to fall asleep. What if Myrkur took hold of her again? Forced her to do some other dark deed?

Instead of sleeping, Silla had desperately pored over a fresh stack of books from Jarl Hakon's library. Now more than ever, she needed to rid herself of this bargain. And Fallgerd had confirmed that there was a way out of it—something that King Hrolf had been too old to attempt. Silla vowed she would not rest until she unearthed it.

But it was difficult to focus when Fallgerd's corpse invaded her mind's eye constantly. She'd taken a life before, but under duress. Fallgerd had been a good man.

Her heartache for Fallgerd had entwined with her sorrow at Saga's absence. Every day, Silla asked Jarl Hakon, and every day, the answer was the same—there was no sign of her. Her sorrow twisted into frustration. It should be Saga here, uniting the jarls of the north. Where *was* she?

More than once, Silla had broken down into a mess of ragged

sobs. During a particularly violent bout, Runný had rushed into her chambers and folded her into her arms.

"I killed him," Silla said, "didn't I?" She couldn't stop staring at her hands. Couldn't stop wiping phantom blood from them.

"We do not know that," replied Runný, though even she did not sound entirely convinced.

Oh, what Silla wouldn't give for it to be Rey's warm chest against her back. With his sturdy presence and his unfounded confidence in her, the impossible somehow felt within her grasp. But by now, Rey would be in those monster-infested woods, risking life and limb for the innocent people in this realm. Clearly he was far too busy to write.

Gradually, Silla's tears had subsided, and she'd allowed herself to be led to her bed. But the moment Runný had left her chambers, Silla had slid out and returned to the stack of books.

This morning, desperate to banish her fatigue, Silla had consumed far too many cups of spiced róa. Rather than curing her exhaustion, the drink had only added a restless, buzzing sensation on top of it. She stared vacantly at a knot in the oak table, her mind a maelstrom of thoughts. A figure standing over her, a knife clutched in hand. *Queen Signe sends her regards.* Myrkur's satisfied smile. *He tried to harm us.* Which was truth? Which was imagined?

Silla's head jolted up. As her pulse jumped wildly, her gaze swung around the room. Had she fallen asleep? How much time had passed? But the hearthfire behind her still crackled away, joined by a soft knocking at the door.

She pushed to her feet. Her head spun, and she gripped the high back of her chair to steady herself. Runný opened the door, granting Lady Tala entry. At the sight of her mentor, Silla braced herself for Tala's admonishments for ransacking Jarl Hakon's grain stores and venturing into Kopa.

"Your Highness." Tala dipped into a quick curtsy before striding to Silla and pulling her into a motherly embrace. It was a surprising breech of protocol from the older woman, but Silla leaned into the hug, closing her eyes. "Thank the gods above you are unharmed," said Tala, smoothing a hand over her hair in a maternal gesture. "Ingvarr told me everything."

Silla's head swung up as she tried to gauge how much Lady Tala knew. Only Jarl Hakon and Silla's inner circle knew about her mother's bargain with Myrkur.

"That the despicable old warrior attacked you," Tala clarified, studying her face. "That it was a miracle you escaped with your life."

Silla pulled back and turned her palms up. No trace of blood. No cuts. No hint of the violence these hands might have delivered. But Lady Tala pulled her hands between hers and squeezed them gently.

"You must have been so very frightened."

Tala's words were a balm to her heart, filling Silla with the sense that she had all the answers and knew just how to make her troubles go away.

A god lives inside me was on the tip of her tongue.

"I know precisely what must be done, Eisa," said Lady Tala.

"You do?"

Tala nodded, gesturing for Silla to take her seat at the table. Numbly, Silla obeyed as Tala waved a pair of servants in. They removed the remnants of Silla's daymeal and placed a fresh bowl of porridge before her.

"First, you'll eat."

Silla's stomach lurched, and she clutched it. "I cannot."

"You will *eat.*"

The motherly tone of Lady Tala's voice—the kind that left no room for argument—was strangely reassuring. Silla could almost hear her foster mother's voice in her ear. *The grains for this porridge were harvested and threshed and sorted, Silla. You must not take this labor for granted. You must be grateful for food when so many go hungry.*

Reluctantly, she lifted her spoon to her lips. Thought of her mother's soft hums. The sizzle of grains in a knob of lard. Somehow, Silla managed to swallow.

"We must forget yesterday ever happened," Tala said as Silla took a second bite. Her voice was firm. Decisive.

"But it did!" Silla could still smell the blood in that room, could still feel it on her hands—

"Do you wish to unite the north, Eisa?"

"Yes," Silla answered without pause.

Tala watched her carefully. "Think of how a scandal such as murder could damage your reputation."

Porridge churned in Silla's stomach as she considered it. Right now Rey and Hekla fought foes in the west. Jarl Hakon mustered men from all corners of the kingdom. Everyone was counting on Eisa to unite the north. This was *her* responsibility—there was no one else.

"Perhaps," mused Lady Tala, "we could tell it differently. It could draw sympathy were it your guard who did the killing."

Silla shook her head vehemently, but it only seemed to muddle her thoughts further.

But Tala was already waving. "Runný, come here."

Reluctantly, Runný pushed off the wall, passing a nervous hand over her braids. Lady Tala had that effect on people. "You understand the . . . complications which would arise should Eisa Volsik be branded a murderer?"

"Yes, my lady," replied Runný, her black eyes flicking to Silla's for an instant.

"Good, my girl. We must maintain the people's trust in Eisa. It would be best if we did not have them looking too closely at the incident with Fallgerd."

Wrong, Silla thought, her porridge threatening to push up her throat. Everything about this felt so wrong—and yet she could see the merit in Tala's words. Her entire purpose here was to meet with the northern jarls—to unite the north in an alliance. Without unity, they hadn't a chance against Rökkur, nor the Urkans to their south.

"When Ingvarr came to me," continued Lady Tala, "I asked him to keep yesterday's events from Jarl Hakon."

"He hasn't told him?" Silla's brows knit together.

"The jarl would not be pleased to hear you've snuck out of Ashfall, Eisa, nor of the bags of grain you took from his stores." Silla's cheeks flamed. "Telling the jarl might damage the rapport and trust you've garnered with him thus far. It is, of course, your choice if we tell him or not. Ingvarr awaits your decision."

An uneasy silence hung over the room.

Tala folded her hands on the table. "I propose that we keep your excursion to ourselves. And if anyone does find out, then we tell them this: Runný heard the screams. Rushed into the room to find Fallgerd wielding a knife at the princess. Violence was a necessary evil to save Eisa Volsik's life."

Runný met Silla's gaze across the table. But before Silla could tell her not to do it, Runný answered.

"It is just as I recall it, my lady."

A smile curved Lady Tala's lips. "Good girl," she said, glancing between Silla and Runný. "I'm certain I don't need to tell you that this conversation does not leave this room."

Runný nodded, but Silla only stared into her porridge. None of this sat well with her. Yet none of being *Eisa* sat well with her. Her daily existence was unsettling. Being Eisa was like wearing an ill-fitting gown, and Silla waited for it to get easier—for the morning she'd wake up and it would feel *right*.

Her mind was fogged with exhaustion. It was too hard to think, and Lady Tala was so kind and clever—and she knew how to play the games of politics.

Slowly, Silla nodded her head. A zip rushed through her at Tala's approving smile.

"I'm glad that's settled," said Tala. "Now finish your porridge, Eisa. I have something to show you."

Standing beside Lady Tala, Silla gazed at the cavern wall. After she had forced down the last bite of her porridge—which Silla would begrudgingly admit *had* improved her state of mind—Tala had brought her into the deepest reaches of Ashfall Fortress. Once they passed the cavernous meeting hall where Silla had first met the nobles of Kopa, the carved corridors had shifted to natural, tubular caves. Minerals glinted from rough stone walls, the caverns high-ceilinged and strangely uniform.

"Lava once flowed through here," Tala had explained. Noticing Silla's alarmed expression, Lady Tala merely laughed. "Do not fret, Your Highness. I assure you, these caverns are quite safe. Unlike the Sleeping Dragons, Brími's fire mountain does not slumber. It is well and truly dead."

"Dead?"

"The chambers inside have been empty as long as our history reaches back. In fact, when the Sleeping Dragons last woke, it is thought the people of Íseldur sheltered in Brími's caves."

Green and gold minerals glinted in the cave's walls as they ventured deeper into Brími, the floor beneath them growing ever warmer. At last, the caves widened into a circular space.

"What is this?" Silla asked, breathless.

The space was a strange mixture of natural and human-made. Curious puddling rocks and icicle-like protrusions were interspersed with angular stairs and curved, vaulted ceilings. Arched doorways were chiseled into the walls, and as Silla ducked her head through one, she found an alcove large enough for a family to sleep. Her eyes traced a stone-carved bench, and she guessed these were primitive homes.

"In ancient times," said Tala, drawing Silla's attention back to the central cavernous space, "Kopa was the beating heart of Íseldur." Lady Tala slid her torch into a slot in the wall, and Ingvarr and his guards did the same. "These caves provided a refuge from the hard rains of the spring and the brutal cold of winter. Here, Eisa, you can see the drawings of our ancestors."

As the last of the guards slotted his torch, bright light spilled across the cavern walls. Silla gasped. Shapes and figures were painted from floor to ceiling. Silla wandered closer to examine a simple line drawing of a prowed ship. "Our ancestors drew these?"

"We believe so," replied Tala. "You can see the paintings are simple to start, but as you progress through the cave, the stories grow more detailed."

Silla moved along the wall and saw that Tala was correct. Ornate, scrolling knotwork grew more common a few steps later, symbols and line drawings morphing into elaborate scenes.

"Before the Weavers existed, our ancestors carved their history into the stones. These caves are a secret long held by Jarl Hakon's line. Protected from the Urkans upon their invasion."

Silla could see why. The story of the Ashen was depicted in one scene. Myrkur stealing Malla, Marra, and Stjarna into the darkness of night. Sunnvald growing so angry, He shook the skies. Stardust falling down upon Íseldur, landing on the trees, the rocks, the creatures, and imbuing them with magical qualities.

Her gaze slid to a new scene, showcasing the classes of Galdra. Ashbringers wielding fire and Blade Breakers great strength, a Weaver standing before a loom. Silla studied what had to be a Shadow Hound, reflecting sun on a curious-looking shield of light, then tracked to a lone, crowned figure. The king clutched a stone in one hand, an axe in the other. Brows furrowing, Silla stared harder. The king faced off against a figure of shadows, unnatural creatures crowding around. But the king faced Him all alone as the sun shone down upon him.

The shadowy figure bore an uncanny resemblance to the Myrkur that Silla had seen making a bargain with King Hrolf and her mother. But who was this man facing the god of chaos alone? Was it a Volsik King? Her heart quickened. Could this mural reveal a clue to the mysterious weapon the Volsiks were said to wield against Myrkur? Her eyes traced the scene once, twice, three times, but there were no easy answers to be found.

With a disappointed breath, Silla made to move on. But her gaze snagged on one particular detail—the stone clutched in the king's hand.

"Is that stone blue?"

"Mmm?" Lady Tala appeared at her side. "The stone? Oh yes, that's a halda stone."

"Halda." Silla's mind yanked this way and that, a dozen thoughts colliding at once. "Like the halda tattoos for storing galdur?"

"Aye. When ground into a powder, the stones can serve as a reservoir—"

"But in their natural form?"

She felt Tala's curious gaze on her. "In their natural form, they . . . well, they're stones, Eisa. Without a mind, they cannot harness any galdur that may naturally lie within."

Silla's skin buzzed with excitement, though she was not precisely sure why. "But the stones have a source, I'm certain Harpa told me so. Natural galdur must lie within the stones."

"Might I ask what you're thinking, Your Highness?" Lady Tala watched her curiously.

Mind racing, Silla glanced at Tala. "Why is that king holding on to a stone? Why would he have a weapon in one hand and a stone in the other?"

"I'm afraid I do not know."

Her heart hammered with excitement, answers sliding into place. Blade Breaker, Skraeda had called her, when Silla had thrown her across the room. But Silla had never reproduced the burst of strength, not even with Vig and Harpa's help back in Kalasgarde.

In her mind's eye, Silla saw herself shoving Rey across the field after he'd let the vampire deer attack her. Her hands had fizzed with a burst of energy she hadn't understood. There had been bedrock there, exposed to daylight. Had there been blue minerals threaded into the stone?

The scene shifted, Skraeda's copper braids flying as she collided with a woven room divider. Skeggagrim's home was hewn from stone. And when she closed her eyes, Silla saw the glint of blue minerals in the walls.

She stared at the king—at the blue rock clutched in his palm. She hadn't been able to produce Blade Breaker strength in Kalasgarde because she did not possess the ability. Whatever power Silla had wielded against Rey in that field could not have come from a regular source of magic—for they'd have been blocked at the time by the skjöld leaves.

It is said the Volsiks carry an additional blessing from Sunnvald. A gift with which to defeat Myrkur, Harpa had told her back in Kalasgarde. Could Sunnvald's additional blessing—the one that had the power to defeat Myrkur—have allowed her to unwittingly pull galdur from halda stones?

There was only one way to find out. Silla whirled, striding from the caves with new vigor.

"Your Highness?" asked Tala, falling into stride beside her.

"I'm craving some fresh air, Tala," said Silla. "I think I shall take Dawn for a ride."

CHAPTER 22

Kovograd, Zagadka

Kassandr Rurik was restless, and his beast was only making it worse. Hackles raised, it paced behind his ribs, snarling when anyone got too near. But he couldn't seem to calm it. Today was the council of elders. His father had returned from the oracle, and had been sequestered in his chambers for days. But it seemed he'd come to a decision. Today, the high prince would announce if they'd take a stand against King Ivar or try to broker peace through tributary gifts.

Kass's mind flipped back and forth—on the one hand, the fact that his father had not yet announced a decision gave him hope he'd do the right thing. On the other, he could not forget how his father had crumbled when his heir and eldest son, Radomir, was killed. The high prince had remained behind locked doors for two full moon cycles and had left Kassandr—woefully unprepared and grieving his older brother—in charge.

Today, Kassandr arrived at the council chambers early, climbing the dais and taking the seat to the right of his father's ornate, golden throne. Elisava joined him, a book in hand. Sunlight streamed through three high windows behind them, illuminating the rows of benches that soon would be filled with elders and Zagadkian nobles.

"Do not worry, brother," said Elisava, utterly bored. "All will be well."

Kass's beast growled in irritation. Didn't she understand what was at stake? Not only for his Saga, but for the entire kingdom . . . for their children and grandchildren? These were the Urkans, who slaughtered and raped, who took and took. They would torture the strong and enslave the weak. Would tear down their icons and impose their Bear God upon the masses. Did Elisava not realize they would take her as a bride and force her to bear their children?

Before he could say all of this, his sister snapped her book closed and glared at him with green eyes too much like his own. "Get control of it, Kassandr. Do not let yourself become a target for their hate."

Her words took him by surprise, though he ought to have expected she'd read him as easily as that book. He took a deep breath and let it out slowly. Elisava's gaze returned to her book, and Kassandr's beast abandoned its pacing to lunge and snap in frustration. Kass leaped to his feet, a hand scraping through his hair. "I must go to her."

His sister rolled her eyes. "You must arrive separately, *starshiy brat.** Arriving together only tells the elders how badly you've fallen." Kassandr blinked at that, but Elisava wasn't done. "If they think Saga controls your heart, the elders will not take care when listening to your words."

A low whine escaped him, and it took all of Kass's will not to bolt to the doors. He needed to see Saga with his eyes. Needed to know she was safe—never mind that Rov and half a dozen of his Druzhina watched over her.

"You must control your beast," hissed Elisava.

Gods, but she was right. Today would be a true test of his will.

The door creaked, and Kass's gaze whipped toward it. He found himself holding his breath as a figure entered. But the air rushed out of him as a long brocade jacket came into view, marking the wearer as the first of the elders.

Over the next several minutes, the empty benches filled with

* Older brother.

finely dressed Zagadkians, conversing in low whispers. To Kassandr's great distaste, Oleg also arrived, sneering as he climbed onto the dais and took the seat to the left of the throne. But any irritation directed Oleg's way vanished as Kass caught sight of Rov's twice-broken nose entering the room. And then there she was. His Saga.

Her expression was unreadable, but her air was regal. She wore a gown of brocade gold with heavy, bell-shaped sleeves. A panel of sage green ran down the front, seed pearls stitched along the length of it. Long, beaded earrings dripped from her ears, and a delicate, lacy veil was pinned to her golden tresses.

As beautiful as the Spring Maiden, thought Kassandr, his beast stilling at the sight of her.

The room quieted, all turning to watch the resplendent woman making her way to the front of the room. Rov got her settled on a bench at the front—a seat of honor reserved for the most esteemed of guests.

"My thanks," murmured Kass, unable to tear his eyes away from Saga. "You did well, Elisava."

It was Elisava who'd ensured Saga was suitably attired for this meeting. They'd been holed up in Saga's chambers for many hours this morning, and the result exceeded his already high expectations.

Elisava merely scoffed. "Always, you underestimate me, brother."

Kass opened his mouth for a sharp reply, but his father entered the chambers and a hush fell over the room. Wearing golden ceremonial robes, the high prince leaned on his staff as he walked along the aisle toward the dais. As he neared, Kassandr could not ignore the dark circles beneath his father's eyes.

Kass had a moment of regret. *He'd* done this—had disobeyed his father by boarding that ship to Íseldur. Had brought danger to their doorstep when he'd returned with Saga. But his remorse was fleeting. That knowing feeling deep inside him reassured Kass he had not erred. Honor had demanded he discover Nostislav's fate, and that he ensure Saga Volsik's safety.

And if he were to trust in the thing called fate, then perhaps it had all come to this. Long had Kassandr known that Zagadka must modernize and gain allies if they wished to avoid colonization by the Urkans. And long had his father been resistant to the idea. Perhaps it had always been leading to this, to force his father into action.

Kassandr itched to offer his father a steadying arm as he climbed the dais steps, but he knew this would be perceived as an insult, and so he merely watched as he struggled with his staff. At last, the high prince reached his throne. Lowered himself onto it.

"We are here," said the high prince unfalteringly, "to discuss what must be done." He paused. "The oracle told me many interesting things, but I fear I can no longer trust in her word."

Unease rippled down Kassandr's spine, shock spreading on the nobles' faces.

"It was the oracle who advised we unite with the clans beyond the river." The high prince's tone now had a bite to it. "The *oracle* who proclaimed that he who rides the great winged horse will usher in a new era of peace. Because of this, Radomir is dead. Zagadka's heir stolen."

An elder on the front bench nodded his shaggy head, and Kassandr's stomach gave a queasy lurch.

"Instead, I have consulted with my elder councilors. And after much talk, we have come to a sensible agreement."

Kassandr's heart thrashed in his chest, his beast's hackles rising in anticipation. But a golden goddess rose, and the room collectively gasped. Her veil gleamed in the morning light as Saga kept her head bowed low in true Zagadkian style.

"Yes?" said the high prince in displeased Zagadkian. And yet Kassandr saw the faintest traces of curiosity in his expression. "What is it, Lady Saga?"

The high prince turned to Kassandr, waiting for him to interpret, but there was no need. To say Saga had an aptitude for languages was an understatement. Her mind was astonishing, her determination ruthless. She'd practiced with Kassandr, and when he had duties to attend, she continued with Elisava. And when

Elisava had retreated for the night, she'd dragged Rovgolod in for yet more lessons.

"May I speak to room?" Saga asked in Zagadkian, stirring another flurry of whispers.

Her pronunciation was imperfect, but Kassandr's beast raised its head and howled. The high prince lifted a hand, quelling the crowd's whispers.

"You have learned some Zagadkian." There was no mistaking the note of wonder in the high prince's voice. He relented with a weary sigh. "You may speak your piece."

Saga's demure smile was one Kassandr had seen a hundred times, and the sight of it made him eager. Because this was a smile cultivated in a castle filled with enemies, and beneath it lurked fire. Pride built inside his chest as Saga walked to the dais, ignoring the crowd's outrage.

This time, Kassandr rushed forward, offering Saga his elbow as she climbed the stairs. Elisava muttered something about his eagerness under her breath, but Kass ignored her.

"I thank you for great honor," Saga said with a bow to the high prince, whose expression was now tight.

Kass forced himself to resume his seat, watching as Saga faced the crowd.

"You are unused to outsiders in your country," she said in a carrying voice, "and I thank you for hospitality."

He wanted to snort. She'd been imprisoned in her chambers, and an attempt had been made on her life. Yet still, she faced this crowd without contempt.

"I think I have little time and so I will say harsh truth. You have wasted your time."

Her words carried to all corners of the room, and Kassandr reveled in the unease that followed.

"While you quarreled about my fate, you have missed important fact. Urkans cannot be trusted. They care only for rewards received from Bear God. Before Urkans invaded Íseldur, my parents tried to reach peace. They were deceived and slaughtered in worst way."

Fabric rustled as the elders shifted, but Saga continued.

"Still, you can try buying peace. Maybe for some time you will succeed. But in the end, Urkans *will* come for Zagadka. And they cannot be resisted by broken kingdom."

Kassandr's eyes narrowed. What did she scheme at?

"You must make peace with clans beyond river—"

"It has been tried," interjected Kassandr's father. "Many times."

"We must try more," said Saga, turning to the high prince.

We. Kassandr's heart sang. Here she was, his queen.

"You know nothing of our kingdom!" spat Oleg.

Saga turned. Regarded him blandly. "I know you are not trusting strangers. You furiously guard your island and animal nature. I'm sorry, Oleg, but secret is out."

The air thickened with tension. Saga turned away from a red-faced Oleg and gazed out at the crowd.

"I know are some present who would fight for freedom. I ask you take weapons and ready for battle. We have little time to unite with clans beyond river. Urkans will sail before bay freezes—"

The room erupted at this last statement, men jumping to their feet, shouting terrible things at his Saga. But Kassandr was more fearful of the lupine yellow flicker in Oleg's eye. He'd pushed to his feet and now advanced on Saga's back.

"Lies!" Oleg bellowed, and Kassandr leaped between his brother and Saga.

"She speaks the truth, Oleg," said Kassandr, wishing he could shake some sense into him. "They discovered our animal nature when they stole Nostislav."

"You think I will listen to your *whore*? Think with your head, Kassandr, not with your cock—"

Red swarmed in Kassandr's vision, and before he understood what he was doing, he'd seized Oleg by his fine, golden collar. His beast gnashed its teeth, froth building at the corners of its mouth.

"Say that again, brother," he growled. "My beast hungers for your blood."

"Silence!" boomed the high prince, sending a visceral wave of obedience through Kassandr's body. His beast whined, submitting to his alpha, and Kass released Oleg's collar.

As the room settled, Kass edged toward Saga. Her face looked impassive, but her pulse thundered and her fingers tapped rhythmically against her arm. Kass's hand slid around her waist and he led her to his abandoned chair. She sank onto his seat, and his hand found her shoulder, tapping in time with her own fingers.

Breathe, he urged her silently, his gaze on his father.

"Already, it is decided," the high prince bellowed. "A ship has been loaded with grain and silver. Lady Saga will board the ship and return to Íseldur. This tribute will foster peace with the Urkans. And Zagadka will stay safe."

Kassandr's beast snarled, anger whipping through him. *Cowards!* he wanted to shout, but he sensed Saga's impending panic, and continued the rhythmic taps.

"Father," hissed Elisava. "It is the wrong choice!"

"Contain yourself, Elisava," snapped the high prince. "It is not a woman's place to question her father's decision."

"We must do what is *right,* Father. Will you leave your grandchildren the problem of these Urkans? They will spit on your grave. Curse your very name."

The high prince took two quick steps toward Elisava, but Kassandr's hand shot out, capturing his father's raised palm before the slap could land. "Caution, Father. The nobles watch on."

A vein pulsed in the high prince's temple as he shook free from Kass's grip. "You will hold your tongue, girl," he hissed.

The doors to the council chambers crashed suddenly open, drawing the room's collective gaze. A Zagadkian warrior in full armor rushed down the aisle, and Kassandr recognized the sigil on his breast, placing the man as a wolf shifter within Posadnik Volk's forces. The warrior paused before the dais, bowing his head low.

"Sire."

"What is the meaning of this?" the high prince snapped. His ornate golden coat swirled around him, yet his face had drained of color. "Stand and explain, warrior."

"A message has just arrived from the ocean gate, sire."

The room grew deathly still, but Kassandr's mind ran in circles. *No,* he thought, shoving a hand into his hair. *It is too soon. We need more time—*

But the words the warrior spoke were unstoppable. "The ocean gate lies in ruins. The Urkan fleet has breached the Kovosk River. They will reach the city gates within the hour, Sire."

PART 2

SAPLINGS

A person should tend to the oak
if they want to live under it.

—EGIL'S SAGA

CHAPTER 23

Kovograd, Zagadka

Saga stared vacantly at the crowd before her, fingers tapping frantically on the wooden arms of her chair. Her breaths came in rapid gasps, her heartbeat too quick, and she tried to focus on what was happening in the council chambers around her. The high prince releasing a low, despairing sound. Oleg spitting guttural curses in Kassandr's direction. The nobles and elders pulling at their hair, shouting to their four gods.

Through the mayhem, Saga's fingers tapped.

Too late. She was too late to escape this place and draw Ivar's ire with her. Now the Urkans were here, and King Ivar would take his anger out on Kassandr and the innocents of Zagadka.

"How is this possible?" bellowed Oleg. "The ocean gate! Where are the signal fires, warrior?"

The messenger who'd burst into the chambers shifted on his feet. "W-we believe the guards were killed or captured before the beacon fire could be lit. There was no smoke for the watchtowers to see. Nothing seemed amiss. Everyone—" His voice broke. "—they're all dead or taken hostage. It was only when a merchant ship arrived that the slaughter was discovered and a falcon sent to Kovograd."

Oleg turned on Kassandr. "The blood of those men is on your hands, brother," he snarled. The veins on his neck strained, and his eyes flickered that strange, lupine yellow.

"What orders have you, Sire?" asked the warrior, glancing nervously among the three Rurik men on the dais.

"Orders?" repeated the high prince dazedly. Kassandr's gaze narrowed as his father stared blankly at the chaos unfolding before him.

Saga saw the moment something switched inside Kassandr. He stepped toward the messenger. "Does Posadnik Volk have eyes on the ships?"

The warrior nodded.

"Good. Where are the Urkans this minute?"

The warrior's gaze darted to the high prince before settling back on Kassandr. "They've portaged the Crone's Revenge."

"That is so near!" exclaimed Oleg. "How are we hearing this only now?"

The messenger swallowed.

"He has answered this already, Oleg," said Kassandr. "And we do not have time for useless questions. Have the men from the north arrived?" he asked the warrior.

"Which men from the north?" demanded Oleg.

"The two thousand warriors I mustered from the northern territories," replied Kassandr smoothly. "As a precaution."

Saga exhaled sharply as she felt the first glimmer of hope. Kassandr had mustered warriors. They had the defensive walls. They had her knowledge of the Urkans. Immediately, her senses began to sharpen, and she sifted through the information, seeking their advantage.

"How many ships of Urkans?" Saga asked in Zagadkian.

The messenger's gaze hardened as he looked her way. No doubt this man—and the entire realm—blamed Saga for the Urkans' arrival, and they wouldn't be wrong. But despite the warrior's clear dislike for her, he answered her question. "Almost one hundred."

"Good," said Saga.

"Good?" demanded Oleg. "How can you think this *good*?"

"It means," replied Saga coolly, "that Ivar comes without boats from his father. From Norvaland."

Oleg's hands curled into fists. He whirled to face his father. "There is still time. We must send a delegation. Try for peace—"

"They've destroyed the ocean gate and taken hostages, you fool of a man!" exclaimed Kassandr. "Can you not read their purpose in that? They will never accept peace. We must gather provisions. Prepare for a siege—"

"Enough!" said the high prince in that strange, dominant voice. Immediately, both Kassandr and Oleg bowed their heads, like hounds with their tails tucked between their legs.

"What we will do is this," continued the high prince, slowly, as though he intended for Saga to listen. "We will prepare a delegation to meet the Urkans. Bring to them our large tribute of ore and grain. Propose talks of peace." He looked at the messenger. "Open the outer river gate."

Kassandr's gaze whipped to his father, anger and fear battling in his expression. "Father, that is a mistake—"

"Open the outer river gate," repeated the high prince. "Not for centuries have we welcomed outsiders into our realm. They will see this as a sign of our goodwill."

Saga's stomach twisted into knots. She understood the high prince's desire for peace, but how could he think such a thing would work? Apparently in agreement, Kassandr rumbled, low in his chest. His eyes glowed that vibrant green, tattoos pulsing along the backs of his hands, and Saga wondered who, precisely, was in charge right now.

"I will go," she said softly.

"You will not," growled Kassandr. "I did not bring you here only to hand you over to your enemies at the first threat." He turned to his father. "*I* will join the delegation."

Anger and irritation battled within Saga. Again, he stole her choice. Again, he imposed his own will upon her.

The high prince turned to his eldest son. "You will not, Kassandr." His voice turned cold and cutting. "You are my heir, and I cannot lose another. Besides, it is *you* who got us into this mess. You have done enough."

A low whine came from deep in Kassandr's chest, and Saga felt a fleeting moment of pity. But she swallowed it back and stepped forward. "Let me talk to King Ivar. Let me tell him face-to-face what happened in that hall."

The high prince surveyed her with cold detachment. "I would not hesitate to send you," he said in slow Zagadkian. "But our opening of the gates is a show of goodwill, and we must keep some leverage to trade for hostages."

The high prince gestured to someone on the floor, and an elder approached. His fussy ceremonial robes fluttered as he climbed the dais steps, then bowed uncertainly before the Zagadkian royals.

"Elder Bogdan," said the high prince, "I wish for you to entreat with the king of Íseldur."

A tremulous breath escaped the old man, but he stood and met the high prince's eyes with remarkable steadiness. "It will be my great honor, Sire."

"Good," said the high prince. "You will offer them grains and ore to depart our lands. And once all the hostages have been released and all but one of their ships have left Zagadkian waters, then we will deliver Lady Saga to them."

Elder Bogdan nodded, and the high prince continued his instructions in Zagadkian too rapid for Saga to follow. Numbness crept through her, and she moved to the windows to look out over the strange, beautiful city of Kovograd. Hundreds of turfed roofs peeked up from within the city's defensive walls. How many people went about their day, unaware of what was coming? How many lives would be irrevocably changed today? Soon the Kovosk River would be dotted with a hundred prowed ships. Soon the air would fill with the hammer of drumbeats and the bellow of war horns.

Soon, there would be bloodshed. Saga could feel it in her bones.

Kassandr Rurik stood upon the fortress gate tower, staring out at the Kovosk River. Men scurried about atop the outer river gates, readying them to open. His beast snarled beneath his rib cage. How could his fool of a father have ordered the outer river gates opened to the Urkans? It was like welcoming a predator right into their nest. Kassandr took comfort in the fact that his father had not ordered Saga handed over—*yet.*

It was also small comfort that the inner river gates remained sealed. As thick as a man is tall and ten times as high, the inner gates linked to the formidable defensive walls surrounding the city. Yet still there were vulnerable people outside their protection—the pier and fish market and the farmlands surrounding the city.

"Kovograd's walls have never fallen," said Oleg from beside him, as though reading Kass's thoughts.

"They have never faced a foe like the Urkans," Kassandr muttered in reply.

His gaze landed on the ships being readied at the pier. He scowled at the pleasure barge most frequently used by Oleg and Elisava for lazy days on the river. Today it would hold twenty finely dressed Zagadkians, headed by Elder Bogdan. Inwardly, Kassandr cringed. The barge was showy and ornate when what they needed was a show of strength.

"It should be you on that ship," muttered Oleg, following his gaze. "Handing back the whore. Begging for their forgiveness."

Kassandr's beast growled, the tattoos pulsing along the backs of his hands. "She is better than you will ever be, Oleg," he snarled, snatching his half brother by the collar.

"Your quarreling shames me," said their father, approaching from behind. Still clad in his ceremonial robes, the man looked entirely unprepared for war. "Our kingdom faces great strife. We must unite against it."

"Much like Lady Saga has said," replied Kassandr, turning her unexpected words over in his mind.

You must make peace with clans beyond the river.

But she did not understand the bad blood between their two peoples. And with Urkan war horns now sounding on the wind, time was clearly not on the Zagadkians' side. Kassandr cast a sidelong look at his father, whose pale-green eyes gazed out to the river. "What did the oracle tell you, Father?"

"It does not matter what she said."

Kassandr turned to face him head-on. "I think it does."

The high prince sighed, refusing to meet his son's eye. "My heart demands I do everything in my power to foster peace. It is my sworn duty to keep my people safe."

"And what the oracle said—" Kassandr didn't need to finish his question. It was obvious whatever the oracle had told his father further endangered the people of Zagadka.

Kassandr felt a moment of guilt. This was all happening because he'd gone against his father's orders and joined the delegation on the voyage to Íseldur—because he'd stolen Saga away from the Urkans. His impulsive choice had lost him Saga's trust and might cost his kingdom everything.

"Perhaps they will accept our terms," said Oleg wistfully. He clutched the wall, leaning closer, and for a moment, Kassandr pitied his half brother. After today, Zagadka's innocence would be long gone. No longer would they believe their gods and secrets would keep them safe.

He opened his mouth to say something, but the wail of a war horn had him snapping it shut. The horns and drumbeats grew louder by the minute, and soon Urkan longships would drift into view. The Zagadkian delegation would welcome King Ivar and Prince Bjorn upon their ridiculous pleasure barge. Would try to buy peace with ore and grain and the promise of Saga Volsik.

"Excuse me," said Kassandr, "I have work to do."

He left his father and half brother in the gate tower and strode along the covered walkway leading to the keep. Just as he pulled the door open, Kassandr collided with a slight figure hovering in the doorway. His hands wrapped around Saga's elbows, steadying her before she could fall on her arse.

"Saga," said Kass, hands skimming up the backs of her arms. "A pleasure to run into you."

Saga's lacy veil had fallen askew, and she tore it from her head and threw it on the ground. His beast purred in appreciation—her fire was strong today. Good.

"They won't surrender, Kass," she hissed, glancing at the door leading to the defensive walls. "You know this . . . *meeting* is only a ruse."

He nodded with a frown. "I do not doubt it."

"We must gather provisions. Ready ourselves to fight."

A slow smile spread across his face at her use of the word "we." "At last," he said, his grin growing wider, "here she is, my queen."

Her expression grew thunderous.

"Come," he said, before she could reply. "I will show you what *we* have already accomplished together."

Kass led Saga to the military wing of the fortress, which bustled with activity. Apprentices sharpened blades and pikes while weapons masters passed out armored jackets and pointed helms. The warriors paused their work, gazes hardening as they looked upon Saga. Kassandr's beast let out a low, warning growl, and the men bowed their heads in submission, then turned back to their tasks.

It wasn't long before they entered his war chamber. It was a small, functional room, with unadorned walls and a floor of packed earth. Kassandr's posadniki—chiefs from the eastern territories of Zagadka, each of whom was loyal to him alone—had gathered around the table over a map. But as Saga and Kassandr entered the room, all conversation halted.

The posadniki straightened, then dipped their brows in deference.

"Rise," said Kassandr, waving a hand in irritation. He slowed his Zagadkian, hoping Saga could follow. "Morzh, an update?"

The broad-shouldered man stepped forward. His drooping mustache bore an uncanny resemblance to the walrus tusks the warrior sported when he shifted into his animal form. "We've fifteen boatloads of seaweed, as you requested, Sire. My warriors have been busy threading it into the nets, and many are ready to be strung from the walls."

"Good," replied Kass, watching Saga from the corner of his eye.

"You—" She shook her head in disbelief. "Ocean plants . . . You listened?"

"Of course I listened," he shot back. "It is as I have said. Who better to learn about our enemies from than the one who lived with them?"

Her blue eyes searched his face. He wanted to grab her shoulders and give her a good shake—when would the woman realize how clever she was? Instead, he turned to his next posadnik. "And the hides, Volk?"

The man who stepped forward was tall and lean, his eyes an amber yellow, which he maintained when shifting into his wolf form.

"The pelts have been gathered, Sire. They've been soaked and draped over the armory, the fortress, and the walkway roofs nearest to the river."

"Clever," murmured Saga. "Skins also will provide excellent protection from fire." If Kassandr wasn't mistaken, he heard a note of admiration in her voice.

Kassandr moved to the next man, whose hair tufted around his ears much like his mountain cat's. "Grigorii, tell me of the sand."

"The barge arrived from the coast last night, Sire. My warriors have worked tirelessly to portion it into barrels and distribute them throughout the city. Buckets have been hauled to the stockade walls; great barrels to the courtyard."

"Sand for extinguishing fires?" Saga guessed.

Kassandr nodded. "As you have noted, the Urkans favor their firepots filled with oil and pitch. Sand is the only antidote."

Her disbelief and wonderment shifted to determination before his very eyes, and Kassandr had the maddening realization that no one had ever shown this woman how great her potential was.

"Is there fiery pots here? For Zagadka?" asked Saga.

The corners of his lips tugged down. "Some. I fear not enough." He could see her beautiful mind at work, yet he still was not prepared for the words she spoke in Zagadkian.

"I will finish. Maybe I can find helper." Those blue eyes fell upon him, and the tongue of his beast lolled to the side. "Do you have additional—" She paused in search of the Zagadkian word, then shifted to Íseldurian. "Pitch, or oil, or even wax."

"What have you in mind, Winterwing?" he asked in her language.

A beautiful blush suffused her cheeks. "Boil it. And when the berserkers set their ladders in place, cast it down upon them."

His beast howled in agreement. She thirsted for their blood, hungered for their misery, just like him. "What else?" urged Kassandr. He wanted to absorb each violent thought in her head. To set upon these Urkans with the vengeance wrought from her beautiful mind.

"Is there time to open the land gates? Grant the city's protection to those who live beyond?"

"It is done," Rov called out, sauntering into the room. A thin sheen of sweat misted his brow, but otherwise, the man held his trademark casual demeanor.

"The firepots you mentioned," Saga said, "how many do you need?"

Kass shook his head in delight. "My wicked little bird wishes to give to the Urkans a taste of their own ale."

"A taste of their own *medicine.*"

Kass waved a hand and switched to Zagadkian. "Grigorii and Rov will show you the room where they are made and how this is done."

"Elisava," said Saga, in stunted Zagadkian. "Tell to her bring women to . . . help with fiery pots."

Each minute her confidence grew greater, and with it, Kassandr's hope. The Urkans were coming, but they expected to find an unprepared nation and frightened woman.

Kassandr sent Volk to fetch Elisava. He turned to Saga, who readied to leave the room with Grigorii and Rov. But she paused.

Looked up at him. With his enhanced hearing, it was impossible not to hear the blood rushing through her veins; the irregular beat of her heart. It took every ounce of Kassandr's will not to gather her in his arms, not to kiss her like he had in Askaborg's gardens. But that would not win back her trust. Only patience could do that. Only time.

"Be safe," she said softly.

"And you," he replied.

Their gazes held. But they were soon wrenched apart by screams from above. Kassandr's feet were moving before he could think, carrying him up a staircase and down a corridor. Soon he was bursting onto the defensive wall. Another scream, projectiles thudding against the protective roof. Kassandr braced himself for the scent of smoke, for the sound of crackling flames.

Instead, a metallic tang met his nose.

"Blood," he hissed. Another scream had him racing along the defensive walls leading to the gate tower where he'd left his father and Oleg.

The Urkan fleet now dotted the river—a hundred prowed ships crawling with warriors. Before, it had been merely a warning, a thing that had not yet come to pass. But now that he laid eyes on the Urkans, everything became real. Kassandr's heart pounded as he stared at the largest of the fleet, trying to see King Ivar's blond head of hair.

A wail from the turret had him tearing his gaze away. There he found his father and brother huddled on the tower's floor. Kresimir and his retinue stood around the high prince and his son, shields raised protectively as heavy objects battered down from above. Thank the four gods, Kassandr's kin were unharmed, but he jolted back as a projectile split through the timber roof and crashed onto the walkway.

Kassandr stopped, staring at the missile.

Not a missile. A human head.

He was not proud of his first instinct. *You see?* Kassandr wanted to gloat. *Why did you not listen to me—to Saga—when we warned you of the Urkans?* They were selfish and petty thoughts to have in such dire times, and as Kassandr's gaze slid about the gate tower, he felt nothing but pity for those present. Oleg twisted to retch on the floorboards, Kresimir's face white as candle wax. And his father stared blankly, clutching something to his chest.

"Father," Kass hissed. "There is only one way forward now. We must get to the war chamber. Mobilize our warriors."

But as the high prince's retinue parted, the item in his father's hands came into focus. Elder Bogdan's lifeless eyes stared up at Kassandr, his face twisted into fear and agony.

"They've killed them," said the high prince dully. "They've killed them all—Elder Bogdan and the rest of the delegation. Every hostage taken from the ocean gate."

"Is something in mouth."

Kass whirled, a low growl coming from deep within him. There stood Saga in the gate tower's doorway, as human heads rained down on the fortress from above. She was still clad in the ethereal gown, and looked out of place among the soldiers rushing about. Kassandr's instincts urged him to usher her back into the keep. But hadn't he wanted this? For her to work alongside him? And so he swallowed his irritation and snatched Elder Bogdan's decapitated head from his father's grip. He pried the elder's broken teeth apart and worked a wad of parchment from his mouth. Kassandr unfolded it carefully.

"What does it say?" demanded Oleg, jostling to his side and yanking the note from his hand.

Oleg's face drained of color, one hand flying to his mouth.

"Their demand is this," read Oleg, "that the river runs red with our blood."

CHAPTER 24

Kopa, Íseldur

The air held a bitter chill and her muscles ached, yet Silla could not wipe the smile from her face as she slid from Dawn's saddle. She, Atli, and a combined assortment of his retinue and her guards had ridden up a snaking pathway for an hour or so until they reached the rolling, snow-covered meadows atop Brími.

Brittle yellow grasses protruded from the snow, interspersed with bursts of blue. *Stjarna's lilies,* Silla heard her foster mother say. *They bloom only after the first fall of snow.* The lilies, she decided, were a reminder of resilience—or perhaps a reminder that beautiful things could thrive even when all else had perished. Silla smiled like a fool. With fresh air in her lungs and a rousing wind on her cheeks, her mood was so bright that Myrkur burrowed ever deeper within her.

Ever since Myrkur's great expenditure of energy on the day of Fallgerd's death, He'd been remarkably quiet, slumbering deep within her. Silla had foolishly hoped He'd be permanently incapacitated, though somehow she knew it would not be so easy. Her fears were confirmed this morning, as she'd sensed Him beginning to stir.

She had to be quick to do this without His notice. Runný, Ingvarr, and the rest of Silla's guards milled about with Atli's retinue near the trail's edge, but Silla and Atli had ridden farther into the meadow before dismounting. Dawn nudged her elbow, and Silla turned toward her, pulling an oat treat from the folds of her fur-lined cloak.

"I've missed you so much, girl," she whispered, stroking Dawn's cheek as the horse chomped on the treat. "But I hear you've been grazing in Jarl Hakon's sheltered pastures. I bet his grass tastes better than the best grass you've ever had. Have you made friends with the other horses . . ."

Silla trailed off as snow crunched and a figure appeared by her side.

"Did you say something?" asked Atli Hakonsson, lips quirked. He was clad in the finest fur cloak Silla had ever seen, and it draped asymmetrically, revealing the thick weapons belt secured at his hips.

"I . . . was talking to Dawn." Silla knew she should probably be embarrassed, yet she was too distracted by the view from so high. "You truly *can* see all the way to the ocean!"

For a moment, she forgot about all the challenges before her and simply took in the beauty. To the north, snow-covered, toothy mountains stretched for leagues until they met the sea. To the south, the city of Kopa was nestled into Brími's embrace, the Hvíta River and Black Road snaking through the landscape beyond it.

Silla found her gaze drifting south, toward Sunnavík. The Weaver had hinted that Saga's thread had diverged some distance from Silla's. Was that why they hadn't heard from her? Silla reached inward for the curious sisterly bond through which they'd communicated, but it remained still and silent. At first, Silla had thought it muted by the hindrium, but what if that was not true? What if she couldn't feel Saga because her sister was gone from the realm of the living?

With a deep breath, Silla shook her head and reminded herself why she'd insisted on coming up here. While Atli might think she simply wanted some fresh air, Silla had ulterior motives. She needed to find natural halda deposits so she could test her theory that the Volsik bloodline gift allowed her to pull raw power from the minerals.

Silla strode purposefully toward a windswept patch in the meadow. But her foot caught on a snow-covered stone, sending her sprawling. "Sor—" She caught herself before she could finish apologizing to yet another rock.

Atli gripped her elbow and hauled her to her feet. Silla's gaze fell once more upon the patch and her heart leaped at the glint of blue minerals. Eagerly, she swept the rest of the snow free, revealing a swath of blue-veined stone.

"These are halda minerals, correct?" she asked excitedly, tracing the threads with her gloved hand.

Atli peered over her shoulder. "Aye. The deposits are plentiful in these parts."

Silla chewed on her lip, choosing her next question carefully. "Do you use them? Halda stores, that is." Atli, Silla had learned, was a Blade Breaker, while his brother Eyvind was an Ashbringer like her.

Atli tapped the bracers at his wrists. "I prefer to wear my stores. I know some Galdra have imbued halda into the hilts of their weapons."

Silla took Atli's hand, twisting it this way and that as she examined the finely wrought bracer strapped to his wrist. It seemed to be made of the same leather-like material as the lébrynja jacket Rey had gifted her, though carved with elaborate knotwork and adorned with gleaming blue stones.

"Rey has his tattooed." At the pang of emotion in her chest, Silla quickly changed direction. "How do you pull your galdur from the bracers?"

"It's hard to explain," Atli said, squeezing her hand gently. She hadn't realized her palm was still in his hand. Silla blinked and stepped carefully back. Had she imagined it, or was that disappointment in Atli's expression? He cleared his throat. "It's an intuitive thing," he continued, "much like expression."

Silla hummed in thought, then slowly pulled her glove off and dropped to her knees. Her bare fingers skimmed along the deep blue lines of the halda minerals, and her eyes fell shut as she searched for the quiet corner of her mind that she'd discovered in Kalasgarde. Myrkur shifted behind her rib cage, and anxiety spiked through her.

She had to be quick—had to do this before He regained His strength. With a deep breath, Silla refocused.

Had it not been for all the hours she'd spent practicing expression and the weaving of her galdur, Silla might have discounted the small sensation beneath her palm. It was the feeling of potential—a promise of something that *could* be. Before she'd been forced to take hindrium doses to guard her Ashbringer power, Silla had felt something similar in the pool of galdur resting behind her breastbone. But while her source had always had a shape to it—a flavor, perhaps—what she felt in this stone was altogether different. It felt raw. A little wild, perhaps.

Beside her, Atli cleared his throat. "The halda must be ground into a powder for you to use, Eisa."

"I don't think so."

"What do you mean?"

"Please hush," Silla said curtly, then sighed as the feel of the halda's power slipped from her grasp. She pushed to her feet, then wandered toward the next patch.

"Will you tell me what you're trying to accomplish?" Atli asked, rushing to keep up with her.

Silla pursed her lips and glanced his way. "I'm testing a theory," she said in a low voice.

"That . . . halda stones are cold?"

Irritated, Silla dropped to her knees beside the next patch of halda stones. In this moment, she missed Rey more than ever, and wished she had someone in whom she could confide. Could she trust Atli? Silla glanced toward the guards and retinue warriors, then looked up at Atli's curious face. *Let us be friends*, he'd said, and gods, but Silla could use one right now.

"I believe I can . . . sense the galdur inside these stones," she said in a rush. At his blank expression, Silla continued. "No one understands the gift Sunnvald bestowed upon the Volsik bloodline, but twice now, I've experienced curious bursts of strength."

"And you think—"

"I think I might have pulled galdur from halda minerals without realizing it."

Atli's brows rose in wonderment, but after a long moment, he dropped to his knees beside her and helped her swipe snow away. For the next hour, they traipsed about the meadow, Silla placing her hands on stone after stone. By the time her fingers were chilled to the bone, she knew beyond certainty that she could sense *something* in those stones. But her attempts to pull the strange, untapped energy to herself had yielded nothing.

Eventually, she could sense nothing beyond the wind and how gods damned cold her fingers were. Atli wrapped his elegant cloak around her shoulders as Silla's teeth chattered. It smelled like cedar and salt, and while it was nice, it wasn't *hers*.

The pair made their way back to Dawn, and as they began the ride down the mountain, she was glad beyond measure for Atli's cloak. Beside her, Atli directed his warhorse along the trail, handling the hot-tempered beast with ease, while Eisa's queensguard were split—half ahead and half behind her.

The trail zagging down Brími grew steeper with each pass. To her left were sheer stone cliffs, jutting toward the skies. To her right, the bluff plunged downward, dotted with black volcanic boulders. And at the very base of these bluffs was the city of Kopa.

"It's stunning," she said, examining the tiny black buildings, looking much like a toy town.

Atli looked over his shoulder, locking eyes with her. "Aye, 'tis a lovely view." Sunlight caught on his onyx waves, casting shadows beneath his olive cheekbones, and for a moment, Silla thought he did not mean the city. But as soon as the thought had arrived it left, and Silla shook her head. Her emotions were all over the place today.

"I forgot to share," said Atli, "that I've had word from Eyvind."

Cold flooded Silla's veins. "Oh?" she asked, her voice a little too high.

"Their group arrived in Istré, or what is left of it. They planned to enter the woods, oh, what would have been two days' past."

Silla's mind whirled. Two weeks and not a single letter had arrived from Rey. She'd grown increasingly worried for his safety. But Eyvind had written Atli with no mention of harm. So why hadn't Rey written her?

A hundred scenarios flitted through her mind—Rey, once more with the Bloodaxe Crew, remembering where his place truly ought to be. Perhaps the distance between them had given him new clarity. Perhaps he'd realized that Kalasgarde had been an illusion, that Silla and Rey didn't fit together in the real world. *You're making too much of it,* she argued with herself.

But the lack of letters stung worse than she cared to admit. A single blasted letter—three little words would even suffice. *I miss you.* Silla exhaled in irritation.

"Everything all right?" Atli inquired, glancing over his shoulder. "I assumed you'd already know of this."

"No," she replied, failing to keep the bitterness from her voice. "I've not heard any of it."

Atli's brows drew together, and he seemed to understand. "Galtung is good at his job," he said at last. "And this one has proven stubborn. I'm certain he's immersed himself so deeply he's . . . temporarily lost track of things."

Silla pressed her lips into a thin line. "Perhaps." Desperate to change the subject, she said, "I've heard a second jarl and his retinue have arrived for the feast."

"Aye, Geirmundur and his lot," said Atli with irritation. "Wasted no time in drinking through three barrels of mead."

Silla huffed. "Jarl Geirmundur," she recited, trying to pull the name from the depths of her sleep-addled mind, "of the Geirroth dynasty. Holds the lands west of Kopa to the Nordurian border. His wife is Lady Gunhild—"

"Brynhild," Atli interjected.

Silla exhaled, irritated with herself. "Do you know, Atli, I can recite the nine different methods used to make breads. I know which herbs and mushrooms are safe to forage; how to make five sólas stretch for a month. But I cannot, for the life of me, recall all these names." For a moment, she longed above all else to go back to those simpler times.

Atli chuckled, and Silla was glad it was not in mocking. "I can help you," he offered. "Let us sit together at the feast. We could . . . have a signal. You can stomp on my foot if you forget a name, and I'll cough it into my dining linen."

"Gods, Atli, that would be divine," Silla exclaimed. "Please, that would ease my worries so very much."

Atli grinned back at her. "Consider it done."

A crack from above had Atli's warhorse snorting, then dancing to the side. Silla could not see around Atli's large form, but an incoherent shout raised the hairs on her neck.

"What did he say?"

The ground began to rumble, a high, splintering sound coming from above.

"Rockslide!" shouted Atli. "Retreat!"

Silla yanked on Dawn's reins, whirling her around in time to see Runný doing the same. Keeping her body low to Dawn's back, Silla tried to stay close to Runný's mare as they raced back up the trail. But Runný was an experienced horsewoman, while Silla had only a few months of practice, and there was soon a gap between them. Above, the thunder of the rockslide grew louder, first one stone, then another tripping across the path. Silla reined Dawn up with not a heartbeat to spare—a boulder crashed down and the entire section of path ahead of her broke away from the mountainside.

Dawn whinnied, rearing up for a single, terrifying moment.

"Easy," Silla murmured, sliding from the panicked horse before she could be thrown. "Calm, girl."

But Dawn bolted, leaping over the broken section of trail and leaving Silla trapped by twin rockslides. Another horse raced past her—Atli's riderless warhorse—but then an arm snaked around her waist and Silla was shoved against the sheer rock face. Disoriented, Silla pushed back until she realized Atli had thrown his body over hers and hefted his shield overhead. Stones battered down from above, and the strange press of magic against her skin told Silla that were it not for Atli's Blade Breaker strength, they'd already be dead. He grunted, widening his stance, as Silla's fear surged through her—but no, that was not fear, but *energy*.

A mineral, earthy taste filled her mouth, and she gasped. She pressed her fingertips harder against the rock face, certain that if light shone upon them, she'd see blue veins streaked through. Now Silla was certain—it was the unshaped power of the halda stones flooding her veins. This wild power was eager to be set free—it pushed against her hold, demanded to be released. Had she not spent countless hours mastering expression, Silla would not have been able to grasp it at all.

"Hold on," she told Atli, gripping the power like the reins of a bucking horse.

Rocks hammered down on them from above, but Silla slid her hands along the rim of his shield, clutching with the last shred of her will to the energy coursing through her.

And then she let go.

When she'd pushed Rey in that field so long ago, it had felt like tiny bubbles popping beneath her skin. This was a thousand times stronger. Power surged from her palms in an explosion so violent, it buckled her knees; made her teeth clank together. Atli shouted, his shield wrenched free, but it wasn't only his shield—all of the weight bearing down on them burst free at once. Rocks shot a hundred feet into the air before slamming violently down in a radius all around them. Men shouted; boulders exploded against the bluffs; dust and debris rained down from above.

And then, silence so loud her ears seemed to ring.

The moment stretched on for a small eternity, broken only by the sound of laughter. Laughter? Silla blinked as Atli gripped her shoulders and shook her gently.

"You did it! How—was that what—Hábrók's hairy bollocks, my life flashed before my very eyes, but you *did it*!"

Dazed, Silla glanced about, taking in the enormous radius around her and Atli. The trail was blocked in all directions, but not a solitary boulder remained within five paces of them. And the once-sheer rock face now cratered inward.

"How did you do it?" Atli asked, staring at Silla in astonishment.

Stunned, she fell onto her arse and hugged her knees to her chest. She wanted to scream in delight. Wanted to share in this miraculous breakthrough with Rey. But he was not here, and so she grinned at Atli and said, "I don't know."

As Silla's disbelief slowly faded, beneath it, she began to sense something *other.* Dark curiosity slithered through her veins as Myrkur uncurled from the base of her spine. The god of chaos was suddenly fully alert.

Yes, Eisa, the dark god purred. *How did you do that?*

Silla closed her eyes. Tried to will the god away. But lingering fear clung to her muscles and bones, making it impossible to shake Him free completely.

"My fear," she forced out, to Atli. "It must have helped prime me . . . helped me pull the halda's power . . ."

Do it again, Eisa, begged Myrkur, His keen interest spiraling through her veins. *Let me taste this curious power.*

Silla had not felt the god's presence so strongly since that day in Fallgerd's home. Unease built as Myrkur's emotions entwined with her own. She *needed* this bloodline power. Needed to understand it. Needed to *own* it.

And then she would make every being in this realm bend the knee.

Get out of my head, Silla forced toward Him.

He only laughed. *Let me play with this power, and perhaps I'll consider it.*

But Silla was not the same girl she'd been in Svangormr Pass—she now understood the consequences of handing her power over to Myrkur. *Never,* she told him.

His laughter rattled her spine and sent fear spiking through her. *We shall see,* He said, before setting to prodding and scratching at the corners of her mind. Silla braced against the unnatural feel;

tried to fortify her mental defenses to keep Him out. But as voices reached her from beyond the crater, her focus shifted outward.

"Over here!" someone called.

Heads popped up from above—Runný. Kálf. Several members of Atli's retinue.

"They're all right!" someone shouted.

"The horses?" called Atli.

"Safe!" Runný said, grinning wide. "Everyone is accounted for."

Relief coursed through Silla's veins as reality settled in. That could have easily gone another way—they could have been buried beneath tons of rocks, every one of them dead.

But they'd survived.

And better than that, she was certain she'd just wielded her bloodline gift.

CHAPTER 25

The Western Woods

Hekla was growing used to the scrape of prickles down her spine and the crawling sensations beneath her skin. In the Western Woods, it felt like the trees had eyes and the forest had a pulse. The sickness of the trees and the dead underbrush only added to the eerie feel. Yet on their group walked, for days upon days.

After their battle with the mist and its Turned beasts, Rey's excitement about returning to Kopa was a palpable thing. And when he'd handed leadership to Hekla, the moment had felt strangely weighted—like he was handing over more than just the mission.

Now it had been several days since Rey had departed, and Hekla was still shaken from their encounter with the wolfspider. For years, she hadn't let her discomfort with spiders keep her from doing her job. But the sheer size of that spider paired with the sound of its voice inside her skull had thoroughly flustered her. She could not afford to let it do so again.

Instead, she refocused her thoughts on the task ahead of them. Mad though it sounded, she could feel energy gathering in the forest, like the culmination of a great storm. It was too much to consider all the moving pieces at once, and so she fixed on what was directly ahead of them: a trek across the Western Woods to reach the dormant half of the Forest Maiden.

As the days wore on, Hekla grew convinced that the stories Rey had told her of the Forest Maiden were true. It was undeniable that she exerted some magic on the forest—they traveled far more quickly than what was natural, as though the woods folded in on themselves. This skill of the Forest Maiden's was rather helpful, with the caveat that it drained her.

The Forest Maiden spent most of her time slumbering in a small sling that Thrand Long Sword insisted on carrying around his neck. His strange devotion had Hekla wondering if the Maiden had Thrand under her thrall—he did seem the kind of man to be seduced and led to an untimely death.

Now Kritka was perched on her left shoulder, gnawing on a hard heel of bread, as he had for hours on end. Her temples had begun to throb earlier in the day, and the incessant gnashing of his teeth was not helping one bit.

Must you do that? Hekla sent through their bond, stepping over a fallen tree branch while dodging an oozing black mushroom.

Do what? asked Kritka, rotating the bread between his little paws.

You've been eating all day!

The squirrel assessed her with beady black eyes. *Kritka must bulk up for winter.* At Hekla's bewildered look, he clarified, *To keep warm and fed during cold months.*

She sighed, then batted at a brittle pine branch, sending parched needles skittering to the snow-dusted forest floor.

Kritka senses Protector is angry.

As I've told you a hundred times before, I'm not the Protector.

Are Protector's mates not chasing to her liking?

She nearly tripped over a rock. "What?" she demanded aloud, causing several heads in their party to turn her way. "Nothing." Hekla waved her hands and waited until their attention drifted elsewhere.

What mates? she demanded inwardly.

The red one and the one who lingers behind.

Hekla glanced over her shoulder, locking eyes with Gunnar.

White teeth flashed against his black beard, and she quickly looked away. A few warriors ahead of her strode Eyvind, bundled in his red cloak. Hekla turned her glare upon the squirrel.

If mates are not chasing to Protector's liking, perhaps Protector should encourage them more, Kritka carried on, his russet tail twitching.

Malla's tits, rodent, what are you going on about?

When a female squirrel goes into heat, she leads the males on a chase, Kritka explained. *Many males take up the hunt. But the one who gets there first performs the mating strut.*

Ahead of them, Eyvind held a pine bough up to allow their group to pass. Hekla's heartbeat quickened as she neared, and when he opened his mouth as though to speak, her eyes darted anywhere but on him. She heard his frustrated breath. Felt his searing gaze upon her cheek. He'd tried half a dozen times to explain himself to her, and each time, a hot panicky feeling arose within. She'd fled like a coward. Hekla knew she was being childish—that she couldn't avoid him forever. Still, she didn't exhale until she'd ducked beneath the branch and put space between them.

Protector's heart beats rather quickly near the red mate, observed Kritka.

Hekla's prickly defenses rose in an instant. *He broke my trust. He's betrothed to another woman.*

Kritka was silent save for the scrape of his teeth against hard bread. *Kritka does not understand. Is it not natural for males to mate with many?*

Her irritation reached a breaking point. Hekla plucked Kritka from her shoulder, then whirled on a startled Gunnar. "I need a break from him," she grumbled, handing him the squirrel.

But even without the squirrel on her shoulder, the throb at her temples did not subside.

When Hekla tripped over a moss-covered stone for the third time that hour, she raised her hand, bringing their party to a stop.

"It seems as good a place as any to set camp for the night," she muttered, looking around.

There wasn't truly a *good* place to camp in these gods forsaken woods, but the relieved looks among their crew made Hekla glad of her decision. Each day that she led this crew of warriors, her confidence grew a little more. She knew this job better than anyone else, and taking full control of it felt like a natural thing.

Hekla dropped onto the forest floor and pulled provisions from her sack. They were down to salt cod rations, and as Hekla chewed on the tough, briny meat, she tried to imagine it was the kind of fare Silla had once cooked for the Bloodaxe Crew.

Eventually, their group split off—some warriors fetching deadwood for their nightly fires, others searching for water. For the first two nights, Eyvind had stayed up, ready to produce flames with his Ashbringer skill should the mist attack. But by the third night, the man was practically sleeping on his feet, and it was clear this setup would not work anymore. That night, they'd lit a perimeter of small campfires around their bedrolls. Two men sat on watch, buckets of water on hand to douse errant sparks. It was a fine balance to maintain, keeping themselves protected without setting the woods aflame.

Gunnar soon ambled back into their makeshift camp, a bucket of water in each hand and Kritka perched on his shoulder. The squirrel clutched a portion of salt cod between his tiny paws, and Hekla suppressed the urge to remind Gunnar their priority was to make these portions last—not fatten up a squirrel for the winter.

"Came across a pool," Gunnar said, a gleam in his dark eyes. "Perhaps we could return to it later, *alone.*"

Hekla's flat gaze was all the answer Gunnar should need. He was remarkably persistent, as was Hekla's hesitation to trample this new, bright version of him. She knew she ought to give the man an answer to his marriage proposal and put an end to this, yet she couldn't bring herself to do it. And though she hated to admit it, a small part of her enjoyed being at the center of Gunnar's and Eyvind's ridiculous attentions.

While an intimate visit to the pools with Gunnar was certainly not on her mind, the idea of scraping the grime from the socket of her prosthetic sounded divine. And so Hekla picked herself off the ground and gathered her remaining energy to trudge in the direction Gunnar had come from. She passed several of Eyvind's men along the way, greeting them with curt nods.

They'd proven to be good, loyal warriors, and she sensed she'd earned their respect when they'd fought together in Istré. To be sure, she'd had to prove herself to them—and break Thrand Long Sword's ribs—but such was the life of a woman warrior. She had to work twice as hard as the men, and twice more on top of that because of her prosthetic arm.

At last, the dense tree canopy opened up, a still, glassy pool reflecting the constellations above. The woods were so quiet, the water so enticing. After a glance over her shoulder to ensure she was alone, Hekla stripped down to her undertunic.

Lowering herself onto a flat stone overhanging the pond, Hekla dipped her prosthetic arm into the water, rubbing the forest grime from it. She then twisted the arm off, sighing as she dipped her residual limb into the cool liquid. It had been too many weeks since she'd been able to prepare Silla's poultice recipe, and her skin around the anchor joint was once more patchy and irritated.

As she soothed the burning itch, Hekla examined her moonlit reflection. The same brown eyes looked up at her, framed by the same dark, slashing brows. Her olive cheekbones were more pronounced than they had once been, and there was a weariness in her face that told of many long days just like this one. Yet Hekla collected each small mark on her skin like a badge. Once there had been a time when wrinkles and scars weren't guaranteed.

A snap from somewhere behind her had Hekla glancing over her shoulder. But still, shadowy woods were all that met her eyes. The trees were so eerie in their quietude; she had to shake off a shiver before turning back to the water.

She frowned at the small ripple marring the surface of the pool and distorting her reflection. Then—movement beneath the surface. And Hekla realized she no longer looked at her own likeness, but that of a yellow-eyed woman beneath the water.

Time slowed as the woman's face twisted into a snarl. And then she burst from the pool, all sharp teeth and lank hair and corpse-gray skin.

Hekla screeched, rearing back, but her left hand slipped on the rock's surface. Webbed fingers snatched at her braid and hauled her toward the pool. Hekla groped for her prosthetic arm, but she could not reach it—nor could she reach the dagger sheathed in her boot. How could she have let her guard down in this, of all places?

As Hekla fought against the thing's immense strength, horror spread through her. The creature had the feel of something ancient—something older than even the trees in this forest. And her eyes—a pale yellow rather than ember red—placed her as something entirely different from the draugur and Turned creatures they'd encountered so far.

Water hag, her mind oh-so-helpfully provided.

The fetid stench of pond water invaded her senses, and she devolved into desperation, clawing with the blunted nails of her left hand against cold rubbery skin. With a sudden rush, her head plunged into the water. She knew she ought to hold her panic at bay—to save as much air as she could—but a torrent of bubbles poured from her nose. Hekla punched at the water hag; clung desperately to the rock above the water with her legs.

Suddenly, the hag's grip on her hair relented, and the creature reared back with a jerk. Blood spread like ink through the water and the hag wrenched a dagger free from her shoulder. Where in the gods' burning bollocks had that come from? With one final snarl of bubbles, the creature darted into the pool's dark depths.

Hekla shoved her head above water and sucked in a deep breath of air, but a grip on her hips hauled her onto her back. She collided with the hard stone, a band around her waist pinning her in place. Hekla fought like an overturned beetle, but could not free herself from the shackle.

"Be still, Hekla. I have you."

All her fight died in an instant as she recognized Eyvind's voice. Gasping for breath, Hekla sagged against what she realized was not, in fact, the stone, but Eyvind's firm chest. She couldn't bring herself to care—couldn't shake that creature's haunting yellow eyes from her mind, nor drive the smell of the pond from her nose. For a moment, she lay atop Eyvind, staring up at the star-filled skies as she heaved for breath.

Then she pried his fingers free from her waist and rolled onto all fours.

Eyvind was on his feet in an instant, hauling her up and into his arms like she was a gods damned damsel in distress. "You've been hurt," he said with worry, cradling her tighter to his chest. Hekla thrashed against him, but his grip was unyielding. "Do not exert yourself, Hekla. Let me look upon you."

Hekla's body warmed at his words, and she growled in frustration. How, after everything, could Eyvind still have this effect on her? "Release me, Hakonsson, or those'll be the last words you speak," she snapped.

His hazel eyes hardened, but his grip slowly softened, and a moment later, Eyvind placed her gently on her feet. He produced a flame in his palm, the light revealing the worry in his eyes.

"Let me look."

Emotion caught in her chest, and she found herself swaying toward him. With a defeated sigh, Hekla relented. Eyvind stepped forward, firelight dancing across his irritatingly handsome face as he prodded at the scratch marks at the base of her neck; at the bare patch where the creature had yanked the hair from her scalp.

"See?" she mumbled. "I'm fine. Nothing Sigrún's ointment won't fix."

Eyvind stepped back, his concerned expression turning stern. "You removed your arm? And what happened to your weapons?"

She deemed his questions unworthy of an answer and pointedly looked away. Hekla searched for her defenses. Tried to pull them back into place.

"You were fortunate. A moment later and I'd have been too late."

Hekla rubbed the stinging wound on her neck.

"You should not be unaccompanied in these woods," said Eyvind, low and deadly serious. "I do not care who you bring with you, but do not lower your guard."

She ought to be glad that someone cared enough to look out for her. Instead, anger simmered in her gut. She was so gods damned angry—with Eyvind for his deception. With herself for letting her guard down.

"Do not trouble yourself with my safety," she hissed.

Eyvind's jaw shifted, and he turned away, but only to fetch her prosthetic arm. As he handed it over, Hekla noted that his tunic, wet from holding her to him, now clung to him like a second skin. The fact that she noticed such details only made her anger burn higher.

"I *will* trouble myself with your safety," said Eyvind. "In fact, it is no trouble at all. It is instinct. It is *need,* Hekla, much like breathing or sleeping—"

"Enough!" Hekla snapped, twisting her prosthesis back into place. Her skin prickled and her blood boiled, a thousand angry words building on her tongue. But as she met his hazel eyes, her anger deflated to hurt. She couldn't bear to talk about all that had happened—not yet, and certainly not *here*. But she had to make him understand. "Perhaps you should turn this *instinct* of yours toward your betrothed, Hakonsson."

"If you'd let me explain—"

"Stop!" Panic surged to life in her chest, and Hekla backed away. "I need space, Eyvind. If you mean any of the words you've just spoken, you'll respect my wishes."

"Hekla." There was weight to her name. Meaning in each syllable.

But Hekla couldn't endure the ache of it.

Turning her back on Eyvind Hakonsson, she retreated toward camp. And if Hekla was glad to hear his near-silent steps trailing her, she would never tell a soul.

CHAPTER 26

Sunnavík, Íseldur

Jonas's breath clouded in the stagnant air of Askaborg's pits as he massaged the pain from his thigh. Around him, warriors sparred under Volund's watchful eye, but as the war chief's gaze fell Jonas's way, he quickly straightened. Since he'd climbed from Askaborg's dungeons to its barracks, the pain in his leg had subsided some. Still, last night he'd dreamed of an axe being driven into his thigh and had woken to an explosion of pain from his frostbitten limb.

Jonas squared off against his partner, a barrel-chested beast of a man. Based on the tattooed claw marks and the man's impressive stature, he seemed to be ex-Klaernar. Jonas tried not to think what the man might have done to be expelled from the King's Claws.

Jonas watched as his opponent's gaze fell on his wounded thigh and cursed inwardly. He knew better than to show any weakness—particularly among warriors like these. Volund clapped his hands, barking out orders, and Jonas launched at his opponent before he could target his weak leg.

"What's a pretty boy like you doing here?" grunted the man as he parried a blow.

Jonas drove forward with speed and vigor, pushing through the pain radiating up his thigh. It was the dozenth time he'd been asked since he'd found himself in Volund's warband. While having a handsome face had its perks in the regular world, here among the Corpse Bringers, it only put a target on Jonas's back.

At the end of each training day, Volund pitted warriors against one another in no-holds-barred matches. Unlike during practice, their weapons were not wrapped, and the matches continued until the loser could no longer stand. The first day, Volund had immediately found Jonas, with an ugly, malevolent smile. "Pair the pretty boy with Horfi," he'd told his underlings.

An enormous, black-bearded brute was soon standing opposite him, clutching twin handaxes. But Horfi, like Volund, made the mistake of judging Jonas based on his looks. It was nothing new to him—Jonas was used to having to use his fists to demand respect. This *Horfi* was no different. True, Jonas took a few blows and a slash to the forearm. But by the end of the match, he held both of Horfi's handaxes, and his boot rested on the lout's rib cage.

Forcing his mind to the present, Jonas found an opening and swept his opponent's feet out from under him. The warrior landed hard on his back, and Jonas retreated to allow him to regain his bearings. He gazed around the stone-hewn arena where King Ivar had once pitted his pet bears against Volsik supporters.

The men of the Corpse Bringers were nothing like his brothers and sisters of the Bloodaxe Crew. Their code of honor was more fluid, ever-changing like the weather. Jonas had learned that the bulk of these men were discharged from King Ivar's warbands or plucked from prison cells. A select few had joined voluntarily, seeking a warrior's purse.

And curiously, the creatures Jonas had fought in his initiation battle trained alongside them as well. Draugur, he'd learned they were called, and though the sight and smell of them repulsed Jonas, he could not help but watch in curiosity. Strange robed acolytes carved marks on the creatures' foreheads each morning before calling out various commands and scoring the draugurs on their ability to obey.

Volund proclaimed they readied for war; that while the king fought in Zagadka, it fell upon them to keep peace in the realm of

Íseldur. But as Jonas looked at the murderers and rapists plucked from prison cells—at the mad-eyed berserkers too violent for even Ivar's warbands—he did not trust Volund's words one bit. There was more to this crew, of that he was certain.

The bars on his windows and guards at each garrison hall exit as good as confirmed his suspicion that the only way out of this warband was on the corpse cart. Still, Jonas always kept a watchful eye, searching for any opportunity. At the first chance, he planned to escape and regroup. There would be other ways to avenge his brother without the queen's help.

"Line up to greet our queen!" bellowed Volund in a bizarre moment of coincidental timing.

Anger churned in Jonas's gut. *Not my queen,* he wanted to sneer. But he knew better than to say such things aloud.

Instead, he joined the other warriors in formation. A moment later, an entourage of warriors strode into the pits, clad in the queen's livery. And there, in the middle of them, was the queen's slight figure. The queen and her guards crossed the floor of the pits, then climbed the steps between spectator benches to the royal dais. Jonas glared at the queen's back. Though still clad in mourning black, today she'd forgone the veil. As she settled into a seat of honor, Jonas caught his first glimpse of Queen Signe's face. She was younger than he'd expected—likely less than ten years his senior.

An elbow landed in his ribs. "I'd have a crack at her," muttered his sparring partner with a leering grin.

Jonas sent a scowl the man's way. "I'd like to see you try to get within ten paces of her."

But as he stared back at Signe, he was struck by her beauty. Along with her white-gold hair and glacial blue eyes, she had skin as pale as moonlight. She was utterly out of place among the Corpse Bringers, and he wondered what business a queen had in a place like this.

It was the fierceness in the queen's eyes that Jonas found most striking of all. Even from across the arena, he could tell she was no docile creature—this was a woman of ambition. Yet he could not forget that she'd refused to hear him. How she'd thrown him into this pit of vipers.

Jonas turned his attention back to Volund, who barked orders for the warband to break off into pairs. Again, he faced off with his large opponent, and they raised their wrapped blades. And a moment later, Jonas surged at the warrior as though he were the curly-haired woman who'd ruined his life.

Calmness fell upon Jonas at once. With a sword in his hand and the battle thrill in his veins, he almost felt like his old self. Jonas lost himself to the familiar movements of his body, throwing himself into it until his muscles ached and sweat dripped from his brow. Minutes, or perhaps hours, passed, but at last, his opponent lay panting and disarmed on the packed-earth floor of the arena.

"Did I wrong you in a past life, warrior?" he wheezed, making no move to stand.

Jonas opened his mouth to reply, but he felt a prickling sensation on the back of his neck. Wiping the sweat from his brow, he turned, his gaze finding the queen's at once. She sat on the protected dais, watching him with an unreadable expression.

Jonas held her gaze, perhaps too boldly. Yet he could not forget how easily she'd dismissed him. How she'd refused to hear what he had to say. How she'd thrown him in this warband of thieves and murderers.

And so Jonas gave the queen a mocking bow.

Then he turned his back on her.

CHAPTER 27

Kopa, Íseldur

"Deliberate?" repeated Silla, trying to comprehend what Atli Hakonsson had just revealed. "Surely it cannot be true?"

But Atli's expression bore no hint of amusement.

"If the rockslide was deliberate," she murmured, "then it must have been another attempt on my life." Her mind spun as she tried to make sense of this.

They were seated at a table in Atli Hakonsson's private quarters, a pair of wine goblets before them. Candlelight cast a serene glow through the space, catching on a vase of Stjarna's lilies and the finely embroidered table linen beneath them. When Silla had first entered the room—after Ingvarr and Runný had deemed it clear of threats—she'd found this an oddly intimate setting. It hadn't helped that Atli was dressed in one of the most resplendent tunics Silla had ever seen, that his hair was styled in an elaborate warrior's braid and his beard freshly oiled. But with her guards leaning against the wall behind her, and Atli's retinue lounging on the benches near the hearth, they were far from alone. Besides, she reassured herself, the discussion of assassination attempts warranted a private setting.

Silla shook her head incredulously. "You're certain?"

A look of concern settled on Atli's face, and he reached across the table to take her hand. Restlessness filled Silla as she pondered how to take her hand back without offense. But Atli's next words shook the thought clean from her mind.

"There were deep grooves on the ridge where boulders once would have sat. There is no chance these stones dislodged on their own. Someone *pried* them loose."

Laughter skittered down her spine. *Still, they try to kill us,* whispered Myrkur, pumping anger through her veins.

Since she'd caused that explosion to free herself and Atli from the rockslide, the god of chaos had been alarmingly active. Her awful dreams were more vivid, the cravings sliding through her veins more potent.

Atli's thumb swept across the back of her hand, and Silla jumped, yanking it back. She blinked, trying to refocus. "Does this mean Ivar has allies in the north?" Silla frowned. "I didn't ask for this. I always say *please.* I'm somewhat tidy. I even rescue spiders and set them free outdoors."

We're a threat, dear Eisa, purred Myrkur. *We have the power to topple kings and queens.*

There is no "we," Silla shot back, then winced as the dark god forced visions into her mind's eye. Silla and Myrkur sat on a throne in Askaborg Castle, a crown on their head. They would string the vile Urkan king and queen on those pillars—would flay the skin from their bodies—

You aspire to be queen, whispered the dark god. *Let me in, Eisa, and together we can accomplish it.*

Nausea roiled in her stomach, and with great effort, Silla pried the dark god's talons loose from her mind. She drew her gaze back to Atli.

"Spiders?" he repeated, brow crinkled in amusement.

"What?"

"It's only . . ." Candlelight flickered in Atli's eyes, intense as they roamed her face. "I'm certain they do not wish to kill you for poor manners."

"No, I suppose not."

"You represent change," said Atli. His gaze lingered on her mouth for a moment before flicking back to her eyes. "Perhaps they wish for things to stay the same."

"Someone with power, then," Silla mused. Frustration gathered in her stomach. She'd run over the suspects in her mind time and time again—the troublesome Jarl Agnar, who had yet to reply to her multiple letters; Helgi, angered that she'd spurned his advances.

Signe sends her regards— Silla had been unable to shake these words, spoken by the dark form standing over her in Fallgerd's home. Had it been merely a dream? Or had someone truly spoken those words?

You know it was no dream, snarled Myrkur, and anger spiked sharply inside her. Silla reached for her goblet of wine and took a hearty gulp.

Atli's voice, thankfully, cut through her swirling thoughts. "I hope this news has not soured you against the evening meal?"

"You must understand, Atli," said Silla with a raised brow, "attempts on my life are no new thing. If I let it turn my stomach, I'd scarcely ever eat."

At last, Atli's stern expression cracked, and an amused smile curved his lips.

He waved two fingers and servants bustled in, carrying fresh jugs of wine and platters of food. A trencher of roast rabbit was laid on the table, the delicate scent of juniper reaching Silla's nose. Platefuls of barley cakes and blistered carrots, pots of butter and clotted cream were all arranged. Eilif refilled Silla's wine, her eyes silently asking permission to taste it.

Silla nodded, every muscle in her body tight as a bowstring as Eilif sipped her wine, then proceeded to taste small morsels from each plate on the table. Only after she'd curtsied and left did Silla release her breath.

Better her than us, whispered Myrkur, and Silla bristled with irritation. Hadn't the god of chaos anything better to do? She forced her mind to winter-blooming lilies; to Vig's booming laugh. Myrkur hissed, slinking lower inside her, but Silla could still sense Him. It was growing increasingly difficult to force Him down entirely.

"Have you seen Galtung?" Atli asked casually.

Chest clenching tight, Silla reached for her wine and took a long sip. "No." She could not meet Atli's gaze. "I've received no letters."

"It was not the letters I referred to—" Atli dropped the rabbit flank he'd reached for, his gaze growing intent. "Do you not know?"

"Know what, Atli?" Icy fingers of fear spread through her.

"Rey has returned from Istré. Has he not—" Atli's voice trailed off, a piteous expression filling his face.

Silla's fear quickly morphed into pain as understanding settled.

Rey was back.

And Atli-gods-damned-Hakkonsson knew it before she did. Silla's mind spun with confusion and hurt, but Myrkur's anger soon eclipsed them both.

The man is a deceiver, whispered Myrkur. Gods, had she not just shut Him out? How had He already slithered back?

Leave me, Silla screamed in her mind, but the god of chaos only laughed.

Her insides twisted with betrayal and anger, and she no longer knew which belonged to her and which belonged to the god of chaos. Silla's anchor to this world of Galdra and politics—the one man she thought she could always depend on—couldn't even bother to let her know he'd returned. Kalasgarde now felt like years ago, like a dream she could hardly recall. And wasn't it a dream in so many ways—a refuge from reality, where only she and Rey had existed?

Whatever was written in her face, Atli seemed to read it. "I didn't mean to upset you, Eisa. I thought you knew—I assumed you'd seen him."

"It's nothing," she muttered.

Nothing is what you are to him, whispered Myrkur.

Nothing was what she needed. Silla took a deep drink of her wine, then wiped a droplet from her mouth with the back of her hand.

She froze, then groaned. "I suppose that wasn't up to Lady Tala's standards."

Atli chuckled. "Let me assure you, I'm not bothered by Lady Tala's standards in the least." He put his elbows on the table and bit into the rabbit flank. Juice dribbled down his chin, and he wiped it with the back of his own hand. "Does this make us even?" he asked, after swallowing.

Silla's chest squeezed at Atli's attempt to ease her discomfort.

If you want the queenship for yourself, you must have more ambition, Eisa, whispered Myrkur. *This man's name alone demands respect from the nobles. It would be a smart partnership to amass more power.*

Silla tried to shake off the dark god's words, but they sank into her all the same. Atli was kind and protective; a man of good house who knew this world inside and out. And there was no doubt that he was handsome. Chiseled cheekbones, full, smiling lips.

He wouldn't lie to us, purred Myrkur. *He wouldn't break promises.*

There was one problem.

Her heart beat for only one person.

Tears pricked Silla's eyes. She was spinning around, losing all sense of herself. Who was she? Not Silla. Not Eisa. Just a confused woman, desperate for a break from it all.

Gods, what she wouldn't do to lose herself in her skjöld leaves right now. In their absence, Silla would make do with wine. Reaching for her goblet, she was helpless against the seductive pull of numbness. Silla tipped it up, draining the last of it before waving for the cupbearer. Soon Silla had her chin propped on her hand, swirling her freshly refilled goblet. The wine was working its magic already—delicious warmth smoothing the jagged edges of Rey's broken promises. Smothering the dark god's incessant words. Smothering everything, truly.

She cocked her head, sending Atli a loose smile. "I hear your little brother has been chasing after my best friend."

Atli raised his goblet, a conspiratorial smile on his lips. "Tell me what you know, and I'll do the same."

Silla lifted her own goblet, then did just that.

—∞∞∞—

It took every last shred of Rey's will to remain seated before the enormous obsidian fireplace in Jarl Hakon's private quarters. Hakon paced before it, the ostentatious buckles on his boots clanking with each step, and his expression growing more thunderous with every lap of the room. But Rey couldn't bring himself to care what the jarl felt. His thoughts were entirely consumed by Silla.

He'd have gone to her already, but the moment he'd dismounted in Ashfall's yard, Jarl Hakon's men had swarmed him. Before Rey knew what was happening, Horse was swept away to the stables, and he was being led urgently to the jarl's chambers.

Running a weary hand along his untrimmed beard, Rey wondered how much more of his time Jarl Hakon planned to waste. After driving Horse as hard as he dared on the road from Istré, he was restless. For days, they'd paused only for food and water, with only the briefest spells of sleep. And though the grime of travel felt much like a second skin, it was not the prospect of a bath that had him on edge.

It was *her.*

He needed to see her. Wanted to hear every small thing that had happened in his absence. He wanted to hear her hum, to braid her hair, to fold her into the Silla-sized pocket between his shoulder and his side. Rey needed to wipe the sight of draugur and Turned beasts from his mind and remind himself what he fought for.

But Jarl Hakon only continued his pacing, as though Rey's time didn't matter in the slightest. Rey had already told Hakon everything that had happened—of the village of Turned draugur, gone to the mysterious place called Rökksgarde; freeing the Forest Maiden who'd sent him and Hekla on separate missions.

"I'm here to fetch Eisa," he'd told the jarl, "and to muster as many warriors as I can to do battle in the heartwood."

The jarl's expression had shifted from disbelief to outrage at this newest revelation. "You cannot take Eisa Volsik to the Western Woods! This will ruin all of our plans."

Rey's gaze was hard and flat. "Would you prefer to watch every person you love turn draugur, Jarl? I have looked into their eyes, and can assure you—death is far preferable."

Jarl Hakon began pacing, driving Rey's agitation to new levels. "The feast of the Shortest Day approaches, and many jarls have begun the journey—some have already arrived! We cannot present Eisa Volsik to them without the woman herself."

Rey released a long exhale. "Then I suppose it is a small comfort to you that we have agreed to meet under the infected tree when Marra is next at her fullest."

The jarl threw his hands in the air. "How long is that?"

Rey pursed his lips as he calculated. "Seventeen days. Twelve when you account for travel time—"

"Twelve days?" the jarl sputtered. "*Twelve days?*"

Rey wanted to shake the man. It was nearly two weeks! "I thought you'd be happy this plan allows time for Eisa to attend your feast."

Jarl Hakon grew still at that. "Will *you* attend the feast?"

That was not the question Rey had anticipated. Clenching his teeth, he watched the jarl carefully. Was he imagining it, or did Jarl Hakon seem displeased? As a flush built beneath the jarl's fine tunic and climbed up his neck, Rey understood—clearly his early return had disrupted one of Hakon's schemes.

But the jarl resumed his pacing. "Surely you understand diplomacy cannot be accomplished in a single evening! It takes careful negotiations, and these take time."

Rey sighed in irritation. He was not in the mood for political talk on the best of days, but today it drew his ire even more. "It will be a difficult task indeed," Rey said through his teeth. "But if anyone can accomplish it, I expect it would be you, my lordship."

"Be careful, Galtung," the jarl bit back. "Your tone nears mocking."

Rey ran a frustrated hand through his hair. He'd forgotten how much he despised these games of words. Rey always said the wrong thing. He was too blunt. Too terse. There was a reason he preferred to spend his days on the road. "I apologize, Jarl Hakon. I meant no disrespect."

Hakon nodded curtly, then turned to the sideboard and selected a jug. "Wine?"

"I thank you, but no." As the jarl poured himself a goblet, Rey pushed to his feet. "If you'll excuse me, Jarl, I must—"

"Wait!" The jarl's voice had a desperate edge to it, one that gave Rey pause. He eyed Hakon, leaning against the sideboard and tapping his rings against the jeweled goblet. "I am glad you've returned safely to us, Galtung. My son—" Hakon frowned into his wine, apparently uncertain how to finish his sentence.

Rey cocked a brow. "Eyvind is . . ." *a lovesick puppy?* ". . . doing a valiant deed. Without his Ashbringer skill, the group would be at the leech's mercy in the Western Woods."

Hakon sighed. "I do not like to think of him in those woods."

"He's finishing the task you set him, my lordship," said Rey, carefully. "I think it an admirable thing."

And as the jarl scowled absently into his cup of wine, Rey was finally able to slip from the room.

Rey felt like a man newly freed from the gallows as he set course for Silla's chambers. He wanted to hear her gripe about the lack of pockets in her gowns and tell him about the strange dream she'd had; wanted to count the freckles on her nose and trace the scar beside her eye.

Gods, he was turning soft.

But Rey's happiness was short-lived. Upon his arrival at Silla's chambers, her maid Hild informed him she took the evening meal with Atli Hakonsson. The name shattered his moods in an instant.

"Atli *Hakonsson*?" Rey repeated with such loathing that poor Hild took a step backward. "My thanks," he muttered, turning on his heel.

His insides twisted as he strode through the corridors, phantom whispers and laughter echoing in his skull. He'd warned Silla to be careful who she trusted, but Rey ought to have gone farther. Been more specific. Now he was viscerally aware of why Jarl Hakon had ushered him into a meeting immediately upon his return. How could he not have anticipated that the jarl would push Atli as a husband to Eisa Volsik?

Because he was a fool. Rey should know better than to feel any sort of kinship toward Jarl Hakon. Never mind that he'd been good friends with Rey's father—that he'd fostered Rey through countless seasons while he trained with Eyvind and other Ashbringers. To a man like Jarl Hakon, his bloodline would always come first.

Rey's ground-eating strides had him in Atli's wing with astonishing speed. Guards milled outside the jarl-to-be's door.

"Galtung?" asked Kálf, stepping forward. "You're back sooner than—"

"Is she in there?" Rey demanded, unable to keep his ire at bay.

Kálf scowled at his tone. "Aye, but—"

Rey shouldered through the guards.

"Runný and Ingvarr are acting as chaperones," Kálf called out.

But Rey was already pounding on the door. "Silla!" he bellowed, anger coursing through him. If it had been anyone else in that room with her but *him*—

Rey raised his fist to pound again, but the door flew open, and Atli's dark gaze met his. Rey had made it his business to avoid Eyvind's pompous older brother as much as possible, but as Atli propped an arm against the doorframe to bar his entry, there was no avoiding the arse. Atli Hakonsson's arrogant face still begged to be rearranged, his eyes gleaming in silent challenge.

Rey's hands curled into fists. "Where's Silla?"

"Do you mean *Eisa*?" Atli's mouth twisted up in mock confusion, before settling into a smarmy smile. It was a smile that sent Rey back in time. A smile that made him feel small and weak. Rey wanted to do what he hadn't all those years ago. Seize Atli by the collar. Slam his fist into his jaw and wipe that smile right off his face.

"Is that Rey Rey?"

His body stilled at that voice, his heartbeat steadying. Silla's curly head peeked out from under Atli's arm, and before either man knew what was happening, she'd ducked under it and thrown herself at Rey.

As her arms and legs wrapped around him, a delighted laugh spilled free from her. It was like standing in a sunbeam in the middle of winter. Rey closed his eyes. Let his anger melt away. Home. He was home.

His hands hooked under her thighs and he pulled her up until his lips could meet hers. And perhaps Rey's kiss was more claiming than it ought to have been.

Mine, he told Atli-gods-damned-Hakonsson, like a complete cave dweller. But Rey couldn't care. As his tongue dipped into her mouth, he pulled back.

"You taste like wine." A *lot* of it. Now that he realized it, she smelled like it, too.

He turned them toward the torchlight, illuminating her glazed eyes and bright-red lips. Rey's heart lurched and the urge to punch Atli filled him once more. Had he plied her with wine? Tried to take advantage?

But Silla's fingers slid into his beard, a lopsided grin on her face. "I must trim it."

A chuckle shook loose from him, and Rey rested his forehead on hers. "No sharp objects for you tonight. Perhaps after you sleep this off."

She lay her head on his shoulder, burrowing her face into the crook of his neck. "I missed you so much, Rey Rey."

One of Atli's guards snickered, and Rey sent him a thunderous look before carrying her away from the onlookers. Her queensguard thankfully had the good sense to trail them at a distance, allowing him and Silla a modicum of privacy.

"I missed you, too, Sunshine," he whispered into her hair, uncaring that she clung to him like a squirrel to a tree. "I have you," he whispered into her ear. "And I'm not letting go."

A choked sound came from her, and worry twisted in Rey's gut as a tear slid along her cheek.

"What has happened?"

She kept her face buried in his neck, unbothered, apparently, by the road's grime on his skin.

"I'm so tired," she murmured.

His hand slid up and down her back. "Then you must sleep."

A thousand questions pricked his mind—about all that had happened in his absence—but Rey knew now was not the time to voice them.

They reached her chambers, and Rey cast Runný a look that had her whirling on the other guards. "Sweep the room and then get out."

"But—" began the leader of Jarl Hakon's appointed queensguard—Ingvarr, if Rey recalled correctly.

"Any intruder will have to get through me," muttered Rey, sending the man a look that had him scurrying into the room.

At last, the guards waved them into the chambers and Rey carried a yawning Silla in. He laid her on the bed, smoothing her curls out behind her.

"I dreamed of you like this," he whispered, but realized it was not quite how he'd imagined it. In his dream she'd not had dark circles beneath her eyes, nor such tightness at the corners of her mouth. She was beautiful all the same, and as her eyelids fluttered shut, Rey found himself reaching for a coil of hair. He pulled it taut. Let it spring back.

"Gods, I missed you," he said.

"You've a strange way of showing it," Silla mumbled.

Rey's heart lurched. "What?"

But her breaths had grown rhythmic, her face so peaceful, and Rey knew she was now deep in the realm of sleep. He pulled off her slippers and stockings, then drew a blanket over her, examining her all the while for some clue to the meaning behind her words. There were none to be found.

"Sleep," he said wearily, climbing onto the bed beside her. Rey slid his hand into hers and squeezed it tight. "I have you, Silla."

CHAPTER 28

Silla dreamed of enormous trees; of tangled roots and pulsing heartbeats. She sensed each happening in the vastness of the woods; each gasping tree, each suffocating plant. The life force upon which she fed grew ever thinner, ever weaker, and so she unfurled more tendrils beneath the soil—sent them sprawling to join with plants beyond the borders of the woods.

With a satisfied sigh, she sipped from these new plants and used their energy to call to her children. Grimwolves and wolfspiders and bears gathered, each animal a vessel for her progeny. The humans, though, she did not summon. No. The humans were needed elsewhere. Hundreds—thousands—of beasts soon amassed around her, snarling and snuffling, hungering for the blood of her enemies.

Soon, she crooned in a feminine voice, pulling and twisting the threads of their will. *Soon you will battle. Soon you will spill blood. And then, my children, you will feast.*

Silla was filled with the sudden sense of being caught where she was not meant to be.

You! gasped the being, tearing her out like an errant weed. Silla's vision wobbled for a moment, but as it steadied, she became aware of her surroundings. Before her, the vast, misshapen tree she was certain she'd just inhabited. And behind her—Silla gasped at the tree's children. An army of red-eyed creatures, too many to count.

Get out! boomed Myrkur's voice, deeper than the tree's, and from everywhere at once.

Silla woke with the smell of mold in her nose and cold sweat slicked on her brow. Beside her, Rey slept on his stomach, a tattooed arm stretched toward her.

Stop meddling, came Myrkur's whisper, drawing her mind back to that dream. Glowing red eyes and the monstrosity of a tree . . . and the god of chaos banishing her . . . The god's anger was still palpable, thrumming through her veins, and Silla tried to understand. Had that truly been just a dream? Or had Myrkur inadvertently given her a glimpse of His plans?

You saw nothing I did not allow you to see, snapped Myrkur, His wingbeats fanning her anger higher.

Your irritation tells me otherwise, Silla replied in her mind. She rolled onto her back, then winced as her temples throbbed with the beginnings of a hangover. Despite this, she felt a surge of boldness. *Why haven't you taken my life yet, god?*

The god did not answer, but darkness unspooled low in her stomach.

A life for a life, she taunted. *Just take it.*

I told you, Eisa, a life yielded is not what I want.

His cravings slid through her blood, filling her with the need for power—the need to make all others bend the knee. Visions blurred in her mind. A river of corpses. A throne of bones. Shadows wrapped around her like a cloak.

You hunger for power, she realized.

You want it, too, Eisa, purred the dark god. *I sense it in your thoughts. Feel it in your blood. Imagine what we could achieve together.* More visions arrived. She would be more than a queen—she would be a *goddess.* No one here would dare lie to her. Should they break their promises, she would break their spines.

And yet she sensed something buried beneath—the faintest traces of fear.

You're trying to distract me, she accused. *What don't you want me to see?*

The dark god writhed in anger, and Silla waded through the murk of her thoughts. *You grew more vocal after I pulled galdur from the rock-slide.*

Myrkur screeched, rattling her bones. But His fear had sharpened above all other emotions, and Silla decided to test her theory.

You are curious about my bloodline gift, she thought, *because it has the power to undo you.*

No, snarled Myrkur, but she could taste the lie. With a growl of rage, the dark god burrowed down beyond her reach, leaving Silla blissfully alone with her thoughts.

The god had all but confirmed her theory, and Silla's pulse skittered with excitement. The secret to defeating Myrkur flowed in her blood.

She turned to Rey, excited to tell him, but paused. Black lashes fanned against his brown cheekbones, and Silla found it unfair that the man could be so handsome, even in sleep. A rueful smile curved her lips as she realized she'd stolen the bulk of the blankets, and that Rey clung to a mere corner. With a sigh, she folded the blanket over him, tucking it carefully around his sides.

Her chest ached at the sight of this man, but the ache was chased by a pang of uncertainty. He hadn't written to her, hadn't come to find her for *hours* after his return. Last night, her mind had been so wine-addled she'd thrown herself at him without a second thought. But in the light of day, realization was settling. It seemed that their feelings for each other weren't matched.

Silla needed to clear her mind. Needed to *think.* With a sigh, she climbed from the bed. And after pulling on the gown Hild had left out for Eisa, Silla strode from the room.

Rey woke in slow increments. His mind was sluggish, his body aching, and he knew he'd pushed too hard on that last day of travel. But not reaching Kopa—not seeing Silla—had simply not been an option. And thank the gods he'd arrived when he had. Because Silla had been drunk and in Atli Hakonsson's private quarters.

The insecurity he'd kept buried for years had reared its ugly head. But with morning had come clarity. It was over. He'd returned, and had disrupted Jarl Hakon's schemes to push Silla and Atli together. Today was a new day, and he had much to accomplish. It was time to move forward.

He rolled toward Silla, only to find the other side of the bed empty and cold. The lurch in his stomach was softened by the fact that the blankets she'd stolen were now tucked all around him. But she hadn't woken him—hadn't nestled into the Silla-sized pocket between his arm and his ribs and drooled all over him.

You have a strange way of showing it.

Her words from last night rang loudly in his ears. At the time, he'd brushed them off as drunken nonsense, but now, paired with her absence, Rey knew something wasn't right. He threw off the blankets and dressed quickly. Kálf and some of Hakon's appointed queensguard lounged in the hallway but straightened as Rey exited.

"Well met, *Rey Rey,*" beamed Kálf.

Rey growled in irritation. "Where is she?"

Kálf nodded down the corridor. "At the chicken house." As Rey stalked off, he called out, "Aren't you going to stay and chat, *Rey Rey*? I want to hear all about Istré—"

Rey stormed through Ashfall's corridors and out into the yard, and as the barn that housed the jarl's chickens came into view, that gods damned hearthfire in his chest ignited. Based on the horde of guards lingering by the doors, Silla was still inside.

"Runný." He nodded at his old friend. "Any news from Kalasgarde?"

"Well met, Galtung," said Runný. "Had a note from Vig a few days' past. The chasm remains sealed. Harpa yelled at him for disrupting her Weaving. The ice spirits have taken to following Snorri about. Oh, and there's been a fresh hatching of chicks."

Rey nodded, but his mind was elsewhere—was inside that barn. "Is she in there?"

"Aye."

Rey entered the barn, wandering past rows of chicken roosts until he found Silla at the far end. With a fur-trimmed cloak secured over an elegant purple gown, she looked out of place in the barn's squalor. Yellow chicks clustered around the bench she sat on, one nestled into her palm. As Rey neared, the chicks peeped in alarm, and Silla's eyes darted up.

She smiled, but Rey knew her well enough to know it wasn't her true smile. Something was definitely wrong. What had happened? Who had dimmed the light in her eyes? The chicks on the barn floor scattered as he made his way to the bench and settled beside her.

"How do you feel?" he asked, reaching over to stroke the chick in her palm.

"I shall never drink the red-colored wine again," Silla said ruefully.

Rey huffed a laugh. "I suppose the chicks help improve your moods?"

"Do they yours?"

Rey eyed the little yellow fluff balls, who'd once more converged around Silla's skirts. "Loath though I am to admit it, they do."

"I come here each morning," she said, smiling at the chick cupped in her palms. "Well. First, I visit Dawn—she's perhaps a little *too* well fed in Kopa—but after that, I come here. The chicks help me think—help me fill my bank of hearthfire thoughts."

Rey peered at her from the corner of his eye. Sitting in the barn, surrounded by baby chickens, for a moment, it felt like they'd gone back to a time when things were just a little easier. When it had been the two of them in a shield-home in Kalasgarde, with Runný's borrowed chicks tottering about.

He slid his hand into his pocket. "I meant to give this to you upon my return, but last night did not go according to plan."

Perplexed, Silla set the chick down on the barn floor and took the item from him. She blinked, then choked out a sob. "My rock! My heart-shaped rock—where did you get this?"

Rey stared at the strange, gray stone. He supposed if one squinted, it might look like a heart. "The Bloodaxe Crew's wagon burned to the ground in Istré, your satchel with it. But when I dug through the rubble, I found the stone and thought, surely there's a *reason* you hauled this rock across the arse end of the kingdom."

Silla's thumb smoothed over the rock's surface, her eyes glassy. "My father," she said softly, "my *foster* father, Matthias, gave this to me the day before he died."

She flinched, then shook her head. "The god, He's . . . grown louder. More active. It's hard—" Silla pressed fingers to her temples, but did not continue.

Rey watched her with preternatural stillness. "What is it?"

"It's only"—her voice seemed far away—"sometimes, I do not know truth from lie. What is my own emotion and what is His. Sometimes I don't know who I am anymore. Like I'm losing myself in this place." Silla turned to him, finally meeting his eyes and letting Rey see it all. The weight of bearing her mother's bargain all alone, while striving to be Eisa. And in that moment, Rey would have given anything to take the burden from her.

"I missed you," she whispered.

"I missed you, too," he replied, sliding his thumb along the smooth skin of her jaw.

But she drew back and said softly, "Then why didn't you write?"

The hurt on her face was like an axe in his sternum, and Rey would do anything to banish it. But her words made no sense to him. "What do you mean?" Silla looked away, but he gently pulled her chin until her eyes met his once more. "I wrote to you, Silla . . . *every day*. Did you not get the letters?"

She blinked furiously, clearly befuddled.

"No."

"No?" Anger blazed to life inside his chest, and he gritted his teeth. "I swore to you I'd write, Silla, and I did, every gods damned day we were apart."

"And yesterday?" There was a note of disbelief in her voice, but far greater than that was her anger. Rey was relieved to hear it. "Why did you not come to me upon your return?"

"Jarl Hakon hauled me to his chambers and forced me into a pointless, hours-long meeting." Rey's gaze hardened.

"You wrote to me." This time it was only confusion in Silla's voice. "I thought—"

"Tell me." Rey's mind was reeling, trying to understand. How had this happened—and how could she think he didn't write?

"I thought you'd changed your mind." Her voice was small, but the words slammed into him with the force of a maelstrom. "I thought with space, you'd realized . . ."

He picked up where her voice had trailed off. "You want to know what I realized?" Rey slid an arm around her back, scooping her onto his lap. "I realized how much had changed in Kalasgarde. That leading the Bloodaxe Crew no longer felt right."

Silla blinked at him, and this time, when he smoothed a thumb along her jaw, she did not pull away.

"I realized what a mistake I'd made in abandoning you in Kopa, with so much on your shoulders. *Frightened together,* Silla, I promised you that. And breaking that promise haunted me each day we were apart."

"Oh," she said, clearly dumbfounded. And then she softened against him, her warmth seeping into all the cold crevices inside his chest.

"Oh," he repeated stonily. His hand slipped beneath her cloak and his knuckles brushed up her spine. "I don't understand why my letters didn't reach you."

Rey's mind raced for an answer, and it didn't take long to find one. Who had diverted him from seeing Silla? Who was displeased by Rey's early return? This *had* to be Jarl Hakon and Atli's doing. Rey's anger burned to life. They thought they could walk all over him, simply because of their rank—thought they could take *her*. But they were mistaken if they thought Rey would ever allow such a thing to happen. This wasn't over, not at all. But it could wait.

His anger at the Hakon men burned strong, yet the feel of his woman after so many days apart was stronger.

"I missed you," he murmured into her hair, before drawing a deep pull of her scent.

Silla was silent, and it pained Rey that for all this time she'd thought he'd broken his promise to write. He opened his mouth to beg for forgiveness, but she beat him to it.

"How *much* did you miss me?"

Rey drew back at the mischievous note in her voice. Then his blood heated with desire.

"I'll show you," he muttered, glancing around. Rey hefted Silla into his arms, chicks tottering away as she squealed in surprise and he strode through the chicken house. Spotting a small door exiting the main part of the barn, Rey kicked it open to reveal a small room. Against one wall was a desk of sorts, scattered with papers, while ledgers and tomes were stacked on a shelf opposite. Rey sent the records scattering from the desk with a sweep of his hand, and after laying Silla down on the surface, he yanked the door roughly shut behind them.

"Rey!" protested Silla.

But as he turned toward her, he let his mask of control slip for a moment, showing her the full breadth of his hunger. "Yes?"

She propped herself up on her elbows, pupils spreading wide with need. But the mischievous quirk of her lips told Rey she had something up her sleeve. "Clean that up," said Silla, in a voice of soft command.

It was a test, and he knew it, but Rey needed to atone—needed to prove his devotion to her. Besides, he was so gone for this woman, he'd probably light himself on fire if she asked it.

Slowly Rey dropped to his knees before her, then gathered the strewn papers without taking his eyes from hers. "What else?"

Silla licked her lips, and Rey's whole body throbbed. "Take off my boots."

It was pure torture to gently loosen the ties on her deerskin boots when every muscle in him yearned to rip them off. He cupped her calf as he slipped the second boot free, fingers reaching for her stockings.

Silla tutted. "I recall no mention of my stockings."

Already, Rey was hard as granite, but the lilt of her voice had him growing somehow harder. He forced his fingers to still, gazing up at her over layers of silken skirts.

"You know I'd not kneel for anyone but you," he said, in a hoarse voice.

Her lips tilted up as a stockinged foot landed on his shoulder and pushed him gently backward. "Undress for me," commanded Silla, shimmying up to a sitting position on the edge of the desk so she could watch. Her dark eyes were glazed as her teeth sank into her lower lip.

Rey's control was held by the very finest thread, but he pushed to his full height and reached for his belt. The buckle clanked loudly inside the small space. Silla's pulse fluttered madly at the base of her throat, her gaze roaming all over his body. He shucked his lébrynja jacket as slowly as he could, giving the maddening woman a taste of her own medicine.

"Hurry up," she muttered, leaping off the desk and striding to him. Her fingers slid beneath his breeches, and Rey couldn't help the tremor that ran through him. But she only reached for the hem of his tunic to yank it upward. She was too short to get it over his arms, and Rey let her struggle for a moment before finishing the task.

Silla's fingers traced the tattooed dragon wing along his collarbone before she jerked back. And as she returned to her perch on the edge of the desk, Rey knew he'd scored a point in whatever game this was.

He toed off his boots and stockings, then slid down his breeches. And as they hit the floor, he could tell Silla was nearing her own breaking point. The proof of his desire jutted evidently from his body, and he stood before her, letting her look her fill.

"What else do you command of me?" he asked.

"Stockings—" she choked out, lifting one foot.

Once more, Rey dropped to his knees before her, taking her calf reverently into his palm. A shudder ran through her as his fingers teased the edge of the stocking. But the moment his fingers touched her soft skin, Rey's careful control snapped clean through.

"Fuck it," he muttered, wrenching her legs apart and rucking up her skirts.

"Rey!" she exclaimed, falling backward.

He buried his nose at the apex of her thighs, nuzzling her inner leg until she cried out. Rey drew back and looked up from where he knelt between her legs. "Let's get this clear, Sunshine. You might one day rule this kingdom, but I will *always* be in charge in the bedroom."

"We're in a barn—"

He slid his tongue through her center, and Silla's words broke off in a breathy moan.

"Y-yes," she pleaded.

"Who is in charge?" he demanded.

"You!"

Satisfaction pooled in his gut. "Later," gritted Rey, "we'll have a proper conversation, Silla, and you'll tell me why you doubted my feelings for you."

A whimper escaped her as he jerked her legs roughly up, and bundled them over his shoulders. "But for now," he rasped, nipping her sensitive skin, "let me prove to you just how much I want you."

And he showed her with the expert strokes of his tongue; with the claiming way his mouth worked her. Rey showed her the flaming heat of his desire until she too was burning with want. His grip on her thighs was bruising, his pace relentless, but he could not stop until he'd wiped each and every shred of doubt from Silla's mind.

Her whimpers and pleading whispers were the sweetest music to his ears, and her still-stockinged feet slipped down his back, trying and failing to find something to grip onto. But the more she pleaded, the more Rey slowed his pace, prolonging this moment for as long as he could.

"Rey."

"Not yet, Silla," he tutted, kissing her inner thigh, as Silla's feet, hooked around his back, tried to pull him to where she wanted him. "I'm still making my point." He was painfully hard, yet he thrived on control and enjoyed this method of torture.

Working first one finger, then two in tandem, Rey brought her to the brink, then pulled back, smiling as her wail of frustration filled the small room. He pushed to his feet and reached for the fastenings of her gown.

"Too many gods damned layers, Silla. I need to see you *now*. It's been too long."

It took all his restraint not to rip the gown from her, and he grunted in satisfaction as it finally slid free. She was gorgeous and his eyes roamed greedily over her.

"Rey," she pleaded, reaching for him. He considered prolonging this game of control, but even Rey had his limits.

The air thrummed between them as Rey hauled Silla to the edge of the desk and positioned himself at her entrance. With a single swift motion, he sheathed himself deep inside. A curse fell from his lips at the silken heat of her. And based on the pleasure-dazed look in her eyes, she was right there with him. Rey drew all the way out.

"Let me make this clear to you, Silla." He thrust back in.

"I wanted to tell you about every strange gods damned cloud I saw." Thrust.

"I spent my days dreaming up names for your future chickens." Thrust.

"Did I miss you? No. I obsessed about you, every minute we were apart." Thrust.

"My every thought circled back to you. I missed the feel of you. The smell of you. I even missed your incessant humming."

"I don't hum—"

But Silla cried out as he climbed onto the desk and began to move in earnest. Rey covered her mouth with his own to stifle her cries, but the desk thumped against the wall with each thrust, and he soon gave up. Let the guards hear them. Let the whole city hear them.

It wasn't long before her inner muscles began to pulse, and Rey thanked the gods because he couldn't last much longer. The desk rocked back and forth with their motion, and he wondered if it would hold. But he couldn't stop, wouldn't stop, not even if the world crashed down around them. The feel of her was so exquisite, for a moment the edges of his vision darkened.

Silla's sharp cry pushed him over the edge, and a groan wrenched free from the deepest part of him. With one last thrust, he buried himself deep inside of her and grunted. His vision burst with starlight as he shuddered in release. Sounds all around him grew muffled and for a moment, he was weightless—he was falling.

But a shriek from Silla had his instincts rushing back. They *were* falling. Rey took the brunt of their weight on his arms, still wrapped around Silla, as they landed in a pile of splintered wood. They lay there for a silent moment, as understanding settled into place. The gods damned desk had collapsed beneath their weight.

Silla laughed first, but it wasn't long before Rey joined in—deep laughs coming straight from his belly.

And as he looked down at her, Rey was flooded with warmth. Because this time, her smile was true.

CHAPTER 29

Kovograd, capital of Zagadka

Standing atop Kovograd's outer defensive wall, Kassandr Rurik's grip tightened on the hilt of his sword as he watched the scene unfolding below. The frigid breeze rustled his hair, carrying the stench of blood and shit. Above, ravens circled in the skies, ready to feast.

The battle was currently held to the river, though that would shortly change. Half of Zagadka's fleet was on the water, warriors spilling onto the decks of the Urkan fleet in wolf and mountain cat forms. Trebuchets on shore hurled rocks and what few fire flasks they'd managed to assemble, while Morzh and his legion of walrus shifters gouged holes in hulls. But the Urkan fleet was well built, and had many defenses of its own—protective shields and smaller ballistas, not to mention the bloodthirsty berserkers.

The Zagadkians simply did not have enough ships or warriors to keep the battle on the river. And it wasn't minutes after Kassandr had this thought that the first of the Urkan ships anchored at Kovograd's outer docks.

Unused to the business of sieges, Kassandr's beast loosed a long, low growl. His animal nature urged Kassandr to leap from the walls and charge into battle. Throats would be torn, Urkan blood spilled. But with more and more warriors arriving by the minute, victory would be short-lived.

Patience, he urged his beast. *We must be clever.*

After they'd exhausted their supply of decapitated heads, the Urkans had split their fleet in two. On the water, Urkan ships rammed against the inner river gates, demanding entry into Kovograd city. Zagadkian warriors flung stones from catapults mounted on either side of the gates and fired flaming arrows down from above. But Kassandr's focus was on the vessels now docking at the outer moors. Warriors seeped from the prowed ships and poured along the docks.

Kassandr had pulled the Zagadkian warriors stationed at the outer moors and had ordered the area evacuated hours ago. The tower bell tolled loudly, citizens streaming from the city streets to the safety of Kovograd fortress. There, they were protected by both the city and the fortress walls. Fitted with outward-facing pikes, arrow slits, and murder holes, each was built upon earthen ramparts, with walkways and turrets protected by roofs. The Urkans would not have an easy time summiting either set of walls. But there was the ever-present fear lingering in the back of Kass's mind. The glaring weakness his Saga had seen at once.

Kovograd's walls were made entirely of wood.

On land, the Urkan warriors pulled ladders from their ships and rushed at the city's land gates. But as Kassandr watched their land-based foes, they quickly split off into two groups. The first, to his consternation, jogged *away* from Kovograd's land gate. He scowled, wondering what they schemed at.

The second group of Urkans paused just out of his archers' range. The plains leading up to Kovograd city's land gates were kept barren for scenarios exactly like this. While merchant tables and tents had begun to crop up around the gates in more recent years, Kassandr had ordered them cleared out the moment the Urkan ships had been sighted. Now there was nothing to shield the Urkans—not a tree nor a boulder to conceal them.

Across the field, a bear-skinned warrior brushed his knuckles to his nose and took what appeared to be an enormous breath. Kassandr's eyes narrowed as the warrior gave his head a rough shake, then howled at the sky. It seemed he'd taken his berskium powder, giving him the battle frenzy the Urkans were so famous for.

His own beast howled, begging to be let out, but Kassandr urged its patience. *The time for carnage is near,* he told it.

Having taken their berskium, the entire regiment now bashed their axes against shields, snarling and baying at the sky.

Kassandr gazed along the defensive wall. Behind the line of archers stood his Druzhina—his personal retinue—clad in full armor. He found Rov and Grigorii—even Oleg had come. Emotion thickened in Kass's chest as they stood on the precipice of the battle of their lives.

"If the Urkans think such displays will cow us, then they do not know Zagadkians at all!" he bellowed, pounding his chest. "The eyes might be afraid, but the hands are doing! We fight for our motherland! We fight for our freedom! And we fight so our children and grandchildren will not!"

The Zagadkian warriors along the wall voiced their agreement—a barrage of animalistic growls and snarls, yips and bellows. It was the sound of his people, and Kassandr had never been so proud to be one of them. For a single, weightless moment, he was certain every step in his life had been leading him here.

And then the moment was broken. Their enemies surged across the field, laddermen flanked by shieldmen and fierce axe-wielding warriors.

Heart pounding, Kassandr raised a fist. Feathers rustled as arrows were fitted.

"Fire!" he roared the moment the Urkans came within range.

Archers unleashed a flurry of arrows. Screams split the air, men stumbling and crashing to the ground. They were quickly trampled by their brethren, with more storming from the docks to join the charge.

"Again!" Kassandr barked.

More arrows flew, more men fell. But ladders were now thudding against the palisades, berserkers scrambling up.

"Forks!" shouted Kass.

Rov led a wave of warriors forward, hooking pronged instruments under the ladders. With a hearty shove, the ladders tipped backward, warriors screaming as they lost their grips and fell. Those who survived the fall were crushed by others clambering for their turn at the ladder.

The air filled with screams and snarls and the thunder of battle. Kassandr bellowed orders to target new laddermen, to drop rocks on the shield walls assembling around the base of the ladders.

His beast clawed against his rib cage, howling in indignation. Where was the honor in this type of battle? He much preferred to look his enemy in the eye as he delivered their death. But this was no tournament, and it was not merely Kassandr's own life at stake. Thousands of innocent people sheltered behind these walls.

"Oil!" shouted Kass, making room for a pair of apprentices shuffling forward with a cauldron between them. With a grunt, they heaved the cauldron onto the wall and tipped it on its side. Steaming oil gushed down, hissing and spitting. The shield wall below fractured, men rolling and howling, tearing at their skin, and though it was far from delightful, Kassandr allowed himself a small smile.

Something at the far end of the field caught his eye. A sail had been trussed up between trees, feet scurrying about behind it. But as more ships docked and hundreds more berserkers streamed onto the battlefield, Kassandr could not afford to give the strange sail another thought.

A sharp, splintering sound scraped down Kassandr's spine, and he whirled toward the river. He quickly spotted the source of the sound—a large Urkan warship had just crashed into the inner gates.

Kassandr assessed the chaos on the water. Half a dozen Urkan ships had capsized, but he saw twice as many walrus corpses bobbing on the surface. Ivar's archers had arrows nocked, firing them into the river. He cursed under his breath, hoping Morzh and the bulk of his walrus shifters had managed to escape; that they could rest and regroup.

Another large vessel raced toward the river gates at alarming speed, the Urkan oarsmen paddling furiously. It struck with a sickening crack, the wood of the gates groaning long after. Zagadkian warriors flung stones from atop the gates, and they crashed through the hides shielding the oarsmen. Screams tore from the ship, and it wobbled side-to-side but did not sink. Kassandr's gaze flew to a cluster of warships waiting their turn to ram into the gate. How long would it hold?

"Volk!" he shouted. "What is the delay with the boat?"

Volk appeared by his side, perspiration dotting his brow. "We had troubles navigating the back channel and had to portage, but it is done. There." The wolf shifter pointed to a small ship, barely visible through thick grass.

Kass finally drew breath. "This must work," he muttered.

The ship edged closer to the Urkan fleet. But Ivar's watchmen soon caught sight of it, arrows raining down on the Zagadkian oarsmen, who steadfastly refused to abandon their task. Kass murmured a silent prayer to the four gods on behalf of these brave men.

Closer the Zagadkian ship edged, progress slowing as Ivar's archers picked the oarsmen off.

But it was close enough. "Fire!" bellowed Kassandr.

From the tall grasses, archers stood, a torch-wielding warrior quickly lighting their arrows. Kass gripped the wall in anticipation as the fire arrows streaked through the sky. The oarsmen leaped free of the fire ship, Urkans bellowing as they realized what was happening.

But it was too late.

Arrows landed, one after another, fire catching quickly in the dry brush piled atop the ship. Soon the entire boat was ablaze, a river-bound inferno drifting ever closer to the Urkan fleet. Kass was now grinning, bracing himself for the culmination of this operation—when the flames reached the contents of the cauldrons.

An explosion rocked the air, shaking the walls and knocking warriors on their arses. But Kassandr gripped the wall, laughing like a fool at the scene upon the water. A perimeter of burnt and overturned Urkan ships encircled where the fireship had been moments ago. Warriors floundered in the water under the weight of their chain mail, while berserkers rushed to douse the flames of a dozen burning ships. But as Kassandr's gaze found the largest warship—the one housing King Ivar and Prince Bjorn—he frowned.

It was unmarred.

Commands were shouted, too far off for Kassandr to hear. A prickle of unease slid down his neck as he watched the warriors abandon their efforts to extinguish the fires. Instead, they took up the oars. Started rowing the flaming ships toward the inner river gate.

A cold pit of dread opened in Kassandr's stomach.

"They will burn the gate!" he shouted. "Stop that ship!"

Volk loosed a piercing whistle, and the reserve fleet waiting in the back channel surged into the river. But as Kassandr's gaze jumped from the Zagadkian fleet to the flaming ships drifting toward Kovograd's timber gates, he knew they'd be too late.

"Curse the one who built this city entirely of wood!" he bellowed. His beast raged, howled, battered against him. All the while, Kassandr's mind raced for another plan.

But it was time. Kassandr already felt the shifting of his flesh, the lengthening of his limbs and backbone. Spines burst from his flesh, claws tearing through his knuckles. Kassandr rolled his neck, then stood on his hind legs. And tilting his beastly head back, he loosed an earsplitting howl.

Kassandr took in the glorious moment when the berserkers paused their frenzied attempts to climb their ladders. Gazed up at him with dawning horror. For in that moment, they beheld his animal nature, and discovered the secret Zagadka had long hidden away.

Behind him, Kassandr's brothers and sisters in arms shifted into their animal forms. The confusion and disbelief on the faces of his enemies made Kassandr smile wide.

Then he leaped from the stockade walls.

And at last, his beast tasted blood.

The scarf tied over Saga's nose did little to quell the foul smell of the dim, flameless room. A dozen or so women sat silently in chairs, spooning horrid ingredients into ceramic flasks before carefully passing them to their neighbor. Saga, leader of this grim operation, had placed herself at the end of the line. Her mind was numb with all that had happened but she was glad to have something to busy her hands.

Elisava passed her a flask filled with putrid-smelling rock salts, ashes, tree resin, and lard, and Saga slid the stopper into place with all the control she could muster.

"The warfire," the mountain cat shifter Grigorii had informed her, "will catch under sunlight. You must keep it in darkness, sealed within the flask." According to Grigorii, the mixture within the flasks would catch on almost anything—water included. It certainly sounded effective against the enemy, though Saga wished it weren't such a danger to handle.

The women Elisava had brought to her were all members of Zagadkian nobility, yet the fact that none were afraid to get their hands dirty immediately endeared them to Saga. Nonetheless, there had been more than one cutting look sent her way. There was no question they blamed her for the danger now surrounding their city. But Elisava had reminded the women that in this room, they had the power to help Zagadka's warriors. And with that common goal, a tenuous peace had settled.

"It's the last of the lard," said Elisava glumly. She pushed to her feet and arched her back. "The butcher shall soon arrive with more, but it is a good time to wash and take a meal." She looked about. "We must return to our task as quickly as possible."

The women nodded, quickly filing out of the room. Saga remained in her chair, frowning at the basket of fire flasks. She'd counted just over fifty, and yet it didn't seem nearly enough. She'd seen the Urkan war vessels anchored on the Kovosk. All afternoon, shouts had carried from the stockade walls, the entire fortress shaking at intervals. How could fifty fire flasks truly make a difference?

A hand fell upon her shoulder and squeezed gently. "You must rest and eat some food," said Elisava in slow Zagadkian.

An impulsive thought pushed forth in Saga's mind. "Should we send word," she asked, eyeing Elisava, "to the clans beyond the river?"

A long weary sigh. "It is a waste of time. They will never come for us."

Saga thought of the book back in her chambers. Of the legion of winged horses flying over a battlefield of fierce shifters. "But once they did."

"We must keep our minds on what we can do here and now," said Elisava. Her voice was hard, so unlike the carefree woman who'd flitted into Saga's chambers all those weeks ago.

Saga nodded numbly. "I shall deliver the fire flasks, then tend to my needs."

As slowly as she could, Saga lifted the basket and departed the room. The shouts from above sent her heart racing, but Saga kept her panic at bay by counting each step she climbed.

A thunderous boom shook the fortress walls, startling Saga so badly she nearly missed a stair. It was utter mayhem above. Footfalls pounded on timber, warriors shouting in rapid Zagadkian. Saga understood enough to know the inner river gate was on fire. Fear twisted her stomach in knots, and she held on to the wall for support as she labored for breath. The telltale signs of her panic were creeping up, but Saga couldn't let it grab hold of her now.

Lives counted on it.

She focused on one step at a time, until she reached the doorway to the defensive walls. With a deep breath, Saga pushed through it.

Her feet faltered, heart racing ever faster, but she recognized the high prince's right hand man Kresimir and made her way toward him. After Saga explained the contents of the basket, Kresimir raced off to deliver them to the city gates. With a reassuring glance over her shoulder to confirm that the keep's door was just a few steps away, Saga strode to the nearest turret. She gazed over the city toward the defensive walls. Was Kassandr atop those walls, overseeing their defenses? Or had he jumped into the battle teeming on the plains? Worry twisted in her gut.

Saga's gaze drifted to the inner river gate, and as she took in the blazing inferno, her breaths shallowed. Her fingers tapped against the turret's wooden walls as she surveyed the Urkan fleet, now retreated to a safe distance. Once the fleet breached those gates, they'd have access to the whole city of Kovograd.

Saga stared at the largest warship, cold slivers lodging in her spine. Ivar Ironheart was on that ship, orchestrating the deaths of these innocent Zagadkians. He would kill them all, then drag Saga back to Íseldur—back to Signe.

Punished, echoed Magnus's voice, ravens screaming overhead. Saga's fingers tapped feverishly as she tried to calm her racing heart. But a new, terrifying voice met her ears.

"You should not be here," said Oleg in slow, measured Zagadkian.

Saga whirled to find Kassandr's half brother, thick arms folded over his chest. Tension corded Oleg's neck, his eyes flickering a lupine yellow as he turned to look at her. Before she could react, his retinue strode into the turret, blocking her exit. Her arms were seized and Saga was dragged toward Oleg.

Lights danced in her vision as she struggled for breath. Trapped. No exits.

"Tell me why I should not throw you from these walls," came Oleg's far-off voice.

Saga's fingers found her palms, and she focused on the feel of them tapping gently. Once. Twice. Three times. Saga drew in a breath. Forced words from her lips. "I am . . . no enemy," she managed in stunted Zagadkian.

Oleg seized her collar and shoved her against the timber walls. In the courtyard below, Zagadkian soldiers rushed about, the chaos too great for them to notice her plight.

"You have damned us all!" shouted Oleg, lifting her higher and shoving her backward along the gap between turret wall and roof. The blunt wooden planks scraped along her back as Oleg shoved her farther. Above her were open skies, below her, the courtyard.

Saga couldn't think. Couldn't breathe. But rather than the paralysis her panic often brought, Saga was now filled with savage energy. She'd survived the sacking of Askaborg by the Urkans. Had survived Magnus branding her in those stables. Saga had survived Oleg's cowardly attempt to have her killed once already. She would not go like this—not at this man's hands. She screamed and kicked, fought like a wild creature.

"Oleg!" roared a new voice—a voice Saga had not anticipated. "You will put our guest down." She was lowered onto her feet, knees buckling and sending her to the turret floor. She closed her eyes. Drew in deep breath after deep breath. Tapped her fingers in a frantic rhythm. Saga wasn't certain how long her panic gripped her, only that when she finally opened her eyes, the world swayed—and she found the high prince crouched before her.

When last she'd seen him, he'd been clad in fussy, ceremonial robes. Now he wore the same pleated, leatherlike surcoat as the rest of his Zagadkian warriors.

"Tell me," said the high prince slowly. His green eyes were filled with fear and remorse. "Tell me everything you know about our enemy. I'm ready to listen."

CHAPTER 30

Kopa, Íseldur

Silla had faced many new changes since her arrival at Kopa, but she wasn't certain she'd ever adjust to the relentless fussing over her appearance.

Oh, stop it, she wanted to say as Hild repositioned a particular pin for at least the third time. But though Silla doubted an errant braid would cost her the northern jarls' swords, she recognized that the girl was only doing her job. And there was something to be said for those who gave it their very best effort.

So Silla smothered a yawn and let her thoughts drift to the night ahead. Her *debut,* Jarl Hakon had called it. Eisa Volsik would be officially presented to the most powerful families of the north. She'd been preparing for this night for weeks, a fact that had her nerves on end.

It is an opportunity for us to amass power, purred Myrkur.

Why do you even want that? she demanded, against her better judgment.

I do so love to play, whispered the god, sending a shiver through Silla. She focused on the moons stitched into the cuffs of her gown, trying to shut Him out.

These jarls will come to our cause, or we will bend them to it.

With an irritated huff, Silla closed her eyes. She thought of dimples; a broken desk; the fact that Rey was back in Kopa. Myrkur hissed, His grip on her relenting. But she knew He was only biding His time.

The dismayed cries of her queensguard signaled Rey's arrival. As the door swung open, Ingvarr's plaintive voice reached Silla's ears.

"You must leave your weapons at the door—"

But it slammed shut, muffling whatever else he planned to say. Silla smiled wide as Rey's boots thudded on the floor. It was clear his mood was as bright as a thunderstorm, and she must be mad, because she found it positively endearing.

"You don't need twenty-seven guards beyond your door, Silla, not now that I'm back."

Her smile spread wider. "I'm glad to see you, too."

"I—" sputtered Hild, eyes going wide as Rey lumbered closer. "I think that will do." And then she scurried off.

As Rey stepped into view, Silla understood why the girl had been so eager to leave. Clad in a dark-blue tunic that revealed the halda tattoos coiling up his throat, Rey had folded his thick arms over his chest, and his *axe eyes* were sharper than Silla had seen in a while.

His expression was so stern, she could not help but laugh. And as Rey's scowl deepened, warmth spiraled through her. Gods, but she was glad to have him back, even if they'd each been busy with separate tasks throughout the day.

"Quiet, woman," he muttered. "At least I'm not clad in red this time."

"We match," said Silla, smoothing a hand along her gown's bodice. Midnight blue, it shimmered with golden stitchings of suns and stars and moons. A white fox fur stole hugged her shoulders, and a delicate crown of steel and gold was woven into her hair.

Silla felt Rey's gaze rake from her toes to the top of her crown. Hild had applied kohl around her eyes and a pigment to her lips. When Silla had stared into the mirror, she'd been dumbstruck. This was a woman of grace and beauty. This was *Eisa.* She paused for Rey's reaction, but after a weighted moment, he only looked away.

"What is it?" asked Silla, stepping forward and clasping his hand.

His gaze swung back to hers, torchlight catching the golden embers in his brown eyes. A muscle in his jaw twitched, as though he chewed on words he did not wish to voice. "It's only—" He sighed. "—sometimes I wish we could go back to the shield-home, when it was just the two of us."

She slid her arms around his waist and pulled him into a hug. "I've felt the same," she admitted. "Everything is so . . . *complicated* here."

Myrkur stretched, sending new thoughts spiraling through Silla. *I'm starting to question my own thoughts and emotions,* she wanted to scream. *I'm starting to question my ability to know a lie from truth.*

Rey eased away from her. "There is much we must speak of before the feast," he said, clasping her hands in his.

The worry in his voice had Silla's stomach twisting. She knew Rey had been to the falconry tower to investigate the missing letters, but she'd asked him to look into correspondence from Saga. "Was there word?"

"No word." Silla's shoulders slumped as Rey led her to a bench near the hearth. Where was her sister? Had her letters been stolen as well?

Saga is dead, whispered Myrkur. *I would sense her if she were in these lands.*

"Quiet," Silla snapped, then cast Rey a guilty look. "He's . . . vocal."

Rey watched her silently, the worry plain on his face. But as Silla made to sit down, Rey's arms shot out, and he pulled her onto his lap. "Better," he whispered, sending a warm shiver down her spine. "If He bothers you tonight, you squeeze my hand. I'll make excuses and whisk you away."

"You'd love that, wouldn't you?" Silla teased, though her voice came out flat.

"No. In fact, each time the god speaks in your mind, I think of a new creative way I'd make Him pay."

Useless taunts from a useless mortal, sneered Myrkur, causing Silla to wince.

"I despise that you've had to deal with Him alone." Rey glowered and pressed on. "I need you to tell me everything that happened in my absence."

And she did. Silla started with her attempts to find a way to rid herself of Myrkur, and Rey's expression darkened with each failure—the books, the Weaver, and last of all, Fallgerd.

"Are you certain the old man died at your hand?" he demanded, turning her hands over to examine them. "Did you have any nicks on your palms? What did the blood around his body look like?"

Silla blinked up at him. "I—I did not think to look. I know only the feeling of Myrkur's satisfaction and the sight of blood on my hands." She shuddered, and he stroked her spine gently.

"Tell me more."

She continued on, describing the attempted poisoning and the landslide, and with each word, Rey's arms tightened around her further. But as Silla detailed the events of the landslide, including her suspicions around her bloodline's gift and her ability to pull galdur from the halda stones, he blinked in astonishment.

"We must hone this skill," he said softly, kissing her palm. "I fear you will need it."

Yes, purred Myrkur. *Let us play with it, Eisa.*

Silla exhaled in frustration, refocusing on what Rey was saying.

"I did not return merely for a visit. I came to fetch you."

"*Me?*"

"It seems," said Rey, "this job with the mist has always involved you." And with a sigh, Rey relayed everything that had happened in the forest—the Spiral Staves carved into the trees; the Forest Maiden's awakening and her call for the Protector. Silla gasped when Rey revealed that the grimwolf she'd encountered in the Twisted Pinewoods—the one that had slaughtered the Battle Thorns warband—was none other than Kritka, servant of the Forest Maiden, who'd been searching for a Volsik heir.

Myrkur growled low, anger sharpening Silla's senses. She drew a deep breath, trying to keep her mind on task. "And the Forest Maiden believes that my gift—this strange ability bestowed by Sunnvald—will banish the leech from the woods?"

"Unfortunately, yes."

Myrkur shifted, peering upward. *We must play with this power of yours, Eisa*, He purred. *You won't defeat my progeny without it.*

Silla's spine stiffened, but Rey buried his nose in her neck. His touch caused warmth to bloom inside her, and the dark god to skitter away.

"There's more," Rey murmured against her skin. Silla's fingers scraped along his scalp, and he leaned into her touch. "I need to muster a great number of warriors. I'm told the leech has a considerable army guarding—"

"The tree," finished Silla, the dark dream she'd had the night before haunting her anew.

Rey's spine straightened as he stared at her intently. "In the heartwood, yes. The leech is thought to reside inside the tallest hjarta tree. How did you know?"

"A dream," she said, gaze growing distant. "I believe it was an accident . . . that Myrkur did not mean for me to see it . . . but I *have* seen it." The god hissed, flooding her with a wave of anger, but she focused on the feel of Rey, steady and warm. "A misshapen tree and an army of undead creatures surrounding it." Silla swallowed. "We will need *many* men."

Rey's grip on her relaxed, and Silla sensed a great weight lifting from his shoulders. Did he think she'd refuse the Forest Maiden's call? That she'd leave him to deal with such a task alone?

"You must go to Atli," she said. "Ask for his help in mustering men. He has great sway over Jarl Hakon—"

Her words broke off at Rey's preternatural stillness.

"What is it?"

"We must discuss the missing letters," said Rey in a voice of gravel.

Silla exhaled, running a finger along the embroidered neckline of his tunic. She'd gone over this a dozen times in her mind and only one person made sense to her.

"It was Kaeja," she blurted, right as Rey said, "It was Atli Hakonsson."

Silla blinked, then stared at him. "No," she murmured, shaking her head. "It cannot be Atli."

"You don't know him like I do."

"But he's been such a support in your absence. Besides, I told Atli I was with *you,* and he assured me his interest was only in friendship—"

Rey's fingers dug into her hips, and she could practically feel the rage rolling off him. For a moment, his anger felt like more than missing letters. Like there was some history between them that she didn't understand.

Secrets, whispered Myrkur. *He keeps things from you.*

Silla shook Him off. Chose her words carefully. "How can you be certain?"

"I have no proof, but . . ." Rey's jaw hardened as he drifted into thoughtful silence.

"What about Kaeja?"

He was silent for a moment, then shook his head. "It *has* to be Atli."

A memory coalesced in Silla's mind. "Atli *did* bring up Eyvind's letters in conversation—twice, in fact. Each time, the reminder that you hadn't written was like a knife in my heart—"

Her words broke off at the growl rumbling from Rey's chest. Silla slid a hand along Rey's newly trimmed beard, checking for uneven strands. "It does not matter," she said, stroking his jaw. "You are here now."

"It matters *very much.* They made you doubt my feelings for you. They're trying to drive a wedge between us. But it is more than that, Silla. They think their rank permits them to treat others as though they're dispensable." Silla lifted his hand from where it rested on her hip and entwined her fingers with his.

"I do not disagree. But we must be cautious, Rey. Right now, we need unity, as well as Atli's sway to muster warriors. Let us put the missing letters behind us for the greater good—"

Rey's chuckle was low and dark, but he brought her knuckles to his lips and pressed a reverent kiss there. "I will put it behind me once I've had a little talk with Atli."

A shiver rolled through Silla as she took in the coldness behind his eyes. "He never overtly—"

Rey shook his head. "Of course not. It is not his way. The man is a serpent and a schemer—"

She cut him off with a kiss. "We must retain a good relationship with House Hakon," she warned. "Please, Rey. If you're to speak with Atli tonight, let it be about the battle in the heartwood. Let it be about mustering the warriors we need."

"Very well," said Rey. His eyes softened, his gaze growing tender. "Tonight is your night."

For a moment, Silla wanted to abandon all plans of the feast—to drag him to the bed and repeat what they'd done this morning.

But something flickered in Rey's eyes. "To be clear, Silla, I *will* get to the bottom of the missing letters."

Silla sighed heavily. "But first, the feast of the Shortest Day. At the very least there shall be good food to be had."

Rey grumbled something inaudible into her hair.

"You do not like the fineries of Kopa?"

He drew back and surveyed her through narrowed lids. "I like them just fine. It's the people I find intolerable. There's a reason I preferred my time on the road, doing the Uppreisna's tasks."

Worry gathered within her. "Please be . . . kind tonight, Rey."

He huffed a dry laugh. "I shall try, though you must know the people of Kopa make this a difficult task."

"I mean it, Reynir," she said, poking him in the chest. "I've worked so hard to make a good impression tonight. And your *axe eyes* do not exactly inspire goodwill and trust."

His scowl only deepened, sending a tremor through her body. "Though if you want to bring them into bed afterward," she whispered, "I'd not be opposed."

"We could skip the feast and go straight to bed," he rasped, fingertips digging into her hip.

“Later,” she promised, heat unfurling inside her. “After.” Her hands slid along his jaw, pulling him down to her—

A knock on the door had her jumping to her feet.

“It’s time!” called Runný from the corridor.

Rey let out a long-suffering sigh.

Silla chewed on her lip, taking in Rey’s miserable expression. “If you wish, you can stay behind—”

“I will go,” he asserted.

“Very well.” Slowly, she pulled him up from the bench and led him to the door.

CHAPTER 31

Silla's head began to pound as she, Rey, and their retinue of guards approached Ashfall's great hall. The enormous oak doors were thrown wide, raucous laughter escaping from the room beyond. Her pulse picked up, and Silla tried to calm herself by repeating Lady Tala's advice from their meeting earlier in the day.

Show your backbone and be sure not to smile too much. Kindness and compassion will not win the jarls' respect. Show them a queen they can believe in.

This advice did nothing to temper her nerves, as none of that was intuitively *her*. For a moment, she was filled with frustration. It should be Saga here, charming the nobles. Winning their fealty. Myrkur seized this frustration. Amplified it. Was Silla to do all of the work, only for Saga to slip in and enjoy the fruits of Silla's labors?

She paused in the corridor, trying to control her emotions. Trying to loosen the dark god's grip on her. Frustration would get her nowhere. She *had* to find a way to slip into Eisa's skin. Too much was riding on winning over these jarls.

You must not fail, whispered Myrkur, slinking around her spine and displacing her frustration with a jolt of anxiety.

Rey caught her elbow. "All right?" he asked, eyes roaming her face. She nodded tightly.

I won't convince anyone to bend the knee with you toying with my emotions, Silla told the god of chaos. *If you want the jarls' fealty, then keep your thoughts to yourself tonight.*

Myrkur bristled. Then, to her surprise, the god crept deeper inside her. *Very well, Eisa,* He whispered, *if it gets us power, then so be it. But if you fail tonight, I shall have to take measures into my hands once more.* And with that chilling statement, the god of chaos seemed to vanish entirely.

Silla blinked at the disorienting feeling of having her mind to herself. Beside her, Rey was rigid as stone, but she was glad beyond measure to have him there as they approached the great hall.

Jarl Hakon appeared in the doorway clad in a crimson tunic; the jewel-encrusted cuffs in his black beard caught the torchlight. But Silla paused a dozen paces away, her heart racing as she considered what fate awaited her. Once she stepped into that room, there was no turning back.

"We could escape back to Kalasgarde," Silla whispered to Rey. "Check on Vig and the chicks, and leave Jarl Hakon to do all the politicking."

"We could."

She shifted uneasily, willing her racing heart to calm. "But first . . . I suppose . . . I must do this."

Rey's hand slid into hers and gave it a gentle squeeze.

"I'm glad you're here," she whispered.

His gaze pricked along her skin. "As am I."

Together, they approached the great hall. Jarl Hakon beamed, taking her by the elbow. "You look like a queen, Eisa," he said with a warm smile. His gaze slid to Rey, irritation flashing. "I hope you don't mind if I borrow her."

But Silla shook free from the jarl. "Rey will enter with me," she said in her most *Eisa* of voices.

Jarl Hakon's shocked expression lasted the span of a few heartbeats, but then he was waving Rey forward and signaling to someone within the hall.

"Introducing Eisa Volsik, daughter of Svalla and Kjartan Volsik, second heir to the throne and princess of Íseldur!" bellowed a crier dressed in House Hakon livery.

The great hall was filled with hundreds of nobles dressed in their finest for the feast of the Shortest Day. Jarl Hakon led Silla and Rey between dual rows of feasting tables decorated with sprigs of mistletoe and greenery. Candlelight flickered from antler chandeliers, making the golden stitching of her gown glint. And as heads dipped low in deference, *Silla* was no more. For the first time, she truly *felt* like Eisa.

Jarl Hakon led them to the high table at the front of the room. There stood Atli, watching with sparkling eyes. Her gaze skipped to Lady Tala, looking regal in a purple gown, then to the assortment of gray-bearded jarls filling seats of honor. She followed Hakon around the table, then turned to face the room. Eisa's heart pounded vigorously, her palms slick with sweat. But Rey's hand was an anchor of calm at her back—steadfast and unmoving.

"Eisa Volsik lives!" shouted Jarl Hakon. "Let us raise a cup to this blessing." He lifted his goblet, and Eisa found her own to do the same. "We have much to celebrate on this Shortest Day! Skál!"

The crowd drained their goblets, then erupted so fiercely that it left Eisa stunned. Her hand flew to her chest as she took in tear-filled eyes and nodding heads, men who pounded fists on the finely dressed tables, and silk-clad women whose hands clapped together with astounding enthusiasm.

They looked at her and saw Eisa. They saw her parents and grandparents—a legacy that had been stolen not only from her, but from them all. And in this moment, everything she and Lady Tala and Jarl Hakon had been working toward became real. All the names she'd struggled to remember had faces. They were real people with love in their hearts—love for this kingdom and what it could be. And for the first time since arriving in Kopa, Eisa admitted to herself that she wanted this. Wanted the throne. Wanted to lead these people into a different sort of era. A better era. The realization terrified her. Was this another thought planted by Myrkur? But the dark god was nowhere to be found.

Eisa was shown to her seat, a fresh goblet of wine placed before her—after Eilif had tasted for poison, of course. It took Eisa a moment to realize she was seated between Atli and an unfamiliar blond man. There was no place set for Rey at the table. She turned to the jarl with pure, incinerating anger.

"Someone," she said tersely, "had best set a place for Galtung on my right." Hakon's brows rose, and he nodded heartily. Soon servants were scurrying about. The blond man—*another* jarl's heir as it turned out—was moved down the table. A chair appeared from nowhere, plate and goblet and serveware set on the table. Only then did Eisa settle into her chair with Rey beside her.

"You've already captured their hearts," whispered Atli from her left.

Eisa examined Atli from the corner of her eye. Rey was certain he was responsible for the missing letters, and the thought made her insides burn with betrayal. She'd thought Atli a friend and confidant—a rare ally in this new and confusing place. But the stunt with her entry painted Jarl Hakon and Atli in a new light. It had seemed a move orchestrated to shame Rey and position Atli as a potential marriage match.

Behind her, she could sense a heated look exchanged between Atli and Rey, and again she had the strange inkling that these two had some history she did not understand. But tonight was too important to get pulled into such trivial matters.

Eisa watched on as a group of burly warriors hauled the yule log into the hall. Lady Tala had explained that the most majestic tree was selected for this ritual, and that this year, Sunnvald's runes had been carved into its trunk. The northlings burned this offering to the Sun God in thanks for Eisa Volsik's return to them. Eisa felt tears prick her eyes as she watched the warriors heave the log into the enormous obsidian fireplace, sending ash and sparks billowing.

Jarl Hakon was back on his feet, as were many in the room. "Now," bellowed the jarl above the clamor of jovial feasters, "let us eat!"

Servants bustled into the room bearing platters of feasting food. They began with trays of smoked trout and bowls of root vegetable soup, and progressed quickly to the main event: a boar roasted specially for this occasion, accompanied by chicken legs and braised lamb.

Rey eagerly heaped his plate with some of each, then proceeded to steal from Eisa's plate. She struggled to comprehend that there was more, but of course there was. Baked apples with clotted cream and small, round honey cakes were brought out, and Eisa got retribution by stealing Rey's dessert for herself. Finally, steaming cups of spiced wine were distributed, warming her down to her toes.

Once the plates were cleared, she was more formally introduced to the jarls at the high table and lost the better part of an hour in conversation. It was blissful to have her mind to herself, and as everything she'd practiced with Lady Tala came to her with ease, Eisa's confidence only grew. She could do this. She *would* do this.

After conversing with Jarl Geirmundur—and recalling his wife's name without Atli's help!—Silla returned to her seat to find Rey having left to relieve himself. Eisa reached for her goblet of spiced wine but stiffened as she became aware that she and Atli were alone. Jaw tightening, she kept her gaze trained on the greater room.

"Your demeanor tonight makes it clear Galtung has convinced you of his . . . theory," said Atli, snatching his goblet and swirling it.

"What do you mean?"

"He cornered me today and went on and on about some . . . letters he thinks I've stolen." Atli rolled his eyes. "Sounds like he wants to blame someone for his own shortcomings."

"Then you deny it?" Eisa flashed a smile at a passing jarl, then returned to studying Atli's expression for any hint of deception.

"I swear it to you, Eisa. I had nothing to do with Galtung's missing letters."

"And your father?"

Atli drank deeply from his goblet, then placed it down with unnecessary force. "My father might have suggested I court you, but he would not be reckless with Eyvind's welfare. What if there'd been a warning in those letters? A plea for help?" Atli shook his head, and it was clear he was both irritated and a little hurt by her accusation.

"I'm sorry," she huffed, guilt festering inside her. Rey had been so certain Atli was the culprit, and she . . . she'd been swept up in his gusto. But if it wasn't Atli or Jarl Hakon, then was it Kaeja's doing?

"I suppose Galtung has told you of our history," said Atli, a note of bitterness in his voice.

Eisa sat up straighter. "What do you mean?"

"Old rivalries. You know how such things go."

Eisa wanted to remind him she'd grown up moving from town to town and that she hardly knew how *anything* went. But she sensed there were things left unsaid.

Atli took a long drink of wine and frowned. "It was . . ." He sighed, sliding a hand along his warrior's braid. "You know of his history with Kaeja?"

Eisa's gaze raked through the crowd, picking out Kaeja's vibrant blue gown with ease. Rey had just ambled back into the hall, and it was clear Kaeja had spotted him. Eisa's brows dropped low as the black-haired beauty sidled up to Rey and slid a hand along his arm. She'd made no secret of wanting him back. Had she stolen the letters to cause strife? But Rey only scowled and shook Kaeja's hand free.

"He's told me of their entanglement," she said cautiously.

"Did he tell you she was with me as well?"

Eisa's gaze whipped to Atli. "No."

A rueful smile spread across Atli's face, but it was edged with a certain . . . sadness. "I do not like to speak of it, but I feel you, above all else, are owed the truth. And if Galtung hasn't enough honor to tell you, then I shall do it for him."

A cold pit opened up in Eisa's stomach.

"He was dealt a blow in the sparring grounds that he deemed unfair. And so, I suppose he thought it retribution, stealing Kaeja away from me."

"Stealing . . ."

"He lured her to his bed when she was mine."

Eisa felt herself making a decidedly unqueenly face. "Atli," she started, then sighed. "I thank you for sharing this with me, and am sorry you were hurt. But . . ." She sorted through her words, choosing them wisely. "But Reynir Galtung would never force a woman, which can only mean Kaeja went of her own free will."

It was clear no matter how carefully chosen, Eisa's words had not landed softly. Atli's gaze turned sharp, and his chair scraped across the floor as he pushed to his feet.

"Atli—" she started, discomfort twisting in her stomach.

He bowed stiffly, avoiding her gaze. "Excuse me. I require some air to clear my mind."

And with that, Atli departed.

As he returned to the feasting table, Rey turned over Silla's suggestion in his mind. The very thought of approaching Atli Hakonsson was appalling. Never mind the fact that this job was *Rey's* responsibility, the thought of asking that arsebadger for help made his stomach sour. Atli would wield his rank as a weapon. Would take control and relish ordering Rey around. But they had scarcely a week to muster hundreds of warriors. There was no time to waste.

"How fares your friend Vig?" asked Kaeja, suddenly by his side. He shook her off, continuing his amble between the feasting tables to reach Silla.

As Kaeja caught up with him, Rey shot her a flat look. "Why are you talking to me?"

A laugh fell from her poisonous lips, the same that had spewed so many lies. "As ill-tempered as ever, I see." Her blue eyes gleamed with mischief—the same eyes that had once dazzled him. There was no doubt Kaeja was still beautiful. Yet when Rey looked at her now, he felt nothing but irritation. "Merciless on the battlefield and in conversation," she teased.

"What do you want, Kaeja?" He could sense the feasters glancing their way and it made his skin itch. Were they talking about him?

Kaeja's nails tapped against her wine goblet, and Rey couldn't keep his gaze from sliding back to the high table. Silla looked like a goddess in that gown, stars and suns and moons radiating in the torchlight. And based on the expressions of those in the hall, they were equally enchanted. A gray-bearded jarl had slid into Atli's vacant seat, engaging Silla in conversation.

Kaeja followed his gaze. "Why wasn't there a place set for you beside her, Rey?"

"You know why," muttered Rey, snatching a goblet from a passing servant and taking a hearty gulp. A pair of nearby nobles bowed their heads together in quiet conversation, and he glared their way.

"I simply cannot watch you suffer like this." Kaeja sighed. "You know this is only the start. There will be council meetings, diplomatic trips, and more feasts than you can imagine. All the while, Eisa will be up there with them. And you, Rey, will be elbowed farther and farther into the shadows. Sent about the realm to do the Uppreisna's dirty work."

Rey whirled on Kaeja. "Keep your venomous thoughts to yourself," he hissed. "And if I hear you've stirred more trouble with Sill"—he flinched—"*Eisa,* I'll have you hauled away from Ashfall on a donkey cart."

Kaeja opened her mouth to reply, but her gaze caught on something at the front of the room—Atli, meandering through the great hall. Rey drew a deep breath, trying to quash the disdain that rose in him whenever he saw the Hakon heir. He readied himself to swallow his pride and weather his discomfort. Rey would speak to Atli about mustering men for the heartwood, but he only did so for Silla, and for Íseldur.

Atli wove through the crowd, taking a goblet of wine from a passing servant. He seemed to search the room, and as his gaze landed on Rey, he changed course. Smoothing a hand along his artfully styled warrior's braid, Atli sauntered up to Kaeja and Rey.

"Well met, Hakonsson," Rey grumbled, glancing across the room. Silla watched with worry, though the graybeard beside her prattled on.

"If it isn't two of my favorite people," said Atli, a smarmy expression on his face. "Well met, Kaeja."

"You can go climb a tree in a lightning storm," Kaeja muttered.

Atli chuckled low at that.

"And you, Galtung? Suppose you're off the Uppreisna's leash now that your identity has been revealed. What shall the hound do without a hare to chase?"

Rey's hand tightened around his goblet. "Funny you should ask." His every instinct urged him to abandon this conversation, but Rey gritted his teeth and steeled himself in place. "I would ask for your . . . help."

Atli's black brows lifted. "Shall I fetch a healer to check my ears? I could have sworn you just asked for help."

Gods, but Rey hated this already. "I need warriors, Hakonsson. Hundreds of them, and quickly, to do battle in the heartwood on the next full Marra."

Atli blinked.

"And you need my—"

"Help. Aye." Rey could sense more gazes swinging their way. Could feel the whispers building in the room. Gods but this was his idea of torture. Rey would rather bathe in the eternal fucking flames than ask this man for help, especially after Atli had tried to turn Silla against him.

Atli glanced at the high table where his father and Silla sat, then back at Rey. A slow, scheming smile crept across his face. Atli lowered his voice. "You know, Galtung, while you were gone, I truly got to know Eisa. The evening meal you disrupted last night was only one of many."

Anger burned to life in Rey's veins, and again his intuition urged him to abandon this conversation. But Atli, it seemed, was merely getting started.

"We've gotten rather close, Eisa and I. And I do not appreciate you poisoning her against me with your false accusations." Atli leaned closer. "I did not steal your gods damned letters."

Rey's pulse thrummed in his temples, his hands curling into fists. The fire coursing through his veins now licked up his spine with increasing fervor.

"I'll help you, Galtung," said Atli coolly. "But only if you drop to your knees right here and beg."

Red misted Rey's vision, and he seized Atli by the tunic and hauled him up until his boots dragged against the floor. "Listen to me, you serpent," he said in a low, dangerous voice. "There will be no begging."

Atli's smarmy smile deepened at that. "Tsk, Galtung, such a temper you have. When will Eisa realize your true nature and come crawling to me? What do you think, *Kaeja*?"

What little control Rey had left snapped clean through at that. He drew back his fist and slammed it into the jarl-to-be's pretty face once. Twice. It was long overdue, and for a moment, he relished the delayed justice.

But a choked sound from nearby had him dropping Atli to the ground. Rey turned and blinked. Silla had made it halfway across the hall, then stopped, her face flushed with anger and embarrassment. The feast-goers whispered among themselves, all eyes on them. Games of combat were a common enough occurrence at *rural* feasts. But this was Kopa, and Rey had just punched Jarl Hakon's heir before the northern jarls Silla was trying to impress. His insides burned as he saw the embarrassment plain on her face.

She turned and fled the room.

"I cannot decide if you're clever or a kunta, Atli," murmured Kaeja.

Rey couldn't bear to see Atli's smug expression—couldn't confirm that he'd just played right into Atli's schemes. Gods, but he was a fool.

Rey shouldered through the crowd, cursing under his breath. He'd planned to be a pillar of silent support for Silla tonight. Instead, he'd as good as swung a greataxe right through their plans.

Rey jogged into the corridor, feet faltering as he passed a couple entwined in an alcove. They broke apart, torchlight illuminating Liv Eriksson's flushed face, and a spill of black braids he recognized well.

"Runný?" Rey's feet faltered as Runný whipped around, her eyes widening as they locked with his. She opened her mouth to say something, but Rey ran on, granting the women a few more moments of privacy.

He rounded a corner just in time to see the star-speckled train of Silla's gown disappearing through a door midway down the hall. Rey reached the doorway quickly, yanking it open with too much force. It banged against the wall, echoing down the hallway. But as he stepped into the terraced courtyard, the violent thrashing of his heart eased just a touch.

Lunar-blooming plants glowed all around him, climbing up the volcanic black stone walls and spilling from barrels. Everywhere he looked, ethereal white flowers had unfurled, lifting to the moons. His chest constricted as he found Marra, already half full.

But then his gaze fell on the lone figure seated on an obsidian bench. Her gown pooled around her, suns and stars and moons glinting in the moonlight. Silla had kicked off her slippers and pulled her knees to her chest. Cautiously, Rey approached, ducking beneath an arch of wild brambles, hundreds of cup-shaped flowers illuminating it from within.

She turned her face toward him, resting her cheek on her knee. His tongue suddenly felt too big for his mouth, uncertainty filling him.

"You don't trust me," she said.

A hot, panicky feeling grew inside him. "That's not it—"

She sighed. "Don't lie to me, Galtung. You're worried I'll leave you for Atli."

Rey's old instincts told him to flee, to deflect—anything to avoid talking about this. But he held himself in place and said, "You don't know him like I do."

"You're right, I do not, Rey. Because you haven't revealed a word about your history." She tilted her head up and gazed at the stars. "It has not been easy for me here, Rey. I do not fit in—I was not raised like these people. Atli and Lady Tala, and perhaps Liv, are the only ones who've welcomed me—who've made me feel like I could belong. And now you—you've *embarrassed* me, Rey."

Shame stung his cheeks, but it didn't stop him from voicing the thought that he'd been unable to shake for days. "Tell me he didn't try anything when I was gone."

She pushed to her feet, planting hands on her hips. "You sound like Jonas!"

Rey blinked in surprise.

"Did you know what he said to me on the Road of Bones? Jonas told me he didn't want me to speak to you anymore!" Her voice was rising, echoing off the stone walls of the courtyard.

"I would never ask that of you, Silla," Rey tried, his stomach wrenching at her unexpected ire. "Only that you are cautious around him."

His words seemed to go right through her. She was pacing now. "You undid all the goodwill I've tried to cultivate with the northern jarls tonight. I told them of your honor and integrity and now"—she shrugged—"now I look like a horrible judge of character at best, a liar at worst."

Glowering, Rey wiped a luminescent spore from his tunic. He felt just as he had all those years ago. Small and weak. An object of ridicule. "I don't need their approval."

Rey could not meet her burning gaze.

"We need unity, Rey. We need warriors to fight in the heartwood."

"I did what you asked," he said stubbornly. "I asked Atli for help. You see how well that went!"

"This is too important to risk on petty squabbles!" Silla shot back.

Rey glowered stubbornly at the wall behind her.

"I need you to trust me, Rey."

His fist tingled with the remembered feel of Atli's jaw. "I trust you. It is *him* I cannot trust."

"Well, you'll have to. I have no choice but to be around him, and I've made it clear to Atli where we stand." There was a finality in her voice that told Rey this was a battle he'd never win.

Something ingrained deeply within him pushed back. *Stop being a coward and fight for what you want. Fight for her.* Rey scrubbed a hand down his face. "You're right." He turned toward her. Swallowed his pride. "Once again, I've let old ghosts haunt me. How can I make it right?"

Silla cocked her head to the side. "You can tell me what really happened with Kaeja. Atli told me—"

Rey felt himself grimacing. Felt old humiliation flare hot within him.

But Silla continued. "Atli told me you stole Kaeja from him as retribution for some . . . wrong in the sparring grounds. But his words did not fit with what I know of your character."

Shock rippled through him, and Rey stared at her. Never before had he felt such unwavering support from another—never had he met someone who knew him so well, she could glean truth from lie. But of course she was different. Silla had never been like any other he'd met.

It took him a moment to regain his ability to speak. "Aye," Rey choked out. "It was he who . . ." He scowled. "The blame does not lie on Atli. It was Kaeja who went to his bed willingly—"

"That's what I told him!" Silla exclaimed.

A wry smile twisted his lips. Rey took her hand, drawing her closer. "Kaeja went to his bed while she was still with me. She kept it from me, lied right to my face, and I was too much of a fool to realize." His jaw hardened as he thought of it. "Everyone knew, and no one said a thing. I found out later, it was all they could talk about among themselves. They gossiped about Kaeja and Atli rutting behind my back. My humiliation served as their entertainment. Eyvind had been sent out for the season, visiting the northern reaches of the Hakon lands. He found out soon after returning and immediately came to tell me."

Silla squeezed his hand, urging him on.

"I thought—" Rey paused. Tried to find the strength for what came next. "I thought I loved her. Thought we would be wed one day. Needless to say, I couldn't leave this place soon enough."

Silla laid her chin on his chest, staring up at him. "She didn't deserve you."

The ache inside Rey grew and spread, but he didn't flinch away from it. He opened himself wide; let Silla see that old vulnerability. "In the barn, you said you felt like you're losing yourself in this place. And I feel—" He paused. Shook his head. "—like I cannot *find* myself in this place, with these people."

Wordlessly, Silla slid her hands around his neck and pulled his forehead down to hers. "I don't know what's been said to you to make you feel unworthy." She kissed him softly. Slowly. Then drew back. "But you are worthy, Reynir Galtung. There is no better man to have by my side. I will tell you every day, until you feel it as strongly as I do."

All the night's tension eased from his bones as her words seeped into his blood and warmed him through. The glow of moonlight and lunar-blooming plants caught on her crown and the golden stitches in her gown. Rey's chest ached at the sight of her—she'd never looked more like a queen than in this moment.

He walked them back to the bench, then pulled her into his lap. Rey's lips dipped to hers, and he lost himself in the taste of her, the tickle of her hair against his skin, the soft sounds coming from them both. For a moment, they were the only two people in the world, just the pair of them and the moonlight and the luminescent plants all around them. Their kiss grew frantic, Rey's hands sliding around her backside and hauling her against him. He wanted her, desperately, here in this garden of moonlight.

But a throat cleared from the doorway. Rey drew back, staring at Silla's dark, dazed eyes. For a moment, they stayed like this, just the two of them. But the throat cleared again, and they whirled to face Runný, half a dozen guards around her.

"Sorry to interrupt," said Runný, sounding genuinely regretful, "but Eisa's presence is requested in the hall."

Silla and Rey sighed at the same time. Then their eyes met in amusement.

"Well," she said, taking a step back and smoothing her disheveled hair. "I suppose I must . . ."

"I'll join you in a moment," said Rey, adjusting his breeches.

Silla rocked back on her heels, then nodded. And as she strode toward the door, Rey inhaled deeply. The night was cool and quiet, a sharp contrast to the hot emotions he'd felt in that hall. No matter how right it had felt, Rey knew it had been wrong to punch Atli. He had to find a way to leave the past behind him. To find his place in this world of queens and jarls. Because Silla was right. The consequences of failure were simply too dire.

CHAPTER 32

Kovograd, Zagadka

A firepot streaked over the fortress walls, heading straight for the grassy courtyard.

"Fire!" shrieked Saga, hovering in the keep's doorway. A dozen Zagadkian women rushed across the courtyard, pails of sand clutched in hand. The clay pot broke and an explosion shook the air, flames spraying across grass and packed earth with the flammable liquid. Saga's handmaiden, Alasa, got there first and emptied her bucket of sand over the foot-high blaze.

"Not too much!" Saga called out, her stomach knotting. They had to preserve their resources. Two days had passed since the Urkans first landed, and it was clear they were settling in for a siege.

Elisava appeared by Saga's side, peering into the courtyard beyond. Alasa's companions had joined her and together they stamped rogue flames out.

"More firepots?" asked Elisava, worry creasing her brow.

Saga nodded solemnly. It was the dozenth Urkan firepot this hour to breach the walls of the fortress. Ivar's ships had broken through the inner river gate, granting them access to Kovograd city, and putting them in better range of the fortress walls.

"The healer's station?" asked Saga.

Elisava wiped her brow with the sleeve of her dress and sagged against the doorframe. "More warriors stream in by the hour."

Saga chewed on her lip, unable to keep Kassandr and Rov from her thoughts.

"Not them," said Elisava, apparently thinking the same thing. "They hold the city gates. For now." Elisava needn't say the rest. Even with the forces Kassandr had mustered from the northern territories, the Zagadkians were badly outnumbered.

A member of Saga's makeshift fire brigade approached, tilting her bucket to show how little sand remained. "You can replenish on north of yard," Saga replied in slow Zagadkian with as kind a smile as she could manage.

In truth, she was unused to this—to people looking to her as though she knew what to do. Saga wanted to shout at them that she didn't know—that her name might be Volsik, but it didn't mean she was built for such things as this.

"Rovgolod tells to me," said Elisava in cautious Zagadkian, "that the Urkans have more tricks in their sleeve. The sail on the far end of the battlefield conceals something, but our spies cannot get near to it. Do you recall anything they might have said in Íseldur?"

Saga closed her eyes. Tried to drive the sounds of battle from her ears. Imagined herself sitting by Bjorn as he prattled on about nonsensical things. Karthian steel and ore deposits in the bogs and nothing, nothing, *nothing*!

Frustrated, Saga shook her head. "I cannot recall—"

Shouts from the walls had Saga searching the skies. They landed on a projectile, larger than the others had been, and heading straight toward the—

"Stables!" she shrieked, watching in horror as the firepot crashed into a bare patch of turfed roof. There hadn't been enough water-drenched hides to cover all the roofs and walls of the fortress; and after saddling the horses for mounted combat, the Zagadkian guards had apparently deemed it a low priority.

But as the firepot cracked open and bright flames ripped across the stable roof, Saga knew not all creatures had been evacuated. A panicked whinny from within confirmed her fears. Havoc was shackled in there.

Before she had time to reconsider, Saga was moving across the courtyard. It did not matter that she was beneath wide-open skies; did not matter that Elisava's screams chased her. Any panic she might feel was overshadowed by her dire need to get to those stables.

Saga shoved open the doors and slipped inside. Darkness engulfed her, though firelight expanded with every rapid beat of her heart. The flames ate widening holes in the roof, and Saga knew she had to act quickly. Through smoke-stung eyes, she spotted the farrier's station, and Saga rushed forward to snatch a driving hammer. After pivoting, she charged toward Havoc's panicked sounds.

It wasn't long before she saw him. The turf roof above the pen was all but consumed, the flames now burning down the timber walls. Rage twisted in Saga's stomach as she took in the stallion's white coat, pocked with raw burns where embers had landed.

The stallion reared, his wings spread wide and fanning the flames into increasing furor.

"Don't!" Saga called out, and as the creature noticed her, he stilled for just a moment. Before she could second-guess the madness herself, Saga scrambled into the enclosure and found herself face-to-face with the winged horse.

What are you doing? she asked herself as the beast grew frantic, thrashing against the pair of chains securing his hind legs.

"Easy," she tried, her gaze trailing along the chains until it reached the anchor loops securing the horse to the stable floors. Saga threw herself at them and began hammering furiously.

Havoc shrieked, rearing back. Yet perhaps some deep-rooted intuition told the stallion Saga was here to help, as he did not aim to strike her. Heat lashed against her skin, tears streaming from her stinging eyes, but she did not pause. The iron was already weakened from the stallion's panic, and as a crack splintered the loop, Saga's hope swelled. Her arms were weak, her lungs burning, yet still she hammered until the chain wrenched free.

The stallion reared again, but Saga did not flinch. Perhaps it was the unrelenting panic churning through her body or something deeper that told her this creature meant her no harm. She crawled to the second chain anchor.

"You! Will! Be! Free!" she shouted as she drove the hammer down onto the chain, fueled by her rage at the injustice of this creature's captivity. The stallion gave a sudden leap, and the chain snapped through.

Saga scrambled backward just in time. Havoc's wings spread wide, the inferno glinting in his iridescent white feathers. Ink-black eyes peered at her for a moment before the stallion crouched low, then launched into the air.

Havoc crashed through the skeletal remains of the stable roof, sending burnt beams and a flurry of embers crashing down into the pen. A hay bale beside Saga burst into flames, and she knew she had but moments to get free. But as she crawled over the enclosure, Saga's feet faltered. Flames now raged in every direction.

She shielded her face from the unbearable heat, her lungs choking on thick smoke. Saga's panic spiraled to new heights. Was this how it ended? In fire and smoke?

But a voice penetrated the roar of the fire.

"Saga!"

Crouching low to the ground, Saga craned her ears. "This way, Saga!" Unthinkingly, she darted toward the sound. Rounding a pillar, Saga came face-to-face with a sight that would have made her weep if tears weren't already streaming down her face from the smoke. There was Elisava, sheltered beneath a soaked hide. Behind her, dozens of members of the fire brigade surged into the stables, flinging water and sand on the fire within.

They'd created a safe pathway leading outdoors.

Saga nearly sobbed in relief as she reached Elisava, the wet hide cutting through the heat in an instant. Elisava hauled her toward the stable doors, and soon they were falling to their knees in the courtyard, coughing and gasping for breath.

A torrent of angry Zagadkian assaulted Saga's ears, and she

turned toward the sound. Elisava held the same disapproving expression as when she chastised Rov, and something about this made Saga's lips pull up at the corners.

"Are your brains pickled? You risked your life for that murderous beast, you crazy fool of a girl! It is not worth it!"

The fire burning in the stables had been contained, but it was too late—the beams and framing collapsed to the ground. Ash and smoke billowed skyward, but as Saga gazed up, it was a white form she searched for.

And when she did not see Havoc, her smile only widened.

Hours later, bells tolled through Kovograd, mournful and tired as the city itself. News had spread through the fortress: The Urkans had retreated for the night, returning to their camp on the banks of the Kovosk River.

Now Saga dragged herself through the corridors, not quite certain if she was heading toward her chambers at all. A guttural sound ricocheted through the hallway, and Saga paused as the hairs on her arms lifted. The sound came again, and this time she recognized it. Before she had time to think, she was rushing down the corridor.

Men shouted, growls shaking the walls. And then, a howl—the same she'd heard in the hull of that ship. Saga was now running toward the chaos and screams of men. A door slammed and Rov's frustrated voice reached her ears.

"He cannot be eased!"

Saga rounded the corner and skidded to a halt before Rov and Kass's Druzhina. Their armored coats were smeared with mud and gore, exhaustion etched into their faces. One battered-looking warrior sagged against the wall, nursing a fresh gash in his arm. Another was sprawled on the floor, feeding a bandage through a tear in his breeches. And as Rov turned to Saga, a wound shone red against his brown cheekbone.

"What is not . . . so?" she stumbled in Zagadkian.

Rov scowled at the door, answering her in Íseldurian. "Is nothing, Printsessa. You must not trouble yourself with such matters."

But the shattering of glass and a low, mournful howl from within the room had her stepping closer. "It is Kassandr? What has happened?"

Rov ran a hand down his haggard face. "He is . . . not himself."

"What has happened, Rov?"

"Is . . . trapped," he said. "No one can calm him. Bring back to himself."

Saga chewed on her lip, staring at the door. "I will try."

Rov's laugh was anything but amused. "Printsessa, no, you cannot—"

"He won't harm me." Saga was surprised at her certainty—she felt it in the very marrow of her bones.

"Is not in control—"

"He won't hurt me," repeated Saga, sending her most assertive gaze at Rov. "Let me try. And if I succeed, then you and the Druzhina must go and get some rest."

Perhaps it was due to exhaustion, or perhaps it was the determination he read in Saga's eyes, but Rov relented with a dramatic sigh. Muttering in unintelligible Zagadkian, he retrieved a key from his pocket and slid it into the door.

Then Rov paused, sending Saga a sidelong glance. He pulled a dagger from his hip and held the hilt toward her. Saga stared at it blankly, but her mind replayed those gruesome sounds in the gallery—Kassandr ripping out throats and tossing men as though they were made of straw.

She pushed the dagger back to Rov. "What good will a blade do against him?"

Rov's mouth hardened into a thin line. "Is madness. Kassandr will carve out my entrails and wear them as a necklace." But at Saga's unrelenting stare, he sighed. "You are certain?"

She nodded.

And with that, he turned the key and eased the door open. Saga kept her movements slow and steady to avoid startling the beast as she entered the room, but she could not suppress her gasp as she took in the space. It looked as though a windstorm had crashed through it. A heavy table was upended, its chairs reduced to kindling. Clothing was torn, the walls and floors gouged with claw marks, and shards of glass scattered the floor.

And there, with his back to her, was the beast. Saga stared. His back was broad and covered with wolf-like fur, with bony protrusions bursting along the length of it. These spikes were as long as her hand and curved to sharp points, and Saga's gaze traced their path down his spine where they gradually diminished, giving way to a barbed tail. There was something decidedly wolf-like about him, and yet so much more that was entirely *other*.

Saga felt her pulse in her wrists, her knees, her temples. His tail lashed back and forth, breaths sawing heavily in and out from him. Saga had a moment of trepidation, wondering if the smoke from the stables had addled her mind.

But she took another step forward, then slid the door closed behind her. The click of the latch was loud in the silent room. Tufted ears pricked.

And then hundreds of pounds of snarling beast charged at her.

He was all blood-flecked fur and hard muscle, pointed teeth and jagged claws—a predator designed to maim and kill. Saga's body reacted as though she were prey, screaming at her to flee, to take cover before this beast ripped her limb from limb. But those green eyes anchored her in place, forcing her to stand her ground.

Those eyes belonged to Kassandr. And Kassandr would *never* harm her.

His once-gray muzzle was matted with blood and pulled into a vicious snarl as he lunged at her. Saga tried not to look at the gleaming fangs, instead focusing on those eyes—Kassandr's eyes. They were mad with bloodlust, flooding her with apprehension. What if she'd miscalculated? What if his beastly nature could not identify her? But then she saw the flash of recognition.

The beast's claws gouged the floorboards as he tried to slow the momentum careening his enormous form across the room. He came to a stop bare inches from her, and Saga finally released her breath. Crouched on his long forelegs, the beast stood eye-to-eye with Saga, and for a moment, they simply stared at each other. He was so near that she could smell him—wet fur and the iron scent of blood—so near she could now see how his muscles clenched and unclenched with each labored breath.

"What is it?" she asked, aiming for soothing, but landing on something sharper. Saga hadn't a clue of what she was doing—she didn't know if he could even understand her.

Kassandr jolted, and a whine came from low in his chest. It was clear he was in discomfort, but she could not tell if he was in pain.

"Come to the bed. Let me look at you." Saga took a cautious step forward, but as that barbed tail lashed to and fro, she stopped.

The whine shifted into a growl, and he resumed his pacing.

Saga released a frustrated sigh. "You must rest, Kass."

The beast continued prowling about.

"Get on the bed, Kassandr. Now." Part of Saga wanted to laugh. In some other life, those words might have an altogether different meaning.

Without waiting for him to comply, Saga marched to the bed herself. Wincing as her soot-stained garments dragged along the fine linens, she crawled to the middle of the bed and reclined against the carved wooden headboard. The scent from the bedding hit her senses—herbal and woodsy, with the faintest traces of sweat—and for a single, dizzying moment, she was acutely aware of whose bed this was.

Saga gave herself a mental shake and patted the blanket. "Bed, Kass."

His eyes filled with something that looked an awful lot like fear, and in that moment, Saga understood. "I know you won't hurt me, you obstinate man. Now get on the gods damned bed."

Slowly, his long, angular forelegs drew forward, thick muscular hind legs powering him toward her. Another cautious bound forward, and then he slowly . . . *carefully* . . . climbed onto the bed. As he crawled toward her, Saga's heartbeat picked up. Kassandr was a large man, but his beast was nearly twice as large. In this form he easily took up half the bed.

With slow, deliberate movements, Kassandr eased himself down, laying his head on her lap with a soft whine. She nearly gasped at the weight of him—nearly made a joke about such a large head for such a mindless man—but Saga knew it was not the right moment.

"You're trembling," she murmured, her fingertips grazing the thick tufts of fur around his ears.

The clench and release of his muscles continued, and an idea struck Saga. Gathering her courage, she found the joint of his shoulder and began tapping in a gentle rhythm.

After the explosion she'd caused in Sunnavík, Saga had told Rurik she had not been in control. And his reply?

I understand. More than you know.

"This has happened to you before," she murmured, continuing the taps. He nuzzled deeper into her lap, eyes squeezed tightly shut. "Perhaps I am beginning to understand you better." The muscles beneath her fingers shuddered, and a wave of empathy flooded her. She, too, understood how it felt to be helpless against her body's own reaction. How vulnerable he must feel right now.

Saga began to hum. It was a silly song her mother had once sung to her, but it made her think of kinder days. And she could have sworn Kass's agitation eased just a touch by the time she reached the second verse. She continued to hum, her fingers tapping against Kass's shoulder for several minutes. Gradually, his tremors quieted, his breaths growing more rhythmic. And as he loosed a long, contented sigh, she regarded him.

In her previous encounters with this side of Kassandr, she'd been too frightened to examine him closely. But now, with him sprawled across her lap, she let herself look. He was not all teeth and claws and spiny protrusions, she realized. His fur was an assortment of grays and whites, even a few soft browns along the top of his wolf-like snout. Delicate black whiskers framed his muzzle and sprang from above his eyes—eyes that gazed right back at Saga, filled with what looked like . . . shame.

"I think you're rather striking," she whispered.

Saga hesitated, then slid her fingers into the thick fur on his neck, surprised at how soft it was here compared with his shoulder. She gave him a gentle scratch. A low rumble came from his chest, and Saga blinked. But this was no growl—it was softer and far more steady.

"Are you *purring*?"

The sound only intensified, vibrating through her, and soon Saga grinned like a delighted fool. She grew more bold, her fingers rubbing behind his ears and down his neck, searching for the places he liked the most. But eventually, the purring faded, and she realized his eyes had fallen shut. Asleep. Kassandr had fallen asleep with his head on her lap.

With a sigh, Saga prepared to extricate herself so she could return to her chambers. But a wave of exhaustion struck her. She did not even know which wing she was in, nor how to get back to her chambers.

"I'll just close my eyes for a moment," she told herself. Saga leaned back against the headboard. Let her eyes fall shut. Sleep found her mere minutes later.

Kassandr woke to the telltale throb in his skull that told him he'd given too much to his beast—had stayed too long in that form. His muscles ached, his body wrung out, but the scent in his nose had him alert at once. Looking up, he confirmed that his current pillow was, in fact, Saga Volsik's lap.

Everything rushed back.

His Saga had faced him down when his bloodlust was at its worst. She had used the taps and stroked his fur; had eased his pain and discomfort. In the past, the only way to calm him from such a state had involved entrapping him in a bathhouse with sedative herbs applied to the hot rocks. Hours, it sometimes took, before the tranquilizing steam took hold. How had she done it?

His beast stretched in contentment as Kassandr stared up at her face. In sleep, his Saga looked so peaceful. But the ash and dirt coating her face told of long, trying days, as did her gray and torn dress. And yet she was the most beautiful thing he'd ever seen.

Slumped against the headboard, Saga held her neck at an uncomfortable angle. Kassandr lifted his head from her lap and, as gently as he could manage, eased her onto the bed beside him. Her eyelids fluttered, unintelligible mutterings coming from her lips, but his Saga soon settled.

Kassandr placed his bare chest to her back and curled himself around her. One arm draped over her hip, his hand clasped around her wrist. Gods, he could snap this wrist with barely a thought—could have easily killed her last night. She'd been so brave to face him.

Her hair tickled his nose, her scent not quite overpowered by smoke. Inwardly, his beast purred contentedly at her nearness. *Mine,* it said.

Ours, Kass corrected, but paused. Something about that word didn't feel right.

As Saga's rhythmic breathing filled the room, Kassandr probed this strange unease. He pulled a lock of ash-stained hair between his fingers, examining the singed tips. Rov had reported that Saga had exhausted their supplies making fire flasks. She'd tasked Elisava with setting up a healer's station, while she herself had rallied a fire brigade. And apparently, she'd run into the burning stables to free the murderous winged horse. His beast's purrs halted at that, a low snarl rumbling through him.

Kassandr had taken her from Íseldur to keep her safe. But Saga had been in danger for days now—*would be* in danger so long as she remained on the isle of Zagadka.

His unease grew and spread, and his beast released a soft whimper. What was this strangeness? It was a nervous feeling, as though he could not relax. But then the word crystallized in his mind, and Kassandr couldn't shake it.

Regret.

Did he . . . *regret* taking Saga from Íseldur? Immediately, Kassandr rejected the notion. Always, he'd lived his life by intuition—he chose swiftly and decisively, and did not waste time on trifling emotions like regret. There was only forward. Only the future.

Saga rolled over, and reluctantly Kass relented his grip. Her eyelids fluttered open, and she stared at him for a single, sleep-addled moment.

"*Dobroye utro, moya koroleva,**" he said softly.

Saga's blond brows drew together as she pondered the Zagadkian meaning, and it took every shred of his will not to take her into his arms—not to kiss her as he had in those gardens in Sunnavík. She'd done a selfless thing for him last night, and he did not want to frighten her off.

"You are . . . well?" she said in stunted Zagadkian.

He nodded.

She looked at him, a question in her eyes. "It has happened before? Creature . . . troubles?"

With a resigned sigh, Kassandr nodded again. He switched to Íseldurian. "You might notice my animal form differs from others. Not a wolf, but something . . . other. Is rare affliction falling once in generation. And I am lucky recipient." He hoped his sarcasm was obvious.

Saga seemed to ponder his words, her teeth sinking into her soft lower lip. Gods, she was adorable like this, all sleep-mussed and docile. "But you lose control," she said after a minute.

Kassandr's gaze roamed her face. "Aye. My beast is strong. Has great power. But with this strength comes problems. He is . . . difficult to control. But you, Saga, tamed my beast, and for that I am grateful."

* Good morning, my queen.

Her gaze had settled on his chin, and Kassandr wondered what she was thinking. Did she understand now, how he knew of the taps? Did she now see that he, too, was prisoner to his body's response? Kassandr watched curiously as the black of her eyes spread.

"I can do it again." Saga's gaze snapped up to his. "If you wish it, I mean."

His beast gave an appreciative howl, a smile spreading wide on Kassandr's lips. "I wish it."

The moment was broken by a harsh knock at the door which had Kassandr and Saga jolting up. Rovgolod did not wait for permission to enter—the irritating man barged right into the room. Rov's dark eyes jumped from Saga to Kassandr, his brows raising a hair's breadth.

"What is it?" demanded Kassandr, his beast growling in displeasure.

"Siege tower," barked Rov. "The Urkans, they— Behind the sail, they have constructed a siege tower unlike anything I have ever seen. As tall as five men stacked high and covered with iron plates. Battering rams and catapults and cover for a hundred archers."

Kassandr was silent for several long moments, his mind racing in search of a plan. There was a weakness to every weapon. He needed merely to find it. But as he sorted through all the ways they might best an enormous, iron-plated siege tower, he was forced to reckon with an unsettling truth.

They were woefully unprepared for a weapon like this.

It was then that Kassandr knew: The city would fall.

CHAPTER 33

The Western Woods

For Hekla, the days blended together as they traveled through the Western Woods toward the grove housing the second half of the Forest Maiden's consciousness. The forest was dense and thick, the essence of the leech ever-present—from the faint lingering rot that hung in the air to the brittle foliage drained of color. The only sign of animals was the occasional flap of wings. When investigated, more often than not the culprit was a Turned raven with torn, leathery wings. Maddeningly, the ravens only watched with their glowing ember eyes, screeching angrily when Sigrún fired an arrow their way.

To pass the time, Gunnar had taken up Ilías's old role as camp prankster. The snake-like vine he'd left in Thrand's bedroll had drawn the exact response Gunnar had wanted—after sliding into bed, Long Sword had shrieked like a little girl and leaped to his feet. After five minutes had passed with no sign of a serpent, Long Sword's tale had only grown taller.

"As thick as a tree trunk and slimy as an eel," he'd insisted, gesturing to the darkness. "Fortune shines upon me, lads—had it bit me, I'd be food for the ravens." And after that, even Eyvind had taken to shaking out his bedroll at night while Gunnar snickered from behind his flask of brennsa.

Perched on her shoulder, Kritka continued his quest to "bulk up for the winter," gnawing on any provision he could get his paws on while dispensing terrible love advice.

Leaving food in red mate's nest will show that Protector cares, and *females are known on some occasions to perform the mating strut as well. Kritka can show Protector how it is done.*

The Forest Maiden slumbered more often than she was awake, a fact that Kritka attributed to the severe energy drain that came from reshaping the woods. Thrand had added increasingly elaborate modifications to the Forest Maiden's sling—higher sides to act as a windbreak, a pillow made from his spare tunic.

On they walked as their rations dwindled and their blisters grew. Hekla heard the grumbles of Eyvind's men—saw the wariness in their eyes. They'd signed up for a battle, not to traipse endlessly through the woods.

Slowly, the doubts grew in her mind. Was she leading them on a fool's quest? Would the Forest Maiden truly be able to muster creatures to aid in their battle? Would Rey be able to gather enough warriors in Kopa? And how would Silla be able to defeat this vile, parasitic leech that seemed to have infiltrated each plant—each blade of grass—in this forest?

Even Eyvind's laughing hazel eyes grew more somber, though she felt them track her every movement. Felt the words he wished to speak piling up between them. It was impossible not to recall how well the man had learned her body in the span of an evening—even harder to forget the feeling of sharing her innermost secrets with him. Slowly, she felt herself softening to the idea of hearing him out, and the realization terrified her.

Hekla had to remind herself on a daily basis that he'd deceived her the entire time—Eyvind Hakonsson was betrothed to another. The thought drew her ire without fail. Did the fool think she'd never discover it? That Hekla would happily be with him while another woman took his name?

One night, after leaving Kritka to bury his dinner, Hekla headed out to collect firewood. As she walked, she heard Eyvind and Thrand speaking in low tones. It was wrong for her to listen, and yet, she could not help herself.

"I'm giving her space as she's requested, but I can't help feeling like there's something more."

"Perhaps it is time for a grand gesture," Thrand was saying.

Already, Hekla did not like the sounds of it.

Thrand spread his arms wide. "You must write her a poem."

"A poem?" Eyvind's voice was rightfully filled with skepticism.

"Aye. A skaldic rendition to woo the thorniest of roses."

Hekla wrinkled her nose.

"*Fair maiden of the slaughter arm, let me plunder thy golden ring with my battle spear—*"

Eyvind snorted. "Battle spear?"

"One-eyed serpent of the breeches. Boar sword. Hammer of thy seed."

Hekla heard Thrand's soft *oof* as Eyvind landed a blow of some kind. "You'll get me butchered!"

Scowling, Thrand rubbed his shoulder. "I've had great success with my poetry."

Hekla could only imagine what kind of brainless woman would fall for such things. Eyvind's sigh was comically loud, and for a moment, Hekla's lips curved up. But then she remembered the last time she'd overheard these two, when she'd discovered that Eyvind was betrothed.

As though really trying to drive home the point, pain speared up her residual limb. Her pains had grown worse throughout this trek through the woods. It was probably due to her exhaustion, but each stabbing sensation seemed a reminder of all that was at stake, each low throb a reminder of why she'd created her rules in the first place.

No soft sentiments.

Do not spend the night.

And no matter what, she would never again let a man have power over her.

With her thoughts put firmly back into her skull, Hekla kicked off the tree and continued down the trail.

Kritka was curled against her neck when they came across the horde. Hekla's focus was trained on the tree roots along the trail rather than her surroundings. But when she nearly ran into Sigrún's back, and the squirrel's surprise caused him to claw her shoulder, Hekla's senses quickly sharpened.

"What is it?" she whispered, trying to see around their group.

Human draugur, signed Sigrún. *A lot of them.*

Hekla made her way to the front of the line, edging up beside Eyvind. They stood on the forested edge of a cliff, looking out over an endless expanse of pinewoods below.

"Down there," whispered Eyvind, his heated breath on her cheek making her pulse accelerate.

But as Hekla caught motion in the forest below, her heart pounded for a different reason. Slowly, the figures distinguished themselves into a horde of draugur. There were more than a hundred undead men, women, and children moving like ants among the trees.

Hekla's hand slid to the hilt of her sword as she watched the draugur heading south.

"They're unaware of our presence," hissed Thrand, who'd emerged on her other side. The Forest Maiden slumbered peacefully in the sling hanging from the warrior's neck. "This is our chance to take them out," Thrand continued. "To stop them from reaching their destination—"

We must not be diverted, Kritka chattered in Hekla's mind, and she repeated the squirrel's thoughts aloud.

Thrand shifted in agitation. "It has been too many long days spent marching. Too many days of doing nothing."

A whispered chorus of agreements joined him, and the air seemed to thicken with the hunger for battle. Hekla felt it herself—felt her hand tightening once more around her sword's hilt. But she paused. "We cannot afford to lose a single warrior," she told them. "And aside from that, we do not wish to draw the leech's attention onto us."

Group cannot be diverted, said Kritka in her mind.

Hekla forced her grip on her sword to loosen as she repeated the squirrel's orders to the group. She wanted to descend into the valley. Chase down the horde. Spill their foul black blood on the forest floor—

"It is likely a trap," murmured Hekla, trying to shake the battle lust from her mind. "The leech wants to lure us away from our quest."

"And why should we not grant those poor souls the long death?" demanded Thrand.

Hekla scowled at the lout. "We agreed to see this quest through, Long Sword. After we complete our task with the Forest Maiden, you can slay all the draugur your heart desires."

Thrand glanced at the slumbering Forest Maiden and sighed. Then he jostled the warrior to his left. "You heard the woman!"

One by one, the warriors turned away from the horde.

And on they marched.

CHAPTER 34

Kopa, Íseldur

Silla sat at the head of the long table, counting the collective number of beard rings in the room to calm her nerves. Jarls lined the table, heads bowed in quiet conversation, and it was impossible to forget that these were the most powerful men in the north of Íseldur. She'd met them last night; had conversed with many. But in the aftermath of Rey and Atli's confrontation, her nerves were frayed. Did they think her weak for fleeing the hall? Think her a poor judge of character for Rey's outburst?

The ostentatious décor in Jarl Hakon's private meeting hall did not help her nerves. A bronzed human skull glared at her through ruby eyes from a pedestal in one corner of the room, while a bear's hide—complete with taxidermied head—was stretched on the wall behind it.

Last night, bolstered by the crowd and the Shortest Day traditions, she'd felt like Eisa. Today, though, she was back to Silla. And unfortunately, Myrkur fed on her insecurities and further agitated her nerves. She'd tried to explain to Him that she'd made strides in bringing the jarls to "their" cause last night, but the god was unimpressed that they'd not yet bent the knee. Impatience prickled through her body, and He refused to leave her mind to herself.

Rey sighed irritably from beside her, and Silla wholeheartedly agreed. While Atli had taken his seat a few minutes ago—glaring at

Rey through a black eye that made her frown—Jarl Hakon had yet to arrive.

The jarl plays his games of control, whispered Myrkur, making her flinch. *When he arrives you must put him in his place. Shame him for his tardiness to show the others who is truly in charge.*

Silla hated that a part of her agreed with the god. These were Jarl Hakon's plans. She was naught but a figurehead for his schemes, a name the jarls could rally under until Saga took her rightful place. And yet Silla was growing increasingly aware that this was not what *she* wanted. Was it not her duty as a Volsik to play a greater role? She wanted a seat at the table, making decisions that could better the lives of those in this kingdom.

Or did she? Was this ambition truly her own, or did it belong to Myrkur? Confused and rattled, Silla turned to Rey. At the warmth that she felt upon seeing his face, Myrkur hissed and loosened His grip on her spine.

"All right?" asked Rey. He sat to her left, glowering at the skull decor.

"Fine," Silla replied, managing a small smile. "You?" She inclined her head toward Atli, silently asking, *Have you made amends?*

Rey grumbled something unintelligible that made frustration flare in her gut. She had enough on her plate without worrying about his childish grudges.

Silla's knee bounced as she waited for Jarl Hakon's arrival.

Backbone of steel, rang Lady Tala's voice in her ears. *Give them a queen they can believe in.*

But how did she quell her racing heart? How did she stop her palms from sweating? Here sat the northern jarls of Íseldur—those who owned the land and controlled vast warbands to protect it. Their dynasties ran back centuries, their deeds sung by skalds around the kingdom. And then there was her. Silla. A girl raised in poverty. A girl who'd gone to bed with an empty stomach more times than she could count. A girl who'd recently served men, just like these.

They are only men, purred Myrkur. *And they are only mortal.* A sudden hunger grew in the pit of her stomach—the yearning to sit on a throne. To wear a crown. To make the men in this room kneel before her . . .

Rey's hand slid onto her lap, and he squeezed her thigh gently. Myrkur snarled, wings unfurling in agitation. Rey seemed to have a knack for knowing when Myrkur was giving her trouble, and gods, it was lovely to have an ally in this internal fight.

Silla's hand slid beneath his palm and she tangled their fingers together, but before she could say anything, Jarl Hakon finally strolled into the room.

"I see everyone has arrived!" he exclaimed, arms spread wide.

Deep inside her, Myrkur rattled in displeasure, a poisonous dislike for Hakon gliding through her veins. Hakon settled in the high seat to Silla's right, then addressed the room.

"I thank every one of you for braving the winter elements to join us for the feast of the Shortest Day. It was an honor to share my table with you, and I trust that you ate and drank your fill." He planted his hands on the table and leaned forward. "Now we must turn our conversation to the true reason we've come together." Hakon looked at the jarls around the table. "Ivar wages war on the Zagadkians. The timing of this attack, paired with the sudden reappearance of Eisa Volsik, tells me one thing: The gods themselves want us to take Íseldur back."

A chorus of *ayes* spread around the table.

He schemes, muttered Myrkur. *He is an opportunist. He uses the Volsik name for his own gain . . .*

Silla squinted as she tried to focus on the jarl's words.

"Now you've had the opportunity to meet Eisa Volsik; to confirm that she's returned to us," continued Jarl Hakon, gesturing at Silla.

The motion triggered an avalanche of emotions inside her—frustration that she was meant to sit demurely and let this man use her name; yearning for a greater role; anger that she'd let this all happen.

Unaware of her inner turmoil, Hakon continued. "With the Urkans distracted by war, we must act quickly to solidify our northern alliance."

"Where is Jarl Agnar?" asked one of the men—Jarl Holger, if memory served.

Hakon made a sound of irritation. "Killing my people along the eastern border," he muttered. "I've written the boy, have sent emissaries to entreat with him. I even went so far as to offer him a valuable family heirloom as an offering of peace—but he simply *won't* acquiesce. I've stopped trying to understand his motives. They make no sense to me."

Lies, hissed Myrkur.

"My letters did not help, then?" Silla asked.

"If they ever made it," muttered Rey, and Silla could have throttled him.

Atli grumbled something under his breath that drew a fierce glare from Rey. Anger burst to life inside her.

They act like children, whispered Myrkur. *Stand up, Eisa. Take control of this table.*

With a calming breath, Silla pressed on. "I wrote to him thrice. Have you not heard back?"

"Afraid not, Your Highness," said Jarl Hakon, while shooting a pointed look at his heir that seemed to urge him to behave. "It's looking like we cannot count on Agnar to join our alliance."

As silence stretched out in the room, Myrkur coiled ever-tighter. Talons kneaded; anger and frustration built low inside her. How dare these jarls not leap at this chance—not immediately bow to their rightful queen? With a ragged exhale, Silla managed to shake Myrkur's grip.

"Forgive me, Jarl Hakon," said the one named Jarl Holger, "but I'm trying to understand. You're asking us to risk the wrath of Ivar Ironheart to overthrow the Urkans—a feat never before accomplished in any Urkan colony, I might add—"

Jarl Hakon lifted placating hands, silencing the murmurs of agreement with Jarl Holger's statement. "I ask you to stand up for what is right—"

"But the long winters," said one of the jarls. "Our resources are already stretched so thin."

"As are mine with the violence on my eastern borders!" exclaimed Jarl Hakon. "Yet still, I know in my heart—in the very marrow of my bones—that the timing is right. Too long have our people suffered. Too long have the innocents been slain on those pillars. This is our best chance since those bear-worshipping kuntas landed on our shores—"

While I admire his ambition, this man is a threat to your rule, Eisa, whispered Myrkur. *You must speak . . . make these men understand who is truly in charge . . .*

Silla tried to blink Myrkur's suggestions away, and yet His claws sank into her. This time, their grip was firm. Unshakable. She jolted to her feet and stared fiercely into Jarl Hakon's perplexed eyes until he got the message and sat. Anger burned low in Silla's gut, growing and churning with each hammering beat of her heart. The words she and Lady Tala had practiced for so long suddenly seemed entirely too soft. She needed to make these men *understand.*

"The Urkans murdered my parents," Silla began, in a voice of sharp edges. "They stole the throne. They've committed atrocities across this kingdom." Her desire for vengeance grew hotter and higher. "This *cannot* stand. They must pay for what they have done."

Silla looked around the table, meeting each jarl's eye. Her blood sang with the righteousness of this moment. This was her birthright, and she would take it.

More, Eisa, purred Myrkur. *Show them!*

"Jarl Hakon has spoken highly of the honor each and every one of you holds," she continued. "Does your honor not demand vengeance for the deaths of King Kjartan and Queen Svalla? Does your honor not demand King Ivar meet the same fate as my father? We must put him to a pillar, pry back his ribs, and drape his foul lungs from his body."

At the perplexed looks that met her, her voice grew louder.

"And what about the *child* they put to the pillar in my place? If not my parents, then surely that innocent girl, who had seen but four winters, deserves retribution?"

When her statement was followed by silence, Myrkur hissed with displeasure, sending a wave of blistering anger through her. Silla slammed a fist onto the table. The torchlight flickered black for a fraction of a moment, and Jarl Holger recoiled at whatever he saw in her face.

"We have waited long enough! Salvation will not fall into our laps—we must *seize* it for ourselves. Band together against our common enemy in a northern alliance. We will slaughter one of theirs for each life stolen. Blood for blood. Together, we will make them pay!"

As Silla's words registered—as the jarls stared slack-jawed—panic rippled through the wall of incinerating rage. These were not her words. These were *His.* And yet they'd felt so good to speak. Had felt so *right*. Silla sealed her lips shut to prevent more from coming, but her temples throbbed with the need to spill blood—the need to hunt down her enemies and make them pay. She would make it slow . . . make them hurt as they'd hurt her parents . . .

Good, Eisa, whispered Myrkur, wings fluttering gently. *You spoke well.* His approval fulfilled every longing she'd ever had and she yearned for more, thought of every conceivable way she might get it . . .

A warm hand slid into hers, jolting her from her thoughts. Rey pulled her down into her chair, eyes steadily holding hers. She anchored herself in his gaze and in the warmth of his hand. Myrkur hissed, but slowly, gradually, those talons loosened by subtle degrees.

Hakon's nervous laughter met her ears. "What Eisa means to say is that a northern alliance would solidify our friendship and strengthen us all. United against the Urkans, we would be unstoppable."

Through the tension in her skull and the restless fire in her veins, Silla looked around the table, ready to meet the jarls' eager gazes.

They would come to her, one by one. Drop to their knees and pledge fealty. But they only looked at her with skepticism and doubt.

Myrkur snarled in disapproval, and the desire to spill their blood pushed forth once more. She would collect their jarldoms as her own. If they would not bow, then they would *break*. Silla tried to push to her feet, but Rey grabbed her hand and yanked her back down.

"You must understand, Your Highness," said Jarl Holger, glancing apprehensively her way, "I think I speak for every man at this table when I say that a Volsik belongs on the throne. We long to push the Urkans from our kingdom and to restore Íseldur to what it once was. But to do so, we must be careful and clever. And the facts are that without Jarl Agnar, this alliance simply won't work."

Myrkur thrashed about in wrathful indignation, Silla's heart churning madly in her chest.

She glared at Jarl Holger as he turned his gaze on Jarl Hakon. "Agnar controls the ports at Kunafjord, and he has many hundreds of warriors oathsworn to him. Without them, we will be no iron fist of resistance—we will be but an open hand."

His statement hung heavily in the air, several jarls nodding in agreement.

Coward! bellowed Myrkur in her mind. *Fool of a man! We will cut you down first!*

Silla gripped Rey's hand tighter, fighting against the urge to leap to her feet. Throw herself across the table, and squeeze the life from Jarl Holger. She desperately focused on Rey's thumb rubbing circles on the back of her hand. The dark god thrashed deeper, seething.

"Then we need Jarl Agnar." The words came from Rey, and Silla blinked in surprise.

"You have written and sent emissaries?" Holger asked Hakon.

"Aye."

"Perhaps we might try with a more neutral party?"

Jarl Hakon was silent for a thoughtful moment, before his gaze fell on Rey. "What about Rey Galtung—"

"Father," interjected Atli, "you cannot entrust *him* with such a task—the man has the temperament of a bear!"

Children! seethed Myrkur, His anger rising anew. Silla squeezed Rey's hand so tightly he glanced her way. But words were building, and Silla could not hold them back . . .

"Rey will not go," she said tersely. "He's needed here—"

"It does not matter," interjected Rey. She had the sensation he was trying to prevent her from talking, and slowly swiveled her gaze to him. "I've already sent men to the borderlands to entreat with Jarl Agnar."

Schemer! hissed Myrkur, turning His gaze upon Rey. The god's wings flapped violently, spurring her anger back to life. *More secrets! More withheld truths! This man is no ally of ours, Eisa.*

Betrayal and anger and dumbfounded confusion roiled in Silla's blood. She longed to scratch her nails down his skin. Gouge his eyes from his skull. As she turned to Rey, concern flickered in his expression. "You did *what?*"

A muscle in his jaw feathered, but his thumb continued its soft, reassuring circles on the back of her hand. But Silla didn't want to be comforted and she yanked her hand free.

Rey's gaze hardened. "Someone was tampering with your correspondence, so I took it upon myself to determine whether your letters to Jarl Agnar ever arrived. Hef, Kálf, and Erik have gone to investigate, and if possible, I asked them to entreat with him." Rey's hard gaze slid to Jarl Hakon, whose face was slowly turning red. "I mean you no dishonor, Jarl Hakon, but I won't take any risks where Eisa is involved."

The jarl and Rey exchanged sharp words, but Silla was too busy weathering the storm of emotions inside her. She wanted to spill their blood. Wanted to show them that she was no placeholder queen. *Why did he keep this from you, Eisa?* seethed Myrkur. *We cannot amass power with this man at our side!*

Silla closed her eyes, trying to control her rapid breaths, yet the sting of Rey's withheld truth made it difficult.

"It was merely a precaution," Rey said carefully. She sensed his gaze on her, but was too angry to meet it. "I was only planning to tell you if they discovered something of concern."

She homed in on his words. Tried to drag them into her mind. *He did not want to burden us,* she told Myrkur. *He did it to protect us.* But the god only snarled, rejecting the notion.

"Well." It was Holger's voice, from the opposite end of the table. "It seems we shall have to wait to hear Agnar's response."

"Which means," said Rey, "we can turn our attentions to another matter of urgency."

Stand up, Eisa! screamed Myrkur. *Let me in and we'll show them . . .*

Silla could not open her eyes. Could only breathe through Myrkur's displeased tantrum. She did not trust herself not to stand and unleash a verbal tirade like before.

Silla sensed Rey standing. Addressing the table. "An enemy gathers in the Western Woods," he began, but she tuned him out. Placed a chasm between her and this room. *Stop him,* hissed Myrkur. Anger and bitterness burned inside her. Frustration and the thinnest thread of fear that these mortals would ruin all her plans.

Distantly, she heard Rey detailing everything that was happening in the Western Woods. The leech draining life from the trees, using it to create spawn in the form of undead creatures. He told of the empty village and the draugur being mustered to a place called Rökksgarde. He told them of the Forest Maiden's awakening and her prophecy of a battle in the heartwood. "And so," he concluded, "we ask for warriors to join us in the woods to do battle on the next full Marra. We'll need to depart no later than eight days from now."

"Forgive me." Jarl Holger chuckled nervously. "Surely you did not just tell us—"

"That a poisonous mist is turning the good citizens of Íseldur into the restless dead?" Rey laughed caustically. "Yes."

Speak, Eisa, pleaded Myrkur, sending a visceral wave of anger that had her gasping. *Let me in!*

As she sensed the room's attention, her eyes fluttered open, only to find the jarls exchanging wary glances. Inside her, Myrkur clawed, trying to regain control, and it took all her might not to scream with rage.

Her fingers itched to wrap around Rey's throat and squeeze. To show him what she thought of his keeping secrets from her. But a servant suddenly burst into the room.

"F-fire!" he exclaimed. "Fire in the hall! We must evacuate now!"

The words hung in the air for a moment before pandemonium broke out. Jarls leaped to their feet, jostling for the door, while the scent of smoke grew more potent by the second. Cries of alarm flowed in from the hallway, but for the first time since this cursed meeting had started, Silla felt a wave of relief. She could get out of here. Regain control of herself.

Myrkur thrashed about, screaming in rage. Rey, thank the gods, was at her elbow, calmly pulling her toward the exit. At least one person in this room had some sense in their head.

But even amid the tumult—even amid Myrkur's angry rantings—Silla retained enough clarity of mind to know one thing for certain.

Today's meeting had been an utter disaster.

Silla's wool-wrapped sword flashed through the air in the sparring yard, yet it did little to quell her frustrations. The fire in Ashfall Fortress—caused when a serving thrall had knocked over a candle—was extinguished before extensive damage could be done, but the meeting with the jarls had been canceled. Jarl Hakon had rescheduled for the next day, tersely urging Silla to rest and regroup. What he hadn't spoken aloud was written plainly enough across his face.

Her performance at that meeting had been reprehensible.

Thankfully, after an hour of conspiratorial rants that had her pacing restlessly, Myrkur had seemed to wear Himself out. Now she sensed Him curled low inside her, dark wings tucked in tight. Yet the restless energy persisted inside Silla. She could not shake how Myrkur had shaped and molded her words in that hall. The things she'd said—the things she'd *felt*—haunted her. The god of chaos was doing what He did best, causing strife and unrest among the mortals, and she was furious with herself for letting Him control her like that.

A cry from above had Silla craning her neck, shielding her eyes from the winter sun's glare. Her stomach hollowed out when she saw it—perched high on a spire sat that gods damned black hawk.

"Get out of here!" she shouted, waving her sword in the air. "Leave me alone, you wretched creature!"

Boots crunched in the snow behind her, and Silla whirled to find Rey approaching. And based on his expression, he'd seen the entire exchange.

"What?" Silla pushed a stray lock of hair from her face and sent him a challenging look. "I'm not mad!"

"I said no such thing."

"I can see it in your eyes, *Reynir.* You think I'm unfit, just like those jarls!"

Rey stepped closer to grip her elbows. "I do not think you're unfit, and neither do the jarls—"

"He manipulated me," she whispered frantically, burying her face in his tunic. "He pulled on my emotions . . . whispered things in my ear. I cannot do this, Rey—I cannot live like this!"

"I know. We must renew our search for a cure."

How? she wanted to scream. Her search for a cure had taken her through countless books—had rendered the Weaver comatose and had cost Fallgerd's life. Silla had exhausted every avenue she could think of and was running out of hope.

Rey's arms were a reassuring weight as he held her to him. But Silla wasn't ready to let him soften her anger. She wanted to bathe in the flames of her burning wrath. Wanted to break and burn things to the ground. Silla shook free from his grip and pointed the wool-wrapped tip of her sword to the middle of his chest.

"Spar with me," she challenged. Rey pursed his lips as he stared at the sword, then leveled her with a hard look.

"Very well."

Silla paced restlessly as Rey wrapped his sword, and when he turned, his face was set in grim determination. Warmth fluttered deep inside her, and for a moment, she was back in the snowy yard of their shield-home—before everything had gotten so gods damned complicated.

"I won't apologize for sending those men to Jarl Agnar," said Rey, surging forward. Silla parried his blow, glad that her restless emotion was finally channeled into something.

"I will *never* apologize when it comes to your safety, Silla." Rey ducked under her lashing sword, then delivered an upward swing in return. She blocked it without a heartbeat to spare.

Rey leaned between their locked swords. "I have already proven I'm willing to kill, to torture, to do whatever dark deeds I must to keep you safe. You'll just have to get used to that."

"Stubborn man," she muttered, shoving him back and finding her stance.

Rey's eyes burned like the hottest embers of a fire. "For you, always."

"Always," she repeated. The word felt somehow heavier than all the rest, as though it held meaning. As though he'd almost named this thing they'd been dancing around for some time.

Capitalizing on her momentary distraction, Rey drove forward in a vicious series of blows. Her sword fell to the ground, and Silla was left ducking and dodging, looking for an opening. She saw it when he drew up short—the fool of a man feared hurting her. With a shout, she threw herself at him, tackling him around the waist.

Silla knew he let her take him down to the ground, but she was too far gone to care. Rey landed hard, and though he'd retained his grip on his weapon, Silla pinned his sword arm beneath her knee. She straddled his upper chest, and the position sent heat blazing through her.

"Stupid sparring sessions in Kalasgarde," Silla muttered. Her body now seemed to confuse sparring practice as the precursor to something altogether different. And based on Rey's smoldering eyes, it had the same effect on him.

Silla's moment of victory was short-lived. The air shuddered with magic, and a thin ribbon of smoke peeled up from Rey's palms. The smoke slithered toward her, coiled along her arm, and caressed her shoulder.

"Cheater!" she accused, writhing as the smoke prickled the sensitive skin on the back of her neck.

"Opportunist," he said cheerfully.

She squealed as the smoke delved down the collar of her jacket. And then everything happened quickly. Heat surged into her body. The taste of smoke burst on her tongue. And suddenly, the ribbons of smoke were pouring from *her* palms.

Rey's eyes widened. "What—"

The heat guttered out, and the smoke evaporated into thin air. Silla felt hollow—felt empty. She blinked at her palms in astonishment. Where had it gone? What had that been?

Her eyes met Rey's as he stared at her in wonder. "What was that?"

Yes, purred Myrkur, opening one eye and peering up. *What was that?*

"I felt—" Ignoring the god, she stared at her hands, the heat of Rey's smoke lingering in her veins. "—*You.*"

Confusion marred Rey's expression, but Silla was consumed with giddy excitement and her mouth crashed into his in a fierce kiss. He hummed, lips moving against hers as he kissed her right back. But he rolled them with a sudden burst of energy, and then it was Silla pinned to the ground, with Rey straddling her hips.

"Explain," he ordered.

Silla bit down on her lip, momentarily distracted by that stern voice of his. Her anger had burned out, leaving something more smoldering.

"You took it, didn't you?" continued Rey. "My galdur—it was as though it was suddenly siphoned straight from my blood."

Silla nodded. "I do not understand it. You were tickling me with your smoke, and I desperately wanted to get away, and then . . . then suddenly it was in *my* veins." She stared up at him. "It feels so different from my own . . . so hot and . . . and I tasted smoke . . ."

"You've done it before," said Rey. "When I had you restrained in the bed. Do you recall? You freed yourself from my smoke, and I did not understand it—"

"Kaeja!" exclaimed Silla. "In the sparring yard, when I escaped her Harefoot speed, she called me a *thief.* I thought she meant I'd stolen you, but now—" Silla's mind careened wildly. Could it truly be?

It was Rey who finally voiced it aloud. "You can pull galdur from more than mere halda stones." He looked up at her reverently. "You can pull it from human Galdra. Perhaps you can pull it from all of the Ashen."

Myrkur chuckled, yet it was quiet. Smothered. The god was exhausted, which meant this was the perfect time to investigate this curiosity.

Rey climbed to his feet and offered her a hand up, a wicked gleam in his eye.

"Do it again."

CHAPTER 35

Sunnavík, Íseldur

Hunched over his plate, Jonas bit into a chicken leg and pretended he was not surrounded by murderers and rapists. During his time as a so-called member of the Corpse Bringers, he'd made a point of keeping his head down, and he always sat alone. The last thing he wanted was to get to *know* these people. He was merely biding his time until he could escape this vile warband.

Warband. The concept was a farce. This was no gathering of common minds—no brotherhood like the Bloodaxe Crew. This was a collection of the worst of Íseldur, forced together and prevented from leaving. But Jonas wouldn't let the barred windows and dour-looking guards keep him from breaking free from this place. Sooner or later, he'd find a way out.

After picking the chicken bone clean, Jonas sopped up the juices on his plate with a heel of bread. At the very least, the fare here was better than Sigrún's shite cooking. When dining in the garrison hall, it was impossible to tell there was a grain shortage. But it was no secret that the riots in Sunnavík had worsened, the death toll climbing higher this week.

King Ivar was not terribly popular among his people. Any hopes of a quick victory in Zagadka had been quashed; and any hopes that the fleet would return to Íseldur with boatloads of Zagadkian grain were long gone. Word was, the king had settled in for a siege, leaving his kingdom without provisions for the winter. Jonas was no ruler, but even he knew it wasn't the wisest move.

Movement to his right had Jonas lifting his head. Straggly blond hair and a patchy beard had his eyes playing tricks on him once more. For a moment, it was Ilías approaching—Ilías with a tray clutched in bruised hands. The din of the dining hall fell away as Jonas's heart grew wings. But then the light shifted, and the warrior's likeness with it. Jonas's cursed heart crashed into his rib cage.

It was the young warrior who'd been imprisoned in the cell next to his.

Jonas's despair was so crushing it left him breathless and blinking at his plate as he tried to gather himself. How could this keep happening? How could he have let himself believe, even for a second? Ilías was *gone.* Jonas would never see him again.

He schooled his face into a scowl as the young warrior set his bowl on the long table and climbed onto the bench across from him. The man's eye was swollen shut, his face mottled with bruises.

"Jonas, isn't it?" asked the man. "I'm Freki." He extended a hand, but Jonas only stared at it.

How this warrior had escaped death during his trial for the Corpse Bringers, Jonas did not quite know. All he could say was that what Freki lacked in bulk, he made up for in speed. He'd been able to lure the undead creatures away from one another and had used a board pried loose from the dais to bludgeon them. The arena had fallen as silent as night as Volund had reluctantly welcomed the young man into the Corpse Bringers.

But Freki had not fared so well in Volund's fighting games. When he was pitted against the brutish Horfi, not a single warrior among them had wagered on Freki, and they'd all been proven right. Jonas had forced himself to watch, and now he relived the vile brutality, staring at the ruins of Freki's face.

Rolling his lips together, Jonas dropped the last of his bread onto his plate. He could not be seen with this warrior. Could not afford to offer even a shred of kindness. Wordlessly, Jonas pushed to his feet, then hesitated. He planted his hands on the table, holding Freki's pitiful gaze. The young warrior's good eye widened, and he recoiled in fear.

"Let me give you some advice," Jonas said in a low voice. "You see an opportunity to escape, you take it. Get out of this place before they kill you."

And with that, he stalked out of the garrison hall to return to his lodgings. The winter sun had long since set, and torches lighting the hallway were sparse, so Jonas did not see the man until he stepped from the shadows.

"Jonas Svik?"

Jonas frowned, eying the wasp sigil on the man's crimson livery. "Who asks?"

"The queen requests your presence."

He folded his arms over his chest, irritation prickling through him. "For what reason?"

The messenger bristled. "That is the queen's business." He turned on his foot, gesturing for Jonas to follow.

But Jonas hesitated. His bitterness toward the queen had not yet softened. Because of *her*, he was in this hellish place. She'd refused to hear him out that day at the pier. Some part of him wanted to punish her right back. Yet as the messenger's shadow vanished down the corridor, Jonas sighed. Deep down, he knew he had little choice in obeying the queen's command, and so after a moment, he followed with long strides.

They exited the garrison hall and made their way across the sparring grounds. On the opposite end, a pair of burly warriors guarding the doors to Askaborg proper stepped aside, allowing them entry.

Jonas had to remind himself to close his mouth as he gazed at the luxurious tapestries and intricate stonework on the castle walls—a far cry from the cold, utilitarian garrison hall. His mind whirled in search of a reason for the queen's summons. What could she possibly have to say to him? They walked for several silent minutes until at last they paused before a large oak door.

Jonas's feet faltered as the door swung inward, revealing a cavernous space. A high, vaulted ceiling was supported by arched pillars, but more startling was the fact that it was all white and gold—from the marble floor and dual, gilded hearths to the cream draperies and ivory furs in each corner.

The lone disruption in this sea of white and gold was the figure in mourning black, seated by the largest of the hearths. Queen Signe held a goblet between long, slender fingers, as she regarded him blandly.

Jonas trailed the messenger toward the queen, his unease growing with every step. On the battlefield, he was in his element. But here, before the queen, Jonas was acutely aware of all his shortcomings—the sweat and grime clinging to his skin, the tear in his breeches, and his unkempt beard.

Signe lounged in a gown of black silk, her white-gold braids woven into a steel crown of claws. The queen's gaze lifted to Jonas, and she studied him in silence.

"You're meant to bow," hissed the messenger as the queen's brows lifted expectantly.

Though his instincts protested—this woman was the cause of his current misery—Jonas forced himself to bow low in deference. As he straightened, he examined the queen's pale face. Jonas considered himself a master at reading women, but this one—this *queen*—was completely inscrutable.

"Sit," said the queen, gesturing to the seat opposite her own.

Reluctantly, Jonas did as she bade, hoping the filth on his leathers didn't mar her pristine furs. Signe waved two fingers in the air. A cupbearer rushed forward and poured wine into a goblet, and all the while, the queen's unnerving gaze never left Jonas's face.

"Jonas Svik," she murmured, once the cupbearer had left. "Do I make you uncomfortable?"

"No." He held her gaze, trying desperately to prove her wrong.

But her lips curved into a smile that did not reach her eyes. "Liar."

Jonas took a sip from his goblet, then blinked. The few samplings of wine he'd tasted in his life had been acidic and sour. But this one played across his tongue like a hundred splendid musical notes.

"It's good, isn't it? One of the few good things to come from our

Zagadkian *friends.*" There was no disguising the queen's sarcasm in the last word.

Jonas wasn't certain if he was meant to answer, and so he let his eyes roam to the gilded fireplace. *How many sólas would the grating fetch?* he couldn't help but wonder.

"You have talent on the sparring grounds."

Jonas's gaze snapped back to the queen, that foolish, impulsive bow rushing back to the forefront of his mind. He'd let his anger get the best of him that day in the pits, and now, he felt a moment of regret. "My thanks," he said woodenly.

The queen took a sip, then set her goblet down. "Word of your prowess reached me from Volund, so I came to see for myself. Imagine my surprise when I realized you were the same man who cost me Svangormr Pass."

Jonas's hands tightened around the arms of his chair as he struggled to hold the words back—to explain that they'd *had* Eisa Volsik when the avalanche had struck.

"I wrote to Kaptein Ulfar," she said casually, yet he felt her studying his every move, his every reaction. "I understand you came to him in Kopa. That you told him you *knew* the pair we sought."

The birchbark etching of Reynir Bjarg and Silla Nordvig—*Eisa Volsik,* he corrected himself—flashed in his mind. "Aye."

"The kaptein expressed his doubts in your story."

"Kaptein Ulfar is an incompetent fool," snapped Jonas, then closed his eyes in regret.

He braced himself for a reprimand, but was met instead with soft laughter. "Aye, but he is," said the queen. "I had him flayed and left for the wolves." She sipped her wine casually, as though she hadn't just uttered the most hair-raising thing Jonas had ever heard. The queen's eyes locked onto his, sending a jolt straight through him. "Do you know how *hard* it is to find competent people?"

Jonas wasn't certain if he was meant to answer. He held the queen's gaze, and for the first time in years, he felt faint traces of fear.

The queen continued, unperturbed. "I've been thinking, Jonas, that perhaps in my anger, I was rash to dismiss you. What say you to that?"

Jonas swallowed. "I would say you are a wise and humble queen."

"Humble?" The queen laughed. "It might be the first time I've ever been called such a thing. Drink, Jonas." Signe nodded at his goblet.

Jonas took a large, nerve-calming gulp.

"Tell me, warrior, do you truly know her?" The queen's gaze had an eager edge to it. "Eisa Volsik."

The wine in Jonas's stomach soured at the name. "I thought I did."

Signe's white-gold brows rose as she leaned forward in her chair. "Tell me everything."

Jonas hesitated, reaching for his wine. Some part of him knew he stood on a threshold; that he could walk away from this meeting and find an opportunity to escape. Jonas could put this all behind him. Start fresh. But the pendant hung heavily beneath his collar, his grandfather's words ringing loudly in his ears.

Family, respect, duty.

And so, after a long draught of his wine, Jonas began. He told the queen a brief version of it all, starting with the woman who'd climbed into the Bloodaxe Crew's wagon. He paused to collect himself as he detailed her role in his brother's death, and finally, Jonas ended with the avalanche that had nearly taken his life.

By the time he was done, the queen's eyes had sharpened to deadly points. "She cost you your brother." The queen unexpectedly leaned forward, taking Jonas's hand in hers. "*You* understand." She paused for a moment. "I lost my Yrsa to Saga Volsik."

Jonas squeezed the queen's hand in gentle reassurance. Of all the people in Íseldur he might feel a sense of kinship with, Queen Signe was the last he'd guess. "I do understand."

The queen slipped her hand back, then got to her feet. Her black skirts swished on marble as she paced back and forth. "The Volsik sisters are heartless *monsters.*"

"Aye, but they are."

“So . . . kind and *caring* on the surface,” continued Signe. “But it’s only a ruse. Beneath it, they are cold, selfish beasts who take and take and *take.* They think of no one but themselves.”

Jonas had been numb for so long that the anger licking in his chest was disorienting. “Exactly.”

The queen paused as her gaze met his. “I know we’ve just met, Jonas, but I feel a sort of kinship with you—we have so much in common. Can I trust you?”

“Aye.”

“This must not leave this room.”

“It won’t.”

The queen licked her lips. “There are those in Íseldur who support the Volsik sisters. These supporters are like weeds, growing in each corner of the kingdom. But they do not know how many hands I have to pluck them.” A malevolent smile curled Signe’s lips. “Eisa is in Kopa, trying to rally the jarls of the north against my husband. But she does not know I have a spy in her midst, reporting her every pitiful attempt.”

Jonas’s heart thumped in his chest as excitement churned through his blood.

But the queen’s smile fell. “Eisa is slippery as an eel, as you’ve discovered. Already, she’s escaped three attempts on her life. Tell me, Jonas. Tell me what you know of her. Give us some edge that we might use against her.”

Jonas reached for his goblet and took a hearty drink. And then he told the queen everything he knew.

CHAPTER 36

Kovograd, Zagadka

The night Saga soothed Kassandr's beast was the first in a stretch of many. By day, Kassandr pushed himself to his limits on the battlefield, giving, as he said, "too much to his beast." This meant that by night, he was trapped in his beast form, dangerous and impossible to control. The thought of abandoning him was abhorrent at best, and so Saga came to soothe him. They lay on the bed and she tapped his shoulder, singing softly until he fell into slumber, or shifted back into human form.

At first, Saga tried to justify her actions to herself as returning a favor. Kassandr, after all, had helped her through her panic on many occasions. But at some point, her reasons ceased to matter. Her feet simply carried her to his room; her mind was too exhausted to fight against it. What did anything matter, when tomorrow might be their last?

This was now the fourth consecutive night that Saga found herself standing at Kassandr's closed door. It was silent inside. A strange combination of smoke and cabbage soup clung to Saga's skin, and her muscles screamed with exhaustion. A day spent scurrying from one task to the next was a far cry from her usual pastimes—reading and drawing and keeping to the shadows. Amid a siege, the shadows were simply not an option. There was always something to do, be it ladling cabbage soup or grinding poultice herbs. And there was always someone coming to her with questions. Saga still wanted to laugh when they looked at her as though she had the answers. But to her great surprise, she often did have *something* to tell them. And each time she helped mitigate a problem, her budding sense of pride grew a little larger.

Midmorning, thick gray clouds had rolled over the city and sent flurries of snow down upon them. It had been a blessing in disguise for the Zagadkians, as the snow melted and soaked the hides and seaweed draped on Kovograd's fortress and city walls anew.

"Old Man Winter has come to our aid," a kitchen worker had proclaimed.

Indeed, the Urkans had pulled back on their relentless warfire assault as the snow dampened the fire's effectiveness. This had allowed those sheltering within the fortress walls a moment to breathe. But only a moment, and then they shifted their focus to healing and feeding the constant stream of cold and injured warriors. Each time a new figure limped through the doorway, Saga had searched for a familiar set of green eyes. Yet the entire day had passed and there'd been no sign of Kassandr.

Her hand now hovered over the latch, the need to know if he was all right prickling through her. With a quick breath, Saga opened the door.

The room was lit, everything precisely as it had been that morning. Unbidden, Saga approached the bed. Ran her hand along the furs. He should be here by now. Had harm befallen him?

"Where are you, Kassandr?" she whispered, the knots in her stomach tightening.

The logical part of her reminded Saga the foolish man had stolen her and brought this danger to his kingdom. But the illogical part of her could think only of how dim the world would feel without him.

Saga sank onto the bed, closing her eyes, as his scent surrounded her.

It wasn't a few minutes later that a growl shook the fortress walls. Saga's spine straightened in recognition. The menacing sounds grew nearer, men's shouting voices joining in. And before Saga knew what was happening, Kassandr's beast form was shoved into the room, that vile snare looped around his neck. The snare released him, then the door slammed shut. Her heart hammered violently as the latch slid into place.

And then Saga was alone with the Beast of Zagadka. He bayed and snarled, throwing his enormous body against the locked door. She knew she ought to be afraid, but the only emotion Saga felt was relief.

He was *alive*.

The beast grew suddenly preternaturally still, and she knew he'd sensed her.

"Kassandr?" she said softly, and his shaggy, snarling maw whipped toward her. "Come here. Let me help you."

A low whine came from deep within his chest, and this time, he needed no convincing. His gnarled claws tapped the floor as he hobbled toward her, and as he neared, she gasped. Blood matted his fur, and not all of it was from his enemies.

"You're injured," said Saga. The beast climbed onto the bed, smearing red across the fine blankets as he crawled toward her. As though he'd used his last vestiges of strength, Kassandr collapsed, the full weight of his head landing hard on her lap. His muscles spasmed, and he flinched as though in pain. But tonight, there was more than his anger and pain. There was a profound sense of weariness that made it clear today's battle had been hard.

Saga's fingers drifted to the joint of his shoulder, and she began the rhythmic taps while humming softly. Gradually, Kassandr's muscles eased, and she sensed his humanity drifting back. And after some time had passed, the air suddenly shuddered. Kassandr's spines and claws retracted, fur transitioning to smooth human flesh. Soon a very naked Kassandr Rurik lay on the bed.

Saga blinked, then averted her gaze, though the sight of him was imprinted on the backs of her eyelids. Curled on his side, Kassandr's limbs were long, his shoulders broad, and every inch of him looked hardened from hours with a sword in hand. Saga's hands flexed with the urge to skim her fingertips through the dusting of dark hair on his firm, golden chest. Yet somehow, she managed to keep them to herself.

"My Winterwing," murmured Kassandr, rolling on his back and staring up at her. "Once more, you have come to my rescue." The man was completely exposed to her—and utterly unbothered.

Against her better judgment, Saga snuck another glance. But rather than what was between his legs, her gaze snagged on the countless wounds along his arms and torso.

"You're hurt!" Saga shimmied out from beneath him, then fetched a pitcher of water from the sideboard. "Come here," she ordered, patting the edge of the bed.

"*Yesli moya koroleva potrebuyet etogo,**" purred Kassandr, rising up on his knees and—

Saga slammed her eyes shut. "Gods above, Kassandr. Cover yourself, I beg of you."

"Is not kind of begging I hoped for, but I will obey all the same."

Saga's cheeks were on fire as the mattress moved and fabric rustled.

"I am covered," said Kassandr.

Hardly, Saga wanted to scoff as she took in the loose breeches belted at his waist. She approached, dipping a scrap of linen into the water jug. Slowly, she stepped between his spread legs. Her skin buzzed at his nearness, her heart pounding at the expanse of bare chest before her. For a single, dizzying moment, she imagined what that bare chest might feel like pressed against her own. How the weight of him might feel atop her. But his wounds were seeping, and she quickly dabbed at one with the linen. Her fingers grazed dangerously close to the place on his chest she'd imagined touching just moments before, sending her heart beating in sharp, fast strikes. Saga glanced up at Rurik, and could tell from his tired smile that he could hear her racing heart.

"What happened today?" she asked, to divert his attention from her body's foolish response.

* If my queen demands it.

"City walls have fallen." Kassandr's voice was uncharacteristically flat, and Saga did not like it one bit. "Urkan siege tower is . . ." He shook his head. "Impossible. Their archers pick off my warriors while hiding behind the iron plates. Is dishonorable way to fight."

She swallowed, dabbing at a nasty wound on the thickest part of his shoulder. "And King Ivar?"

Kassandr harrumphed. "It is said he fights with bodyguards always around him, but I have not yet seen. Please, Saga, tell to me of your day. I do not wish to think of battle. I want only to hear your voice."

Her eyes lifted to meet his, and Saga was suddenly feverishly hot. How easy it would be to drop the cloth to the ground. To slide onto the bed and pull him over her. Saga's gaze fell to his lips, and it was as though a string in her belly grew taut, urging her forward. Somehow, she caught herself before she did something reckless.

"I served cabbage soup for hours." Saga tore her eyes away from his lips, but they only landed on his chin. Kassandr hadn't shaven in days, and Saga was disappointed to find that her favorite cleft was now buried beneath the beginnings of a beard.

"I can smell so," said Kassandr.

"What?" asked Saga, ripping her gaze upward.

"I can smell the soup on you."

Saga scowled at him as she dipped the linen into the pitcher, then squeezed it out.

"Do not worry, always it has been my favorite of meals," Kassandr quipped. "To me, you smell delicious."

Saga prattled on. "I had the fortress stores restocked before—" *Before the city walls fell,* she did not say. "I can assure you, Kovograd Fortress has enough *medovukha* to last five years."

"You do not know how we Zagadkians can hold our drink," teased Kassandr. "I am certain it will not last so long as you think."

Because the fortress will fall, Saga thought grimly, *and all the* medovukha *with it.* She bit down on her lip, focusing on cleaning a long, shallow cut along Kassandr's side.

"I am glad," he said in a rough voice, "you came to me so many nights. It seems you alone can tame my beast. He slumbers now, right here." Kassandr tapped the center of his chest with two fingers.

"I'm glad as well," she said softly. "Has it caused you . . . troubles? Your beast?" Saga cringed, her skin prickling with remorse. "I'm sor—"

"Many times."

Her gaze darted up, locking on his vibrant green eyes. But where she so often found a certain wildness, she now saw something softer. Vulnerable, perhaps. Maybe this is what prompted her to press on.

"What I saw in the red room, with your father." Saga wasn't sure quite how to phrase it. "Are you often punished for your . . . nature?"

His sigh was long and weary. "When I was a child, yes. My animal form and disposition were not what my father wished for in a son. He thought my beast could be tamed by Kresimir's whip."

Saga abandoned her linen, staring at him in horror. "Your *father* is the beast," she said venomously. "What a horrible thing to do to your own son. And your mother? Where was she through all this?"

He cocked his head to the side, as though her reaction was not what he'd expected. "My mother died when birthing Elisava, long before my nature became large problem. During those years, my father was wed to Oleg's mother, who—" He sighed, his gaze growing distant. "—who lost no sleep worrying on me."

"It was wrong." Saga gripped the cloth tightly. "All of it. You cannot help your nature."

For the first time since she'd arrived in Zagadka, she was filled with a sense of shame for her actions. "I'm sorry."

"Is no fault of yours."

"Not for your horrible father, Kassandr, for my . . . *reaction* to you." Her brows pulled together. "You have always seen me for who I am and I . . . I reciprocated in a rather shameful way."

He smiled sadly. "Is not unusual. But now I think—" He paused. "—I *hope* you have seen my beast will never harm you."

Saga nodded, then swayed on her feet.

Kassandr's fingers dug into her hips—when had they landed

there? "I think you, too, are very tired, my Winterwing." He pulled her closer, and she placed steadying hands on his shoulders. What would happen if she leaned a little closer? Pressed her lips to his?

"Kassandr," she said, caught somewhere between a protest and a plea.

"Shh," he said, burying his nose in the crook of her neck. "Let me hold you. Just for a minute."

A wet slap told Saga the linen she'd used to clean his wounds had fallen to the floor. She leaned into his touch, arms sliding around his neck. Saga let herself forget all the horrors of the past days and relented to a moment of comfort. With his arms around her, with his face buried in her neck, she felt safe; felt cherished; felt for one moment like everything would be all right.

Saga did not protest as Kassandr lifted her in his arms and set her down on the bed, nor when he arranged himself behind her. Her eyelids were so heavy. Saga was asleep within a minute.

The next day, Saga winced as a kerchiefed woman tended a burn on her forearm. The healers had taken over in the fortress great hall, rows of pallets filling the central space. Four enormous wooden statues of their seasonal gods watched over the wounded while silken tapestries glinted from the walls.

Looking around the room made Saga want to cry. People were dying—lives irrevocably changed—all because of the explosion she'd caused back in Íseldur. Yes, Kassandr had taken her against her will; yes, she'd been prevented from speaking with the Urkans. But still this guilt festered, as did the desperate need to put things right, no matter what—

She tried to stop these thoughts in their tracks, and it was a great comfort to Saga that she didn't have to look far in this room to find hope. It was there in each small corner of the great hall, where those who could not fight found ways to help. One group worked to cut and sterilize linens for use as bandages. Others clustered around an enormous pestle, grinding herbs and birch bark for poultices. Still others slipped about the room, providing food and waterskins to anyone in need. So many Zagadkians had stepped up, no matter how unglamorous the task.

The healer prodded her wound once more, and Saga clenched her teeth against the pain. She'd lost count of how many errant sparks had singed her skin since the Urkans had invaded. But this wound was far worse than a rogue ember. With the city walls fallen, the siege tower now steadfastly lumbered through the streets toward the fortress. Word had carried that Kassandr's warriors held it at midtown, but it was little comfort. The catapult atop the siege tower was within range of the fortress walls.

Now, rather than the small firepots flung by the ship-bound trebuchets, they had to contend with enormous explosive barrels. The one responsible for Saga's wounds had landed near the field kitchens, where she'd been shoveling soup into her mouth. Bodies had flown, leaving people writhing in agony while trying to extinguish their burning clothes.

Saga knew she was lucky to have been shielded from the worst of it. Yet still, she gritted her teeth as the healer pried out the fibers seared into the wound.

"What is it between you and my brother?" asked Elisava in slow Zagadkian, emerging from the shadows between the statues of Old Man Winter and the Spring Maiden. In recent days, Elisava had forgone her elegant brocade jackets in favor of a simple linen kaftan belted over breeches.

"Nothing." Saga said this as much to Elisava as to herself, as a reminder. Yes, she'd been sharing his bed, but it had been out of convenience. And if this lie was flimsy, Saga refused to acknowledge it.

Elisava's arched brow told Saga she didn't believe it, either. "Between us cannot be anything," Saga said, putting steel in her voice.

She felt Elisava's curious gaze on her skin. "Why?"

"He stole me!" Saga exclaimed, hissing as the startled healer ripped the garment from her wound. Despite her conflicting feelings toward the man, she could never forget that he'd lured her from her cage, only to entrap her in a new one. Even if deep down she knew it was not so simple as that.

But Elisava only sighed. "Kassandr has always been . . . overbearing in his caring. His meaning is right, but his methods are not."

It was mad to speak of such things with the dead and dying all around them; with the growing inevitability of what was to come. As the siege tower inched closer to the fortress walls, it was no longer a question of if, but when, they too would fall.

The healer was now packing a cooling blend of herbs and honey against the wound, and Saga felt relief from the itching burn for the first time in hours. "Forgive me." Saga exhaled as the healer wrapped strips of clean linen around her arm and tied them in place. "I am tired."

An explosion rocked the keep, shouts tearing from the courtyard. More and more barrels had landed beyond the fortress walls, where the citizens of Kovograd now sheltered from the Urkans. Saga had tried long and hard not to think of what fate would befall them when the walls fell, but now it was impossible not to. Everyone in this fortress would be killed or worse, and Elisava . . . Saga glanced at Kassandr's sister, whose eyes were wide with fear. Would this beautiful, headstrong woman be taken as Bjorn's bride? Forced to watch as her family was slaughtered? Broken down as her kingdom was unmade, stone by stone.

Saga wouldn't wish what she'd endured upon her greatest enemy. Watching everything her mother and father had worked for in Íseldur torn away; each kind face she'd grown to love in the palace slaughtered for sport; Ivar's men mimicking the pleas of Saga's mother as she'd begged for her life . . .

Wrath built low in Saga's chest, and she wrenched free from the healer's grasp. Outdoors, mayhem was unfolding, the toll of bells joining the din. And it was here, amid the tumult, that Saga had a moment of clarity. She would not allow this to be Elisava's fate. She knew what she had to do.

Saga pushed to her feet, then faced the Zagadkian princess. "Do fiery pots remain?" But Elisava's face had drained of color, her green eyes wide and shining. "Fire flasks, Elisava!" repeated Saga, in sharp Zagadkian.

Elisava seemed to come back to herself. She reached into her pocket and pulled out a small, stoppered flask. "If they tried to take me . . ." Elisava could not finish, but Saga understood well enough. A fiery death was far preferable to falling into the Urkans' hands. With a hard exhale, Elisava placed the flask in Saga's palm and folded her fingers around it. "You must take it. I will find another."

Saga met Elisava's gaze and swallowed. "My thanks." She blinked furiously. "You were kind. I—I wanted to have longer together. Tell your brother—"

"Saga," said Elisava, eyes widening, "what do you intend to do with that flask?"

Saga slid the fire flask into her pocket. "What I must."

And with that, she turned on her heel. Let her feet carry her through the corridors. Saga's mind pulled the details she'd overheard between Rov and a wounded wolf shifter. A postern—a back exit to the fortress—could be found in the northern wing. Saga walked through the fortress as though she were dreaming. Found the tower the man had mentioned. The door was unmanned, which was no surprise to Saga, as all capable warriors were now on the battlefield. She drew a deep breath. Pushed the door open.

And stepped into a hellscape.

Beyond the fortress walls, berserkers clashed with shifter warriors, the monstrosity of a siege tower looming in the distance. Her gaze darted from the arrows flying from the body of the tower to a barrel being loaded on the catapults up top. Saga's hand closed around the fire flask in her pocket, and she took a single, angry step toward it.

No, she told herself. This flask was intended for Ivar.

The screams and clash of steel and those ominous tolling bells all jumbled inside Saga's skull. She gasped for breath as her heart raced impossibly fast. The telltale signs of her panic quickly swamped her, and Saga took a few moments to catch her breath. When it was clear that would not happen, she forced herself to take a step.

One foot in front of the other, rang in her ears as she took a second step.

The air was thick with smoke and blood, sweat and excrement. A few paces away, the greataxe of a berserker whizzed through the air, embedding into the neck of a wolf shifter with a wet *thwack*. A whimper slipped from Saga's lips, but she took another step.

Overhead, a barrel launched from the siege tower, sailed over the fortress walls, and landed with a ground-shaking explosion. The impact rumbled through the ground and into her bones.

Her teeth ground against the too-rapid beat of her heart, and she reminded herself of all that was at stake. One step at a time, Saga skirted the edge of battle. Her progress was painstakingly slow, and twice she fell to her knees, certain she was drowning. But each time, she got back up. Put one foot in front of the other.

By the time she saw the warrior's red beard, Saga could scarcely see through the lights dancing in her vision. The berserker warrior howled, a gleam of madness in his eye as he hefted his greataxe above her. But Saga was so startled by this warrior's presence that she could not look away.

"Thorir?"

The warrior faltered, his mad blue eyes assessing her, and Saga still wasn't certain it was actually Thorir until the man's disbelief shifted to a cunning grin.

"Lady Saga." Thorir hooked his axe into his belt.

"Thorir," Saga panted. Her breaths were shallow, white dots looping in her vision, but she forced the next words past her teeth. "Take me to King Ivar. I surrender."

As Thorir bundled her over his shoulder and carried her through the streets of Kovograd, Saga relented to her panic at long last. Her vision warped as she tried to breathe; her heart pounded so fiercely she was certain she'd perish before ever arriving at Ivar. Saga tried to relax into it. Tried to let it wash over her. But this disturbing procession through the streets made it impossible. Hands groped at her tunic and hair as more warriors joined the march. Berserkers tilted their heads to the skies, howling in victory as the lost princess of Íseldur was led to their king.

"Saga Volsik!" shouts rose up. "It's her! We have her!"

She imagined Kassandr's fingers on her shoulder, tapping gently, but her mind soon jumped to the words her sister had spoken in her mind so many weeks ago. *This is only kindling, building me up.* Saga's hand closed around the flask in her pocket, ensuring that the stopper remained secure. *And soon it will be time for them to burn.*

She was jostled about, burly warriors on either side of her ensuring she could not flee. They spoke foul words, hurled the most vulgar of insults, but Saga had found a strange sort of peace in what she was about to do. The fire flask rested inside her pocket, and soon she'd unleash it upon Íseldur's king.

At some point, they reached the Urkan war camp, and Saga found herself standing before an enormous tent, Ivar's berserkers flanking her on all sides. Saga stared, resigned, at the Urkan flag flying above the tent. The tent flap rippled.

And then *he* emerged.

Ivar Ironheart wore a crown of steel on his silver-streaked head, his brown eyes just as hard as she remembered. But as Saga took in the glossy red burns covering half of King Ivar's face and his once-long beard now singed short, she blinked at the realization—*she* had done this to him during that explosion in Sunnavík. Morbid satisfaction pooled in her gut.

King Ivar's scowl deepened at whatever he read in Saga's expression. Then he strode forward and cracked his palm across her cheek. Saga's head snapped to the side, and she stumbled to her knees.

"That," snarled Ivar, "is for trying to kill me."

Berserkers hauled her back to her feet, and Saga braced for a slap in Yrsa's honor.

But Ivar only growled, "I'd have far worse for you, were it not for your mother."

"Signe is *not* my mother!" Saga shouted, her anger a sudden blazing thing.

Ivar's palm cracked across her other cheek, and Saga fell once more, tasting iron in her mouth. She chastised herself for goading the king when she needed to speak her piece. "It was me," she croaked, standing yet again. "I tried to kill you. The Zagadkians had nothing to do with it."

Ivar spat on the ground. "I do not believe you, girl, but it matters not. Their fate is set. We shall not rest until every one of them is dead or in chains."

Saga blinked back tears. It was much as she'd expected, yet still, she'd held out hope. Her hand slipped into her pocket. Curled around the smooth surface of the fire flask.

It had come to this.

Saga would not return to Íseldur—would not fulfill her promise to Eisa—but at the very least, she would ensure King Ivar did not return, either. As Saga made to pull the fire flask from her pocket, she paused. Something white floated down on the breeze. At first she thought it snow, then perhaps a bird. But when she realized it was a single, iridescent feather, Saga's mind went completely blank.

The sky above her darkened.

Thorir shouted his surprise, the other berserkers growling in warning. Saga gasped as an enormous white figure swooped down from above. It was a flurry of anger matching her own; a storm of lashing hooves and beating wings. The creature screamed, one of those lethal hooves crashing into Ivar's back and sending him sprawling. Berserkers shouted as the horse struck warriors down and trampled those who were too slow to flee.

And Saga found herself face-to-face with Havoc.

Even through her shock, Saga recognized what this was—an alternative she could never have anticipated. Her mind's eye showed her the book she'd found in her room—showed her that page depicting an aerial legion of archers riding on winged horses. The clans beyond the river. All it would require was climbing onto Havoc's back and flying through wide-open skies.

So much open space. No exits. What if she fell apart? Lost her grip and plummeted to her death?

Then she thought of Kassandr, fighting tirelessly on the battlefield. Kassandr, who'd do anything to keep his people safe. Kassandr, who'd seen Saga's potential all this time. With his help, she'd faced so much already.

And in this moment, Saga knew there was no going back to the girl she'd once been.

Boosting herself up on the backs of the fallen, she threw herself onto Havoc. Ivar screamed, his berserkers shaking off their surprise. A dozen warriors charged toward them at once, and Saga clutched the stallion's mane, heart hammering with vicious strikes. They'd soon be in the air.

Fear is a thing to be felt, not obeyed, said Kassandr in her mind. So Saga took a deep breath and hung on with all her strength.

Havoc launched into the sky. And for the first time in her life, Saga was airborne.

CHAPTER 37

Kopa, Íseldur

Rey's nerves were on edge as his spoon scraped the bottom of his bowl. He leaned back in his chair, his gaze falling on the curly-haired woman seated across from him. Today they took the daymeal alone in her chambers as Silla conserved her strength for their upcoming meeting with the jarls.

She'd been uncharacteristically quiet all morning, a fact which made Rey want to punch the wall. It was clear the god was growing more active, twisting Silla's thoughts and whispering inside her skull. It drove him mad that there was nothing he could do to lift the burden from her shoulders.

Silla buried a yawn in her sleeve, then met his eyes with annoyance. "Bother," she muttered. "A queen doesn't yawn, according to Lady Tala."

Rey's eyes narrowed. "And I suppose a queen doesn't piss, either," he grumbled. As far as he was concerned, Lady Tala could go and jump into the Hvíta River. What did a battle-hardened jarl care for rules and etiquette?

Silla's eyes widened. "Absolutely *not*!" But she propped her chin on her fist and cocked her head to the side. "According to Tala, I must never insinuate such bodily needs. But if it absolutely must be broached, I'm to say I must *pass water*."

Rey's face pulled into a grimace, causing Silla to burst into laughter. But suddenly she flinched, then fell silent. Immediately, Rey sat up a little straighter.

"What did He say?" he asked with cutting calm.

For the past few days, Rey had studied Silla's every move—each small expression—and he'd learned the signs that the god of chaos was present. A flinch. A sharp word. And most chilling of all, the occasional dark flicker in her eye that hinted someone else peered out at him.

Silla reached across the table and slid her hand into his. Rey gasped—her palm was ice-cold. Instinctively, his thumb rubbed circles on the back of her hand.

"Dimples," Silla muttered, and he knew she recited her hearthfire thoughts. "The ice crystals that form in the air when it's really cold. The winterwing bird's song."

Her palm seemed to warm by the barest degree.

"The handaxes I picked up in Sunnavík," Rey contributed. "The way you drool when you sleep."

"At least I do not snore!" Silla shot back.

"But you *do* steal all the blankets."

The tension in Silla's shoulders eased as her lips curved into the hint of a smile. "My thanks. It seems He's rather . . . enthusiastic this morning." She returned her focus to her half-eaten bowl of porridge.

Tension coiled in Rey's gut. He knew their time to muster an army was tight, but his concern for Silla's well-being was growing by the hour.

"Should we reschedule our meeting?" Rey asked cautiously.

"No!" Silla snapped, in a way that told Rey it was not all her. "We've rescheduled once already. Too long have we waited. It must happen today."

Unease crept across Rey's skin as he watched her eat. They had to free her from this gods damned bargain, but how? The Weaver Silla had visited was still bedridden, and Fallgerd was dead. All that remained were the piles of books they combed through day after day. It was like searching for a single snowflake in an enormous snowdrift. How would they find answers? How would they cure her?

He dragged his hands across his thick curls, before folding them behind his head. Rey was used to being a leader. To having complete control. But when it came to the bargain living inside Silla, he felt completely helpless.

"After we meet with the jarls—" he began.

"We must practice drawing out my bloodline gift," Silla finished for him.

Rey frowned as she smothered another yawn. "Perhaps you ought to rest. Last night you—" He broke off as the memory of her voice rang in his ears. A voice that was not her own, speaking in tongues. "It is clear you had dark dreams. I think rest is in order."

Silla slapped a palm on the table, her eyes flashing black for the fraction of a heartbeat. "We haven't time to rest," she said sharply. "I must play with this bloodline gift. Learn all I can of it."

Trepidation crept across his skin, leaving goosebumps in its wake. Rey held himself rigid as stone, wondering if these were Silla's words, or if they were Myrkur's. Gods, but he hated this.

How was Silla to practice this bloodline gift of hers to prepare for the battle in the heartwood with a shard of the god of chaos monitoring her at all times? They'd been fortunate that Myrkur had exhausted Himself in the wake of the unfortunate meeting of jarls, as it had left Silla's mind to herself for several hours.

During those precious hours, they'd discovered that Silla could pull magic not only from halda stones but also from other Galdra. After she'd inadvertently pulled Rey's galdur, she'd repeated the move countless times. Then Silla had called over Runný and done the same with her light-bending skills.

"I can see . . . *threads*!" Silla had gasped, vanishing before Rey's eyes.

After Silla mastered vanishing, Runný showed her how to form a shield of curving light. Then Silla had called Hef over, and learned to wield his Blade Breaker skill. By the end of the day, they'd learned

Silla could most easily pull from those who were primed. But with a little extra effort, she could draw straight from Rey's source.

"Why do you think you could not feel this bloodline gift before now?" Rey asked cautiously. It was a fine line between understanding this gift and revealing too much to Myrkur.

Silla tapped her spoon against her bowl. "I think," she finally said, "my Ashbringer source is so bright and vibrant and . . . *loud* . . . that I could not sense this other ability. Only now that my Ashbringer source is smothered with hindrium am I able to sense these more subtle cues."

Rey hummed in agreement, but then turned toward the door as someone knocked. "Come in!" he called out, hoping it wasn't the irritating one called Ingvarr.

Thankfully, it was Runný, no doubt here to usher them to their meeting with the jarls. But her drawn expression had Rey immediately on his feet.

"What is it?" snarled Silla. Rey could have sworn the torchlight flared black for a second.

"Refugees," said Runný, gaze darting from Silla to Rey in alarm. *Is she all right?* she asked with her eyes. Rey shook his head subtly, *no*. Runný swallowed, then continued. "Hundreds, I'm told. They've been gathering at Kopa's gates all morning."

"Refugees?" asked Silla, and to Rey's great relief, the words seemed to be truly her own. "From where?"

"From the countryside." Runný's dark eyes met Rey's. "They bring word of a mist with a beating heart."

"Why are they gathering at the gates?" asked Silla. "Has Jarl Hakon refused them entry?"

"Aye," answered Runný. "He claims he hasn't the resources to feed them."

"He *has*," snapped Silla, and this time, Rey was certain the flamelight beside him blazed black. "I have seen that man's grain stores with my own eyes. You will take me to him, Runný."

Trouble, thought Rey, trailing Silla from her chambers. He had a bad feeling about this day.

—∞∞∞—

News of the refugees seemed to enliven Silla. She quickly took charge of a group of servants—remembering each of their names with enviable ease—and ordered that any empty room in Ashfall Fortress be readied. Within an hour, she had the kitchens preparing a dozen enormous cauldrons of stew and countless batches of griddle cakes; the stablehands collecting spare blankets and clothing; the healers gathering in Ashfall's great hall, ready to see to any sick and injured.

The meeting with the jarls was postponed once more. Jarl Hakon hovered nearby and tried to interject, but he was uncharacteristically cowed by Silla today. Rey was certain he'd seen those dark flashes in her eyes, and given that Hakon was privy to Myrkur's bargain, it was likely the jarl was simply afraid to object.

Atli, to his begrudging credit, took orders from Silla with impressive ease, and was soon putting out a call for any available lodgings in Kopa. Pride bloomed in Rey's chest as he watched her lead—as he watched the jarls who'd seemed ready to dismiss her the day before witnessing the true Silla in action.

Rey didn't have to watch carefully to see the signs of Myrkur—Silla flinched frequently, her words growing sharp. Despite this, she seemed to hold Him back. As the line of hungry, exhausted refugees snaked from Ashfall's gates and down through the streets of Kopa, Silla insisted on standing by a cauldron, ladle in hand. She spooned stew into wooden bowls, greeting each beleaguered villager with a smile and reassurance.

Rey stood by her side, handing out flatbreads while trying not to frighten the refugees with his *axe eyes.* As the sun reached its low peak in the winter skies, stories flowed into the city, matching what he and Silla had told the jarls just a day before—mist crawling across the countryside, Turning all creatures in its wake. There were tales of nightmare creatures and human draugur, of the moldering stench that clung to them. Now, more than ever, Rey was reminded of his purpose, and of those who'd pay should he fail to muster an army.

Today he would swallow his pride and go to Atli—would go to any jarl who'd hear him out. He'd do what it took to get Atli's help in mustering men, even if it meant dropping to his knees and begging.

Hours passed, and the line gradually dwindled. The cauldrons were scraped dry, the platters of flatbreads emptied, and winter's early darkness fell over them. Silla swayed on her feet, exhaustion etched into her face, but as Rey wrapped a stabilizing arm around her shoulders, he caught sight of a figure watching from the shadows. It was an opportunity he had to take.

Rey waved Runný over. "Take her to her chambers and make sure she lies down."

As Runný led Silla away, Rey strode toward the man in the shadows. There, leaning against Ashfall's black stone walls, was Jarl Holger, his impressive gray beard reaching midway down his chest.

He tried not to show his deep discomfort in approaching the jarl. For the last five years, Rey had been the blade, or as Atli put it, a hound on the Uppreisna's leash. What right had he to make an ask of this jarl?

But as he took in the brutal scar on Holger's pale cheek, Rey told himself that this was not the kind of jarl who lounged by the hearthfire and let others do the work. He could do this. He could ask this man for help.

Reaching the wall, Rey extended a hand.

Holger accepted it and gave it a sturdy shake. "I cannot decide why you look so familiar," said Holger, examining Rey's face in the torchlight.

Rey forced his limbs to relax. "I'm certain we've never met, my lordship." The words felt clumsy on his tongue, and Rey stumbled over what to say next.

But realization had settled in Holger's face. "You're a Galtung."

A premonitory ache grew in Rey's throat. "Aye," he croaked.

"I knew your father," said Holger, stroking his long beard. "We fought shoulder to shoulder when—" The jarl sighed, sorrow settling in his face. He did not need to finish the sentence for Rey to know he thought of the Urkans' landing. The battle his father did not return from.

"He was a good man, your father," continued Holger, before launching into a story about the chaos they'd caused behind Urkan lines.

As Rey listened, his discomfort eased just a touch. Holger did not speak to him as though he were lesser, and they had common ground. As the jarl wrapped up his story, Rey prepared to make his ask. A better man would play the dance of words—would ease into things—but it was not who Rey was. Instead, he broached the topic with the subtlety of a broadsword.

"I would call on your history with my father, Jarl Holger. You've seen the refugees. Have heard the tales they carry. We need good men to fight with us in the Western Woods."

Jarl Holger chuckled softly, staring up at night's first stars. "In these matters, you're direct. More like your mother than your father, I suppose." The jarl exhaled heavily, and Rey felt the man choosing his words. "I have seen the refugees. I have heard their tales. I've also heard tellings of giant serpents in the north." The jarl paused. "Strange happenings indeed. Alone, they might merely be oddities. But together . . . together they tell an alarming story."

Holger laid a hand on Rey's arm. "I tell you this in honor of your father, and because I respect that you're not the sort to play games." Jarl Holger's jaw hardened. "This is where I stand. I arrived with doubt in my heart—doubt that the girl Hakon had unearthed was truly Eisa Volsik. But the moment I saw her at the feast, I knew she was who he claimed. I can see it in her eyes and her hair; in the scar beside her eye; and, strangely, in the way she moves her hands when speaking. For a moment, I thought that at last our prayers had come true—that Íseldur had hope of becoming whole once more."

Rey braced himself for what came next.

"But I sense something dark in her—something she keeps from us. And I cannot place my faith in a leader, no matter their name, when they hide truths from me. I will send a warband to fight with you in the woods, Reynir Galtung, but I do it for *you*. For your father. And for this strangeness I sense sweeping across our lands."

Rey was filled with a mixture of gratitude and worry. He wanted to explain about Myrkur—about Queen Svalla's bargain gone awry. But it was not his truth to share, and so he forced a smile. Clasped Jarl Holger's hand again.

"My thanks, Jarl Holger," said Rey.

And as they turned toward the fortress entryway, for the first time in weeks, Rey felt the stirrings of hope. Holger had spoken to Rey as an equal. Had taken his request seriously. And Holger would send warriors, which would certainly help sway the other jarls. Rey might just muster the men he needed to do battle in the heartwood.

But as they walked beneath Ashfall's portcullis, Runný came rushing forward, a look of panic on her face.

"What is it?" demanded Rey, the fine hairs on his arms lifting.

"Eisa," said Runný, gaze darting everywhere. "She's gone missing."

CHAPTER 38

A dull ring began in Rey's ears as Runný's words penetrated his skull.

"What," he ground out, "do you mean Eisa is *missing*?"

How could she be missing when he'd seen her only moments ago? Rey's conversation with Jarl Holger could only have lasted ten minutes. But a lot could happen in ten minutes—things he refused to consider.

"She seemed fine." Runný ran a hand down her face. "We cleared her chambers, and she went inside. But then we heard her shout and feared an assassin had gained entry to her rooms. The door was barricaded, and by the time we got inside, she was gone."

The ring grew louder, blocking out all else. Runný's mouth was moving, yet her words no longer reached him. There was only anger and bone-deep fear.

"Do you think an assassin took her?" Rey asked in a hoarse voice. "But *how*?" He shook his head. "It does not matter how. They can't have gone far. We must comb the fortress."

"Ingvarr leads a search party in the northern wing," said Runný.

"Then we shall take the south," said Rey, striding through Ashfall's entry hall. Runný's soft footsteps came from his left, but Rey faltered at the heavier gait on his right. He paused. Faced Jarl Holger.

"You needn't join us, Jarl," said Rey carefully.

"On the contrary," said Jarl Holger, "I think that I must."

Rey, Runný, and Jarl Holger examined the southern wing in detail. They searched the library, the stables, the caverns beneath the fortress. They searched the kitchens, the servants' quarters, the great hall. Silla was nowhere to be found. Gradually, Rey's anger was eclipsed by fear, his mind showing him different scenarios in which she'd been harmed.

But as they rushed from the great hall, a male scream echoed off the corridor walls. Rey veered toward the sound, shoving through the double doors that led to a garden courtyard. It was the same garden he'd chased her to during the feast of the Shortest Day, the lunar-blooming plants just beginning to unfurl. It took Rey's eyes a moment to adjust, and another to make out the figures before him.

Silla, looming over a terrified Ingvarr, a long-bladed hevrít in hand. Ingvarr tried to scuttle backward, but as he tripped over his own feet, Silla attacked. Her movements were too quick, the blade lashing out like a serpent, and immediately Rey understood. There was no assassin. Myrkur had gained possession over Silla. There was no time to ask *how.* Silla brought the knife down, the blade missing Ingvarr by a bare inch.

"Silla!" Rey bellowed, storming toward the pair.

His feet faltered as Silla turned toward him, head cocked. Unkempt curls blocked her eyes from view, but Rey knew it was not Silla who peered out at him.

"What happened?" he murmured, panic thrumming through him. How had Myrkur gotten ahold of Silla? His gaze fell to the hevrít gripped in her hand. It was steel, not the lethal blade of black fire, which made him exhale a relieved breath. At the very least, the hindrium guarded Silla's Ashbringer skill.

"I discovered her here, sleeping!" rambled Ingvarr, scrambling away from Silla. "I woke her and she . . . she *attacked* me!"

Rey's mind whirled, trying to understand. Hadn't Silla mentioned she'd fallen asleep before the incident with Fallgerd?

"Kill," growled Silla, in Myrkur's voice of shadows and darkness.

"Kill him. Finish him." Silla stalked toward them, and Ingvarr retreated farther.

But Rey held his ground, raising a placating hand. "Silla. I don't want to hurt you."

"Kill," hissed Myrkur.

Rey got his first look at Silla's eyes—utterly black with no whites to be seen, just as they'd been on that mountainside. She'd been lethal, a creature of death, and Rey had been forced to strangle her until she'd passed out. Bile rose in his throat at the prospect of having to do it again.

"Come back, Silla!" said Rey sharply, drawing his sword.

Silla only raised Ingvarr's stolen hevrít and advanced on him. He yanked on his galdur as quickly as he could, but it was too late. Silla launched at him, and Rey could do nothing but parry her blows. Her strength was astounding—each blow reverberating down his arm—but her speed was terrifying.

Rey was forced to retreat until the backs of his knees hit a stone bench. Instinct had him ducking beneath a hissing blade. It sliced through a climbing plant, sending leaves and vines flying. Before he could right himself, Silla's knee smashed into his nose. Cartilage and bone crunched, blood gushing down his face, and Rey bellowed in pain. But he channeled that pain into his galdur. Tendrils of smoke burst from his palms and wrapped around her torso.

But Myrkur grasped at Rey's power and yanked it away.

"No!" bellowed Rey, as smoke churned from Silla's palms . . . and a smile of pure malice spread across her face.

"What is this?" asked Myrkur, as Silla stared at her palms. Rey could feel her pulling from his source . . . gathering more and more smoke to her being. He closed his eyes. Tried to clamp down on his magic to no avail. Myrkur would drain him empty. Use Rey's own magic against him.

With a cry of rage, he charged at Silla, driving his shoulder into her stomach and sending them both crashing to the ground. Startled, Rey felt Myrkur's grip on his magic stutter, then fall away. They scuffled, Rey trying to pin her down with his bulk. Her nails gouged into his neck, and he shouted in pain, his momentary surprise all she needed to wriggle free. But Jarl Holger and Runný both threw themselves at Silla, and Atli was suddenly at Rey's side, blowing into a flute-like implement. A quill shot through the air and embedded in Silla's arm.

"No!" screamed Myrkur as Silla thrashed about. But her movements grew more feeble with each passing breath, and Silla's head soon lolled to the side.

"Kill," Silla murmured, but the word was slurred, drawn out. Her knees buckled, Jarl Holger and Runný supporting her weight.

Rey pushed to his feet, pain radiating from his broken nose; from the wound on his neck. Atli handed him a pocket linen, and Rey pressed it to his gushing nose. Heart in his throat, he approached a limp Silla. Her eyes were open but disoriented, her muscles bled of all their strength. His gaze fell to her palms, and Rey grew preternaturally still.

Blood oozed from slash wounds in the middle of her hands, and he knew in an instant they were defensive in nature.

"Ingvarr?" Rey demanded, barely recognizing his own voice.

"He's gone," said Atli, appearing by his side. "You don't think—" Atli's expression darkened at whatever he read in Rey's eyes. The jarl-to-be turned and bellowed at his retinue. "Find Ingvarr and apprehend him."

As the warriors bolted from the gardens, Atli dropped to his knees beside Rey. "What do you need, Galtung?" There was no trace of malice in the heir-to-be's voice. No hint at the hostility Rey normally felt.

"Bandages," Rey managed.

Soon clean bandages were in Rey's possession, and he used them to wrap the wounds on Silla's palms. He caught sight of the quill in her arm and pulled it out to examine.

"A sedative," explained Atli. "It shall work itself out in half a day's time."

"Thank you," said Rey, meeting Atli's gaze, "for incapacitating her." In this moment, Rey could not convey the gratitude he felt at not having to strangle Silla as he had in the mountain pass, but Atli seemed to read it in his expression. The jarl-to-be inclined his head in a subtle nod.

Rey closed his eyes. His mind spun, trying to understand all that had happened, but he knew that without Ingvarr, there was only one other who had answers.

He prodded the broken bones and cartilage, and, after a deep breath, shoved his nose back into place. His shout of pain echoed off the courtyard walls, but Rey climbed to his feet and leveled his gaze on Jarl Holger.

"Now," said Rey, resignation settling into his bones, "I suppose you know what it is she hides."

He could not read the expression in Holger's eyes, nor did Rey want to imagine the fallout from this. Instead, he turned his gaze on Runný.

"Bring her back to her chambers," Rey growled. His fingertips found the stinging wound on his neck and he winced. "And shackle her to the bed."

"Tell me how to release her from the bargain," Rey hissed in a low voice, as close to Silla's ear as he dared to venture.

Hair was plastered to her forehead, and her head lolled to the side. Every part of Rey despised seeing her like this—hands and feet shackled to the bed, sweat-slicked brow, her breaths raspy and labored. He had to remind himself that the healer had deemed her well; that Myrkur must be expending tremendous energy, and sooner or later, He'd lose His grip.

The healer had properly bandaged Silla's hands, then determined that she was in a state of *wakeful sleep.* How in the gods' ashes one could be awake in sleep, Rey didn't know. What he did know was he could not grant the god of chaos the slightest of opportunities. And so Silla would remain sedated and shackled to the bed—both for her own safety and to protect others.

A quiet tension filled the room. Runný and Atli had returned to the chambers with Rey and now sat by the hearth, combing through the books stacked nearby. Rey, meanwhile, could not bear to leave Silla's side. Not while this monster had her in his thrall.

"You should thank me," slurred Myrkur. "Without me, she'd be dead beneath that mountain of snow."

Rey wanted to punch the wall. Wanted to scream at the top of his lungs. Instead, he gathered every last shred of his composure. "I'll thank you," said Rey, "when you release her from the bargain. *A life for a life,* you said. Take anyone's life. Anyone *else*—"

Myrkur's laugh fell from Silla's lips, unnatural and eerie, and Rey pushed away from the bed to resume his pacing.

"Pitiful mortals," taunted the god. "So beholden to your hearts. Tell me, warrior, would you give your life for hers?"

"Aye," said Rey, without hesitation.

Myrkur tutted. "Unfortunately, you do not hold my interest."

Now Rey did drive his fist into the wall—a foolish mistake, as the volcanic stone split his knuckles. He cursed and shook out his hand, but Rey was glad for the pain—it was far more tolerable than what lay on that bed. Each glance at Silla felt like a hand reaching through his ribs and squeezing his heart. Each word from Myrkur was like knives in his skull.

It was hard to stay hopeful in moments like these. Because even when the god's grip on Silla faded, the fact was, irreparable damage had just been done. Jarl Holger had witnessed Silla's possession, and Rey did not want to consider the repercussions. Would he withdraw his offer of warriors? Would he poison the other jarls against their cause?

One week. They had only one week before they rode for the woods. This was the last thing they needed.

A strange scratching noise drew Rey's attention. He strode to the window and pulled back the curtain. Before him was a chilling sight—a black hawk perched at an iron offerings plate, tearing meat from a chicken bone.

The black hawk is a harbinger of death, rattled Harpa's voice in his mind.

"I won't lose her!" Rey bellowed, pounding on the window with his fist.

"Easy, Galtung," said Runný, laying a hand on his shoulder. "That hawk has been here each day, feeding on the offerings left for the spirits and the gods." She sighed. "And the healer said rest is the best thing for Eisa."

But Rey only scowled as the black hawk took flight, the offerings clutched in its talons. He scrubbed a hand down his face and made to turn away from the window, but something curious caught his eye. The corner of the window frame was pried loose, several curly hairs clinging to it. Rey leaned closer. Below the window jutted an ornamental lip of stone.

"I suppose," said Rey, plucking the curly hairs from the window frame, "this answers the question of how she escaped the room."

Runný joined him, staring down at the ledge. "None of this makes sense. Ingvarr was beside me when we swept the rooms. Beside me when Eisa entered and locked the doors. He could not have slipped in."

Rey scowled out the window, his moods as dark as the night. "What happened?"

"I do not know," said Runný carefully. "But I suspect there will be no answers tonight. Get yourself some sleep, Galtung. Morning will bring a better day."

Runný returned to her seat near Atli and continued flipping through her book. A moment later, Rey settled across from them. There was an edge to this silence. An imaginary blade hovering at Silla's heart. The three of them searched for a way to free Silla from the bargain long into the night. But it seemed no answers were to be found.

Rey woke to the clank of chains. Immediately, he surged upright and reached for the dagger under his pillow. Perhaps it had been unwise to share a bed with Silla, but he couldn't stand the thought of her alone. And so he'd arranged himself on the farthest edge, leaving ample space between them. As his gaze now settled on Silla, Rey found her clear-eyed, and exhaled in relief. Myrkur no longer held her in His thrall.

"Rey?" she asked, a panicked edge to her voice. "What is this? What's happened?" She tugged on the restraint again, setting the chains to clatter. Silla paused. "What happened to your face?" She attempted to sit upright, but her manacles caught and wrenched her back down. A whimper escaped her. "Tell me what has happened."

"What do you remember?" asked Rey, prodding his broken nose. It was swollen and tender, and would likely soon be spectacularly bruised.

"I had a bad dream," she whispered, craning her neck to look at her restraints.

Rey followed her gaze to her curled fingers—to the bandages wrapped around her palms.

Silla released a ragged breath. "It wasn't a dream, was it?" Before he could answer, a low wail escaped her. "Oh, gods. Ingvarr . . . your nose . . . did I—"

"No. It was not you." But Rey's words rang hollow, even to his own ears.

Silla's chest rose and fell with rapid breaths, and he knew her mind had gone to Fallgerd.

"Everyone is safe, Silla. No one was harmed."

"But I tried, didn't I?" Her voice trembled, making an ache spread through his chest.

Rey was silent, which he supposed was answer enough.

"I was so tired," she said, collapsing on the pillow and staring at the roof. "I'd kept Him out all day. My mental strength was weakened."

"Let me release you—"

"No! You will keep me shackled to this bed. It is long overdue." Silla drew a tremulous breath.

"It is time I accept the truth: I am a danger to others."

CHAPTER 39

The Western Woods

With her prosthetic arm gripped between her knees, Hekla passed a whetstone along the edge of her claws. She'd grown complacent in her time with the Bloodaxe Crew—had been happy to let Axe Eyes tend her claws as he did any blade he could get his hands on. In his absence, Hekla had taken back her responsibility, and she had to admit, the task was rather soothing. It quieted her mind. Drove out the frustrations that had gathered.

They'd walked for days through the deepest depths of the forest, and everyone's moods were flagging. The Forest Maiden, exhausted by her efforts of speeding their journey, slumbered constantly, but Kritka assured Hekla they made good progress.

The undead ravens continued to stalk them in greater numbers, growing more bold with each passing day. Earlier, a pair of ravens had swooped at Thrand's face—an obvious attempt to surprise him into dropping the Forest Maiden. But it seemed the foul birds had not expected the lethal slash of Thrand's sword. In a matter of moments, their corpses lay on the ground. The rest of the flock screamed angrily from the trees, though they quieted once Sigrún fired a few arrows at them.

They had not encountered the mist again, though Hekla doubted they'd seen the last of it. Yet still, she felt it watching, felt it biding its time. On the long days, Hekla's mind strayed often to Kopa. Had Axe Eyes been successful? Would he be waiting for them in the heartwood? Or would Hekla and her beleaguered crew be on their own?

A shout yanked Hekla back to the present.

"You kunta!" Eyvind bellowed, lunging at a laughing Gunnar and bringing him to the ground.

Hekla pushed to her feet, bewildered. It was no secret these two shared no love for each other, but at least there had been tolerance. Now, as Eyvind drove his fist into Gunnar's jaw, it seemed their emotions had reached a boiling point.

Were they fighting over *her*? Gods, she'd let this go on for too long. It was time to put an end to things.

Hekla rushed forward, elbowing through the warriors gathered around the grappling men. But Thrand put a hand on her shoulder, bringing Hekla to a halt.

"Stop, you man-boys!" she shouted.

Thrand chuckled, brows rising as Gunnar pummeled Eyvind with the speed that had garnered him the nickname Fire Fist. "You know this has long been coming," said Thrand. "Let us enjoy the show."

Hekla scowled as sólas changed hands among the warriors.

"Gunnar has been placing stones in Eyvind's satchel," explained Thrand. "Each day, he's added another. And tonight, when Eyvind dumped the satchel out, there were a dozen of them in there."

Hekla felt foolish to have thought it was she they quarreled over. Gunnar rolled on top of Eyvind, drawing his fist back. But Eyvind caught it and twisted, making Gunnar bellow. The men continued to wrestle, but Hekla's tolerance for it had soured.

"Man-boys," she muttered, returning to her whetstone.

Eventually, the manly grunts and growls fell away to exhausted wheezes. Soon an unexpected sound reached her ears. Laughter.

Hekla rolled her eyes. Gunnar and Eyvind, having exhausted themselves, now lay on their backs, passing a flask between them and guffawing over something. She supposed the pair of them had finished their axe-measuring contest.

At some point, Eyvind stood and pulled his torn tunic over his head. Firelight caught on the toughened muscles of his torso, bunching and flexing as he twisted to examine some blow Gunnar had delivered. Despite her best efforts, Hekla could not seem to look away. His gaze slid to hers, and she felt it like a physical touch.

He was giving her the space she'd asked for, and a part of her hated him for it. Hekla's mind and body were at war, images sliding into her exhausted mind—those muscles moving below her; those hazel eyes looking up at her like she was everything he could ever want.

Break your rule, he'd asked her. *Spend the night with me.*

It was impossible to forget how safe she'd felt in that room with him—how she'd felt more like herself with him than she had in years. But it was only ever a fantasy. Never mind their constant bickering for weeks afterward. Each soft word of praise he'd spoken that night—every sentimental moment they'd shared—was spoiled by the fact that Eyvind Hakonsson was betrothed to another woman all along.

Hekla looked away with a tremulous breath. She didn't care that she was holding this grudge too tight. Did not care that the right thing to do was to hear Eyvind's words. He'd been so patient. Admirably calm. It did not matter. Hekla could not expose her tender heart again.

Eyvind and Thrand had gone to the stream, and Hekla hated herself for noticing. The other warriors milled about within the perimeter of campfires, some playing games of dice, others readying themselves for another night in these cursed woods. Gunnar, it seemed, had won the favor of Eyvind and his retinue with his latest prank, and his laughter came easily as he tossed the dice with a trio of warriors.

She would talk to him tonight, Hekla decided.

And she had her chance a moment later, when, after extricating himself from the game, Gunnar sank down on the bedroll next to hers. He nudged her with his shoulder and offered her his flask of brennsa. Hekla took a long draught, leaning into the whiskey's burn. She'd need courage to do what came next.

"I cannot marry you, Gunnar," she said, returning his flask.

He stiffened. "Why not?"

"I will never marry again."

She felt his eyes on her as the silence stretched on. "It's *him,* isn't it?"

Hekla scowled into the campfire.

"He's not right for you, Hek," continued the obtuse man. "His clothing is threaded with *actual gold*—and have you seen his sword? I swear it to the gods. That's Karthian steel he carries!"

Hekla's scowl only deepened as Gunnar's words settled into her. She knew well enough that Eyvind and she were utterly unsuited, but Gunnar's agreement irritated her.

"Do you know what Thrand told me?" Gunnar did not wait for Hekla's reply. "For Hakonsson's fifth birthday, he was gifted a thousand acres of land. *A thousand!* Do you know how many sólas that is worth?"

When she did not answer, he continued. "I know you, Hekla. You like things a certain way. I can give you stability—a life without rules or expectations. With me, you'd have freedom—something you'd never have with a man like him."

Hekla's mind jerked to another time. It was just after her husband had taken an axe to her arm. She'd dragged herself from the woodshed and collapsed in the neighbor's yard. The old mother there had bound the wound tightly and kept Hekla hidden and abed for the better part of a month. Her survival had been miraculous, but she was not so foolish as to think she could survive such a thing twice.

Upon her recovery, Hekla's first vow was that she'd kill her husband. The second was that she would never marry again. Never again would a man have such power over her.

"You aren't *listening to me,* Gunnar!" Hekla knew that her voice rang too loud—that the warriors in the camp now glanced their way—but she *had* to make him understand. "My answer is *no.* Do not ask me again."

Gunnar pushed abruptly to his feet and stormed into the woods. Hekla waited to feel lighter—to feel some of the burden lifted from her shoulders. But all she felt was exhaustion.

CHAPTER 40

Lands beyond the river, Zagadka

Saga knew the world below her would make a beautiful sight, yet she couldn't lift her face from where it was buried in Havoc's white mane. Her breaths came in ragged gasps, her heart trampling wildly inside her chest, and she clung to the horse with every bit of her resolve. Perhaps the stallion sensed this, for his wingbeats were smooth and even, and he made no rapid changes in direction.

On the flight went like a too-vivid nightmare. Yet the scent of horse and the icy wind whipping her hair rooted Saga firmly in reality.

Hold on, she told herself, her muscles aching. *Just hold on.*

Saga did not even notice they'd descended until Havoc's hooves pounded on packed earth. Gradually, they stilled, and Saga tumbled from the horse's back. She landed on all fours, then heaved every morsel she'd eaten into the long grass.

The horse nickered—judgmentally, Saga thought—and she curled into a ball to protect herself from those lethal hooves. But the sound of ripping grass told Saga that stamping her to death was not currently on the stallion's mind.

She wiped her mouth on her sleeve. Havoc watched with onyx eyes, unimpressed by her antics, and Saga stared right back, trying to collect her thoughts. But iron clanked and her gaze fell to the stallion's hind legs. As she realized the manacles were still strapped in place, Saga's anger burst forth with disorienting force.

"You should never have been caged away," she muttered.

In the bright light of day, Saga could see that the manacle's bolts had loosened and knew it would only take a few twists by hand to remove them. That was, if Havoc didn't crush her skull first.

"Let me unscrew them, will you?"

Slowly, she crawled forward. The stallion merely crunched his grass, watching her with a flat gaze. *Amazing how differently a freed creature could behave,* she thought dazedly. Saga's fingertips slid around the bolt, and she twisted it deftly until the first manacle clanked free. A raw, red patch of skin was revealed beneath.

"I shall have words with Kassandr," she seethed. But Saga's urgency rushed back, her heart lurching at the thought of Kassandr. She had to find the clans beyond the river. Had to convince them to join the easterners in battle, and quickly. She crawled to the second manacle and got to work.

Saga freed Havoc of his second manacle, then pushed to her feet. The horse threw his head back with a gleeful whinny. Then, after stamping the ground, he took off at a gallop, racing across the field with impressive speed.

"Wait!" she cried out, her heart taking off with him. "Come back!" But after cresting a knoll, the stallion launched into the air. Bile rose in Saga's throat as the white form in the skies vanished over distant mountains.

"Oh, gods," whispered Saga, turning to examine her surroundings. Rolling grasslands in every direction, as far as the eye could see. Open skies yawning wide above her. Gods, it was so open, so exposed . . .

A dull ring began in her ears, and Saga tapped her fingers against her shoulder, counting each breath.

What were you thinking, climbing onto the horse's back? Saga wondered. *You've abandoned them, and now the horse has abandoned you, and you'll die all the same, like a coward under open skies . . .*

The ring in her ears reached its crescendo, her heartbeat a rapid staccato. But Saga continued her tappings and remembered to stop fighting against her fear. Instead, she felt it. Let it crest. Its impact was brutal, pulling her under into the frothing, tumultuous seas. She gasped for breath as her heart beat too hard, too fast. But like a wave, it had a cycle. Gradually it lessened, until eventually Saga's panic had washed away.

She lay curled in the grass in the aftermath, wanting nothing but to nap for the rest of the day. But she reminded herself of Kassandr—of all of Kovograd—and forced herself into motion.

"Think, featherhead," she muttered. "What will you do?"

In that chaotic moment in the courtyard, Saga had seen Havoc's offer as a sign from the gods—a chance to beg the clans beyond the river for help. Now, alone on the open steppe, Saga had no idea how to reach them. She searched for Havoc's white form in the skies, and her heart sank when she did not find it. The stallion had abandoned her.

"What did you truly expect?"

With a breath, Saga rose on shaky legs and shuffled in the direction Havoc had flown. As she walked, Saga kept her gaze on the ground; kept her fingers tapping against her shoulder with each step. She thought of the Zagadkian warriors fighting for their lives; of the children and the elderly sheltering inside the fortress. Then she thought of her mother and father—of Ana's little sister—strung on those pillars. She could not let this happen to Zagadka.

Rooted in her purpose, Saga found new strength. She walked across the grassy steppe for hours beneath the bright sun and against the fierce winds. She was clad in breeches and a woolen kaftan, which did little to keep her warm. For the most part, tension thrummed low in her veins, a constant, yet manageable, thing. Despite this, her panic seized control half a dozen times. Saga was forced to her knees. Came back to herself, rolled into a ball on two occasions. Each time, when her vision stabilized, she climbed back to her feet and resumed her journey. What else could she do?

When she first caught the strange thrum in the air, Saga was so depleted, she thought it was a product of her mind. But as the minutes passed it grew into a constant, low-level thunder, and Saga realized it was entirely real. A form in the sky crested the distant mountains, and for a moment, her heart sang, and she was certain that Havoc had returned to her.

But then another form joined it. Another, and five more, until at least a hundred small forms could be seen in the sky. Instinct had Saga searching for a tree, a rock—anything to hide behind. But on the wide-open steppe, there was no escape from the incoming horde.

Trapped! screamed her mind, but Saga rooted her feet in place, reminding herself that this was what she wanted.

The horde rolled on toward her, and as they neared, Saga blinked in astonishment. They were not all white like Havoc, but an assortment of blacks and grays and chestnut browns. Manes snapped like banners behind the striking creatures, and sunlight caught on feathered wings spread wide. Seated atop the winged horses were fearsome-looking warriors in chain mail and feathered cloaks. With kohl smeared across their eyes and long, braided hair secured beneath bronzed helms, at first Saga thought the warriors were merely beardless. But as they neared, she realized.

Women.

Women comprised the entire horde.

The riders landed, the thunder of the skies now reverberating across the entire steppe. The horsewomen directed their horses around Saga, and soon, a storm of hooves and wings encircled her, Saga in the very eye of it. Those nearest to her drew their horses to a stop before leaping down. These fierce horsemaidens had an assortment of complexions—from moonlight-pale to rich mahogany and everything in between.

A tall woman, clad in chain mail and a feathered cloak, approached, unsheathing her blade. She spoke rapidly in a language Saga did not understand. But upon seeing the confusion in Saga's face, the woman quickly shifted to accented Zagadkian.

"What are you doing on our lands, trespasser?" asked the woman, leveling her sword at Saga's breast. A swath of black hair had torn loose from her braids, and the wind blew it across the woman's brown cheeks. As Saga stared into her fierce, dark eyes, she realized this horsemaiden was far younger than she'd expected.

"I come," said Saga, more breathily than she'd have liked, "for asking . . . help. City of Kovograd is attack by Urkans."

"Urkans?" Laughter burst from the black-haired woman. "Let the eastern deceivers fall. It is what they deserve."

Saga's chest constricted further at the woman's remark. "If they fall, Urkans will next aim for you."

The woman's amusement evaporated at that.

"I ask for help," Saga repeated. "Together is chance to win—"

"Enough, girl!" snarled the woman, dragging her sword point up to rest in the hollow of Saga's throat. "Where do you come from to speak so boldly?"

Saga swallowed, trying to quell her racing heart. "Íseldur."

A murmur rose among the clanswomen behind the black-haired woman, their hostility shifting to curiosity. "Íseldur? How did you get here? Our shores are closed to outsiders."

Saga rolled her lips together, trying to choose her words.

"What are you doing on my steppe, foreigner?" said the woman, her words sharpened to a deadly point. Saga's heart skittered, her breaths quickening. She had to be careful. Had to choose the right words, else they might be the last she spoke.

"I ask for—"

"Help," finished the woman, holding up a hand. "Never mind it. You will stand before the clansmother. It is she who will decide your fate."

And with that ominous statement, the woman turned her back on Saga, and her clanswomen closed in.

They patted Saga down and found her fire flask immediately. After Saga explained what the flask was, the horsewomen sought counsel with their leader, whom she'd learned was named

Khiva. Saga watched Khiva examine the fire flask before sliding it into her pocket.

Next Saga was tossed rather roughly onto the back of a chestnut winged horse, a burly, red-haired horsemaiden climbing up behind her. Khiva barked orders in the clanswomen's tongue, and the horsemaiden behind her sighed.

"Give to me your hands," she said in rough Zagadkian, before securing a length of rope around them. Saga glanced desperately about for Havoc, but it seemed the stallion had abandoned her.

"Who is the clansmother?" she whispered to her captor. "Will *she* send help?"

Her captor did not deign to answer, most likely because Khiva's sharp gaze had fallen upon them. Saga's heart was accelerating, her chest constricting. Soon they'd be in the air, and Saga was bound—no escape. No exits. But there was also no turning back. She leaned forward, bracing her forehead on the horse's withers as she thought of Kassandr and Elisava. Of Rov and Alasa. This was for them.

The horsewomen chattered around her, the whinny and flap of wings signaling the horde taking to the skies. Her vision danced with starlight, and she was glad for her captor's freckled arm around her waist as their horse leaped into flight.

And then there were only the sounds of rushing winds in her ears. They were airborne and flying to an unknown location. *Hold on, Kass,* Saga thought over and over, as the seconds stretched into minutes. She wasn't certain when the first whoop met her ears, but she soon learned it signaled that their destination was near.

Saga could sense the horse descending and pried one eyelid open to take in a city of tents. These were no flimsy, temporary tents, but great, sturdy things built on wooden planks and with smoke twisting up from within. Campfires glowed in the looming darkness, and as the scent of sizzling meat reached Saga's nose, her stomach finally felt something aside from nausea.

Children cried out, rushing toward the horsemaidens as they landed on the outskirts of the city. The winged horses lifted their tails, the silver bells braided into their manes jingling as they pranced for the youngsters. At the head of the procession, Khiva bent low, scooping up a young girl and placing her in front of her on the winged horse. But the joy in the children's faces turned to suspicion as they noted Saga, and several began whispering among themselves.

Being back on firm ground made Saga feel somewhat more stable, and she focused on the sights around her to keep her panic at bay. The horses were led to a series of wooden troughs, male horse minders filling them with oats, while others readied brushes and an assortment of grooming implements. The rolling fields beyond were not enclosed by fencing, but Saga supposed there would be no point to a paddock when the horses had wings.

Saga was pulled from the saddle, but the movement jostled her queasy stomach. Her captor jumped back with a cry as Saga bent double and retched. She yearned for the comfort of a roof and four walls—for a break from the ceaseless fear roiling through her. But as Saga wiped her mouth, she found Khiva's hard eyes scowling at her and she reminded herself this was not about her comfort.

"With me," Khiva snapped, and Saga was led by her bound hands through the strange city of tents. The clanspeople gathered in groups around cookfires under thick fur jackets while rabbits and fowl roasted on spits. Children rushed about, bells jingling from their ankles, and a dark form soared overhead. Against her better judgment, Saga craned her neck in time to catch a pair of winged horses taking to the skies.

"What is this place?" she murmured in amazement, more to herself than to the clanswomen. It was jarring to see children playing and people going about their regular lives when only this morning she'd left a place of such misery and despair. Saga bit down on her lip, wondering yet again if she'd made the right choice by climbing on Havoc's back. She could have detonated that fire flask and killed King Ivar. What if she'd missed the chance to turn the tides of battle?

Saga was led to a quiet tent, the flaps thrown back to reveal planked wooden flooring and a fire crackling softly in a central hearth. As she stepped inside and the tent walls surrounded her, Saga's heart immediately calmed, the tension in her chest beginning to loosen. She peered up at a smoke hole cut in the roof, then down at the iron loops secured in the floor. Her mind's eye showed her Havoc, shackled in the stables by a loop much like this, and Saga couldn't help but laugh. What else could she do?

"What is funny?" demanded Khiva. She'd folded her arms, supervising as the red-haired horsemaiden secured Saga's hands to the loop in the floor.

"It is nothing," Saga replied wearily.

And with that, Khiva and the horsemaiden departed, leaving Saga alone in the tent.

Saga curled on the floor, facing the fire as she tried to wrangle her thoughts. Her pulse had eased slightly with the comfort of walls and a roof, but her body tingled with the lingering effects of the day. She was bone-weary and craved nothing but to collapse into a long, deep sleep. Yet time was a luxury Saga did not have. How much time had passed on the steppe? The sun was near setting as they'd landed at the city of tents. Saga had to speak to this clansmother. Needed to convince her to fight for the easterners.

Hours seemed to pass before the tent flap was pulled aside and a trio of women stepped into the tent. Saga struggled to a sitting position and faced the women with as much dignity as she could muster. Immediately, she knew which one was the clansmother. With silver braids that contrasted against her brown skin, this woman's feather-trimmed cloak was more ornate than the others. As the clansmother stepped deeper into the tent, firelight caught on the silver torcs at her collarbones and wrists.

The woman's eyes narrowed as she examined Saga's torn and singed clothing. The clansmother paused a few paces away as her ladies gathered on either side of her. Khiva, Saga noted, scowled from the tent doorway.

"Who are you to trespass on my lands?"

As the clansmother spoke, her cloak shifted, hundreds of iridescent feathers glinting in the light.

"I am Saga Volsik, rightful queen of Íseldur, and no enemy to you."

She did not pause, not even at the flurry of whispers from the clansmother's ladies.

"Kovograd is attacked by Urkans and will fall soon. Men will be killed, women and children taken to other Urkan colonies."

The clansmother watched, her face impassive.

Saga dug deeper, desperate to find the thread that would pull this woman to her cause. "Once, clans came for help of the east—"

"That," said the clansmother, "was centuries ago."

Saga swallowed and tried again. "When Kovograd falls, Urkans will aim next for steppe." She let that statement hang in the air for a moment before continuing. "They will come for horses and lands. And they will come for children."

The faintest flare of the woman's pupils was Saga's only hint that her words had any effect. Still, she shouldered on. She twisted until the scars on the backs of her hands were bared to the clansmother. "Urkans are monsters." Her voice wavered as the ladies leaned forward, studying the screaming bears branded into her flesh. "I once lived among them. Have seen many horrors. Please, listen to my warnings."

The woman stared at Saga's branding marks, silent for a long minute. Saga bit down on her cheek, trying to keep from shouting, from screaming and snarling like a wild thing. How could this woman pause even for an instant, when the blood of innocents spilled and her people were next? How was her answer not immediately *yes*?

"East and west must unite," Saga pleaded, her desperation growing. "Alone, you are not enough. Urkans have power you cannot imagine." She thought of the siege tower and the thousands of warriors. "Your horsewomen could break battle . . . expel Urkans from lands . . ."

The clansmother lifted a hand, and Saga fell silent. Her heart hammered in her throat and her skull; emotion clawed at the backs of her eyes.

"The wheel of fate," said the clansmother, "works in mysterious ways." Her dark eyes roamed Saga's face. "I am sorry for what you have faced, queen of Íseldur, but I do not know you. How can I send my warriors into battle at the word of a stranger?"

The throb in Saga's skull built to a deafening crescendo. "Please," she begged. "I—I will give to you *anything.* They will *die.*" Her mind spun with dizzying force. "*Please.*"

But the clansmother turned. "The east deceived us before. There is nothing that can convince me to trust them again." And with that, she departed.

"Please!" shouted Saga, Kassandr's face flashing in her mind. "They cannot die!"

Movement in the tent's corner drew Saga's gaze. There lingered Khiva, watching her silently. But after a moment, she followed the others.

And as the tent flaps slid shut, Saga's sob broke free.

CHAPTER 41

Kovograd, Zagadka

Kassandr's body ached as never before as he slashed and parried, retreated and surged forward. His Druzhina flowed around him, bending and parting like water. Guarding his flank, they relentlessly cut down berserker warriors as Kassandr lost himself to the frenzy of battle. Fat snowflakes had drifted downward all day, giving the battle a strange, muted feel. But everywhere he looked, red spattered the blanket of white.

Darkness fell, and the moons rose, and Kassandr became aware there were fewer Zagadkian warriors at his back. His Druzhina was falling.

But on he fought, not a man, nor a beast, but a being of destruction fueled by stimulant teas and battle thrill. Through the buzzing in his veins; through the battle haze shrouding his mind, Kassandr knew one thing for certain. The Urkans were set to win this battle.

Though time was lost to him, the moons told Kassandr it was sometime past midnight. Now fighting in his human form, he'd forced his beast away for the time being. In the early evening, Kass had lost his humanity, had lost his control, had lunged and snarled and tried to kill anything that got too near—be it friend or foe.

Rov had fetched the snare, and it had taken half a dozen men to drag Kassandr back to the fortress. But Rov had been unable to find Saga to help ease Kassandr. And in the end, he was thrust into a bathhouse, the healer's potent herbs drifting up from the steaming rocks. They'd rendered him senseless for several hours, and when Kass had woken, he'd been in his human form. Now his beast was confined, but it raged behind his rib cage, demanding to be let out.

When the Urkan warriors did not retreat with the last light of the day, Kass knew in the marrow of his bones that the battle would end tonight. He'd savored Saga's presence as she'd slumbered beside him, but he wished he'd known it would be the last time. Perhaps he'd have said something different. Done something different. Perhaps he'd have found the courage to apologize for all the sorrow he'd brought to her life.

The Urkans could taste victory and drove forward with more vigor. The siege tower hurled barrel after barrel at the fortress walls and the buildings behind it, and Kassandr knew they were beyond what the nets of seaweed and soaked hides could protect. There were too many sparks; too many gods damned barrels.

Any warrior who could fight was now on the battlefield. Any who could fire a bow or pour buckets of boiling water—women and the far-too-young included—were now stationed atop the walls. Kassandr hazarded a glance over his shoulder, trying to regain his bearings. But the flurries were too thick, the battlefield too chaotic, and as a berserker lunged at him from his left, Kassandr slammed his blade into the man's armpit.

As he hauled his sword free, crunching snow signaled Yuri Rovgolod's arrival.

"It is done?" asked Kassandr, pausing to wipe cold sweat from his brow. As night had fallen, so too had the cold, and his dampened hair was now frosted white.

"Rovgolod?" he demanded.

"Elisava leads the elders and the injured into the tunnels," Rov panted, driving his shield into the gut of a charging warrior. Kassandr finished the stunned man off with a brutal slash to the neck. Steam rose from the wound as hot blood met frigid air.

"Good," said Kassandr, then paused. "What is it?"

Rov's face held a strange expression. "If I am to die, then I will own my truth," Rov proclaimed, slashing his blade through an Urkan's neck. As he turned to face Kassandr, his brown skin was flecked with blood, but his smile was wide. "I am in love with your sister."

Kassandr blinked, then lunged, intercepting a warrior coming for Rov's flank. "My sister?"

"She is the most beautiful woman in Zagadka. Most pleasant disposition—"

"You are certain you speak of *Elisava*?"

Rov's smile had somehow grown wider, and though it was mad, Kassandr grinned right back. "I am glad for you, my brother," he said, slapping Rov on the shoulder. "Will you take the Rurik byname and become my brother by marriage?"

But Kass's smile suddenly faltered. "You made no mention of Saga. She too is in the tunnels?"

Rov's expression tightened.

"And *Saga*?" Kassandr repeated.

"She has not been seen for many hours."

Kassandr's beast smashed against his ribs in a burst of searing anger. Not seen. Not *seen*? "What does this mean?" growled Kassandr.

"It means," grumbled Rov, sinking into a defensive stance as a trio of berserkers lumbered forward, "that she has not been seen. Nothing more and nothing less. I am certain she is well, Kassandr."

Kassandr's mind whirled for an explanation. Saga's transformation over the past days had been remarkable. She'd gone from cautious and fearful to a woman his people turned to. Kassandr's pride had grown with Saga's increasing boldness, but this latest development had him worried. Had she pushed too far? Gone from bold to reckless?

Again, he glanced toward the fortress's defensive walls, difficult to view through the snowfall. "She is not atop the walls?" he barked at Rov while trading sword blows with a slavering Urkan.

Rov slammed the rim of his shield into a berserker's mouth, sending teeth flying. "Not," he agreed.

Kassandr blinked rapidly, trying to understand, but inside, his beast grew more and more frenetic. Where was his Saga? Where *was she*? His beast snarled and yipped, desperate to be free of its cage as his mind tormented him with dozens of possibilities of what might have befallen her.

Beside him, one of his best Druzhina—a warrior who'd been with Kass for eight years—fell with a cry of agony. The man's voice joined the screams of the wounded and dying, as his people were cut down around him. Kassandr threw himself at the Urkan who'd killed his man, stabbing and hacking with rage and sorrow.

Through the thick flurries of snow, a barrel soared through the air, landing with bone-rattling impact. The toll of a bell and screams from behind him told Kassandr its mark had been true. Yet still, nothing could quell the shock he felt as he glanced over his shoulder. The barrel had collided with the fortress bell tower—the crown jewel of Kovograd city, and the largest entry gate into the fortress. The seaweed and hides, even with a layer of snow upon them, did little to stop the flames, which now spread along the roof and ate down the timbered walls.

For the first time since the Urkans had landed, Kassandr felt true despair. This was all wrong. His people were falling. His home was burned. And Saga was missing.

His sword found purchase in the joint between an Urkan's snarling bear shoulder plates and breast armor, and the warrior crumpled to the ground. The rage of Kassandr's beast nearly clouded his vision, but through it he caught sight of a smaller figure with a familiar face.

With a shout of fury, Kassandr barreled toward Prince Bjorn, cutting down warriors without mercy.

"Kassandr!" shouted Rov behind him, the rest of his Druzhina scrambling to keep up.

Kassandr's anger burned as it had never before. He cut down Urkan warriors with alternating swings of his sword and cunning slashes of his dagger. He was death incarnate, the feeder of the wolves and ravens. Tonight they would feast, not only on his countrymen, but on the corpses of his enemies. Blood rained down on the snow, and Kassandr saw the moment the princeling recognized him. Bjorn's pale, freckled face pulled into a look of pure terror.

At thirteen winters, Bjorn was too young to be in this battle, too young to be blamed for any of this. Yet Kassandr knew if he captured the prince, it could change the tides of battle.

But a familiar red-bearded warrior stepped between them, smashing Kassandr's plans to ruins. Half a head taller than any warrior on the battlefield, Thorir the Giant's armor was spattered with blood and gore.

"Kassandr Rurik is mine!" bellowed the giant, thumping his chest plate with the broad side of his blade. "We have unfinished business."

Kassandr gritted his teeth as Prince Bjorn was ushered away, any hopes of a ransom along with him. Rov and his Druzhina gathered around Kassandr, panting with the exertion of hacking their way to him.

"We must return to Zagadkian lines," heaved Rov. "We have gone too deep."

But Kassandr only squared his feet. "It is time I finished the red troll man," he growled. "You will not interfere, Rov. But keep the Urkans away so I do not take a knife to the back."

Rov grumbled in frustration, but he soon fell back with the rest of the Zagadkian warriors.

Wiping the melted snow from his face, Kassandr reached for his bravado. "You lost the last time," Kassandr shouted to Thorir in Íseldurian. "You are eager to lose again?"

Thorir took a menacing step forward. "I am eager for vengeance. You see, warrior, I don't lose with a sword."

Kassandr's jaw hardened, but there was no time for anything but to block Thorir the Giant's longsword from taking his head. Their steel blades clashed with bone-jarring force. Kassandr reacted quickly, kicking out low, but as his foot connected with Thorir's armor it did not so much as budge the larger warrior.

"The battlefield is my kingdom," growled Thorir as they exchanged blows. "Here you won't win." He drew a dagger, then twisted to deliver a brutal backslash to Kassandr's shoulder.

Though the armored jacket protected him from the worst of it, the blade slashed into his flesh. Kassandr hissed, his beast howled, and they threw their collective force into a flurry of attacks. Thorir was on the defensive now, barely keeping up with the preternatural speed Kassandr's beast granted him. A nearby Urkan tossed his shield to Thorir, who caught it and charged forward.

Kassandr whirled to the side, tutting. "I see you are again needing favors from others. It seems they still know you cannot defeat me."

Thorir recovered with startling swiftness, slamming the metal rim of the shield at Kassandr's face. Kassandr raised his sword and braced it with both hands against the shield. He gave it a hefty shove, forcing Thorir to dig his boots into the packed snow.

"Tell me what you did to Magnus," gritted Thorir. The giant of a man dropped the shield and retrieved another dagger, ducking beneath Kassandr's sword and slashing at his leg.

The tear of fabric and searing pain from his left thigh had Kassandr lurching back.

"You killed him, didn't you?" growled Thorir. "Else you'd have claimed ransom."

A grim smile spread on Kassandr's lips, and he knew his eyes had flashed a warning green. "You're more clever than you look," he taunted. Thorir dropped his dagger and grabbed his longsword in a two-handed grip, hefting it overhead, but Kassandr danced out of range.

"Come here," growled Thorir. "You dishonorable son of swine."

Kassandr's smile grew. "I have called my father worse to his face."

"You like to play games," snarled Thorir. The large man's eyes flashed as he adjusted his grip on his sword. "I can play, too."

"Please do not overtax yourself, Thorir. There are battles yet to fight."

"A shame," said Thorir, driving forward, "that Lady Saga is not here to help you this time."

At the mention of Saga's name, shock jolted through Kassandr's body and his foot slipped on packed snow. Thorir capitalized on Kassandr's shock, aiming a powerful backswing right at his neck. Kassandr ducked, lifting his arm with not a moment to spare. The blade struck his bracer, severing through the fortified material and into his forearm.

Kassandr bellowed in pain, but Thorir's words of Saga kept him lucid. "What did you say?" demanded Kassandr.

Thorir's smile was cruel and mocking, and he raised his longsword up for another two-handed swing. Kassandr bounded back, and the sword hammered deep into the snowpack.

"She went to Ivar," grunted Thorir, freeing his sword and righting himself. "She surrendered herself."

Kassandr shook his head vehemently. "You lie."

Thorir's laugh was cruel and mocking. "Ask anyone. She pleaded for Íseldur. Begged King Ivar to withdraw. Of course, he would never agree to such terms. Her head is now mounted on a pike at our war camp."

The battle seething around them seemed to fade away. The rage of Kassandr's beast bled into his body, and he knew in an instant that he could not hold it back. The air thickened with the magic of his shifting. "You wish to know Magnus's fate?" His bones cracked, claws and spines bursting free from his skin. "He drove me to such anger I tore out his throat."

Thorir's eyes widened, and he stumbled backward. But it was too late—Kassandr was already airborne. And as he tore the throat from Thorir the Giant, the last human thought that entered his mind was that perhaps the man did lose with a sword after all.

CHAPTER 42

Sunnavík, Íseldur

Jonas followed the queen's guardsman through the torchlit corridors of Askaborg, while wondering if the finely wrought sconces were made from gold or only forged to look like it. Each night for the past week, Jonas had found the queen's man waiting for him after the evening meal, always with a summons from Queen Signe.

After relaying all he knew of Eisa Volsik to the queen, Jonas had expected her to lose interest in him. But still, the requests came. Perhaps the queen had found an unexpected ally in him—someone to share in her anger and hatred. Sometimes she spoke of her daughter Yrsa, slain by Saga Volsik, and sometimes she asked Jonas about Ilías.

Jonas was surprised to realize that at some point during the week, he'd stopped assessing the guards at each exit of the garrison hall. His longings to escape this place had lessened substantially. It certainly wasn't due to any improvement in the warband. Volund was still a brute, his morals nonexistent. The war chieftain believed that by culling the weakest from his crew, his warband grew stronger. But the way Jonas saw it, to lead by fear was no way for a headman to build trust among his warriors.

The draugur were hauled into the pits each day by their iron collars, spitting and snarling like wild beasts. But the moment an acolyte carved a strange-looking rune into their foreheads, their demeanors grew instantaneously placid—at least until the acolyte gave the order to attack.

Now the Corpse Bringers warband was expected to square off with the vile draugur. Jonas had to wonder where these corpses had come from. They seemed too fresh to have come from the grave. But he'd learned that in this band, it was best not to ask too many questions.

With each passing day, Jonas became more certain that this warband had nothing to do with keeping peace in the realm. Murmurs abounded of a place called Rökksgarde, where the next phase of their training would begin. Yet the lack of firm details raised Jonas's hackles.

Logically, he knew he should probably resume his attempts to flee this place, yet the queen and her continual summons held his curiosity. Where was this "friendship" going, and what would happen should Jonas see it through?

Tonight, as he entered the queen's private drawing room, he immediately realized something was different.

"Jonas," said Signe, lounging in her preferred chair near the hearth.

"Your Highness." Jonas bowed low, but as he straightened, he blinked at the queen. "You're not in mourning."

She was clad in a gown of pure white, with an ivory mantle clasped at her delicate throat. Candlelight caught on the glacial pearls hanging from her ears, and the steel crown upon her brow. Her lips lifted with the hint of a sad smile.

"Today," sighed the queen, "I forgo my mourning attire to celebrate my sister's birthday."

"I did not know you have a sister," said Jonas, hesitantly approaching.

"How could you?" laughed the queen, and he thought he caught the hint of a slur in her words. "She's long dead." Signe gestured for Jonas to take the seat across from her, and he did so carefully. "Today, my darling Eylín would have seen thirty-six winters. Let us raise a cup—" She paused, realizing Jonas had no cup, then waved at a servant.

A cupbearer appeared and filled a goblet for Jonas before vanishing like a whisper.

"Let us raise a cup," Signe repeated, lifting her jeweled goblet. Reluctantly, Jonas did the same. "To Eylín," said the queen, "the best of us all. The most selfless. The most *beautiful*."

There was a sarcastic edge to the queen's voice that gave Jonas pause, but he quickly murmured in agreement, then sipped from his goblet. The queen's blue eyes had a glazed look to them, and he wondered how long she'd been drinking by the fire.

"Did you know," said Signe, "*Eylín* was meant to marry Ivar?"

"Oh?"

"'Tis true. She was to marry Ivar, and *I* was to be slaughtered with the rest of my siblings. The Urkans only need one daughter, you see." The queen's brows pulled together as she stared into her goblet. "A shame she had a terrible fall from the castle tower. It was an awful thing, to see her limbs splayed out at such angles."

Jonas swallowed thickly and let the queen continue.

"Eylín died on what was to be her wedding day. And then it became *my* wedding day."

"Did she—" Jonas shut his mouth before he could voice the question.

"Did she jump?" Signe drew in a deep breath, then let it out slowly. "I suppose if she had, she'd have been cleverer than me. Sometimes I think marriage to Ivar is a punishment worse than death."

Jonas's skin prickled as he waited for her to continue. But the queen eyed him, clearly weighing a decision.

"I can trust you, can't I, Jonas? Yes." She nodded to herself. "I *can* trust you. You've shared so much with me."

The words seemed meant to convince herself, rather than him, and Jonas sat uneasily quiet. The queen took a long drink from her goblet, tongue darting out to catch a drop of wine from the corner of her lips. Signe set the cup aside and leaned toward Jonas. "Eylín didn't jump," she whispered conspiratorially. "I pushed her."

The queen's drunken confession rocked Jonas to his core. Why was she telling him this? In some cases, it was a benefit to know secrets about one's ally. But this was the gods damned queen, and she could have him killed with a snap of her fingers. And she *had* just revealed herself to be a killer.

Signe was gazing at her hands, as though mystified that they might have done it. But something sharpened in her expression. "I suppose I should not have told you that."

"Your secret is safe with me, Your Highness," said Jonas, his heartbeat kicking up a notch.

The queen's nails tapped against the carved arms of her chair as she stared at him. There was a warning in her gaze, a silent knife to his throat. His heart pounded harder, faster. He needed to say something to put her at ease . . .

"I understand," said Jonas, his voice slightly hoarse. "I, too, know what it is to have the blood of my kin on my hands."

And before he knew what was happening, Jonas spilled the details about his abusive father. Of how he'd killed him in retribution for the murder of his mother. But by the time the last words fell from him, the queen's posture had eased, and Jonas knew he'd done the right thing in telling her. She'd shared something deeply personal, and with it came a sense of instability. His confession was simply rebalancing the scales. Placing them back on even ground.

Signe shook her head slowly. "You understand," she said softly, something flickering behind her eyes. "In this world, it is kill or be killed." Her gaze locked onto his, as though fortifying this new bond.

Jonas nodded, though something in her words didn't sit entirely right. It was one thing to deliver death to an evil man, and altogether another to push an innocent woman from a tower. But there was no force in this kingdom that would convince Jonas to voice such thoughts.

"Should I have simply rolled over and let the Urkans slaughter me?" The queen laughed, though it sounded far from amused. "Still, it was a . . . regretful thing to have to do."

"I understand," Jonas repeated numbly. "I will mourn my brother until my last breath. But it is my father who haunts my dreams. Whose words slither into my mind."

The queen pushed to her feet. Sauntered over to him. Lifted Jonas's goblet and pressed it to his lips. Gripping the arms of his chair in surprise, Jonas obligingly sipped.

"You understand," whispered the queen, setting the goblet down. Her face was now an inch from his, and she slid a finger across his lips, capturing a droplet of wine. "How is it that you *always* understand?" Jonas hardly dared breathe as the queen stared at him, perplexed.

And then she pressed her lips to his.

She tasted like wine and honey, and her lips were soft as silk. For an instant, Jonas forgot just who she was, losing himself in this moment of vulnerability. They'd shared their burdens with each other, and with that came a sense of weightlessness.

But shock jolted through Jonas as he recalled just who he kissed. Queen Signe was married to a violent man—a king, no less.

"Wait," he said, drawing back. The queen's gaze grew thunderous as she stared back at him. "The wine," he said quickly. "You're intoxicated. I cannot take liberties—"

"I can handle my wine far better than most." Signe ran a hand up his biceps, and indeed, her words were clear.

Despite all the logical reasons he ought to end this, Jonas was a hot-blooded man with a pair of eyes. It was impossible not to note the queen's beauty. And if she wanted comfort in his arms, who was he to deny her?

Jonas swept the queen onto his lap. And then he kissed her in earnest.

Hours later, Jonas lay in the queen's bed, staring dazedly at the ivory canopy above. It had to be made of silk, imported from some isle to the south, and it was delicately sculpted into the shape of a flower. He stared, dumbstruck, at this elaborate canopy, pondering how he'd climbed from the dungeons to the queen's bed in a few short weeks. But then Jonas decided some things were better not examined too closely.

The queen lay curled against his side, her breathing soft and rhythmic. But as a draft whispered through the room, Jonas carefully extracted himself from her slumbering form to set another log in the fireplace.

"Leaving so soon?" asked the queen, a sour note in her sleepy voice.

Jonas paused, then looked over his shoulder, satisfied to find her gaze homed in on his backside. "Only livening the fire, *my queen,*" he said softly. "Does that please you?"

Her scornful expression shifted into something softer, a slow smile curling her lips. "What would *please* me," she purred, "is something to nibble on. I've rather worked up an appetite." Signe looked at him expectantly. Did she intend for *him* to fetch it? After a brief internal struggle, Jonas padded to the doorway.

Beyond it, he found a pair of unsmiling guards, who looked at him with disdain as Jonas relayed the queen's request. After a long-suffering sigh, the smaller of the two wandered off, and Jonas slid the door shut. He turned back to the bed, eyeing the queen's naked form. She was lithe, and with her alabaster skin and white-gold hair, she looked like an ethereal creature not of this realm. Jonas prowled toward her, his intentions clear.

But the queen waved a hand at him, saying, "Not now."

Jonas blinked furiously at her casual dismissal.

"Come here, Jonas," said Signe, patting the bed beside her. "Sit."

His teeth snapped together at the command, and it took every ounce of his will to obey. Reluctantly, he sat on the edge of the bed.

"I *did* have a matter in mind when I summoned you to my chambers last night," she said, gaze trailing across his chest. "Before we were . . . diverted by other things."

Jonas nodded slowly.

The queen's glacial-blue eyes met his, and he could not read the expression behind them. "What do you think is the purpose of Volund's warband?"

His brows dipped low at the unexpected question. "Are you asking if I believe what I've been told?"

The queen nodded.

"Do I believe that our purpose is to protect Íseldur while the king fights in Zagadka?" He shook his head. "I do not think it true."

The queen seemed pleased with this answer. She leaned forward and placed a hand on Jonas's forearm. "And what do you think the warband's purpose *is,* darling?"

He licked his lips, choosing his words carefully. "I think you have your own plans for the Corpse Bringers."

The queen nodded to herself, as though confirming some suspicion. "I can see your ambition. I can feel your anger. You're a talented, cunning warrior. We have so much in common, you and I." Her fingers massaged his forearm softly. "Tell me, Jonas, what do you want? *Truly* want?"

He need not even think about it. Wordlessly, Jonas reached for the talisman hanging from his neck and pulled it over his head. He handed it to the queen, allowing her to examine the three interlocked triangles.

"Family, respect, duty," he said softly. "These are the Svik family values. All I seek in this world is to restore my family's honor. I must avenge my brother's death and buy back the family lands that were stripped from us." It was strange. The sense of conviction he normally felt had grown somewhat muted. Perhaps it was only that Jonas had spoken these words so many times.

The queen pressed the talisman back in his palm, then folded his fingers over it. Her eyes met his, and he felt it all through his body.

"What if I told you," said Signe, "that you could do better. You could have all that, and more. A jarldom—a rank of power. You could have your family lands back *and* gain authority over those who wronged you."

A hot, hungry feeling pumped through Jonas's veins. All his adult life, he'd only yearned for what he'd lost—had never imagined he could do better. But with this queen beside him, the world seemed more like a feasting table.

"Do you want that, Jonas?"

"Yes."

"Good," said Signe, pulling him toward her on the bed. "I have need of good men. Cunning men. Warriors who can see beyond the battlefield to the greater picture."

As Jonas crawled to her, Signe's eyes roamed hungrily across his straining biceps.

"And our plans have just begun," said the queen, coming up on her knees and running a soft hand along the planes of his chest. "Soon we shall head north to Rökksgarde and unite with Maester Alfson. Do you recall the Chosen warriors who accompanied you to Nordur?"

Jonas thought of the strange warriors who'd been able to render themselves invisible. The queen's Chosen, they'd been called, an elite branch of warriors with special gifts. "Aye," he said, letting his own hands wander along the queen's pale skin.

"They were only the first of Alfson's experiments. In Rökksgarde, our warband will start the next phase of training, transforming into something great . . . something *unstoppable.*" Signe's fingers slid into Jonas's beard. "After you complete the ritual in Rökksgarde, you'll be promoted to Volund's second, but it is only the start." A smile curved her soft lips. "Stay this path with me, Jonas, and you'll be granted power beyond your wildest imaginings. Together, we will avenge your brother and my Yrsa's deaths. The Volsik sisters cannot live."

She drew back, her ice-blue eyes blazing. "What say you to this?"

Jonas's fingertips drifted up the bumps of her spine. "I think," he said softly, "I find your passion quite catching."

The queen leaned forward, finally bringing her lips to his. "Good," she whispered against him. "I've found I'm rather hungry for something other than food."

With a warrior's speed and strength, Jonas rolled Signe onto her back and pinned her to the mattress. "What does my queen command?"

"Make me scream," she whispered with dark delight.

CHAPTER 43

Kopa, Íseldur

The hours dragged on, but Silla only grew more resolute in her choice to remain shackled to her bed. She'd let her condition go on in secret for too long—she ought to have locked herself away in the aftermath of Fallgerd's death.

Now she was simply too tired to keep the god of chaos from slithering into her mind. She dreamed His dreams; heard His curious mutterings. Myrkur was always prodding, always searching, and Silla knew He was trying to understand her bloodline gift and how it had the power to undo Him. She'd thought that she could hold Him off—that she had more time. But now, she was forced to accept the truth.

She was slowly losing herself to Myrkur.

For the hundredth time, Silla wondered how things had gone so badly. She'd failed at being a silent placeholder queen. Had ruined Hakon's plans to rally the jarls and Rey's chances of mustering warriors. Gods, what had she done? Saga would never have made such a mess of things.

Atli and Runný sat near the hearth, frantically flipping through tomes as though the answer to all Silla's problems would suddenly emerge. The silence in the room made Silla want to scream. It was no weightless, easy silence, but a dangerous, unsettling kind. Each passing breath brought them a moment closer to the doomed battle at the heartwood. How was she going to vanquish this mist when she did not have her own thoughts to herself?

You must convince them to release you, Eisa, whispered Myrkur. *If we want the throne, we must act quickly. The jarls cannot leave before they've sworn themselves to us—*

Silla squeezed her eyes shut and tried to push the god away. But no matter how many hearthfire thoughts she forced into her mind, Silla could not find a shred of optimism. It was like a vital part of her had died; like her light had been smothered by Myrkur's darkness.

Atli slammed a book shut with obvious irritation. When he'd first arrived in the morning, Atli had droned on about everything and nothing for several long minutes, until Silla finally demanded that he give her an honest report. It was not good news. Jarl Holger, it seemed, was not ready to raise his banners for Eisa Volsik, and the other jarls were following suit. The lone bright spot in this dismal news was that Holger would still send the men he'd promised to the heartwood. But none of the other jarls had made such an offer.

"Holger has ordered his horses readied," Atli finished, wearily. "He plans to ride home on the morrow."

Atli had settled near the hearth with a book soon after, and Lady Tala had taken his place by her side. She'd examined Silla's pallor and tutted over the manacles clasped at her wrists. But then Tala had fluffed the pillows and ordered a window opened to allow fresh air into the chambers. Broth was brought up, and Tala offered to spoon it into her mouth, but Silla's stomach roiled at the sight of it.

"Has there been any sign of Ingvarr?" Silla whispered, the wounds in her palms throbbing angrily. Rey had explained that such marks could only have been left when defending herself, and that Ingvarr had fled before he could be questioned. Had Ingvarr attacked Silla, and Myrkur retaliated? And did this mean that Ingvarr was the assassin?

But there were too many questions—too many holes that needed filling. For one thing, Ingvarr had been far from Silla's cup on the day of the attempted poisoning. When questioned about the day of the rockslide, Runný could not recall Ingvarr's position. It had been too chaotic, and their group was fractured by the slide.

Lady Tala shook her head with a tight smile. "There has been no sign of him, I'm afraid, but you needn't worry. You must focus on restoring your health. Come, take some broth."

Tala lifted the spoon again, the thin liquid quivering upon it. Bile rose in Silla's throat again. "Later," she said weakly. With a frustrated sigh, Tala set the bowl aside then began prattling on about the inroads she and Ladies Liv and Kaeja had made with the jarls' wives.

Silla was glad when Tala finally took her leave until she realized she was now alone with Myrkur and her toxic thoughts. The god of chaos breathed in her bitterness and exhaled it in greater potency. She'd come to Kopa with hope and determination, but now she felt shattered and on the very brink of ruin.

There was blood on her hands.

Poison in her mind.

Why are you so stubborn, Eisa? whispered Myrkur, His claws sliding into her mind, kneading and molding it as He saw fit. *Are you not intrigued by all that we could accomplish together?*

Silla sighed, too weary to shove Him out.

All you need to do is let me in. Grant me access to your bloodline gift.

Images flooded her mind—legions of undead creatures and black-veined Klaernar; berserker warriors banging weapons against their shields. An enormous black dragon circled the skies above, and all the while, raw, unbridled power thrummed through Silla's veins. *You could have it all, Eisa,* whispered Myrkur. *The throne. Íseldur's undying loyalty. A reprieve from your pitiful mortal struggles. All you need to do is yield your Volsik power to me.*

The door flew open and crashed against the wall, sending Myrkur's depraved images scattering from her mind. Rey stormed through the doorway, a strange look upon his face. Deep inside her, Myrkur hissed in displeasure.

"What is it?" asked Runný as she and Atli gathered at Silla's bedside.

"This!" There was a note of triumph in Rey's voice, and his hand was curled into a fist. Rey's dark gaze homed in on Silla. "You hadn't any cuts on your hands when they found you in Fallgerd's home. There were only smears of blood on your gown and hands."

Runný nodded vehemently.

"Fallgerd suffered a dozen stab wounds," continued Rey. "If you'd killed him, Silla, you'd surely have cut yourself."

Silla's gaze roamed his face as she tried to understand.

He shook his fist once more, and for the first time, Silla realized he held a small scrap of fabric. "I visited the undertaker," he said, a mad sort of gleam in his eyes. "While preparing Fallgerd's body for burial, he found this in his hand."

Rey held the scrap near enough for Silla to study it. A swath of red fabric was embroidered with threads of gold in the image of a dragon's claw. Shock jolted through her in recognition, but Atli's dark voice beat her to it.

"This is my house sigil." Atli's olive skin flushed red with fury.

Rey kept his focus trained on Silla. "Someone else was in that room, Silla," he said gently. "The dark form you saw was real."

Tears blurred her vision.

"You didn't kill Fallgerd," he said in a low, dark voice. "This fabric proves someone else was there. Imagine that this *someone* entered Fallgerd's home. Tried to kill Princess Eisa. But Old Man Fallgerd interrupted them, and they turned on him instead."

"I didn't—"

"No. You didn't. I suspect that Fallgerd's killer then turned his blade on you—that was the dark form looming over you. But you screamed. Startled them away."

The despair in Silla's chest was displaced by a feeling so potent it sent Myrkur skittering deep within her. Hope. "But the blood on my hands—"

"Came from the weapon. They used your hevrít; placed it back on your lap to frame you."

She hadn't killed Fallgerd.

But who had? Silla forced her thoughts back to that horrid day.

Ingvarr had hauled her to her feet and carried her from the home. She'd stared at his uniform, desperate for calm. Had noted the róa stains. The torn corner of his sigil.

"It *was* Ingvarr," she whispered. "Ingvarr killed Fallgerd."

Victory swelled in Rey's chest as Runný and Atli raced off to search through Ingvarr's quarters. He and Silla were alone in the room.

"I have Atli's sedative in my pocket," said Rey, staring at Silla's fluttering pulse. Her eyes were set with determination, yet uncertainty still lurked beneath.

He slid the key into the manacles and they clicked open, releasing her wrist. Rey took it in his hands and massaged the red indentation. His eyes met hers and held them. "I won't hesitate to use that sedative. And I surely won't let you near my nose again."

Rey had seen his reflection—two black eyes and a new crook across the bridge of his nose. It looked ghastly, and yet it was nothing he hadn't suffered before. As he released the rest of Silla's shackles, he felt as though he could finally breathe. He'd spent hours chasing down leads, questioning anyone who'd been near Fallgerd's home on that fateful day. Rey had been too late to examine Fallgerd's body before it was buried. But when the undertaker had passed Rey a satchel with the old man's bodily possessions, his irritation had quickly shifted to exhilaration.

That scrap of fabric changed everything.

And as he'd watched understanding light Silla's eyes, he realized how much Fallgerd's death had weighed on her. He hoped this news loosened the dark god's grip on her just a touch.

Silla now held the scrap of fabric up to the light. "I should have known," she said softly. "Ingvarr's attire is normally pristine. But the day of Fallgerd's murder, as he carried me back to Ashfall, it was stained and torn." Silla's gaze turned steely. "*Queen Signe sends her regards.* That's what he said."

"So Ingvarr is working for the Urkan queen." Rey massaged Silla's wrists, running over everything he knew about Ingvarr. "He was appointed by Jarl Hakon to keep you safe. Now it seems he might actually have been tasked with ending your life."

"Ingvarr was with us on the day of the rockslide," mused Silla. Her eyes met Rey's. "Do you think Jarl Hakon knew Ingvarr's motives?"

Rey bit down on his back molars. Jarl Hakon was a schemer to be sure, yet of anyone, he stood to benefit from Eisa Volsik's return. "That landslide endangered his heir's life," Rey said slowly. "And Atli's reaction just now"—he shook his head—"he was genuinely shocked."

"I should like," said Silla, climbing from bed, "to look at Ingvarr's quarters myself. Perhaps there is an explanation—a motive to be found." She snatched a gown draped on the back of a chair, then slid it over her head. Within minutes, she was dressed in a gown and boots, her hair braided back. But most beautiful of all was the brightness back in her eyes.

"May I?" asked Rey huskily. In his hands was the thigh sheath he'd gifted to her all those days ago. At her nod, he dropped to his knees before her, one hand sliding under her skirts. He slid the strap in place. Pressed a kiss to her knee. And let the silken skirts fall to the floor.

As he stood, he noted the color in her cheeks—the determination in her eyes. But as her gaze settled on Rey, they softened.

"You never gave up on me," she said.

The very thought made anger kindle inside him. Rey slid his hands over her hips. He tugged her against him, then tilted her chin up. "Never," he said through gritted teeth.

Silla's fingers slid around his neck, and she pulled him down until his lips hovered just above hers. "Frightened together," she whispered against him. "Somewhere along the line, I forgot about our promise." And then Silla kissed him deeply, gripping his jacket while pushing up on the tips of her toes.

A groan built low in his throat as he held her to him, no traces of cold, no traces of anger—of the vile god still lurking inside her. "Always," Rey said. It was strange how this thing between them grew stronger, even as the world fell to pieces.

With a sigh, Silla drew back, though her eyes held a dark promise. "Now," she said with a mischievous smile. "Shall we have a little search through Ingvarr's quarters?"

And as she flounced from the room, Rey couldn't keep the smile from curving his lips. Today, he would get answers, even if he had to tear them from Ingvarr, kicking and screaming.

To Silla, the afternoon passed in a whirl before grinding to a halting stop. Ingvarr's guards had gone into an uproar, insisting that he was a man of good name and morals.

But their protests had quieted as evidence emerged from Ingvarr's chambers: plans for Fallgerd's home; a pry bar with rock dust upon it; and most damning of all—the surcoat with a torn sigil. The scrap of fabric found in Fallgerd's hand fit perfectly in the space.

Perhaps the biggest surprise of all was the collection of sedative quills found in Ingvarr's chambers. According to Atli, these quills should be housed in the maester's apothecary. Further investigation unearthed remnants of crimson thread—the precise kind used to secure correspondence to messenger falcons. And after turning Ingvarr's room inside out, they found one of the missing letters—one from Eisa to Jarl Agnar—stashed beneath his mattress.

"Why would he keep it?" asked Silla, confused.

It was a good question—one that Rey seemed to puzzle over for some time. "Protection," Rey had finally answered, which only made Silla's head spin faster. "The only logical reason not to burn it is if this letter was damning to someone else."

"I do not understand."

"I think," Rey said carefully, "Ingvarr was doing someone else's bidding. It would make sense. Why would a queen correspond directly with a guard?"

"It's only more questions," Silla said with a sigh.

She ran over the facts in her mind. All evidence pointed to Ingvarr as both Fallgerd's killer and the one who'd triggered the rockslide. Ingvarr also seemed the culprit for Silla's missing letters. But how had Ingvarr poisoned Silla's wine when he'd been stationed well across the room? And if someone was indeed directing Ingvarr, then who?

It was midday when Atli delivered the news they did not want to hear. Ingvarr had been found.

And he was dead.

Though Rey had advised against it, Silla insisted on being brought to the body. In the far back corner of one of the stables, his corpse was sprawled in the hay. The hilt of a blade protruded from his chest, Ingvarr's hand clasped around it.

It is what he deserved, hissed Myrkur, writhing with anger.

Silla flinched, though she was glad to know Ingvarr's death could not have been by her hand—not when she'd been shackled to the bed or in Rey's presence for the past several days. Ingvarr's once-pale skin was now a grayish hue. It was clear he'd been dead for several hours.

"Pity," muttered Rey, cracking his knuckles. "I'd have liked a few minutes alone with him."

Silla pressed her fingers to her lips, sorrow flowing through her. "He took his own life."

Better his than yours, whispered the god.

"Perhaps," Rey said carefully. "Or perhaps we're only meant to think that."

Eyes wide, she turned to him. "What do you mean?"

"I mean," said Rey, "perhaps someone in this fortress was willing to kill Ingvarr to keep him from talking."

CHAPTER 44

Lands beyond the river, Zagadka

Saga Volsik was delirious with fatigue, yet refused to give in to sleep's pull. Her cheek rested on the tent's timber floor, and she'd curled herself around her tied wrists. Beneath the ropes, her skin was rubbed raw. For hours now, she'd tried to loosen her binds, but the horsemaidens clearly knew their way around a knot.

"Please!" Saga cried into the darkness. "I'll do *anything*!"

Her voice was hoarse, her throat scratched raw. Saga's hope had extinguished hours ago, yet she refused to give up. But in the silence, Saga could not keep her mind from drifting to the east. Was she already too late? Was the fortress still standing? Did Kassandr Rurik still breathe?

This last thought made her despair grow deeper and higher. Kassandr *couldn't* be dead, because she'd never met someone so alive. In this dark, silent moment, Saga was filled with the desire to tell him that he was right. That the girl he'd taken from Askaborg Castle hadn't been ready to walk freely in this world. But the girl she was now—the queen he'd shown her she could be—was ready. She wanted to show him what he'd done for her. She wanted to *thank* him.

But it was too late.

Her eyes burned, a tear rolling off the bridge of her nose and spattering the floor. Saga couldn't even be mad at herself for crying. Because she was only just realizing how dreary the world would be without Kassandr in it. But it wasn't just Kassandr; there was also Elisava's fire and Rovgolod's lazy humor.

The tent flap burst open, and Saga scrambled upright. There stood a silhouette, barely distinguishable from the darkness. For a moment she thought this a phantom vision, but the thud of Khiva's boots against the floorboards told her it was real.

"You are honest?" came Khiva's low voice in Zagadkian. "You swear you do not lie to me?"

"Why would I lie?" croaked Saga. "What I said was truth."

"My mother," said Khiva, "holds a grudge tighter than a horse to its apple."

Saga blinked at the revelation—the clansmother was Khiva's mother?—but she dared not move for fear she'd break this strange spell.

"I will not sit idle if what you say is true. I will not risk the children of my clan for my own pride." Khiva crouched low before Saga, a long-bladed knife gleaming in the darkness as she lifted it between them. Saga's pulse thrummed at the sight of it.

"I promise you, queen of Íseldur," Khiva warned, "should I discover treachery, you will find this blade buried in your neck."

A laugh fell from Saga, part disbelief, part pure madness. "If I deceive you, I'll bury it there myself, Khiva."

Khiva huffed. "You are bold, I will give you that."

Saga smiled a secret smile. What would Kassandr say to that? Perhaps his brashness had rubbed off on her. She could only hope some of her caution had transferred to him.

"I have two dozen horsewomen, armed and ready," said Khiva in a low voice.

Saga tried to quell her rising disappointment. Two dozen horsewomen were nothing to scoff at, and yet she'd hoped for more—for hundreds.

"I could not muster more without alerting my mother. She has ears all over this city, always listening and reporting back to her. But if we move swiftly, we can avoid her detection."

The blade shicked through Saga's bonds, freeing her wrists.

"Come. You will disguise yourself in this armor." Khiva proffered a shirt of chain mail, a pair of buckskin boots, a helm, and a feathered cloak, then helped Saga slip into them. Saga allowed herself a moment to examine the attire. She looked like a warrior—like a woman to be feared. And in that moment, she felt it.

They exited the tent, Saga's new boots crunching on a layer of freshly fallen snow. Slowly, she looked up. A few lazy snowflakes drifted down in the dark skies, and beyond them lay a blanket of stars. Saga gazed up as they walked, spellbound by the sheer number of them. Had she ever seen stars so vivid as this?

"Stjarna, light my path," she whispered to the Mother Star before scurrying after Khiva. The cookfires were long dead, the citizens who'd once gathered around them having long ago retreated to their tents.

"We go to the fields," Khiva whispered. "There the horses have been readied."

Saga's heart swelled with gratitude for the brave horsemaidens willing to hear her warnings—willing to look past their strife with the easterners and provide aid. After several long minutes trailing Khiva between shadowed tents, Saga saw the expanse of a snowy field come into view, punctuated by two dozen dark figures and their winged horses. Her heart thumped in anticipation, and she wondered if flight would be less frightening in the dark of night. A horse nickered, another mouthing at the snow, and then Khiva was tugging her toward a black stallion. There was no more space in her heart for fear, and no time to be afraid.

"You will ride with me," whispered Khiva, cupping her hands to help Saga onto the horse's back. But no sooner had her snowy boot landed in Khiva's palms than a voice cut through the darkness.

"My own daughter deceives me!" came the clansmother's voice.

Khiva swore, then straightened her back.

"You have freed my prisoner!" At least twenty horsemaidens had gathered around her, arrows nocked and trained toward Silla and Khiva. "You've colluded with others to undermine my rule!"

Hopelessness eddied in Saga's blood, but her anger boiled forth with startling force. This woman would hold her grudge against the easterners while they died—would put her children and grandchildren and each glorious winged horse on this steppe at risk.

"She wishes to fight!" Saga shouted with such fervor, Khiva startled beside her. "As do all these brave women! Their eyes are open to what you refuse to see, clansmother. Come with us. See what the future holds."

People had begun to gather, drawn from their tents by the commotion.

Good, thought Saga. Let them all hear what threat loomed nearer and nearer. Her Zagadkian grew more fluent as she fell into the speech she'd practiced with Elisava. "The Urkans murdered my parents and stole my throne! They dismantled my kingdom stone by stone until all bent the knee to their Bear God and king. I know these people! I was raised by them. They take and they take and they *take,* until there is nothing left, and then they move on to the next isle! How long after the east is pillaged before they turn their eye on your clans?"

Cries rose up at her blunt words, and though Saga did not understand their tongue, she guessed they did not like what they'd heard. There was a tumult as more clanspeople were drawn by the noise. One of the horsemaidens was jostled to the side, and Saga heard the distinctive twang of a bowstring.

"Arrow!" shouted the maiden.

Saga was no warrior—today was the first time she'd ever set foot on the battlefield—and yet she sensed that the arrow flew straight for her. Shock held her frozen in place as death whipped toward her upon a fledged arrow.

But an enormous beast crashed down from above, knocking the arrow clean out of the skies. Havoc landed with an earth-shaking thud, then reared back with a scream of rage.

For a moment, Saga could not speak against the thundering in her skull. But then she stepped toward the infernal creature. "Where have you been, you wretched horse?"

The crowd had grown still, but before Saga could question it, the winged stallion knelt low and bent his wing. She hesitated for only a moment before clambering atop him and gazing out at the clanspeople.

"I will not lose another minute quarreling while east is slaughtered!" she shouted. "I invite anyone who wants to help—"

Saga's voice broke off, and she gazed around in confusion—from the clansmother, whose eyes were wide, to Khiva, dropped to one knee and staring at Saga in wonder. Slowly, the rest of the clanspeople followed suit, until every single one of them knelt before her. The clansmother was the last to drop to her knee, bowing her head in deference.

"She has tamed the untamable!" shouted Khiva, banging a fist against her chain mail. "She is the great warrior of whom the oracle spoke!"

Saga's mind replayed Kassandr's words. *One day a great warrior would climb atop Havoc's back and usher in a new era of prosperity.*

Had this oracle foretold the prophecy to the clans as well? Saga would laugh off such a ridiculous notion were she not so desperate for their help.

"Let clans and east unite as once was!" shouted Saga. "I ask for swords and arrows! Let us rain death on Urkans! With your help, we will force them away!"

Her words rang out across the silent steppe. But then Khiva stood and drew her sword, lifting it into the sky.

"For our children!"

A resounding cry rose up, lifting Saga's spirits. Havoc hoofed at the snow, and she could sense his restless energy—his need to take to the skies.

The clansmother stepped forward, silver braids gleaming in the moonlight. She eyed Saga not with admiration, but with a resigned sort of acceptance.

"I will join you, tamer of horses."

The rest went quickly from there—horses were readied, armor was donned. And within twenty minutes, a horde of three hundred horsewomen had gathered behind Saga on the snowy steppe.

Khiva directed her stallion beside Saga and reached into her pocket. Saga stared in shock for a moment at the fire flask held in her palm. "You might need this, queen of Íseldur."

With a murmur of thanks, Saga slid it carefully into her pocket.

The clansmother edged up on Saga's other side, watching her with stern, dark eyes. "What say you, horse tamer, to my warrior maidens?"

Again Saga felt herself in the strange position—hundreds of fierce horsewomen looking to her for an answer. This time, it was easy to push her uncertainty aside.

"To battle!" shouted Saga.

"To battle!" the clansmother called in reply, the roar of the horse-maidens lifting into the skies and carrying across the snow-swept plains. Saga's heart hammered ferociously in her skull as her hands curled tightly into Havoc's mane. Somehow, under darkness of night, the steppe felt a little less open; the skies less broad. Though she fought against the urge to bury her face in Havoc's neck, Saga managed. And as the winged stallion launched into the skies, she looked east, toward the city of Kovograd.

"Hold on, Kass," she whispered into the wind. "We're coming."

CHAPTER 45

Kovograd, Zagadka

The moment Kassandr Rurik tore the throat from Thorir the Giant, chaos erupted within the Urkan ranks. The berserkers that Rov and his Druzhina had held back broke through, desperate to spill Kassandr's blood after he'd slain the mightiest among them.

In his beast form, Kass nursed injuries in his shoulder and thigh, and his forearm leaked an alarming amount of blood. He and the others fought in their animal forms—Rovgolod and Volk sleek wolves; his Druzhina a trio of mountain cats, a pair of wolves, and an elk with sharpened antlers. They fought, tooth and claw, for their country. For their honor. And in Kassandr's case, for vengeance.

As much as he tried to see Thorir's words as mere taunts, Kassandr could not forget the fact that Saga had not been seen for the better part of a day. He could imagine her doing this, his brave, beautiful Saga—throwing herself at Ivar's feet and begging for mercy for Zagadka.

Thorir's words burrowed under his skin, spreading until Kassandr's heart was a blackened thing, churning rage and sorrow in equal amounts. With his kingdom burning and Saga lost, he had nothing to lose, and he fought like it. He lived in a world of reds and oranges—reds on the battlefield, where his claws spilled blood across the snow; oranges from the hungry flames consuming Kovograd's walls and fortress.

The flurries of snow had eased, but as Kassandr looked around, he realized how deep into the Urkan lines he'd pushed while trying to reach Prince Bjorn. Now they were too near to that gods damned siege tower. It loomed over them, the arrows—impossible to see in the darkness of night—delivering silent death. One sliced through the air, missing Kassandr's neck by a hair's breadth, but as a scream came from behind him, he knew it had found purchase. They needed to retreat.

He growled low, a command to his Druzhina to follow him, but as Kassandr turned, he realized there was no escaping this death trap. Urkan warriors teemed all around them in impossible numbers, all semblance of order and battle tactics vanishing.

Behind him, the blackened beams holding Kovograd's mighty tower splintered, and the bell gave one last tremendous toll as it crashed to the ground.

Kassandr released a low, mournful howl.

His home was burning, his friends falling on the battlefield all around him. Every reckless choice he'd made in the past months flashed in his mind—sneaking to Íseldur against his father's wishes; burning his boat when he was not ready to leave Íseldur; kissing Saga in those gardens and taking her to his country against her will.

This last one haunted him above all else. How arrogant he'd been for thinking he could keep her and all of Zagadka safe. Kassandr wished he could see her one last time. That he could look into her eyes and tell her how sorry he was. But it was too late.

Sorrow pulsed through him as realization landed. He'd thought he was doing the right thing by taking a stand against the Urkans, but now he knew better. Kassandr was no savior of the future generations—he was the downfall of his people.

An arrow clipped his shoulder, the sharp hot pain yanking him back to the present. A fresh surge of Urkans crashed into battle, and Kassandr felt the weariness in every muscle in his body. His parries were too slow, his blows too weak. A black-bearded berserker charged for Kassandr, great axe hefted overhead, and he wondered if this was it—the moment death stopped flirting and came for him in earnest.

But a snarling gray figure barreled into the Urkan, sending the man sprawling into the bloody snow. It was Oleg's wolf form, and Kassandr wondered if he'd ever been so glad to see his half brother. He did not allow himself to dwell on it—the berserker was twice Oleg's size and quickly rolled on top of him. Before Kassandr could reach him, Kresimir's grizzled mountain cat leaped onto the pair, sinking teeth deep into the berserker's neck.

Blood spurted, and Kresimir shook the man with a savage snarl, allowing Oleg to escape from beneath him. But the berserker's blade hacked down once, twice, three times, sending the mountain cat stumbling away. Kresimir yowled, then sprawled on the snow, his lifeblood seeping from multiple gashes.

Kill, snarled Kassandr's beast, launching on the vile Urkan and finishing what Kresimir had started. *Kill. Kill. Kill.*

Beside him, Volk yelped as an arrow embedded deep in his throat. Sorrow and horror mingled inside Kassandr as he watched his chieftain's lifeless body crumple to the ground. More arrows rained down, the animalistic shrieks telling Kassandr that many had met their mark. *Where is your honor?* he wanted to shout. The archers cowered behind that gods damned siege tower, picking the Zagadkians off.

Something inside Kassandr snapped through, and instead of running away from the siege tower, he turned and charged toward it. But as he leaped at an Urkan warrior, Kassandr saw the man's dark eyes fix on something behind him and widen in surprise. A shadow passed across the moons, the distant cry of an animal meeting his ears, but Kass focused on raking his claws through the berserker's throat. As he set his sights on the next warrior, that berserker turned tail and ran. Kassandr pushed through his puzzlement, hunting the man down and tearing him to the ground.

The strange animal cry grew louder over the din of battle, and

Kassandr paused amid the carnage. His enhanced hearing recognized it at once—this was no animal, but the distinctive, all-female war cry of the clans beyond the river. He whirled, then stumbled in astonishment at the sight that met his eyes.

A legion of winged horsewomen descended upon the battlefield with bow and blade. And at the front of the group was a golden-haired woman. For a moment, Kassandr felt weightless, as though the ground beneath him had fallen away. But then he was firmly rooted on solid ground.

Saga was *alive.*

Nothing made sense. She was clad in horsemaiden's armor, a feathered cloak rippling behind her as she rode upon the murderous winged horse. But it didn't have to make sense, because his Saga was *alive,* and not only that, but she'd brought help when they needed it the most.

Saga broke off from the rest of the horde, directing Havoc toward the siege tower. Horror calcified in Kassandr's chest. There were too many archers . . . it was too dangerous. He roared his warning into the skies, but Saga did not falter. Arrows zipped up, but the winged horse was too quick, twisting away and, in one case, kicking the arrow right out of the skies.

Protect, Kassandr's beast snarled, and he crouched low to launch himself over the teeming battle. The white stallion swooped, wings spread wide as he glided over the siege tower. Saga leaned to the side of the horse, and it seemed there was something in her hand—

And he understood. Kassandr loosed a savage snarl, calling his men to him. Together, they twisted away from the siege tower and loped over the berserkers staring slack-jawed at the winged horses. He didn't look over his shoulder to see the moment the fire flask slipped from Saga's hand and bounced down the stairwell into the belly of the siege tower, but Kassandr heard it. The explosion was swift, and though it did not have the same force as the barrels, its aim was fatally true.

He glanced over his shoulder to see smoke pouring from the

siege tower, the screams of men growing to a crescendo. Flames licked up the sides of it, warriors throwing themselves to their deaths as they tried to escape the flames. And through the smoke, he could just make out a small blond figure enfolded into the aerial horde of helmed clanswomen.

Saga had escaped.

Kassandr lifted his maw into the skies and howled with every ounce of his being. But he hadn't the time to stand in his wonderment. As an opponent lunged at him, he turned to greet the man with fang and claw. His blood pumped with renewed vigor, hope a buoyant thing in his chest. Kassandr's world grew wholly red as he became an instrument of death. He could feel it in his bones, could smell it in the air—the tides of battle had just turned in Zagadka's favor.

And it was all thanks to Saga.

Over and over, Kassandr showed each foul Urkan what it meant to face the Beast of Zagadka—what he thought of their coming to take what was not theirs. At some point, Rovgolod appeared on one side, Oleg on the other, and they fought a path into the thickest throng of berserkers. All the while, the winged horsewomen swooped down with speed and ferocity, delivering death with hooves and blades and arrows.

It wasn't long before the flaming siege tower splintered and crashed to the ground. But the moment Kass saw the Urkans turn and flee was one of the sweetest in all his life. Kass and Rov chased them down, felling every last berserker they could. A beleaguered fleet of prowed ships rowed furiously away, the winged horses haranguing them from above, forcing the warriors to cower under a wall of shields. An hour ago, death had seemed certain, and now . . . now it was over. He could hardly believe it.

All this time, Kassandr had wanted Saga to see her potential—to show her fire and her heart to the world. But this warrior queen was beyond his wildest imaginings. How she had managed to convince the clans and to gather a horde of winged horsemaidens, he could not imagine.

His gaze swept the skies and the field of death all around him. The horsemaidens had formed a queue at the Kovosk River, rapidly filling buckets and passing them back along the line to those who took to the skies. Over and over the horsemaidens flew above the burning fortress, dumping bucket after bucket onto the flames.

And then Kassandr saw *her,* just beyond the horsemaidens. Helm clasped at her side, Saga shielded her eyes from the glare of the rising sun as she searched the snowy battlefield for something—or someone. Kassandr gave a triumphant *whuf,* and then he was loping toward her, his chest too small for his heart. In that moment, his exhaustion was long forgotten; his injuries no longer pained him.

At last, Saga's gaze fell upon him, and her lips formed his name. But the horsemaidens had also spotted him, and they closed around Saga, arrows trained on him. Kassandr skidded to a stop with a whine, his claws gouging deeply into the snow. A low warning snarl slipped from his maw, and it took all his will not to claw through the horsemaidens to get to his Saga.

"Don't shoot him!" Saga cried out, pushing her way through. "Khiva, stand down!" She put her hand on the shoulder of the tall horsemaiden whose glare was the sharpest. The woman did not drop her bow, but her stance eased just a touch. And then Saga was breaking free; was running, throwing herself at his beast form . . .

She landed with startling force, and between his injuries and complete exhaustion, Kassandr nearly toppled over. But as Saga's arms slid around his neck, all his pain fell away. This moment was better than he could ever have dreamed. She buried her face into his gore-smeared fur, muffled words falling from her lips.

"You're alive," and, "We did it," and, most inexplicably, "Thank you."

Unable to speak in his beast form, Kassandr relented to nuzzling against her, scenting her for injuries. He found none. She was safe. She was alive. And she'd saved the city—likely the entire kingdom.

As Saga unwound her arms from his neck, Kassandr reared on his hind legs, lifting his maw to the skies and howling in triumph. Nearby, Rov joined in, and then Oleg, and then the whole of the battlefield howled in unison, the war cries of the horsewomen weaving in last of all.

He looked over the battlefield, lit by the rising sun.

It smelled of blood and smoke.

Looked like chaos incarnate.

Yet it felt like a new day.

CHAPTER 46

Kopa, Íseldur

Standing in the caves deep beneath Ashfall Fortress, Silla tried to distract herself from her nerves by studying the murals painted on the walls. But no matter how hard she stared at them, she could not shake the thought from her mind—*everything* was riding on today's meeting. Two days remained before she and Rey would ride to the heartwood, and aside from thirty warriors Atli had pulled from their reserves, and the fifteen Jarl Holger had committed to send, they had otherwise failed in mustering the necessary forces.

Myrkur's possession of Eisa had been catastrophic to their plans. Not only had they lost two precious days, but tales had spread among the jarls, and they readied to depart Kopa. To have them leave without committing to Eisa Volsik, nor to sending warriors to the heartwood, was a failure beyond measure.

But then a letter had arrived with the most unexpected news. Jarl Agnar was coming to speak with her. After Rey had sent Kálf to investigate what precisely was happening on Hakon's border, they finally had an update—and it was a good one. Jarl Agnar would secretly venture onto Hakon lands to meet her. It was enough to make hope flare brightly in her chest. Myrkur cringed, slinking deeper inside her.

"They're late," muttered Rey, glancing down the tunnel.

"They had a long distance to travel," Silla reminded him.

She slid her palm into his, smiling at the warm scrape of his calluses. Silla had recited hearthfire thoughts all morning. She'd taken a long bath and had requested her favorite foods for the daymeal. She'd visited the refugees and ensured they were well settled in Ashfall. And once they'd returned to her chambers, Silla had showered Rey with kisses and soft touches until he'd tumbled them into the furs. Suffice it to say, she was doing everything in her power to keep her moods bright and the god of chaos at bay.

A cough echoed down the passageway, and Silla whirled toward the sound. Kálf ambled forward, torchlight catching on his brown scalp and thick black beard. Silla rushed toward him, surprising the man with a firm hug.

"Now, that's a warm welcome," Kálf said with a grin as Silla stepped back.

"You did it," she whispered, breath catching as her gaze slid over Kálf's shoulder to a pair of warriors she did not recognize. With tunics bearing House Agnar's blue eagle worn over chain mail, there was no question who these men were.

"Well done," said Silla warmly, as Erik and Hef appeared. She shook their hands firmly as Rey kept his gaze on Jarl Agnar's warriors, who'd entered the cavern and now swept the space for threats.

"Clear!" shouted one, and then Jarl Agnar himself was striding around the bend.

Silla had known the man was young, but she hadn't realized just how young. His brown skin was smooth, only sparse hints of a beard peppering his jaw. Agnar's shoulders looked slender even beneath the heavy armor he wore. But as he strode toward her, the jarl's eyes held a challenge—as though daring her to question his abilities. Silla could relate, and immediately liked him.

She straightened her spine and smiled at the jarl. "Welcome," she said, extending a hand.

The young jarl accepted it, meeting her eyes with honor and respect. It was hard to believe *this* was the man causing so much chaos on Jarl Hakon's borders.

"I am glad to meet you, Jarl Agnar," Silla continued. "How was your journey?"

"We traveled at a hard pace," said Agnar, turning to inspect the sprawling caverns. "I am eager to put this matter behind me, as you can imagine."

Silla kept pace with Agnar as he strolled to a nearby alcove and examined it.

"I am in your debt for granting my warriors safe passage on your lands," she told Agnar. "And I am grateful beyond measure that you heard their words with an open heart." Silla took a deep breath and continued. "I tried to write to you, but someone intercepted my letters. I suspect they have also been tampering with Jarl Hakon's correspondence. Have you received any from him?"

Jarl Agnar's gaze whipped toward her. "I—no." He shook his head, confusion plain on his face. "I've received no letters from House Hakon, nor any reply to those I've written."

Silla nodded to herself. "Then it is as I suspected. Tell me what is really happening on the eastern border."

Jarl Agnar smoothed a hand down his tunic. "It started small. Farmsteads burned down, grain stolen, petty deeds done by petty men. But when an entire village was set alight and men wearing Hakon livery were seen fleeing, retaliation was necessary."

Silla chose her words carefully. "Jarl Hakon denies any involvement. According to him, your warbands set a village on *his* lands alight."

Agnar's brows drew together. "'Tis not what his emissary relayed to us."

"It's . . . not?" Silla's mind whirled as she tried to understand.

"Who was this emissary?" asked Rey, suddenly at Silla's side. "Reynir Galtung," he added, extending a hand for the young jarl to shake.

"A woman calling herself Valdasson. She came with a hundred warriors in House Hakon livery."

Silla cast Rey a confused look, but his brows were drawn in concentration. "Valdasson," he murmured. "Why does that name sound familiar?"

"*I* do not know this name," said Silla slowly. "What did she look like?"

Agnar was silent in thought for a moment. "She looked to have seen fifty winters. Reddish hair, a very . . . regal sort of air about her."

"Valdasson," said Rey, a note of discovery in his voice. "A jarl with a small tract of land. I recall the name because he lost a large sum to Gunnar in a game of dice but paid only in a promissory note. When he went to collect months later, Gunnar said the jarl had died and his widow refused to honor the wager."

Cold slid through Silla's veins as the facts settled into place. She knew a jarl's widow—one with auburn hair. Her eyes met Rey's, and she could tell he'd come to the same realization.

It was Lady Tala.

"No," murmured Silla absently. Could it be? "What did this woman tell you, Jarl Agnar?" she forced out.

The jarl watched her carefully, uncertainty in his voice. "That Jarl Hakon claimed the maps were drawn up wrong in my father's time. That all lands within five miles of my eastern border were his by right. And that my people had ten days to vacate before his men would force them to do so."

Silla's heart pounded in her skull, a vicious wrath rising within her as Myrkur snarled. She funneled hearthfire thoughts into her mind, desperate to keep the god at bay and keep her mind as her own.

"There is no way those are Hakon's terms," said Rey. "He tries to *unite* the north, not divide it."

"That emissary was not acting under Hakon's orders," said Silla, trying not to let the bitter sting of Tala's betrayal grant Myrkur any power. "If my hunch is correct, she follows *Signe's* command."

"Q-queen Signe?" stuttered Jarl Agnar.

I'll admit, whispered Myrkur, *I'm rather impressed with Signe.*

Silla blinked. *You sound as though you know her*, she shot back, against her better judgement.

Myrkur only chuckled, ducking away before Silla could gage His emotions. Rey touched her elbow and Silla refocused on Jarl Agnar.

"I—sorry." She shook her head. "It seems the queen has been rather busy. Not only has she tried to have me assassinated several times, but she's been stirring up chaos in the north. Intercepting not only my letters but those of Jarls Hakon and Agnar as well." Silla's gaze fell on Agnar and hardened. "Enough is enough."

Silla thought back on all of her interactions with Lady Tala, seeing them in new light. Tala, seated beside her the day her róa cup had been poisoned. Tala, coming to Silla after Ingvarr's botched attempt on her life, urging her to keep Fallgerd's death quiet. Tala, whispering advice to Silla that had only made her question herself. Her blood chilled further as she recalled Tala coming to her while she was shackled to the bed, trying to feed her broth. She'd been too nauseous to take it. Had it, too, been poisoned?

Let me in, Eisa, crooned Myrkur. *Grant me access to your bloodline gift. We can make her pay. We will make it hurt.*

Jarl Agnar's voice thankfully diverted her attention. "When your retinue arrived at the borderlands, I suspected treachery," he confessed. "I wondered if you lured us into a trap on Jarl Hakon's behalf. But the way your men spoke of you . . . I'll admit I was intrigued. And now that I've met you, I feel hopeful. You've gotten to the bottom of our issues. You treat your warriors with respect. And you alone have the ability to topple Ivar's hold on the north of Íseldur. To bring peace to these lands."

Peace, laughed Myrkur.

Silla's jaw hardened, but an idea struck her. She strode across the cavern, beckoning Jarl Agnar to follow her. "I will be honest with you, Jarl Agnar. I fear this conflict with Lady Tala will be the first of many battles." Silla paused before the mural, staring at the Volsik king facing down a horde of demon creatures. "Dark days are on the horizon, and if we wish to survive, we must unite."

Silla watched the young jarl, waiting for some reaction. But he only nodded solemnly, staring at the mural. She drew a deep breath and prepared for what came next. This had to work. They were out of time.

"Do you know, Agnar, I believe we are much alike. Like you, I am used to being underestimated. It is, in some ways, my greatest weapon." Silla turned to the mural, examining the Volsik king alone in his battle against Myrkur. She'd thought she had time. Thought she could wait for Saga. But now she understood.

I will stand up to Tala and the jarls, she thought, *and then, I will stand up to Myrkur.*

You can try, mortal, taunted the god of chaos. *But you will fail.*

If I fail, thought Silla, *at least I have tried.*

Silla and Agnar spoke in hushed tones for the better part of an hour as she relayed her plans. By the time she left the cavern, the sting of Tala's betrayal was smothered by a blanket of hope.

Rey's hand slid into hers, giving it a gentle squeeze. "Do you realize what you've done?" She turned to him, alarmed, but a smile curved his lips. "You just won Jarl Agnar to your cause."

She squeezed his hand back.

"And you did it," said Rey, "simply by being Silla."

Confidence and hope mingled in her chest. But Silla focused her attention on what must come next.

"We have work left to do," she said.

By the time they returned to Silla's bedchambers, the sister moons had risen under winter's early nightfall. She walked to the windows. Snowflakes fluttered softly down, blanketing Kopa's peaked roofs, and her gaze fell to the smallest of the sisters, now swelling toward fullness.

It was a reminder she did not need that only two nights remained before they departed for the heartwood. Silla's heart gave a panicked leap. What if her plans failed? What if she and Rey had to ride to the woods with naught but Jarl Holger's warband?

Silla blinked furiously at the moons, serene in the star-speckled skies, and felt a moment of outrage. All her life, she'd left offerings for the gods and the spirits; all her life, she'd been dutiful in her worship. How could the gods be so silent while Myrkur wrought havoc? Where was Sunnvald, father of the gods? Where was Malla, goddess of love and battle?

My brother does not bother himself with you mortals, whispered Myrkur. But as a cloud drifted from the largest of the moons and the moonlight intensified, Myrkur hissed and burrowed deeper.

"Is it true, Sunnvald?" Silla murmured, gripping the window linens.

"What?" asked Rey from across the room.

Silla spun away from the window, shaking her head. "It's noth . . ."

But her words trailed off. A moonbeam now flowed through the glass windows, like a beacon lighting a path for her to follow. Breathless, Silla trailed it across the floorboards to where it landed on a stack of books—one of many that Runný and Atli had been combing through. Heart pounding, Silla approached the stack and examined the book at the top. It was a collection of old mythologies gathered from the northern reaches—Karthia, Íseldur, Norvaland, and the like—and as Silla flipped it open, it fell to a particular page.

"What is it?" asked Rey, appearing by her side.

"Perhaps the gods have not abandoned me," Silla said, glancing back at the window. The moonlight indeed led a path to this very book. "Perhaps I've forgotten to watch for their signs."

Silla probed inwardly for Myrkur, and was surprised to find Him buried away, somewhere deep. Had the moonlight repelled Him? She could not say.

Silla settled on the floor in the moonbeam's path, and began to read. The Karthian fable told of a man named Tuiren, who engaged in a betting game with a mysterious stranger. The drunken Tuiren made an increasingly astonishing series of wagers, not the least of which included his wife. Given the man's apparent lack of wits, it was no surprise to Silla when Tuiren lost, nor when the stranger revealed himself to be a god.

Tuiren, apparently realizing the error of his ways, begged the god not to take his wife. And when the god declined, Tuiren challenged him to combat to reclaim his wife. And so he fought the god, which, Silla would admit was romantic. But being impaled on a nature god's antlers was rather less so.

She stared up at Rey, trying to understand. "Tuiren lost a wager with a god. Is a wager not rather like a bargain?"

"Wait," said Rey, lifting a hand. "Perhaps we should wait—"

"He's not listening." Silla probed again for Myrkur, then grinned. "The moonlight—I think it has warded Him off." As she realized she had her mind to herself, excitement thrummed to life inside Silla.

"King Hrolf was simply too old to attempt. That's what Fallgerd said." She tapped her finger on the image in the book. "He was too old to battle the god."

"I do not like where this is going," said Rey warily.

"I understand it now." Silla walked to the window, never stepping from the moonlight's path. She turned and faced Rey. In this moment, with her mind her own, Silla felt more like herself than she had in weeks. "This is how I will banish the dark god from my body."

"How?"

She shook her head, incredulous. "I must challenge Him to battle."

CHAPTER 47

The Western Woods

Hekla pulled cobwebs from her grimy hair and grimaced. She needed a bath. Needed a horn of ale. Needed the comfort of a warm, feathered bed. Instead there was only more grayish trees, more brittle needles crunching underfoot, more red-eyed ravens, trailing them through the dreary forest, and more tension in her stomach as Hekla worried about their timing.

Their timeline to reach the Forest Maiden's other half had been tight to start with. But then they'd encountered an impassible ravine, and had wasted a day skirting around it. Kritka claimed they were now back on track, but it did little to loosen the knots in Hekla's stomach. She'd ordered their crew to walk through the night. Had allowed them only a few scant hours of rest. They had a quarter moon left before the battle, and had not yet reached the other fragment of the Forest Maiden.

Hekla had nearly wept tears of relief when the Maiden predicted they would reach her second grove today. They walked at a punishing pace through the dead woods, a stream burbling peacefully nearby. Perched on Hekla's shoulder, Kritka nibbled on a pilfered strip of smoked elk, ever dedicated to bulking up for the winter.

So slow you two-leggeds are, the squirrel said inside her mind.

"You're awfully whiny for someone who's been lounging on my shoulder," Hekla grumbled aloud. The exertion of the past days had made her phantom limb ache worse than ever, and it put her increasingly on edge.

It is not much farther, chittered Kritka, eyeing a fresh cobweb strung from a skeletal tree. *We must keep moving. I sense strangeness about these parts.*

Hekla cringed at the cobweb, then whirled at a disturbance to her right. A pair of Turned ravens regarded her from a dead tree, a third one landing a few branches above them. Hekla craned upward, gazing at the overcast skies through the clawing branches. A dozen or more Turned ravens flew above, sending shivers down her spine.

Yet on they walked at this relentless pace. It was another two hours before Kritka drew them to a halt. He leaped from Hekla's shoulder and bounded down the trail.

Here! the squirrel chittered. *The grove is just through there!*

A Turned raven swooped down at Kritka, jagged talons barely missing the squirrel as it darted back to Hekla. As the squirrel climbed her like a tree—a sensation she'd never get used to—another raven swooped down, and then another. Suddenly dozens of Turned ravens descended from above, settling on dead trees surrounding the path.

"That's not alarming," mumbled Eyvind, turning in a wide circle. Glowing red eyes watched on, and if Hekla hadn't thought the woods eerie enough before, now she certainly did.

"Blades," Hekla commanded, unsheathing her sword while eyeing the ravens. But the birds merely watched as their group approached the Forest Maiden's grove.

"Do you hear that?" Thrand asked, casting a nervous look over his shoulder.

Hekla's ears strained, but all she heard was the increasingly loud rush of the stream beside them—was there a waterfall nearby?

"I cannot hear it," said Hekla.

"There it is again!" exclaimed Thrand. "It's like a *clackclackclack.*"

Kritka lifted his face from where it was buried in Hekla's neck and released a flurry of squirrel nonsense.

Thrand nodded vehemently at the chittering sound. "Aye, small warrior."

Then Hekla saw it. Prickles rushed down her spine as she stared in disbelief. A gleaming silken web stretched across the path, blocking their way into the grove.

And at last she heard what Thrand had—a rapid series of clicks that could belong to none other than the enormous wolfspider who called himself Gjalla.

The Turned ravens surrounding them began to caw.

"Shield wall!" Hekla shrieked, but it was too late. Gjalla charged out of the woods and lunged at the rear guard. Massive, gleaming fangs impaled the warrior as though he was not wearing the finest armor.

Kritka leaped from her shoulder and cocked his head to the side. Magic shuddered through the air, the scent of wet dog filling her senses. The squirrel's limbs elongated, his russet fur shifting to gray. And where a moment ago a squirrel had been was now a grimwolf the size of a small horse.

Eyvind was suddenly by her side, Gunnar on the other, and Hekla forgot all about avoiding them. Their group formed a loose shield wall, protecting them from an overhead attack. Hekla scrambled to form a plan. They were roughly twenty warriors against the spider, but they'd walked right into his trap. Trees were tightly packed on either side of the trail, and the beast of a spider obstructed the path they'd been traveling. She glanced over her shoulder, where retreat was blocked by the thick, sticky web.

"Can you blast that web away?" Hekla asked Eyvind from the corner of her mouth.

"Not without risking the Forest Maiden's tree beyond it," he shot back.

Gjalla quickly flung the rearguard warrior aside, then advanced. With the spider's missing forelegs, the beast's gait was lumbering.

Gjalla has waited many days for you to come, chittered the spider inside Hekla's mind. *Soon you will be trussed in our web, waiting for our mother to Turn you. She wants you in her army, clawed mortal.* The spider clicked disapprovingly. *She thinks your strength would be useful to her cause.*

"I'd rather die than be used as the leech's doll," muttered Hekla.

Kritka's lips pulled back in a savage snarl, and Hekla urged him mentally to hold back for now. "We must target the underbelly," she told their group quietly.

"It is too dangerous," Eyvind replied.

Of course it was dangerous—they'd have to get directly beneath the spider. But what else could they do?

Their conversation was cut short as the spider let out an earsplitting shriek and jabbed forward. A fang struck Hekla's shield with such force that she stumbled back, fortified, thankfully, by the warriors behind her. But her shield had cracked clean through, and Gjalla's other fang had struck another of Eyvind's warriors. Kritka shrieked, lunging at the spider's fang, but the creature was too quick. With a gleeful chitter, Gjalla hefted the warrior into the air. Blood spattered down on the shield wall as the man screamed in anguish, wriggling to get free.

The ravens cawed as horror and revulsion churned in Hekla's stomach, her mind splintering much like her shield. Gjalla flung the warrior at their group with tremendous force, driving men to their knees as the bones of the dying warrior crunched.

Protect the Forest Maiden, Hekla ordered Kritka, *and try to rid us of that web*. She was relieved when the grimwolf obeyed without protest.

Cries rose up as Gjalla surged down, fangs scrabbling against shields while the force of the spider crushed them. Hekla frantically searched for a plan, but they were trapped between the spider and his web; she noticed only the crash of water from what had to be a nearby waterfall.

A waterfall.

Hekla focused with all her might, spinning a plan together. They could not flee into the forest without breaking their shield wall, yet they needed a diversion. Could she? No. It was a ridiculous, dangerous idea.

But Gjalla fell upon their huddle again, fangs piercing through another wooden shield and into a warrior's chest. Gunnar tried to capitalize on this moment of distraction, slamming his sword between the shields. Yet his blade connected with tough carapace, and Gjalla yanked the other warrior free from their group.

They were trapped on this trail in shield wall formation. Were being picked off, one by one. This could not continue. She could not let Gjalla reach the Forest Maiden. Hekla took a deep breath, then spoke to Kritka in her mind.

Stay with your mistress and help Thrand perform the ritual to free her other half. I will find you again when I can.

You must not— Kritka replied in her mind. But Hekla was already drawing a deep breath. Readying to launch herself into the woods—

The cries of Turned ravens left Hekla momentarily stunned. Eyvind, evidently having the same idea as Hekla, had broken off from their shield wall and now rushed into the woods. The spider's fangs gnashed together as Eyvind paused. Turned. Waved his sword about.

"What is he doing?" demanded Thrand Long Sword.

"Trying to lure it away," Hekla said, her heart in her throat.

Gjalla took one step off the trail, his gleaming red eyes darting from Eyvind to the huddle of warriors. But as Eyvind shouted at the spider, Gjalla's choice was made. The enormous spider crashed through the underbrush in pursuit of Eyvind. For a moment, Hekla simply stared. And then, she *moved*.

Going after him wasn't a question in her mind. It was instinct. It was fate.

"Cut through the web!" she shouted at Gunnar, launching into the brush. "And whatever else happens, protect the Forest Maiden!"

Grip tightening on her sword, Hekla didn't wait for Gunnar's inevitable protest. She moved with as much stealth as she could through the underbrush, never taking her eyes off Hakonsson. They'd reached the stream, Eyvind now waist-deep. Gjalla launched into the waters and threw himself at Eyvind with a loud, screech that sent goosebumps up Hekla's arms.

As Gjalla's lethal fangs stabbed into the frothing, swirling waters, Eyvind vanished from view. Horror built in Hekla's chest as the spider jabbed downward again and again. A scream tore from her throat as she leaped between dead bracken and dried moss, sword raised in hand.

Eyvind's head broke the surface of the waters just downstream of the spider, but Gjalla surged at him with impossible speed, chitinous fangs clashing against Eyvind's steel blade.

But the current was too strong, the river rocks too slick, and Eyvind's feet slipped out from under him. His head vanished beneath the seething waters once more, and again Gjalla became a flurry of limbs and fangs. The water bloomed red, and Hekla was sprinting—was *screaming*—but Gjalla was relentless in his assault on Eyvind.

There was no time to think. No time for revulsion or fear to grip her. Hekla threw herself from the stream's edge onto the spider's turned back. Momentum sent her careening along Gjalla's tough, slick thorax, and just before she tumbled off the other side, Hekla's hands folded around a thatch of coarse hairs.

Gjalla reared back with an ear-piercing shriek that rattled Hekla's skull. But she did not relent—she held on tight as the spider thrashed about. And while no one would call her pious, in that moment she prayed to the Sun God Himself.

"Sunnvald, keep Eyvind bloody Hakonsson safe," she gritted out. "So I can wring his neck myself." Hekla unsheathed her prosthetic's claws and slammed them through the spider's thick carapace. With her grip more sure, she climbed toward the spider's wriggling feelers.

Gjalla writhed about, trying to knock Hekla free from his back, but her claws held firm. Slowly, she climbed higher on the spider's thorax. At last, she reached the top. Her gaze slid from Gjalla's thrashing feelers to the glowing red eyes just beyond. With the claws of her right hand embedded in the spider's thick cuticle, she unsheathed her hevrít with her left, then brought it down over and over—as many times as she could manage before Gjalla finally knocked her free. Hekla flew through the air, then plunged into the frigid waters, her head colliding with a rock and knocking her momentarily senseless.

But as Gjalla's fangs struck through the waters and clipped the edge of her thigh, Hekla's wits surged back. Pain speared from her leg as she floundered on slick river stones, her gaze searching frantically for Eyvind all the while.

Hekla's heart gave a panicked lurch as she saw him just downstream—floating face down.

"Eyvind—" Her shout quickly turned to a gargle as she dove underwater to avoid Gjalla's lashing fangs. Bubbles gushed from her nose as she kicked and clawed her way along the riverbed. Her lungs ached, her thigh throbbing as though it had a heartbeat, yet her only thought was of Eyvind—she *had* to get to him.

When her chest felt as though it might burst, she finally broke the water's surface, gasping and choking. Hekla cried out as she saw Eyvind, mere paces away. Desperately, she crashed through the waters and flipped him onto his back. Her gaze roamed over his face for any sign of life.

But a shadow crossed the sun, and Hekla was dimly aware that the crash of the waterfall was now near deafening. She looped a loose arm around Eyvind's neck, holding him face up, then gazed up at the wolfspider. Gjalla chittered angrily, black blood seeping from at least half his eyes.

You foul, bothersome creature, the monster screeched. *Gjalla does not care that Mother wants to keep you. We will relish your death.*

"Unfortunately, you wretched beast," Hekla shouted, barely able to hear her own voice above the crashing water, "you'll have to wait for another day."

Her hold on Eyvind tightened as the stream beneath her vanished. And then they plunged over the waterfall's edge.

PART 3

ELDERS

A rotten branch will be found in every tree.

—THE SAGA OF OLAF HARALDSSON

CHAPTER 48

Sunnavík, Íseldur

Jonas looked around the musty room with distaste. Though braziers were arranged in each corner and a plush bed was set beneath the lone window, it was far from the opulence he'd grown used to in the queen's quarters. Not only that, but the room was in an abandoned tower in a seldom-used wing of the castle.

But with King Ivar's impending return to Íseldur, Jonas and Signe's encounters had been relegated to whatever quiet corner of the castle they could manage. The queen was surprising in her ardor, and it was matched by Jonas's own.

It was more than the fact that she was a queen—more than her enticing beauty. Jonas and Signe had forged a connection. It had started with their shared hatred of Eisa Volsik and only grown and expanded with each passing visit. The queen, it seemed, was starved for affection. Had lived too long in a loveless marriage. And Jonas, too, craved company after losing his brother and the Bloodaxe Crew. When he was alone with the queen, it felt for a moment like he had regained just a fragment of all that he'd once had.

And he'd be lying if he said there wasn't something alluring about burying himself inside the queen of Íseldur. There were the promises she'd whispered into Jonas's ear—that he'd be granted power and status, that he'd be able to avenge his brother, and so much more—but there was also the forbidden aspect of their affair. It was one thing to meet with the queen in her private quarters. But with the king's forthcoming return, Jonas found himself even more enamored.

Footfalls from beyond the doorway met Jonas's ears, and it was no surprise when the door swung open on groaning hinges. One of the queen's personal guards ducked through the doorway, surveying the room before glaring at Jonas with steely eyes. It was clear the man was no fan of Jonas's. But it was equally clear he would say nothing of the queen's indiscretions.

The guardsman ducked out, and a moment later, Queen Signe entered and closed the door behind her. She wore a silk ivory robe, tied at the neck with a golden ribbon.

"You look like a gift waiting to be unwrapped," murmured Jonas. He wasted no time, surging forward with need that surprised even himself. Jonas had the robe fluttering to the floor in a matter of heartbeats. Beneath it, the queen wore a nightdress so thin, he could see every part of her.

"Lovely," he growled in her ear, placing rough kisses down the smooth column of her throat. "Far too lovely for a brute like me." It was one of many games they played together.

"Take me all the same," she urged, and Jonas pushed her backward until they tumbled onto the bed. "But you must not leave marks for my husband to find—"

Jonas ignored her, dragging his teeth along her collarbone while sliding her nightdress off her shoulders. He knew the forbidden aspect of their meetings was an aphrodisiac to the queen as well. In the dazed aftermath of one of their sessions, Signe had confessed to Jonas that Ivar hadn't warmed her bed since the birth of her youngest son, and that the burns her husband now sported repulsed her.

He tended his queen in all the ways he knew how, making sure she was loud enough for her sullen guardsman to hear. Soon they lay on the furs, limbs entwined and breaths heaving. In the aftermath, Signe was much like any other woman. Soft and tender, fingertips trailing along Jonas's bare chest. In this state, she was stripped down to what Jonas suspected was her very barest self. And he found himself wondering what kind of a person Signe might have been were she not queen.

He gave himself a mental shake.

"Volund will take you to Rökksgarde in two days," said Signe, breaking the silence. "There you'll continue your training. But I must stay in Sunnavík."

Jonas lifted his head, meeting her gaze. "I thought you were to accompany us?"

A sad smile crossed Signe's lips. "I will join you in time for the ritual ceremony. But first, I have matters to tend to in Sunnavík."

"What kind of matters? Do you need my help—"

Her fingers pressed into his lips, silencing him. "I need you in *Rökksgarde*, Jonas." She sighed. "I will join you the moment I am able to. If all goes well, our forces shall soon be marching north."

"North? Beyond Rökksgarde?"

"My, but you are certainly full of questions today," teased Signe. "And here I'd thought you'd have other plans for those lips."

Jonas blinked, trying to quell his irritation. He rolled Signe onto her back, though his smile was brittle. "As my queen wishes," he purred before climbing down her body.

An hour later, Jonas whistled a tune as he made his way back to the garrison hall. While he normally kept to the defensive walls to maintain a low profile, tonight he craved fresh air, and so he took a stroll across the sparring grounds. Stars speckled the winter skies, and the smaller of the sister moons was nearly full, her light catching tiny snowflakes drifting lazily down.

For a moment, Jonas was filled with the strangest sensation—contentment. He had a woman whose company he actually enjoyed and a plan to avenge Ilías's death. For the first time in weeks, Jonas's thoughts weren't consumed with all that he'd lost.

A low, keening wail drifted across the yard, making Jonas's feet falter. Moonlight spilled through the sparring grounds, catching movement on the far end.

"Cry, little Freki," came a voice Jonas immediately recognized. The brute, Horfi.

His gaze narrowed as he made them out—the much larger Horfi towering over Freki's smaller form. As Freki bent double, Horfi drove his knee into his jaw with a sickening crack.

"Fight back, weakling," taunted Horfi, grabbing Freki by the hair and delivering a sharp slap across his face.

"Leave me be!" begged Freki, squirming to get out of Horfi's grip.

"Not until you learn to fight like a man."

Fight like a man, rang in Jonas's ears, sparks on the dry tinder of the wounds left by his father. *Fight like a man,* his father had said, delivering blow after blow until his world had gone black.

Jonas knew he should keep walking. That this was none of his business. But in that moment, Ilías's face filled his mind's eye. What if Jonas hadn't been there to protect his younger brother all those times? Wouldn't he have wished someone else had intervened?

His hand curled into a fist, Freki's distressed cries ringing in his ears.

Jonas wasn't certain when the decision was made, only that his feet were suddenly striding across the sparring grounds. He threw himself at Horfi. They crashed to the ground, Horfi's shout of surprise ringing out in the night. But Jonas paid him no heed. There was only his fist cracking into Horfi's jaw. The warrior's head snapped to the side, blood and teeth spraying from his mouth.

"Fight like a man?" Jonas snarled. He lifted Horfi's head by the hair and slammed it into the ground. "Do you feel like a *man* when you pick on those weaker than you?" He slammed it again. "Does it make you feel *large,* warrior?" Again, he slammed Horfi's head into the ground.

The red hazing Jonas's vision dimmed just a touch, the battle thrill churning through his blood gradually dissipating. Jonas raked the hair from his brow, turning back to Freki, and again, for the hint of a moment, it was Ilías he looked at.

"Are you all right?" Jonas demanded, climbing to his feet.

"F-fine," stumbled Freki. The young man's cheekbone was split, his eye swelling shut. But it would have been far worse had Jonas not intervened. The thought made anger flare to life once more in Jonas's stomach. "If he ever bothers you again, you let me know," he told the young warrior.

"Is he—" Freki's eyes were wide as he stared down at Horfi's prone form.

Jonas glanced at the fallen warrior. Blood pooled beneath the man's skull, his eyes wide and unseeing.

"Fuck," muttered Jonas.

A strangled sound broke from Freki, drawing Jonas's glare. The young warrior took a fearful step back.

"Go back to your quarters," barked Jonas. "If anyone asks, you saw nothing. I delivered those bruises to your face." He swallowed, the thought making him nauseous. Jonas's temples began to throb as he considered the fallout. This warrior was Volund's tool. There would be consequences for Horfi's death.

Jonas was dimly aware of Freki turning toward the garrison hall doors. "Go to the healer," he told the young warrior. "Ask for a poultice of mountain arnica."

Freki paused at his words. Then without another word, he vanished into the hall.

The throb at Jonas's temples intensified as he stared at Horfi's lifeless body. He could have kept walking. Could have gone on with his life. Now he'd risked all he'd been working toward—his standing in this warband; Volund's approval; perhaps even his relationship with the queen.

And yet, Jonas could not bring himself to regret it. His knuckles were split and aching, his mind in turmoil. And yet, in his heart, Jonas was at peace.

In the deepest part of himself, Jonas knew that he'd done the right thing.

He gave his head a shake, then returned to his quarters.

CHAPTER 49

The Western Woods

Hekla woke with mud in her mouth and twigs in her hair. She rolled onto her side and retched up the contents of her stomach, which, apparently, included water, mud, and more water. When there was nothing left to expel, she struggled to a sitting position.

"Fuck," muttered Hekla. She braced herself against bent knees and stared at the empty sleeve where her prosthetic arm ought to be. Her insides wrenched at the realization that it had come off. Teeth clattering with cold, she scanned her surroundings for any sign of her arm—wet, muddy riverbank beneath her; lazy river meandering beside her; the distant crash of the waterfall—

The waterfall. Oh, gods.

"Eyvind!" she shouted, clambering to her feet. Thinking of the monstrous things lurking in the woods, she unsheathed a dagger from her boot.

Silence met her ears.

"Eyvind!" she bellowed even louder, scouring the riverbank for any sign of the warrior. The last thing she remembered was plunging over those falls, but based on their distant sound, she must have drifted some way downstream.

She broke into a run, the soft riverbank impeding her progress.

Hekla reached a bend in the river, and the silt thankfully shifted to river stones. And there he was, sprawled on the shore. Eyvind's face was tilted to the skies, one arm flung out, as though reaching toward her.

"Eyvind," she gasped, running. As she splashed through a shallow tributary, her foot caught, and the dagger went flying as Hekla fell to her knees. But she was on her feet in an instant, and by Eyvind's side in another.

Hekla lowered her ear to his lips. A faint puff of air against her skin had her exhaling in relief, but his breaths were shallow and his lips tinged blue. Hekla wrangled her emotions into place, knowing she had to stay calm—had to work quickly. Her gaze fell to the red-slicked river rocks beneath Eyvind, and she examined the warrior for injuries. She discovered a shallow, oozing wound on the side of his temple and a slash into the fleshiest part of his biceps. But when Hekla's hand reached Eyvind's side, she gasped.

Blood pulsed from a jagged wound the length of her hand. Bile rose in Hekla's throat, but she swallowed it back.

"All right." Hekla knelt back, raking her hand through her hair. "All right. You're still alive, which means nothing vital was struck."

She clumsily shucked off her lébrynja jacket, cursing the lack of her prosthetic arm. By some miracle, the blades in her battle belt had held in place, as had her survival pouch. Hekla unsheathed another dagger and cut a swath from her woolen tunic, which she balled up and held firm against Eyvind's seeping wound.

Hekla surveyed her surroundings. They were on a pebbled bank in the river's curve, sheltered from the wind. She knew that when darkness brought the biting cold, they'd need something more to keep them warm. But with Eyvind's wound, she could not risk moving him, and so she'd have to make a fire right here. Hekla propped the makeshift bandage in place against Eyvind's side using a rock, then pushed to her feet.

"Don't die on me, Hakonsson," she barked, before running into the woods.

Half an hour later, Hekla had a small fire crackling on the river's shore. She supposed she ought to be grateful to the leech for sucking the life from the trees; between the dried moss and deadwood, it hadn't taken many strikes of her firestone to get it lit.

Now, using her teeth and left hand, she worked on pulling Eyvind's wet clothing from him so the fire's heat could reach his skin. Hekla wondered if this was some dark joke of the gods, forcing her to haul this man's breeches off, but as her fingertips brushed his cold, clammy thigh, she cursed. If the wound didn't kill him, the cold very well might.

Setting her sights on his tunic, Hekla worked with maddening slowness, peeling each fiber from the wound in his side. When it was fully revealed, she stared at it, feeling sick. It was deep and jagged, with tiny stones and river muck lodged inside it. Hekla pinned the makeshift bandage back into place with the rock, then set to work.

She pulled the medicinal supplies from her survival pouch and stared at the curved needle and thread for several measured heartbeats. Her mind drifted to that terrible night following Ilías's death, when Rey's wound had required sewing.

You'll have to stitch it, Hekla had told Silla. *I cannot with my hand.*

Now she gritted her teeth and blinked furiously. How could she stitch a wound with only one hand? But one glance at Eyvind's pallid complexion and blue lips had her jumping into action. "You must figure this out," she told herself, "or he will die."

To Eyvind, she whispered, "This will hurt, Hakonsson."

And on an exhale, she pulled the bandage away. Methodically, Hekla began cleaning Eyvind's side: a cycle of flushing it with preboiled water from her waterskin, then wiping it through with a swath of her tunic. Throughout the process, Eyvind moaned and writhed. Yet he did not wake, and for that, Hekla was eternally grateful.

When the wound was clear of muck and debris, Hekla sat back

on her haunches and eyed the sewing kit. "You can do this," she muttered, picking up the needle in her left hand and staring at it. "You *must* do this."

Hekla slid the needle into the leg of her breeches to hold it in place, then wet the thread. It took her several tries, and many muttered curses, but when she managed to get the thread through the needle, her heart flared with excitement.

Using her dagger, Hekla cut a long length of thread, then heated the needle over the fire until it glowed red-hot. And then she set her sights on Eyvind. Shimmying onto her stomach, Hekla braced her residual limb on the ground.

"You'll owe me for this, pretty boy."

With slow but decisive movements, Hekla sank the needle through the bottom edge of the wound, and then the top. Twisting, she repeated the motion until she was back to the start. Transferring the thread to her mouth to keep it taut, Hekla used her left hand to tie it off. As the knot caught on the flesh, pulling the edges of the wound together, Hekla's heart filled with hope. Could she actually do this?

Hekla had to do it all over again for the second stitch—thread the needle, heat it, shimmy on her stomach, and perform the stitch. Over and over, she repeated this process, until she reached the other side. Hekla knew she could not sew the wound as tight as a two-handed person. But after tying the last of the thread off, she rose and examined her work. Her stitches were uneven, but it was enough—the wound had stopped seeping. Hekla bit down on her lip with a small measure of joy. It was better than she'd guessed she could do.

Hekla added it to the long list of *fuck you*s she'd compiled for her former husband.

Quickly, she dressed the wound, applying layers of moss and securing it all in place with a long strip of linen. By the time she was done, Eyvind's lips were blue. Goosebumps covered every inch of his exposed skin, and Hekla knew they were not in the clear yet.

He was near the fire's warmth, but it was winter in the northern reaches—they needed a shelter. Thankfully, this section was on a river bend and driftwood was plentiful. Hekla collected load after load, dumping them near the edge of the forest. Next, she linked her battle belt with Eyvind's, then strung them between the roots of a felled tree. Hekla then propped the driftwood against them.

When she laid the last piece of flattened wood in place, she was ready to collapse from exhaustion. But she couldn't—not yet. She dashed back into the forest and found a long, sweeping branch at the base of an evergreen. It took her a few minutes to snap the branch clean, but soon she was dragging it back onto the beach.

Carefully, she positioned Eyvind on the tender boughs, then began the painstakingly slow process of hauling him up to the shelter. By the time Eyvind was protected beneath the driftwood roof, with a fresh fire burning low before him, Hekla's limbs tingled with exertion. The battle thrill had long faded. She barely managed to peel off her clothing and string it on their shelter's roof before collapsing onto the evergreen boughs beside Eyvind.

His skin was cold as ice.

"You'd better pull through, Hakonsson."

Hekla pressed her cheek to Eyvind's back and counted the beats of his heart. And it wasn't long before she succumbed to sleep.

CHAPTER 50

Kovograd, Zagadka

Saga stared vacantly at her reflection in a round of polished metal as Alasa combed her hair. She'd already dressed—not in Zagadkian silks, but in the horsemaiden's armor Khiva had provided on the steppe. It was absurd to think it had been mere days since she'd sat in that tent, certain that every Zagadkian she cared for would die. Now the Urkans had been driven away, the city of Kovograd and its fortress saved from complete decimation.

The fires were extinguished, and warriors combed the battlefield, pulling the wounded from the rubble and executing any surviving Urkans they discovered. Elisava had turned to Saga for help in restoring order in the chaotic aftermath of battle. With so many mouths to feed, the cellar needed restocking, the wounded needed tending, and builders needed to be fetched to pull down fire-ravaged sections of the fortress. And Saga had lost herself in this daily work.

But today felt different. Kassandr had sent a message informing her that a meeting would be called today. Saga had forgone her fine Zagadkian silks in favor of breeches and buckskin boots, and as she watched her reflection, she felt empowered. Gone was the girl who yearned to hide away in the shadows. Here was a woman, ready to do whatever it took to bring help to her kingdom.

A knock at the door made her bright mood falter.

Alasa stood, but before she had time to open the door, Kassandr Rurik strolled through it.

"Once again, you fail to catch me unclothed," muttered Saga in Íseldurian.

"One day perhaps I will be lucky," he quipped back in Zagadkian.

As Saga caught sight of him, her heart did leaps and kicks. He'd scrubbed the soot from his face and had recently shaved, his arm now bandaged and in a sling. Yet as the man swaggered into her chambers, she caught the brightness in his eyes and knew that his beast still lingered near the surface.

Once, this would have instilled fear in her heart. Now she felt a strange wave of fondness.

"I have brought the daymeal for us to enjoy over today's Zagadkian lesson." Saga's gaze dropped to the tray held in his good hand.

"Must we?" she protested, though she lost the battle against her smile.

"We must," he agreed, sliding the tray onto the table before collapsing into the chair with a pained breath.

Alasa secured the last of Saga's braids into a crown, then dipped into a curtsy and slipped from the room. And then they were alone.

Saga planted herself in the chair across from Kassandr, her heart riotous inside her chest. The exhilaration of seeing him whole and hale on the battlefield had burned away, leaving in its wake something softer and quieter—perhaps a little delicate. Now that they'd succeeded against their common enemy, Saga was not quite certain where they stood.

If Kassandr felt the same uncertainty, he did not show it in the least. Saga followed his lead, tucking into the daymeal. As it turned out, the meal consisted of salted cod and stale bread, yet somehow it tasted like feast fare. The Urkans were gone. Zagadka was safe.

For now.

Kassandr spoke casually of what he'd been so busy with over the past days—that he and his Druzhina had done their best in identifying as many Zagadkian remains as they could so the families could claim the bodies and proceed with funeral rites. The Urkans were afforded no such luxury. Their weapons and armor were collected by fortune hunters prowling the grounds. Their corpses were being stacked with wood and hay into makeshift pyres that would soon burn day and night.

As he spoke, she couldn't keep her gaze from snagging on his cleft chin. She'd thought she'd never see that chin again, and now she couldn't look away. Zagadkian rolled off his tongue as he gestured dramatically with a piece of stale bread. As she watched him, tingling warmth spread throughout her body, and Saga vaguely wondered if she'd caught a fever during her journey across the river.

Kassandr's voice grew muted as Saga became lost in her thoughts. The man before her was more clever than she'd ever imagined, and she now saw each of their interactions in a new light. It was glaringly obvious that his Zagadkian lessons had been for more than just teaching her the language. He'd coaxed information from her, then used her intel to organize the Zagadkian defenses. And Saga was suddenly struck with the realization—Kassandr Rurik had believed in her even when she herself had not.

You, Saga, are a queen without her crown, he'd told her all those weeks ago. At last, she truly felt it.

"Thank you," she blurted. Her cheeks heated as she realized she'd interrupted him. Kassandr raised a brow, those green eyes glinting in amusement and making her insides grow even more flustered. "Thank you for—" Saga shook her head, words beyond her current grasp.

"For being so handsome?" The corners of his mouth curled up. "Is my pleasure."

The strangeness swirling inside her body coalesced into irritation at once.

"No? For . . . my clever wit? Or perhaps my patience when teaching such a slow student."

"Your arrogance is unmatched," she muttered, tearing another strip from her salted meat.

Kassandr leaned back. "But I cannot forget that you, Winterwing, have called me *striking*."

Saga's sharp reply was interrupted by the door swinging open. Yuri Rovgolod sauntered inside.

"Does no one wait to be let in?" Saga grumbled, but she quickly stood. "Rov, your nose—" She hissed in sympathy as she examined the new bump in Rov's nose, bracketed by twin black eyes.

"Sword hilt on battlefield," replied Rov in a nasal voice. "I will add to collection of many ways it has broken."

"Broken nose is no match for the pain of my arm," muttered Kassandr, unimpressed. "Where does your sympathy for me hide, Winterwing?"

"We have no time for sympathy, Kassandr," said Rov. "Your father calls for a meeting in the courtyard, since council chambers are now ashes."

At the thought of meeting outdoors, her panic throbbed to life. Yet somewhere between rushing across the courtyard with buckets of sand and riding a winged horse to the lands beyond the river, Saga had gotten used to the low-level thrum of fear. Standing under open skies would probably always make her heart take off at a gallop and her breaths come more shallow. But new confidence brimmed within her.

The eyes were afraid, but the hands were doing.

And with that, Saga strode from her chambers, the men at her heels.

The courtyard was filled with an assortment of horsemaidens and Zagadkians eyeing one another with suspicion. Saga glanced from Khiva, horsemaidens huddled around her as she spoke rapidly in their clan's tongue, to Oleg, scowling with a swollen right eye. Zagadkian nobles and elders milled about, though they'd forgone their ceremonial garb in favor of armored jackets. At the farthest end of the courtyard stood the high prince, head bent in conversation with the clansmother. Saga blinked. What she wouldn't give to be an insect listening in on the ruined wall beside them.

After a single, fortifying breath, Saga entered the courtyard,

Kassandr and Rov flanking her. The crowd immediately hushed, making the rapid beat of Saga's heart feel even more pronounced. She kept her gaze fixed on the high prince as Magnus's voice echoed in her skull.

You deserve to be punished.

But it was weaker, this voice, and far less effective than it once had been. Magnus was dead. The Urkans had been driven away. And Saga was not the girl she'd been that day in the stables when Magnus had branded her hands and deemed her property. Her hand found the feather she kept in her pocket, and as her thumb stroked along the downy barbs, Saga's heart calmed just a bit.

Saga nodded at Khiva and the horse maidens gathered around her, then at Elisava and the noblewomen with whom she'd constructed fire flasks. She glimpsed Alasa and other servants who'd assisted the healers and helped extinguish fires, and as she caught sight of Havoc, soaring high in the skies above, Saga's heart was suddenly so full, she feared it might burst.

She'd been brought to this kingdom against her will. Now she was struck with the realization that Kovograd felt more like a home than Askaborg had in many long years.

With a shaky breath, Saga joined the high prince and clansmother by the ruins of the bell tower. Each looked to have aged a decade, yet their eyes were filled with fierce determination. Good.

"Sire," she said, dipping into a curtsy. "Might I speak to the crowd?"

The high prince eyed her with a new respect. She'd been pleased at his response to the horsemaidens, welcoming them into the fortress with unrestrained emotion. It had felt like a momentous occasion as the high prince had shaken hands with the clansmother; as he'd ordered his retinue to fetch whatever provisions the horsemaidens were in need of. Saga was glad to see the high prince did not think himself above such shows of gratitude.

"You may," said the high prince with a small smile.

With a deep breath, Saga climbed atop a large boulder in the rubble, giving her height and allowing her voice to carry.

"People of Zagadka!" she called, the speech she and Elisava had practiced for days now flowing smoothly from her tongue. "You fought valiantly and restored peace to your isle. Thanks to your efforts, Urkans were expelled!"

War cries rose up from the fearsome horsewomen, while the easterners thumped swords against shields and breastplates. Saga waited for the din to quiet before she continued.

"I know is tempting to enjoy this victory. But we must not forget that King Ivar will return with even bigger numbers."

All jubilance evaporated in an instant.

"How do you know this?" snapped Oleg, glowering from the front of the crowd.

"Above all else," said Saga carefully, "Urkans are thirsty for Bear God's blessing. This loss will disgrace Ivar. He will seek to regain his honor." She cleared her throat before continuing. "They are not yet truly vanquished."

A murmur rose up from the crowd, and Saga felt the stares of the clansmother and the high prince boring into her.

"What we faced is small part of Ivar's power. You see, he sailed without his father's fleet. Once King Harald arrives in Íseldur, Ivar will have hundreds of ships—thousands of warriors—"

Saga's breaths shallowed as a raven cried far overhead, but as her thumb stroked the feather in her pocket, it eased just a touch.

"Now you have seen Urkans with your own eyes! You have seen their war contraptions and battle frenzy. You have seen destruction of Kovograd River and land gates! Now you know what we fight against."

The horsewomen and Zagadkians held identical expressions of astonishment as Saga's unnerving words settled.

"But!" cried out Saga. "You also have seen proof Urkans are not invincible! Your victory proves they can be vanquished!"

"What is it you're dancing around, queen of Íseldur?" asked the high prince with cutting calm.

Saga did not blame him for his wary expression.

"I ask," said Saga, her gaze drifting to the clansmother, then back to the high prince, "for you to come to Íseldur. Join with my people. Together, we have chance against Urkans. Together, we can eradicate this evil."

The high prince's face grew bone white, while the clansmother's turned a violent shade of red. The pair exchanged a look that told Saga that, for once, they were in complete alignment.

The clansmother's gaze hardened as she turned back to Saga. "We cannot simply cross an ocean!" she protested. "Our horses cannot fly such a distance. Are you suggesting they travel by *boat*?"

In truth, Saga hadn't thought quite so far ahead, but she did not let the clansmother know it. "I am eager to discuss such matters with those who know best," she said carefully.

"We have just survived the impossible!" interjected the high prince. "We are surrounded by devastation. I simply cannot afford to send valuable resources across the ocean—"

"Perhaps," said Kassandr, speaking for the first time, "we cannot afford *not* to, Father. You saw those berserkers. You see what they've done to the might of Zagadka." He gestured to the ruins all around them. "How do you think we will fare upon their return?"

Khiva stepped forward, encouraged, apparently, by Kassandr's boldness. "Thus far, the tamer of horses has not spoken an untruth. She knows things we cannot—she knows this enemy better than all else!"

"You would go to this isle of ice and fire?" asked the clansmother, aghast. "You would lead your horsemaidens into danger on unknown soil?"

"I would die to keep a collar from the necks of our children, Mother. To keep our horses free and protect peace on the steppe." Khiva nodded, resolute. "Everything I have seen in this city tells me the tamer of horses is a truthful and wise leader—a woman worth following."

Khiva approached Saga, dozens of horsemaidens following.

"I have discussed with my women, and we have agreed to follow you." Saga's heart hammered as Khiva and the horsemaidens dropped to one knee. "We pledge to you our swords and horses.

That is close to one hundred horsemaidens who will travel across the oceans with you, tamer of horses. We would see these bear-warriors vanquished before their greed consumes our world."

Saga's rapidly beating heart now swelled with gratitude.

"I cannot abandon my clans in the middle of winter," the clans-mother protested. "But perhaps I can put them to use. With access to the ore mines in the east"—she glanced at the high prince briefly—"we could prepare armor and weapons in our mountain forges. We can ready ourselves should the time come—" The clansmother's voice trailed off.

It was not a promise to join the war, but it was a door opened. A possibility. Saga jumped down from the boulder to clasp the clans-mother's hands before bowing her head.

"I thank you, clansmother." She turned to Khiva and, after a moment of hesitation, wrapped the startled horsemaiden in a fierce hug. "And I thank you, Khiva, for your trust. I do not take these words lightly."

Saga stepped back, willing the tears burning behind her eyes to stay put.

"I need more," said the high prince, rubbing his temples. "I need details—a plan. What do you propose?"

Saga turned to him. "King Ivar will take this loss badly. I suggest that you send with me warriors to Íseldur; that we strike before Ivar recovers."

"Our city has burned, our fortress destroyed!" exclaimed Oleg. "Father, we need those men—"

To Saga's great surprise, the high prince raised a hand, and his son fell silent. "Continue."

Saga swallowed. "North." The last she'd heard from her, Eisa was in the north, and Saga could not shake Ana's comment that the rebel chieftains opposing Ivar hailed from the same region. It seemed a promising place to start. "I propose we sail to north of Íseldur. Find Eisa and join with her. Perhaps *alone* we do not have swords enough to fight Ivar and his father. But together with those in Íseldur . . . he would not expect it."

Oleg's face had reached crimson now. "Father, surely you are not considering—"

Another wave of the high prince's hand, before he stepped onto the boulder and stared out at his people. "Saga Volsik," he said in a loud, carrying voice, "might have brought the Urkans to our doorstep sooner than expected. But she has also saved us. Without the timely help of the clans beyond the river, Kovograd would have fallen. A Usurper would sit on the throne, and we would be dead or enslaved. For that, she has earned a boon."

Hope pumped through Saga's veins as the high prince glanced from Kassandr to her. The corners of his lips pulled up. "We will lend you our swords," said the high prince of Zagadka. "But I have some conditions."

Saga licked her lips. "What are they?"

"One," said the high prince, lifting a finger, "you will swear to this alliance before the altars of our four gods."

Saga was already nodding along.

"Second." The high prince lifted a second finger. "You will join your bloodline with ours through marriage."

Saga's stomach hollowed out as she stared at the high prince, dumbfounded.

"Father—" growled Kassandr, but his father cut him off.

"You may choose among our eligible nobles. My son Oleg—"

"Have you knocked your head, old man?" sputtered Oleg.

"—is of marrying age," said the high prince, lips pressed together as though this amused him. "And Elder Fedar is in need of a second wife."

Despite herself, Saga's gaze followed the high prince's. Elder Fedar stroked his long gray mustache pensively.

"Of course, there is always my heir." The high prince sighed. Saga blinked furiously as her heart hacked against her rib cage.

"Father," interjected Kassandr, before launching into a flurry of Zagadkian too rapid for her to follow.

Saga's mind raced, her pulse too quick to sustain. A month ago, the thought of marrying Kassandr had been reprehensible. But everything had changed. And now that she'd witnessed the Urkans' wrath firsthand, other things had shifted in her mind. There was so much at stake—the safety of Zagadka, and that of her own realm. This was bigger than her.

She drew a deep breath. Faced the high prince.

"I will do it," she said, with forced nonchalance. Inside, her heart twisted and flipped and rolled in loops. "My choice is Kassandr."

Meeting Kassandr's eye in this moment felt a lot like granting him a victory, and right now, she could not bear to do it. Instead, Saga turned on her foot and strode from the courtyard. After entering the fortress, she sagged against the wall, drawing deep breaths. She waited for the walls to close in on her. Waited for the voices to shout in her mind. *Trapped,* they'd say. *No exit.*

But as the minutes slid by, her mind was strangely quiet.

CHAPTER 51

Kassandr's beast thrashed restlessly within him, as it had since his father had made his insidious demand of Saga. She had saved their people from the Urkans and had fostered the first step toward peace with the clans beyond the river. As far as Kassandr was concerned, his father ought to be falling at her feet. Giving her anything she demanded.

Instead, he'd strong-armed her into a marriage with Kassandr.

I will never marry you.

Her words burned through his skull, setting fire to his veins. Once he had wanted this—desperately so. He had to admit there was still a part of him willing to have her by whatever means necessary. *Perhaps,* this part of him said, *she will grow to love you.*

No, another part of him countered. Not this woman who'd been held captive all her life—who saw marriage as yet another cage.

Now he stalked through the remnants of Kovograd Fortress, his mood darkening with each step. He lost himself to time, but eventually, Kassandr found himself rattling Saga's locked door. It wasn't long before Alasa unlocked and cracked the door open, eyes widening before she dipped into a curtsy.

"My lord," said Alasa, not moving from the doorway to allow Kassandr entry, "she is indisposed at the moment."

"Who is it?" called Saga from within the room.

"Kassandr," he replied, trying to keep his voice steady as his beast howled and scratched, desperate to get to her. "I must speak with you."

Alasa shook her head, knuckles white where they gripped the doorframe. "You mustn't. It is improper—"

"Let him in," said Saga, to Kassandr's great surprise. Reluctantly, Alasa stepped aside, allowing Kassandr entry. But his feet soon faltered, and he damned near choked on his own tongue.

Steam rose in undulating waves from a large wooden tub set near the hearth. And there, within that tub, sat Saga Volsik. Her bared back faced him, and his eyes hungrily traced the curve of her shoulder, then jumped to a bead of water sliding down her spine. Saga's hair was still woven into a crown of braids, and it took all of his restraint not to cross the room to her and unbind it.

"You may leave, Alasa," said Saga. On the surface, she seemed like a woman in control, yet the slight waver in her voice betrayed her.

"My lady—" objected Alasa.

"Do not worry after my virtue, Alasa," Saga replied, her voice more level now. "He is, after all, my betrothed."

Kassandr's beast howled, and his lips curved into a lazy smile. But the circumstances of their engagement surged back to mind, and his smile fell away. Kass was dimly aware of the swish of Alasa's skirts. The *thunk* of the iron latch. But more than anything else, he was aware of the sound of rippling water as Saga moved within the tub.

He cleared his throat. Tried to recall why he'd come.

"I suppose," said Saga, "you've finally caught me unclothed."

Kassandr made a nonsensical, garbled sound. He shook his head, trying to clear his senses.

"You do not need to marry me," he finally forced across his lips as his beast snarled and his body tried to hold the words back. "I will give to you the help you ask for. I will go to Íseldur with you, and will bring strong warriors. We will fight with you all the same."

Her spine grew rigid, and he wanted to drop to his knees behind her. Knead the tension from her shoulders.

"Now you *do not* wish to marry me?" she bristled.

"It was wrong what I did." The words wrought shame and a deep sense of remorse. "To take away your choice. To think I know what is best for you. I should have asked for your decision and respected it, even if I did not like it."

Her intake of breath was so faint, a man with ordinary hearing would have missed it.

"I wish only for your happiness." Kassandr clenched his fists to keep himself rooted in place. "And so I will go to my father and . . . *force* him to do what is right."

She was silent a long moment, and Kass pictured her chewing on her lip in thought. When at last she spoke, her words rocked him to his core.

"And if I do choose it? To marry you?"

For a moment, time seemed to stand still. His beast gave a triumphant howl, blood pumping hot through his veins. And for the first time in weeks, Kassandr allowed his old fantasy to replay in his mind's eye. Saga by his side, sharing the daymeal each morning. Saga, sitting on a throne beside his, her clever wit strengthening his kingdom. Saga, tangled in the furs of his bed, writhing beneath him . . .

A sharp breath escaped him, and Kassandr realized he'd been silent for far too long. "What are you saying?" he asked.

"I'm saying," she said, toying with the water, "that perhaps you're brash and drive me absolutely mad. But I've been betrothed twice before and I find you far preferable to my other promised husbands."

Kass's brows dipped low at the reminder of Magnus Hansson and Bjorn Ivarsson. His beast's hackles rose, a fierce wave of protectiveness thrashing through him.

Mine.

He shook his head, trying to clear it. He'd allowed such thoughts to drive him before, and it had been the wrong choice. Now he knew better.

"Not good enough," he growled, hating himself just a little. "Your reasons are lacking."

Saga turned her face to reveal her profile. Kassandr's eyes roamed over her tilted blue eyes, the slant of her jaw, the elegant arch of her neck, and desire surged through him with dizzying force.

"What if," Saga whispered, "I told you that I admire your character?"

His knees nearly buckled. "My character?"

She nodded, though the corners of her lips tugged down. "It was despicable of you to take away my choice, Kassandr, and I do not know if I've yet forgiven you." The rising steam eddied with her exhalation. "Perhaps it is a comfort to know that you had my best interests at heart."

His beast ran circles inside his chest.

"I suppose I understand you better now," continued Saga. "And though sometimes you make the most wretched of choices, I've found your character to be remarkably steady." She lifted a shoulder in a delicate shrug. "I find that an admirable trait in a husband."

Kassandr turned her words over. Looked for hidden meaning. "Winterwing," he said, his voice a low rasp. "Are you telling me that you . . . like me?"

"'Like' is too strong a word."

Kass could not help his cocky grin. "You have a fondness for me."

"I tolerate you. You will make a tolerable husband."

A low chuckle escaped him. Her words were playful, teasing even. And though they were not bold proclamations of love, they hinted at something. Forgiveness. A chance to start anew.

He shoved a hand through his hair, his mind awhirl. Kassandr had come to this room to release her from the shackles of marriage, but he'd never considered she might want it for herself.

"Very well," he said softly. "If you do not object, then I suppose it is agreed." A sly smile spread across his lips. "Shall we seal it with a kiss?"

Saga snorted. "That never was a Zagadkian tradition, was it, *Rurik*?"

He shook his head, then realized she could not see him. "No. But how can you blame me for trying?"

"Very well," said Saga, her voice a near whisper. "Let us seal it with a kiss."

Kassandr might have lost his mind, for he did not remember surging forward, only that he suddenly found himself kneeling on the floor beside the tub.

Claim! snarled his beast, the need to mindlessly rut barreling through his veins. Kassandr yanked on its leash, trying to cage it away. But the sight of Saga Volsik reclined in that tub had knocked all the sense from his skull.

A better man would have kept his eyes on hers, but Kass had never been known for his self-control. His eyes dipped to her knees, hugged to her chest. She held them with a white-knuckled grip that made him frown, and a shred of his wits returned to him.

"We need not—"

"I *want* to," she interjected.

Kassandr hardly dared breathe for fear he'd frighten this beautiful creature away—this lovely woman who would soon be his wife. He trained his gaze on the fluttering pulse in her throat, longing to scrape his teeth along it, to sink into her flesh with his claiming bite—

Instead, he leaned forward, bracing his forearms on the edge of the tub, and took her mouth in a rough kiss. Saga, to her credit, only faltered for a moment before her lips moved against his. Fire blazed through him, burning up all his plans for caution. Kassandr leaned farther forward, but Saga did not slink back. Instead, she melted against him, filled all the broken places inside him.

A whimper came from Saga's throat, and it spurred him on. Kassandr leaned farther forward and cupped her face as he showed her with his lips just how good they could be—she his queen, and he her protector. Her *husband.* His elbows had dipped below the waterline in the tub, but he couldn't care, because Saga's fingers clutched at his wrists, holding him in place. She was barely keeping up with the strokes of his eager tongue, and Kassandr had to remind himself that she was unused to this—that he should go slowly. But this was his Saga, and he'd yearned for her for so very long.

Kassandr was painfully hard, his cock straining against his breeches. And gods, but he longed to pull her from the tub. To splay her legs wide on the furs before the hearth and bury his face between them. What sounds would she make when he made her come? He had to find out.

But not yet.

As Kassandr broke the kiss, he felt he deserved an award, for it had taken every last shred of his will. He eased back just a touch, though he was still leaning over the tub. Saga's blue eyes were glazed, her cheeks and lips flushed, and for a moment they stared at each other, breaths mingling in the steam.

"More," whispered Saga, pulling on his hands—trying to bring his lips back to hers.

"Soon," he said, his voice rough as broken stone. "We must save something for our wedding night."

It gave him immense pleasure to watch her eyes darken—to give the maddening woman a taste of her own ale. After all, she'd been driving him mad with want since the day he'd met her. Now she, too, would suffer.

His beast was livid, railing against the sudden appearance of Kassandr's self-control, and resisting its call to claim was the hardest thing Kassandr Rurik had ever done.

"I will care for you, Winterwing," he promised her in a low voice. "I will cherish you. I will protect you and stay by your side. Each day I will work to earn back your trust." He studied her face in exquisite detail, noting the droplet of water clinging to long, black lashes; the tiny freckle just beside her ear.

He pressed one last, lingering kiss to her lips, and then he forced himself to stand. His beast pounded against the cage of his chest, urging him to go back, but Kassandr forced himself to take one step toward the exit, then another. He wasn't sure if he breathed until there was a closed door between him and the naked form of Saga Volsik.

Kass sagged against the wall, bracing himself against his beast's tantrum. Gods, but he was in trouble.

CHAPTER 52

Kopa, Íseldur

Silla smoothed the leather-like scales of her lébrynja jacket as Hild held up a round of polished metal for her to examine her reflection. Her curls were woven into a thick braid that fell down her back, and her eyes were free from kohl. Gone were the fine garments and ornate jewels, exchanged in favor of an armored jacket and functional breeches. The woman staring back at her was no longer Eisa. Today, she would introduce the jarls to Silla.

Yet the dark circles beneath her eyes and her pallid complexion spoke of Myrkur's ever-tightening grip. And as she stared at her reflection, darkness flashed in her eyes—so brief, she might think she'd imagined it.

Together we will make them bow, hissed the dark god. *Once you are on the throne, Eisa, we will rule it together.*

Silla frowned. *What makes you think I would ever want that?*

She sensed the dark god's satisfaction. *You cannot hide it from me,* He taunted. *I hear it in your thoughts. Taste it in your blood.* Hunger surged through her. A desperate want. *Where is Saga? Would you work so hard to gain the fealty of these nobles only to have her claim it? It is you who should be on the throne.*

She tried to shake off Myrkur's odious presence. Tried to ignore His provoking words. But it was impossible to do so when there was a kernel of truth to what He said. Silla was forced to admit that she did want the throne, though not to rule as He would have it. She wanted to make choices that would help Frida and her shelter home; Eilif and her ailing sister; the refugees unsettled in the north.

Let me in, Eisa, purred the god, her yearning growing more potent, *and we will have the throne.*

"No," she said aloud, ignoring Hild's perplexed look as she snatched the heart-shaped rock from her dressing table. Immediately, memories of her foster father surged forth and her ears rang with the remembered sound of Matthias's voice, calling her *Moonflower*. Myrkur recoiled, filling Silla with satisfaction.

She stared at her reflection, smiling as she slid the heart-shaped rock into her pocket. Silla drew a deep breath. Tonight was their final chance—to gain the warriors they needed in the heartwood and to earn the jarls' trust. Armed with a plan and a few small defences against the dark god, Silla knew there was a chance, even if slim.

"Ready?" asked Rey, appearing by her side.

"Not truly," sighed Silla, finding one last errant lébrynja scale and smoothing it flat, "but let us get on with it all the same."

Rey's large hand slid into hers, and when he looked at her, she was both warmed and strengthened by his presence. "Together," he whispered.

"Together."

The pair of them turned in unison, and as they exited her chambers, Runný and the rest of her queensguard moved into formation around them. Their pace was unhurried as they navigated Ashfall's tangled corridors; as they descended stairwell after stairwell into the deepest parts of the fortress.

They approached the enormous oak doors Silla had nervously entered so many weeks before, and she reflected on how different she now felt. Her pulse still pounded, and sweat still beaded on her brow. But as the double doors opened before her, she was filled with a sense of certainty. No longer was she trying to be someone else. Today, she was simply Silla.

Rey squeezed her hand, and when she glanced at him, Silla was surprised by the eagerness she found in his eyes.

"Are you . . . *excited,* Galtung?"

His lips curved up into an almost-smile. "Only for you to show them who you truly are."

"An apologizer to rocks," she teased.

"A resilient woman with a heart of gold. The best in this entire realm."

I will relish watching others underestimate you, he'd told her all those weeks ago. His words, then and now, reached to the deepest parts of her, making something tender unfold inside her chest. This man and his unwavering belief in her.

Myrkur hissed with disgust, slinking lower. With her mind to herself, Silla pushed up onto her toes and kissed Rey softly. *Thank you,* she told him with her lips, *for believing in me. For building me up when so many would tear me down.* Silla ended the kiss quickly but sent Rey a look that promised more later.

They entered the hall side by side. Silla had given the jarls an earlier time than the rest. She wanted to ensure that their little games of power—tardiness high among them—had time to play out. She also wanted them to sit with their peers—the stablemen and kitchen women, the refugees from the west. And perhaps Silla wanted the jarls to squirm a little as they wondered why one section of the benches remained glaringly vacant.

As the light of the braziers illuminated the many hundreds of people seated, Silla tried to ignore the butterflies swarming in her belly. She glanced into the crowd, waving at Hild and Eilif before nodding at Jarl Holger. Silla's gaze skimmed quickly past Lady Tala before landing on Jarl Hakon, whose expression looked simultaneously curious and irritated.

He conspires, hissed Myrkur, pumping anger and hatred for Hakon through her veins.

Silla squeezed Rey's hand, and his thumb caressed her knuckles in answer. *Dimples,* she recited, *large hands. Trimming his beard.* The dark god retracted, and with Him, her anger.

But as she brimmed with self-satisfaction, Silla caught Rey nodding at Atli and nearly choked on her own saliva. It seemed that sometime during Myrkur's possession of her, Rey and Atli had found a tentative sort of peace. Indeed, Rey had informed her that he and Atli had been working to muster forces to join them in the heartwood. Unfortunately, with the bulk of Hakon's men stationed at the eastern border, it was not a straightforward task.

Silla and Rey climbed the dais stairs, then waited for her queensguard to fan out on the floor. Once they were all in position, she drew a deep breath and began.

"I thank you for coming," Silla said to the crowd. "I know this is an unusual summons. But the fact is, we live in unusual times." She cleared her throat, readying herself for the next part. "I see not all have arrived. Kálf, will you let our guests of honor into the hall?"

Whispers rippled through the crowd as attendees craned their necks toward the double doors. Kálf threw them wide, and Jarl Agnar strode into the hall with his two dozen warriors. The room collectively gasped. Jarl Hakon leaped to his feet, an angry flush creeping from beneath his bejeweled collar. As the jarl's hand strayed to his hip, Silla was glad all weapons had been left at the door.

You've shown Hakon, preened Myrkur. *Now he sees who holds the power!*

Despite reminding herself that they were all on the same side, it was impossible not to feel a measure of satisfaction as Jarl Agnar and his men crossed the hall and settled into the vacant expanse of benches. It was *she* who brought these warring factions together. *She* who would restore peace.

"There is a snake in our midst!" Silla called out, a giddy feeling rising as she took in the shocked expressions in the crowd. Myrkur wriggled gleefully. "One who conspires against me."

The crowd fell deathly silent, jarls and peasants glancing around with equal confusion. Jarl Hakon sat down hard, glancing around at his peers with a hint of worry.

"Someone in this very room has tried to kill me *four* times."

And they will pay, whispered Myrkur, the desire for vengeance surging through her veins. Rather than shoving it down, Silla let it flow. Reveled in this moment.

She wanted the culprit to squirm a little longer, but unfortunately, they hadn't time to waste. "Lady Tala," called Silla, "would you like to explain yourself?"

Tala looked around with a tittering laugh. "A jest? How humorous!"

But the silence seemed to thicken the air, and Lady Tala's expression soon shifted to anger. "Surely you do not accuse *me* of those attempts on your life?" she sputtered. "I was not even present for the rockslide!" When Silla's expression did not falter, Tala's face turned crimson. "After all I have *done* for you . . . after I've taken you under my wing . . ."

Myrkur cackled wickedly inside her, and despite herself, Silla smiled malevolently as she gazed at Tala.

"Would you like to explain," she said loudly, "how your son holds the deeds to Ingvarr's family lands? Did you force him to do your bidding, Tala? Threaten to evict his family if he did not comply?"

She's frightened, preened Myrkur, as Tala's eyes widened. *Keep going.*

Silla complied. "Or perhaps you'd like to tell Jarl Hakon what truly happened at the border mediations?" Hakon's gaze slashed Tala's way. "Or shall Jarl Agnar speak for you?"

"What have you told her, Jarl Agnar?" demanded Lady Tala, sending him a thunderous look. "This *child* is a proven liar, Your Highness. You cannot trust a word he speaks—"

She is the liar! countered Myrkur, and Silla had to seal her lips shut so as not to shout it out.

"This is the woman," called Jarl Agnar, "who came to our mediation on your behalf, Jarl Hakon. A so-called neutral party. But from her tongue came threats and the declaration that you'd laid claim to my borderlands."

"Preposterous!" exclaimed Jarl Hakon, leaping to his feet. "Your men came onto *my* lands and set fire to several villages—"

"In retribution for the fires *you* set on mine!" challenged Agnar.

More, begged Myrkur. *More chaos. More strife!* The god was feasting on the conflict in the room, and Silla had to battle back His urges. Her hand slid into her pocket and wrapped around the heart-shaped stone. Immediately, the god cringed back.

Silla brought her focus outward once more, where the two jarls stared at each other for a long, tense minute.

"Is this true, Lady Tala?" asked Hakon, his gaze sliding toward her.

"Of course not!" Tala ran a shaking hand along her auburn braid.

Tell them, Eisa, urged Myrkur, His glee a palpable thing. *Show them the letter.*

Silla pulled the square of parchment from her pocket and unfolded it carefully. "'Your coffers will be replenished with fifty thousand sólas when Eisa Volsik lies dead,'" she read, her heart pounding vigorously, "'and fifty thousand more should Jarls Hakon and Agnar march against each other. Burn this note after reading. Yours, Queen Signe.'" Silla's eyes met Tala's across the room. "A pity you did not burn it, Lady Tala."

"Where did you get this letter?" sputtered Tala. "Did you—did you search my quarters?" She glanced desperately about. "It is nothing but falsehoods! Planted to place guilt upon my innocent shoulders—"

We have her, Eisa. Let me in and we will show her—show them all *what happens to deceivers.*

Silla shook off the ominous request, focusing on Lady Tala, whose eyes darted frantically to Jarl Hakon. "You must believe me, Jarl Hakon. I relayed your request for peace just as you asked—"

Jarl Hakon's face had turned a furious shade of red. "It is no secret that your house suffered financial mismanagement long before your husband's death, Lady Tala," said the jarl. "As a token of my friendship to your late husband, I've held a place for you in my court, but I can see now that you've abused it for your own gain."

Spill her blood, wheezed Myrkur. *Kill. Destroy. Show them what it means to cross a Volsik!*

Silla massaged her temples, trying to keep her focus on her former mentor.

"No!" pleaded Tala, glancing about as though searching for an exit. "Please, Hakon, you must believe me—"

But Jarl Hakon only looked to his retinue and nodded. The crowd gasped as Hakon soldiers pushed to their feet.

This woman must be punished, Myrkur cried. *She made you twist yourself to fit her standards, Eisa. Toyed with you while plotting to take your life.*

The god had a point. "Aside from the attempts on my life, I wonder how many of your lessons were designed to ensure my failure?" Silla found herself asking.

"*You* are the one spouting lies!" exclaimed Lady Tala, her anger reaching a boiling point. "You ought to be grateful! How dare you smear my good name—"

Strike her down, seethed Myrkur, wrath burning through her veins. *Squeeze the breath from her lungs. Let me in, Eisa!*

As Silla ran her thumb frantically along the heart-shaped rock, Tala darted away from one of Hakon's warriors as he tried to seize her arm. Just as it looked like she'd reach the walkway, Lady Tala stumbled, falling hard on her stomach.

"Oops," said Kaeja, pulling her foot back from where she'd tripped Tala. And as Kaeja's blue eyes met hers, an incredulous laugh came from Silla.

Hakon's men swarmed around Tala and secured her wrists in manacles as Myrkur chanted inside Silla's skull. The god was enjoying this spectacle just a little too much.

Lady Tala could have maintained her dignity had she let them lead her out of the meeting chambers quietly. Instead, she went like a spitting cat.

"The Volsik Dynasty is filled with wolves!" hissed Tala as she was hauled to her feet. "The queen has plans! She will be a just leader and usher in a new era in this realm!"

Do not let this slander stand, Eisa! pleaded Myrkur. *We must act swiftly and without mercy—*

But the chamber doors slammed shut, muffling Tala's voice and making the dark god writhe angrily. Silla's fingers flew to her temples, and Rey seemed to notice. He stepped nearer, the press of his boot against hers made the dark god hiss.

Still, it was difficult to concentrate through Myrkur's tantrum. Silla grabbed Rey's hand. Focused on the feel of his thumb rubbing circles on the back of her hand. And finally, she was able to turn her attention back to the crowd. Jarl Hakon stared furiously after Tala before turning abruptly to Jarl Agnar.

"I suppose my letters never reached you?" said Hakon, striding toward him with one hand outstretched.

Agnar accepted Hakon's hand and shook it firmly. "No. And I suppose mine never reached you?"

"No." A brief pause, and then, "I can assure you, Jarl Agnar, I have no interest in your borderlands. In fact, I have a parcel of land along the northern coast that has grown cumbersome to manage. It is rocky and infertile, but the waters are thick with whales. Perhaps with your fleet of fishing vessels, you could make use of it?"

Agnar's eyes widened for a fraction of a second, reminding Silla of just how young he was. "That would be—" He cleared his throat. "—I would accept, and offer you in return half of our catch."

Two matters settled, thought Silla. The realization that she'd restored peace on the border caused satisfaction to shimmer all through her. And knowing this emotion to be her own, Silla grasped onto it. Refused to let it go.

Myrkur growled, trying to resurface, and she again focused on the feel of Rey's thumb drawing circles across her knuckles. She thought of the shield-home, of sitting on the bed while Rey untangled her curls. The god cringed deeper, and Silla blinked back to the present, only to realize the entire room was watching her.

"I am glad to see friendship restored between your families," she forced out, bracing against Myrkur's furious attempts to push forth.

"There is more we must speak of," she said, glad to have practiced this speech, as she required all her mental strength to keep the dark god at bay. "I called you here today in *this,* of all halls, to signify a fresh start. This is the very place where countless plans have been hatched by the Uppreisna, and so it seems a fitting location to usher in a new age. An age where we stand shoulder-to-shoulder—east and west, Galdra and not, peasant and jarl—axes in hand and hearts in alignment. I like to think of it as the Dawn of the North."

An enthusiastic cheer rose up from the crowd, and Silla blinked in startled gratification as the dark god was driven further down. She let the sound billow through the high-ceilinged chamber—let the hope and optimism of these people loosen Myrkur's hold. After a moment, she held up a hand and continued.

"You all know me as Eisa Volsik, but long before that, I was Silla." Her eyes found Hild's, and her insides grew buoyant. "I grew up with very little. Earned calluses and blisters through long days in kitchens. I love animals to a fault, can make nine different types of bread, and I've been told I drool in my sleep, though I choose not to believe it."

A murmur arose in the crowd, and Silla caught Hild and Eilif sharing an amused smile. She latched onto the warmth that bloomed inside her. Used it as a weapon against the god of chaos. Silla reached into her pocket and pulled out the heart-shaped rock, lifting it for all who were present to see.

"My foster father gave this to me." Pride and love and a multitude of other emotions blossomed inside her. "Some of you might know him as Tómas, others as King Kjartan's bodyguard. But to me, he was Matthias. He raised me to be kind and hopeful. I've been told these are not qualities one needs in a leader. That you need someone stern . . . a queen who can strike fear in the hearts of your enemies."

Silla smoothed her thumb over the rock's surface. Myrkur thrashed deep within her, but He was distant. Smothered. It made her smile. "That, I fear, is not me. Instead, I can bring a willingness to dig my hands in and work—to fight alongside you. And above all else, I bring an eagerness to learn from those who know better.

"I am not too prideful to share that I am better suited to some tasks than others. Some would see this as a weakness, but I choose to see it as an opportunity. I am here today to ask for your help. I do not care how many bushels of grain your land can produce, nor how far back your lineage reaches. Your rank does not concern me. Only the courage in your heart will matter when we face Myrkur's creatures at Rökkur."

While the jarls knew of Rökkur's threat from their meeting, the rest of those present did not. Silla found herself holding her breath, allowing a few moments as whispers rippled through the crowd. But she could not give their fear space to sharpen. Could not relent her hold on Myrkur.

Silla's gaze found Jarl Holger's in the crowd. "My honesty has been questioned, and I will tell you now, Jarl Holger, you were not wrong. I thought that in order to gain your trust, I must hide parts of myself. Instead, it has only planted doubt in your minds."

Rey's hand slid once more into hers, and they held the heart-shaped rock between their palms. It gave her the strength to say what she must. "Now I share with you the truth: I have not been well in my time in Kopa. My mother, Queen Svalla, made a bargain with the god of chaos, and the bargain now lives within me."

She saw disbelief in the faces of the crowd, and Silla did not blame them one bit. Yet as Myrkur clawed back some ground in her consciousness, she forced herself on.

"A shard of Myrkur lives in my body and each day He grows stronger. I've hidden this away, afraid you'd lose faith in me. But in doing so, I've only weakened the bonds of trust. So now I share my whole truth with you, as well as my plans—tomorrow I will leave for the heartwood of the Western Woods. There, I will vanquish the leech and break the bargain my mother made."

Myrkur roared deep within her, his displeasure pushing forth. But Silla focused on the faces in the crowd, landing on Agnar's encouraging expression.

"Rökkur is indeed coming—the twilight of days. It begins with the long winters and ends with fire raining down upon us. You might have heard of Myrkur's serpent offspring slipping through the crevices in the north, and the deadly mist that has forced so many from their homes in the west. This leech is Myrkur's progeny, which has climbed from His realm through the deep roots of a hjarta tree.

"Each day, the god of chaos gains more anchors to our realm," continued Silla. "But there is hope. The mother serpent was vanquished; the crevice through which she entered our realm sealed. Do you know what that tells me?"

The room was silent, but Myrkur was riotous. Anger lashed through her veins and pounded at her temples. Clearly the god did not wish for her to reveal His plans.

"It tells me that our fate is not set—it can be rewoven. But we must act quickly. Tomorrow, we ride for the heartwood in the Western Woods. And when Marra is fullest, we will do battle against Myrkur's progeny and the Turned creatures it has spawned. We need all the help we can get. No longer can we afford to be complacent on this issue. I ask for your swords—"

Silla gasped as Myrkur railed against her, sending sharp strikes of pain through her skull. But through her inner tumult, she was vaguely aware that several figures had stood from the benches. Jarl Agnar and his two dozen warriors walked across the floor toward the dais. The crowd watched on as they dropped to one knee and bowed their heads.

Jarl Agnar's voice was loud and carrying as he spoke. "Eisa Volsik has proven herself an honorable and truth-seeking leader. House Agnar pledges their swords to you."

The lightness in Silla's chest expanded, dulling the pain in her skull and easing the unruly beat of her heart. She smiled broadly, tears shining in her eyes. Both Silla and Agnar knew how it felt to be underestimated, and so it felt fitting that the young jarl would be the first of her oathsworn.

But it surprised her to see the next jarl to step forth—Jarl Holger, who'd witnessed her possession by Myrkur and had confided to Rey his distrust of Eisa. The grizzled warrior dropped to one knee, his retinue of battle-hardened warriors at his back.

Her insides turned light and fluffy, warmth suffusing all of her limbs. Myrkur thundered within her, trying desperately to regain control. But Silla's smile only widened. She had the upper hand. And as more jarls crossed the floor, she knew she'd keep it.

The rest of the jarls came forth. Hild and Eilif joined them, the stablehands, the refugees, and more. Atli stood, leaving his father to join the others. And soon, Hakon joined them as well. Hundreds of people, bending the knee. How many warriors would that mean for the heartwood? Silla could not say. It would have to be enough.

Tears of hope filled her eyes as she looked over the bowed heads. She'd done the impossible—had rid herself of the traitor in their midst, had united the jarldom, and had gained the swords needed for the battle of the heartwood—all while a shard of her enemy lived inside her. Myrkur snarled within her, but He was buried deep.

And she could not help but think it—if she could do all this, perhaps she could break the bargain, too.

CHAPTER 53

Kovograd, Zagadka

Saga's fingertips skimmed the lace neckline of her wedding gown as she tried to quell the worry gathering in her stomach. She could hardly believe it was truly happening. Of course it was happening. She'd had *days* to put an end to the preparations, should she have chosen to do so.

Instead, she'd busied herself overseeing preparations to leave the isle. Given the abysmal state of the Zagadkian naval fleet, merchant and fishing ships had been commandeered for the voyage and fitted with stalls to carry one hundred winged horses. Word had arrived from the clansmother that the ore from the eastern mines had arrived and smelting was under way, with two hundred new swords expected to be forged before the ships sailed to Íseldur.

Aside from their continued morning language lessons, Saga had seen little of her betrothed during this time. Kassandr and Rov worked tirelessly to muster the best of their warriors to fight in Íseldur. Somehow, they'd convinced the high prince and Zagadkian elders to send two shiploads of grain along with them, a detail that had rendered Saga speechless. She knew the long winter in Íseldur would be dire, and that this grain would bring some much-needed hope.

In short, Saga's hands and mind had been so busy, she'd scarcely had time to think of this day. But now, it was here, and there was no avoiding it.

Today, she would marry Kassandr Rurik.

A flutter low in her chest was quickly overshadowed by a twist in her gut. She didn't *have* to do this; Kass had told her as much. One word, and she'd be on a ship bound for Íseldur, Zagadkian warriors at her back. His offer to fight for her regardless of marriage had meant more to Saga than he'd ever know.

But the fact was, her decision to marry him was not solely for her kingdom. For thirteen years, Saga had been engaged to Bjorn, and her engagement to Magnus had felt even longer. She was no fool. She knew that the moment she returned to Íseldur, her hand in marriage would once more become a bargaining tool.

And Saga was done being used in such games.

But no matter how often she repeated her good, logical reasons for marrying Kassandr, there were also . . . intangible motivations. Saga could no longer deny the truth: Her husband-to-be was appallingly handsome, and the curl low in her belly whenever she saw him could no longer be ruled an illness.

Saga's fingers went to her lips, still tingling with the remembered feel of Kassandr's mouth. He'd kissed her in the tub with such reckless abandon, and she'd returned it with equal fervor. Her body awakened beneath his touch, as though she'd never truly been alive until she was in his arms.

The door groaned open, and Saga jumped in fright.

"It's time," said Alasa, stern and unsmiling.

Saga took one last look at her gown, then strode from the room.

She soon learned that the process of marriage in Zagadka was no simple affair. It began in the red room, with Elisava and her handmaidens burning birch sticks all around her.

"Birch," Elisava explained, as the smoke drifted over Saga's skin, "is sacred to the Spring Maiden . . . she who is goddess of love and fertility and patroness of marriage."

Next, the women took up a song, flocking around Saga and gathering her hair into a single, long braid.

"Into your hair we braid good intentions that you will carry with you into your marriage," said Elisava.

With the collective sound of their voices surrounding her—with the countless hands tending to her—Saga's throat grew thick with emotion. Eisa should be here, on this of all days. If only she could reach her, if only she could talk to her . . .

Strand after strand of pearls were layered around Saga's neck, and an ornate, beaded headdress set upon her brow. Bells dripping from each side of the headdress tinkled against yet more strands of pearls. Elisava painted Saga's lips a bright red before handing her a bouquet of berry sprigs.

"Spring Maiden?" Saga queried, recognizing them as the berries that had once garnished her plate.

Elisava nodded, her green eyes shining as she examined Saga from head to toe. The noblewomen surrounded her, fastening a white fur cloak around Saga's shoulders.

"Perfect," announced Elisava with a decisive nod.

When Saga stepped out of Kovograd's fortress, she blinked at the sight that met her eyes. The courtyard was still a mess of rubble, though crimson ribbons were now strung from the ruins, punctuated with sprigs of greenery and silver bells. Flames crackled in golden braziers, lighting a pathway cleared through the detritus and toward, Saga presumed, her husband.

Her feet faltered as the weight of this moment sank into her, and she took smooth, slow breaths, trying to quell her racing heart. Elisava and her ladies held the hem of Saga's gown, trailing her down the steps. Shifting her bouquet to one hand, Saga tapped with the fingers of her other against her shoulder as she followed the path around the bend.

The roof of the royal forge was collapsed in on her right, but the blacksmith and his apprentices had gathered outside in fine crimson tunics. They held candles in their hands, their baritone voices singing a low song.

As the path curved, a group of fortress servants came into view. Alasa stood at the front of the group, but Saga recognized many others as members of her fire brigade. Like the blacksmiths, they were dressed in their finest, clutching candles as their voices twined into the song. She sniffled but managed to send a watery smile their way.

On they walked, passing soldiers and kitchen workers and the townspeople of Kovograd. It was not lost on Saga that the pathway she walked was the same she and Kassandr had taken during their language lessons. Her heart raced as the temple's red flag and the wooden icons rose before her eyes. The singing grew louder, coming from the direction of the temple, and as the throng of elders and nobles came into view, Saga's breathing shallowed.

She spotted the clansmother and Khiva, surrounded by horse-maidens, and the high prince, who'd donned ceremonial robes. An arch had been erected before the temple tower, grasses and winter berries woven through it, and beneath it was placed a vibrant rug. And then she saw her future husband.

The blight upon her life.

And the man who'd shown her what heights she could truly reach.

Kassandr Rurik would look dashing wearing a sack, but seeing him clad in a Zagadkian kaftan that emphasized the breadth of his shoulders and brought out the green in his eyes, Saga was so distracted she nearly tripped on her own feet. His gaze raked from her head to her toes, as though he could not decide where it should land. But as it returned to her face, his eyes gleamed with new intensity. There was possessiveness in that gaze, so sharp she felt it on her bare skin.

Next to Kassandr stood Oleg, looking as though he were in physical pain. It was clear he'd rather be anywhere but here. Saga stifled a smile.

The song suddenly shifted, growing somehow more beautiful. Saga could not catch the words, and yet she felt the meaning—

a blessing from all those gathered to the new couple. Saga handed her bouquet to Elisava and stepped onto the ceremonial rug. As Kassandr took her hands, his eyes burned like emerald fires.

"*Krasavitsa,**" he murmured.

"I can understand you now," she said softly in reply.

"Good." Kassandr brought the scarred flesh on the back of Saga's hand to his lips. For a moment, she was transported back in time to the gardens in Askaborg where he'd first seen those scars. From the very start, this man had never looked away from her—not even when she'd tried her best to hide.

Elisava and her women arranged Saga's skirts and veil behind her, then stepped back. The high prince led them through a prayer, then instructed them to bow to the statues of each Zagadkian god—north for Father Winter, south for Brother Summer, east for the Spring Maiden, and west for the Autumn Crone. Then Saga Volsik and Kassandr Rurik stood before each other repeating words fed to them by the high prince. Saga's heart beat so ferociously, she scarcely knew what she said.

Finally, Kassandr stepped forward, and Saga's stomach began to dip and twirl. This man, whose face looked to have been carved by the gods, would be her *husband.* His fingertips skimmed along her cheek as he leaned down toward her. Saga lifted onto the tips of her toes, eager to meet him halfway, and then their lips met, and it felt as though pure, molten gold flowed through her veins.

Saga's eyes fell shut, his touch making the ground beneath her feet seem to tilt. But he was pulling back. The crowd was quietly clapping. It was over.

Dazed, Saga turned to the crowd, who called out blessings to the couple. The high prince presented them with a loaf of salted bread—much to Saga's confusion—which Kassandr accepted proudly before handing it to Oleg. Kassandr slid his hand into hers, sending Saga's heart skittering. His hand was warm and rough with calluses,

* Beautiful.

but as he squeezed hers gently, Saga's nerves eased just a touch. With the widest grin she'd ever seen, Kassandr lifted their joined hands into the air, and the crowd cheered.

And with that, Saga was married.

The marriage feast lasted long into the night, with countless boisterous toasts. Yuri Rovgolod praised Kassandr's virtue—lies, Saga knew without a doubt—and hoped they were blessed with "one hundred children." Elisava recounted with glee Kassandr's first failed proposal, when Saga's response had been to stab him in the shoulder. According to Elisava, this was the day she'd known Saga would make an excellent sister.

The high prince looked remarkably pleased with himself, and made more than one speech praising his new daughter for "saving the city" and "taming my unruly heir." Saga's constant inclusion as a part of this grand family made something catch in her chest. Logic told her to remain wary—that Oleg had tried to kill her, and the high prince would have handed her to the Urkans. Yet still, it was a lovely feeling to be enfolded into a family when, for most of her life, she'd been kept at arm's length.

Or perhaps she'd merely consumed too much *medovukha,* the Zagadkian mead, which flowed a little too freely.

Elisava, at some point, planted herself on Rov's lap. The battle, Elisava had explained, had put things into perspective, and Saga couldn't help but smile as she watched the pair flaunt their burgeoning love.

Khiva and her horsemaidens had eagerly joined the feasting celebrations. As the *medovukha* flowed, the uncertainty between the horsemaidens and the nobles softened before Saga's eyes. She spotted one horsemaiden teaching a noblewoman their war cry, while another tried to drink the woman's husband under the table. And to Saga's great pleasure, the clansmother sat to the high prince's right, their heads frequently bowed in quiet conversation.

So far, the wedding had been a surprisingly pleasant experience, though she wished she'd had just a little time with her new husband. Aside from the ritual where they'd fed pieces of the ceremonial loaf to each other, she'd interacted with him very little. Each time Kassandr returned to her, he was soon entrapped by some old friend, an elder, a relative. But this did not keep his heated glances from reaching her, setting her insides aflame. Saga tried to quell her nerves as she conversed with numerous guests, glad for her growing Zagadkian vocabulary.

Gradually, the candles burned low and Saga's ladies gathered around her, ushering her from her husband's side and out of the feasting hall.

"We must prepare your marriage bed," Elisava whispered conspiratorially.

Saga's heart once again found its rapid rhythm. The thought of sharing a bed with Bjorn had been abhorrent. With Magnus? Terrifying. But with Kassandr . . . altogether new feelings stirred inside her. She was flustered and nervous and intrigued all at once.

The women led her to Kassandr's chambers, anointing the room with birch smoke. But it wasn't until Elisava produced a garment made just for Saga's wedding night that her nerves began to fray. The gown was stunning—white as snow and embellished with seed pearls. It was also transparent, leaving very little to the imagination.

With soft, tinkling laughs, Elisava and her ladies departed, leaving Saga all alone in the room.

CHAPTER 54

Saga's pulse thrummed as she waited for her husband to join her in the bedchamber. Lying on Kassandr's bed in her sheer dressing gown, she stared at the canopy, visions of spoons and honeypots flitting in her mind. Saga wished she knew more of what, precisely, to expect of her wedding night. True, she'd read many romantic tales, but the books from the Southern Continent tended to use flowery words to describe the act.

Arms folded over her stomach, Saga tried to ease her sharpened nerves. Where was Kassandr? How long would she have to lie here? And how long would the act take?

Male laughter had Saga jolting upright. That wasn't Kassandr. Sounds of drunken singing met her ears. Good gods, was there a *crowd* of them? She gaped down at her transparent gown, then quickly fetched a pillow to cover her most prominent bits.

The singing grew louder, setting her teeth on edge. She could make out Rovgolod's voice and—was that Oleg? Saga's brows knitted together. How much *medovukha* had they consumed that even *Oleg* sounded jovial?

The door flew open, Kassandr's broad back to her as he warded off a throng of wedding guests. By some miracle, he managed to slam the door shut.

"If any fools try to come into this room," he shouted through the door, "I will cut off your leg and draw pictures with your blood!" The air vibrated with that strange, unnatural sensation that Saga now knew to be a sign of his beast.

"We must ensure consummation—" came Oleg's muffled voice.

"Come, Oleg!" bellowed an extremely inebriated Rov. "Our duty is done. Kassandr is delivered to his bride. Let us find some fun. The horsemaiden they call Khiva looked much in your direction."

Saga choked on a laugh, but then Kassandr was sliding the lock into place and turning toward her. She clutched the pillow tighter to her chest, staring at her husband.

Her *husband.*

"My wife," drawled Kassandr, a lazy smile on his lips. He sniffed the air, then found the remnants of burnt birch sticks lying on a chest and nodded to himself. "What are you doing there?" he asked, his gaze landing on the pillow she clutched to her breast.

"I'm ready to consummate our marriage," Saga announced, settling back on the bed and staring up at the canopy.

Kassandr strolled to the edge of the bed, and as he looked down at her, Saga watched him lose the battle against a smile.

"What is it?" she asked, cheeks flushing. Did he not like what he saw?

Kassandr reached for her hand and pulled her toward the edge of the bed. Saga clung to the pillow like her life depended on it.

"Scarcely have I seen you tonight." He pressed a kiss to her scarred hand, sending heat jolting straight down her spine. "Come. Have drink with me. Bring pillow if you wish it."

Kassandr strode to a table on the far side of the room and worked his armored jacket loose, revealing his wedding kaftan beneath. He draped the jacket over the back of a chair, then poured the contents of a clay jug into a pair of cups. Reluctantly, Saga padded across the room to join him.

Kassandr handed her a cup, those emerald eyes ever-burning as they dragged from her bare feet, along the pillow clutched against her sheer dressing gown, then finally landing on her face. Flustered, Saga brought the cup to her lips and sipped what proved to be *med-*

ovukha. It went down smoothly, warming her stomach and softening her nerves just a touch.

"Tell to me what you are thinking," said Kassandr, reclining.

Saga flopped onto her chair, the pillow still clutched to her chest. "I don't know—"

"Do you regret the wedding?"

Her gaze slashed to his, and she caught the faintest traces of vulnerability there. Perhaps his casual air was not so effortless after all. "No."

"Good."

Saga studied his face. "Do you?"

Kassandr sipped his *medovukha.* "How can I regret a thing I have yearned for, for so long?" His words brought a flush to Saga's cheeks, but her attention snagged on their subtle edge.

"You do not like how your father made it happen, then?" Saga guessed, watching him over her cup.

His jaw flexed, answer enough.

"Kassandr," she said softly. "In case it isn't clear to you, let me put it plainly: I chose this. I chose you."

His green eyes heated, but they dropped and narrowed. "Then *this*—" He nodded at the pillow clutched to her chest. "—what is this?" A slow smile crept across his lips. "Is that clever mind of yours thinking too much, Winterwing?"

"Perhaps," she breathed, the flush now creeping down her neck.

"Hmm. And what can I tell to you to put it at ease?"

"I—I do not know."

Kassandr sipped his *medovukha,* his eyes never leaving hers. "Would it help if I told to you all that I want to do to you?"

Her heart kicked up a rapid beat, and damn it, but she hated that he could hear it.

His brow cocked up. "Ah. I see you *are* curious."

Saga scowled into her *medovukha* as Kassandr's amusement wafted across the table and rankled her further. It was unfair that he had this effect on her, and even more so that he could hear her body's response. She had the sudden urge to do something to bring the scales back into balance.

Impulsively, she released the pillow. It landed on the floor with a soft *thunk*. For a single, weightless moment, Saga felt unmoored from her body. Swallowing, she crossed one leg over the other, then reclined in her chair in an attempt to replicate her husband's nonchalance. And then she boldly locked eyes with him.

Kassandr grew preternaturally still as his gaze roamed over her transparent dressing gown. The black pupils in his too-bright eyes spread wide, his grip on his cup tightening until his knuckles whitened.

"Perhaps I am curious, *husband,*" she managed. Victory flared in the pit of her stomach, but Saga soon felt a moment of trepidation—rather than rebalancing the scales, she felt suddenly like prey.

A wolfish smile curved his lips, and Kassandr ran a hand along his jaw. "My delightfully wicked wife. I like this thing, Saga. It makes me want to—" He exhaled, shaking his head.

A mix of curiosity and anticipation prickled through her body. She tried to maintain her nonchalance, but her eyes betrayed her, falling to Kassandr's mouth. "What?" she asked. "Makes you want to *what?*"

Green eyes met hers, sending heat spiraling through her body. Those eyes transfixed her. Enthralled her. Commanded her to rise.

Who was she but to obey?

As though in a dream, Saga rounded the table. Whereas before the table had concealed her lower half, now Kassandr could see all of her. A look of feral intensity filled his eyes as he took her in, sending warm, pulsing heat all through her. Saga closed the distance between them before sinking down on his thick, sturdy thigh. This near, she could see the soft hairs curling at his nape; a faded scar running at the edge of his temple.

"Tell me," she whispered.

For an instant, Kassandr held himself rigidly still, as though he were on the very knife's edge of snapping. But then he let out a low, dark chuckle and leaned closer, until his breath tickled her ear.

"Why don't you use your imagination?"

A soft sound escaped her as Kassandr brushed a tentative knuckle up her spine.

"You want to kiss me," Saga guessed.

He shook his head slowly, gaze fixing on the hollow of her throat.

"You . . . want to touch me."

His fingers stilled just below her ribs, and he dipped lower to scrape his teeth along her earlobe. Saga gasped with sudden understanding.

"You want to *bite* me."

Kassandr drew back, running his tongue along his teeth. "Does that frighten you?"

"Yes."

"But it excites you."

She swallowed.

"The thought of my claiming bite makes your pulse flutter. I can see it. Right . . ." His tongue slid along the hollow of her throat. "Here."

Saga's head tilted back as she felt the wet heat of him all through her body.

"And the same thought makes me harder than steel." He tilted his hips, and it was impossible for Saga to miss the proof of just how much he liked this idea. "But do not fear it, Winterwing. Tonight is not time for such things."

Kassandr suddenly stood, effortlessly lifting Saga into his arms. She placed a steadying hand on his chest, blinking as a low rumble from deep within vibrated her palm—the delightful purr of his beast. And to her great shock, the sound made desire pool sharply inside her.

Kassandr set her down on her feet near the bed. The emotions and sensations swirling in her body were disorienting, and Saga gripped his kaftan to keep her balance. And then his lips were coming down on hers. His mouth was hot and slick, yet his hands were tender as they cradled her hips.

Touch me, his kiss seemed to say, and she did.

As Saga's fingers began to explore, the low, pleased sound from the back of Kassandr's throat was the sweetest praise. A heady sense of power filled Saga. *She'd* drawn that noise from him—had made his heart race with such speed. How could she get him to make that sound again?

As her fingers slid up his chest and around his shoulders, they brushed against his nape. A shudder ran through him, and Kassandr groaned, deepening the kiss. Saga had the sudden impression that Kassandr's two sides were at war, and that his humanity was hanging by the very finest thread. And as she had back in Askaborg's gardens, she wondered what might happen when his control snapped clean through.

"Do you like that?" she whispered. Her fingers skimmed along his nape once more, and she was rewarded with another tremor. Confidence bloomed inside her chest. "What else do you like?"

Kassandr's grip on her hips tightened, and he buried his nose in the crook of her neck with a growl. Her head fell back, the sensations swirling inside her building with each heartbeat. "I want—"

Want. It was the only thought she could name. Pure, visceral, unrelenting *want.*

"I want, too, my Winterwing," rasped Kassandr. It was only when the backs of Saga's legs hit the bed that she realized he'd been walking them backward all this time. "But tonight is not about what I want. Tonight, *my wife,* is all about you."

"Me?" she asked, dazed. Her skin was aflame, burning through all rational thought.

"You," he agreed. "If you wish it."

"I wish it!"

His chuckle was like the softest caress. "First, I will unbind your hair," he breathed, turning her toward the bed. Kassandr unwound her braid with torturous slowness. Shivers rushed all through her, and Saga wondered when the feel of his fingers in her hair had taken such an erotic turn.

"Kassandr," she whined impatiently.

His gentle fingers untangled the last of her braid, and Kassandr swept the spill of golden hair over one shoulder. Saga heaved for breath as his fingers found the buttons at the back of her dressing gown.

"And now I will remove this . . . impractical garment."

"Impractical," she echoed.

"Terribly," he agreed. Yet despite his jovial nature, she could sense him struggling with the buttons.

"You can rip it," she whispered.

His fingers stilled.

"Rip it, Kassandr," she urged. "I can't take another minute—"

Saga gasped at the sharp tear of fabric, and the sudden rush of cool air along her back. Kassandr's breath sent goosebumps across her nape. With agonizingly slow speed, he slid first one shoulder of the gown off, then the other. The garment fell to the floor in a puddle of embroidered silk, and Kassandr's breathing ceased altogether.

"May I look at you?" he managed at long last.

Slowly, Saga turned and met Kassandr's gaze. The feral intensity in his eyes was startling to see, and he was silent for so long, she shifted uneasily.

"You are perfect. A goddess among women."

Saga clasped her fingers before her, and Kassandr's gaze grew yet sharper. "You know that, do you not?"

"It's only—"

"What."

"I'm not used to hearing such things."

A growl built low in Kassandr's chest, setting the hairs on her arms on end. "Those people." He buried a hand in his dark hair, mussing it deliciously. And when his gaze landed back on hers, it was utterly possessive. "I will worship you until you feel like the goddess you are. I will break down every doubt those vile Urkans planted in your head and build you up anew. And Winterwing—" He stepped so near, she could feel the warmth of him on her bare skin. "—I will make you feel very good."

"Oh—" was all she could manage from her befuddled mind.

Kassandr eased her onto the bed, then crawled over her before kissing her until she gasped for breath.

"Wait," she protested, breaking the kiss. "You." Her hands grappled for his kaftan. "I want to see you, too."

The mischievous smile that had caused her so much trouble settled on his face. And then Kassandr was reaching for his wedding kaftan. Buttons popped and fabric ripped, and in the span of three heartbeats, it lay in a heap on the floor.

"Impatient man," she teased, but then all humor drained from her as the expanse of his bare chest met her eyes. She'd seen this sun-kissed skin before, but never had she been bold enough to touch it. Now she slid her fingers through the dark dusting of hair on his warm, firm chest, but paused as black tattoos pulsed beneath them. She'd wondered how far his tattoos went, and now Saga had her answer.

"I would not advise that," warned Kassandr, his eyes fever-bright. "My beast is very eager to claim you."

"Claim . . ." Saga thought of the bite, and damn it, but her pulse did flutter at that.

"Not tonight, Winterwing," soothed Kassandr, his large, capable body sliding over hers. The friction was maddening, driving her need to dizzying heights. "Tonight, you need soft. Tonight, you need to be worshipped."

The rough tips of his fingers slid along her stomach, lower, lower . . . Saga gasped.

"You are wet for me already, *malen'kaya ptichka,**" he said on a groan.

His fingers made soft circles, and oh gods—they were the best fingers, the most clever fingers in the whole world. Saga saw stars behind her eyelids and was vaguely aware of her back arching off the bed.

* Little bird.

"Don't st—"

Saga inhaled sharply as Kassandr slid first one, then two fingers inside her. Her eyes flew to his, and the sight of him watching her with such hunger made everything tighten inside her. Now she realized that the pleasure she'd felt earlier had been a surface-level thing. With his fingers inside her, everything was deeper and taller and so much stronger. Saga was vaguely aware that he studied her every moan, that he adjusted his fingers and the pressure he applied, until she writhed beneath him, clutching at his arm. Words spilled from her lips as her vision tunneled, and she knew that whatever she was climbing toward was tantalizingly near . . .

The moan that escaped her was embarrassingly loud, and Saga tried to cover it with her hand. But Kassandr pried it gently away.

"Scream, *moya koroleva.**"

It was at that moment that the breath seized in her lungs, the tension coiling inside her body unspooling in a sudden rush. Pleasure shuddered through her, and a low, guttural sound came from her chest. On it went, for a small eternity, where Saga was nothing but a thing of light and sound and complete sensation. It felt much like it had when she'd come into her magic—like for one moment, she understood every working of the world. But then it burned away, leaving in its wake an empty husk. She had no thoughts, no worries, no Urkans to vanquish or seas to cross. She was only Saga.

And he was Kassandr, staring down at her with a look of male satisfaction.

But the arrogance quickly melted to something softer. "I chose you, Saga, the first time you showed to me your fire," he whispered with unexpected tenderness. "In gallery, when you told to me *I am no one's pet.*"

"I'm—not," she mumbled, trying to catch her breath.

"I would apologize for my behavior that day, but we both know I'm not sorry."

She slapped him lightly on his chest, and he chuckled. But as he

* My queen.

brushed against her thigh, she became aware that he was left unfulfilled. Saga reached tentatively for him, but his hand encircled her wrist.

"Later." There was an edge to his voice. A warning she wanted to ignore.

"But—"

He captured her other hand as it reached for the hot length of him. "Trouble," he murmured, his eyes a little wild.

"It is only fair—"

"It is enough for me to hear your sounds," he said softly, before pressing a kiss to her lips. "It is enough for me to look into your eyes as you find pleasure. Today you have shown much bravery." Kassandr rolled onto his side, not taking his eyes from hers for even a second. "We have time, my queen, to savor one another. To play and to learn."

Saga turned toward him, tucking a hand under her cheek. And then she allowed herself to stare at him.

Her husband.

The title had once felt like a shackle, meant to bind her further. But not this. Not with him. For the first time in her life, Saga was excited to discover the unknowns of the future. Because the gods knew life with this man would never be dull.

"Time," she murmured, smothering a yawn. It was a thing she'd once taken for granted. But after the harrowing weeks they'd endured, she'd gained new appreciation for it.

"You must rest," Kassandr said softly, tucking a lock of hair behind her ear. "Tomorrow, we sail."

Saga's eyelids had grown heavy, but they jerked open at that. "Tomorrow?"

A lazy smile curved her husband's lips. "Is my wedding gift to you, my beautiful wife. Tomorrow we sail for Íseldur."

CHAPTER 55

The Western Woods

Hekla dreamed of trees so tall, they scraped the skies; of wolves the size of horses. She strode into the grove that marked the heart of the woods. Life and pure vigor flowed all around her. For a moment, she could see every minute happening in the forest: the way the hjarta tree on her right gifted nutrients through an underground labyrinth to the sapling on her left; the raven who knocked cones from the canopy, scattering seeds below; the insects tilling the soil and the mushrooms feasting on the detritus of the forest.

But then she saw it all reverse—the hjarta tree pulling life from the sapling until it became a brittle skeleton of itself. Then came the mist—and the raven's form was breaking, shifting, re-forming into something new. Misshapen wings, glowing red eyes, talons that longed to tear into flesh.

She woke with a start, the decaying scent of the woods heavy in her nose. But there was also something else—*someone* else. Eyvind. Her cheek pressed against the firm muscles of his back. In sleep, she'd curled further into him, seeking the heat of his body.

As Hekla shifted, a symphony of aches rose up within her—sharp and hot from the wound in her thigh, dull and throbbing at the base of her skull. River stones and pine needles dug into her hip, and her stomach growled loudly. But none of it mattered, because the skin against her cheek was warm.

Eyvind had survived the night.

Consumed by emotion she refused to examine, Hekla wriggled herself up into a sitting position. Carefully, she peeled back Eyvind's bandage and inspected his wound. Morning light filtered through the open end of their shelter, illuminating the swelling, reddened skin along his side. Her stitches were uneven, and not perfectly tight. But the bleeding had stopped and Eyvind's breaths came in a slow, even rhythm.

Blinking furiously, Hekla climbed to her feet. Goosebumps broke out across her skin, making her overtly aware that she was completely nude. She climbed over Eyvind and added several pieces of wood to the fire before assessing the clothing she'd laid out the night before. Though cold to the touch, the thinner woolen layers had mostly dried. Eagerly, she climbed into her clothing.

"Liked you better without it," mumbled a voice.

Hekla's gaze darted to Eyvind, and then she was rushing, falling to her knees, words tumbling from her. "Thank the gods," and, "I didn't know if you'd make it through the night," and, "Don't you ever do that again, you reckless arse."

Eyvind squinted at her with a dopey smile. "Awful lot of trouble you've gone to just to see me naked."

Hekla was too glad to hear his voice to let his words irritate her. "You frightened me."

Eyvind's smile fell to something softer. "I'm fine, Lynx."

She flinched at the name. "What were you thinking, trying to bait that spider away—"

"I could read the plans written all over your face. Perhaps you are jealous I got there first."

Eyvind grunted as he tried to rise to a sitting position, but Hekla was there, looping an arm around his shoulder.

"Let me help you." Hekla eased him upright while trying not to look down at his extremely naked body. "Better?" she asked.

Eyvind nodded, watching her intently. "Where's your arm?"

Hekla glanced down at her undertunic, right sleeve hanging empty. "I-it was lost in the water," she said glumly. Being without her arm—without the added protection of her claws—felt like a part of her very being was missing, but Hekla tried for a flippant air. "Pity, we've been through much, that arm and I."

Somehow she knew he saw straight through her words. "We'll find it," Eyvind assured her. And a foolish part of her was delighted at his use of the word "we."

Giving herself a mental shake, Hekla fetched a waterskin and portion of salt cod, then handed them to Eyvind. For a moment, they chewed in companionable silence, Hekla trying to ignore the warm prickles rushing down her spine. It was impossible to forget that she knew the stories of his scars and the wobbly dragon tattoo on his naked torso. Even more impossible to forget the pleasure that body had wrought from hers.

Instead, she tried to focus on the miraculous—Eyvind had survived the night; he was now sitting up *and* eating. Hours ago, this had felt impossible.

"Where are the others?" he asked.

Hekla's jaw hardened as she tried to gauge the time. "It's been a full night, plus half a day. By now they'll have freed the Forest Maiden's other half and be well on their way to the heartwood."

"It is just the two of us, then."

"Mmm." She kept her gaze on the fire, but felt him watching her.

"All I had to do to get you alone was to be impaled by a maneating spider and go over a waterfall."

She refused to smile at that, but could not keep her gaze from sliding his way.

"Hekla, I've tried to give you space, but—"

Panic sliced through her, and she pushed abruptly to her feet.

Eyvind's exhale was long and heavy. "I thought your anger was directed at me, that you only needed time. But now I realize I was wrong. This has gone on too long for that."

Her stomach was twisting itself into knots. “Stop,” she whispered, pressing fingertips to her temples.

But the fool persisted. “What happened between us frightened you—”

“Stop!”

Her words echoed off the trees surrounding the riverbank, but the sound was no match for her thundering heartbeat. She couldn’t do this. Couldn’t speak of it.

Hekla snatched Eyvind’s dried undertunic and flung it at him. “Get dressed.” She turned her back to him, refusing to glance his way. “Do you think you can walk?”

“Aye,” he said, his disappointment making her insides wrench tighter.

“Good,” she forced out. “We’re out of time. Three nights remain before the full Marra. It might be impossible to catch the others, but still, we must try.”

Eyvind’s breaths grew labored as he tried to work his tunic over his head. A pang of worry struck Hekla, and she turned—keeping her gaze above his shoulders—to help him slide it on.

“My breeches,” he mumbled somberly, and she felt like she’d kicked an injured puppy. “Could you help with those, too?”

Hekla’s teeth clamped together. “Fine,” she seethed. As she helped him pull his breeches on, Hekla’s body and mind were at war with each other. Why couldn’t she do this? Why couldn’t she hear him out?

Because, her stupid, logical mind informed her, *you’re afraid you’ll forgive him*.

After a minute or two of careful shifting, Eyvind belted his breeches in place, and Hekla helped him stand.

“Your handiwork?” he asked, nodding at the blood-matted side of his tunic.

“Aye.”

“Impressive,” said Eyvind. “Very well.” He sighed. “Lead the way.”

They trudged along the riverbank, glancing frequently at the sun to ensure they traveled due north. Their pace was slow, and they rested often. Hekla checked the gash on Eyvind's side, replacing the moss and tearing the last remnants of her overtunic to prepare fresh bandages.

The pair quickly gave up on the concept of boiling their water, as they had no pot with which to do so. Thankfully, the river's flow was far quicker than the thin lazy brooks elsewhere in the woods. Still, Hekla and Eyvind had shared an apprehensive look before taking the first sip. A day soon passed, though, and neither fell dead, nor did they suffer any maladies.

As darkness fell, Eyvind kindled a fire with his galdur, and they curled side by side for warmth at night. Whether by his Ashbringer skill or something else, Eyvind held the heat rather well. And sandwiched between him and a campfire, Hekla fell into an easy sleep.

The woods were wholly empty, and even more unnerving.

"Where are the ravens?" Hekla asked. Two days had passed since they'd gone over the waterfall, and her hopes of catching the others were dwindling by the hour. "Where is that . . . feeling that the leech is watching?"

Eyvind crouched by the river, filling their waterskins. His wound was healing nicely, his strength rebounding more each day. Now he glanced at the indigo skies peeking through the canopy above. "Perhaps it has called its attention elsewhere."

Frustration rolled through Hekla as her gaze fell on Marra. One day. A single day remained before the full moon. They'd be too late.

A helpless sort of anger rushed through her. This was *her* job—the one she'd spent countless days and sleepless nights laboring over. To think she wouldn't be there to help fight the monstrous tree and its undead army was absolutely maddening.

Hekla jabbed their campfire in frustration, sending sparks skyward. With a sigh, she sank back on her left elbow to prop her boots next to the flames.

"Cold?" Eyvind handed her a waterskin then sank down beside her.

"Only my toes," Hekla lied. The farther north they traveled, the colder it got. She stared into the flames, her body and mind alike exhausted, but as Eyvind reached for her boot, she jerked away. "What are you doing?"

Eyvind raised a thick black brow, his hazel eyes dancing in the firelight. "Warming your toes." Reluctantly she acquiesced, and he pulled her boot free. As his hand—unnaturally warmed with his Ashbringer galdur—made contact with her foot, Eyvind cursed under his breath. "Mulish woman," he muttered, warmth seeping into her ice-cold toes. Hekla nearly moaned with the pleasure and pain of it. "Are you truly so stubborn you'd rather lose a toe to frostbite than ask for my help?"

She bit into her lip, scowling into the fire. Yet she felt him watching her, silent frustration filling the air.

"I can't do this anymore!" he said with a sudden burst of anger. "I can't pretend I'm happy. Can't pretend you were nothing but a roll in the furs, Hekla.

"I thought myself a patient man, but you drive me to absolute madness! I think of you constantly. Dream of you at night. And each morning I awaken to this quiet, distant version of you, I lose my mind just a little more."

Hekla stared at him in stunned silence.

"The truth," said Eyvind, "is that I've been betrothed to Liv since I was a child. The other truth is that Liv has no interest in me . . . in men, at all." He hesitated. "It was not my secret to tell, but when I was in Kopa, I got permission from Liv to share this."

Hekla stared into the fire, refusing to meet his gaze.

"I'm sorry," he said, thumbs pressing into the arch of her foot. He sighed. "You know I hate to waste the present by speaking of the future. But in this, I erred. Greatly."

Hekla bit down on her cheek, desperate not to let his words affect her.

"It was my duty, as my father always told me, to marry Liv," continued Eyvind. "I was willing to go through with a loveless but companionable marriage if it meant strengthening our ties to her family. Until I met you."

Hekla grasped for the anger she'd held for so many weeks, despising herself as she felt it softening.

"My father," continued Eyvind, "has planned my entire life, and I was desperate enough for his affection to go along with it. But then Istré happened, and everything changed."

Despite her best attempts to stop it, Hekla's gaze darted to Eyvind's. His hazel eyes were so expressive—had always been effortless for her to read. Now his remorse was plain to see.

"You," said Eyvind, "changed everything. Hekla, you've taught me what it means to truly live free. What it means to *stand* for something. I cannot go back to a time when I let my father shape my life. And so when I returned to Kopa, the first thing I did was end my betrothal."

Hekla blinked, incapable of hiding her surprise. Despite herself, pride swelled in her chest. She knew this was no easy thing for Eyvind—that he'd longed for Jarl Hakon's approval all his life, and breaking his betrothal would be yet another blow to their relationship.

She searched his face for the spoiled, arrogant lordling she'd first met in Istré, but she found an earnestness that made her chest ache. Hekla tried to find the hurt that his lie of omission had caused; tried to remember all the reasons this would never work.

"I will never marry again, Eyvind." Her voice came out hard and sharp, a last desperate weapon to ward him off. "Don't waste your time on me."

His thumbs stopped on the ball of her foot. "Why would you think," said Eyvind, "that any time spent with you was a waste?"

The pull of his gaze was magnetic, the emotion in her throat building with impossible force.

"A privilege, Hekla. That's what I call time spent with you. An honor."

Hekla felt as though the ground had just been ripped from beneath her—as though she was helplessly falling toward peril. Because that's what this was, was it not? Her husband had also been handsome—had spoken honeyed words to her. She'd loved him so fiercely. Had thought he was her dreams come true. But he'd only been a monster who'd gambled all their money away and beaten all the soft, hopeful parts of her into submission.

Pains from her missing limb seized her with sudden fierceness. Hekla gasped, every muscle in her body taut with agony. How could something that wasn't there hurt her so gods damned much?

"What is it?" asked Eyvind, setting her foot down. "Hekla, what can I do? How can I help?"

"You can help," she gritted out, "by giving this up." Pain sizzled through her like a fierce summer storm, and she sucked in air through her teeth. "You and I will never be."

Her eyes slammed shut, in part to brace against the agony in her body, but also to avoid what she might find in Eyvind's expression. There had been a time when Hekla had spent her life fearing these pains and doing everything in her power to avoid them. But today, she was glad for them. They were the reminder she needed of just what was at stake in these games of the heart.

The phantom pains blazed through her in a matter of short minutes, but as she emerged from their haze, Hekla felt more like herself than she had since she'd met Eyvind Hakonsson. Eventually, her eyes fluttered open, meeting a pair of bright hazels. But rather than the hurt she'd expected to find, Hekla found something altogether worse.

Eyvind looked at her with a tenderness she did not care for. "Lynx," said the gods damned fool, "you can use those claws of yours all you wish. Can't you tell I'm not going anywhere?"

Hekla stared in disbelief as she tried to understand. Was he mad? Had he lost too much blood? But his words sank into her, softening all her defenses. The pain had left her wrung out and exhausted—

had probably addled her mind. It was the only explanation for what she did next.

Hekla reached out. Curled her fingers around Eyvind's collar. And pulled his lips to hers.

The feelings she'd tried so hard to smother surged forth with new fire, suffusing every part of her body with heat. She whimpered against him, then was swiftly furious at herself for letting him hear the effect he had on her. It was dangerous, she knew, giving a man such power. But at the moment, Hekla was lost to the sensation of his lips against hers.

Being vigilant of Eyvind's wound, they sank against each other, then carefully lowered themselves on the smooth river stones next to the fire. Her body tingled in response to his kiss—to the gentle brush of his fingers up her side—and she marveled at the way the feel of him brought her back in time. Back to another riverbank where she'd met this handsome stranger and had confessed to him things she'd never told a soul.

But Eyvind suddenly tensed and broke the kiss.

"What?" she gasped.

"Did you hear that?" He pushed up to a sitting position, hissing as his wound undoubtably pained him.

Hekla's senses sharpened in an instant. Slowly, she sat up and examined the dead bones of the forest. All was silent and dark, but then—*movement.*

Days they'd been trekking along this river, and they'd not seen a solitary creature. To see something now sent alarm flaring through her. Hekla and Eyvind clambered to their feet and drew their weapons, staring hard into the forest. The shadows shifted and merged, a low growl rattling the air.

Hekla braced herself for glowing red eyes—for the nauseating stench of the Turned beasts. Her heart beat an edgy rhythm as enormous lupine forms emerged from the woods—grimwolves. She counted the forms, giving up somewhere after twelve.

One grimwolf, perhaps two, they stood a chance. But with more than a dozen, their odds were hopeless. Her heartbeat was riotous inside her skull as the wolves prowled slowly closer. A glance over her shoulder dispelled any hopes they had of fleeing across the river—more wolves descended from the bank behind them.

"We're surrounded," she whispered, searching desperately for a plan.

"They're not Turned," Eyvind muttered.

And she saw it was true. The wolves' eyes glowed yellow in the last light of their campfire; their coats were thick and glossy; and only a single row of fangs was bared. But each was the size of a small horse, and those gleaming canines were designed to tear into flesh. It was clear these grimwolves were not friendly toward humans.

A large, white wolf at the front of the pack lunged forward with a warning snap, and Hekla and Eyvind scrambled backward. The wolves bared their teeth, creeping forward. Where had they come from? Why weren't they Turned? It did not matter—Hekla knew they didn't stand a chance.

But then came a new sound—a higher-pitched yip. The wolves' ears pricked, and one of them barked in reply. And soon the wolves lifted their snouts to the sky, the air filling with a discordant chorus of yowls.

"What is happening?" whispered Eyvind.

"I don't speak wolf, do you?" muttered Hekla, not daring to loosen her grip on her weapon.

Movement in the shadows, and then, disbelief. Because bounding from the woods was a form she knew.

Tears pricked her eyes. Hope unfurled in her heart.

"Kritka," Hekla breathed. And as the wolf came nearer, she saw something dangling from his maw. It gleamed in the moonlight, and Hekla nearly fell to her knees.

Clutched in Kritka's jaw was her prosthetic arm.

CHAPTER 56

Wind whipped through Hekla's hair as she clung to Kritka for dear life. She winced as the grimwolf leaped over a fallen log, jostling her on his back. Her arse would be black and blue by the time they rejoined the Forest Maiden and their warband. But it didn't matter. With the woods zipping past and her prosthetic arm snapped back into place, Hekla was filled with more hope than she'd felt in days.

They might just make it to the battle of the heartwood.

Eyvind yelped beside her as the grimwolf he rode upon lurched around a tree, nearly unseating him.

Your mate yelps like a pup, teased Kritka, launching them over a small stream and onto the opposite bank.

"Not my mate," Hekla muttered, her teeth clanking together with the impact. A dozen curses climbed up her tongue, but Hekla would not let them free.

You smell of him, said Kritka in her mind. *Did you finally breed?*

"No!"

Why not? Did he not perform the mating strut to your satisfaction?

"I am not speaking of this with you right now," she grumbled.

Though irritated by Kritka's invasive questions, Hekla thanked the gods the grimwolf had arrived in the very nick of time. She and Eyvind had stood dumbfounded as Kritka greeted what Hekla now knew to be his pack. The wolves had nuzzled against one another, greeting him with licks and excited yips. To go from facing near-certain death to that level of . . . well . . . *cuteness* had been rather a shock.

Eventually, Kritka had turned his attention on Hekla, bounding toward her and damned near knocking her to the ground. Through their mind-to-mind connection, he'd filled all the gaps in Hekla's knowledge.

After being fully awakened, the Forest Maiden had called all her living creatures to her—including the grimwolves she'd sent beyond the woods in search of the Protector. And once their warband had been fortified with several new arrivals—bears and other beasts who'd fled the woods to avoid being Turned—Kritka had snuck back to the waterfall to find Hekla and Eyvind. He'd found their scents and tracked them along the river, and in a moment of striking good fortune, he'd found his bonded human *and* his pack, all in the same place.

The wolves' joyful reunion was short-lived. Kritka had relayed the urgency of their situation—one day remained before the full moon, and they needed to get to the north of the woods quickly. He'd ordered Hekla to climb on his back, and a shaggy, black grimwolf had begrudgingly allowed Eyvind to do the same.

Now they loped through the woods with a pack of thirty grimwolves, and Hekla's blood sang with anticipation. Soon they would reunite with their group and be one step closer to finishing what they'd started.

"How much farther is it?"

First, we must pass beneath the black arch and skirt the skarpling burrows.

Hekla scowled at the vague reply, though she supposed she should expect nothing less from a wolf.

On they ran, ducking low under branches and leaping over stones, until Hekla's heart soared and her cheeks hurt from smiling. It seemed as though the trees bowed away and whispers of encouragement chased them. The frosted ground was soon dusted with snow, growing gradually deeper until Kritka's paws sank up to the knee.

It wasn't long after that they were reunited with their crew.

And what a crew it was. Hekla's eyes widened as she took in the Forest Maiden's creatures—grizzled cave bears and ivory frost foxes, quilled skarplings and mountain reindeer. There were hundreds of them, all gathered in the grove, predator and prey, standing side by side, unified by their singular goal. Clusters of what Hekla presumed to be forest spirits—tiny and verdant winged women—zipped about overhead, keeping order in the ranks.

"We might stand a chance," Hekla murmured as she slid off Kritka.

"Hekla!" Gunnar started toward her, but Thrand Long Sword got there first, tackling her in a hug so fierce, she thought her ribs might crack.

"You're alive!" he said, swaying her from side to side before releasing her so Hekla could greet Sigrún. Over her Bloodaxe sister's shoulder, she saw Gunnar helping Eyvind off his wolf's back.

"You kept her safe," Gunnar grunted.

"I believe," Hekla said haughtily, "I kept *him* safe, thank you."

"Aye, she did," came Eyvind's voice, gruff with emotion. "I owe her my life."

"I suppose that makes us even," said Hekla, unable to keep her mind from the explosion in Istré's square. Eyvind had shielded her with his fireproof cloak, saving her life. Hazel eyes met hers, and it was like a loose thread unraveling inside her. What would have happened had the wolves not interrupted that kiss? Perplexed, Hekla looked away.

And blinked in surprise.

The Forest Maiden had grown and changed, now standing as tall as a human. Her green-tinged skin held a tree bark texture, and a bushy white fox tail peeked out from behind skirts of moss and grass. But it was the pack of grimwolves rolling on the snow around the Forest Maiden that shocked Hekla most of all. The Maiden threw herself into the enormous pile of wagging tails and lolling tongues.

"My children," the Forest Maiden laughed, scratching ears and soft bellies. "My babies. You're returned to me."

For a moment, their group forgot about the obstacles ahead of them and allowed themselves to enjoy this small miracle. Gradually, their laughter faded as their minds drifted to the hours and days ahead.

The Forest Maiden climbed to her feet, fox tail twitching, though a smile stretched wide across her face. The forest spirits zipped around her antlers, making it seem like a swarm of large green insects buzzed about her head.

"You have fled your homes," said the Maiden, gazing at the animals gathered in the grove. "You have hibernated and hidden and lain dormant until conditions were right. And now the time is upon us. Tonight is our chance—perhaps our *only* one—to reclaim the woods as ours once more. No longer will we wither in our dying forest, helpless as the leech Turns our kin against us. Tonight, we will take it back."

The grove erupted in animal sounds—braying reindeer and yipping foxes; howling wolves and growling bears—all entwined with human war cries. It livened Hekla's blood. Readied her for battle. So many days and weeks had led to this confrontation, and now it was nearly upon them.

"Let us fly!" bellowed the Forest Maiden, her voice booming like thunder. "Let us fight! Let us take back the woods!"

Kritka appeared by her side, and Hekla climbed onto his back, her left hand sliding into his fur and clasping on tightly. She was dimly aware of the rest of Kritka's pack presenting themselves to Sigrún and Gunnar and Eyvind's warband.

And then they were gone, loping toward the heartwood on the backs of grimwolves.

CHAPTER 57

The Black Road

Silla rode from Kopa with a warband of roughly four hundred warriors. After the northern jarls had pledged themselves to Eisa Volsik, plans had come together with disorienting speed. The battle-ready jarls, including Agnar and Holger, had readied their retinues at once, while the older jarls had agreed to send their retinue warriors in their stead. And to Silla's surprise, a number of Kopa's citizens and refugees had volunteered to join them in the woods.

Silla had tasked Rey with organizing their warband for battle. Jarl Hakon, meanwhile, arranged parties to collect provisions from the abandoned villages to feed the increasing number of refugees who flooded into Kopa daily.

Now seated in Dawn's saddle with Rey and Horse by her side, it felt like Silla had gone back to far simpler times. But with Atli Hakonsson and Jarls Agnar and Holger riding ahead of them with Volsik banners, it was impossible to forget what trials awaited them in the heartwood—the deepest and oldest grove in the Western Woods.

There was the matter of the so-called leech—a foe that apparently Silla alone had the skills to best. There was the army of Turned creatures guarding it. And then there was the shard of the god of chaos living inside her.

After Silla's triumph in the meeting hall, Myrkur's excitement only seemed to grow. To this point, the god's motives had been easy enough to understand—He wanted to, as He called it, play. He also wanted access to Silla's bloodline gift. But what could the god of chaos gain by them going to the heartwood? This she did not understand, a fact that unnerved her greatly.

Their warband rode at a steady pace and was on track to reach the heartwood by the full Marra. Each night, they made camp. Tents were erected, fires lit, brennsa passed hand to hand, while the stories flowed. They were blessed with many bright-mooned nights, and Silla was able to confirm that when bathed in moonlight, Myrkur burrowed deeply away. With her mind blissfully to herself, Silla took advantage, meeting the brave warriors who followed her into battle against this unknown foe; not only professional warriors, but blacksmiths and field workers and the like. She made it a point to sit at a new fire each night; to hear their stories and learn their faces.

She spent hours sparring with Runný and Rey, Kálf and Hef, practicing the art of pulling their galdur into her veins. Silla knew well the burn of an Ashbringer, and was growing used to the intensity of Hef's Blade Breaker strength.

Runný's Shadow Hound galdur was the strangest of all. When Silla pulled on Runný's power, she gained the ability to see and manipulate thousands of shimmering threads. It was a simple matter of bending these threads of light to make herself invisible, or twisting them another way to create a shield. Over and over, Silla practiced with their powers by night; in combat and on horseback. If this bloodline gift was the key to defeating Myrkur, then she needed to master it.

Myrkur slithered restlessly through her veins during the long days of riding, wavering between excitement to reach the heartwood and begging Silla to let Him in. The dark god's emotions were overpowering and utterly maddening.

But there was something that Myrkur did not understand: After all she'd weathered with the skjöld leaves, Silla was no stranger to hungering for things that were no good for her. Like giving in to her addiction, granting the dark god access to her bloodline gift was an easy, instantaneous choice that would forever change her. The realization made her strangely grateful for her struggles.

And yet it was not easy. The god's cravings intensified each day, sometimes growing so potent that they drove her to her knees. He showed Silla her darkest desires—all the different ways Signe and Ivar could be slaughtered; the crown being lowered onto her brow; the entire Kingdom of Íseldur under her thumb. They would bow to her—bend the knee to her. And she would make those who'd turned their backs on the Volsiks pay for their dishonor—

Silla shook her head, trying to physically dislodge the thoughts from her mind. It was the fifth day since they'd ridden from Kopa, and the Black Road leading to Istré was covered in a white blanket of snow. Silla focused on the thick, white snowflakes drifting down from the sky, lifting her face upward and opening her mouth. And as a single snowflake landed on her tongue, her insides shimmered like the flames of a hearthfire, making Myrkur recoil and hiss.

"All right?" asked Rey, watching her from atop Horse.

Silla nodded wordlessly, not trusting herself to speak. But knowing that he was beside her—that Rey would be strong for her when she could not—made the hearthfire in her chest grow just a little stronger.

There was something familiar about their surroundings, and as they rounded a bend, Silla understood why. The gates of Istré had once stood before them. Now they were naught but a snow-covered mass. This, she realized with startlement, was where she'd found that birch-bark etching identifying Rey as the Slátrari. The place where her path and Rey's had become irrevocably entwined.

"Well," said Rey glumly, gazing at Istré's ruins, "I suppose it's time for the next part of the plan."

After Hekla had relayed the ordeal of her horse being Turned and attacking her, their group had decided it would be best to leave their horses at the border of the woods. Five refugees had been appointed to care for the horses, Ashbringers among them to ward off the mist should it attack.

Silla dismounted, and after pressing a kiss to Dawn's muzzle, she looked deep into her mare's dark eyes. "Be well, Dawn," she said softly. "Be kind to the other horses. Don't nip at your caretakers. And when I return to you"—*if I return to you,* she refused to amend—"I shall give you all the oat treats you could ever wish for." Dawn nuzzled against her, her eyes dark and solemn, as though she understood the gravity of this moment.

When at last they reached the edge of the woods, Silla paused, taking one last look over her shoulder. The fire mountains loomed dark in the direction from which they'd come, and she wondered if she'd ever see Kopa again. With that dismal thought, she entered the Western Woods.

Silla was glad for the soft deerskin boots that warmed her feet, as the snowdrifts were deep. As she trudged through the forest, Silla could have sworn she felt its pulse—weak and labored. *Volsik,* the air seemed to whisper, urging her forward.

Even beneath the drifts of snow, it was clear this forest was not as it ought to be. What foliage they could see was either dead or an ill-looking gray, and there was a notable absence of birdsong. As they walked, the jovial banter fell away to quiet tension within their warband. The woods grew denser and darker, but a strange, unnatural presence grew stronger. Silla felt it in each sickly tree and gray blade of grass protruding from the snow. They walked for hours, perhaps a full day, and this dark, oppressive presence of the wood grew more burdensome.

But beneath the heavy-handed darkness was something softer. *Volsik,* the woods gasped through the gloom's strangling hands. Leaves she did not see rustled with winds she could not feel, and snow-covered brambles seemed to lean away from the path, as though aiding their travel.

Silla sensed the heartwood well before she saw it. Here was something more ancient than all—more ancient, perhaps, than

Myrkur Himself. She wanted to go to it, wanted to see the wonder of the great elder trees, but that would ruin the plans they'd so carefully crafted.

They paused in the greater forest, just beyond the heartwood. The snow here reached up to their knees, and the trees in this part less dense than at the outer edge, letting the day's waning sunlight cast long shadows. As the warriors drank from their waterskins, Rey and the jarls gathered around Atli to go over their plan for the final time.

"Shadow Hound scouts will go in first," whispered Atli, waving two of his men forward. "They will skirt the border of the heartwood grove and report back to us."

Their group watched on as Atli's Shadow Hound scouts pulled their specialized masks into place. Rey had explained he'd had the Tailor create these masks, with the aim of keeping the mist's miasma at bay. But just in case the masks did not work, the warriors had torches strapped to their backs and orders to light them at the first beat of the mist's heart. The Shadow Hounds flickered out of view, but Silla couldn't help but worry the effect was lost—with knee-deep snow revealing their every trudging step, these warriors were far from invisible.

"We break off into three groups," Rey said quietly, looking each man in the eye. "Agnar with masks and torches to ward off the mist. Atli and Holger with longswords to take on the Turned creatures. Remember, you must take their heads." They nodded solemnly. "And Silla—" Brown eyes found hers, and Silla's heart pounded faster. "I'll be by your side. Your queensguard will have your flank. You focus on that tree, and we'll keep you safe."

She nodded, holding his gaze. This was it. Days of travel—weeks of preparation—and they would finally do battle in the heartwood. Silla thought of all the refugees flowing into Kopa, and of all those who hadn't escaped in time. This was for them—to keep the citizens of Íseldur safe. To keep this leech from Turning any other creature in this realm. At this thought, Myrkur shifted deep inside her, and she was suddenly aware of how distant He'd grown over the past several hours.

The worry she'd pushed aside now niggled back. Was He scheming at something?

"Where is Hekla?" Silla whispered. They peered into the forest in search of movement, but there was none to be found.

"If she is here, my scouts will find her," said Atli, his tone so assured that Silla almost believed him. "And if she is not, we must wait. Our plan will be strengthened by her forces and the element of surprise."

Trying to calm her racing heart, Silla stared at the strange lumpy forms of the winter forest, young trees and the underbrush buried beneath feet of snow. How different the forest looked in winter. Sounds were muffled, a tranquil feeling settling over them. And a curious, sickly-sweet odor hung in the air.

She opened her mouth to remark on the smell, but motion from the corner of her eye diverted her attention. Silla squinted, trying to understand what, precisely, she saw. The woods were dim and shadowy in the last light of the day, but gradually the black figures distinguished themselves.

"Turned ravens," hissed Rey, unsheathing his sword.

Indeed, they were ravens, though not as they ought to be—their movement was too quick, their motion abnormal, and as she took in the red glow of their eyes, Silla shivered. This, she thought uneasily, was not the kind of good omen she'd hoped to see.

Silla pulled her mask up over her nose, the piney scent of the imbibed herbs permeating her senses.

"We may not have a choice in awaiting your scouts, Atli," Rey whispered, working his own mask into place. "It seems the leech has sent scouts of its own."

Atli's archers waded forward through the thick snow, then sent a silent flurry of arrows into the woods. Several ravens were felled, but one of the birds miraculously avoided the arrows, and it swooped down on their warband on torn, leathery wings. Silla's gaze locked onto what it clutched in its talons.

"Rey," she whispered, watching in horror as Rey's longsword hacked the unnatural creature in two.

Black blood spattered down, but as the raven corpse landed, the object it held sank into the snow. Silla reached down for it, then dropped it with a gasp.

"Eyeball," she managed, blinking furiously. "And fresh."

"Shite," muttered Atli, staring intently into the woods. She could tell he searched for any sign of the men he'd just sent in.

"We have a problem," said Rey ominously. "Those ravens flew straight for us." His gaze slid to Silla, and he swallowed. "They knew where we were."

Laughter from deep inside her rattled Silla's rib cage, and her worry sharpened into fear. "Something is wrong," she whispered, her eyes finding Rey's. "Myrkur has been silent—" But before she could finish her thought, a shout rang out from the rear of their warband, and she soon saw why.

Snow swished around them as the strange lumpy forms of the forest began to *rise.*

"Swords ready!" bellowed Rey, stepping between Silla and the hulking form causing a small avalanche before her. Silla drew her own blade, heart in her throat as the snow tumbled free, revealing a pair of glowing red eyes. A black, wet nose. A maw drawn back, revealing two rows of fangs.

"Turned grimwolf," she whimpered. At last, she understood the sickly-sweet smell. Myrkur's strange quietude. The Turned army was *here,* all around them, buried beneath feet of snow.

The woods erupted with violence, Myrkur cackling within Silla. On her left, Hef's sword hacked through the air with Blade Breaker strength. It sliced clean through a leaping mountain cat, severing the Turned beast's body in half. Black blood spurted, releasing a moldering stench that the masks did little to quell. On her right, Kálf's whip of fire cut through the neck of a Turned fox, sending it sailing through the air. Silla's hand was on her own sword, gripping it tightly, though her retinue let no foe get near enough for her to use it.

The Turned moved with unnatural speed and frightening ferocity, unaffected by the bite of swords, and seemingly unimpeded by the thick snow. The only way to end them was to take their heads—a feat that was far easier with a rabid fox than it was for the enormous slavering bears. Silla hacked a swooping raven out of the air, then whirled at a grimwolf that was lunging at Rey.

Atli intercepted the beast, hacking until the thing's head lay still in the snow.

"We must push into the heartwood!" bellowed Rey, death incarnate as he cleaved a bloody path through a throng of Turned beasts.

Atli's men trudged forward through the snow, bolstering their forces, and after several laborious minutes, they'd opened a gap in the circle of undead creatures.

"My men will hold them back," panted Atli, wiping black gore from his face. Rey nodded, seizing Silla's elbow.

"Into the heartwood!" Rey ordered.

And Silla *ran.*

CHAPTER 58

Silla's retinue fell into formation around her as they trampled through the snowdrifts and into the heartwood. To her right, Rey twisted his smoke to melt a pathway through the snow. To her left, Runný flickered out of sight with her Shadow Hound skill, while Kálf's fire whip sizzled in the wintry air. Thankfully, the abundant snow would keep the woods from becoming a tinderbox.

On they ran, the trees stretching higher, while the snowdrifts grew shallower, sheltered by the mighty canopy above. And soon they were in the heart of the Western Woods. Groves of enormous hjarta trees scraped the skies with their branches and burrowed to the deepest depths of the earth with their roots. Their girth was so great, it would take half a dozen warriors linking arms to encircle them, and Silla found herself wondering what ages these elders might have seen; what stories these trees could tell.

For a moment, she felt humbled.

Mortal like the rest of you, spat Myrkur, and that was enough for Silla's senses to swarm back.

Where have you been? she demanded. *What are you hiding from me?*

Why ruin the surprise? purred the dark god.

Trepidation filled her. Why had Silla not questioned His growing silence?

Shaking her head, Silla pushed on. The plight of these trees was clear as daylight—leached of color and their life-giving magic. Around the base of them was a graveyard of the plants they'd once nurtured—skeleton saplings and bone-dry ferns. The life had been sucked from them . . . fed back to the leech that coughed out the malevolent mist.

As Silla ran, she had the strangest sense that the giants of the forest urged her on. *This way,* the trees seemed to say, an invisible hook in her belly pulling her forward.

It was more open among the hjarta trees than in the dense outer woods where they'd been ambushed, and as warriors spilled into the grove behind her, Silla heard Atli's bellows as he wrangled his warriors into a shield wall. Ferocious yowls and shouts of men rent the air as Atli and his warriors held the undead beasts at the entrance of the heartwood, allowing the rest of the warband safe passage into the grove.

Silla longed for her sword of frostfire, yet she'd ordered Runný to dose her with triple the hindrium this morning. She could not risk Myrkur accessing her Ashbringer skill again; could not risk that weapon being turned on her own kind once more.

At last, Silla and her queensguard broke into the central grove of the heartwood, the clamor of battle in quick pursuit.

"The tree," growled Rey. He placed his palm to his sword, heating it until it was red-hot. As a Turned grimwolf leaped at them, Rey drove his heated sword clean through its neck. Black blood spattered the snow, the putrid scent of decay filling the air.

"Tree," Silla repeated, turning until she finally laid eyes upon her adversary.

There stood the most enormous tree she'd ever seen. This, Silla knew in an instant, was the first infected tree—the one housing the so-called leech. Its trunk was twisted and lumped with burls; branches sprawling outward like a many-limbed creature. There was no sign of color, only gray bark and dark needles, blackened sludge dripping down its trunk.

This was the cause of so much misery—the near death of this forest, the slaughter of entire villages. As Silla screamed with anger, her feet crunched on snow, but they skidded to a halt as an enormous creature stepped out from the shadows. Silla gasped as a pair of corpses fell from the spider's pinchers, landing in the snow with a brutal *whumf.* She recognized their livery at once—here were Atli's Shadow Hound scouts, missing their eyes.

Silla swallowed back her rising bile, studying this new foe. Its missing forelegs matched Rey's description of the spider they'd battled in the Forest Maiden's grove so many weeks ago, yet now several of its eyes oozed a putrid liquid. It chittered, assessing Silla as though deciding which part of her to feast on first.

She is mine, Myrkur whispered. *Take the others.*

And before Silla could react, the spider stepped clean over her and came down on her retinue. Behind her, Rey bellowed and Runný screamed, and Silla had to remind herself they could hold their own in battle. Gritting her teeth, she set her sights on the monstrosity of a tree.

"Greetings, you foul parasite," she muttered, advancing. Her heart thudded, palms slick with sweat, but she covered her fear with extra bravado. "Our meeting is long overdue."

Thus far, Silla had largely managed to keep her training with her bloodline gift hidden from Myrkur, but given that the moons had yet to rise, there was no hiding it from Him now. With a deep breath, Silla dipped her hand into the pouch belted at her hips and pulled out a raw chunk of halda stone.

Behind her, steel crashed against carapace, and within her, Myrkur tittered with glee. Silla ignored it all, forcing her focus into that stone. With an exhale, she pulled the raw power from the stone into her veins, letting the unshaped energy surge through her until it grew unbearable. She bent her knees, bracing against the force, holding it as long as she dared. Her heart raced; sweat beaded her brow. And then Silla expressed. The wild, untamed power burst from her palms in a torrent of energy and shot across the grove.

It struck the tree like a bolt of lightning, the sound shaking the ground and echoing through the woods. Snow and debris flew through the air, obscuring Silla's vision. But as it settled, her stomach lurched. The tree remained standing. Slowly, she stepped closer, stomach clenching at what she saw. The halda's power had not so much as scratched the bark.

A shiver rolled down Silla's spine.

Let me in, Eisa, purred the god with a prickle of excitement. *Together we shall destroy the leech.*

Silla paused. *Why would you want that?* she demanded of the god. *The leech is your child!*

I have many children, replied Myrkur. *Let me in and I'll show you how to defeat the leech.*

The fact that the god was willing to sacrifice His progeny to access her bloodline gift only made Silla more certain that she must not let Him in. "Never," she grunted, bracing against the force of the dark god's cravings. Behind her, the battle raged. Atli and his warriors had retreated into the grove, joining the greater warband in their fight with the Turned creatures. But Rey and Silla's queensguard still battled the monstrous spider.

"Lend me your strength, Hef!" Silla called out, unsheathing her sword.

She said a silent thanks that her loyal guard was able to extract himself from the battle. Hef appeared at her side, offering his bare forearm for Silla to clasp. Closing her eyes, she searched for that Blade Breaker energy burning through his veins. The moment she found it, Silla called it to her, reveling in the brutal strength surging through her blood. With a scream of rage, she rushed at the tree, swinging her sword with her borrowed Blade Breaker strength. But the blade only rebounded, jarring her arm so hard, her grip on it faltered.

Silla shook her arm and retrieved her sword, all the while glaring at the tree.

Kálf came next, lending her his Ashbringer skill, but as Silla lashed the tree with a whip of flames, it did not so much as scorch the bark. Then came Rey, but his smoke neither charred nor caught on the tree's unnatural wood.

Worry gathered in Silla's stomach, the din of battle making it difficult to think. She'd tried the halda stones; both Blade Breaker and Ashbringer skills. Runný's invisibility and light-bending shield would do nothing against it. So how . . . *how* did she kill this foe?

You cannot kill it, taunted Myrkur, the dark god's arrogance flooding her veins. *But I can. Made from Sunnvald's own heart, it cannot be defeated by light, but of its own darkness.*

Sunnvald's heart, thought Silla. *What does this mean?*

The hjarta trees were created by my brother's ashes, replied the god of chaos. *And their infected form cannot be defeated by Sunnvald's magic. Only my own will defeat the leech.*

"You're lying." Why would He tell her this? It felt like a trap.

I'm not.

"I do not believe you."

A vision flashed in her mind's eye. A book came into view, age-worn pages depicting this very tree. And scrawled below it were the words Myrkur had just recited: *Made from Sunnvald's own heart, it cannot be defeated by light, but of its own darkness.*

So you see, Eisa, purred the dark god, *the only way to destroy the leech is to let me in. Grant me access to your bloodline gift, and I shall braid it with my own magic. Together, we shall destroy it.*

Silla suddenly understood Myrkur's silence leading up to this. He'd been biding His time for this very moment, when He'd force her to choose between vanquishing the tree and guarding her bloodline gift. Granting Myrkur access to her bloodline gift might destroy the tree, yet Silla knew from Svangormr Pass that it would also endanger every person in this grove.

She stood before the monstrous tree, battle raging all around her. It was an impossible choice.

But what if there was another way? Silla's heart raced with a new idea. If the tree *was* only vulnerable to Myrkur's power—could she use her bloodline gift to siphon His magic and use it against the leech? It was impossible. And yet . . . it was an opportunity too great to resist. Because if fortune and skill aligned just right, perhaps Silla could both vanquish the leech *and* free herself from her mother's bargain.

Dropping her sword, she drew her dagger, then slashed it through her palm.

What are you plotting, little Eisa? Myrkur demanded.

But Silla didn't answer. Working swiftly, she dipped her fingers into the pooling blood and drew a series of lines and circles on the blackened trunk of the infected tree. She'd seen her mother scrawl these patterns a hundred times in her nightmares; never had she thought she would do so herself.

Silla drew a deep breath. Gathered her courage.

"Dark One," she shouted, "I call to you!"

CHAPTER 59

Each violent pound of Silla's heart echoed in her skull, drowning out all else in the grove. The hjarta trees towering above her, the battle seething behind her—everything ceased to exist. Silla adjusted her mask as black muck oozed from a burl on the misshapen tree, but as frigid air suddenly rippled through the grove, she knew the god of chaos had answered her call.

A black shadow formed at the base of the tree's trunk, swirling and climbing upward before coalescing into the shape of a man. As the spikes of Myrkur's crown jutted from His head, Silla was nearly driven to her knees by the overwhelming presence of the god. This was nothing like the shard of Him she carried within her—a mere echo compared with the power before her.

This was a *god,* through and through.

Silla locked her knees in place and braced herself. Behind her, cries of alarm told her the others in the grove could see Him as well. The shadow rippled, and Myrkur's laughter was no longer confined to her skull, but came from everywhere all at once.

"Little Eisa," He cackled. "It was not so long ago that I met your mother like this."

Anger rushed through Silla, and she grappled for the reason she'd called Him. "I would like to make a bargain," she forced out, goosebumps prickling up her arms and down her spine.

"A bargain," repeated Myrkur, bored. "Do not tell me *a life for a life,* Eisa. Not when I already hold your life in my palms." Silla's lungs seized in a demonstration of the god's power. Her hand flew to her throat, eyes blinking frantically as she tried to remember how to draw air into her chest—

Myrkur cocked His head to the side, and the feeling subsided at once.

Silla gulped a deep lungful of air, trying to clear the dancing lights from her vision.

"If you wanted me dead," Silla panted, "you'd have done it weeks ago."

Myrkur's shadowy form rippled on the tree bark.

"But you haven't," challenged Silla, "because it vexes you that you do not understand that which has the power to undo you—my bloodline gift."

For a moment, Myrkur was unable to conceal His cravings—they bled from the tree into the air all around her. He wanted that gift. Needed to understand this weapon that His brother Sunnvald had granted the Volsik bloodline . . .

It took all of Silla's will to force the next words through her lips.

"I, Eisa Volsik, challenge Myrkur, god of chaos, to battle." Her legs felt weak, but she soldiered on. "You will pick a mortal avatar from among the Turned creatures to fight me in single hand-to-hand combat. If you win, you shall have access to all of my magic, including Sunnvald's bloodline gift. But if *I* win, my mother's bargain will be considered fulfilled. That includes," she added fiercely, "the bargain living inside both me and my sister, Saga."

The shadow on the tree rippled, the clamor of the battle so distant in her ears. Her shoulders rose and fell on rapid breaths as fear and panic writhed within her. Had she truly just challenged a *god* to combat?

"You surprise me, little Eisa," purred Myrkur, dragging her from her thoughts. "It has been many years since a mortal has done so." The shadow cocked His head, Myrkur's longings for her bloodline gift growing potent. "Only the two of us," He said at long last. "Should anyone try to harm my avatar, I shall be granted victory. Do you agree to this?"

With a deep breath, Silla nodded.

"And Eisa," said Myrkur, His shadows rippling on the tree, "none of this first blood nonsense. If we fight, we do so until one of us can no longer stand."

Silla's mind was numb, her body shaking. It was madness, it was impossible, and yet, it was the only way. "I accept," she said.

"Good," said Myrkur. "I, too, accept. Let us battle."

The ground beneath her feet rumbled, the air around her shifting. The burden of Myrkur's presence flitted away from the tree, and the shard of Him living inside her grew suddenly muted. Silla understood—the god had chosen His mortal avatar.

Instinctively, she turned toward the god's presence, but she gasped as she took in the battle raging in the heartwood. Rey and her queensguard had driven the spider back, but it now wrought havoc on the battlefield. Droves of Turned creatures fought their warband, and it was clear the numbers were not in their favor. Each warrior fought multiple Turned beasts at once, and as a Turned mountain cat tore into a House Agnar warrior, worry tightened in Silla's stomach. Where was Hekla?

Silla's gaze snagged on a Turned bear. As it lumbered through the battle, she realized it was *enormous*—at least as tall as two men. Its grizzled brown fur was torn in patches and oozing black blood. And this, she realized with a sudden chill, was Myrkur's chosen avatar.

"A bear," Silla muttered. "Why is it always a bear?"

But she squared her shoulders and reminded herself of her plan. If only Myrkur's magic could kill the leech, then there was only one thing she could do. Silla would have to get close enough to the bear to lay hands upon it and siphon Myrkur's magic into her veins. And then she would unleash it upon the tree.

Warriors flew through the air as the bear cut a path of carnage toward her. Rey and Hef dropped into twin defensive stances.

"Stand down!" Silla shouted. "This is *my battle* with Myrkur. If anyone harms that bear, He shall win."

Rey whirled on her, fear and anger etched into his face. "What did you do, Silla?"

She swallowed. Met his eyes and tried to make him understand. "The only way to destroy that tree is through Myrkur's power."

Rey's sword hung limply at his side, and she watched as understanding settled into place. She waited for him to scold her—for him to tell her it was too dangerous. Instead, his jaw shifted before he began barking orders at her retinue.

"Hef, Kálf, Runný, keep the Turned creatures away from this tree."

Silla's heart felt too large for her chest as she watched Rey organize her queensguard into place. She was struck by the sudden realization that this man believed in her ability to fell a *god*. It was that same unfounded confidence he'd had when he'd let a vampire deer attack her on the Road of Bones; when she'd expressed her galdur for the first time; when she'd rallied a room of jarls and nobles to her cause. He'd believed in her all those times, and he'd been right. Why should he be wrong about her now?

She could do this. She could defeat Myrkur.

Silla squared her shoulders. Shook out her body. And after drawing her sword, she sank into a defensive stance.

"Sunnvald, protect me."

A warrior's body flew through the air and crashed into an elder tree.

"Stjarna, light my path."

The bear broke away from the teeming battle and trudged through the clearing toward her. Rey and her queensguard edged away, allowing it a clear path to Silla.

"Malla, grant me courage."

Myrkur's avatar paused ten paces away from her, the god's dark presence filling the air with promise.

"Marra, grant me wisdom."

The beast rose on its hind legs and roared at the sky. This was no natural sound of a bear—it came from all sides of her, above and below—from within her skull.

Are you ready to play, Eisa? purred Myrkur, His glee and battle thrill charging the air.

"Ready to take that ugly head from your shoulders."

And with that, the god of chaos attacked.

CHAPTER 60

Reynir Galtung had never been so terrified in his life. He batted at a Turned raven trying to gouge out his eyes, as the screams of men falling to undead creatures filled his ears. The leech's Turned army had them surrounded; Silla's warband was impossibly outnumbered and impeded by the snow. But none of that mattered while Silla battled the god of chaos.

"Fuck," he muttered, swallowing his fear as he stared at the two lone figures facing off near the tree. Silla looked so gods damned small before the Turned beast. But her face was drawn with complete focus as she ducked the enormous bear's slashing paw. With impressive movement, Silla twisted, hacking upward and burying her sword deep in the bear's armpit.

The creature opened its maw wide, but no sound came out. Instead, the air vibrated with a premonitory warning.

"Duck!" bellowed Rey, and Silla threw herself to the ground not a heartbeat before black flames poured from the bear's mouth. They scorched a nearby hjarta tree, and Rey muttered a thanks to the gods that the wet wood prevented it from catching flame.

But the sight of those black flames chilled Rey to the bone. Black flames, like the sword the enthralled Silla had wielded against him in Svangormr Pass. Black flames, like her sister Saga had used to decimate the great hall in Askaborg Castle.

And if what Silla said was correct—that only Myrkur's power could destroy the leech—then she would need to wield these black flames for herself. But first, she had to get close enough to the bear to pull the dark god's power into her veins. It was impossible, and yet Rey knew better than to underestimate this woman.

She needed *something* to give her an edge. Rey scowled at Myrkur's avatar, assessing its movements. "He's just shown you His tell!" he called out. "Next time the air vibrates like that, you know what He'll do."

Silla did not so much as glance his way, but the bear turned with a warning snarl. The air grew suddenly heavier; more difficult to pull into his chest. Panic lashed through him, and Rey fell to his knees, clawing at his chest. His need for air grew more desperate—

All at once, the feeling subsided and air surged into his chest. Rey clambered to his feet, anger burning to life inside him. It should be *him* facing the god. He yearned to hack off that bear's head—to flay its chest open and peel back its ribs. For weeks Myrkur had tormented Silla, and gods, but Rey wanted to make Him hurt.

Eerie, cackling laughter rattled the air, and though the bear's back was to him, Rey sensed the god's attention. *Such delicious anger you have, lover of Eisa,* purred the god inside his skull. Rey's whole body shuddered at the reverberant sound. *Little good it will do you now.*

Rey's grip on his sword tightened, blazing with fury as he watched Silla and the bear circle each other. He was vaguely aware of Hef battling an undead mountain cat just a few paces behind him, but Rey knew he could trust in the queensguard. Right now, Silla needed his eyes on that bear, studying His movements.

I will cut her down before your eyes, and you won't be able to do a thing about it, taunted the god. *Or perhaps I will Turn her draugur and keep her as my pet.*

"You need an obstacle to slow Him!" shouted Rey.

Silence, mortal! shouted Myrkur. The sound scraped down Rey's spine and left him gasping once more. But he gritted his teeth and examined the bear with keen eyes. Black blood oozed from the creature's armpit and several wounds on its shoulders, but like the other Turned creatures, it seemed completely unbothered.

"Keep your eyes on His nostrils!" he called out. Silla said nothing, but the tilt of her head told Rey she was listening. "They flare before He lunges—"

Irritating mortal! roared the god of chaos, constricting Rey's lungs. *Do you want to play?*

"Fight . . . me," Rey wheezed, desperate to lift this burden from Silla's shoulders . . .

Very well. The bear seemed to smile—if a bear could do such a thing. *I'll send you a playmate.*

As air rushed into his lungs, Rey unsheathed his sword and advanced. But a thud from behind the bear drew his attention. Another soon followed. Another in a rhythm that had Rey's stomach twisting in recognition.

A heartbeat—and it came from the infected tree.

A burl protruding from the side of the tree burst, and a cloud of white spores seeped into the air. The tiny particles whirled and twisted, joining together into a cloud.

"The mist," muttered Rey, with a curse. Another burl exploded, more spores spewing from the tree. Rey strode toward the tree, giving Silla and Myrkur a wide berth. Then he wrenched his galdur forth and shoved smoke into the air as quickly as he could. Already, a tendril of mist tried to slither past him to reach Silla.

None may touch my avatar, snarled Myrkur inside Rey's skull, *but it was never specified that Eisa cannot be touched. If the mist reaches her, your precious shield-maiden will be Turned draugur. I fear that will end our battle rather quickly.*

Silla danced back from the mist and stumbled over a rock. A ripple of dark glee filled the air.

Tut tut, ally of Eisa. You'll have to be faster than that.

Silla and Rey exchanged a weighted look. And with a quick nod, they turned their focus on their respective opponents.

There was, after all, only forward.

The dark god screamed, and then the bear and mist charged in unison.

CHAPTER 61

Contrary though it was, in the midst of battle, Rey felt most at peace. There was no space for the past; for anger or bitterness or ill-tempered thoughts. There was only the here and now.

But as Silla battled an undead fire-breathing bear and Rey defended her against a foe that could not be pierced by sword, his mind scattered in a dozen different directions. The air vibrated once more, and from the corner of his eye, Rey watched Silla dive aside before a burst of black flames could reduce her to ash.

Focus, Rey urged himself, expressing his galdur with more force than usual. The power churning from his palms was nearly unbearable—a torrent of smoke and ash on the knife's edge of his control. Sweat beaded his brow, snow melting underfoot, the power surging from him dangerously hot.

With a flick of his wrist, Rey split his smoke into wisps to match the white mist striking out toward Silla from all sides. Rooting his feet into the packed snow, Rey sent his charring tendrils at the mist with all the force he could muster. Mist and smoke collided, steam hissing where they met.

Fury rattled the air—Myrkur and the parasite in that tree all at once—and Rey shoved harder, trying to drive the mist back. The bear roared, and Silla shrieked, Rey catching movement in his periphery as she flew through the air. He shouted in frustration, hating that he could not be of more aid to her. Yet more movement had him turning—a rope of mist snaking over the snow toward Silla. Fear fueled Rey's galdur as his smoke shot out, driving the mist back.

Ally of Eisa, I expected better of you, taunted Myrkur inside his skull. *You are slow and dim-witted.*

"My grandmother has called me far worse," Rey grunted. To Silla he muttered, "You'll need to take Him by surprise. A quick, powerful flurry of attacks."

Silla rolled beneath a swiping paw, body colliding with that gods damned boulder. The tree behind it vibrated, showering snow down from above. Concern knotted in Rey's gut as Silla brushed snow from her face and the undead bear lumbered ever closer.

"What kind of pitiful god are you, anyway?" taunted Rey, hoping Myrkur could not hear the edge of panic in his voice. *Shake it off,* he urged Silla silently, exhaling as she gingerly climbed to her feet.

"Where is the honor in fighting the smallest among mortals?" Rey shouted.

Honor, laughed Myrkur inside Rey's skull. *How amusing you think I care for such things.*

Rey couldn't shake his worry as he tracked Silla's movement from the corner of his eye. Her motions were apprehensive—still far too cautious. A single swipe of a paw and she could be lying dead on the forest floor. And yet no swipe came. As the bear and Silla circled each other, and Rey corralled attempt after attempt by the mist to reach her, he realized what was happening.

Myrkur was toying with her.

I've decided I won't kill your precious Eisa, hissed Myrkur. *Instead, I'll have her Turned draugur. And then I shall turn the little Volsik on her lover. She shall feast on your flesh. Suck the marrow from your bones.*

"If I'm to die," grunted Rey, "having my . . . *marrow* . . . sucked does not sound like the worst sort of thing."

Displeasure rolled off Myrkur in waves. *She will feed on your entrails and eyeballs! Tear the lungs from your body!*

Sensing the mist slinking around his periphery, Rey changed the trajectory of his galdur and drove it back. In a move Rey recognized well, Silla lunged forward. Swung her sword upward with impressive speed. The undead bear snapped its fangs at her, but Silla was already spinning away, her blade stained black with blood.

A hit, thought Rey, but it was not a hit she needed. Silla needed to get near enough while avoiding those lethal claws. Using her momentum, Silla suddenly darted toward Rey. He tried to parse what she needed from him, but he was diverted by another cord of mist slithering into the clearing. He shoved his galdur at it, then gasped. Silla's cold hand had landed on his wrist, where smoke spilled in a dozen different directions. Immediately, the galdur crackling through him was siphoned away, and his storm of smoke evaporated.

Panic surged into Rey as the mist broke free from his hold. But one glance at Silla and Rey knew what had happened. She'd wrangled his galdur to wield against the god's bear avatar. Rather than the orderly wisps Rey had managed, it was now a disordered torrent of smoke.

"Silla!" he shouted as the mist surged all around them. Finally, she expressed, blasting the massive frenzy of smoke at the beastly form of the god.

Rey had scarcely enough time to draw a breath—to feel her release her grip on his galdur. It billowed back into his veins, and he'd barely seized it before flinging it outward without precision. He couldn't look to see if Silla had managed to subdue the bear, not while it took every ounce of his strength to keep the mist at bay. But her whimpered, "No," told Rey enough.

A moment later, the bear ambled straight through Rey's smoke, fur singed black, but utterly unbothered.

As Rey's smoke battled with the mist, the scent of mold and ash and scorched loam filled the air. Rey's limbs trembled with the force of his exertion—with the will required to keep the wall of smoke in place. Embers snapped, smoke hissing where it met the mist. The surrounding snow had melted away, and patches of grass had caught alight. Keeping his focus on the mist, Rey stamped the flames out.

Myrkur laughed, His dark delight filled the clearing, oozing through Rey's veins. Rey gave his head a shake, trying to free himself from the god's thrall.

Dear Eisa, purred the god, *that was quite fun.*

Rey's brows dipped down, sweat sliding into one eye and blurring his vision.

Let's do it again.

"I can do this all day," snarled Silla, and Rey wasn't sure if he wanted to laugh or cry. She'd pulled so much galdur from him; he could now feel the dry bottom of his source. Rey glanced over his shoulder in search of another Ashbringer. Kálf's skill manifested as a whip, but they needed a gods damned wall to drive the mist back . . .

"Hef!" Rey hollered, catching sight of the man. "Get me another Ashbringer!"

"On it!" shouted Hef, darting into the fray.

Silla lunged into battle with the god of chaos once more, and Rey focused all his wits on keeping the mist out. But he felt his smoke thinning, gaps where the mist slunk through. He pulled smoke from other places in the wall to plug these holes, but it only created new weaknesses.

"Hurry up, Hef," Rey muttered under his breath.

Silla sailed through the air to his left before crashing onto sodden grass. "Get up," muttered Rey, prodding at his dry source, then the halda stores tattooed on his chest. Empty—he'd reached the end of his galdur, and though he had his sword, it would do nothing against the mist.

He couldn't let go, not without risking every warrior in this clearing being Turned, but his galdur was faltering and starting to fade . . . Rey gritted his teeth, assessing Silla from the corner of his eye.

And then it happened.

His smoke sputtered, then failed. Immediately, the mist surged forth and swarmed all around him. It was like being plunged underwater, only in reverse. Inside the mist was a world of chaos and discordant sound. Cloudy forms charged at him. Immediately, Rey knew these masks would do nothing to keep it out, and held his breath. His world became a haze. Bright lights danced in his vision—he needed to breathe but could not let himself.

But then came a blast of orange—the mist hissing. Retracting.

"Get away from them, you foul fucking gutter sludge!"

The forest swam back into view, and Rey finally drew breath as he caught sight of Silla. Thank the fucking gods, she'd climbed back to her feet and was raining a flurry of blows at the Turned bear. But who had driven back the mist and saved Rey from joining the ranks of the draugur?

He whirled to his savior.

There stood Eyvind Hakonsson. The man's beard was grizzled, his clothing filthy and torn. But the orange flames pouring from Eyvind's wrists were a sight for sore eyes.

"Fire Breath," Rey wheezed in mingled relief and exhaustion.

"Soot Fingers," Eyvind replied in kind. "I'm here to save your sorry arse."

CHAPTER 62

Hekla whirled in a full circle, taking in the roiling battle in the heartwood. Everywhere she looked, undead forest creatures clashed with mail-clad warriors. The snow was sprayed with black and red blood, the moldered scent of Turned creatures heavy in the air. Silla's warriors were impossibly outnumbered, and it seemed Hekla and her crew had arrived in the nick of time.

The Forest Maiden and her beasts surged into battle, cheers of relief rising up from Silla's beleaguered warband. Hekla watched in disbelief as a reindeer gouged a vampire deer, allowing a knot of warriors to take the vampire deer's head. Nearby, forest spirits clustered around a Turned mountain cat, disorienting the beast and giving a nearby warrior the chance to drive his blade through its neck. Beside her, Gunnar bellowed before charging into the fray with Sigrún on his heels, but Hekla took another moment to assess where she was most needed in the battle.

Her gaze jumped to Eyvind's older brother Atli, battling side by side with a black-haired youth. On the farthest edge of the clearing, the Kalasgardian Galdra wielded their magic—bushy-bearded Kálf lashing his fire whip at undead ravens, while pale-skinned Hef snatched a Turned fox clean from the air and yanked the head from its shoulders with his Blade Breaker strength.

Above the din of battle, the mist's heartbeat thundered, and Hekla traced the sound to its origin—a giant aberration of a tree.

Her blood chilled at the sight of the thing. Its trunk was thick and gray, bark bulging with various burls. She watched in disgust as one of the protrusions burst and white spores belched from it. They mingled together, forming a cloud, which whipped out toward . . .

Hekla gasped as she recognized the figures squaring off before the monstrosity of a tree. Silla, small yet nimble, battling an enormous Turned bear. But Rey—he'd collapsed on the ground, a familiar figure standing above him. Flames poured from Eyvind's palms, driving the mist back.

Her heart clenched tight, and Hekla started forward, ready to defend Eyvind's flank as she had in Istré. But she made it no farther than a step before a yelp had Hekla whirling.

An enormous Turned wolfspider towered over her.

As she took in the spider's five ruined eyes, a smile formed on her lips, but it quickly fell. Because cradled in Gjalla's feelers was the silk-wrapped body of a creature she knew all too well.

Protector! pleaded Kritka, his voice so quiet over the din of battle.

"Kritka," Hekla hissed. Nausea roiled in her gut, but anger quickly overtook it. "Release him!" she bellowed, raising her longsword.

If you want the beast, chittered Gjalla inside Hekla's skull, *then come and get him.*

Hekla's vision tunneled, a scream building deep inside her chest. This monster had tried to kill her. Had very nearly ended Eyvind's life as well. And now it had taken Kritka.

This ended. Now.

She glanced over her shoulder, confirming that Eyvind had warriors at his back. And then her scream broke free as Hekla tore after the spider.

CHAPTER 63

Silla's limbs quivered with exhaustion, her mind frantically churning through options. Her blast with Rey's borrowed smoke magic had been meant to subdue the undead bear, but all it had managed was to singe the beast's fur. She needed to get near enough, but how? Those claws were lethal and far faster than a mortal bear's.

Rey had collapsed nearby in the grass, but a new warrior had taken his place to keep the mist at bay. *Eyvind,* she thought distantly, eyeing the fire pouring from his palms and shoving the mist back. Yet the awful burls continued to grow and burst, black sludge and endless mist pouring from within; that maddening heartbeat drumming on. Would the leech ever reach the end of its stores?

Silla's muscles ached with exhaustion, her forearm throbbing where the bear's claws had torn through her lébrynja jacket. She was dimly aware of her queensguard all around her—Hef, battling two vampire deer at once; Kálf and Erik battling droves of Turned foxes and grimwolves; and Runný guarding their backs, wielding her curious reflective shield to repel the surging creatures.

On Silla battled, her energy waning as she searched for any path to victory. She knew Myrkur could end her with barely a thought—she could feel Him feeding on the chaos all around them. He was enjoying this. And though she knew the god toyed with her—that He'd shown her but a fraction of His strength—Silla had no choice but to keep fighting.

Silla ducked beneath a surge of black flames, heat searing through her jacket. But the bear had paused to loose the flames, and shock rippled through her. The bear stood upright. Here was her chance. Silla couldn't allow herself to second-guess it.

Time seemed to slow. The last rays of sunlight poured through the trees as Silla threw herself onto her stomach and slid on the wet grass. Black flames powered above her, unbearably hot. Her hair singed . . . her skin seemed on fire, but this was her only chance.

She gritted her teeth against the agony of the flames blazing inches above her. With a scream of rage, Silla channeled her anger at this god for the misery He'd put her through; for the bargain He'd tricked her mother into; for the way He'd preyed on her great-grandfather.

Time sped back up, the world becoming a blur.

Silla stretched one hand out and clamped it onto the bear's lower hind paw. Its fur was coarse, the smell horrific, but Silla found the place of peace in her mind and let her senses stretch out, reaching, searching for . . . nothing. Where was Myrkur's magic? She could not sense it.

It took her a moment to realize the black flames had burned out, and by the time she did, it was too late. The bear crashed down onto all fours and swatted her.

It was a casual gesture, a mere flick of the paw, but it was laced with the power of a god. Silla flew through the air and crashed to the ground with jarring force.

For a moment, she lay there. Let herself pretend she hadn't just lost all hope. Then she heaved herself up onto shaky feet and tried to comprehend. She'd done the impossible—had laid hands on the bear—and yet there'd been no galdur for her to siphon. Tears gathered in her eyes as the bear loosed a long, low growl.

"No," pleaded Silla, despair thrashing inside her. She couldn't siphon the dark god's magic—she couldn't even *sense* it.

Of course she couldn't. Silla now realized what she ought to have known from the start. Myrkur's magic was not the same as what flowed in her veins; as what shimmered inside each magical creature in this realm. They were the Ashen, created when Sunnvald's ashes fell upon the world. Myrkur was the opposite—a being of disorder and destruction.

The bear prowled toward her with lethal intent.

Now you understand, Eisa, growled Myrkur, taking a step forward for each one Silla retreated. *You've made a bargain you cannot win.* And in this moment, she sensed something had changed. Gone was the god's amusement—His contentment to toy with her.

Here was His satisfaction.

The full force of Myrkur's presence assaulted her, and Silla felt herself fracturing, cracks spreading like spiderwebs through all her defenses. She reached for her hearthfire thoughts—for the faintest thread of hope to grab onto. But like a dam broken, Myrkur's barrage was a wild, unstoppable thing.

It was fun while it lasted, purred Myrkur, the bear's rancid breath meeting her nose. *Surrender your bloodline gift to me.*

You'll have to win it, as we agreed, Silla pushed back, staggering against Myrkur's relentless assault on her mind.

The god's fury lashed through her, battering her from within. *I am winning, dear Eisa. I will tear you apart, one thought at a time. I will break you from within. Turn you into a useless shell.*

More power flowed into her, and she felt herself splintering. Whereas the shard of Myrkur which had lived inside her had prodded and scraped at her mind, now the god of chaos ripped through it with talons. Silla screamed, clutching her head, and fell to her knees with the force of His onslaught.

I thought you'd be more like Signe, He seethed. *I thought you'd see our potential together. Do you not have ambition? Do you not crave the queendom for yourself? I can make that happen.*

Silla gasped for breath. Wrangled her words. *I would not have the fear of my people*, she barely managed. *I would have their love.*

Disgusting, Myrkur hissed, but Silla sensed that for the first time, He finally understood. It was never a matter of biding his time, nor a matter of finding the right incentive. Silla simply would never partner with Him.

Do you know what will happen once you're gone, Eisa? Myrkur cackled, and the sound was like needles piercing her skull. *With no Volsiks left in the realm, Sunnvald's so-called weapon to oppose me will be gone. I'll be unstoppable.*

"No," repeated Silla, but this time it sounded far more like a plea.

It's too late for begging, growled the god of chaos.

And with a godly burst of darkness, Myrkur consumed her.

CHAPTER 64

The scream tore from Hekla's throat as she charged at Gjalla. Horror and panic battled within her as the spider twirled Kritka with frantic speed, further enshrouding him in silk, and somehow, muffling his pleas with it. The grimwolf let out one last plaintive yip, but it was quickly silenced as his air was sealed off. Gjalla dropped Kritka to the ground, the silk-wrapped bundle writhing to get free. Hekla had to get to her wolf, had to cut him free from his binds before he suffocated—

But Gjalla's fangs stabbed downward, and she dove out of their path with barely a heartbeat to spare. The force of the spider cratered the snow and ground beneath it, the whole of the woods shaking with the impact. Gjalla chittered in rage, ripping his fangs free and launching at her.

Hekla kept her gaze on the writhing white mass that was Kritka, just beyond the wolfspider's back legs. She was not fast enough to make it, but she was foolish enough to try it all the same. Gritting her teeth, she charged forward, then threw herself on her stomach, saying a silent prayer as she slid on the snow toward Kritka's bundled form. But her momentum came to a jarring halt as one of Gjalla's six remaining legs slammed down and caught the edge of her lébrynja jacket. Hekla's grip on her sword loosened, and the blade spun across the snow.

The spider clicked with apparent glee as she thrashed against his hold, unable to reach her sword. But it seemed the vile creature had forgotten about Hekla's *other* weapon. She thrust her claws into the joint of his segmented leg, and the spider reared back with a vicious screech. Shouting her anger, Hekla heaved against the leg until her jacket pulled free.

Then she was scrambling across the snow, desperate to get to Kritka. His movements were weak, his muffled yelps so feeble. She knew she didn't have long.

A sudden gust of air had Hekla rolling. Gjalla's fangs slammed deep into the ground, sending snow powdering the air and shielding Hekla's view. A great shadow blocked out the last light of day. Again, Hekla sensed an impending strike; again, she rolled. But this time, as her back hit the snow, Gjalla's leg slammed into her stomach. Air punched from her lungs and pain blazed through her as something cracked—a rib or two had certainly just broken.

Your fortune has ended, gloated the spider. *You won't sneak your way free this time.*

Pinned like an insect on her back, Hekla blinked up at three glowing red eyes—at the fangs gnashing down, down, down . . .

The last time she'd faced certain death, Hekla had been at peace, glad to die with a sword in her hand. Now hazel eyes filled her mind. A black lupine nose nuzzled against her palm. She heard Silla's laughter and saw Axe Eyes sharpening her prosthetic's claws.

A scream built in her throat as Hekla drove her claws upward. Steel and carapace smashed together. Hekla shrieked, pain radiating down what remained of her limb as Gjalla's fangs grappled and yanked at her prosthetic arm.

The spider screeched in anger, and time seemed to slow. She twisted her limb to the side, and as the anchor clicked, she gave a hearty shove. Unhooked, her metal arm slid free, and Gjalla stumbled backward with the surprising shift in momentum.

The enormous weight lifted from her chest, and Hekla clambered to her feet, ignoring the pain radiating from her residual limb and broken ribs. Gjalla scuttled about, trying to regain his balance.

But before the beast could regain his senses, Hekla staggered forward and, with her left hand, scooped her sword up from the snow.

Unleashing a scream of pure, visceral wrath, she slashed her sword upward.

Burrowed it deep into the spider's soft underbelly.

Wrenched it forward with every bit of her strength.

Black ichor poured from its wound, an earsplitting screech wrenched from the spider as he tipped to the side. Hekla dodged a twitching leg and dragged her gaze from the dying spider to the silk-encased bundle lying still on the snow.

"No!" Hekla choked out, digging through her pain to reach Kritka's side. She fell to her knees, unsheathing her dagger before slashing through the spider's silk.

Please, she pleaded through their mind-to-mind connection. *Kritka, wake up!*

But no answer returned to her.

Black canine lips were stark against the white spider's silk, yet they were utterly still. Swallowing back a sob, Hekla worked her blade carefully, widening the hole. Soon Kritka's entire muzzle was free.

"You're alive," she whispered, a plea to the gods as she pulled the sticky silk away from his face. "You're alive. You're *alive.*"

The battle raged nearby, and Hekla was vaguely aware of Kritka's pack guarding her from the Turned creatures as she worked to free their kin. It was painstaking, but at last she was able to slice down the length of his binds and free him entirely.

Kritka rolled onto his side. The grimwolf's eyes remained closed, but as his chest rose with steady breaths, Hekla's sob broke free.

Protector, came Kritka's voice, feeble in her mind.

"You're alive!" Hekla buried her face in Kritka's scratchy fur.

A grimwolf's howl met her ears, then another and yet another. Hekla knelt back on her haunches, gaze swinging around the clearing. One by one, Kritka's pack lifted their heads to the sky and howled in triumph.

But the swell of victory in Hekla's chest was short-lived. As her gaze roamed across the battlefield, it landed on her curly-haired friend, stumbling backward. Hekla watched in dawning horror as Silla fell to her knees, clutching her head.

As Rey howled in rage, Hekla knew her friend was in grave danger.

CHAPTER 65

Silla was buried in darkness and drowning in despair. The dark god was in every corner of her body, each crevice of her mind. She clawed against His hold, tried to bring herself back to the light.

No, she pleaded, thinking of Rey and Hekla and all of Íseldur—of Saga and her promise they'd meet one day. The names expanded like bubbles in her chest, and for a moment, Silla held on to hope. She only needed to try harder—to fight with more vigor.

Your stubbornness would be admirable, whispered Myrkur, *if it weren't so bothersome.* One by one, the bubbles burst, leaving her emptier than before.

Silla just needed to hang on a little longer. She grasped for the last shred of her control, but it was hopeless. Futile.

All you had to do was surrender to me, purred Myrkur, kneading her spine with His talons, lulling her with gentle beats of leathery wings. *Such a waste of potential.*

The dark god's words were weighted, and her mind was buckling beneath the force of them. She collapsed to the ground, the last of her free will sliding through her fingers.

And then she knew. She'd never stood a chance. Myrkur would win this battle.

CHAPTER 66

Nausea boiled in Saga's gut, though it was not due to the wide-open skies all around her. It was Eisa—Saga *had* to get to her. Gripping Havoc's mane, she pressed her chest lower to his sleek form as he sailed through the salt-tinged air.

Must get to her, she thought frantically, the tug of Eisa's mind growing stronger with each passing heartbeat.

Saga had felt the familiar pull of Eisa the moment Íseldur's shores had come into view. She'd also felt that other *thing*—the dark creature nesting deep within her. Immediately, Saga had bristled. Never again would she listen to that voice. Never again would she let it feed her deepest, most heinous desires.

But Eisa. Something was wrong.

Kassandr had found Saga unfastening the sling that secured Havoc in his stall on their merchant ship.

"I have to go to her," she'd explained to her husband's wordless question. "She's in trouble."

Kassandr had chewed on his reply, then to Saga's great relief had simply nodded. "You will bring me with you," he ordered. And though Havoc had snorted indignantly as the Beast of Zagadka climbed onto his back, her stallion seemed to understand the urgency of this moment.

And so they'd taken to the skies, Kassandr shouting to Rov that they'd meet them at the port in Kunafjord. Saga said a silent apology to Kass's long-suffering second in command, who pulled his hair while shouting foul Zagadkian curses at Kass.

As Havoc carried Saga and Kass over angry frothing seas and closer to Íseldur, her Sense had grown stronger. And with it came awareness of something new—a pool of power behind her breastbone. Cautiously, Saga probed it, trying to understand. Was this the heart of her magic? If so, what was that other thing . . . the dark thing that had spoken in her mind in Askaborg's great hall? It was silent now, but she shuddered to think what it might do should it wake.

As they at last flew over a rugged beach, Saga's breaths grew more even.

She was back in Íseldur.

Below them, the Western Woods sprouted upward, and Saga gasped at the state of the forest—the trees gray, spindly things, starving and parched. And in the very farthest distance, a column of smoke churned into the skies.

"There!" she shouted to Kass. After retching several times into the ocean, he'd been uncharacteristically quiet. Kassandr Rurik's stomach, it seemed, was not so ironclad as the grip he held around her waist.

On they flew until Saga's hands were numb with cold and her stomach seethed like a swarm of angry bees. It was the farthest she'd ever flown on Havoc, yet with Kass behind her and her sister before her, she was bolstered with strength. Over and over, Saga reminded herself that fear was a thing to be felt. Still, her heart raced and her breaths were shallow.

Time ceased to have meaning—perhaps they flew for one hour, perhaps it was six. But gradually the column of smoke grew nearer. The sun had set in the west behind them, and the moons began their Rise in the east, directly before them. And as Saga gazed at the smaller of the sister moons, she realized Marra was full. Hope sparked in her chest.

Saga had always been drawn to Marra above all the other old

gods. *Goddess of healing and knowledge,* Saga heard in her mother's voice. *Marra is often called Peacebringer.* A full Marra felt like a good omen—not that Saga believed in such things.

Havoc whinnied as a harsh sound climbed above the howling wind.

"Battle," growled Kass, his grip on her waist tightening. "I do not like this—"

"You don't *need* to like it," Saga snapped. "Eisa is down there and I have to find—"

Her words broke off as she felt something she hadn't in many long weeks—thoughts seeping freely into her mind. It was a strange sensation, foreign yet familiar all at once, but as the thoughts grew in strength and intensity, she braced herself against their onslaught.

. . . *Die, you sack of rotten meat* . . .

. . . *I wish I'd had longer* . . .

. . . *Must get to her. Must reach her* . . .

Saga shoved her barriers into place as the battle came into view. She blinked in shock. Monstrous versions of forest creatures fought hundreds of warriors. Saga spied a green-skinned woman with antlers battling a pack of vampire deer; grimwolves lunging at a horde of undead mountain cats. She gasped as the great drum of a heartbeat met her ears, carrying with it the scent of mold and blood. It made no sense, but the part of her linked to her sister told Saga that Eisa was down there, and she was in danger.

Saga's heart raced even faster, her stomach turning over. Danger all around. If she landed, there would be no exits . . .

But Eisa needed her.

"What is that?" muttered Kassandr, and she followed his pointing finger.

There stood the largest of all the trees in the grove, its bark moving like liquid. She watched in horror as a lump emerged on the gray-black bark, growing and swelling until it burst and white mist seeped into the air. And there, a few paces from the tree, stood a warrior with flames pouring from his palms. This Ashbringer warrior alone, it seemed, held the strange cloud at bay. The man's face was lined with exertion, and it looked as though he might not hold on much longer.

"Something unnatural is afoot," said Kass. "Winterwing, I do not like this—"

But Saga was not listening—her gaze jumped from the Ashbringer to a large, dark warrior, bellowing as he charged across the grove. There was something familiar about this warrior, something Saga could not place. But then she saw *her,* and nothing else mattered. Dark-brown hair, pale skin, black armor worn beneath a wolfskin cloak. Saga's sister was on her knees, eyes squeezed shut as she clutched her temples. A monstrous bear loomed several paces away.

"Eisa," she whispered.

Saga reached out to her sister, not with her Sense, but through the mysterious sisterly bond they'd used to communicate. She found her, but gasped. Eisa's thread was so weak . . .

Havoc landed with jarring force, hooves pounding the snow hard enough to send monsters scattering and Saga half climbing, half tumbling from the saddle.

"Get behind me," growled Kassandr, the press of his magic filling the air. Fabric ripped, and she knew he'd shifted into his beast form behind her. Havoc shrieked, hooves lashing out at a lunging grimwolf.

"To the sky, Havoc!" Saga called. With a begrudging snort, the stallion obeyed.

Saga pulled a dagger from her boot as Kassandr unleashed himself upon the grimwolf. Ignoring the carnage unfolding around her, Saga turned back to her sister. The bear was still several paces away, but Eisa had fully collapsed in the snow, her body convulsing and her thread a bare wisp.

"Eisa!" pleaded Saga, all thoughts of self-preservation fleeing her. Trusting Kass to guard her from the bear, she rushed to her sister. Saga dropped to her knees, then pulled Eisa's head into her in her lap. "I'm here, Eisa—"

Saga, hissed a voice inside her skull.

"No," mumbled Saga, reeling. It was the voice she'd heard at her engagement feast—the one that had pulled her darkest cravings forth. "You won't sway me this time."

A wave of glee nearly knocked her to the ground. *Oh, but I will,* purred the voice. *I will take your sister's life and keep you as my thrall . . .*

For years, Saga had been weaving her mental barriers to control her Sense, and it came to her now as easily as breathing. She reinforced her walls with stone and steel, the creature's displeasure a low grumble deep in her chest.

Saga caressed her sister's cheek. "You promised, Eisa," she whispered, reaching once more for that strange, sisterly intuition. "You promised we would meet one day. Come back, Eisa. Help me keep that promise."

The thinnest, fraying thread of Eisa seemed to remain, and Saga entwined her own self around it, braiding them together to reinforce it. Images jolted through Saga—a dark, knife-wielding figure above her; a man stabbed dead on a bench; blood and flesh beneath her fingernails. Dark cravings slithered through Saga's veins. *I am winning, dear Eisa,* they purred. *I will tear you apart, one thought at a time.*

Understanding dawned on Saga. The voice she'd heard in her skull—the one who'd promised they'd have fun together—had lived inside her sister as well. And now it had a hold on Eisa. Would try to take her from Saga, just when she'd found her.

"You won't have her!" Saga screamed, holding her sister to her as she shoved all her will into Eisa's mind.

Saga could have sworn she saw Eisa's eyelids flutter, and though it might have been a trick of her mind, she let it fuel her hope all the same. She was dimly aware of Kassandr in beast form nearby, ripping the heads from monstrous deer and mountain cats as they lunged her way. But she tried to ignore him—tried to focus on the sister before her. With a deep breath, Saga gathered her energy and pulled from the pool of power shimmering behind her breastbone.

"Get out!" she shouted. And with the full force of her will, she shoved again.

This time, she *knew* she saw Eisa's eyelids flutter. Saga felt the thread of her sister become firmer, stronger, resisting the force that tried to fray through it.

Stop! shouted the voice—in her skull, in the woods all around her.

But Saga would not stop. Would never give up when it came to Eisa. She pulled all the memories she had of her sister, imbibing them with love and thrusting them at her. Saga showed Eisa their mother making silly voices as she told the girls bedtime stories, and the time their father had paused an important meeting to allow his girls to climb into his lap and tell him about the newborn fawn they'd spotted on the grounds. Saga showed Eisa the flíta in the royal gardens, their father's belly laugh, their mother's wild curly hair.

She sensed that *thing* pulse with fear, but all that mattered was bringing Eisa back to her.

Release her! bellowed the dark presence, the ground shaking with its fury.

Eisa's threads grew thicker, stronger, her eyelids fluttering more strongly now, and Saga did not relent her grip. She held her power, entwined with Eisa's, and continued pouring all her love through the bond.

Saga was so focused on her sister that she did not see the bear charging at her with impossible speed. Kassandr launched himself through the air, but he was too late. The bear collided with her. Saga lost her grip on Eisa and went skidding across the snow. Her skull collided with a large boulder, and for a moment, her vision was a blur of dancing lights. Disoriented, she pushed to her feet.

A shame, growled the dark thing, its voice coming from everywhere all at once. *We wrought such havoc in Askaborg together.*

The bear stepped over Eisa's prone body and prowled toward Saga.

But if you won't relent your hold on Eisa, then you'll have to die.

Time seemed to slow as the bear crouched, preparing to leap upon her. Saga's eyes blurred with tears as she stared down certain death. At least she would die fighting for something worthy. At least she would go with her promise to Eisa made true.

"We're not done, Myrkur," came a voice of steel.

And Saga could have wept, for there stood Eisa, sword in hand. Her eyes were clear, the whites bright, and beside Eisa stood a pale-skinned woman warrior with dozens of long black braids, yanking up the sleeve of her armored jacket. Through her strange sisterly bond, the name Runný flitted through Saga's mind.

The bear unleashed a savage growl that shook the very realm. The white mist held at bay by the Ashbringer broke through with sudden force, surging up the bear's nostrils. Saga felt the power flowing into the bear from everything all around them—the infected tree, the undead creatures—all the darkness in this grove channeled into the creature.

The raw power in the bear was so staggering, Saga's vision seemed to haze. Yet she did not miss her sister's hand on the woman warrior's arm. Saga pushed through her addled mind for that thread of Eisa, still braided with her own, and she felt her sister's power change. Suddenly, Saga was acutely aware of the light all around them—minuscule wriggling tethers they could control with their mind. Shadow Hound, her mind supplied, and Saga realized these were the building blocks of light. The tethers shifted, re-formed, became a great mirrored shield.

Runný backed away from Eisa, and everything happened so quickly—black flames erupted from the bear, surging right for Eisa. Saga screamed. Warriors on all sides shouted in dismay. The black flames struck Eisa.

And bounced off the reflective shield.

Saga's scream died in her throat as the jet of black flames rebounded off the strange, invisible force, striking the bear and the infected tree directly behind it. An earsplitting crack had Saga clapping her hands over her ears, and she sealed her lips shut as snow and wood dust powdered the air. But as the debris settled, she saw that where the bear had once stood was now a pile of blackened, steaming gore. And behind it, the monstrous tree was rent in two.

Saga looked about in stunned disbelief. The undead creatures were breaking—were fleeing from the woods. A war cry rose up as warriors chased them. Kassandr was suddenly before her in his beast form, scenting for injuries.

Saga patted him absently as her gaze found her sister's. Eisa swayed on her feet, looking just as incredulous as Saga felt. But as those brown eyes locked with hers, a jolt ran through Saga.

For years, she'd dreamed of that horrid day countless times: Of the arm snaking around Saga's waist and wrenching her from little Eisa's grip. Of those brown eyes, widened in terror. "Don't leave me!" Saga had screamed as Eisa was pulled away. It was the day she'd lost her entire family. The worst day of Saga's life.

But as she looked upon her sister now, there was no trace of fear in Eisa's eyes. Instead, there was wonder and joy. An enormous smile spread across Eisa's face, and it was the best gods damned dream of Saga's life. Her sister was smiling. Something inside her began to heal at that.

Her *sister*!

And then Saga was rounding past Kassandr and running at Eisa. Tears flowed down her cheeks as she laughed and shrieked. She tackled Eisa to the ground, wrapping her arms and legs around her. Eisa hugged her back with equal vigor, and Saga's heart was so full she thought it might burst. She was laughing, crying, repeating the same words over and over.

"My sister!" Saga shrieked. "That's my sister!"

CHAPTER 67

Rey's ears rang in the wake of the explosion. Paired with the absence of the tree's thundering heartbeat, he was disoriented, almost dizzy. But then he laid eyes on her. Silla. Gods, she was on her feet. Had destroyed the infected tree *and* defeated the god of chaos in a duel.

When she'd crumpled to the ground, all Rey's fears had been made real. He'd thought he'd lost her. And for those long torturous moments, he'd experienced what life was without her. Dark and grim; devoid of light and laughter.

Now Silla stood with eyes clear and wide, and Rey felt the broken shards of himself reassembling. Everything felt different. Everything was so clear. She was the other half of him, his light and hope, his reason for breathing. She was his lone hearthfire thought, and he would shelter her warmth as long as she'd let him.

Rey needed to get to her. He wanted to tend the wound on her cheek; wanted to bundle her in blankets and feed her sweet rolls. He would bring her chicks every morning. Would make each and every one of her hearthfire thoughts come true. His limbs moved without thought—he shoved warriors aside, desperate to reach her. But before Rey could reach Silla, another figure charged at her.

"My sister!" shrieked Saga Volsik, tackling Silla to the ground.

Rey watched, dumbstruck, as the sisters embraced, rolling on the ground while laughing and crying. He'd seen the winged horse land in the clearing but had been too deep in the throes of battle to see much else. Now he tried to shake the haze from his mind—tried to comprehend what had happened.

Snippets of memory flared behind his eyes. Runný, hauling Silla to her feet. Silla had grasped Runný's arm. Formed a reflective shield. Rebounded Myrkur's black flames at Him. Rey's mind blurred.

Nothing made sense. Saga Volsik was here, hugging her sister. The impenetrable tree was now cracked clean down the middle, and the undead monsters had broken, chased from the grove by Jarl Agnar and his men.

"That's my sister," sobbed Saga.

Emotion caught deep in Rey's chest. After seventeen years, the Volsik sisters were reunited. Rey would not interrupt them, but he lingered nearby, keeping a watchful eye for danger.

To his left, he caught sight of Hekla falling to her knees before a prone figure. "Hakonsson, you gods damned fool of a man. You tore your stitches! Do you know how long they took me?"

He could not hear Eyvind's mumbled reply, but as Atli joined Hekla, Rey's gaze shifted to another scene unfolding in the grove. The Forest Maiden strode toward the broken tree, a dozen grimwolves surrounding her. She looked as she had when last he'd seen her, only now human-sized. But with her green skin, antlers sprouting from her brow, and a fox tail bristling behind her, she looked every bit like a thing of myth and legend.

The Forest Maiden approached the split tree, and Rey watched in fascination as she placed her hand upon the ruined bark. The Maiden closed her eyes, almost as though listening for a pulse. Gods willing, life would never flow in that damnable tree again.

Her lips moved in an inaudible murmur, and Rey watched in fascination. Mushrooms of all shapes and sizes sprouted before his eyes—white clamshells unfurling like shelves up the tree; delicate, frilled mushrooms bursting from the bark. Upward they blossomed until they covered every surface of the tree.

Rey could sense them beneath him as well, burrowing in the soil and encasing the tree's roots. He blinked in astonishment as the mushrooms feasted on the tree's corpse before his very eyes.

For a single moment, Rey could have sworn he felt the pulse of the forest and a deep understanding of the complex thread work in the soil. He felt the parched, gasping trees all around him, finally able to draw breath. Death was all around them—skeleton saplings and brittle bracken; bone-dry grasses and graves of insects.

But as the mushrooms consumed the dead tree, Rey felt wonders happening beneath the soil—minuscule threads weaving into a web, nutrients from the dead tree flowing through them like blood through a vein. As the strange underground network reached dormant spores and seeds, they germinated with the burst of nutrition. As the web reached the other great hjarta trees in the grove, they were infused with life.

In this moment, Rey understood that the forest held its own sort of magic. The dead would feed the living. The elderly would nurture the seedlings. Life would return to these woods. In time, it would be all right.

"*Married!*" Silla exclaimed, and Rey's deep connection to the woods snapped free. Dazed, he turned to Silla. She and her sister had disentangled and settled themselves cross-legged on a cloak. Silla's smile was bigger than Rey had ever seen, warming him clean through.

But then he caught sight of a large form approaching the pair. Rey's sword was drawn in an instant.

"Not another step forward," he growled, the tip of his blade pressing into the middle of the man's bare chest. Rey scowled, his gaze drifting downward, then swiftly snapping up. "Where are your breeches?"

The man's eyes flashed a dangerous green. "Is . . . casualty of battle," the warrior said, shrugging. "I suggest you put away your sword before I tear hands from your body and use them to decorate my wife's horse."

Inky-black markings pulsed on the man's tanned skin, further raising Rey's hackles. He expressed a thin ribbon of smoke, covering his concerningly low reserves with extra bravado. "I'll roast you like a spring rabbit before you can try."

"Kassandr," came a woman's voice. "Oh, gods, you impossible man." A cloak flew through the air, smacking the green-eyed warrior on the side of the head.

Saga Volsik appeared by the man's side and eyed Rey coldly. "Unhand my husband." Shocked, Rey's gaze flitted between Silla's sister and the green-eyed warrior who was apparently her . . . husband?

"So protective, my *wife,*" said the man, grinning like a wildcat as he pulled the cloak around his shoulders. "It seems almost like you care for me."

"Just cover yourself before you get frostbite," Saga muttered.

Silla's hand slid around Rey's elbow, and she gently pulled his sword away. Rey discarded it in an instant, his hands moving to cup her jaw. "Sunshine," he rasped, inspecting her for any signs of injury. There was a cut on her pale cheekbone, an egg-shaped swelling behind her ear. She hissed as his fingers probed her shoulder and thigh, but she had no broken bones. No deep wounds in need of stitching. She was a gods damned miracle.

Rey pressed his forehead to hers and asked the question he dreaded most. "Do you feel Him? Do you feel Myrkur?"

She wrapped her hands around his wrists, holding him to her. "No," she whispered. "He's gone."

Rey met her eyes with a tremulous exhale, then kissed her because he couldn't bear not to. "You did it," he breathed, between kisses. "I knew you could—"

But the clearing of a throat made the pair break apart. Silla and Rey turned sheepishly toward Saga and her husband.

"Is sister of my Saga!" exclaimed the green-eyed man, the cloak now belted at his waist to cover his most prominent parts. The half-naked warrior's smile somehow widened as his gaze landed on Silla. He took Silla's hand in his and brushed his lips against her knuckles. "I am Kassandr Rurik of Zagadka," the man continued, "son of high prince and husband of Saga."

"Tone it down, Rurik," muttered Saga, rolling her eyes.

"Nice to meet you," said Silla, her cheeks flaming red. Rey wrapped a proprietary arm around Silla's shoulders and pulled her tight to his chest. Looking over her head, he and Kassandr Rurik locked eyes, and the gleam that Rey found there told him this man was trouble.

"Oh!" Silla glanced up. "This is Rey! *My* Rey."

Rey met the Zagadkian warrior with a warning glare, but the man smiled back, unperturbed. Rey's gaze then slid to Saga Volsik. With her blond braids and blue eyes, at first glance, there were few similarities with Silla. But the pert nose and the slope of cheekbones were shared by the sisters.

"We've . . . actually met," he told Saga. "I'm of the Galtung line. You might not recall, but you played with my brother Kristjan in Askaborg's gardens."

Saga blinked. "The Galtungs . . . yes, I remember your family." But her eyes narrowed. "And I most certainly recall the incident at the fountain."

Silla's hand went to the scar at the corner of her eye, while Rey felt that long-suffering twinge of guilt that she'd fallen from that fountain under his watch. He also felt Saga's gaze on him, stern and assessing. He had the distinct impression she was trying to decide whether he was good enough for her little sister.

"The gods brought Rey and me back together," explained Silla, excitement sparkling in her voice. "I hid in his wagon, and he tried to kill me, but then I blackmailed him to take me north—" Silla broke off as Saga's glare on Rey intensified. "I have much to tell you, as I suspect you have to tell me." Silla grew silent, her eyes shining with unshed tears. "I cannot believe it," she whispered through her smile.

The caution in Saga's face melted away, and she closed the space between them, embracing her sister tightly. "I cannot, either." Saga lifted her blue eyes to Rey's. "Thank you for keeping her safe. *This* time," she added.

A laugh broke free from deep in Rey's chest. Saga Volsik was an older sister through and through. Perhaps they'd get along, the two of them.

Silla released her sister and smiled at Kassandr. "And you, uh, Lord Rurik?"

"You may call me Kass," Saga's husband said jovially, eyes dancing.

"I've always wanted a brother," said Silla cheerily. Her gaze darted to his bare chest, then quickly back up. A nervous laugh fell from her lips. "Let us find you some clothing!"

And as Silla tugged Kass away, the pair chattered eagerly. Rey and Saga exchanged weary glances that each said the same thing: This would be a very long ride back to Kopa.

CHAPTER 68

Kopa, Íseldur

Silla sighed contentedly as Rey picked a comb gently through her freshly washed curls. A fire crackled in the hearth nearby, and the feel of Rey behind her was absolutely divine after so many days spent apart. He let out a sound of displeasure, working the comb through a stubborn knot.

Rey's chest brushed against the back of her nightdress, and the friction set Silla's skin alight. Gods, but she'd been away from this man for too long. But tonight, Rey was back in Kopa. Back in her bed. And Silla's patience was quickly fraying.

All told, they'd lost roughly a third of their warband in the battle of the heartwood, and it hurt Silla deeply to think that each one was a father, a brother, a sister, or a mother who would not come home to their family. Yet their sacrifice was not without merit. They'd defeated the leech and had prevented its poisonous mist from spreading and creating any more Turned creatures. But it was impossible not to think of all those who'd already been Turned. To wonder how many draugur had traveled to the place called Rökksgarde, and for what purpose.

Still, Silla had returned to Kopa with Myrkur's bargain broken. She was free from His dark whispers, from His twisted influence. She no longer had to dose herself with hindrium to protect her Ashbringer source. And reuniting with her cold, wintry light had been a moment of pure joy.

The biggest prize of all wrought from the battle of the heartwood was Saga. The sisters had flown on Havoc back to Kopa ahead of their group—a fact that both Rey and Kass had initially opposed. But with Saga's condition, days upon days spent traveling outdoors would be too taxing, and besides, Silla would let nothing come between her and getting on that winged horse. When Rey and Kass had seen the conviction on the sisters' faces, they'd begrudgingly relented.

Silla would admit her heart had squeezed with delight when she'd laid eyes on Havoc. True the stallion did not care for her attempts to sweet talk him, but Havoc had allowed Silla to climb onto his back behind Saga. Soaring above the Western Woods and gazing out over the snow-swept lands of Íseldur had been a moment of absolute freedom.

There had been much fanfare upon the sisters' arrival in Kopa, but Silla had quickly ushered Saga into her chambers, where they'd remained sequestered ever since. They'd exchanged stories of the strife they'd each faced, laughing and crying at each high and low. And then Silla had begged for stories of their parents—of the castle she'd been too young to recall. She collected each story like a treasure, and when Saga had offered to draw their parents, Silla had been overcome with emotion.

She owed her life to Saga. Once again, when she'd found herself in the darkest of places, Saga had extended a hand in help. Again and again, Silla mulled over the strange effect of braiding their power together. It was clear this channel between them allowed more than just communication. She had *felt* Saga—had seen her sister's memories in her own mind. And Silla had felt Saga's love like the warmest hug. Yet she wondered about this bond and what power it might reveal.

But now Silla finally had time alone with Rey. Each pass of that comb wound her up even tighter, the maddeningly gentle way he handled her hair only worsening things.

The next tug at her roots broke her patience clean through. Silla brushed her toes against Rey's calf, back and forth, back and forth. But the man was dedicated to his task. She blew a wayward tendril from her face. Then another idea struck her. Silla dipped her shoulder, wiggling it until Rey huffed in irritation.

"Be still, woman, I'm nearly done."

But it was enough—the loose collar of her nightdress had slid free. She waited for Rey to notice the bare skin of her shoulder; waited for the wet heat of his tongue to slide along it.

Nothing.

Her brows snapped together as he continued to pick at a stubborn knot. She bristled with frustration, then pulled forth her Ashbringer galdur. A smile curved up as the familiar cold press of her magic filled her veins. Her forearms glowed with pure white light, and her chilled breath clouded the air. Gods, but she'd missed this skill of hers.

Silla found the crevice in her mind that controlled her expression and gently pulled at it, allowing a slow release of her light into the air. Rey's comb stilled, and victory swelled inside her. Silla herded the motes of light toward his bare foot, using the softest of touches to make them dance along his skin.

He gasped, goosebumps pebbling beneath her cold light, but his skin did not frost, nor did he jerk his foot away. She'd practiced this lighter touch in the days since her return to Kopa, and hoped that in time she could use her Ashbringer skill as adeptly as Rey did his smoke.

As though he could read her thoughts, the scent of smoke pricked Silla's nostrils. An undulating charcoal tendril drifted over her shoulder before entwining with her light and lifting it away from his foot. She loved to watch their magic play together; loved watching the contrasts of dark and light, of ice and fire. It was strange, she thought, how such different elements could complement one another so well.

Rey's smoke thickened, its heat quickly melting away the icy motes of Silla's light. And then the smoke was changing direction, sliding along her bared arms and leaving pinpricks of heat. With a gasp, Silla writhed away, but—trapped between Rey's body and his smoke—there was nowhere to go. The press of Rey's chest to her back sent desire spiraling into her center.

"I was nearly done," grumbled Rey, mouth directly next to her ear, "but since you cannot keep your galdur to yourself, now you'll have to suffer the consequences."

"What consequences?" Silla asked breathlessly as his smoke entwined her wrists.

With a quick twitch of his fingers, Rey's smoke hauled her up from between his legs and over onto her stomach. Face pressed into the furs, Silla was disoriented as the binds around her wrists pulled upward until her arms were pinned above her head. She managed to turn her head toward Rey and blow some wayward curls away from her face.

Rey had discarded his tunic, revealing an expanse of warm brown skin that contrasted the deep blues of his dragon tattoo. Silla didn't know where to look first, but her gaze soon fell to where he strained against his breeches.

"Your hair," warned Rey, "will be mussed."

His heated look made Silla's body clench down on empty air. "Make it thorough. Hopelessly tangled."

"You want that?" he asked dangerously. "To be all tangled up?"

She nodded emphatically, then gasped as his smoke rolled her over once more. Now she lay on her back, wrists twisted over each other. More smoke wrapped around her ankles, wrenching her feet apart and rucking her nightdress up. A delicious shiver rolled through her as Rey crawled closer, then rose up on his knees to examine her splayed form.

She was utterly at his mercy, and the predatory gleam in his eyes told her he knew it, too. But as his ember-bright eyes met her own, Silla saw the question there. They both knew that with her bloodline gift, she could free herself from her binds if she wanted. Yet after weeks of fighting against Myrkur—of refusing to surrender to Him—there was something thrilling in letting Rey take full control.

"Do you want this?" he asked.

Silla nodded before he'd finished speaking, then moaned as the delicious weight of his body sank over hers.

Bracing himself on his elbows, Rey cupped her face and stared down at her, the gold flecks in his eyes blazing with heat. The thin layer of her nightdress separated them, and she shifted, impatient to be rid of it.

"Always so eager," he mused, the vexing man holding himself still. "Do you want me to take care of you, Sunshine?"

She nodded, squirming against him. The proof of his want was pinned against her stomach and impossible to ignore, but the man had pulled his mask of control into place, and Silla shivered with anticipation. Slowly, he brushed a lock of hair from her face.

"You'll have to earn it, Silla."

And then he brought his lips to hers. Rey's mouth was so soft, his kiss controlled. Gods, but she wanted to shatter his composure—to drive him to wild, reckless abandon—but there was something so freeing in surrendering all control to him.

Her soft whimper drew a grunt of satisfaction from Rey before he drew back. Arms caging her in, he hovered his face just above hers. This close, she could count the dark eyelashes framing his eyes; see the place where she'd nicked him while trimming his beard. A giddy feeling rose up inside her. She adored this man with his glowering looks. The way he took charge. The softness he showed only to her.

"Silla—" he murmured, and she sensed there were words he could not quite give voice to. Rey shook his head, then shifted his weight to the side. His eyes never left hers as a callused finger slid inside her.

"Fuck," he muttered, so soft she barely heard him.

She canted her hips toward him, desperate to get closer. An irritating smirk pulled up the corners of Rey's full, beautiful lips. He watched her with such intimacy as his fingers worked inside her, stroking and building her into a panting, writhing mess. Her back arched off the furs, her hands and wrists twisting against her binds, but they were held tightly in place. She was helpless against the onslaught of pleasure—powerless as every muscle in her body seemed to tighten . . .

Just as his fingers stilled. Pulled free.

"Rey!" she whined as he placed openmouthed kisses all down her throat.

"I told you," he muttered, teeth scraping along her collarbone, "you'll have to earn it."

On he continued his games as the moons climbed higher beyond the windows. Sweat misted her brow, her body aching for release. Finally—*finally*—he had mercy on her. Silla broke, warm shivers radiating out from her center until they reached every part of her being. Every taut muscle fell lax with satiated relief, and Silla heaved for breath.

As her consciousness slowly came back to her, Silla felt the smoky binds at her ankles expanding up her legs, along her stomach. She whimpered, twisting away from the hot prickles, but as the scent of smoke intensified, she blinked down to see her nightdress burning to cinders before her very eyes. Silla opened her mouth to protest, but it was over before she could make a sound. Rey's smoke evaporated, though the binds at her wrists and ankles remained.

The smoke at her right ankle pulled up, twisting her over at the hips. Arms pinned above her head and twisted half on her side, Silla had her legs scissored apart. It was obscene to be positioned like this, every inch of her on display, but one look over her shoulder had desire building sharply once more inside her.

On the surface, Rey might look like a man in control. But the little signs said otherwise—the sharp intake of breath; the clench and release of his shoulders.

"I've wanted you like this," he admitted, pushing down his breeches and taking himself in hand, "for a long time, Silla."

Words had vacated her. There was only the soft, floaty feeling she got when he looked at her like this. The way he couldn't resist touching himself while looking at her.

"Look at you," he murmured, kicking off his breeches before crawling over her. "All twisted up for me."

"You," she agreed, wishing she could pull him down to her. The slow slide of his skin against hers would surely drive her mad.

She had only a moment of anticipation before he pushed inside her. The stretch of him was delicious, always on the very edge of pain, yet never quite fully there. Rey rocked, gentle but relentless, until he reached the deepest part of her. A sound escaped him, strangled and harsh. Curling himself over her body, Rey rested his forehead on her cheek, like he needed a moment to adjust as well.

"All right?" he whispered, and she nodded in reply.

With his body cocooned around hers, she felt so cherished. So protected. So *loved.* But with his hot breath steaming her cheek and the possessive slide of his hand down her neck, she also felt desired. And the thought that this stern, deadly warrior would show this side of himself only to her made her dizzy with joy.

But then Rey began to move, and all thoughts fled her mind. In this new position, he reached different parts of her. She was helpless; unable to do anything but feel. He started with slow, experimental thrusts, but soon pushed himself upright, clutching her hip while moving in earnest.

Rey's eyes held a glazed, lost sort of look as he stared at the place their bodies were joined. His thumb soon found the sensitive part of her, rubbing in tandem with his short, determined thrusts. Silla's pleasure spiked upward, and an orgasm broke through her like a sudden, brutal storm. Through the sharp bites of pleasure, she heard Rey's low muttered curses, a sound that only prolonged the sensations.

"Beautiful," he murmured.

Candlelight caught on his coarse curls, crowning him in light. He looked like a king, reigning over his subjects. But his eyes blazed with visceral want, every line in his body now drawn up taut, and Silla knew this was a man holding on by the very finest thread. With her delicate inner muscles, she clenched down around him, dark delight filling her at his hiss.

"Not yet, you wicked woman," he muttered, pulling out. "I've waited too long."

Silla frowned, her lax, satiated body suddenly so empty. But it wasn't a heartbeat later that the smoke was once again tugging at her ankles, rolling her onto her back. Her thighs were spread wide, knees bent and pressed into the bed. Gods, she thought she couldn't have another, but the way Rey rearranged her just how he wanted only made her body throb for him.

His hands came down on either side of her head, smoothing her curls away so they would not pull. The way he handled her—reverential yet demanding—made her melt beneath his touch. Her trust in him was absolute, and she did not take her eyes from Rey's as he placed her legs against his shoulders. She gasped as he pushed inside her, hitting a spot that made stars scatter across her vision.

Garbled praise fell from Rey's lips: "Beautiful," and "Take it," and "It's yours." His long, measured strokes quickly descended into a fevered pace, his words shifting to grunts. There was something so delicious about the way he used her body—the way he took what he wanted and gave so much in return. Pleasure built, low and deep-rooted, and though it felt impossible, she knew she would soon break apart again. Perhaps there was no limit with this man.

The unbridled passion in Rey's eyes fell to something more tender, and suddenly the pressure was gone—Rey released his grip on her thighs and wrapped them around his hips. His body came down on hers, the hot slide of his firm chest against her sensitive breasts driving her mad. Rey cradled her face, bringing his lips down to hers in a soft, reverent kiss.

"I can bend you any way I want, Silla," he whispered between kisses, "but I want you most of all like this."

The heat and pressure at her wrists vanished, and Silla wanted to cry out at its loss. It had been exciting—a thrill to place her trust in him like that. But as Rey threaded his fingers with hers, his intimate gaze set her skin alight. Heat unfurled in the deepest part of her being, and Silla let her adoration for this man pour from her.

"I like you like this, too," she whispered. "I think I might even love you."

The words spilled from her, completely unfiltered. She hadn't meant to say that—hadn't known she felt it until this very instant. But suddenly she couldn't bear not saying it. Silla tilted her head and fit her lips against his.

"I love you, Reynir Galtung," she breathed against his skin. "I had to say it. And it doesn't matter if you return the—"

His finger pressed into the divot of her lower lip, cutting her words short. Silla blinked up at his gaze, burning with the heat of a thousand suns.

"Is it *love* when all you really want to do is feed her sweet rolls and wrap her in a blanket and care for her so she's never wanting for anything?"

An incredulous laugh fell from her.

"Is it love when every gods damned thought circles back to her; when you see her and it feels like your heart beats outside your own gods damned body; when you plot murder anytime another man looks her way?"

Silla found herself smiling so wide her cheeks hurt.

"*Love* is too tame a word for what I feel for you, Sunshine."

Heart pounding in her chest, words eluded her.

Reynir Galtung smiled, that dimple carving into his cheek. "Have I rendered you speechless?" he teased. "I suppose there's a first time for everything—"

"You *love me,*" she repeated, ignoring all the rest. "Even after I used your full name."

He kissed her softly, drawing back for a moment. "Only you can use it."

"I shall abuse this privilege," she vowed.

He kissed her more roughly, and she laughed against his mouth. But when he drew back, all traces of amusement were gone. *I love you,* he told her with his eyes, rocking inside her.

I love you, too, she told him back, squeezing his hands tighter.

Their lips crashed together, each of them pouring in their passion and love and utter adoration. Rey's movements were choppy, his tempo quickly building, and Silla's unfulfilled pleasure from earlier barreled back into her. The tension built to dizzying levels, and then she was arching, inundated in wave after wave of exquisite sensation. The pleasure ebbed and pulsed until it had reached all through her.

Above her, Rey made a guttural sound, burying his nose against her neck as he found his own release. They lay in a tangle, twitching with the aftershocks as they tried to catch their breaths. After a long moment, Rey pushed himself up, then blinked. He rolled his lips together, as though trying to suppress a smile.

"What?" asked Silla.

"Your hair." Rey laughed throatily. "It's certainly tangled."

Silla patted her mangled hair, a smile spreading wide as she stared up at the man she *loved.* "You can apply a treatment of bear grease to it later."

She made to pull him back down for another kiss, but Rey jerked back at a sudden scratching sound.

"What–" In the span of a heartbeat, Rey had leaped from the bed, retrieved his sword, and was striding–bare-arsed–to the source of the sound. Silla scrambled after him, wobbly as a newborn faun as she pulled a fur around her shoulders.

Rey hauled the curtain back, and together they stared into a pair of beady black eyes.

"The black hawk," murmured Silla, peering through the glass. Her heart pounded as she tried to seek meaning from the bird's presence. But without the god of chaos lurking in her blood, it seemed rather less ominous.

Rey reached for the window opening, lifting his sword, but she placed a hand on his wrist. "Wait," said Silla, stepping closer. The hawk scraped its yellow beak along the glass, and for the first time, Silla realized the offerings plate was empty. "It's only hungry."

She felt Rey's incredulous stare as she padded to the table where the leavings of their evening meal rested. Silla picked up a plate and carried it to the window. After hauling the pane open, she offered a leftover roast chicken leg to the bird. The hawk snatched it with its razor-sharp beak and, with a soft, throaty sound, took to the skies.

Silla turned back to Rey and shrugged.

Reynir Galtung shook his beautiful head. “Only you could tame the gods damned herald of death.”

Silla shrugged and set the plate aside. “I suppose I’m used to befriending the surliest of beings.”

His brows shot down, and he leveled her with his fiercest *axe eyes.*

“Come now, *Reynir,*” Silla cooed, sauntering toward the bed. “Bring that glare back to the furs.”

CHAPTER 69

Hekla batted Eyvind's hand away from where it squeezed her thigh under the feasting table, then winced as pain twinged from her ribs. Eyvind's gaze whipped her way, and she felt him assessing her with concern.

"I'm fine, Hakonsson," she muttered, breathing through the pain. "My broken ribs are healing." It was true. With diligent application of Sigrún's ointment each day following the battle in the heartwood, her ribs were well on the mend. Still, it would be several weeks before they were truly healed.

As for her prosthetic arm, well, Hekla had pulled it from Gjalla's fangs to find it mangled beyond repair. It was silly, she supposed, to grow attached to a non-living thing. But this arm had saved her life on multiple occasions. And so she'd been a little sentimental about its demise. Hekla had buried it in the heartwood with murmured words of thanks.

Now her sleeve hung empty as she waited for the Tailor to finish crafting her new prosthetic arm with his strange, textile-manipulating magic. The Tailor's promise of extra sharp parts and a few new tweaks had done much to assuage Hekla's dismay at the loss of her old one.

Eyvind was also healing up rather nicely, though the man had milked his injury for all it was worth. From making Axe Eyes fetch his ale to asking Hekla to adjust his blanket, he'd become a thorn in everyone's side. Though a part of her itched to defy his ridiculous requests, another part couldn't bear to have him suffer. And so, thus far, she'd begrudgingly relented.

Though she felt Eyvind's smoldering looks, Hekla had managed to extract herself from conversation before he could bring up their interrupted kiss. Deep inside, she knew everything had changed on that riverbank, even if she wasn't ready to admit it.

You can use those claws of yours all you wish, Eyvind had said. *Can't you tell I'm not going anywhere?*

She had time. He wouldn't rush her. And the thought made nervous flutters erupt low in her belly. She did not know what this was—what *they* were—but for the time being, that was all right.

When Eyvind had insisted she join him in House Hakon's seats of honor, Hekla had nearly declined. But the curl of Jarl Hakon's lip had made up her mind for her. It was clear Eyvind's father thought her a terrible match for his son, and something about this had rankled Hekla enough that she'd taken the damned chair.

Now Hekla sat with Eyvind on her left, Gunnar on her right. She should feel on guard seated between the pair, and yet a casual sort of acceptance had settled between them. Of course, it could be the black-haired beauty on Gunnar's right who made the seating arrangement tolerable. *Kaeja,* the woman had introduced herself, before laughing at each of Gunnar's horrible puns.

Eyvind's former betrothed, Liv, sat at the far end of the table, laughing with Runný, and Hekla found herself smiling at the pair. It was strange to see different worlds colliding, and even stranger to be done with the job in Istré, when it had been her solitary focus for so long. Hekla still had nightmares of the mist swarming her; of a giant spider looming over her. It was jarring to go from the horrors of the Western Woods to the fineries of Ashfall. To be seated among the most powerful jarls in the north, though . . . that, she could get used to.

Eyvind's hand slid over her thigh, squeezing once more, and Hekla turned toward him, blinking as slowly as she could.

"Your recovery," she drawled, "has been miraculous."

A cocky grin spread across Eyvind's face, and despite her good senses, Hekla's insides frolicked at the sight. "You healed me with your divine beaut—"

Hekla's boot came down on Eyvind's foot before he could say more. "You spend too much time with Thrand Long Sword."

Eyvind chuckled, but their bantering was cut short as the double oak doors to the council chambers swung inward. Everyone stood as Silla flounced in. She was clad in a vibrant emerald dress, golden embroidery glinting in the torchlight, though Hekla's lips curved into a smile as she noted the battle belt strapped at her friend's hips. Beside her, Rey strode in, his gaze scraping over every inch of the room. Ever on alert, Axe Eyes was, but Hekla had never seen him more protective than when Silla was by his side.

Next came Saga Volsik, her blond hair a soft contrast against the black gown she wore. Hekla's gaze landed on the back of Saga's hand, tapping against her husband's arm in an even rhythm. Hekla scowled at the burn marks she found—snarling bears branded onto the backs of Saga's hands. A pitiful, insecure man had done this, Hekla knew in an instant, and she made plans to discover the culprit's identity.

Saga's husband was certainly a fine looking warrior, and their entry was met with applause. Days now, Saga had been holed up in her chambers with Silla as the sisters got to know each other. But her absence had caused whispers to float through the fortress—some claiming that Saga was not real, that she was only a ploy to unite the north.

Hekla couldn't help but smile at the adoration written plainly on Silla's face as she and her sister took their seats at the head of the table. Cupbearers swirled into the room with jugs of ale.

"Let us raise our cups," said Silla brightly, "to the return of the Volsik heir. Daughter of King Kjartan and Queen Svalla, sister of Silla—"

Saga cleared her throat and sent her sister a look that seemed to say, *On with it.*

"Let us raise our cups to my sister!" said Silla. The room did just that. Cups and goblets were raised, the joy of Saga's return so great it was felt in the air. And then they drank.

Silla grimaced as she took a sip, then set her cup down and faced the room. "As you've heard," she said, voice rising above the chatter, "thanks to the brave warriors who joined in our cause, we were successful in the heartwood. The leech was defeated, the infected tree destroyed, and the deep roots in the grove have been fortified by the Forest Maiden. We will continue to monitor the hjarta trees, but with the Forest Maiden's bolstering magic, it is unlikely that another leech should be able to enter through their deep roots."

Silla's hand went to her chest. "My mother's bargain with Myrkur was broken." She looked to her sister. "And the most unexpected gift has been granted us. Not only has Saga returned to Íseldur, but she's brought someone with her."

Silla gestured to the green-eyed man, but before she could say more, Saga pushed to her feet. Silla blinked, then sat down, her expression faltering for just a second.

"Allow me to present to you my husband," said Saga. Her voice was slightly deeper, and perhaps a little more stern than Silla's. "Meet Kassandr Rurik, heir to the throne of Zagadka."

Whispers rippled through the room, curiosity brightening the jarls' eyes.

"As you know," continued Saga, "King Ivar's fleet sailed to Zagadka and lay siege to the city of Kovograd. He succeeded in nothing but uniting the Zagadkians against him. Now we've brought a large warband to Íseldur, along with a cavalry of winged horses and two boatloads of grain."

At first, there was silence and stunned disbelief. But as Kassandr Rurik nodded in agreement, those present seemed to finally understand. Support. Swords. An airborne cavalry. Still, it was perhaps the mention of grain that drew the cries of relief around the table.

"This aid comes from Zagadka with a request," Saga continued over the chatter. "Together, we turn our sights on Sunnavík."

Saga glanced at her sister, and Silla's expression held a moment of doubt as she slowly rose to her feet. Silla cleared her throat, then spoke to those present.

"Queen Signe has schemes beyond those of her husband. She's rounded up and experimented on the Galdra; has set Lady Tala against me. And I believe she gathers forces at a place called Rökksgarde." Silla paused, her brows furrowing. "When we went to draw answers from Tala, we found her dead in her prison cell. Her corpse"—Silla's nose wrinkled—"was swarming with wasps. This must be Signe's doing."

Saga's gaze hardened as she picked up the thread. "Too long," she said, "have Signe and Ivar sat on their stolen thrones. Too long have they persecuted our people for the gods they worship. For being born with galdur flowing in their veins.

"It is time," concluded Saga, "that we take back our kingdom."

A cheer rose up, jarls standing and bashing their fists on the feasting table. The energy in the room was palpable, impossible to resist. Soon Hekla was on her feet, hooting her agreement.

Silla raised a hand, and the room gradually quieted. "But we have much to accomplish, and many hurdles before us. Though we've won some small victories against the god of chaos, there is more for us to do. We must find the place called Rökksgarde and discover Myrkur's plans. We must keep vigilant, and we must, under all circumstances, ready ourselves for the very real possibility of Rökkur.

"Once, long ago, our ancestors sheltered in the caves behind Ashfall. I propose that we ready them, should we need them once more." Silla's gaze slid to Eyvind's older brother. "Atli Hakonsson has agreed to take on this enormous task." Saga's expression seemed to sharpen as she glanced between Atli and her younger sister, and Hekla had an inkling that she hadn't been privy to this part of the plan.

"We must gather our troops," Saga cut in. "We must assemble our allies. Surely there are jarls to the south who'd join our cause?" Saga looked around the table, her gaze lingering on each man in turn. "I'll need you to contact your allies and friends. We'll need every warrior willing and able to have a chance at defeating the Urkans. Already, Ivar's father's fleet has sailed from Norvaland, and they shall arrive any day. We'll need to be cunning if we wish to defeat them, but it is more than mere cunning we'll need."

Those at the table nodded in agreement, their gazes turning to Silla as she picked up where her sister had left off.

"The Urkans believe in individual glory," said Silla. "They believe a hero is the one who spills the most blood on the battlefield. I am ready to dispel such thoughts among our warbands—to prove that unity is a far greater weapon. Were it not for my sister's bravery, I'd have fallen to Myrkur in the Western Woods. Were it not for Hekla's teachings, I'd not have escaped the Klaernar. Were it not for Rey, I'd have died at least a hundred times by now."

Pride welled in Hekla's chest. Not pride at being mentioned, but pride that she'd done something—left a mark on this world.

"We must use the Urkans' self-centered beliefs against them. We will harness the power of the collective. That means setting aside our differences and our own interests for a time. Because the only way we will drive the Urkans from our shores is if we come together.

"But for now," said Silla, a smile spreading wide as she gazed at Saga, "we must celebrate this bright spot amid the gloom we've recently faced. Let us raise another cup to the return of my sister." She raised a golden goblet, looking around the table as the others did the same. "And to these new bonds forged with the Kingdom of Zagadka."

Hekla raised her cup, emotion welling in her. Silla had done the impossible—had quelled the bickering among the jarls, had vanquished the leech and banished the dark god from her body. As she watched her friend tip back her cup of ale, Hekla was filled with wonder and gratitude to be in the presence of such a woman.

But then Silla winced, setting the goblet down. Her gaze met Hekla's across the table, unimpressed. "Still tastes like tree sap to me," said Silla.

Hekla threw her head back and laughed.

The doors to the meeting room slammed open, her laughter dying off abruptly. Rey and Sigrún shot to their feet. Gunnar gaped in open disbelief. And Hekla blinked hard at the gray-bearded figure in the doorway. Was this a phantom vision? Surely it had to be. What other reason had *he* to be here?

Kraki, former leader of the Bloodaxe Crew, staggered into the room. His face was gaunt, his hair and beard wild and askew. And his pale-blue eyes held a deranged look.

"What is it?" demanded Rey, moving around the table and reaching his former mentor just as Kraki's knees gave out. "What has happened?" Hekla joined Rey, Gunnar, and Sigrún a moment later.

The four remaining members of the Bloodaxe Crew stared down at the once-formidable leader, now a thin, rambling mess of a man.

"Awakened," mumbled Kraki, disoriented. "It's happened. It's awakened."

"What are you saying?" asked Rey, easing Kraki to the ground.

"Kiv is no more," said Kraki, gaze roaming wildly from face to face. "Barely escaped . . ." When Kraki's eyes met Hekla's a chill settled into her bones. "It's happened," he rasped.

"What happened?" she asked, against her better judgment.

"The dragon."

The room fell silent, Hekla's ears ringing at Kraki's words. Surely she'd heard him wrong. Surely it could not be. But Kraki spoke four little words that changed everything.

"The dragon," he said, "has awoken."

EPILOGUE

Ale spilled down Ivar's chin, dripping into his beard. Cursing, he lifted the hem of his tunic to dab it dry, but the motion sent pain spearing down his back. Ivar bellowed, ale sloshing from his cup and all down the front of his tunic. He let the cup fall, holding himself so still he scarcely breathed.

Ursir's Bollocks, but that damnable winged horse had ruined his back. And though he'd had the very finest of healers tend to him, Ivar swore the injury was only worsening. Could be, he supposed, that he'd ignored the prescription for bed rest and abstinence of ale.

It was absurd, of course, for the man to have even suggested such a thing. In the wake of his retreat from Zagadka, Ivar had no choice but to show strength. Besides, the Norvalander fleet would arrive any day, and Ivar could not show any hint of weakness to King Harald. Though his father was nearing his seventh decade, he'd yet to show any signs of aging. But of course, his father had never weathered an assassination attempt, nor encountered an aerial cavalry of monstrous winged horses.

Loath though he was to admit it, the other reason Ivar avoided bed rest was that it would only feed Signe's ego. Already her gloating looks were impossible to bear, each one seeming to say, *I told you to wait for your father.*

Ivar ground his teeth at the thought of it. The pain in his back dulled with each passing heartbeat until it was finally bearable to move. Ivar gingerly climbed from his chair and retrieved his empty cup while cursing himself for sending his cupbearer away. He simply couldn't bear the humiliation of anyone seeing him like this. Ivar refilled his cup with ale and lost himself to his thoughts.

Curse those Zagadkians and curse his former foster daughter. When Saga had stood before him on Zagadkian soil, he'd read the surrender plain on her face. But that horse! That god damned cursed abomination of a creature had come from nowhere, lashing out with those iron hooves. His back twinged with remembered pain.

Ivar's fist clenched around his cup. He'd been far too merciful when Saga had been caught kissing that wretched Zagadkian in the gardens. And what was wrought from Ivar's mercy? An attempt on his life!

To think how near Ivar Ironheart had come to death in the explosion of the great hall. What shame it would have wrought not to die in battle. Ursir might well have denied his entry to the Sacred Forest.

No matter. Saga could hide behind the wooden walls of Kovograd and fall like the rest of them. The Norvaland fleet would arrive. They'd rally. Storm Zagadka. And then Ivar would grind each and every feral Zagadkian into the ground and claim their isle.

The door to his chambers scraped open, and Ivar whirled, then hissed in pain.

It was Eldrún, his favored concubine, who slunk through the door. "My king," she purred.

Ivar exhaled, trying to wipe any lingering traces of pain from his face. "I didn't summon you," he grumbled, turning away. Ivar drained the contents of his cup in one gulp, then set it down on the table roughly.

"It has been several days," said Eldrún. "I missed you."

In his mind's eye, Ivar saw the low cut of Eldrún's gown showcasing the ample swell of her bosom. He hadn't called for her, but Ivar was not one to let opportunity pass him by.

"Bring the wine," he ordered, settling onto the bed with a wince. She'd have to ride him carefully, else he'd not be able to walk for days.

"Yes, my king."

Ivar's moods were lifting already. With her sweet disposition and simple nature, Eldrún had quickly become his favorite. And while his other concubines pouted for jewels or fine gowns, not his Eldrún. There were no games of the mind with this one, no hurt feelings when he sent her away. She was even and true and so willing to do whatever he demanded.

Eldrún set the wine pitcher and a pair of goblets down.

"Unbind your hair," ordered Ivar, unable to take his eyes off Eldrún as she worked her blond tresses free from their braids.

"Dress." She blinked at him with long-lashed eyes, sliding her gown off one shoulder, then the other. All the blood in Ivar's body rushed south as the dress slid down to her waist, held in place only by the fastenings at her hips.

"Belt."

Eldrún released the belt, and the silk puddled on the ground around her. She stepped toward him, long blond hair covering her nude form from his view. His gaze landed on the pulse at the base of her throat, hammering with curious intensity.

And then everything happened too quickly for Ivar to follow. Eldrún was upon him, a blade slashing toward his chest with impossible speed.

With a shout, Ivar's hand shot up, pain biting into his palm as he caught the blade before it could pierce his heart. But Eldrún moved with inhuman speed—had already drawn a second blade from Ursir knew where. Ivar jerked away, but the blade plunged deep into his shoulder. He bellowed, rolling onto the woman and driving his fist forward. But rather than her head, it hit the empty blanket, and Ivar cried out as pain pierced his side.

Ursir's Flaming Paw. How was this woman able to move with such speed?

"Guards!" he shouted, lunging at Eldrún, who'd leaped from the bed. Daggers sang through the air, each aimed directly at his heart. Ivar ducked and dodged, his body an inferno of pain. A growl built in his throat as he shouted for his guards again. Where in Ursir's name were they?

Ivar barreled at Eldrún, but she dodged him, again with that impossible speed. Momentum carried her to the wall, but she kicked off it, sailing back through the air toward him. Ivar's warrior senses had caught up with him, and he ducked low, catching her leg. He slammed Eldrún to the ground, satisfaction welling in his chest as she was momentarily stunned.

"Who sent you?" he demanded, bringing his face low to hers.

But Eldrún swung her head forward, her forehead crashing into his nose with startling force. As his vision wavered, Ivar's grip on Eldrún loosened and she scrambled free.

He whirled in time to see her launching onto the bed, retrieving a fallen dagger. Ivar had never witnessed speed like this, not since . . .

"No," he growled, ducking beneath the flying dagger. Images filled his mind's eye—of a battlefield seventeen years ago. King Kjartan's warriors moving with unnatural speed. "Harefoot." Ivar picked up a fallen chair, batting another flying dagger out of the air.

"You're a god damned Harefoot," he growled, charging at Eldrún while wielding the chair. "You are Galdra!"

Ivar's blood ran cold as the future the Weaver had foretold to him so many years ago rang in his ears. *You will fall by galdur's hand.* The thought was momentarily dizzying, giving Eldrún a chance to evade him. She kicked off the enormous wooden headboard, striking Ivar's right side.

He staggered but managed to seize the woman by the neck. With a roar, Ivar shoved her against the wall so hard that bones snapped and the stones rattled. "Who sent you?" he bellowed, spittle landing on Eldrún's face. Her lifeless face.

Ivar cursed, realizing he'd get no answers—he'd broken her neck. He released Eldrún, and she crumbled to the floor, limbs splayed at odd angles.

Pain surged suddenly from all over Ivar's body—back, shoulder, palm, side. He pulled the dagger free from his shoulder with a grunt, then he paused. Blinked at the hilt protruding from between his ribs. For a moment, Ivar simply stared, dumbfounded. He knew from years of battlefield experience that he could not pull this dagger free himself—a healer would have to do it.

"Guards!" he bellowed, before releasing a foul string of curses. He was going to have them all bound and whipped; publicly humiliated for their failings. Ivar staggered to the bed, snatching a goblet of wine from the table and tossing it back.

The door scraped open, and Ivar's pulse leaped.

"Darling?" asked his wife, striding toward him. "I heard your shouts. Where are your guards? Oh!" With her cream-colored gown and white-gold hair, Signe looked like a spirit drifting toward him.

Lights danced in Ivar's vision, the pain now so great he did not know where it started and ended. "Stabbed," he grunted. "Need. Healer." Ivar gasped as a wall of pain slammed into him.

"Yes, darling," said Signe, his shield-maiden here to protect him. She eased him onto the bed. Cooed softly as she swept the hair back from his brow.

Signe's blue eyes met his, and Ivar felt a wave of tenderness toward his wife. She was the mother of his children. A queen who'd stood by him despite all his shortcomings. Ivar knew he hadn't been the best husband. Perhaps he would try harder.

"A shame," said Signe, "that you killed dear Eldrún. It's hard to find such dutiful followers." As her words landed, Signe's hand curled around the hilt of the dagger.

"N-no," Ivar wheezed.

The queen's lips curved up into a smile, and she yanked the dagger free. Shock and confusion and utter panic assaulted Ivar as his lifeblood rushed out of him. But the delight dancing in his wife's eyes told Ivar enough.

He tried to shout. Tried to form words.

"Shh, darling," said Signe with a demure smile, smoothing another lock from his brow.

Outrage and loathing battled within Ivar, all while the lights in his vision grew and spread, globbing together. Signe leaned down.

Pressed a kiss to his cheek. She hovered above him, those glacial-blue eyes studying his face.

Ivar wanted to reach out. Wrap his hands around her neck. Snap it as he'd done to Eldrún. But all he could manage was a feeble flap of his hands.

"Hush now, darling," whispered Signe, "I want to watch as the light fades from your eyes."

Pronunciation Guide

Many of the words and names in this book are derived from Old Norse and/or Icelandic; *ð* and *þ* characters have been converted to *th* and *æ* to *ae* for readability.

Bjáni – byan-ee
Dúlla – doo-la
Eystri – ay-stree
Flíta – flee-ta
Hevrít – hev-reet
Hjarta – h-yar-ta
Hver – kvehr
Hvíta – kvee-ta
Íseldur – ees-el-door
Klaernar – klite-nar
Kunta – koon-ta
Lébrynja – lyeh-bryn-ya
Myrkur – mihr-koor
Nordur – nor-door
Reykfjord – rake-fyoord
Róa – roh-a
Signe – sig-nuh
Skjöld – shkuld
Skógungar – shkoon-gar
Slátrari – slow-trar-ee
Stjarna – styat-na
Sudur – soo-door
Urka – oor-ka
Vestir – vest-eer

Glossary

Ashbringer – a type of Galdra who wields fire magic

Berskium – a powder mined near Reykfjord and taken by the Klaernar to maintain their large stature and strength

Bjáni – fool (an insult)

Blade Breaker – a type of Galdra capable of great strength

Brennsa – fire whiskey

Dúlla – doll (a term of endearment among women)

Draugur – also called the restless dead; an undead creature

Eisa Volsik – a former princess of Íseldur thought to have been murdered by King Ivar

Eystri – the easternmost territory of Íseldur

Flíta – phoenix-like butterflies whose wings light up when they fly; in their old age, they burst into flames, and a caterpillar emerges from the ashes

Galdra – a magic-wielding person, also called Ashen; outlawed by King Ivar

Galdur – magic itself

Gothi – a priest of the Ursinian religion

Hábrók – the god of battle, honor, luck, and weather; one of the old gods of Íseldur

Harefoot – a type of Galdra capable of great bursts of speed

Halda – a magical stone that can be ground into a powder and used to store excess galdur

Hevrít – an Íseldurian long-bladed dagger

Hindrium – a specialized metal that inhibits Galdra from accessing their magical source

High Prince – the ruling monarch of Zagadka

Hóra – whore

Illmarr – a scaled vampire of the sea; it can be lured by eel blood and felled by rowan arrows

Íseldur – kingdom of Ice and Fire; the island nation where this book takes place

Ivar Ironheart – the new king of Íseldur who usurped the throne from King Kjartan Volsik seventeen years ago

Kalasgarde – a town in the north of Íseldur, located in Nordur lands

Karthia – an isle to the south of Íseldur

Kjartan Volsik – the former king of Íseldur, murdered by King Ivar using the blood-eagle method in the pits of Askaborg Castle

Klaernar – King Ivar's specialized soldiers, also known as the King's Claws

Kopa – a large stone city in the northern parts of Eystri territory

Kunta – cunt (an insult)

Lébrynja – specialized, lightweight armor made of tiny leather-like scales and worn by the Bloodaxe Crew

Malla – the goddess of love, war, and death; one of the old gods of Íseldur; also, the name of one of the moons

Marra – the goddess of knowledge, healing, and peace; one of the old gods of Íseldur; also, the name of one of the moons

Medovukha – a Zagadkian alcoholic beverage similar to mead and made from fermented honey

Myrkur – the god of chaos and darkness; one of the old gods of Íseldur

Nordur – the northernmost territory of Íseldur

Norvaland – the isle northeast of Íseldur, it was overthrown by Ivar's father, Harald, who now sits on the throne

Nostislav – childhood friend of Kassandr Rurik's; the man he searched for in secret while in Íseldur

Posadnik – regional representative of the Zagadkian royal family (plural posadniki)

Reader – a type of Galdra capable of sensing threads of thought

Róa – a hot beverage served in Íseldur, made from the bark of the róa-bush

Rökksgarde — an unknown location where Maester Alfson and Queen Signe are gathering an army

Rökkur — the twilight of days; it is foretold in legend that the volcanos will erupt and bring death and fire to Íseldur

Saga Volsik – a former princess of Íseldur, she was seized by King Ivar and raised as his ward; she was betrothed to his son Prince Bjorn

Sbiten – a hot Zagadkian beverage made with spices

Seasonal gods – includes the Spring Maiden, Brother Summer, the Autumn Crone, and Old Man Winter. These are the gods worshipped by Zagadkians

Shadow Hound – a type of Galdra able to bend and manipulate light; are capable of invisibility and creating reflective shields

Skald – a poet who composes a type of Urkan poetry, often exaggerating the deeds of kings past and present

Skarpling – a small, mouse-sized creature with quills on its back

Skjöld – a dried leaf taken to treat headaches

Skógungar – a forest walker; a peaceful tree-like creature that lives in the Western Woods

Slátrari – "the butcher"; a murderer who burns people from the inside out

Smith – a type of Galdra capable of manipulating the bonds of this world and creating new structures from them

Solacer – a type of Galdra capable of sensing and modifying emotions

Sólas – Íseldurian coin currency

Svalla Volsik – the former queen of Íseldur, she was murdered by King Ivar, her body impaled upon a pillar in the pits of Askaborg Castle

Stjarna – "mother of stars"; Sunnvald's wife and the goddess of weaving, fertility, and guidance; one of the old gods of Íseldur

Sudur – the southernmost territory of Íseldur, it houses the capital city

Sunnavík – the capital city of Íseldur, where Askaborg Castle is found

Sunnvald – the Sun God; the god of fire and might; king of the old gods of Íseldur

Thrall – an enslaved person; in the Kingdom of Íseldur they are most often brought in from Norvaland and marked on their inner wrist

Uppreisna – a secret organization of Íseldurians whose aim is to overthrow Ivar Ironheart

Urka – a large nation to the east of Íseldur where the line of Urkan Kings originated

Ursir – the Bear God worshipped by King Ivar and fellow Urkans; belief in Ursir has been imposed upon Íseldurians

Vampire deer – carnivorous deer that hunt mammals and drain their blood

Vestir – the westernmost territory of Íseldur, it houses the Western Woods

Wolfspider – a large spider covered in shaggy gray fur

Weaver – a type of Galdra capable of Weaving the threads of the past, present, and future into a tapestry

Zagadkia – the mysterious island nation to the south of Íseldur

Acknowledgments

From learning about medieval Russia to the mycelial networks featured in this book, I don't think I've ever had so much fun doing research for a book.

While the hjarta trees in *Dawn of the North* are magical trees gifted by Sunnvald and able to share nutrients with their neighbors, the truth is, these trees (and fungi) exist in our world. Thank you to *Finding the Mother Tree* by Suzanne Simard and *Entangled Life* by Merlin Sheldrake for introducing me to the amazing world of mycelial networks. Originally, a fungus was going to be the Big Bad in this book, but I just could not vilify such amazing organisms. Instead, the leech "hijacks" the mycelial network and uses it for its own gain.

Other books that helped shape this book included *Russian Folk Belief* by Linda J. Ivantis, *Reimagining Europe: Kievan Rus' in the Medieval World* by Christian Raffensperger, and *Russian Magic Tales from Pushkin to Platonov,* edited by Robert Chandler.

Thank you to my agent, Jessica Watterson, for being such an amazing cheerleader, for fighting so I don't have to, for seeing the worth in these books. Thank you to my editor, Shauna Summers, for taking a chance on Silla and the Bloodaxe Crew, for helping me juice up the romance (all of the romances, I should say), and for helpful discussions to get me unstuck!

Thank you to my team at Penguin Random House, Mae Martinez, Brianna Kusilek, Taylor Noel, Megan Whalen, Meghan O'Leary, Christa Guild, Fritz Metsch, and Saige Francis.

Thank you to my beta readers for helping me wrangle this complicated story into something that reads so much easier, Maggie, Elayna,

Kelli, Bree, Sasa, and Brittany. Thank you to Angelina and my sensitivity reader through Penguin Random House for your thoughtful comments on Saga's agoraphobia. Thank you to Tanya and Rebecca for help with the Russian translations. Thank you to my dear friend Mallory for your step-by-step instructions (and diagram!) for how Hekla would stitch up that wound.

Thank you to my amazing PA Molly for keeping things going when I go into "gremlin mode." Thank you to my author friends for keeping me sane in this career, which could so easily feel isolating: Nisha, Elayna, Daniela, Penn, and Sasa.

And thank you to my family: To my parents, who still share my books with every family member they see (much to my chagrin). To Z for your gap-toothed smiles, and K for your bravery and talent on the stage. And to Ben, who believed I could do this whole "writing thing" before I believed in it myself.

About the Author

DEMI WINTERS is the author of romantic fantasy books featuring softer female leads, grumpy heroes, and immersive worlds. Lover of all things fairy-tale, fantasy, and romance, Winters lives in British Columbia, Canada, with her husband and two kids. When she's not busy brainstorming fantastical worlds and morally gray love interests, she loves reading and cooking.

demiwinters.com
TikTok: @demiwinterswrites
Instagram: @demiwinterswrites

About the Type

This book was set in Hoefler Text, a typeface designed in 1991 by Jonathan Hoefler (b. 1970). One of the earlier typefaces created at the beginning of the digital age specifically for use on computers, it was among the first to offer features previously found only in the finest typography, such as dedicated old-style figures and small caps. Thus it offers modern style based on the classic tradition.